Meet the Colemans of Texas, the

TEXAS RICH

BILLIE:

"I love Moss, Mother. He's going to ask me to marry him, and I will. And if he doesn't ask me, I'll wait for him, forever if necessary. I love him!"

MOSS:

"No, Billie, you can't wait here. I want you up there with me. You're married to a flyer, and I want you to know what it's like. Don't you trust me?"

THAD:

"I'm not preaching, Moss. I'm telling you a fact. Remember, I met that little girl you married and I always thought she was too young for you. Don't make her grow up the hard way."

(more)

AGNES:

"I scraped and scratched to give you a good life, Billie. This is our one chance at security, and even if you're too stupid to see it, I'm not."

JESSICA:

"Darling, Billie, this is the way we do things here. You're a Coleman now, and you have to accept our ways. That's why Moss sent you to us."

SETH:

"I want a grandson, Aggie. And it had damn well better be a boy this time around. You're the girl's mother. If I were you, I'd make sure she understands."

MAGGIE:

"I'm sick of the Colemans, just plain sick to death of the whole lot of us. I can't wait till I can leave home and breathe some other kind of air. Air that the Colemans don't own."

RILEY:

"It wasn't a performance. It's the way I felt. We don't belong in Vietnam, Pap. And if you tell me we do, I'll tell you you just want to sell more planes to the government."

SAWYER:

"I'm not just any woman, Grandpap. I'm a Coleman woman."

Also by Fern Michaels
Published by Ballantine Books:

ALL SHE CAN BE

CAPTIVE EMBRACES

CAPTIVE INNOCENCE

CAPTIVE PASSIONS

CAPTIVE SPLENDORS

CINDERS TO SATIN

FREE SPIRIT

TENDER WARRIOR

VALENTINA

VIXEN IN VELVET

TEXAS RICH

Fern Michaels

Copyright © 1985 by Fern Michaels

All rights reserved under International and Pan-American Copyright Conventions. Published in the United States by Ballantine Books, a division of Random House, Inc., New York, and simultaneously in Canada by Random House of Canada Limited, Toronto.

Library of Congress Catalog Card Number: 84-91077

ISBN 0-345-31374-7

Manufactured in the United States of America

BALLANTINE BOOKS • NEW YORK

Library of Congress Catalog Card Number: 84-91707

ISBN 0-345-31374-7

Manufactured in the United States of America

First Edition: April 1985

In loving memory of Alfred P. Anderson, husband and father.

"Oh! I have slipped the surly bonds of earth...put out my hand and touched the face of God."

—John G. Magee, Jr.

ACKNOWLEDGMENTS

Recently I had the opportunity to visit the tiny dot in the Pacific known as Guam. I found it to be a land of warm smiles, laughing eyes, blue skies, and what seemed like perpetual sunshine. To compare this beautiful, progressive paradise to Hawaii and Palm Beach would not be unjust. Like Riley and Otami my heart shattered when it was time to leave.

Because of the devastation created by Typhoon Karen on the island of Guam it was necessary to take certain liberties in my early descriptions of specific locales and buildings. All references are true and accurate to the rebuilt Guam.

I particularly want to thank Louise and the entire Crisostomo family along with Mary James, Astrid Hertslet, and Ben Blaz for being so generous with their time and making my visit so memorable. My sincere thanks to all of you.

Fern Michaels

PART I

The crisscross-patterned lace curtains, which should have been silk organdy but were rayon instead, billowed in the soft May breeze. The chitterings of birds and new green scents drifted into Billie Ames's room. She drew in her breath, savoring the tantalizing fragrances. Spring was her favorite time of year and this year it had seemed such a long time coming. In thirty-seven days she would graduate from high school. Adulthood. Grown-up. She bent to tie her saddle shoes, brushing impatiently at her ash-blond hair, which fell over her eyes, and frowned. Multistriped shoelaces and white anklets? Some grown-up! She should be wearing nylon stockings and heels, not these remnants of girlhood. But the war had been on in Europe for some time now and since the attack on Pearl Harbor last December, Billie had wondered if sheer stockings would go the way of the passenger pigeon: extinct. Not that it mattered, because they were beyond the limits of her clothing allowance anyway. Lots of women wore leg makeup and drew seams on the backs of their legs. But only pagans and Philistines did such things, declared Billie's mother. And Agnes Ames rarely, if ever, admitted she was wrong.

Billie's thoughts circled back to graduation. When she flipped the tassel of her mortarboard from one side to the other it would be the beginning of her last free summer and then off to Penn State. She'd already signed up for a major in English, because she had to pick something, but the truth was she hated the whole idea. What Billie wanted, really wanted, was to go to a good design and textile school. Agnes said that wouldn't be seemly. The best schools were in New York City and young girls just didn't live there alone. Not nice girls, at any rate. Later, after Billie had her degree, she could fool with such notions.

But Billie suspected the real reason was that the cost of design school was prohibitive. She wished she knew more about the family finances. Were they comfortable or merely keeping their heads above water? Agnes said that was hardly the concern of a young girl. Study, socialize with "acceptable youngsters," and dress well. That was Agnes's credo, and it always ended with: "Then you'll marry a young man from an old mainline family and your future will be secured. And always remember that no man wants used merchandise. Virginity is your most prized possession. Guard it well!" It was hard not to giggle when Agnes began preaching.

Sighing, Billie buttoned the straps of her jumper, which she'd made herself. It was such a beautiful shade of lavender and it had huge pearl buttons on the shoulder straps and two smaller ones on the patch pockets. Instead of hemming the skirt, she'd fringed it. She was the only girl in school with a fringed skirt, so far. By next week there would be at least twenty others; she was certain of it. Billie Ames enjoyed being something of a style setter.

Virginity. Agnes put great store in preserving it. Temptation was something to be fought and conquered until one's wedding night.

Billie sighed again, this time more deeply. Temptation wasn't a problem for her. She had no steady boyfriend, didn't want one, either. And the boys she knew were certainly not worth wasting her virginity on. They had pimply faces, sloppy clothes, and bicycles with chipped paint and chains that always slipped off when they rode double. There was nothing at all romantic about them! Besides, most of the boys had nothing except the war on their minds, hardly able to wait for graduation when they could enlist and prove what big men they were. Girls were only secondary to the German and Japanese armies.

Billie's world was simply too narrow, she thought. She wished she had more opportunities to travel, see things, do things. Even her trips downtown had been severely limited by Agnes ever since the arrival of military personnel. She thought of all the young men in their uniforms and grinned wickedly at her reflection in the mirror. The navy uniforms were the best, especially now in the warmer weather when they'd switched to whites. The men looked so dashing and debonair, like Tyrone Power or Errol Flynn. Imagine walking into her senior prom on the arm of a tall dark navy man! That was another thing. She didn't have a date for the prom. A dress . . . but no date. Agnes was beginning to worry, Billie could tell. But a senior prom was special, and you had to go with someone special. Several boys had asked her, but she'd declined. Even she, with all her romantic notions, didn't really expect the white knight to come charging down Elm Street to swoop her off to the dance. . . . Yet surely something or someone better would come along. At the last minute, she could always snag Tim Kelly. Ungainly Tim, who would make chopped liver of her feet on the dance floor. Still, he was a basketball captain and would make a respectable escort. Another sigh. Being one of the prettiest girls in the graduating class, and one of the most popular, didn't ensure romance.

A glance at the clock on her nightstand told Billie she'd have to hurry and she experienced a small skitter of excitement. She loved Saturday afternoons and the matinee at the Loews Theatre. It meant she could leave her sewing and piano lessons behind for a few hours. Saturday afternoon meant walking downtown with her two girlfriends and meeting the gang at the corner. No one paired off, exactly, but they did walk side by side down the tree-lined streets. They were friends, and after this summer they'd all go their different ways. Billie decided she wouldn't miss them, not the way some of the kids said they would. She'd be going off to a new school, where she could pick and choose her own friends, new friends. Ones that wouldn't have to pass Agnes's muster. Friends that might or might not be "acceptable."

Billie closed the lid of her tinkling music box, a Christmas gift from her father when she was four years old. She looked at it fondly for a moment. She would not take it with her when she left for college; nor would she take the photograph of her parents smiling on the last day of their honeymoon. For an instant she felt a twinge of disloyalty. Her father had died before she and Agnes moved into Grandmother's house on Elm Street. One day he was there and the next he wasn't. It wasn't as though she missed having a father, not exactly, but in some ways she did think of herself as deprived. It made her different from the other girls, whose fathers sat on Sunday afternoons reading the newspaper and took them out for a driving lesson in the family automobile. She wouldn't want Agnes to know she'd left the music box or photograph behind. If worse came to worse, she could pack them at the bottom of a trunk in the attic and leave them there. Billie felt better immediately. She was a good child. A dutiful daughter. And she was still a virgin, which was more than some of the girls at school could say. Already there were whispers that Cissy had given her all to an army corporal.

Billie ran a brush through her thick blond hair, pinned it back with two heart-shaped barrettes, then closed the door on her pink-and-white bedroom. "Mother, I'm leaving now," she called to Agnes from the foot of the stairs, then she waited.

Some people could walk into a room; others could make an entrance. Agnes Ames just appeared. One minute she wasn't there and the next she was. It always amazed Billie.

She managed to keep her voice just a notch above conversational—Agnes said shouting was unladylike—as she went through the weekly litany for Agnes's benefit. "We may stop for a cherry phosphate after the show. If we do, I'll be home by five. If we decide to go for hamburgers, I'll be home by five-thirty. The boys like to see the newsreel a second time. So it may be six at the very latest. I have my purse and enough change to pay for myself and enough for a phone call. I'm wearing my best underwear and I only put cologne on my wrists, not behind my ears. I polished my shoes and buffed the white part."

Billie smiled at her mother and stood still for her silent inspection. Agnes's dark brown gaze snapped and clicked as it monitored her daughter. From long experience Billie recognized the invisible signal that said she had passed standards. "What are you going to do this afternoon, Mother?"

"Today is Saturday. I have to clean the two front bedrooms. Our roomers are out, so this is the best time. Miss Carpenter is working overtime at the Navy Yard today. She certainly must make a princely wage." This might be the time to think about raising the room rent a little, Agnes thought, maybe a dollar or so a week. Or perhaps she could offer breakfast and charge three dollars more. . . . God, how she hated this penny-pinching! "Miss Addison is away for the weekend. Did she pay you for hemming her skirt, Billie?"

"Yes, Mother. And there's another for me to do this week."

"Good. We don't want to be taken advantage of, do we? I still haven't resigned myself to opening my home to total strangers. Of course, what else could I do? I'm as patriotic as the next person and, considering the housing shortage in Philadelphia and having the space, I couldn't very well not, could I?"

"They're both nice ladies," Billie said. "They're quiet and they don't mess up the bathroom." She hoped Agnes wasn't having second thoughts about taking in roomers, because now there always seemed to be a little extra money.

Agnes Ames was tall and thin, stylishly so. Her expertise with the needle proved that clothing need not be padded or flounced to make a garment appear custom tailored. Today she wore a beige-and-brown street dress with a wide chocolate sash. Adorning her long aristocratic neck were her grandmother's pearls. *Severe* was a word that came to mind when one thought of Agnes Ames. Just as the pearls were always around her neck, so there was the calculating expression in her eyes. She had good clear skin, thanks to Pond's Cold Cream and Dream Puff Powder. They were the only cosmetics she allowed to touch her face, aside from lipstick. Agnes never wore rouge: that was for wantons and streetwalkers. She preferred to pinch her cheeks. She did her own hair, out of necessity and frugality, and had become expert at using Nestle's thick green wave set and the metal clamps that guaranteed a tight crimp. Small, imitation pearl clip-on earrings completed the outward appearance of Agnes Ames.

She poked her long thin arms through the holes of a pinafore-style apron, which she wore to save her dress. "Yes, they are quiet and neat, aren't they? However, that was not happenstance, Billie—I was quite careful in choosing them and it always pays to have a clear-cut understanding from the beginning." Switching to Billie's plans for the afternoon, Agnes asked, "Are all of you going to the matinee?"

Billie took her cue. "Carl, Joey, Chester, and Tim. Bernice, Barbara, Dotty, and myself. That's all."

Agnes rolled the names over on her tongue. Hardly old Philadelphia mainline society, but they were acceptable. No old money there, but a lot of new money, most of it profits of war. New money could be offensive, almost threatening, because it had to be earned. Old money was comforting, a state of being.

"Enjoy the movie, Billie. I'll hold dinner. Something light. Perhaps some of that new lettuce from our Victory garden. There are still four eggs left on our rations." Agnes's lip curled when she mentioned the Victory garden and food rationing. Billie suspected that the careful tending of the garden out back was less an effort of patriotism than an outward sign of Agnes's driven desire to be like everyone else, only better.

"It sounds fine, Mother. Don't work too hard. Perhaps I should stay home and give you a hand."

"Nonsense. You go out with your friends. I'll be done in no time. If it weren't for this ridiculous war, decent people would still have cleaning help. It seems anyone who's able to give a full day's work has gone on to greener pastures at the Navy Yard or in factories. Help is so difficult to find."

After Billie had left, Agnes looked about the small living room. It was neat, tidy and gleaming. Agnes liked soap and water. With her daughter out of the house this might be a good time to move Billie's things downstairs to the study. There was no sense letting an extra room go to waste, and they certainly could use the money it would bring. By Tuesday the room could be rented. She should have done it long before this. It never occurred to her that Billie might object. Billie never objected. She was such a good child. The study had a window seat where Billie could sit and read for hours. No one could ever point a finger at Agnes and say she wasn't doing her duty for the war effort. It wasn't her fault she didn't have a son to give for her country. Renting out her spare rooms and having a Victory garden were her contributions.

Agnes wrapped a bandanna around her head to protect her wave and went about getting her cleaning products in order. Oxydol, Old Dutch Cleanser, and a supply of rags. A feather duster under one arm, the mop in the other, she climbed the stairs. It was such an awful way to spend a Saturday afternoon. She should be taking a leisurely tea at someone's house and talking about what was on everyone's minds, the war. She'd love to be a hostess at a formal tea and serve thin cucumber sandwiches. Instead, she was cleaning rented bedrooms and a community bathroom. She didn't want this kind of life for Billie; she didn't want it for herself, either.

Billie walked alongside Tim Kelly. There was something different about the sandy-haired Tim today. His tall thin body looked ready to explode. Whatever it was, the other boys were in on it, too.

"If you walk any faster, you'll meet yourself coming," Billie teased.

"You always say that, Billie." Tim laughed. "You just take short little steps. How come you aren't wearing your penny loafers?"

"Because I polished these and I wanted to show them off."

Tim laughed again. "I like girls who wear silk stockings and high heels," he teased.

"You can't get silk stockings anymore because they need

every bit of it to make parachutes," Billie countered. "The best you can get is nylon, but they cost a fortune."

"Cissy always seems to have enough money for them, and don't they look great on her!" Tim started smacking one fist into the palm of the other. He didn't seem to notice that at the mention of the notorious Cissy he had gained everyone's attention. "You aren't going to believe what I did yesterday. You just won't believe it!"

The girls stopped in their tracks while the boys laughed. "If it's something dirty, Tim Kelly, we don't want to hear it," one girl said excitedly.

"Yes we do." Another giggled.

"No we don't!" Billie said firmly.

"Well, you're gonna hear it anyway. I signed up. I went and did it. I didn't even tell my parents yet," Tim said proudly.

"Oh, no," Billie whispered. Suddenly she wished they could all be little kids again, roller-skating down Elm Street, setting up lemonade stands. Tim was the first of their bunch to enlist and it seemed an omen of things to come, judging by the awe on the other boys' faces.

"I leave a couple of weeks after graduation. I'll be eighteen by then," Tim said quietly. "I want to get into it. We all do, don't we, fellas? It's just a matter of time now. We'll write you girls, and you've got to promise to write back. We've decided we want to pay back the Japs for what they did to Pearl Harbor."

"What about college?" Billie asked inanely, still stunned by the news, yet feeling very grown-up now and already mourning carefree childhood.

"Is that all you have to say? Jesus H. Christ! I'm talking about war! About serving my country! I'm going off to fight for the American way of life and for girls like you, Billie! If those Japs can do what they did to Pearl, they could just march across this country and kill us in our beds. Everybody knows how sneaky they are!"

"I don't feel like going to the movies now," Dotty said, sitting down on the low stone wall that surrounded the Cummingses' front yard. The thought of yellow-faced men with bloody fangs marching across the U. S. of A. made her gulp.

"Hey, Dotty, what's the matter?" Carl challenged. "You scared of those Japs? What would you do if they said they'd kill me if you didn't sleep with them? What would you do then, huh?" Carl's eyes glimmered, waiting for his steady girl-friend's answer. Dotty recognized the old no-win predicament. It was a question that usually arose at Brummers Ice Cream Parlor while they were sipping rainbow cokes. If she said she would never sleep with a Jap, Carl would say she didn't care enough about him to spare his life. If she said she'd do *anything* to save him, he'd sneer and question her morals. Either way, a girl couldn't win. The recognition of the dilemma on her face softened Carl. "Don't worry, Dotty, I wouldn't let a 'monkey man' lay a finger on you. I'd kill myself first." Tenderly, he placed a hand on Dotty's shoulder.

"Let's go downtown to the Navy Yard instead," Tim suggested. "We can hang around outside and watch the ships in the harbor." The girls' eyes lit up. It was certainly better than trying to figure out what had gotten into the boys. Once they were there, the boys would meander around acting like big shots and talking about the ships, and the girls could watch the uniforms.

The boys led the way while the girls hung back, huddling as they walked. "Does anyone have any rouge or lipstick?"

"I have some Tangee. It's not very good, pink coral, or something. It was all I could sneak off my sister's dresser."

"It's good enough," Dotty encouraged. "We'll just use lots of it. Just think, we might meet some of those handsome sailors and maybe Carl won't think I'm such a kid if he sees some real men interested in me." She dabbed furiously at her cheeks and lips, watching her reflection in the window of a parked car.

One by one, the girls took turns, to the boys' whistling approval. Then they paired off and walked casually, the boys with their arms flung around their girls' shoulders. Billie felt strange walking beside Tim this way; part of her world was slipping away. The first step in becoming an adult and it had to be learning to say good-bye. Of their little group, the gang, four of her friends from as far back as she could remember were leaving to fight a war. Her mouth was dry and she licked her lips. The waxy lipstick felt thick and greasy. She'd never used so much rouge before. What would Mother say? The problem was where she was going to wash it off? If they'd gone to the movies as they'd intended, she could have washed it off in the ladies' room.

"Do you think the MPs will chase us away?" Billie questioned.

"Not when I tell them Tim already enlisted and the rest of us go down Monday morning," Carl said with more bravado than he felt.

The sight of the Philadelphia Navy Yard frightened Billie. This wasn't a Movietone newsreel; this was the real thing. Battleships, destroyers, cruisers, all with their camouflaged green-and-brown superstructures reaching for the sky. Even from this distance and seen through the chainlink fence, they seemed enormous and ominous. The boys pointed out the classification of each ship, but it all remained a mystery to Billie, who couldn't tell a battleship from a cruiser. Only the aircraft carrier, with its long flat deck, was easily distinguishable from the rest. How could a plane take off from that dock? Worse yet, how did it land? She'd seen the newsreels and marveled at the skill of the pilots. Once she'd heard that from the air the carrier's deck looked like a tombstone. The thought gave her chills.

"How do you like them?" a masculine voice drawled at Billie's elbow. She turned and stared up into incredible, summer-blue eyes.

"They're frightening, but beautiful," Billie said honestly. Handsome. Tall. Beautiful. Simply beautiful. The man, not the ship.

"I kind of like them myself. Especially the carrier. But my favorite is the *Enterprise*. I trained on her. Moss Coleman," he introduced himself. "Lieutenant, junior grade. And you're . . . ?"

"Billie. Billie Ames. Actually it's Willa, but no one calls me that, not even my mother." Now why had she said that? How gauche and immature she must seem to him with her round circles of rouge. She could just kick herself for putting it on. He must be at least twenty-five. Too old for her. Too old for what? All he was doing was talking to her. His brilliant eyes seemed amused and she realized how unsophisticated she must seem to him. His dark hair was almost black against the stark white of his naval officer's uniform. He was as handsome as sin, as Grandmother used to say. His deep tan so early in the year made Billie wonder where he'd been before coming to Philadelphia.

The same amusement was in his voice when he spoke again. "Billie it is. Willa sounds like an old maiden aunt. Do you live here in Philly?"

Billie nodded. "All my life. We live on . . . we live not far from here," she answered, suddenly shy.

Moss stood back for a better look at the girl. She was young, too young. Younger than the girls who hung out at the USO. Soft ash-blond hair framed her face and was held back from her temples by two barrettes. Bright, intelligent hazel eyes were fringed by smoky lashes and naturally arched brows. Her pretty face was smooth-skinned, color marking the high cheekbones. A delicately formed mouth, beneath the lipstick, was generous and yielding, vulnerable with youth. She was a sweet thing, keeping her eyes lowered, her voice soft and shy. His sense of chivalry rose to the surface. If some of his buddies spotted her, she wouldn't have a prayer. They were animals, pure and simple, and the fact that she'd be seen talking to Moss Coleman, Reaper of Virgins, would make her fair game. He'd be willing to bet her mother didn't know she was here or that she wore rouge and lipstick. He grinned. She was innocent. He could see it in her face. Nice bones; good figure. Old Seth would look at that first. Carry on the Coleman line, good breeding, all the shit that went with settling down and marrying the right girl. A closer look made him think she probably didn't know where babies came from, something he could change within two days, three at the most.

His friends constantly kidded Moss about his lady-killer charm and kept track of his score. The latest count since he'd hit Philly was eleven. But these were dangerous times and a man had to take what he could when he could. They offered, he accepted. It was that simple. This little girl standing beside him wouldn't offer. She was what the guys called a good girl. Though some claimed all good girls had wet bloomers.

"So, you live around here. Do you come here often to look around?"

"No. I've only been here once before, on a class trip. I came down with some of my friends. They're around here somewhere. One of the boys enlisted and the others are going down to enlist on Monday. We're supposed to be at the movies," she blurted, looking around for her friends with a worried expression, as though needing to be saved from this stranger in his immaculate uniform.

For the first time in his life Moss found himself uncertain. She was looking at him in a way that made him feel he was being inspected and falling short. His appearance flashed before him. He was perfect: shoes shined, belt buckle polished, all the brass in shining order. Every hair in place, Ipana smile.

Suntan just the right shade. Creases so sharp they could slice bread. It must be his imagination, this dissatisfaction he felt from her.

Moss knew he should leave. There was nothing for him here. "Would you like to see the carrier up a little closer?" he heard himself asking. "I can get you through the gate."

Billie frowned. She remembered her mother's warning of strangers. "Yes, thank you, I would."

Moss cupped her elbow and took her around to the guard at the gate, who offered him a smart salute. He showed his identification and waited while Billie signed in. He watched while she registered her address, 479 Elm Street, and smiled. I have *one* of your secrets, little girl, he thought with satisfaction.

The yard was peopled with sailors and busy work crews, their young faces either wreathed with smiles or studies of concentration. Moss was quick to see the admiring glances that came Billie's way and his hand tightened on her elbow possessively. Battleships and destroyers bound for Europe huddled around the dock. Their decks, dotted with white T-shirts and blue denims, were being scraped and primed, painted and polished, before they took their cargos of men and machines out to sea.

"This is about as far as I can take you. These are great ships, but I'll always think of the flight deck of the USS *Enterprise* as home. There's nothing like the feeling of landing gear touching that deck or of being hoisted backward by the landing hook."

Billie's eyes grew round with admiration. "You're a flyer? You really fly one of those planes and land on that little deck?"

"It's really not that little, Billie." He found he liked saying her name. "I've been flying since I was fourteen on our ranch in Texas and there's more space on a carrier deck than on the old dirt road back home."

There was such naked admiration in Billie's eyes, Moss felt himself blush at his own braggadocio. "I've got to admit to overshooting the landing deck a couple of times, but I've never ditched. That means going over the side, plane and all. Some guys are really good. There's a fella in my barracks who has never made a mistake. Not one."

"That's amazing," Billie said in a hushed whisper. "How long have you been in Philly?"

"A month. I came in from San Diego. That's why the suntan."

There was something bitter about his expression. "That's where I should be now, getting ready to push off for the Pacific."

"Why aren't you?"

"I've been assigned to Admiral McCarter, as his aide. I suppose lots of guys would give their eyeteeth for this duty, but I'd rather be flying." She watched as he lifted his head and tracked a pigeon headed for the superstructure, as though he wished he, too, could just spread wings and fly. Billie was quiet for a long moment, aware of his sadness. It made her almost hurt for him. She reached out to lay her hand on the sleeve of his white tunic.

Moss dropped his gaze to her, seeing her smile and the compassion in her hazel eyes. "My father's an influential man," he told her, something he'd never confided to another soul. "I'm the only son and Pap doesn't cotton to the idea of me flying. He arranged this assignment with the Admiralty." It was there again, the bitterness.

"Couldn't you ask to be reassigned?"

"Yeah, I could, but I couldn't do it to Pap," Moss said quietly. "He hangs a lot on me, wanting me to carry on the family and the business. I could be madder'n hell, but I'm not. He loves me and he's afraid of losing me."

"Texas, you said?" That explained the slight drawl.

"Texas. Austin."

"Then you're a cowboy!"

Moss laughed, a nice easy sound, as though laughing were second nature to him. She liked the way his eyes crinkled at the corners and just the barest dimple showed in his firm, chiseled jaw. "Hardly. Texans don't ride horses to get anywhere. They fly. Seems like most of the people I know have their own planes. Or else they rent them. Just like folks here in Philly hire taxicabs."

Billie couldn't imagine flying anywhere, much less owning her own plane. "All Texans own a plane?" she asked naively.

"Well, not all, but the ones I know do. Say, you've never been up, have you? You've never flown?"

Billie shook her head, following his gaze once again to the birds perched on the carrier. "Never. And I don't suppose I ever will. What's it like?"

Moss took her hand, taking her over to a stack of crates and sitting beside her. "Billie, honey, you're going to be sorry you asked that question." For the next hour Lieutenant (j.g.) Moss Coleman described to Billie the exhilaration he felt when his wheels left the ground. He told her about flying a wrecked old crop duster around the ranch and the way his father had tanned his hide when he'd found out about it. Moss had Billie laughing, exclaiming, shuddering. He sparked her imagination and made her wish that just once she could fly.

"There's a little airport around here where they have planes for hire. I'd like to take you up, Billie, just so you'll know I'm not crazy and everything I've told you is true."

"I'd like that," she answered quickly, cheeks flushed with the anticipated excitement, eyes bright and eager. "Oh, but I don't think my mother would like that— Mother! What time is it?"

Moss glanced at his watch. "Five-thirty."

"Omigosh! I've got to get going." For the first time in hours Billie remembered her friends. They must think she'd gotten lost or gone home by herself. They wouldn't still be hanging around the yard. "It was nice of you to show me around, Lieutenant. I know you must be busy and I've got to start for home. My mother will worry if I'm not home by six." She felt so silly, telling this man that she had to be home by six o'clock. It was so babyish. She felt humiliated by the restrictions, especially since he'd spent the afternoon talking to her as though she were his own age and not an empty-headed schoolgirl.

"Do you see your friends anywhere? You don't suppose they left without you, do you?" he asked, concerned.

"It doesn't matter. I know my way home. Thank you again." Billie began to walk away. Moss was stunned. Girls never walked away from him, not at five-thirty in the afternoon. He was about to speak when Billie turned. "Lieutenant, since you're so far from Texas and your family, perhaps you'd like to come to dinner on Sunday." She almost gasped with astonishment at her invitation. What in the world had made her ask him to dinner? She could already hear Agnes's objections. Still, lots of families invited servicemen for a home-cooked meal. Meal. Food. Oh, God! Agnes was going to complain about the food ration coupons. Still, she'd made the offer and she had to follow up on it. "Four seventy-nine Elm Street. Gray-and-white house."

"Wait a second, Billie. Two miles is a long walk and you'll never make it home in time. Let me see if I can borrow a car and I'll drive you. By the way, thanks for the invitation. Tomorrow's Sunday, you know." He grinned as though he guessed her second thoughts.

Billie flushed under the dazzling smile. "It really isn't necessary. I've still got the money for the movies and I can take a cab if I have to, really."

"I won't hear of it. If I hadn't pulled your ear about flying, you wouldn't be stranded. Please, let me help." He was so sincere, Billie just nodded.

While Billie waited, she contemplated her predicament. She didn't want Agnes to know that she'd spent Saturday afternoon at the Navy Yard, much less that she'd been talking to a military man and had lost her friends. What if someone called or stopped by the house to ask about her? What if Moss came to dinner? He'd surely tell Agnes how he'd met Billie.

Moss returned dangling the keys to a 1938 Nash parked near the guardhouse. Billie felt so grown-up when Moss held the door open for her. Agnes was going to have a fit. Nice girls didn't get into cars with strange boys. Or men. Moss Coleman, Lieutenant (j.g.), was no boy. Agnes wouldn't miss that fact. In spite of herself, Billie was excited and flattered.

"How long will you be in Philly?" Billie asked when Moss had maneuvered through the traffic and swung out onto the main road.

"Probably through the summer. At least, that's the way it looks right now. Or until I can get myself assigned to where the action is. Being an errand boy for a hotshot admiral isn't my idea of doing my part for the war effort. I'm a pilot, Billie, and a damn good one. That's what I want to do."

Billie nodded. She knew all there was to know about a protective parent. Moss interpreted her expression correctly. "You too, huh?"

"It's because I'm an only child. My father died when I was little. I suppose it's natural for a parent to be protective. They want what's best for us." To Moss it sounded like a recital of what her mother must have said hundreds of times. Just the way Seth Coleman had preached to him.

"I've got a sister, but I'm the only son. Pap is up there in years and he's afraid for me. But I can't let his fear rub off on me. Flying is what I do and what I do best. I don't plan to run around for some two-star admiral whose only idea of action is signing papers and drinking scotch. Scotch that I have to procure for him."

"What will you do?"

"It's not what I'll do, Billie; it's when I'll do it! Pap can get me assigned to fat man's duty, but he can't keep me here. I can speak up for myself and there's not a damn thing he can do about it. But I hate to hurt him. He's a great guy and I know how much I mean to him. It's just that sometimes I really feel the weight of that responsibility pressing down on me. Being the apple of ole Pap's eye isn't what it's cracked up to be." Moss could hardly believe he was telling her these things. He was used to keeping his personal life and his problems to himself.

"Turn here. It's two blocks down and then take the next right. Gray-and-white house. I'll say a prayer you get what you want."

Moss almost braked the car. Any other girl would have said she would keep her fingers crossed. This one was going to pray for him. Impulsively, he reached across the seat and took her hand. It felt small and fragile in his. He released it a moment later to shift gears and pull to a stop in front of the house. He glanced at his watch. "Five minutes to six," he announced proudly, as though getting her home on time had been a monumental task.

Billie wondered where her friends were. Were they worrying about her? "Would you like to come in and meet my mother? Oh, but you've probably got other things to do, and I do appreciate your taking the time to bring me home. I'm sorry I've been such a nuisance."

"You, sweet Billie, are anything but a nuisance." He smiled, realizing he'd meant what he said. But Jesus, he didn't want to go in and meet her mother. He loved his mother but other people's made him nervous, especially girls' mothers. Hell, he was here ... maybe she was afraid she was going to catch it and he could help matters. All in the line of duty. "I'd like to meet your mother," he lied.

Billie almost fainted. That wasn't what he was supposed to say. Didn't he know she was only trying to be polite? She didn't wait for him to come around to open the door for her. Instead, she leaped out, smoothing down the skirt of her jumper. Suddenly, the fringe along the hem seemed girlishly silly and trendy, and for the second time that day she wished she were wearing stockings and heels.

Agnes Ames's eyes narrowed when she heard the sound of a car door closing in front of the house. None of Billie's friends drove a car. She parted the lace curtains slightly and peered out. Billie and a navy man. An officer, considering the dress whites. What could have happened? She wouldn't panic. Billie was a responsible child. A serious, responsible child.

"Mother! I'm home. Come and meet someone."

Moss Coleman stood a good six inches taller than Agnes, yet he was immediately aware of her strength, as if she were his height or even taller. It was in the measuring, brown eyes and in the subtle squaring of the shoulders. . . . He'd seen the same signs of character in Seth. Pearls. Why did they always wear pearls? It seemed every girl's mother he'd ever met was adorned with them.

Billie broke the silence. "Mother, this is Moss Coleman. He was nice enough to bring me home so I wouldn't be late. Moss, this is my mother, Mrs. Ames." He waited to see if Mrs. Ames would offer her hand. She didn't.

Billie was beginning to feel desperate. Agnes was standing her ground, staring at Moss with suspicion. "I've invited Moss to dinner tomorrow. He's from Texas and it's been a long time since he's had a home-cooked meal. I knew you wouldn't object," Billie prompted hopefully.

"Dinner. Of course. We'd like to have you for dinner, Lieutenant," Agnes offered.

Moss wondered if Mrs. Ames meant she'd like to have him as a guest or for the main course! But hold on a minute, he'd never accepted the invitation. Somebody was being railroaded here and he thought he knew who. "I wouldn't want to impose, Mrs. Ames," he said in his best-bred Texan, just a shade short of humble. Before he could politely make excuses, Agnes forced something that passed for a smile.

"Fine. Shall we say around two? I want to thank you for bringing my daughter home. It was very considerate of you. She's very young and I worry when she's late." There it was, the gentle nudge, the reminder that he was suspected of being a troll who lived under a bridge and preyed on innocent young girls.

"It was my pleasure, ma'am," Moss drawled. "Billie, thank you for the invitation. I have to get the car back to the yard. Nice meeting you, ma'am."

He still hadn't said if he was coming to dinner and Billie felt wretched as she watched him walk out to the car, Agnes's words about her youth still smarting.

Outside in the car, Moss exhaled a long, gusty sigh. He didn't think he wanted to come to dinner. But Sundays were always so boring you could want to tear your hair out, and it had been nice talking with Billie. If he didn't have anything better to do, he'd show up around two o'clock. If something came up, he'd send a note.

Before Agnes could question her daughter, Billie rushed into a lengthy explanation. "I think it was very nice of him to bring me home, don't you, Mother?"

"Billie, you broke how many rules this afternoon?" Agnes said frigidly.

"Mother, please. Do we have to go into all of this? I'm home, safe and sound. Nothing happened. The lieutenant is charming. He didn't say he was coming to dinner and I'm certain he has other plans, so don't count on it. I'm sorry if I upset you."

Agnes sniffed. It was her usual reaction to Billie's apologies. Once, just once, Billie would have liked to hear that she was forgiven, or at least that her mother understood.

"I think I'll go up to my room and get ready for supper."

"I moved your room downstairs to the study. Mr. Campbell from next door and his nephew helped move down the furniture. I'm going to rent your room. We really have to do our bit, Billie. The housing situation is reaching crisis proportions."

Billie only knew that someone else was going to live in her room, the only place she'd been able to call her own since she was a little girl. "I wish you had told me, Mother. I don't mind the change, but I would have liked to pack my things myself. Did you go through everything? Even my pictures?" Billie felt violated.

"Everything. Go see for yourself. Now you'll have the window seat. You can sit there tomorrow and watch the road to see if your handsome lieutenant shows up for dinner." Agnes smiled.

Billie glanced at her mother. She'd just been bought. Agnes's seeming acceptance of having Moss for Sunday dinner was supposed to soothe the wound of having been moved lock, stock, and barrel out of her room. And she had to accept the terms of truce; otherwise, if Moss did come tomorrow, she could count on Agnes's sulky indifference, which could make Billie squirm as though she had fire ants in her bloomers.

It wasn't fair. It just wasn't fair. At least Agnes could have asked before renting out her bedroom from under her. Billie wandered into the study and looked at the window seat with its velvet cushion. It would be a delightful place to curl up with a book. She had a clear view of the drive and the street.

Perhaps it wasn't so bad after all.

Agnes remained in the hall at the bottom of the stairs, head cocked to one side as though she were listening to a distant noise. The sound she heard was her inner voice murmuring questions concerning Billie. Her perfectly nice and gifted daughter had returned to the house this evening and there was something different about her that had nothing to do with the lipstick or with the artificial blush applied to her cheeks.

{{{{{{{{{ CHAPTER TWO }}}}}}}}}

Agnes Ames bent down to baste the roasting chicken. As with almost everyone else in Philadelphia—and Agnes did aspire to being like everyone else, only better—after coming home from Sunday service the first order of the day was to dress the chicken and stick it in the oven. It was one thing to invite a guest to Sunday dinner and quite another to plan a meal that was acceptable yet not expensive.

The chicken was a delectable golden brown, the bread stuffing savory with herbs. Her practiced eye took in the bowl of garden salad and the fresh string beans, which, being out of season, had cost more than she cared to spend. Mashed potatoes and gravy would be more than enough when she'd added her homemade biscuits. The butter, dearer than dear since rationing, was first allowed to soften, then whipped with ice water to increase its volume, and chilled again. It was one of her little tricks and it worked quite well. Agnes Ames could not abide white, unpalatable oleo. She had prepared a deep-dish apple pie the night before and it would be mouth-watering. If there was one culinary talent she possessed, it was making pies. The secret was using rendered suet instead of shortening, which cost a fortune, for the crust. She did not like to think about the dent in her sugar supply for the sweet dessert.

The music coming from the living room had a mournful sound. That wasn't like Billie. Normally, she'd be playing light, popular tunes after her practicing was done. Once, Agnes had had dreams of her daughter becoming a concert pianist and she'd been told by experts that Billie had the talent. But after learning the prohibitive cost of schooling and lessons and recitals, Agnes had regretfully abandoned the idea and turned her ambitions for Billie along less flamboyant lines.

Agnes listened for a moment. Billie must have learned a new piece. Perhaps it wasn't mournful, just sad. Her thoughts immediately went to the young lieutenant. Moss Coleman frightened her. Or was it the way Billie looked at Moss Coleman? A Texan! No doubt he was a ranch hand—or did they call them cowpokes? And that atrocious drawl! Not for Billie. Definitely not for Billie. She'd been worrying all morning what she would do if the cowboy did show up for dinner and managed, despite her, to ask Billie for a date. Up to now, Billie had always listened to her, always behaved and followed her advice. Agnes's stomach fluttered.

If the lieutenant was still around through summer, what would that do to Billie's chances with Neal Fox? Neal Fox, whose father owned the bank. Neal Fox, who was more than acceptable with his studious habits, family money, and 4F classification. Martha Fox, a member of Agnes's garden club, had eagerly arranged a date for the two youngsters. Comparing the Fox boy with someone like Lieutenant Coleman . . . Agnes shuddered and almost cut her thumb as she peeled the potatoes. She hoped—no, prayed—that the lieutenant wouldn't come for dinner. He had thanked them for the invitation but never actually accepted. No manners. Ignorant cowhand. Agnes supposed this was the way cowboys did things. Neal was the kind of boy who would arrive exactly fifteen minutes early for dinner, carrying a bouquet of flowers for her and a box of candy for Billie. That was the way it should be done. The lieutenant would arrive, maybe, with his hat in his hand, eat three helpings of everything, hold the chicken in his fingers and lick them afterward. She'd been to the movies; she knew cowboys cooked over open fires and ate out of cans. But was the handsome young lieutenant actually one of those? There'd been something about him when he'd met her penetrating gaze. It was as though he'd been trying to figure *her* out. A Texan!

Today would be a good time to talk to Billie about Neal. After their guest left and they were doing the dishes. A nice mother-to-daughter talk. Billie seemed to like that Sunday bit of intimacy. Agnes personally found it especially boring. Her own life was uneventful and Billie's was so placid and predictable that it didn't leave much room for conversation. Usually they ended up discussing a book or the progress of the garden, or exchanging pieces of gossip.

Agnes glanced at the clock. It was one-forty-five. Fifteen minutes till their guest arrived. Billie stopped playing. She closed the piano. She was going into her room. Agnes knew her daughter was perched on the window seat, book in hand, staring out at the road. Waiting for a white uniform.

The telephone rang at three minutes of two. Billie almost broke her neck running out to the hall to pick up the receiver. "Hello," she breathed.

"Billie?"

"Yes." It was him. "Yes, yes, it's me. Moss?"

A low chuckle came over the wire. "I'm sorry, Billie, but I won't be able to come to dinner. The admiral wants to play golf this afternoon and can't find a partner. I'm the best he can come up with. Perhaps you'll invite me another time?"

Billie sucked in her breath. He wasn't coming. Somehow, she'd known he wouldn't. She wanted so badly to see him walk up to her front door. She couldn't remember ever wanting something so badly, unless it was the Christmas she'd wanted a two-wheeled bike. She hadn't gotten that, either. "Anytime," she said brightly, hiding her disappointment. "Our Sundays are open. You don't need an invitation." There. Short of begging, what else could she say?

"That's very kind of you. Please thank your mother. Listen, Billie, if you're ever at the Front Street USO on a Saturday night, I hope you'll save me a dance."

USO. Dance. Save him a dance. "I'll do that, Lieutenant. Thank you for calling," Billie said pleasantly. When she hung up the phone, she forced a smile to her lips. She knew Agnes was standing in the doorway and had probably heard every word. She had to turn and face her mother. Do it. Do it now before your face cracks with the strain.

"Oh, Mother—there you are. That was Lieutenant Coleman. He won't be able to make dinner. He has to play golf with the admiral. I told him he had an open invitation. Was that all right, Mother?"

Relief coursed through Agnes. Neal was still in the running. "Of course, dear. We must do our part, small as it may seem. I'm certain that one day, when he has nothing better to do, he'll drop by for a home-cooked meal."

Billie wanted to run to her room and cry. Cry when things got too bad. But it wouldn't be the same now. Now she was sleeping in the study because her room, a room that had been hers and hers alone, was to be rented! How she had loved it, the small windows under the eaves, the shelves holding all her books. Her music scores in neat stacks, the pictures she'd painted, and her bulging portfolio of designs that leaned against the wall. Now it was all a jumble in the study. A study wasn't a bedroom. She was sick with disappointment.

"Well, since there are just the two of us, we might as well eat now." Agnes turned and went back into the kitchen. "We'll eat in here; no sense going to all the trouble of messing up the dining room, is there?"

Billie followed after her mother, knowing how difficult it was going to be to swallow even one bite. She adjusted her features into a pleasant mask of indifference. It was going to be just another Sunday.

As Moss replaced the phone, his eyes went to the golf bag in the corner of Admiral McCarter's office. The admiral was entertaining a visiting three-star at the Officers Club. Moss's conscience pricked slightly as he made his way down the long battleship-gray hallway. He joined three of his friends who waited impatiently at the curb in the parking lot.

"New York City, here we come!" one of the j.g.'s shouted hoarsely. Moss grinned and climbed into the backseat of the Ford.

He didn't think about Billie Ames again until the next Sunday morning, when he awoke feeling achy and out of sorts. He brushed his teeth and swallowed three aspirin. When was he going to learn that Saturday-night hangovers hung on like leeches and were the ruination of a good Sunday? As long as he was going to be miserable, he might as well salve his conscience and go to dinner at Billie's house.

For a long moment he looked at the pay phone on the wall outside his quarters. Who was he kidding? Last night at the USO, he'd hung about the doorway watching for her. It was only after eleven o'clock, when nice girls like Billie would already be home, that he'd gone out to the local bar to tie one on. Now, he quickly dropped his nickel into the slot before he could talk sense to himself.

Billie picked up the phone on the first ring. She tilted her hat slightly to the side so she could comfortably place the receiver against her ear. She expected to hear her girlfriend's voice.

"Billie?"

When she heard his low, husky drawl, she felt her knees buckle. Her knuckles whitened on the prayer book in her hand. He'd called. Her eyes lifted upward, acknowledging the power of prayer.

Cool and calm. "Lieutenant, how are you? Did you have a nice golf game last Sunday with the admiral?" she asked for want of anything better and needing a moment to compose herself. Lordy, why couldn't she be more sophisticated?

"Golf? Oh, that golf game. Par." His conscience pricked again and he quickly squelched it. His head was killing him and he shouldn't be doing this; he didn't even know why he was doing it. She was a nice girl, a nice young girl, and there was nothing there for him. He remembered how he'd looked for her the night before. "How are you, Billie? Am I calling too early?" He massaged his temples, wondering what time it was.

The low, throaty laugh felt good in his ear. "No, of course not. I've been up for hours. As a matter of fact I was just on my way to church. Another five minutes and you'd have missed me." She waited expectantly.

"Church?" Where people go to pray. Did she pray for him as she'd promised? "Are you Catholic?"

"Yes, I am."

"I'm Catholic also. So's my mother. There aren't very many of us in Texas. Not a very good one, I'm afraid. I don't attend mass regularly." Hell, what was he, really? More agnostic than anything else, he supposed. The day his mother had told him he was old enough to attend services on his own he'd stopped going. Instead of attending the ten o'clock service as his sister Amelia did, he'd hung around the airfield. Seth never went to church.

Billie was unsure of what comment she could make to another of his confessions. Out of the corner of her eye she could see Agnes standing by the front door, waiting impatiently. Did Agnes know who was on the other end of the phone?

Moss saved her from making a reply. "I'd like to come to dinner today, if the invitation is still open."

Moss heard the slight gasp over the wire. "Of course. Dinner is at two. I'll look forward to seeing you again, Lieutenant."

"Do you think you could call me Moss, instead of lieutenant?"

"Of course . . . Moss. I'll see you this afternoon."

"Don't forget you promised to pray for me," he joked.

"I won't."

She dropped the receiver and turned to face Agnes. "Mother, do you know who that was? Lieutenant Coleman is coming to dinner. Isn't that nice?" She adjusted her hat in the front hall mirror, afraid to face her mother's scowl.

"We'll have to hurry dinner through if you're going to visit your girlfriend this afternoon." Agnes made a supreme effort to keep her tone light and conversational. Inside, she was having difficulty resigning herself to the threat of the handsome lieutenant. She'd thought that matter closed.

Billie turned. "There. How do I look?"

Agnes detected a change in her daughter. In the passing of an instant she seemed to have bloomed. She was so pretty, this daughter of hers. In a few years she'd be a raving beauty. Billie had her bones, her carriage. Good, clear skin with soft melting eyes that changed from green to brown to gray. Hazel eyes. Much too good for a Texas cowpoke. Another week or so and Neal Fox would be home from college.

As they walked the four blocks to St. Elias they were regaled with the chiming of the carillon. Agnes was worried. Perhaps a prayer would help. It seemed like such a long time since she'd believed in prayer. She only attended church because it was expected of her; it was the right thing to do and most of the right people were there. Agnes was a convert to Catholicism. That jackass she'd married to spite her parents had insisted she convert and raise the children in his religion. She'd done her duty, but as far as she was concerned religion was just a lot of hokus-pokus. She never held with going to confession and abstaining from meat on Fridays, but, good mother that she was, she'd seen to it that Billie had made her first communion and been confirmed when she was eleven. Once a month she sent her off to confession. How bored that priest must have been listening to Billie's little sins! Communion on every Sunday was a must. For Billie. Billie was a good girl and would stay a good girl. And it wasn't the power of prayer that would do it. That was Agnes's job!

Billie dreamed her way through mass and her mother had to nudge her gently when it was time to go to the altar rail for communion. Her prom was just weeks away. Was it possible to invite someone like Moss Coleman to be her escort? Would he think a senior dance silly and young? She was counting on too much, looking too far ahead. Coming to dinner was one thing; what she wanted and hoped for was another. She had to be patient. She would pray for that, for patience. Still, she'd be the envy of every girl there if she showed up with a tall handsome navy man. A lieutenant, a fly-boy. The girls would drop dead.

In just a few hours she'd see him again. Prickly fingers of excitement ran up and down her arms. She bowed her head and prayed Moss Coleman would get what he wanted, everything he wanted.

Billie sat on the window seat pretending to read, watching for Moss. She'd brushed her teeth twice and kept glancing in the mirror to be sure the breeze hadn't disturbed her hair. It was smooth and sleek, a shining cap of ash blond, curved under in a pageboy. She wished it would fall over one eye like Veronica Lake's, but its own natural tendency to curl forced her to tame it back with a barrette. When the car slid to a stop at the curb, Billie felt positively light-headed. She forced herself to take two or three deep breaths as she did before playing in a piano recital. She allowed the bell to ring before she opened the door and found herself held in the gaze of those smiling summer-blue eyes. She smiled the dazzling smile Moss remembered and his head felt better already.

Agnes walked into the front room and was stunned to see Moss extending a huge bouquet of flowers toward her. "For your table, Mrs. Ames. Billie, the chocolates are for you." This was all wrong. It was Neal Fox who was supposed to bring the candy and flowers. For a moment, Agnes was unnerved. But only for a moment. She smiled her smile that never reached her eyes.

He grinned. He knew she didn't want him here and it didn't make any difference to him. He turned to Billie. "If dinner isn't ready, why don't you show me your garden? I could see from the front that your property goes pretty far back."

"I'd like that. Mother, you don't need me in the kitchen, do you?"

Moss's eyes went to Agnes again. He waited, almost daring her.

"No, you two young people go along. I can manage. I'll serve in twenty minutes." Agnes hadn't failed to notice the time. Moss had arrived fifteen minutes early. Neal Fox was the one who was supposed to have such impeccable manners. She felt confused and irritable as she went back to the kitchen. Stooping to reach under the sink, she rummaged for a suitable vase. The flowers stopped just short of being ostentatious. They must have cost him a fortune. The candy, too. The most expensive there was. And it wasn't a measly little one-pound box. No, it was a full five pounds and tied with a big red bow. How much did junior lieutenants make a month? Not enough to pay for such costly gifts, she was certain. Agnes sniffed. She thought she smelled money. Was it possible that this drawling, brash young man with the perceptive eyes could be something other than a cowhand? She'd quiz him during dinner. Agnes was good at quizzing. Most of the time people weren't aware of just how much they were telling her. She'd somehow underestimated this handsome flyer and she wouldn't make that mistake again.

As she stirred the gravy she watched Billie and Moss through the kitchen window. They did make a handsome couple. What were they talking about? The weather? Hardly. Him? More than likely. Billie was a good listener.

She grimaced. The gravy was lumpy; now she was going to have to strain it.

Dinner was a puzzling affair to Billie. Conversation was rapid and nonstop between her mother and Moss. She'd been worried that Agnes would be frigidly aloof and make the strain of conversation unbearable. Instead, her mother appeared animated and interested. Moss answered Agnes's questions with an exaggerated drawl, all the while wearing a most disconcertingly amused expression. He never spoke that way, Billie thought, when he was talking to her.

"I understand Austin is quite large," Agnes was saying. "Billie and I have never been further south than Virginia. Have you lived there long?"

"All my life," Moss drawled. "So have my folks. This is sure mighty good chicken, ma'am."

So much for his hearty cowhand appetite, Agnes thought. He'd done little more than pick at his food. But she had noticed that he had no difficulty selecting the proper fork and, to her relief, he hadn't tucked his napkin under his chin. Agnes tried again. "I assume your parents still live there?"

"Yes, ma'am. My mother always served her green beans this way, with bits of bacon and onion." His gaze went to

Agnes's narrowing eyes. He smiled, enjoying his success at baiting her. He knew she was fishing for information and he was being polite but evasive.

"Billie, dear, don't you like the stuffing? You aren't eating. Is anything wrong, don't you feel well?"

"I'm fine, Mother." Quickly, before Agnes could dominate the conversation, Billie asked a question of her own. "Tell us about Admiral McCarter. What's it like to work for him?"

Moss laughed. "Boring. All admirals are boring. They sit and shuffle papers when they aren't out on the golf course or having dinner at the Officers' Club. They moan and groan and complain about how lonely it is at the top."

"What is it you'd rather be doing, Lieutenant?" Agnes interjected.

The drawl was more pronounced when he spoke to Agnes. "Well, ma'am, I joined up to fly. And that's what I intend to do, if there's such a thing as having prayers answered." His eyes flicked to Billie and she felt warmed by his smile and by the confidence between them.

"How do your parents feel about your flying? I'd think your mother in particular would be concerned. Of course, I've never had a son, but I'd think your father would be very proud of you. Is he a flyer, too?"

"No, ma'am. Pap's retired, I suppose you could say." He loved the look of frustration on Agnes's face. "My mother was concerned at the beginning, but she said whatever makes me happy makes her happy. She has my sister, Amelia, to fuss over."

He was being too respectful to be considered a smart aleck. Yet he was evading her questions. "I've heard Texans live on ranches. Do you?"

"Live on a ranch?" Moss repeated. "We have a spread. We call it a spread in Texas." He turned to Billie and asked her if she'd like to go to the movies after dinner.

"Yes, I would." Mother, you don't mind, do you?" Billie's tone and the look in her eyes told Agnes she didn't care if her mother minded or not. She was going. It was shocking. Things were going on here. Things she couldn't put a name to and wasn't sure she liked. She'd had such grand plans for Neal Fox and Billie, and she knew now that the girl would never look at the banker's son without comparing him with this exceedingly handsome, if somewhat dull, young lieutenant. She seethed inwardly.

"No, I don't mind." She'd had enough. "Why don't you two leave just after dessert. I'll do the dishes. You can do them next Sunday, Billie."

This Sunday dessert was cherry pie and it was delicious. Both Billie and Moss gulped it down. Agnes served Moss coffee and gave her daughter a glass of milk. Billie was well aware this was her mother's silent reminder that she was a child and Moss was a man; she left the milk untouched.

"The next feature is at four o'clock, Moss. We'd better hurry. I don't like to walk in during the picture, do you?" Not waiting for a reply, Billie walked ahead to the parlor for her purse.

"Mrs. Ames, it was a delicious dinner. It was nice to eat home-cooked for a change. Thank you for having me, and I'll be sure to tell my mother that you use the same string bean recipe."

There was nothing to do except be agreeable. She'd been had. This brash young man had outmaneuvered her. "Thank you for the flowers, Lieutenant. That was very kind of you. We'll have to wait for summer, I suppose, to have flowers from our own garden. Spring flowers are so fragile, wilting and dying almost immediately after they're picked." She was talking too much and he was letting her. When he joined Billie in the front hall, Agnes stared at them for a long moment. He reminded her of a hawk circling its prey and she almost objected when he reached for Billie's hand. She wanted to stop Billie before it was too late. Too late for what? Too late for Neal Fox, for God's sake!

Moss turned, his face half in shadow. "Good-bye, Mrs. Ames. I'll have Billie home before dark." Agnes didn't need to see his eyes; she knew what would be there. Satisfaction. A battle well won.

He escorted Billie down the aisle, careful not to spill the two containers of popcorn. He didn't like two people fishing out of the same box. What was his was his.

Billie sat beside Moss: their shoulders touched. He liked this sweet young girl. She reminded him of his sister in so many ways. Even Seth would approve of Billie. There was something gentle about her, almost old-world. He was beginning to suspect that she was deeper and more complex than she appeared on the surface. She was so young and innocent, without the pseudosophistication that he'd become accustomed to in girls. How had that buzzard back in the house on Elm Street come by a daughter like this? By God, Agnes Ames had to have been cut from the same bolt of cloth as Pap. Traits that he admired in his father were almost unpalatable in a woman. Still, Moss realized the deep vein of loyalty that ran through people like Seth Coleman and Agnes Ames. Loyalty and strength and intelligence. He wouldn't fault her for that.

They sat quietly together watching the newsreel and the cartoon before the main feature. Betty Grable was showing her legs and it wasn't even ten minutes into the movie. Moss reached out and took Billie's hand. For some reason, couples always held hands in the movies. Is that how he was thinking of himself and Billie? As a couple? Billie's hands were soft, just like the rest of her. He knew she was smiling in the darkness. He smiled, too. She was a nice kid. A very nice kid. He wondered when she would be eighteen. Pretty, too. Billie had the kind of beauty that came from within, arresting the beholder. He supposed she was what they called "the girl next door," and he'd heard some guys say that was what the war was about. Moss knew it wasn't. Power, that was the reason for the war. Something people like himself and Pap and Agnes Ames understood.

Another ten minutes into the movie and he leaned over to whisper, "Billie, this is a terrible movie and we both know how it's going to turn out. Why don't we leave and go some place we can talk. I'd like to get to know you better."

"All right," Billie agreed, frowning slightly. She'd told Agnes they'd be at the movies. It seemed whenever she was with Moss she broke another rule.

"Are you always so agreeable?" There was an edge to his voice, as though he were annoyed.

"Only when it's something I want to agree to."

"I've got a blanket in the car. What say we go to the park and sit by the lake?"

Billie's pulses sped. If Agnes ever got wind of this, she'd be very disapproving. Before she could reconsider, she stood up and waited for Moss to lead her up the aisle and out into the sunshine.

It was a beautiful day. If Billie had ordered it from Sears Roebuck, she couldn't have done better. Marshmallow clouds drifted across an incredibly blue sky. The grass never seemed greener, the sun never warmer. The park lake rippled and glistened. It was perfect.

The minutes and hours passed with hardly a notice. Together they sat or reclined on the blanket, talking and talking and talking. She found herself telling Moss things she'd never told anyone. Her desire to go to design and textile school instead of becoming an English or history teacher. How she felt being without a father and how she'd learned to cope with Agnes's protectiveness. When she told him of her aptitude as a pianist, it was a revelation and not a boast.

Moss sprawled out on the blanket, his dark shining head resting in Billie's lap. He reached up and touched a finger to her lips. "No lipstick today," he said, looking up at her. The fringe of dark lashes hemming his eyes cast shadows into the blue.

"Not on Sunday." Billie laughed. "Do you mind?"

"Not on Sunday." He grinned. "I should be taking you home now. I told your mother I'd have you home by dark. By the time we get there it'll be past dark."

"I don't want to go home," Billie told him.

"I don't either."

"Why haven't you kissed me?" she blurted.

Moss laughed. "Did you want me to? Would you like it if I kissed you, Billie Ames?" He tried to keep his voice light and teasing. He'd wanted to kiss her for hours. He could almost taste her, could almost feel her lips soft and yielding beneath his. There was something about this sweet innocent he wanted to leave untouched, undisturbed. He didn't realize he was holding his breath for Billie's answer until she replied.

"I wanted it to be your idea, Lieutenant. Now that I've embarrassed myself by asking, I don't want to kiss you. Come on, we'll be late." Wordlessly, she stood up and yanked the blanket out from under him, folding it meticulously before starting back to the car.

"Billie! Wait!" Suddenly, it was important to make her understand. What exactly she should understand he didn't know. "Look at me when I talk to you. I've wanted to kiss you all afternoon, especially when you had cherry pie right there on the corner of your mouth." He touched her lips with his finger. "I'll know when you're ready to be kissed, Billie. Trust me?"

Billie smiled, his gesture lighting her face. That meant he wanted to see her again. She decided she would invite him not to her prom but to her graduation dance. Perhaps she wouldn't even go to her prom. It held no allure for her now.

They rode home in silence, Moss holding her hand. He

liked the way it felt in his. He liked Billie Ames. He should have kissed her. "I want to see you again. Will you let me?"

"I told you I'd pray for you to get what you wanted."

"How about the USO on Saturday? Does your mother allow you to go there?"

"I've only been there once for a welcoming tea in the afternoon; my mother is a volunteer for the Red Cross. I'll ask her. I think she'll say yes." Even if Agnes said absolutely no, Billie would find a way to get there. She was going to see as much of Moss as she could.

"Okay, I'll see you there, then. Hold on, I'll walk you to the door. We don't want your mother thinking I'm the kind of guy who pulls up and blows the horn and dumps you out on the street."

"Mother would never think that," Billie said loyally, but she knew it was a lie and so did Moss. "I had a wonderful time. Thank you. And thank you for the chocolates."

"Hey, I enjoyed it, too." He realized it was true. He did enjoy Billie's company, was enchanted with it. She made him feel good. She listened and cared and didn't talk too much.

She knew Moss was going to kiss her. It wasn't a soul-searing experience, and rockets didn't shoot off into the night. Instead, the kiss was soft, gentle, with the promise of so much more. More than Moss was ready to give or ask of her. She didn't feel dizzy or weak-kneed. A slow-spreading warmth enveloped her and she wanted him to hold her, just for a moment, just until she could remember that the world consisted of more than Moss Coleman. Her eyes were shining in the porch light. Someday there would be more—she was sure of it—because she would make it happen.

"Good night, Billie. I'll see you on Saturday."

"G'night, Moss. Drive carefully."

His mother was the only one who told him to drive carefully, and then, as if to spite authority, he would drive like a bat out of hell. Tonight he drove carefully, all the way back to the Navy Yard.

Agnes stood in the darkened parlor watching through the lace curtains. Her back stiffened. She'd heard the low, throaty laughter that was Billie's. She'd never heard her daughter laugh that way; it was a woman's laugh. Quickly, she moved to the kitchen, waiting for the front door to open. "How was the movie?" she asked.

"It was awful. Just awful. Neither of us liked it." There,

that was the truth. She simply felt no need or desire to tell Agnes when, where, why, or what. "How was your afternoon, Mother?"

"Oh, I played canasta with the neighbors and I've only just come home. I was going to listen to *Amos 'n' Andy*. Join me?"

"No thanks, Mother, I have to read a couple of chapters for a history quiz tomorrow. I think I'll have a sandwich and get started."

There was no quiz; neither was she hungry. She just wanted to be alone and think about today. She wanted to remember every look, every word, everything about Moss. Saturday was only six days away.

{{{{{{{{{{ CHAPTER THREE }}}}}}}}}}

Agnes appeared in the kitchen to gather her scouring cleansers and wash bucket. Billie stood at the sink clearing away the last of the breakfast dishes. The old wringer washer on the back service porch sloshed rhythmically. "You'll have to hurry along, Billie, if you're going to the movies this afternoon with your nice friends."

All of a sudden she had "nice friends," Billie noticed. "I'm not going to the movies today. I thought I'd stay home and give you a hand. And besides, I want to wash my hair."

At this deviation from her daughter's Saturday routine, Agnes's eyes widened as she waited for the explanation she knew would come. Billie always washed and waved her hair on Saturday night in time for Sunday mass. Billie was struggling with the words. Agnes could sense it.

"Moss invited me to the dance at the USO tonight," Billie said. "I'm going." It was a flat statement, not a challenge.

"You know how I feel about the USO," Agnes countered. "It's perfectly fine for all those boys so far from home and it may be perfectly respectable for all those other girls, but not for you, Billie. When Lieutenant Coleman comes to call, I'll suggest he take you somewhere else, somewhere not quite so controversial."

"He's not coming to call, Mother. I'm going to meet him there. And the only controversy concerning the USO is yours."

"Would it make any difference to you if I said I didn't want you to go?" Agnes pretended to fuss with the cleaning rags and cleansers. This stubborn determination was so unlike Billie that it frightened her.

"Of course it makes a difference. But I'm going anyway." Billie felt her knees quaking and her breath caught in her throat. Never had she deliberately disobeyed her mother, but being with Moss, seeing him again, was almost a tangible need.

Agnes did not speak to her for the rest of the day. The sounds of scrubbing and moving furniture upstairs said all there was to say. There was no supper that night. Billie stood in front of the refrigerator and picked. Agnes was in her upstairs front bedroom, listening and waiting for Billie. She never came. Agnes heard the front door close at 7:18.

The USO was near the Navy Yard, a good walk, and Billie wasn't used to being out at night alone. Thankfully, it wouldn't be dark for almost an hour and she'd be with Moss by that time.

Her heels clicked on the sidewalk, not saddle shoes this time, but the high heels she'd been saving for the prom. Nylon stockings—"Starlight" was the name of the light beige shade—made her feel very adult even though her new garter belt felt a little loose. She'd finished making her dress only yesterday. It was one of her own designs, a soft navy-blue georgette that had cost a fortune at the drygoods. She'd adapted the little Peter Pan collar the pattern called for into a portrait neckline and the intricate puffed sleeves ended in a band just above her elbows. The skirt was full and hung in soft gathers from the tiny waistline, and the taffeta underslip rustled pleasantly with each step she took. Tiny smoke-pearl buttons retrieved from an old dress she'd outgrown marched down the front closing. Agnes hadn't seen it. She would have decreed the style and color too severe for Billie's soft blond coloring, but Billie's sense of color and style told her Agnes would have been wrong. The dress was perfect for her.

Even a block away Billie could hear the strains of Glenn Miller's band coming through the open doors of the USO. Men in uniform hung around outside and the dark armbands of the military police were in evidence. She stopped in the shadows for a moment to run a comb through her hair. Tonight it was pulled up from her ears and puffed over the forehead in a pompadour, allowing the back to fall long and soft to her shoulders. Just a touch of lipstick and powder completed her toilette. Tonight Billie Ames was feeling very far from being a schoolgirl and much closer to the woman she wanted to be, for Moss.

He saw her immediately and ran across Front Street to meet her. He was aware of the change in her and his grin said he knew it was for him. "You're terrific," he told her, looking down into her eyes. He realized how glad he was that she'd come, how relieved. Her hand was warm in his and she smiled up at him, making him feel as though he were the only man in the world. Moss was used to female attention and flattery, but there was nothing of the coquette about Billie Ames. As a Southern buddy would say, she was "gen-*you*-ine"!

The lighting on the dance floor was subdued but not dim. The Victrola attached to speakers played Dick Haymes's "If You Were the Only Girl in the World." Moss held her close, his cheek resting against her brow, and hummed along with the music—the sound was exciting, masculine, in her ear. She never remembered being so happy, so lovely, so much a woman.

Girls and chaperones served punch and cookies at one of the long tables set off to the side of the converted storefront dance hall. Another table held coffee and doughnuts. Khaki-green and navy-blue uniforms lined the walls, swirling skirts and the aroma of toilette water filled the air. No smoking was allowed and Billie had gone to the powder room while Moss went outside for a cigarette. She'd noticed last Sunday that he smoked Old Gold. The aroma of the tobacco clung to him when he again took her into his arms.

As they danced, Moss felt a hand clap onto his shoulder and Billie looked up to see a tall attractive lieutenant smiling down at her. "Thought I'd cut in here, Coleman," the officer said mildly. "Won't you introduce me to the lady?" His accent was crisp, the vowels slightly flat, and Billie fixed him as a New Englander.

For a moment, Moss appeared annoyed. "Billie Ames, Lieutenant Thad Kingsley." Thad stepped forward, forcing Moss to relinquish her into his arms.

As Billie stepped into Thad's embrace she felt his soft gray eyes smiling down at her. He had nice eyes, ready to brighten with laughter and soften his chisled, craggy features. Taller and leaner than Moss, he modified his long steps to accommodate her as they danced.

"You look like the angel from the top of a Christmas tree."

"And you look like one of the posters outside the post office. *'Uncle Sam wants you!'*" she bantered, his compliment pleasing her.

"I'll try to think of that as flattery." He laughed easily, his eyes brightening the way she had known they would.

He seemed to spend a lot of time in the sun; his skin was shades darker than his hair, which was the mellow gold of a summer's day. Billie liked Thad and his quiet way. Sometimes Moss's intensity made her uncomfortable and stirred mysterious emotions within her. Thad was refreshing and had a knack for putting people at their ease.

"Are you from Philadelphia?" he was asking. "It's a nice city and the people have been especially kind to servicemen."

"The City of Brotherly Love," she reminded him. "You're from New England?"

"Shows that much, does it?" He laughed at himself. "Vermont. Top western corner of the state. My family has been there for generations and they actually claim to favor the climate. I prefer somewhere warmer myself. Guess I'll get enough of the tropics if I'm sent to the Pacific."

"Do you think you will?" she asked. An icy finger touched her heart at the thought of all these beautiful young men going off to war. Especially when she thought about Moss leaving Philadelphia.

"Loose lips sink ships," Thad teased, sensitive to her sudden melancholy. "Actually, none of us knows where we'll end up, but I know for a fact Moss is itching to get back to the *Enterprise*, where we trained together. For the moment, I'm assigned to the *Sarasota*, but she's in for repairs."

As Thad took Billie around the dance floor, he looked down at this fresh young thing who was softer than cotton in his arms. What the hell was Coleman doing with her? Little Billie was hardly Moss's type. She was young, too young, and sweet.

Several times during the evening other men cut in on Moss to dance with her. She felt his eyes follow her around the dance floor and it made her feel all shivery inside. "It's time I took you home, Billie. It's nearly ten and I couldn't borrow a car tonight."

"I'll have to meet you outside," she told him. "You know the USO doesn't allow girls to leave with the servicemen. If someone sees us, I won't be allowed back."

"You're not coming back," Moss growled. "I don't like sharing you with other men. You belong to me, Billie." He put his arm around her shoulder and led her outside, ignoring the stares of several girls and servicemen standing near the door.

Outside Billie's front door, Moss took her into his arms. She liked the way she fit against him, liked the feel of his strong thighs pressing through the thin fabric of her dress. He tilted up her chin with the tip of his finger and she saw his dark brows draw together as he looked down at her. It was almost as if he were thinking that he didn't quite know what to do with her. Then he kissed her, a slow, warm caress of his lips on hers. She gave herself up to him, parting her lips, aware of the hard bite of his teeth behind that kiss. There was a power about Moss Coleman, carefully hidden behind those careful manners and tender kisses, and Billie was drawn to it, taking some of it for herself. She heard his soft intake of breath. This was a very different kiss from the first. There was a possession in it and a yielding. His hands cupped the back of her head, prolonging the contact, bringing her mouth to his with a hungry yearning. When his hands slid down her back, resting just above the slender curve of her buttocks, he bent lower to bury his face in the hollow of her throat, nipping the softness of her skin, inhaling the fragrance of her. "Oh, Billie," she heard him say, "you shouldn't let me feel this way about you."

In response, Billie cradled his head against her, her fingertips grazing the crisp dark waves at the back of his neck. "I want you to feel this way, Moss," she whispered, "I want . . ."

The next contact of his mouth on hers was sudden, demanding, and quickly over. "Go inside, Billie, for God's sake, go inside."

He released her so suddenly that it left her trembling, confused, and a little frightened. But if she had never known another thing, Billie Ames knew she had wanted that kiss to go on forever. Before her hand touched the doorknob, Moss had disappeared down the front walk, already lost in the shadows of the overhanging trees.

From the upstairs bedroom window Agnes watched. Because of the porch roof she hadn't seen what transpired outside the front door, but she'd seen Billie and Moss come up to the house. Nine minutes later she watched him streak down the front path.

Agnes watched the relationship between Billie and Moss change from a casual friendship to something deep and warm. Moss came several nights a week after dinner and there were phone calls during which Billie would laugh that new woman's laugh. She knew her daughter was untouched, still innocent. She could read it in Moss's eyes, but the hunger she read in Billie's was disconcerting. Each night when he brought Billie home he would come in for a few minutes. Agnes dreaded those brief encounters when she was forced to look into the lieutenant's eyes for reassurance. Despite her misgivings, which were mostly due to Billie's behavior, Agnes trusted Moss. There was a certain nobility about him, which she suspected would prevent him from taking unfair advantage of Billie's innocence. At least she hoped such was the case. Agnes was not certain of anything any longer, and it was this that caused her the most distress.

Her fond hopes of an alliance between the Fox family and her own were hardly more than a memory. The most she could hope for at this point was that Moss Coleman would leave Philadelphia and leave soon. It was all he talked about during Sunday dinner, which was now a ritual. He hoped to be attached to a fighter squadron in the Pacific. The shadow of pain in Billie's eyes whenever he expressed such desires pierced Agnes's heart. If only it would happen before Billie left for college; then she would have time to recover before embarking on a new life.

This brought a fresh fear to Agnes. She was well aware of the impetuosity of youth and she prayed Moss didn't fill Billie's head with the sense of urgency that was the downfall of so many good girls these days. The uncertainties of wartime, living for today because there mightn't be a tomorrow... it had been more than one girl's undoing. Marriage would never come into the conversation. She couldn't help wondering how many casualties Moss Coleman had left behind. She only knew she didn't want Billie added to the list. Billie was all she had. Billie was Agnes's hope for the future. If only she knew more about Moss, it might ease her mind. He might even have a wife somewhere already!

Billie came home from school and straight into the kitchen. "Mother, I'm home. Did Moss call, by any chance?"

"No. Billie, you haven't given any serious practice at that

piano for weeks. You're not being fair to me. The lessons are expensive and you have to do your part."

"I don't want any more lessons. I'm never going to be a concert pianist and I don't have time for it anymore. Tell Mr. Trazzori I want to stop. Stop, Mother, as in finish. No more. What are we having for dinner?"

"Lamb chops. I managed to get four of them today. I had to stand in line over two hours. I wish this rationing would end." Agnes spoke matter-of-factly, but she was shaken about Billie's decision. Eleven years of study and practice gone to waste because of a cowboy. Even at college Billie would have continued her lessons, but it had been weeks since college was mentioned—the weeks since Moss Coleman had first come to the house. Suddenly Agnes blurted, "Billie, I have to talk to you. You still have two weeks of school left. I received a call this afternoon asking why you didn't attend today. I want an explanation and I want it now."

"Mother, all the marks are in. Really, it isn't important. I was with Moss. We took a ride up to the Jersey shore. There's nothing to be upset about. Why is it so awful to skip school for once? Other kids do it all the time."

"That's just it. You've never done anything like this. Billie, ever since you've met that fly-boy you've changed. You aren't the same anymore, and I don't like what I see. You're spending entirely too much time with him." She hated to ask, fearing the answer, but she had to do it. "Just how fond are you of this Moss Coleman?"

"Mother, I wish you wouldn't ask questions like that. I'm grown now, and it's really none of your business."

"Oh, isn't it my business! It's my business when I have to lie to the school and tell them you've got the sniffles. As soon as I heard you weren't in school, I knew whom you were with and I don't like it."

"I'm a big girl now, Mother, and I can take care of myself. If you're worried that I might...that I might..."

Agnes spoke before she'd really found the words. "It's not you who worries me. I know you're a good girl. But that young man isn't going to wait forever. Billie, do you understand what I'm saying?" There was an edge of desperation in Agnes's tone.

"Don't worry, Mother." Billie's voice had softened in sympathy. If theirs was a more demonstrative relationship, she'd have given Agnes a hug to reassure her. "Moss hasn't touched me. He kisses me good night, but so does Tim Kelly. I wish you'd trust me. You always have before. Why not now? What makes Moss so different in your eyes? Is it because he's older?"

I wish I knew, Agnes thought to herself. "Moss isn't a boy, like Tim Kelly. He's a man, and men have certain needs and desires."

"I really don't want to talk about this." Billie shifted her clear hazel eyes away from her mother. She didn't need to be told about men's desires; she'd already guessed at them, had experienced a taste of them in Moss's strong embrace, in the hardness of his body as it pressed against hers so urgently. Billie had found the echo of those same needs in herself, and Moss knew it. That was why he kept pushing her away, muttering to himself under his breath. He knew that his was the only control.

"I have to work on my graduation dress if I'm to finish it in time. Call me if you need help with dinner." Impetuously, she kissed Agnes on the cheek to take the sting out of her words, then went to her room.

Billie closed the door behind her, wishing it had a lock. Four more hours and she'd be with Moss again. The admiral had taken personal leave and that left Moss pretty much on his own, he'd told her. He'd still have the car tonight and they'd drive down to the park. After that first time they'd never gone to the USO again. He still didn't want to share her with anyone else. His possessiveness made her feel all warm and soft inside. Later, when he drove her home, he would wrap his arms around her and kiss her. Again and again. She shivered when she thought of the way he whispered a groan and grew hard against her. He laughingly called her a tease. If he could have seen her eyes in the darkness of the front porch, he would see her silent dare, the loving challenge to go beyond the limits he had set.

What would she do when he left? The unknown hung over her like a pall. She never told him that she didn't pray for him anymore. Not for his reassignment, anyway. Now she prayed for other things: for him to love her, for him never to forget her.

Moss had agreed to attend her graduation and the dance afterward. He'd wear his dress whites, and the girls were going to die when she walked in on his arm, simply die. Once it would have been important; now it seemed silly and girlish. Now she only wanted to have him to herself, to be alone with him. She knew she was in love. Moss's feelings were still a mystery. He liked her; that much she knew. He enjoyed kissing her and dancing with her and being with her. He'd told her. But when he wasn't with her, did he think of her the way she thought of him?

It was after nine when the phone rang. Agnes laid down her needlepoint canvas and took it on the third ring. "Father Donovan, how nice of you to call," she said quietly, then took a deep breath, almost afraid to hear what he would say.

"Mrs. Ames, I did as you asked. I called Chaplain Franklin at the Navy Yard. I think I told you I was acquainted with him. Chaplain Franklin assures me that Lieutenant Coleman is a very fine young man from a distinguished Texas family. It happens that the chaplain is quite friendly with the admiral's wife. That personal reference concurs with the lieutenant's records—he's not married."

Agnes listened while Father Donovan told her about the Colemans of Texas, her ears perking when he said that the father, Seth, had his fingers in many profitable pies. Oil, beef, aviation, and electronics.

"The lieutenant is well recommended, Mrs. Ames, and has an excellent record. All in all, I don't think you've a thing to worry about where Billie is concerned. I hope this puts your mind at ease. I wish more parents were as concerned about their children as you are. A few discreet questions could save them a lot of grief."

"Father, I appreciate all you've done. You must come to dinner one day soon."

"Anytime I can be of help, just call me. That's why I'm here. Good night, Mrs. Ames."

Agnes's eyes were sparkling like newly cut diamonds when she picked up her needlework again. Beef. Oil. Electronics. Money. Lots of it. Tomorrow she'd go to the main library and check out the city of Austin and what was, apparently, one of its leading families. She snorted in a very unladylike manner when she thought of Neal Fox and his father's bank.

As she stitched along with a bright vermilion length of Persian yarn, listening to the *Longines Wittnaur Music Hour*, Agnes thought that her clever little ploy of attempting to intimidate a cowboy certainly hadn't backfired. She was glad now she'd used her best china and crystal along with her mother's lace tablecloth. At least he could see the Ameses weren't peasants, but examples of good breeding and manners who could hold up their heads with the Colemans of Austin, Texas.

Had Father Donovan said she hadn't a thing to worry about? That was because he hadn't seen the look in Billie's eyes whenever the young lieutenant was near. That look told Agnes all she needed to know. If Moss crooked his finger, Billie would run. He could easily take advantage of her. And if he did, where would that leave Billie? Deflowered at seventeen. She could become pregnant and then what? Still, Agnes had a strong hunch that Moss would keep his head. He knew he was tormenting her; he also knew he held all the cards where her daughter was concerned. But there was something in his eyes that said he played fair.

It was five minutes to ten when Moss and Billie walked through the front door. Agnes was gathering up her needlepoint to retire for the evening. "Good night, Moss, Billie," she said quietly. Not for the world was she going to meet the young man's stare *this* evening. "I have a frightful headache, Billie. Be sure all the lights are out and the door locked when you go to bed." Without another look at either of the young people, Agnes climbed the stairs.

Moss was vaguely disappointed. Of late he'd actually enjoyed his little staring game with Agnes. Something was up. Tonight there was a nervousness and excitement about Agnes that made him wonder.

"It's a shame Mother has a headache," said Billie, "but that means we have the living room all to ourselves. We can listen to the radio or just sit here and talk. You don't have to rush back to the yard, do you?"

Moss's mind raced. He supposed he could stay awhile. The others would wait for him. He'd never told Billie that when he left her most evenings he didn't go back to the base. He didn't have to report in until seven in the morning, so usually he went with the others to an after-hours club. "I can stay for a while. But I'll have to get back soon, early duty in the morning."

Billie sat on the sofa and was disappointed when Moss sat at the other end. Did he think Agnes was going to spy on them? The news report came on the radio and they listened silently. She saw how alert Moss became at the mention of the USS *Enterprise* in the Pacific. H. V. Kaltenborn was speaking.

"Today is June eighth. Less than a week ago a triumph was declared in the Pacific by our naval and air forces off the shores of the tiny island of Midway. It was a day of reckoning for the Empire of Japan, which met with the strength of American aircraft carriers *Hornet*, *Yorktown*, and *Enterprise*. Four Japanese carriers were sent to the bottom. The *Soryu*, the *Hiryu*, *Kaga*, and *Akagi* will never sail into Tokyo Harbor again."

Moss listened with rapt attention. If there was one thing Billie had learned early on, it was Moss's interest in every bit of news. Especially about the war. He could lose track of time when he talked about it. She'd listen with interest until he got to the part where he said he couldn't wait to be reassigned. She always had to bite her tongue to keep from asking, "What about me?"

Moss glanced at his watch. Kaltenborn's news seemed to have shaken him. "I've got to get back, Billie. Tell your mother I hope her headache is better."

"Moss, isn't the *Enterprise* the ship you trained on last fall? Where is Midway? What does it all mean?"

Moss placed his hand on her shoulders, looking down at her. "It means that if I don't hurry and get myself over there, it's all going to be over." He ran a hand through his thick dark hair. "I don't know what to do, Billie. I don't want to go against Pap, but I know I've got to get in there and do my share." His sudden grin relieved the worry lines between his eyes. "Can't let all the other guys have the fun, can I?"

He wrapped his arms around her and kissed her lightly, shifting his brain into what he called neutral, allowing himself to relax. Billie was so soft, so feminine, her lips so tender and gentle, promising more if only he dared to take it. He didn't want to hurt her. Neither did he want to take advantage of her. He cared for her, was enchanted by her, but he didn't love her. At least, he didn't think he did. He couldn't let himself love anyone, not even a nice girl like Billie. Love made too many demands and got in the way of plans and dreams. Seth loved him, too much, and the responsibility of that love prevented him from pursuing something he wanted very badly. He didn't need or want another tie or obligation to anyone, not even Billie.

Besides, she was one of those nice girls who would never understand that a guy could mess around and not want anything lasting or permanent. He'd have to stop seeing so much of her. She was getting under his skin and it was becoming more and more difficult to put honor and respect first. He should see other women, women who weren't so nice and didn't have any false illusions. Women who wouldn't be hurt by an occasional roll in the hay and who wouldn't expect marriage in return for virginity.

When Moss released Billie, he saw the tears in her eyes. "Hey, don't ever cry for me, Billie." And then he was gone.

Billie sat on her bed for a long, long time, warm tears trickling down her cheeks. How could she not cry for Moss? He wanted to be in the Pacific, flying into battle, risking his life. Why couldn't he want her that much? If he did, he'd never want to leave her.

Billie came instantly awake and knew what day it was. Graduation. Her sleepy eyes went to the hook on the back of the closet door where her dress hung. It was beautiful, almost a bridal dress, virginal in its whiteness. The thought suddenly annoyed her. Perhaps she should have threaded some of the eyelet with a colored ribbon or made a colored sash. It wasn't too late; she still had all day. She decided a colored sash was the answer. She'd wear the completed white one for the graduation ceremonies and change to the pastel one for the dance. It would hardly take ten minutes to whip up on the machine. That's what she would do. She wanted to stand out from the other girls, to look just a little different, for Moss.

This was a night she wanted him to remember, herself a vision that he could take with him when he left. How long would she have him with her? Not very long, she realized. For weeks he'd been filled with the news of the *Enterprise* and its part in the battle of Midway. It made Moss "chomp at the bit," as he called it, to get into the fray before it was over. If only it *was* over, all of it; then he wouldn't have to leave her.

Billie felt she didn't really understand Moss Coleman any better than on the first day she'd met him more than a month ago. This was already June. June was a month for brides. Yesterday she'd heard that two of her classmates were marrying before their men shipped out. Simple, hurried ceremonies with only family present.

Billie ached.

By the middle of July Tim would be gone. The other boys would soon follow. Her girlfriends were going off to college and she herself was to leave for Penn State at the end of August. Everyone promised to write everyone, but Billie knew that soon each would find a life and interests of his own. Slowly but surely the letters would cease. Oh, they'd see one another over the holidays or during the summer, but this part of their lives was over. God alone knew when they'd see any of the boys again, if ever. It was sad and it made tonight seem even more special.

There was going to be an all-night party at a classmate's after the dance. Agnes had already given permission for her to stay out until after the champagne breakfast the parents planned to serve. Billie giggled to herself. The poor girl. Billie knew for a fact that most of the couples had other plans. Oh, they'd make an appearance at the party, but then they'd leave. That's exactly what she'd like to do, only she didn't know how to broach the subject with Moss. She knew he'd be bored. Maybe she could suggest driving up to Atlantic City. They could walk on the beach and watch the sunrise. That would be the perfect ending to a perfect night.

Just the thought of spending an entire night with Moss, of lying beside him on a blanket on the beach, was so romantic that she rolled over on her bed and pressed her face into the pillow. Strange things were happening inside her, dark longings and a yearning ache that quickened her pulses whenever she was with him, whenever he touched her. She'd looked in the mirror to see if this change showed on her face. It seemed to be Billie Ames's face but she didn't feel like Billie Ames inside. She ached, her breasts tingled, there was an emptiness in the center of her. She wanted Moss to touch her breasts and fill this emptiness. She wanted it so badly that there seemed to be a bubble of sadness at the back of her throat. Tears were always so near the surface that she found herself biting them back throughout the days until she was with him again. The romance magazines called this feeling passion. But they never said passion could hurt this way.

Moss buttoned the last button on his white jacket. He knew he was going to take a lot of ribbing when he made his way out to the officers' lounge. A high school graduation! That was for sailors.

"Wheweee," Thad Kingsley whistled. "You're gonna throw all those little ladies into a tailspin."

"Smell him!" heckled his buddy Jack. "Smells like he's been in a French whorehouse. All them mamas of all them little girls are gonna have heart palpitations."

"Knock it off," Moss said, grinning.

"Handsome devil, but," said another young officer, wagging

a finger, "it ain't no fun being just a plain old handsome devil unless he's planning on being a sinful handsome devil." The others laughed, enjoying Moss's discomfort.

"How old you say this little gal is? Seventeen, you say? For shame, man, you're robbing the cradle. Pure as the driven snow, right?" Jack cackled.

"Shut the hell up, Jack. Don't you have anything better to do than ride me?"

"Not unless we all dress up like you and stand outside. What say we do that, guys? Maybe some of them little girls will fall all over us and invite us for Sunday dinner. Why should Moss have all the fun? Does that little gal know you been laying every girl between here and New York City?"

"I told you to knock it off—I mean it," Moss snarled. The fun was getting out of hand. Truth always bothered Moss when it was delivered by someone else.

"What are you going to do, sic the admiral on us?" Thad teased. "Come on, guys, let's go find some fun of our own. Coleman has things to do and places to go." To show that it was all in fun, the guys clapped Moss on the back as they left the lounge.

Thad swung around for one last barb. "I want you in by sunup and I expect that uniform to be in the same condition it's in now," he said in what he hoped was a motherly tone. "You hear me?"

Moss laughed and waved as he went out the door.

They were good guys. And if Moss could, he'd pick Thad Kingsley for a brother. Thad was probably the best damn flyer he knew. He was one cool man under pressure and never made a mistake.

Agnes's eyes were unreadable when she opened the door to admit Moss. He looked as if he were born to navy whites. "Come in, Moss. Billie will be ready in a moment." She admired the creamy white camelias he was carrying. "What a lovely corsage!"

Moss stared straight into Agnes's eyes. When he spoke, his drawl was more pronounced. "I'm thinkin' I'll be outa here by September. Leastwise, that's the way it looks now." He watched for her reaction, expecting relief. He frowned. Hell, wasn't that what she wanted? For him to be gone so her little Billie would be safe? That wasn't panic he saw in her face, or was it?

* * *

The small band hired for the graduation dance was making a valiant effort to accomplish the big band sound of Glenn Miller. A young woman was making a fair stab at sounding like Helen O'Connell, to the delight of everyone in the hall. Billie danced with Moss, her head cradled against his chest. She felt so good, so right being in his arms. She'd noticed every female head in the gym turn when she'd walked in on his arm. Even the teachers had cast more than one admiring glance in his direction as he led her around the dance floor.

Agnes stood at the table serving punch from the huge bowl. She preened as she heard the principal beside her acclaim Billie as the prettiest girl at the dance. "And who's the young man with her, Mrs. Ames? It's obvious he's well bred."

"He's Lieutenant Moss Coleman, from Austin, Texas. Confidentially, he's from a very important family, if you know what I mean."

The principal, sensing Agnes's excitement, knew exactly what she meant. Moss Coleman must be a very wealthy man indeed.

"Billie, the band is going to take a break," Moss said against her cheek. "This is a good time for me to check in with Admiral McCarter. Why don't you go over and get some punch and I'll meet you at the refreshment table."

Agnes, standing guard over the punch bowl so none of the more rambunctious students would spike it, saw Billie coming toward her, saw the flush on her daughter's cheeks, the full smiling lips, the glow in her eyes. Billie had a look about her that would throw fright into any mother's heart. A look that said she was full grown and had found the man she would have.

"Mother, are you having a good time?" Even her voice was different, Agnes decided. Warm and vibrant, holding an assurance and confidence. A woman's confidence. Billie was a girl no longer. Agnes had felt that way once, experienced those same tensions and desires, and she knew where they led. Directly to the bedroom.

"It's a wonderful dance and a very special night for you, isn't it, Billie? Especially since Moss thinks he'll be shipping out before September." She pretended not to notice Billie's distress, waiting to hear if Moss had confided his plans or made promises for the future.

"Did he tell you that?" Billie asked, her hands trembling.

"Oh, I'm so sorry, dear. Did I let a cat out of the bag? Yes, he told me just this evening." Agnes stared at her daughter, thoughts ricocheting through her head. Her own hand shook slightly as she ladled out the punch. What a silly little girl Billie actually was. Perhaps she shouldn't have been so protective of her all these years; perhaps then Billie would know how to reach out and take what she wanted. She herself had been much smarter at seventeen than Billie, Agnes thought. She took a deep breath and came to an instant decision. "Take this, dear. You look as though you need it," she said, serving her daughter a cup of punch.

Billie reached for the punch cup and at that instant Agnes's hand flew upward, the bright red drink splattering all over the front of Billie's white dress.

Coming around the corner from the hallway just then, Moss saw Billie step backward, but not in time. Her dress was ruined. He stood still for a minute. There was no point in ruining his uniform. When Billie finished wiping at the deep red stains, he walked forward.

"Oh, Moss, I'm so glad you're here," Agnes said anxiously. "Will you please take Billie home so she can change her dress? Billie, I'm so sorry. I thought you had the cup in your hand. You don't mind, do you, Moss?"

"Of course not." His eyes searched Agnes's. He'd been wrong; it wasn't panic at all. It was fear. A tight smile escaped him as he took Billie past the small, knotted crowds.

Agnes watched them leave. Her glance went to the oversized clock on the wall, somewhat difficult to see with all the crepe-paper decorations hanging above. Ten minutes to drive home, another fifteen for Billie to change, ten for them to return. She would wait. This would be Billie's chance and it might be the only one she'd get. Agnes pushed down all maternal uncertainties. It was a terrible gamble, but she was doing it for Billie's sake. Her daughter was going to be one of the Colemans of Austin. Agnes smiled. And one way or another, she'd be one of them, too.

{{{{{{{{{{ CHAPTER FOUR }}}}}}}}

Moss took the latchkey from Billie's hand and opened the front door. He admired the way she was handling her disappointment and embarrassment. Other girls, he knew, would have fretted and complained about the ruined dress, making the situation miserable for everyone. Not Billie. During the ride home she'd laughed and joked and teased him about being the most popular man at the dance.

"I'll only be a minute. Maybe two." She laughed. "I'm afraid I'm soaked clear through to the skin. Why don't you turn on the radio to keep you company?"

"I'm sorry about your dress, Billie," he told her sincerely. "You were the prettiest girl at the dance. No, not just pretty, beautiful."

Billie felt his words warm her. Now it didn't matter if she had to wear sackcloth and ashes. Moss had said she was beautiful and she felt beautiful when he looked at her this way, with fires glowing behind his eyes.

He watched her disappear into the room off the parlor. After tuning in a radio station, he jammed his hands in his pockets and paced the darkened room. There was a line of light seeping from under Billie's door; he could see it flicker and waver as she moved about inside.

Billie stripped off her dress, knowing she'd find that the red punch had seeped through to her white taffeta slip. Even her skin was sticky and she needed a quick wash. How could Mother have been so careless? She'd need a complete change of clothes, everything.

Moss opened the door to Billie's bedroom; the soft, pink light from the bedstand shafted into the open closet door where he could hear her rummaging. He leaned against the doorjamb, hands stuffed into his trouser pockets, his cap tilted low over his eyes.

Unaware of his intrusion, Billie reached for her terry robe

and stepped out of the closet, humming softly to the tune of "I'll Be Seeing You" playing on the radio in the parlor. Moss surveyed her from the shadow of his cap, seeing the long naked length of her back, her small round rump, and her tapering legs, firm and lightly muscled. Her bare shoulders were dusted with the dark gold of her hair. She turned slightly, affording him a view of her small uptilted breasts with nipples as pink as the inside of seashells. Her waist was tiny and he grinned at her little round tummy, a vestige of girlhood.

Billie shrugged into her robe, gathering it closed with the belt before turning to see him, her face registering surprise. Moss looked at her, his gaze never wavering from her face. It was there, the woman's heat. It had turned her hazel eyes to gold.

A flush of warmth crept down Billie's body, touching embers to her breasts, her belly, between her legs. Still staring into his eyes, she opened her robe, allowing it to slip off her shoulders and caress her arms as it slid to the floor. Just as she discarded the scruffy white robe, so did she cast off her girlhood. It was a woman's arms that lifted to welcome him.

Agnes kept watching the clock on the wall. All around her, skirts swirled and music played. She was oblivious to everything save the passing of time. Nearly an hour had gone by since Billie had left with Moss. Agnes walked to the cloakroom for her sweater. Her step was determined as she left the high school and went out to the street.

Her movements were controlled as she drove her seldom used Studebaker, both hands clutched on the wheel. Instead of coming in from the south end of her block, she drove an extra two blocks so she could swing around and come in from the north and park on the opposite side of the street. There she sat, staring across at the gray-and-white house on Elm Street. Moss's borrowed car was parked in the drive. The house was dark and uninviting.

The light from the outside streetlamp filtered through Agnes's rayon curtains into Billie's darkened bedroom, splashing onto her narrow, girlish bed and puddling a silvery sheen onto their nakedness. She lay close in Moss's embrace, sensually aware of his coarse chest hairs tickling her breasts. His lips nuzzled her neck, trailing familiarly now to the hollow between her breasts and beneath them. He cupped and caressed their swollen firmness and seemed to take such pleasure in them that she wished they were bigger, fuller, for him.

"I don't know what's sweeter, Billie, you or the fruit punch. You're still sticky with it and delicious," he murmured against her flesh, rekindling the throbbing of her pulses. She wanted to be sweet for him. She wanted to be everything for him.

Billie sighed, stretching languorously beside him. She was a woman now. Moss had made love to her and made her a woman. His woman. He'd been so tender with her, so careful, arousing her to such a fever pitch before penetrating her flesh with his that she'd hardly noticed the quick, sudden rending of her maidenhead. Then, as he'd moved slowly within her, she'd felt herself dissolve wetly, her flesh opening itself to him, taking him fully inside her. She'd imagined that she was his canvas and he the artist, painting her with the vivid colors of her awakened sexuality, designing her to his pleasure as he traced intricate patterns along her body with his lips and hands. His wonderful hands. There was not an inch of her unkissed or unloved, and Billie Ames felt she had metamorphosed from a dun-colored caterpillar into an exotic butterfly.

Leaning up on one elbow, Moss trailed a teasing finger from the hollow of her throat down her body to the mossy bank of her sex, still moist and warm from her loving. "It'll be better for you next time, Billie. I didn't want to hurt you."

"You didn't. It was wonderful. I've never felt this close to anyone before, Moss. I love it. I love you."

His only answer was to kiss her, softly, his lips lingering on hers in an intimate caress. She parted her lips, allowing him entrance just as easily as she'd allowed him to enter her body. She was sweet and warm with the aftermath of their loving, but he knew she hadn't come to a climax and this was something he wanted to share with her, wanted to give her. "Being close isn't enough," he breathed. "There's so much more, and I want to show you."

"More? Show me, Moss. Show me now," she insisted, feeling a growing pressure at the center of herself that she knew he alone could assuage. Was it possible to be closer to him than she felt this minute? Was it possible to take a part of him that she could keep for her own and never lose no matter what happened, no matter how far away he would go?

Moss was shaken by her invitation. He had expected to find pleasure in making love to her, but he'd never guessed at the depth of that pleasure or anticipated such uninhibited willingness. She'd been wonderful, accepting his caresses, the possession of her body, offering herself to him as though she were a gift created for him alone. Their eyes met in the dimness, clear and level, heated and eager without a trace of regret or embarrassment. Seeing her lips part in anticipation of his kiss, he lowered his mouth to hers, touching and seeking that special sweetness that was Billie's alone. He felt her fingers graze his back, lowering to his haunches, reawakening his desire for her. At that moment he believed he could never be sated in his hunger. Billie was special, unexpectedly so. She enchanted him with her responses, enthralled him with her eager, unpracticed touch. She was an untapped spring of sensuality and he determined to follow her courses to the deeply hidden source.

Her body turned in his arms, offering itself to his explorations. Her skin was soft, supple beneath his touch. He watched her face as he caressed her breasts, slowly, intriguingly, lowering to her belly, between her parted thighs. The upsweep of her lashes lowered sleepily as she gave herself over to him, trusting him to take her to that place he had promised.

His hand roamed the soft flesh of her thighs, rising upward. He watched her expression of wonder as she moved against his touch and she heard his response to her passion in the catch of his breath and the husky sound of his voice. "I love to touch you this way," he whispered. "I love to watch you surrender yourself to me. Touch me, Billie," he encouraged. "Touch me."

She sought him with her hands, eager to know him, to explore the mystery that promised such pleasure. Her own excitement grew as she realized his delight. The hardness of his sex was somehow vulnerable and tender, throbbing with desire. His body delighted her, tempting her fingers to find the breadth of his chest and the flatness of his belly and the strength of his thighs. The sound of her own heart thundered in her ears as she explored the fragility between his legs and the round firmness of his buttocks.

Moss found himself breathless from her touch, seeing in her eyes that she took as much pleasure in him as he did in her. Her lashes fluttered and the tip of her tongue moistened her lips as though she were about to taste a delicious morsel. He brought his mouth to hers once again, hungering for it, darting his tongue against the silky underside of her full lower lip. His hands never broke contact with her body, fol-

{ 52 }

lowing the rhythmic rise and fall as she pressed herself against him, following his hand, seeking passion's reward.

Billie was ravaged by this hunger he created in her, confused by it, not knowing where it would end, afraid it would. There was an emptiness at her center that craved him, demanded release. There was an exquisiteness in this contact that it was as though she were being fragmented, separated from herself, and nothing existed in the world but her body and his hand.

Moving over her, he placed himself between her thighs, his eyes igniting embers wherever they touched her. The gold spill of her hair on the pillow, her white skin, her gentle curves that were young and appealing, all beckoned to him. His eyes locked with hers as he continued his caress; his passions were fired as she met his gaze with abandon, letting him see the desire that dwelt there and echoed in the trembling of her loins. "Billie, Billie." He murmured her name as if it were a love lyric. "You're lovely, so lovely."

He fed her passions, gentled her desires, and brought her slowly and inexorably to the point of no return, smiling tenderly when she gasped with the sweetness of her release. She climaxed beneath his touch, crying her surprise, rolling her head back and forth as she called his name. He eased the tension in her thighs, pressed his palm into the contractions of her belly, smiling down at her reassuringly and persuading her doubts away. When she calmed, she smiled with the wonder of this discovery he had unfolded for her, and Moss had never felt such a surge of tenderness as he did for Billie at that moment. He wanted to be her lover, to carry her over the threshold of her passions, to explore the mysteries of her sensuality.

"Tell me you want more, Billie. Tell me again how you want me to show you more." His voice was so deep, a rumble in her ears, but she understood and eagerly whispered the words he wanted to hear.

He leaned forward, entering her, gently, so gently, filling her with himself. Her flesh closed around him, capturing him in an exquisite embrace. She caressed the smooth expanse of his back, arched her breasts against his chest. Her mouth yielded to his, deeply, lovingly. She encouraged his embrace, heightened his passions, grasping his buttocks and holding him deep within her. She felt the heat rise again from the contact of their flesh. She felt herself matching the slow sensual rhythm he initiated. She was aware of the building of tension again at her center, driving herself and him once more to that sweet release.

He felt her tighten and become rigid with her climax, her pulsations beckoning him to his own release. He raised himself up, grasping her bottom in his hands, lifting her, thrusting himself into her with shorter, quicker strokes.

Her body was a delight, her responses instinctive, and the expression of complete surrender on her lovely face brought him to the edge of passion and he plummeted over to the other side to join her in the celebration of her womanhood.

Their bodies glistened with the sheen of their pleasure and satisfaction. They lay side by side on the narrow bed, legs entwined, her head resting upon his shoulder. He brought her back from the far side of passion with caresses to her breasts and throat. He kissed her brow and inhaled the fragrance of her hair. His voice was soft and husky as he exulted in the delight he had found in her, enumerating those qualities he found so beautiful.

"I love you," she breathed, nuzzling her lips into the furring on his chest.

"I know you do, Billie. I know." And his answer was a kiss, so gentle and tender that it brought a tear to her eye.

Agnes walked across the front yard, keeping to the grass so her heels wouldn't click on the flagstones, and let herself in through the kitchen door. Laying her purse on the kitchen table, she went into the darkened living room. Frank Sinatra was crooning on the radio. Billie's bedroom door was closed and Agnes drew in her breath when she heard Moss's soft, intimate-sounding laughter and Billie's urgent whispers.

Sitting down on the dark brown Morris chair that had been her mother's favorite, Agnes faced the door to Billie's room and contemplated the quiet sounds she heard from within. She was aware that Moss was in there with Billie and she knew what they were doing.

It seemed strange to Agnes to be sitting out here when any decent mother would be breaking down the door to save her daughter. But, in many ways, Agnes *was* saving Billie—and herself as well. In all likelihood, considering Billie's recent behavior and the glow in her eyes, Moss would have landed her in bed sooner or later. The trick was to turn every disadvantage—such as having a lovestruck daughter who no longer wanted to be a virgin—into an advantage. Deliberately spilling the punch down the front of Billie's dress and arranging for her to be alone with Moss had been a terrible gamble, but so far things seemed to be going just as she'd planned. Taking a deep breath, Agnes waited. The next move in this little game had to be well played and she had to keep her head about her.

Hands folded in her lap, her face expressionless, time had no meaning as Agnes waited. When the door finally opened and Moss, naked except for his white slacks, stepped out, the first thing he saw as the Andrews Sisters sang "Boogie Woogie Bugle Boy" was Agnes glaring at him with icy calm. Billie, her robe clutched tightly about her, bumped into him and saw immediately what had brought him up short.

"Mother!"

Agnes stared first at Billie and then at Moss. Yes, it was a terrible gamble to take. Moss grinned at her, his eyes saying he knew what she'd done. Agnes recoiled slightly, but she knew she'd won. She could feel it in her bones, in every breath she took. Billie was going to be Mrs. Moss Coleman. What was disturbing Agnes at this moment was the knowledge that she hadn't won this little game by outsmarting Moss. No, Lieutenant Coleman had *allowed* her this victory.

As he'd walked out into the living room, Moss's thoughts had been filled with Billie. What an exciting bed partner she was! Willing. So very willing to please. And she was beautiful, in her soft, sweet way. Even now, thinking about it, he could hardly believe her boldness. One minute she'd had the robe on and the next, after seeing him in the doorway, she was lifting those warm tender arms to him, inviting him to be her lover. A wry, satisfied grin was stretching across his face—and then he saw *her* sitting in the chair watching the door. Agnes. He hadn't needed a bolt of lightning to tell him she'd been sitting there for a very long time. And the look in her eyes reminded him of Pap's just after he'd closed a very profitable business deal. In that split second, Moss knew that if he had a chance to do it all over again, he'd do it. Agnes or no Agnes. Billie was worth it.

One of Pap's famous admonishments skittered through his brain. Mothers automatically think in terms of rape; they can never accept that their darling daughters are ready and willing. Their second thought is of bastard children and social embarrassment. Their last—and most comforting—thought is of marriage.

"Close your zipper, Lieutenant," Agnes said softly. "It's getting late. There's no point in going back to the dance. It would be a good idea if you got dressed and left."

Dismissed. Caught just like a kid with his fist in the cookie jar. Moss wanted to laugh. He'd just stolen her daughter's innocence and virginity and she was dismissing him. But Moss knew she wasn't finished with him, not yet, not till she'd gotten what she wanted. He saw her eyes flick to Billie and realized that Agnes would say what she had to say when Billie wasn't around to hear or object. The urge to laugh was so strong that his throat began to tickle. Pap, you old bastard, you didn't tell me there were mothers like this one.

Billie, standing just behind Moss, pulled the belt of her terry robe tighter. The sight of her mother calmly sitting there made her feel faint. Grasping Moss's arm, more to keep herself steady than in any gesture of protectiveness, she protested Agnes's sending him away like a naughty boy. "Mother, this wasn't Moss's fault. I made him do it. I wanted him to and I'm not sorry!" she cried defiantly. "You have to believe me. I love him. You have to understand that."

Moss felt Billie's nails digging into his bare arm. Noble. Little Billie was making her declaration of love and defending him to Agnes. He should be saying all the things Billie was saying. She was stealing his thunder. This time there was no controlling the laughter that bubbled out of him. He put his arm around Billie's shoulder and drew her to him. That little movement, that little declaration of his own, was all Agnes needed. She bit back her smile, lowering her head to cloak her face in the semidarkness.

Billie sat on the edge of her bed watching Moss dress. She needed reassurance; she wanted to hear the words that would tell her he loved her, but she couldn't ask. What would happen once Moss left the house? Would he come back? If he asked her to leave with him now, this minute, she would. Please, God, let him come back. She was silent as she watched him button his white tunic with slow, unhurried hands.

Moss was avoiding Billie's eyes. Her naked love for him was almost more than he could handle. All his life he'd known that when someone loved you that way it demanded something in return. With Seth, the demand had been responsibility and obligation. He refused to imagine what Billie would demand in return. Closer to the truth, it was what Agnes would demand that made him cringe. He knew he had to look at Billie, knew he must take her in his arms. Poor little thing, she looked so frightened. What did she fear most—Agnes's anger or that he wouldn't return her love? Billie had nothing to fear from Agnes. Things had gone exactly the way she'd planned from the moment she'd doused Billie with punch. That left only himself. Love? Not yet.

He gathered Billie into his arms. She felt so good, all warm and soft. He felt himself stiffening. Billie smiled up at him and then laid her head against his chest. How right she felt, how good. She fit just right in the crook of his arm. Think. He had to think. But not here. He had to get out of here. He kissed Billie lightly on the lips, on the tip of her nose, on her closed eyes, and again on her lips. "I'll call you tomorrow, between eleven and noon. The admiral is playing golf then and I'll have the office all to myself. We'll talk. Good night, Billie."

"Good night, Moss," Billie said, choking back a sob. She looked so abandoned and lost and afraid.

"Don't worry, Billie. Things'll work out." He hated to see a woman cry. They got all red-eyed and sniffly and then they had to blow their nose. His sister was forever crying and blowing. Jesus, the things a guy had to tolerate. "Don't cry." The depths of his caring stunned him. Yes, he did care about Billie. "Stay here. I'll let myself out. Call you tomorrow."

Billie nearly collapsed on the bed once she'd heard the door close. She clenched her hands in her lap and waited for her mother. Billie's heart thumped madly all the while she waited. She wasn't sorry for what she'd done. She'd never be sorry. He'd faced Agnes. He'd said he'd call tomorrow. He *would* call tomorrow. Her eyes went to the rumpled bed and the wrinkled sheets. Emotionally drained, she fell back against the pillows and her eyes burned with tears when the scent of Moss's after-shave caressed her cheek.

It had been wonderful, everything she thought it would be. She pleased him, she knew she did; he'd told her. She smiled when she remembered his gentleness, his wildness. She flushed when she thought of her own abandon. How could something so wonderful between two people be wrong? Moss didn't think it was wrong or he wouldn't have made love to her. How she hated now the phrase the kids used. "Doing it." It sounded like two dogs in heat. Moss and she hadn't "done it." They'd made love. Inexperienced as she was, she knew the difference.

Where was her mother? Why hadn't she come into the room to express her disappointment and disgust? To shout, to chastise and issue dire warnings and threats. When the little enamel clock with the painted fleur-de-lis read one o'clock, Billie turned off the lamp and lay back against the pillow Moss had lain on.

Moss drove slowly, savoring the warm summer breezes that blew in through the car window. It had been damn close to a perfect evening. Caught. Caught like two kids behind the barn. He laughed, a rich sound that began in his middle and bellowed out his throat. Damn near perfect. But his thoughts didn't take him beyond the following day. There would be no more nights like tonight. Agnes had allowed him to sample the merchandise and it was to be his one and only. From here on in, he either made arrangements to buy the goods—and this meant marriage—or else removed himself from the situation entirely.

Moss whipped out his ID and idled past the guard at the gatehouse. He had some deep thinking to do. He parked the car, went to his quarters, and changed. Dressed in fatigues, he made his way back to the admiral's office. Now was a good time to take apart the maritime compass on the admiral's desk and put it in working order, as he'd promised. The admiral liked to avail himself of Moss's expertise with anything mechanical, and there was always a radio or clock or something on the car awaiting his attention.

He worked slowly and methodically, and was surprised to find that the sun was rising as he finished. He replaced the antique compass on the admiral's desk and devilishly propped up a sign that read KILROY WAS HERE, complete with the caricature of the little bald guy with a bulbous nose peeping over the fence. The sign struck him as funny and he wondered briefly about the origin of the popular slogan, but instead of laughing he felt like crying. Sitting at an admiral's desk fixing little contraptions wasn't Moss's idea of fighting a war. There was an aching at his center to be airborne, skidding off the flat deck of a carrier and rushing off to face his destiny. There had to be some way of getting out of this stinking assignment. But he couldn't go against his father. Seth was an old man and Moss was the apple of his eye, the old man's chance for immortality, as Pap liked to put it. Seth loved him and in return for that love, Moss owed it to Pap to go along. Seth was set on creating a dynasty, a Coleman dynasty, and his fierce pride demanded that Moss produce future generations of Colemans to inherit the fabulous wealth he'd created out of nothing but shrewd business dealings and a lot of luck. But maybe, just maybe, there was a way to appease Pap and still get what he wanted. To fly. To test his mettle. To pit himself against an enemy and win. Moss wanted it so badly he could taste it, and he worried that it would all be over before he could get in.

Wearily, Moss stepped out into the dawn, heading back to the barracks he shared with other officers for a much needed shower. Reveille was just sounding as he stepped out from the steamy spray and tied a towel around his middle.

"Okay, you wing-tailed bastards, let's get the lead out and move," Thad Kingsley shouted to the men lying sprawled in their bunks. "Let's all look alive like Coleman here. We're looking at navy, men. Real navy. Move it!"

"Knock it off," Moss growled irritably. "I'm not in the mood this morning."

"Get him! Big night last night. High school graduation. Ah, youth! Did you get to keep her out all night? Tell us about it!"

Moss endured the heckling of his friends until Jack Taylor ripped away his towel, hooting and catcalling. "Looks like our man had himself a big night."

Moss was on him like a shot. The men flinched at the sound of his fist hitting Taylor's jaw.

"Jesus!" Taylor complained. "What's gotten into you, Coleman? Can't you take a little ribbing?" He rubbed his swelling jaw. "You can hand it out, so why can't you take it? So who cares if you struck out? You can't win 'em all."

"It's none of your business if I struck out or not," Moss said. "Just stay out of my life, okay? And you better get some ice on that jaw." He headed for the latrine.

Thad Kingsley shrugged. "So the guy's in love. Leave him alone, Taylor. He's got something eating him, and if and when he's ready to tell us, he will."

Thad thought about the little fresh-faced blonde Moss had met at the USO several weeks before and frowned. He hadn't been serious when he'd said Moss was in love, but now he wondered. Could it be that a pretty little thing as sweet and naive as Billie Ames could break through that tough Texan veneer when other, more sophisticated women had failed? Kingsley felt a surge of envy that Coleman always managed to find pie in the sky, and at the same time he almost pitied Billie.

Billie heard the sounds of Agnes preparing breakfast in the kitchen and smelled the inviting aroma of brewing coffee. Just before six o'clock that morning she'd heard their roomers leave for work. Now Agnes and Billie were alone in the house. Now she had to go out and face her mother.

Bravado at seven-thirty in the morning was not something Billie could muster and her hand shook as she poured the coffee. She steeled herself and waited for Agnes to open the conversation. When Agnes nibbled her toast and sipped her coffee, Billie could feel her stomach tighten. She could see Agnes's reasoning. Billie was the guilty one, the offender; therefore, she should be the first to speak. Billie took a deep breath. "Mother, about last night. I know you're disappointed in me. I understand why you would be. I'm not asking your forgiveness; I'm asking you to understand. I love Moss. And none of it was his fault. It was me, Mother. I instigated—"

"Somehow, Billie, that doesn't make me feel one whit better," Agnes said sternly. "It's difficult for me to believe you could be so wanton."

"Mother, I didn't feel wanton last night and I don't this morning," Billie said firmly. "When two people love each other they want to be together. They want to make love." And then they marry each other, Billie said to herself.

"I see," Agnes said coolly. "Have you given any thought to the fact that you may be pregnant? It's been known to happen, you know. What if you're pregnant and Moss is shipped out? He wants to go. He's not interested in spending the duration in the Philadelphia Navy Yard."

"I'll talk to him. Let's not blow this all out of proportion."

"Billie, my concern is you. Nice girls do not go to bed before they're married. I don't want you to be like Cissy. Oh, yes, I've heard the rumors," Agnes answered Billie's surprise. "How that girl's mother holds her head up is beyond me!"

Agnes occupied herself with her coffee cup, carefully hiding her smugness. Everything was going as planned. She had to remind herself to be careful, to say just the right thing at just the right time. She sipped the hot brew, not wanting to admit to herself that Billie's statement had rocked her severely. Strength was not a trait she associated with her lovely daughter. When Moss Coleman entered their lives she'd seen that strength grow and bloom. She mustn't let Billie think she was being manipulated. Agnes sighed, wishing for those easier days when Billie was a little girl and had been so amenable and willing to see her mother's way and adhere to her mother's ideals. Everyone knew that Billie Ames was a talented, lovely girl. Why else would Mrs. Fox have entertained the notion of a match between

Billie and Neal? It was because Agnes had been farsighted, grooming and training Billie for a better life than this one. Carefully now, Billie had to think she was following her own lead. "Billie, you're so young. Moss is older, more sophisticated. You are certainly no match for him. I imagine he's had many women and he's the type to have many, many more. I don't want to see you hurt. Worse, I don't want you used and left behind. That kind of thing can become a habit. Look at Cissy. It's not what I want for you, Billie. It would be best if you didn't see Moss anymore, forget last night, and go on from there."

"No! I love Moss and he loves me. He's going to ask me to marry him and I will. And if he doesn't ask me, I'll wait for him, forever if necessary. I love him!" Tears were bright in Billie's eyes and Agnes felt pity for her daughter. Still, she mustn't allow it to interfere. Billie tossed her napkin onto the table and fled from the room.

Agnes finished her coffee and set the cup in the sink. She marched through the living room to Billie's room and closed the door behind her. "I detest such behavior, Billie. If you want to be grown-up and do the things adults do, then behave like one. I want you to take my place at the Red Cross today. You have to be there by nine and expect to work through lunch. Take a shower and get there as soon as you can. I'll call ahead and tell them you're taking my place. I'm much too upset to go myself," she added, knowing Billie's sense of guilt wouldn't let her refuse. She was right. Again.

The minute Billie had left the house, Agnes called the Navy Yard and asked to be put through to Lieutenant Moss Coleman in Admiral McCarter's office. While she waited, she let her eyes wander to the desk calendar near the phone. She counted the days since she knew Billie'd had her last period. The Moss Colemans of this world didn't believe in things like protection. Agnes would bet next month's ration stamps on that. She swallowed hard, not liking to think of the gamble she was taking. That it was Billie who might be pregnant and therefore Billie who would be taking the risk didn't enter Agnes's mind.

"Admiral Noel McCarter's office. Lieutenant Coleman speaking."

"Lieutenant, this is Agnes Ames. I'd like to talk with you when you get off duty. What time shall I meet you outside the gates?"

Hers was a no-nonsense tone. She meant business. Moss

grinned. She was one hour and fifteen minutes late. He'd expected the call before eight. "Yes, ma'am. I'll be off duty at three this afternoon. Good-bye, Mrs. Ames."

Beef. Oil. Something called electronics. A spread. Acres and acres of land. Money. Respectable money. Power. Prestige. All the things Agnes ever hoped and dreamed for could be Billie's. Billie would share.

Agnes settled herself at the kitchen table and penned off two notes to her roomers. She apologized for such short notice, but she could no longer rent the rooms. She sealed the envelopes and slipped them under the bedroom doors. She felt absolutely wonderful.

The Philadelphia Navy Yard was not one of Agnes's favorite places. As she waited for Moss she watched the activity taking place around her. She was still a young woman by some standards and she had to admit that there was something about a uniform that enhanced a man. For a few brief moments she wished again for youth with its highs and lows. She hastily amended the thought to include "providing I knew what I know now."

The Studebaker was hot and airless and smelled of the brake fluid the idiot at the garage had spilled on the floor mat. She checked her lipstick in the rearview mirror. She wanted to be in command and to be in command one must look one's best.

Moss Coleman walked through the gates at three-forty. Forty minutes late. He didn't apologize or make excuses when he opened the car door and sat down. "Ma'am," he said, smiling a greeting.

"Good afternoon, Lieutenant," Agnes said coolly as she slid the car into gear and away from the gate.

Moss was amused at the situation. If Pap knew, he'd be wetting his pants. Squared off against a woman. At the same time he was finding himself annoyed that she wasn't jittery or just plain mad. She shouldn't be so controlled. He had stolen away her daughter's virginity! She was more controlled than Pap was at times. Agnes Ames was a bitch. Well, Pap was a bastard. He supposed he was a bastard, too, junior grade and working toward first class. Agnes knew he'd make it. He could feel it and almost smell her triumph. That was okay, but he wasn't going to make it easy for her.

"You look fit this afternoon, Lieutenant. This heat is oppressive, don't you think? I'm hoping it will rain so my Victory garden will grow."

"I feel fit, ma'am." He stopped just short of returning the compliment and adding that he thought she looked victorious.

"Did you speak with Billie today?" Agnes asked bluntly.

"She called me from the Red Cross. She said you weren't feeling well so she took your place. My mother always uses a vinegar rag when she has a headache."

"Spare me your little home-grown homilies, Lieutenant, and let's get down to business." She pulled into the A&P parking lot. "I'm not in the mood for coffee and neither are you, so we'll dispense with that idea."

She was reading his mind; shades of Pap. Her coming declaration neither surprised nor offended him. In fact, Pap couldn't have done it better. The lady had what Seth would call spunk.

"I don't think there's any doubt in either of our minds that you will do right by my daughter." Moss knew his shrug irritated Agnes.

"It's quite possible—more than likely, in fact—that Billie will be pregnant," Agnes said flatly. "In your impetuosity last night, I doubt either of you gave any thought to the possible consequences or took any precautions to prevent them. In any case, any doctor could tell you it was the wrong time of month."

Wrong for Billie. Right for Agnes. What was it for him? Less than twenty-four hours and already she had Billie pregnant. There was a lot to be said for seizing opportunity when it knocked. "What is it you want from me, Mrs. Ames? Spell it out so this okey-dokey cowpoke can understand." Moss enjoyed the pink flush that stained Agnes's cheeks. All semblance of his drawl was gone; so was his humor. This was business now. Billie was a commodity. He wished he could hate this old buzzard but if he did, he'd have to hate himself.

"It's not what *I* want from you, Moss; it's what Billie is going to need. In case you aren't aware of it, Billie loves you, is deeply in love with you. You will notice I am not questioning your feelings—at this point they are immaterial. I want and expect you to marry my daughter to protect her reputation and your own as well."

Protect *his* reputation? What was she getting at? Besides wanting him to marry Billie, that is. It surprised him that Agnes could speak so glibly and forwardly about sex and pregnancy instead of alluding to it through euphemisms. Something was wrong here. Agnes was looking like the cat who swallowed the canary and he had a feeling those were his tail feathers tickling her chin.

Moss was about to give Agnes his answer but decided to make her sweat for it. Agnes deserved to sweat. Earlier that morning while tinkering with the admiral's compass, Moss had already made his decision. Certainly he would marry Billie. Aside from the fact that she really was a lovely girl and a surprisingly inventive bed partner, Billie Ames would be the perfect solution to his problems with Seth. Pap was hot spit on carrying on the Coleman line. Billie and a baby would free him of responsibility and obligation and he could ask for reassignment to the Pacific. Billie and a baby would free him from spending the duration in the Philadelphia Navy Yard pushing papers and arranging golf dates.

"I'll ask Billie to marry me tonight," Moss drawled, unable to contain the wide grin that spread over his features.

For an instant, Agnes was taken aback. She hadn't contemplated it would be this easy; she'd expected more of a fight from this tall Texan. She had the uncomfortable feeling that instead of her using him, Moss was using her for his own purposes. However, Agnes was not about to look a gift horse in the mouth. Without another word, she pulled the choke and started the car. As she pulled out of the A&P parking lot, Moss reached forward and turned on the radio, tuning in the ongoing drama of Helen Trent and her trials and tribulations. He lounged back in the seat and stretched his long legs, cap pulled forward so the shiny visor shadowed his eyes. His attitude annoyed her, but then she supposed that's the way they did things in Texas. Texas.

The sky was already darkening when Agnes dropped Moss off at the gates to the navy base. She had driven less than a mile when the cloudburst struck. Cautiously, she steered her car to the side of the road. This was no time to chance an accident, not now, when the golden gates of Texas were ready to open for her in welcome. It took cleverness to lift the Agnes Ameses of this world out of self-sacrifice and privation into the lap of luxury. Coleman luxury. At last she was achieving everything that was meant to be hers since the day she'd entered the world already screaming her head off at the injustice of it all. And it had been unjust, she reflected, all of it, from being born to Maude and Matthew Neibauer, those God-fearing, self-righteous parents, to her sorry marriage to Thomas Ames, made in spite and endured in sour resignation. . . .

Even as a child Agnes wondered if perhaps things would have been different if the Neibauers had not lived on Elm Street in the house Maude had inherited from her mother. Maude had married Matthew, a simple laborer, against her mother's wishes and the whole town knew it. They sniffed through their proper, middle-class noses in disapproval that one of their own should marry beneath her station.

Maude, always high-strung and nervous, anguished daily over what she imagined were intentional slights. Tearfully, she hung her wash at the crack of dawn before the neighbors could see her and be reminded that she did not have a colored woman to do it. Underwear was hung between sheets so it wouldn't be seen and NoWorry bleach was added by the gallon to the wash water. A white wash was synonymous with virtue, according to Maude. Matthew's dirty plumber's overalls were hung in the basement. No need to remind the neighbors he didn't wear a suit and tie. Life, to Maude, was a series of obstacles never to be conquered.

It had been Agnes's job from the time she was very young to clean the house each Saturday morning, before ten o'clock, in case company should come. They never did. In the front parlor she dusted her grandmother's brown horsehair furniture, replaced the crocheted doilies on the arms with freshly starched ones, and polished the whatnot. No one ever sat in the parlor, not even Maude and Matthew. Agnes scrubbed the front porch on her hands and knees and waxed it. She scoured the white columns with Bab-O and waxed them until the gleam could be seen from the bottom of the hill.

Once, her father suffered a back injury and couldn't work for almost an entire summer. They lived off the garden and ate sliced bacon only occasionally. She never complained, even when she left the table hungry, but sometimes she still cringed remembering the threats her parents had made to keep her from telling her few friends that they had no meat.

Friends; how few there were while growing up, and the front porch was the only place she was allowed to entertain them. She could never invite them back to the kitchen for cookies. The kitchen linoleum was cracked, the glasses weren't right, the plates were old-fashioned, and Maude feared the children would report all this back to their parents.

Agnes used to wonder if she'd been adopted. She hoped she was—she hated to think that she shared the same blood with these fearful, passionless people. There was no way she could imagine Maude taking off her pajama bottoms for Matthew, and there was never a sound from their room. It was always as silent as a tomb.

Thomas Ames drew her with his flashing dark eyes and ready smile. It was with him that she found the affection, approval, and easygoing ways she'd needed for so long. Maude was horrified. Thomas simply wasn't good enough. He was lazy, shiftless, a reprobate. The only home he'd known were the tiny rooms over the Twelfth Street saloon. He could never offer Agnes Neibauer a future.

Agnes, however, was much more interested in the very real and very passionate present. Thomas's smile, his gentle nature, intoxicated her. She was determined to have him.

Once, she heard Maude and Matthew fighting. "Why I never listened to my mother I don't know," Maude screamed. "She was right about you! Just like I'm right about Agnes and that Ames boy."

Agnes married Thomas Ames at the age of seventeen in a civil ceremony in Elkton, Maryland. Predictably—it wasn't long after Billie's birth—she came to the conclusion that she'd traded one life for another just like it. Once passion's glow dimmed, she merely tolerated Thomas, forcing herself to share her body with him on Friday nights. When Maude and Matthew died of influenza, she and Thomas took Billie, her few toys, and the cheap living room suite, and moved back to the house on Elm Street. Nothing had changed. Agnes carried on as Maude had done, living the same life and hating every minute of it.

She'd always wanted more, but how did you get more? Prayer wasn't the answer, as any fool could see, and hard work brought no miracles. Power and brains, that's what it took, along with a healthy dose of imagination.

Thomas Ames, husband, father, mediocre provider, died of a lack of imagination. Oh, he'd had it once; that was what had drawn Agnes to him. But time and worry and bills had taken their toll. He had tried his best, that she grudgingly admitted, but he outdid himself the day he took one gasping breath, one last exhale, and died on the kitchen floor. It was over before she could open her mouth in surprise.

She spared no expense on the handsome Springfield metallic

casket. Their neighbors and the whole Parish touched the bronzed metal at Thomas's wake, and their eyebrows rose in respect. Agnes was satisfied. None of them knew how many meatless meals she and Billie had eaten until the casket was paid.

Two hours after the Springfield casket was lowered into the ground, Thomas Ames's scanty wardrobe was packed and delivered to the church poor box. The mattress was turned and fresh linens, the ones embroidered for her hope chest, were put on the bed. She'd then dropped to her knees and thanked God for taking Thomas so quickly. Having to nurse him would have been unjust in a life that was already too one-sided.

The cloudburst was over. Agnes rolled down the window and then wiped the windshield with her linen handkerchief. Everything looked so green. The trees, the shrubbery, even the dress she was wearing was green. Green, the color of money.

It was a glorious day.

{{{{{{{{{ CHAPTER FIVE *}}}}}}}}*

Agnes Ames met with Father Donovan that very evening, even before Moss came to the house. She stretched the truth, just a bit, saying Moss was due to be shipped out any time now, so could the Father please dispense with the banns that should be read three Sundays in a row?

"Dispensation is not given freely, Mrs. Ames," Father Donovan said with a sigh, "but neither is it unusual during these times of war." Little Billie Ames was getting married. How could he refuse this child her precious request? He'd baptized her, confirmed her, and after all, Lieutenant Coleman was a Catholic—on his mother's side, at least. Most unusual for a Texan, the priest thought, but he was naturally pleased. "I'll make the arrangements, Mrs. Ames. It's usual in cases where the banns cannot be announced three Sundays in a row to have them announced in three different churches." He paused a moment. "There *will* be at least one week before the wedding, won't there?" he asked sternly. He was willing to go just so far.

"Oh, yes," Agnes hastily assured him. "Today is Thursday, so this Sunday makes one week. And since the wedding will be next Sunday, that gives us two weeks!" Her mind was clicking with the relentlessness of a metronome. Invitations. Only close friends, of course, and Father Donovan. Caterer. Champagne, something light and elegant. Accommodations . . . the Latham Hotel, downtown. Simple yet elegant. The word that kept coming to Agnes's mind was "small," but then she amended it to "hurried." She wanted this over and done with quickly, before any of the Colemans got the idea of coming up from Texas and talking "sense" to Moss.

The following days were spent on the telephone, readying the house and making arrangements. She explained to friends that "this war" made it impossible to do anything right, but Agnes knew Billie didn't care a whit if it was a formal wedding at a mass or simply repeating vows in the rectory. All she wanted was the ring on her finger that said she was Mrs. Moss Coleman.

Moss had voiced no objections and silently agreed to Agnes's little fabrication that he might be shipped out at any moment. Everyone appeared to be happy. Moss and Billie were to have the upstairs to themselves now, taking over Agnes's room with its big double bed. The roomers were gone, much to Agnes's relief. Everyone would share the kitchen and bath, but Agnes would move down to Billie's bedroom study. Moss would contribute to the household expenses, and of course there would be a nice little allotment for Billie once he went away.

Agnes was in the kitchen, her mind half on the unfinished letter before her and half on what to have for dinner. Her eye fell on the calendar hanging beside the refrigerator. Billie's period should have begun two days ago. Billie was pregnant. She had to be. She was going to bear the Coleman heir and secure her own and Agnes's future.

Billie wandered in and listlessly poured herself a glass of lemonade. She was thirsty yet almost afraid to drink it because her stomach had been so upset these past three or four days. Billie attributed the queasiness to the excitement of the wedding, but when she'd mentioned it to Agnes she'd been shocked to see satisfaction on her mother's face. Surely her own mother wouldn't wish this misery upon her.

"What are you doing, Mother?"

"Oh, I thought I'd write to the Colemans. I think it's about time, don't you? I discussed it with Moss last night and he gave me the address. It's such a long trip for them to make that I thought it would be nice to write about a few of the details so they won't feel left out."

"You didn't say anything to me about it, Mother. Neither did Moss. Why do you always confer with Moss and then I find out what you've decided after the fact? I'm beginning to feel left out."

Agnes stared across the table at her daughter. "You're getting cranky, Billie, and that isn't good for you or the baby."

Billie sighed. "You don't know I'm pregnant. I really wish you wouldn't talk like that."

"All right, let's say you're on edge—does that make you feel better?"

"No. Let's just drop it. I think I'll take a shower and lie down for a while. I feel a headache coming on."

"Is there anything you want me to say to the Colemans?"

"How can I say anything? I don't even know them. I've never even spoken to them, and neither have you. Since you're so bent on doing everything exactly right, Mother, don't you know that it's the *groom's* family who should make the first gesture?"

"Well, *I* know that, Billie, and *you* know that, but perhaps *they* don't know it," Agnes replied defensively. She was well aware of her breach of etiquette and admittedly somewhat unnerved by it. Certainly a family as affluent and influential as the Colemans was aware of its duties and obligations. In fact, this was the only fly in Agnes's ointment: the Colemans might disapprove of Moss's decision to marry; if so, then either they would convince him that he was acting hastily and should cancel the wedding, or they would ignore the situation entirely and never accept Billie or the baby as one of their own.

Billie rubbed her temples and relented, too queasy and achy to argue. "All right, Mother, you take care of it. You usually do. As long as Moss approves, it's all right." It wasn't all right. Why hadn't Moss said something to her? But if he had, it would have been one of those little "don't worry your pretty little head about things like that" speeches. She *was* being cranky, but it was only because she wouldn't be seeing Moss tonight. He had to attend a social function with Admiral McCarter, meeting and dancing with other women. She remembered how Moss had been the focus of female attention at the graduation dance, and even at the USO he'd attracted women like bees to honey. She tried to reason with herself that Moss loved her, that he'd asked her to marry him, but jealous fear bit into her like the teeth of a dragon.

She felt better after her shower, more relaxed. Curling herself onto the window seat, she rested her head on her knees and gazed out at the green lawn and summer flowers through the dark rusty screen, thinking about Moss. She always thought about him; even when she was doing other things, thinking other things, he was always there, like a friendly shadow, smiling down at her. How she loved him! It came from somewhere deep within her, welling, rising like a mountain river during spring thaw, rushing and turbulent until it found its own level. She knew Moss loved her; otherwise he'd never have asked her to marry him, but she guessed it wasn't with the overwhelming, consuming love she felt for him. To Billie, Moss was all that was exciting and beautiful. He was the focus of her passions and the man of her dreams. He was love. If he didn't love with the same devotion and depth, it was all right, she thought. Someday he would. He would grow to love her and she would become his world just as he was already hers. Somewhere in her heart, though, Billie was aware that Moss loved her as much as he could love anyone. It would have to be enough.

A delicious feeling of wickedness rushed through Billie. She dreamed of sleeping in the same bed all night with Moss. She wanted to reach out and touch him, warm with sleep, feel herself turning into his arms and resting her head on his chest. She wanted to awaken in the morning and see him before she saw anyone else, hear the sound of her name on his lips, have him crush her against him, have him make love to her. She hugged her knees to her chest. Life couldn't be more wonderful or perfect if God had stepped down from the heavens and personally handed Moss to her, to keep and to love. If she really was pregnant, it would be wonderful. Moss's baby. Their child. How she would love it. Moss would adore her because she'd given him a child.

A frown puckered Billie's brow. She wasn't certain how Agnes would react to a baby in the house. Babies meant work and confusion, Agnes always said. They demanded and needed attention. Yet whenever Agnes alluded to the possibility of pregnancy, there was something smug and satisfied about her.

Billie was so caught up in her daydreams she almost missed hearing the jangling phone in the front hall. When she realized it wasn't the church bells ringing in the noon Angelus, she scurried to the phone and lifted the receiver. She was breathless.

"Billie?"

"Yes, Moss." He'd called. He wanted to talk to her. How wonderful it was to hear him say her name.

"I can't talk for long. We've got a lot of visiting brass here today. I'm behind in my work and the admiral is edgy. He gets nervous when too many stars are around, especially when they've got more brass than he does."

"Maybe you'll be more sympathetic when you're an admiral," Billie teased.

"Billie, I don't want to be an admiral. All I want is to fly. I want to take my place up there with the rest of the guys."

Billie's heart flopped over. Every day, it seemed, the news was filled with stories of downed pilots. She childishly crossed her fingers to wish that Moss would spend the war with Admiral McCarter. She knew it was selfish of her, but she loved him and wanted to keep him safe. What was wrong with that? "I know. I didn't mean to upset you. I was only teasing."

"I know, honey, but I want you to understand that I could never be happy unless I'm flying. I've told you that all along."

It sounded like a warning to Billie. She'd ignore it. "Yes, you did, and I'm sure you'll get your wish when it's time."

"Hey, Billie, do you still pray for me?" he asked, his voice warm and intimate, sending shivers up her spine.

"You know I do," she whispered. She prayed. She prayed he'd always be safe and never taken from her.

"Good girl. What are you doing today?" he asked. "Will you think of me?"

"All day, every day," she told him, her pulses quickening. She imagined she could see his smile, his thick dark hair brushing his tanned brow, and those summer blue eyes that winked out from under thick black brows. Smiling eyes in an otherwise serious face. "I guess I'll weed the garden and then I'll move some of my things upstairs." She felt herself flush, remembering that just minutes before she had been daydreaming about sharing a room and a bed with him.

As though reading her thoughts, Moss whispered huskily, an intimate sound that made her blood sing, "Will you be moving them up to *our* room? I like having your little-girl things around me, Billie. And then what will you do? I want to know so I can think about you."

"Then I suppose I'll have to help Mother with the arrangements for the wedding." She laughed, gloriously happy. "If she'll let me, that is. She seems to be enjoying each little agonizing detail. Right now she's writing to your parents and seems to think I should do the same. What do you think, Moss?"

"Don't you worry your pretty little head about that. Just let your mother handle it. There'll be plenty of time for you to think about other things besides me." The old girl wasn't letting any grass grow under her feet, Moss thought. Pap, you're gonna whizz in your pants when you get that letter. He hoped Billie wouldn't think to ask him if he'd called his folks. Amusing. It was all so damned amusing.

"Did you know Mother was writing to your parents?" Billie asked hesitantly.

Injured feelings here, Moss concluded. How often he'd dealt with them where Amelia was concerned. Play the game. Lie if you must. "Not actually, but it's not such a bad idea, don't you agree?"

"I suppose so. But Moss, shouldn't you be the one writing to them? You've never said if you called them or what they said about our getting married. Aren't they even curious?"

"Billie, don't worry. Everything is fine. Trust me, won't you?"

"I do, Moss. I feel guilty, I guess, because I told Mother I didn't want to add a note. Lord, she even wants to send a picture of me."

Trust Agnes to come up with that idea. He smiled. Seth would study the photo with a magnifying glass. "A looker" is what he'd call Billie. "We'll call them the day we get married. That way they'll be talking to their new daughter. Tell me you love me, Billie."

"I love you, Moss. I'm miserable when I'm not with you. Tomorrow seems like forever away. I dream about us all the time and what it's going to be like when we're married."

"Good" was all he said. Hell, he had dreams, too. Of taking off from the deck of a carrier and soaring upward into blue Pacific skies. Wing pilot. Squadron commander. Pap, you ain't seen nothin' yet! I've got me a war to fight and you're gonna take care of my wife and baby. Moss knew there was a baby. Even Billie had confessed she was late. It was just a matter of time until a doctor verified the fact. Pap, you're getting a bonus and you don't even know it. Another Coleman. Carry the name, continue the line. It damn well better be a boy—Pap would never settle for less. Moss brought his attention back to Billie. "Tomorrow isn't so far away. Look, honey, I've gotta go now. The admiral is coming up the walk. I'll call you tomorrow and come by for dinner."

"Good-bye, Moss. Think about me?"

"I will, Billie. Now, don't you do anything too strenuous. If you're going outside, wear a hat. The heat is brutal."

The lilt in Billie's voice was like a birdsong. He'd made her happy and that was good. When she was happy she didn't think a lot and if she didn't think a lot, Agnes didn't look for problems.

"I'll do that, Moss. I love you."

Moss leaned back in his swivel chair. Admiral McCarter was nowhere in sight. He wondered how the admiral's golf game was going. If nothing else, he could write some letters. The kind Pap wrote when he wanted something from someone. In this case, Moss was applying for a transfer, listing his first preference as the USS *Enterprise.* He'd get what he wanted; he knew it. He'd graduated top of his class and was known as a good pilot.

Before he'd had a chance to begin, the phone rang four times in rapid succession. He doodled on the blotter in front of him, drawing a sleek plane. His pencil slid over the blotter, honing its lines.

Agnes licked the envelope flap and sealed it. There, it was done. She did not plan to send the letter air mail. The Colemans would receive it after the wedding. Even if they managed to work in a phone call, it would be too late.

Agnes shrugged. Moss was expendable. Once he'd pronounced his vows—she was counting on his sense of duty—and the marriage certificate was in Billie's hands, he could fly off directly to Tokyo as far as she was concerned. It was Billie who was important. Billie and the baby. Of course she was pregnant; she already had the symptoms. And if by some strange chance of fate she wasn't, Agnes would be sure to give them lots of time alone. There would be a baby within the month.

Would Billie make a good mother? She was very young. Agnes didn't know. Agnes didn't care. The Colemans could afford nursemaids and nannies.

Little bumps like those on a fresh-plucked chicken rose on Agnes's arms. She swore she could feel the weight of the Coleman money. First she'd smelled it. Now she could feel it. The heavier it felt, the better she liked it. Billie Ames Coleman. Billie Coleman's mother.

Billie and Moss were married and the day of their wedding was perfect. The sun shone. The garden bloomed. Billie was radiant. Moss was handsome and dashing in his navy whites. Agnes was victorious.

The entire party, including Father Donovan, numbered thirty-five, and the reception was held at the Latham Hotel in downtown Philadelphia. Every time a champagne cork popped Agnes cringed. It was so expensive, even the house brand they were serving. Moss had offered to pay for the wedding but she'd refused. There were *some* things she had to do. This was one of them.

Moss found a quiet corner and for company had taken half a bottle of bubbly and a glass. He watched his beautiful bride as she laughed with her friends and danced with his from the Navy Yard. Thad Kingsley seemed especially attentive to Billie, and Moss was enjoying it. Now that Billie was his, all his, he could afford to be generous. He snickered as he remembered his own jealousy that night at the USO. What he'd said was true. He didn't want to share her with anyone and he'd never taken her there again.

Married. Good God, he was married and had a wife. Moss guzzled the champagne and had to fight to keep from standing on the table and making a toast. Not to his bride, but to his old man. Pap, it was a hell of a wedding. We all got drunk, all but the bride and her mother. We nibbled on strawberries and scrambled eggs and something called crepes. I've got me a wife, you old bastard, and I got her by myself. No picking and choosing. No running her past the Coleman receiving line. His eyes went to his radiant bride. A new Coleman. He held his glass aloft and winked at Billie.

Agnes's party was over. This was *his* time now.

The Hotel Latham was one of the best. The dining rooms were opulent; the little bistro at ground level fashionable and intimate. The service was discreet; carpeted halls muffled footsteps. This was where Billie would spend her wedding night.

It could have been a soddy hut and she wouldn't have noticed, not if Moss was with her.

Outside their room, Moss swept Billie into his arms and carried her over the threshold, his mouth warm and exciting against her ear. "You're mine now, Billie Coleman, all mine!" His arms were strong and she felt small and vulnerable in them, clinging to his neck. He echoed her own thoughts: he belonged to her now, and nothing would ever take him from her.

Their overnight cases had been placed near the bed and roses filled the room. Billie gasped her delight, knowing they were from Moss. A bucket of champagne and two glasses had been placed on the bedstand. Suddenly Billie was shy. It was still daylight. Going to bed was expected. On graduation night the lights had been turned off; their lovemaking had just happened, her passions rising to the surface. Hectic color bloomed on her cheeks.

Moss removed his white tunic. His undershirt emphasized his burnished, tanned skin and snugly fit the contours of his broad chest and manly arms. Peeking above the V neck was a dark curling of chest hairs. His waist was slim, his hips flat, his thighs filled the legs of his trousers. He was beautiful, and Billie felt pale and dun-colored beside him. Why would this beautiful man have wanted to marry her? she wondered. Yet it seemed right that she should find him more physically striking than herself; in nature the male of the species was more colorful and beautiful than the female.

Moss pulled the shades, dimming the room, casting Billie into half shadow. When he turned to look at her he saw the radiance that had surrounded her downstairs in the ballroom had flickered and died. She sat on the edge of the bed, watching him, her chin lifted and her mouth was set as though to keep from crying. He understood and a wave of pity washed over him. She was probably overexcited by the wedding, exhausted by the preparations, and overwhelmed with her new role as his wife. "Let me help you with your dress, Billie," he offered quietly, waiting for her to accept before moving toward her. Ordinarily, Moss was an impatient lover, but with Billie he wanted to take his time; he wanted to arouse her and have her come to him in the wild abandon she had shown in her own little room.

Billie stood and turned her back, letting him work the tiny buttons of her gown. But first he removed her veil and Juliet cap, his fingers smoothing her sleek ash-blond hair, lifting it off her neck to place a kiss that reverberated through her. Tender fingers and loving hands helped her out of her gown, leaving her in her slip. Moss's hands ached with the need to caress her and his body ached with a stronger need as he gazed at her. She was lovely, his Billie, built on delicate, slender lines, her breasts round and perfect for her figure. Her waist was slim above the gentle slope of her hips and soft curve of her thighs. He felt her shiver beneath his touch.

Moss wrapped his arms around her waist, standing behind her, pressing his lips into the hollow between her shoulder and neck. "Don't be afraid of me, Billie. Don't ever be afraid." His voice was warm and loving, cracking the veneer of her shyness. She leaned back against his lean, hard body. "I'll pour us some champagne and you slip into something comfortable," he murmured.

When Billie stepped out of the bathroom into the cool, shade-darkened room, the radio was playing softly and Moss was waiting for her on the bed. She drew in her breath apprehensively, knowing she was being silly; but the sight of his naked chest both excited and intimidated her, until she saw that he was reclining on top of the covers, still wearing his white trousers.

"You're beautiful." He smiled up at her, his intense blue eyes skimming over her nightie. "Come and lie down here beside me. I want to hold you."

Billie crept into his embrace, resting her head against his shoulder. His arms brought her close, warming her skin, giving her solace, demanding nothing. From time to time his lips caressed her brow and he inhaled the fragrance of her hair. He was gentleness. He was understanding. And she loved him.

Street sounds wafted through the windows and seemed in harmony with the music on the radio. The bed seemed strange, longer than her own and wider, alien. The furnishings of the room were impersonal, used by hundreds of other people. Everything was strange, everything was unfamiliar, except the touch of Moss's hand stroking her hair and the clean masculine scent of him and the heat of his body beside hers. Billie turned to that familiarity, seeking reassurance from it, hoping to find the security she did not feel.

He took her hand in his and brought it to his lips, caressing her fingertips, nibbling, tickling her palm with the tip of his tongue. Shyly, she withdrew her hand.

"What's my Billie thinking?" he asked softly.

After a long moment: "I'm afraid. I'm silly, I know, but I'm afraid. You cause such feelings in me, Moss, and they scare me."

"Would it help you to know that you cause the same feelings in me? The very same, Billie."

"I do?" She turned her head, looking up into his face, and saw the truth of his words in his eyes.

"You do. I've never been a husband before, either. I want things to be exactly right. I don't want to disappoint you, Billie. We've been together before, but it was different then, wasn't it? I was Moss Coleman. You were Billie Ames. Now we're married, Mr. and Mrs., and there's a whole life ahead of us. But we're still the same people, Billie. And we can grow together, can't we?"

His words released her fears. He understood. Billie felt such a rush of love for him that she wound her arms around his neck and kissed him, pouring out her emotions in the sweet contact between them. His hand caressed her shoulder; his arm tightened about her waist. "Oh, yes, Billie," he murmured against her mouth, "I want everything to be perfect for you. You do things to me, Billie, in here." He pressed the flat of her hand against his heart.

Billie melted against him, giving herself up to him, rejoicing in the feel of his lips brushing against hers so gently, so very gently. He kissed the curve of her chin, traced the length of her throat and the cleft between her breasts. The ribbons at the bodice of her nightie gave way to his fingers, baring her for his kisses and the easy caress of his hand.

She shuddered with the first wave of passion, closing her eyes and welcoming the sensation. He left her for a moment and when he returned he was naked, the strength of his long legs and firm thighs pressing against hers. He helped her remove her nightie, seeing how she kept her eyes lowered and averted. Tenderly, he lifted her chin, willing her to look into his eyes, to see him, to find what she most wanted to see. He smiled, that slightly askew grin that could turn her heart over in her chest. "My Billie," he whispered, "my beautiful, adorable Billie."

He lay down beside her, drawing her into his arms, kissing her again and again with a passion that was answered by her own. He traced delicate patterns over her face and brow, nibbled at her ears and lowered to the hollow of her throat and

{ 77 }

across the fullness of her breasts, circling but not touching the taut rosy crests, before returning again to her mouth. He savored the young clean scent of her and sampled the sweet taste of her skin. His hands stroked the velvet of her thighs and belly but refrained from going further.

Moss sensed that he was breaking through the barrier of Billie's insecurity. It would be so easy to sweep her over the edge with him, but somehow he knew it wouldn't be enough. Passion was never enough. It was hollow and meaningless unless it was accompanied by some deeper emotion, a lasting commitment, a joining of hands before taking that leap together. He almost laughed at himself; with other women passion had always been its own reward, but not with Billie. He wanted, no, needed her to love him. "Do you want me, Billie? Do you love me?"

He waited for her answer, wanting to hear her commit herself to him. He hadn't wanted to rush her; he didn't want to reveal his own burning need for her that could leave him feeling vulnerable and uncertain. But a deeper need made him insist. "Tell me, Billie," he whispered against the beating pulse of her throat, sending little tremors vibrating through her.

"Yes, I want you. Yes, yes, I love you. I'll always love you," she told him, her gaze melting into his, willing him to know how much she loved him, how much she needed him. "I want you to make love to me," she said in a hungry, husky voice she hardly recognized as her own. "I want you to teach me to make love to you."

Moss was excited by her admission, all sensation heightened. He captured her mouth with his own, evoking a low, sensual groan. He placed her hand on his body, teaching her the rhythm, and he became helpless beneath her touch, awarding to her the power and the control over his desire. He invited her caresses, inspired them. He wanted to please her, to have her find him pleasing.

Billie's eyes shone victorious at this new conquest. His tremors and shudders echoed her own. She smoothed the flat of her palms over his body, delighting in the comparison between the silky thicket of hairs on his chest and the rougher coat surrounding his sex. Her mouth found the pulse at the base of his neck and the ruddy flesh of his nipples that responded just like her own, forming into hard little nubs that teased the tongue and invited her suckling. She tasted and licked, following her whims, excited by her explorations of

{ 78 }

the flatness of his belly and the firmness of his thighs. He gave himself over to her, reveling in the feel of her mouth on his body and rejoicing in the fire that burned in her eyes.

Billie exulted in the power of her sensuality, delighted in the dominion of her femininity. She sought him with fevered lips, possessed him with seeking hands, her own passions erupting and overflowing with the realization that she could give him this pleasure. The unfamiliarity of his sex intoxicated her, beckoning her caress, revealing its strength and yet evoking tenderness with its vulnerability. She wanted to find each hollow of his body, trace every line with her fingers and lips. She wanted to possess him, to make his body as familiar to her as her own.

Moss gritted his teeth to retain control of himself. It would be so easy to give in to this driving need for release. But he wanted to make love to her, to prompt her own driving ambitions for satisfaction. With a groan of regret, he seized her haunches and brought himself on top of her. He returned her caress, answered her hungry kisses. His hands never left her body, smoothing, tempering, yielding, following her sensations and silent demands.

He kissed her eyes, her nose, her mouth, before pulling himself from her embrace to position himself between her parted thighs. His eyes devoured her as she waited for him. Her tumble of soft golden hair shone against the pillow; her skin was bathed in a sleek sheen that silkened the contact between them. She trembled uncontrollably. Fire flickered through her as his mouth moved down her body, and then the fire raged from the most intimate of kisses. Billie felt herself flying upward, like a cinder in an autumn breeze, floating toward the sun. Suddenly the sun was within her, bright and glowing, consuming her reserve and making her part of the universe.

Her body opened to him, needing him, knowing that only he could fill this vast space within her that had once been the sun. His body became a part of her own, completing her.

He watched her face as he moved within her, seeing the passions that he had ignited and that were now consuming him. Sheath and shaft embraced as he drove himself deep within her, thrusting harder, faster, blindly seeking the far side of passion and holding her fast as he tumbled them over the edge.

Billie fell asleep in her husband's arms. The last vestiges of girlhood had been shattered and broken and she had been afraid she would never be whole again. But the fragments had fallen away to reveal the warm, loving woman who lived beneath. This, then, had been her first step into womanhood and Moss had led her to victory.

(((((((((CHAPTER SIX)))))))))

"I don't know, Moss." Billie pulled back on his hand, feet dragging as they crossed the tarmac to the little plane straining in the wind against the wires that anchored her to the ground.

"Come on, Billie. I want to take you up. It's important to me," he insisted, urging her forward. "Look at her sitting out there, just waiting for us. You'll love her. I promise you will."

"No, Moss, please," she pleaded. "Can't I just wait here?"

"No, Billie, you can't wait here. I want you up there with me. You're married to a flyer and I want you to know what it's like. Don't you trust me?"

There was such hurt in his eyes that Billie would have done anything to assuage it. She could never bring herself to cause him pain or disappointment, especially in herself. "Of course I trust you. It's that machine I don't trust. Mother says if God meant for us to fly, He would have given us wings."

"But He did, Billie. Only He didn't attach them to our backs. Those are the wings He gave us. Now, will you stop being a silly little girl and take to the air with your man?"

Billie followed behind Moss as though she were being led before a firing squad.

"She's a beauty, isn't she? She's a PT nineteen, a trainer, and safer than Ivory Soap."

The craft's fuselage was painted a dark meridian blue and her wings, carried low under the main body, were painted a garish yellow. Billie saw nothing of beauty here, only that the cockpit was open to the sky. She knew a terrible fear. "Moss! There's no roof! I'll fall out!"

"Not roof," he corrected, "canopy. And no, you won't fall out. You'll be safely strapped in. You'll love it, Billie. You will."

{ 80 }

Moss was already involved in his ground check. His hands smoothed over the wafer-thin edge of the wings, testing the elevator flaps and trailing beneath to some unseen gadgetry. Billy watched him, eyes focused on those sensitive fingers as they ran over the skin of the aircraft. It was the way a man would caress a woman; delicately, worshipping, exploring.

The hot wind blew relentlessly across the tarmac, ballooning Moss's shirt and ruffling his dark, crisp hair. Her own slacks were flapping violently against her legs and the sun was already burning the tip of her nose. But Moss was oblivious to everything but the craft. He checked something near the tail, and as a final gesture he kicked one of the balloon tires.

"She's in great shape," he declared. "C'mon, Billie, up you go!"

Showing her where to step, Moss placed his hands firmly on her neat little bottom and shoved as she gracelessly climbed onto the plane and then down into the front seat.

"Now tuck your hair up onto your head and put this on." He handed her a leather helmet. "Without a canopy the wind'll blow you to kingdom come. Be sure to pull it down firmly over your ears and watch out for that wire—it goes to the headset and plugs into the instrument panel."

Her fingers frozen with terror, Billie fumbled with the wind-tangled strands of hair, pushing them beneath the leather helmet. Moss was spitting on the inside lenses of the goggles and wiping them with the sleeve of his shirt. "Can't have them fogging up, want you to see what it's all about," he said, handing them to her and instructing her to pull the band at the back of her head to secure them.

She didn't want to do this—she hated it already—but most of all, she hated Moss's condescending tolerance. The excitement lighting his eyes wasn't for her. It was for this garishly painted aircraft that could offer him something she couldn't.

Billie watched with dread as Moss released the guide wires holding the craft to the ground. The space inside the cockpit was small and narrow with barely enough shoulder room for herself, much less a man, but the space beneath the instrument panel was deep and long, built to accommodate long legs. Billie's feet fell far short of the interior bulkhead, where they could have found purchase and helped to brace her against the motion of the plane. She felt as though she were dangling on her seat, frail and vulnerable.

Moss slapped the fuselage twice at Billy's left elbow before climbing into the seat behind her. The few inches of bulkhead separating them seemed miles wide, robbing her of his much needed closeness. When the sudden spurt of engine power turned the prop, slowly at first and then with the alarming speed and thrust of a turbine, Billie's fingernails bit into the palm of her hands. The soft balloon tires bounced them down the runway as they gathered speed, jostling her in her seat, feet reaching for purchase to steady herself. She was unaware of a crackle in her ears until she heard Moss's voice coming over the headset. "Take it easy, Billie. We're almost up and then the going is smooth."

Billie squeezed her eyes shut against the sight of the tarmac speeding beneath the wings. A sudden burst of power, a last bounce, and they left the ground. "Atta girl," Moss was saying, "easy now, easy." Billie hung on to the sound of his voice, taking the reassurances deep inside her. It was the only contact between them and she clung to it. "Give the little lady a nice ride; it's her first time up. Easy, sweetheart, easy."

Billie's eyes popped open behind the protection of the goggles. Moss was sweet-talking the plane! That familiar loving note in his voice wasn't for her at all, but for this damn piece of machinery with her bumpy riveted skin and whorish paint!

"We're going up, Billie. Hold on!" And the nose of the little trainer plane shot upward vertically. Billie gulped, swallowing past the painful lump of fear. Her eyes squeezed shut again and she decided not to open them again until she was once more standing on God's own earth. She felt the wind against the exposed portions of her face, whistling past her ears. The engine vibrated, sending shivers through her body. She held a white-knuckled grip on the edges of her seat, praying that she would live past this moment into the next and the next until she was once again on the ground. A terrible heart-squeezing fear iced her veins and stole her air.

"That's my girl! You're a beauty! A real beauty!" Moss cried, exhilarated.

They were up for more than an hour, Billie clutching furiously to the sides of her seat, her stomach heaving. When Moss finally set the craft onto the runway and taxied to her reserved space on the tarmac, Billie had to pry her stiffened fingers loose, pressing them against her legs in order to work them out of their clawed posture.

She had hated it, every minute of it. Worse, she now understood fully that airplanes were her rivals for Moss's affection. An acid jealousy stirred in her at the realization, as though airplanes were flesh-and-blood women.

After reattaching the guide wires, Moss came to help her out of the cockpit. His face was beaming, wreathed with smiles. "God, I can't tell you how good that was. Every day I don't fly I only feel half-alive!" His hand reached out beyond Billie to once again appreciate the sweep of the wing tip. "You're a sweet little thing," he said. "And you're a sweet little copilot." He threw his arms around Billie's shoulder to hug her against him, leading her with long strides across the tarmac back to the hangar.

When she came abreast of it, she abruptly tore away from Moss and entered the door marked "Ladies." Staggering to her knees, she knelt before what she'd heard Moss call the "porcelain princess" and vomited.

Billie and Moss moved into the master bedroom on the second floor of 479 Elm Street. Privacy was theirs.

June gave way to July and the days were long and hot. Billie was plagued with morning sickness, which she tried to cover by not rising for the day until after Moss left for the Navy Yard. But Agnes had the eyes of a hawk and always seemed to be standing outside the bathroom door just as Billie made her wild dash each morning to retch in the bowl. And always there was the satisfied expression in Agnes's eyes, which Billie mistook for a gloating judgment. "Bad things happen to bad girls." How often she'd heard Agnes repeat that smug little saying as she was growing up. By now her mother should have forgiven her little indiscretion. After all, she was married now. Happily married to a wonderful man.

There was no doubt in Billie's mind that she was pregnant. Still, she never spoke the word aloud. Until a physician made it official, she was simply a young married woman with a delicate stomach. Every so often Billie was aware of how Moss's glance went to Agnes, and sometimes it seemed that they had more in common than she had first realized. Moss didn't exactly defer to Agnes, but he did seem to discuss things with her first. Where had this understanding between them come from? How had it happened? Hesitantly, she spoke of it to Moss, and he was quick to tell her it was her imagination. She believed him.

{ 83 }

Dinner was over—breaded pork chops, to which Moss had added ketchup. He liked to add a variety of spicy condiments to his food, especially to Agnes's plain home-style meals. He liked to sink his teeth into thick rare beef or juicy fried chicken, not a pork chop that had been cooked to kingdom come or an indefinable meat loaf. The pork chops hadn't even been center cuts. Rationing was something that never concerned the Colemans of Texas.

"Whose turn is it to wash, yours or mine?" Billie asked, smiling across the table at her handsome husband.

"You two argue it out. I have a meeting," Agnes declared, rising from the table.

Moss volunteered to dry. He disliked soapy water up to his elbows and under any other circumstances would have refused any kitchen duty at all. At home, they had cooks and house-keepers who handled the mundane chores of living.

Billie liked being alone in the kitchen with Moss, doing all the little things that married couples did. Someday, they'd have a little house all their own and a swing in the backyard for their baby. "I heard the news this morning," she said, scraping the plates into the trash. "The USS *Enterprise* has been assigned a new commander. A Captain Davis. Did you know that, Moss?" Now why had she said that? Why must she persist in punishing herself by mentioning ships and carriers and airplanes and then watch for the eager expression in his eyes?

"Yes, I heard." Christ, he'd give his right arm to be on that ship. Davis. Should he tell Billie now or later? Later always made more sense. Why mention it when he didn't know if Captain Davis would remember him? Just because Davis had been in San Diego while Moss was in flight training didn't mean the captain would go out of his way to honor Moss's request for transfer to the Big E. He had never in his life wanted anything as badly as he wanted out of the Navy Yard and an assignment in the Pacific.

He looked at Billie, who was humming along with the radio as she rinsed the dinner plates. She was all most men would dream of, but Moss knew he needed more than a pretty wife. He needed adventure, challenge; he needed to fly. His gaze lowered to Billie's waistline. Once the pregnancy was confirmed, he'd make his move.

Billie's voice was so soft Moss had to strain to hear it. "They were talking about Midway," she said, her arms immersed in dishwater. "You were talking about it only last week. Remember?"

"How can I forget? The Big E proved herself and closed the argument against aircraft carriers." Always when he talked about carriers Moss's eyes lit from within and his slow, easy drawl quickened to a staccato. Billie felt the stirrings of panic. "Shore-based aviation had only a minor effect on Midway. High-level horizontal bombing is okay for land targets, but it's ineffective against ships at sea. That's why the Flying Fortresses failed where the fighter planes succeeded."

Moss was thinking of the Pacific map hanging in his quarters. He'd bet anything Guadalcanal was next on the Big E's agenda. When he noticed Billie's silence he looked up to see a great tear rolling down her cheek. "Hey, Billie, what's wrong?" He dropped the dishtowel and gathered her into his arms.

She cried softly into his chest. "I was just thinking of all those men and how they died. Moss, if anything ever happened to you, I'd die. I'd just die!"

"Billie, nothing's going to happen to me. Don't cry." He held her, soothing her, comforting her, thinking all the while what a bastard he was because soon, very soon, he'd leave her to join the ranks of the Pacific vanguard.

Routine in the Coleman/Ames household had taken on new life. Billie busied herself with small chores around the upstairs bedroom, trying to make it as inviting as possible. She spent hours standing in line at the butcher shop for something she knew Moss would especially like for dinner. On occasion, she squandered the precious coupons on steak—he'd taught Agnes and Billie just how he liked his steak done, charred on the outside, raw on the inside—and then pleaded an upset stomach at dinner, settling happily for a poached egg. Moss seemed unaware of the sacrifices Billie made, although they didn't go unnoticed by Agnes.

As activities in the Pacific intensified, Moss spent more time at the Navy Yard, sometimes coming home well after midnight and going immediately to bed. While operations for the Pacific were sent directly through the West Coast and not Philadelphia, information did leak through and he was hungry for every morsel. He was well apprised of the escalation of the war in Europe, as it was part of his job, but it was always to the western skies that his attention would drift.

When Moss arrived home late, Billie was satisfied to lie

beside him propped up on a pillow and stroke his dark head. And every night, she'd pray that he would stay at the Navy Yard and not be sent off into battle.

By the first weeks of August, Billie had resigned herself to morning sickness. She had missed her second period and was one week into her next cycle. It seemed to Billie that all of Moss's and Agnes's attention was focused on her belly. It was two days now since Billie had been to the doctor. Agnes had made the appointment. She had to know, and Moss needed to know. Billie told them she had a lifetime ahead of her to have babies.

It was three in the afternoon when the telephone rang. Agnes, who was hovering about in the living room picking lint off the sofa, reached for it on the first ring.

She found Billie in the kitchen drinking lemonade. Billie couldn't remember her mother smiling this way before.

"That was Dr. Backus. He says the rabbit died. That means you're pregnant, Billie. Moss will be delighted."

Pregnant. It was official now. She was going to have a baby, Moss's baby. She should be happy, ready to share in the joy; instead she was a tangle of confused emotions. She didn't think she was ready to become a mother. Not yet. She still wanted to have Moss all to herself. She needed this time with him, wanted it. She would become big and ungainly, uncomfortable and awkward. Would Moss still want her? Would he still be as passionate and demanding in bed? She couldn't comprehend how a couple could make love when the woman's belly was sticking out to here! "You're happy, aren't you, Mother?" Billie asked quietly.

"Certainly I'm happy, for *you*, Billie. And I'm sure that Moss will be just as delighted. You'll see. I think we should wait until after dinner to tell him, don't you? This isn't something you just announce over the telephone."

Agnes was jubiliant. She felt as though a load of bricks had been lifted from her shoulders. It was a fact. Billie carried the Coleman heir. Moss Coleman, Jr. It was done. Now Billie's and her future was secured, regardless of what happened or didn't happen to Moss. The baby's future, too. It was an afterthought.

"Mother, I'm going upstairs for a while. If Moss calls, call me, all right? Even if I'm sleeping."

"Of course, Billie. You do seem a little peaked today. It

must be the heat." It couldn't be anything else, Agnes thought. She wouldn't allow it to be anything else.

Billie lay back amid the mound of pillows with their lace edging. She was feeling an apprehension and dread that she couldn't explain. She should be happy, exuberant. Instead she just wanted to cry. This pregnancy was going to make a difference, she knew it would. No matter what her mother or Moss said. It was going to make a difference. She slept, her pillow wet with tears.

Billie was setting the table when the phone rang. Agnes answered, listened, mumbled something Billie couldn't hear, and then hung up. "Moss won't be home tonight. Take away his plate."

Take away his plate, as though he were already gone. "Mother, why didn't you let me speak to him? Didn't he ask for me?"

Agnes stared at her daughter. It was only natural that she was disappointed, although Agnes would never become used to Billie's romanticism. "Dear, he recognized my voice and he just said to give you the message. I think he was in a hurry. There seemed to be quite a bit of commotion in the background."

Billie sank down into a chair, worry and disappointment dimming her features. "You really are a lucky girl, Billie," Agnes said mildly, disguising her impatience. "You're married to a man in the military and you must accept the fact that he will have duties to perform. Think of all those other wives whose husbands are thousands of miles away."

"What time is it?" Billie asked anxiously. "Let's put on the radio and listen for the news. I just know something awful happened." And then she exploded. "I hate this damn war!"

Moss didn't come home that night. The following night he didn't appear or call. Billie felt a terrible, urgent need to talk to Moss. It had been two whole days. Didn't he miss her? Was what he was doing more important than her and the baby? He didn't even *know* about the baby.

Dabbing her eyes, she went to the phone, dialed the Navy Yard, and asked to be put through to Admiral McCarter's office. An unfamiliar voice answered the phone and explained that Lieutenant Coleman was not at his desk. Was there a message? Billie muttered something that passed for a negative and hung up. She hated the pitying expression in Agnes's eyes that seemed to be saying there were going to be many times like this and the quicker she got used to it, the better. She'd never get used to it. Never.

The next day, just when Billie was anticipating still another night without seeing her husband, Moss staggered up the walk. It was noon; she could hear the Angelus ringing. His eyes were red-rimmed and bloodshot from lack of sleep and too many hours in smoke-filled rooms. His uniform, usually impeccable, was wrinkled and mussed. Kissing Billie briefly on the lips, he shook off her clinging arm. "I need a shower and I could go for a cold beer. I've got three hours before I have to get back and I haven't had any sleep to speak of for two days, and no, Billie, I can't discuss it with you. I should've stayed on the base, but I wanted to see you. Now I'm so damned tired I'm hardly worth your trouble. Get me that beer, won't you?"

When Billie climbed the stairs with a tray holding the beer and a single rose in a bud vase, Moss was asleep. Three hours, he'd said. He looked so tired that it nearly broke her heart. Carefully, so as not to awaken him, Billie untied and removed his shoes and socks. There was a fresh uniform hanging in the closet; and she'd take it downstairs with her and give it a pressing. It would give her something to do. She bent over the bed to kiss him lightly on the cheek, hoping against hope that he'd awaken and take her in his arms. He didn't.

At the bottom of the stairs she met Agnes, who was carrying a small Big Ben alarm clock. "I'll just take this up and set it on the dresser. Your little clock will never wake Moss. He needs a cowbell."

Billie's glance flicked away from her mother to hide her resentment. Moss was *her* husband and *she* wanted to do for him, and she didn't need Agnes's interference. Agnes thought of everything. It was always her decision what they would have for dinner, what mass they would go to on Sundays, what day the sheets should be changed, whether or not the windows should be opened, when and how Moss should be told about the baby. Since her marriage, Billie had experienced a growing sense of powerlessness and inconsequence. Every choice or decision seemed to have been taken out of her hands by Agnes's greater wisdom and experience. It rankled. It was a small wonder that Agnes had not told Moss about the baby.

Billie had been fantasizing about the moment when she would announce her pregnancy to Moss. In the movies the wife always prepared an intimate little dinner and then afterward snuggled into the husband's lap and shyly made the announcement. None of Billie's daydreams were coming true. This was the first time Moss had been home in two days. When could she tell him? On the run, when he had a few minutes for her before rushing back to the base? It wasn't fair. If only she knew what was going on at the Navy Yard...

A feeling of dread stayed with her as she sharpened the creases in Moss's trousers and ironed his shirt. Moss had seemed exhausted but exhilarated. The thought made her queasy.

When Moss's freshly pressed uniform hung on the back of the closet door and his newly shined shoes stood in military line beneath, Billie took the morning paper into the living room. Her eyes raked the columns of the *Philadelphia Inquirer*. News of the war on both fronts leaped at her, but she could find nothing to explain Moss's absence. It was hateful. She wished it would all end so people could get on with their lives.

With nothing better to do, she sat on the front porch and worked the crossword puzzle, her concentration broken by thoughts of Moss lying upstairs on their bed.

When Moss loped down the steps a short while later, he found Billie dozing in the wicker chair. "Hey, is this how you spend your time, lazybones?" he teased lightly. He was already dressed in the freshly pressed uniform and his hair was still wet from his shower and shave. "I've gotta go now. If I get a chance, I'll call you later. Don't wait up for me."

"Moss, wait!" Billie pleaded, running down the walk behind him. "We really didn't get a chance to talk. I have so much to tell you. What's going on at the yard? Why aren't you coming home? Is something wrong?"

"Can't talk now, honey. The admiral'll have my hide if I'm not back on time. You be good and I'll call you later, if I can." He kissed her soundly and drove away. Billie watched after him, feeling foolish and ashamed and damned angry. He still didn't know about the baby.

Moss could see Billie standing on the sidewalk in the rearview mirror. For a brief moment his conscience pricked him, but then his thoughts leaped forward to the yard. Admiral McCarter and big brass from the Pentagon were debriefing West Coast command on the success of the air-sea strike and occupation of Guadalcanal. It was a foregone conclusion that the enemy would attempt to retake the island and reestablish strategic control of the South Pacific. When they did, the *Enterprise* would be there to meet them. Things were moving and Moss was determined to move with them.

Poor Billie, Moss thought. Maybe tomorrow he'd wrangle some free time and take her to the movies. It would be nice to make long, leisurely love to her afterward. Very nice indeed... But it was not bedroom action that he wanted now. Fighting, that was what he wanted. He refused to think of how he and Agnes had used Billie. She was a wonderful girl, soon to be the mother of his child, and she meant the world to him.

When Moss returned to the house on Elm Street, Agnes took one look at him and sat down on the hard kitchen chair. She told him Billie was out back weeding the pole beans. "When do you leave?" she asked quietly.

"Day after tomorrow. I got it, the Big E. She's coming into Pearl for repairs and that's where I'll meet her," Moss said, and realized that Agnes was neither surprised nor upset by his news. She'd been expecting it.

"Before you go out to Billie I want to remind you... she'll want to tell you about the baby herself."

"I won't forget. You know, don't you, that I didn't act on this transfer until I knew definitely that she was pregnant. Now I have to call my father and tell him," Moss said thoughtfully. Call Pap and give him the double whammie. The shock of knowing his son was about to be transferred to the Pacific front would be softened by the news of his first grandchild.

Billie felt herself being picked up off the ground and then turned around to face her husband. "Moss!" The happy surprise that had brightened her features faded into disappointment when she looked into his eyes. "Mother told you!" she accused. "I wanted to tell you."

Moss squeezed her tight, burying his face into her neck. "What difference who told me, little mama. C'mere and give me a kiss. I can't tell you how happy I am!"

Billie's disappointment ebbed with the force of his kiss and his warm arms holding her tight. What difference who told him, as long as he was happy, as long as he loved her this way.

As Moss held her, inhaling her sunshine fragrance, he reminded himself what a bastard he was. Not enough of a bastard to spoil this moment for her, though. His own news would wait until dinnertime when Agnes was there to soften the shock. Tender lovemaking would take the edge off later. He, Moss Coleman, was finally out from under; no one was going to jerk his strings anymore. Not Seth, not Agnes, not even Billie.

Together, arms around each other, they walked toward the house. "We're having roast beef, rare. Mother said it's the only rump roast she ever cooked that could still wink at her."

Moss laughed. They did try to please him, he knew, and he appreciated it. There would be the inevitable string beans made the way his mother prepared them. Small new potatoes with the skins on, fresh biscuits to dip in his gravy, and strawberry-rhubarb pie for dessert. He'd announce his news over the pie—after he finished it. He did love pie. "I can hardly wait until later," he said, leering at Billie. "I haven't been much of a husband for you lately." She grinned and made a grab for his leg, but he was too quick for her. "I'm going to jump into the shower. Help your mother in the kitchen. It's like a steam room in there. Why don't we eat on the back porch?"

"Would you like that?" Moss nodded. "All right, the back porch it is. Mother, we're eating on the back porch. I'll clean off the table and set it. Hurry up, Moss. The gravy cools quickly."

Agnes chattered nonstop through dinner. She felt anxious yet triumphant. It was as if she were conducting a symphony and it was being played chord by chord, note by note, building to the crescendo. She could sense it and so could Billie. It was in her eyes.

Moss laid aside his fork and leaned back in his chair. "You should give my mother the recipe for that pie." There was no easy way. Straight out. Say it. "Billie," he said softly, "I got my orders today. I leave day after tomorrow."

Billie's fork clattered on her plate. She knew it, just knew it. "Where? Where will you go?" she managed to croak.

"Pearl Harbor. The Big E is in for repairs and I'm assigned as a pilot. It's what I want, Billie. I have to do it. Can't you see that?"

Billie lowered her head, her soft blond hair hiding her bitterness. "Even knowing about the baby, you still want to go?"

"Yes. But I don't want to think of you here alone. I've given it thought and I want you and your mother to go to Austin. I can make all the travel arrangements. You'll live with my family until this is all over and I come home to you."

"Go to Texas!" Billie gasped, feeling as though the world were caving in under her feet. She didn't want to leave Philadelphia, leave everything that was familiar to her. She wanted to stay right here, have her baby here, be here when Moss came home.

Moss's eyes linked with Agnes's across the table. "I guess I shouldn't have included you along with Billie without asking you first."

Bitter tears stung Billie's yes. He hadn't asked *her*. The urge to scream was so strong that she choked and reached for her water. Moss was off his chair in an instant, clapping her on the back. Again he looked at Agnes. They were in agreement. It would be all right. Agnes would make it all right.

"You're going to love Texas, honey," he said. "You too, Agnes. You'll have the entire right wing of the house if you want it. I'm calling home tonight and I want both of you to talk to my parents. I don't want you to worry, Billie. Promise me. It's only right that our baby be born in Texas, in my home. You and your mother will have everything you need. It's a big house, Billie. You won't find my family getting under your feet, if that's what worries you. And you'll have the right kind of care for the baby. Neither of you will want for anything."

"I have everything I want right here and now," Billie murmured, lifting her gaze to meet Moss's eyes. "As long as I have you, that's everything to me."

"I know, honey, and the same goes for me. You know that. It's only that I'll feel better knowing you and Agnes have someone to take care of you. And I want my son to know his heritage. You understand, don't you?"

A son, he was saying, Billie thought. What if the baby was a girl? Heritage? What heritage? A ranch somewhere in Texas? Milking cows and planting corn? What was Moss talking about?

Moss realized her confusion and grinned. "Honey, I guess there's something you and your mother don't know about me." He looked at Agnes to include her. "Remember when I said my folks had a spread in Texas? Well, that's true, but I didn't tell you how far it spread. Sunbridge isn't just a little ole ranch, honey. It's an empire, built by my father. Naturally, someday it's going to be mine and our baby's. And it's not out in the sticks, either. Austin is a city, bigger than Philadelphia, with good schools and paved streets, honest," he teased, trying to lighten the situation. "You'll have your own car and anything else you want. But most important, Billie, I'll know someone is looking out for you."

Billie was listening so intently she failed to see the smug

confirmation on Agnes's face. "Tell me the truth, Moss. You put in for the transfer, didn't you? You asked for it. You pulled strings and did what you had to do to get to the Big E, didn't you? I thought all that stopped once we were married."

The truth. When caught with your pants down, always opt for the truth. "I told you from the beginning I'd do anything to get out of here. There's a war on and I want to be part of it. I didn't lie to you, Billie. I never lied to you."

"But that was before the baby. What about me and the baby?"

"Go to Sunbridge, Billie. For me and the baby. You're a Coleman now, and that's where you belong. You'll have everything you'll ever need or want. Give it a chance, honey."

"I don't want or need anything or anyone but you!"

Agnes took over. "Billie, we're going to Austin. It's settled. Moss is right. This is best for you and the baby. I'll be there so you won't feel alone among strangers. And I'm certain you will love the Colemans once you get to know them." Sunbridge. He'd said the name of the ranch was Sunbridge. "It's a good idea, Moss. Billie should be with family at a time like this. What do you think I should do with this house?"

"Put it in the hands of a good realtor and do your business through the mail. My father will handle it for you if you don't want to be bothered."

It was settled. Agnes was as excited as a child at Christmas. Sell the house. Nothing to come back to even once the baby was born. Sunbridge would be her home, too. It was more than she'd dared hope for, but it had all fallen into place. It was perfect and, given time, Billie, too, would see how perfect it was.

"I'll wash the dishes. Why don't you take Billie for a walk? Or ride down to the park; exercise is important for her now."

"That sounds good to me," Moss said with forced brightness. Why couldn't Billie understand? Why did women have to be so emotional? He hated what he was doing to her, but he refused to let himself brood about it. Moss linked Billie's arm through his and patted her hand reassuringly as they walked down the front steps. It would be all right. He'd see to it.

Billie fell into step beside her husband. She had to accept his decision. To fight him would be to alienate him, perhaps lose him, and that she would never do. If she felt betrayed, she would simply have to deal with it. For now, time was precious and she wasn't going to spoil it. Making things unpleasant wouldn't change a thing. Except, perhaps, how Moss would feel about her. Swallowing down her tears, she smiled up at him, a smile that came from her heart.

Moss put his arm around Billie, relieved by her smile. She was so warm and sweet. So endearing, so pregnant. He smiled in return. He'd love her for what she was to him, his wife, the mother of his child. Without Billie loving him the way she did there would be no baby, no way out of the Navy Yard. He'd always love her for that.

It was just before nine when Billie and Moss returned home. Time to call Texas. Agnes watched as Moss shifted from one foot to the other. He was nervous and she realized this was the first time she'd ever seen him so. Usually his brash confidence, just bordering on insolence, carried him through everything. Everything but with his father, evidently.

Moss covered the mouthpiece of the phone. "The operator is having some trouble getting through. There's the time difference, too." When Seth Coleman's voice came booming over the wire, Moss held the receiver away from his ear.

"Moss! Son! It's good to hear your voice. Got a letter not too long ago from a woman who says she's your mother-in-law. We decided to sit on it till we heard from you. What's this all about?"

"It's true, Pap." Moss glanced over at Billie, who was watching him intently. He hoped Pap wouldn't demand explanations he couldn't make. Hell, he'd postponed this phone call too long. He should have called from the yard, where he'd have had relative privacy.

"Why'd you do a fool thing like that? Wartime is no time to get married. A man isn't thinking straight. There's a lot of women willing to give tail without your marrying them!" There was a pause; an idea had just occurred to Seth. "Did you *have* to get married, son?"

"That's about the size of it, Pap," Moss said uneasily, glancing again at Billie, wondering how much of Seth's conversation she could hear.

"What's she like, this filly you married?"

"Aces, Pap. Remember that colt you gave me when I was ten and how I loved her?"

"I remember that you rode her to death," Seth growled harshly.

Moss's eyes clouded. Why did Seth have to be such a

bastard? He'd loved that horse. Zap him now. Get it out. "I'm sending Billie and her mother to Austin. I'm being reassigned to the USS *Enterprise*. I leave in thirty-six hours. I'm going, Pap. It's hands off this time around. The only thing I want from you is to take good care of my wife and her mother. You make sure that my son gets into this world the way he should." The silence on the other end of the phone didn't surprise Moss. Seth was going to chew on that little tidbit for a long time to come.

"That's the third dumbest thing you've done since you got shipped to Philadelphia. If you'd kept your pants zipped, you wouldn't be married. . . ."

"I don't want to hear it, Pap." He forced a smile for Billie's sake. "You're going to have a grandson, Pap."

"It's my *own* son I want right now!" Seth shouted. "Just stay put. I'll get on the phone and call in some favors. Twenty-four hours is all I need and you can forget shipping out."

"Pap, you lift one finger and I'll never forgive you. This is what I want. Leave it alone. I mean it." He waited for silence. He wanted to make sure Pap had heard and was listening. "You're going to love Billie. Think about it, Pap. You're going to be a grandfather." Bait. Throw the old man a little bait and see if he grabs it.

A thick rattly cough came over the wire. Moss could just picture the speculations, the choices, that were running through the old man's head. The baby was going to clinch it. Seth would never chance alienating his son and grandchild. "What's the mother like?" Pap asked.

Moss almost laughed. How could he tell Pap that Agnes was a ring-tailed bitch? "Just like you, Pap. You're going to love her, too."

"Your mother wants to speak with you," Seth said coldly. "Don't hang up when you're done talking to her. We aren't finished yet."

"Yes we are. You just haven't accepted it yet." Moss grinned down at Billie and drew her close. It was done. The old man wouldn't cross him now, not with the heir to the Coleman empire in the offing.

"Mam! It's good to hear your voice. You feeling all right?"

The voice was wavery and tearful. It saddened Moss. "We miss you, son. I'm so happy for you. I'm certain Billie is a wonderful girl and we're going to love her just the way we love you. When will we get to meet her?"

"Soon. Pap will explain it all. Billie and her mother are coming to Austin. Take care of them for me, Mam. Promise me."

"I promise, darlin'. What does this mean? Are you being reassigned? I thought your father took care of that. . . ."

"He did, Mam, but I undid it." Before she could ask any more questions, he handed the phone to Billie.

Startled, Billie swallowed hard. "Mrs. Coleman. This is Billie Ames. No, I mean Coleman." Moss grinned down at her flustering. "It's so nice to talk to you. I'm looking forward to meeting you and Mr. Coleman. I just hope our coming to Austin isn't going to be an imposition."

"Dear child, I wouldn't have it any other way. I'm delighted. In fact, I can hardly wait to get everything ready for you. Billie, I do want us to get on together, for Moss's sake."

"Thank you, Mrs. Coleman. I'll put Moss back on. He wants to talk to his father again."

Moss took the phone. This time there was something different in Pap's voice. Was it acceptance of his reassignment? Never. It was the baby. He'd probably enrolled it in Texas A&M by now. A trust fund and the kid's first pony were already on order. Seth would handle it all. "Send your family on, son. We'll take care of them for you. Take care of yourself, son. You're a damn fool. You know that, don't you?"

"I had a hell of a teacher. I love you, Pap."

"I know you do, son. Knock them on their ass for all of us."

The connection was broken.

In Austin, Texas, Seth Coleman rose abruptly from his oversized desk in the library and went to stand before the long windows that overlooked the back gardens of Sunbridge and the rolling hills of the cattle range beyond. He deliberately turned his back on his wife so she wouldn't see his defeat. The call from Moss had come as a crushing blow. The boy was going off to war and the sudden news of a grandchild was a trade-off.

Jessica Coleman watched her husband, wringing her hands in sympathy. Seth's love for Moss was obsessive and the thought of losing his son to the war was crippling. Jessica loved her son no less, and her fears were just as great; but her love was tender and maternal, without the driving power and possessiveness of Seth's. It was the way Seth loved—or hated—and she had come to accept it years ago, had learned to live with it. And what Seth neither loved nor hated did not exist for him. She, Jessica, did not exist.

"You've got yourself a daughter-in-law, Jess," Seth told her. He turned to face her and she saw he'd come to terms with Moss's decision. "But I've got myself a grandson!"

Billie lay beside Moss, watching him sleep. She needed to commit him to memory, so when she closed her eyes she could bring him back to her and conjure every line, every detail of him. She wanted to remember how his hands felt on her body as he loved her, slowly, completely. Her heart was breaking at the thought of his leaving, but it was a burden she wouldn't ask him to take to war.

She snuggled down against him, taking his warmth, resting her head against his shoulder. It was impossible not to touch him, not to smooth her hand over the breadth of his chest and the flatness of his belly. She loved him, and for this time at least, he was hers.

He stirred beneath her touch and turned his face to kiss her brow. His arms wrapped her in his embrace and he murmured her name. Billie's hand slipped lower, brazenly awakening him, sliding beneath him as he rolled toward her. At least she would have this to take to Texas with her.

{{{{{{{{{ CHAPTER SEVEN }}}}}}}}}

The week-long train trip to Austin, with its stopovers and delays and bone-rattling clackety-clack, was pure torture for Billie. Morning sickness, which continued for most of the day, had struck again within an hour of Moss's leaving. She was nauseated from waking till midafternoon, and then was so debilitated and exhausted that she spent the entire trip in her lower berth with a bucket provided by a kindly conductor. Agnes fussed and clucked for the first two days but gave it up after Billie cried to be left alone to die in misery.

Agnes absented herself somewhat gratefully and dined in style three times a day in the luxurious dining car, where she made it her business to tell anyone who'd listen that she belonged to the Coleman family of Austin. She never considered this a direct lie, leaving it to the listener to assume she was a blood Coleman or to wonder just who or what a Coleman was. Her entire attention was taken up by the adventure of it all; this trip was like an overture to the opening act. Not once did Moss Coleman enter her mind; from the moment he had stepped aboard the transport that would take him to San Diego and then on to Hawaii, he had been forgotten. Moss Coleman had served his purpose.

The Southern-Pacific superliner pulled into the Austin station the morning of August 25, 1942. Billie held her mother's arm and fought down the bile that was rising in her throat. Her eyes were rimmed with purple shadows. Her legs trembled from lying in her berth for almost seven straight days, jarring her spine and increasing her queasiness. She looked gaunt and sick.

"Mrs. Coleman?" A white-jacketed porter approached them, smile gleaming.

"Yes," Agnes answered for Billie, who sank down again on the edge of the lower berth.

"If you'll follow me, Mrs. Coleman, I'll take you to your party. They're waiting on the platform. If you give me your stubs, I'll get your bags and bring them out to the car."

Obviously, the Colemans tipped generously, Agnes thought; this explained the porter's toothy grin. She dug into her purse and extracted the baggage claim stubs. "Come along, Billie. We mustn't keep everyone waiting."

The porter led them to the back of the train and positioned a little stepstool to help them disembark. The capped head and uniformed shoulders of a chauffeur were visible behind a white-haired woman and a tall, bulky-shouldered man leaning on a cane. They stood apart from the station throng.

Billie's eyes met those of her father-in-law and she was sure of what she read in them: So this was the fragile, sickly female that Moss had the misfortune to marry! She turned to Moss's mother and saw compassion and understanding in the soft gray gaze. Billie found herself heading for the woman's outstretched arms.

"You're ill, child," Jessica Coleman said. "You come along

with me. Tita—that's our housekeeper—has a cure for everything, and that includes morning sickness. We'll have you right as sagebrush in a few days." She didn't even have to look at her husband to know he must be thinking that Moss had gotten himself an ox in a ditch when he'd chosen this ashen-faced child to produce the Coleman heir.

Jessica turned to Agnes. "I hope you'll enjoy Sunbridge as much as we do, Mrs. Ames," she said quietly, and Billie recognized the soft drawl that was Moss's.

Agnes's polite response was designed to make perfectly clear right from the beginning that her coming to Texas had been Moss's idea entirely—it had seemed to ease his mind before he went away, and so, of course, she'd been prompted to oblige. This Agnes said without gushing, without any display of emotion. Her manner was subdued, exactly correct. Seth observed the performance and remembered Moss's remark when asked what the mother was like: "Just like you, Pap." Well, here she was. Agnes Ames in her severely tailored suit and small black hat atop her chestnut curls. A woman of few words and with a no-nonsense look about her. Seth approved. He looked at Billie and thought how unfortunate it was that Moss's tastes didn't run along the same lines.

"Why don't you take the little gal to the car, Jess," Seth suggested. "Poor li'l thing looks about done in. Mrs. Ames and I will be along shortly. Carlo," he addressed the chauffeur, "take care of the baggage."

Seth took Agnes's arm as they walked behind Jessica and Billie. "I wonder if you'd mind if we let Jess and your daughter go ahead to Sunbridge. I'm going to the office and we can take a company car home from there." Seth had no intention of riding forty miles in a car with a retching mother-to-be and this was as good a time as any to get to know Agnes.

"I wouldn't mind at all. Billie is hardly fit company these days. The baby, you know."

Seth forced a smile and his blue eyes beneath the thick gray hair glittered in a way remarkably like Moss's. Agnes watched to see if he carried the cane for effect or out of need. He did walk with a slight limp, but not enough, she thought, to warrant the cane. There was nothing of the invalid about this tall, powerful man, whose eyes seemed to see everything and whose words said only half of what he meant. Agnes already felt completely comfortable with him but she knew instinctively that hers was the exceptional reaction: Seth Coleman would be intimidating to most women and especially someone as young and naive as Billie.

Agnes missed nothing, from the uniformed chauffeur to Seth's white custom Stetson to Jessica's expensive silk-blend suit and Stone Marten stole. When the baggage had been stowed in the trunk of the luxurious black Packard, Agnes climbed in the backseat, beside Jessica and Billie; Seth sat in front, with Carlo.

"Jess, Carlo will drop Mrs. Ames and me at the office. There's something I have to sign. We'll follow you in one of the company cars."

"Perhaps Mrs. Ames is tired and would prefer to go directly to Sunbridge," Jessica said, offering Agnes the opportunity to decline Seth's arrangement.

"Nonsense!" Seth declared.

"Actually, I had a very good night, Mrs. Coleman. I'd be delighted to accompany Mr. Coleman to the office and follow later."

Jessica smiled and nodded.

"She's Jessica and I'm Seth," her husband growled from the front seat.

"And I'm Agnes," she replied, mimicking his tone.

In spite of himself, Seth grinned. So the old girl could give as good as she got. Perhaps there was hope for the daughter after all. Perhaps in a few years she'd lose that soft edge and smarten up, be more like her mother. He was going to enjoy having Agnes about, Seth decided, as he decided most things, instantly. The women in his household were just too soft, too easily brought to tears. Agnes would be a refreshing change.

Agnes had been expecting Austin to be a frontier town, like in a western movie, but she couldn't have been more wrong. They drove down wide-paved streets, between sidewalks almost as wide. The downtown shopping area, while less developed and hectic than New York, certainly could rival Philadelphia's. The long black Packard came to a stop before a tall building with a pink Italian marble façade. Engraved in the lintel over the brass-and-glass revolving doors was the name *Coleman*. Agnes was impressed but kept her counsel, as though she were used to associating with people who owned their own skyscrapers. Remembering Billie, she said, "You will be all right, won't you, dear? I'm certain I'll be joining you before long."

Billie, her eyes closed against the bright sunlight and the motion of the car, simply nodded. She'd be glad when Agnes left the car, taking the overpowering scent of her Tabu perfume with her.

"Billie will be fine, Agnes," Jessica reassured her. "We're heading straight home and I'll put her right to bed. Seth, why don't you take Agnes out to lunch? It will be well past noon before you'll be able to get out to Sunbridge, anyway."

"I'll do that, Jess," Seth said politely. Why did Jess think people needed three squares a day to survive? He could remember a time when if he ate once a day, he could consider himself lucky.

Billie slept the forty-odd miles to Sunbridge and Jessica found herself patting Billie's arm. She wanted to gather the young girl close to her but was afraid to disturb her.

Billie Ames Coleman, Moss's wife, her son's wife, and within her she carried Moss's child. Her own honest-to-goodness grandchild. There was a time, so long ago, when she was as bright and hopeful and young as Billie. Time and Seth had changed that.

She was being bitter, something she usually reserved for the early hours of the morning when she awoke in her bed, alone. A body had a right to feel bitter at such times. Was it too much to ask to have affection and tenderness and perhaps just a tiny dose of companionship at her age? She wished fervently she could point to a time, a place, when things had changed between herself and Seth. If she had to choose, it would be the day of Moss's birth. She'd done what was expected, given him a son. His *first* son, he'd declared, the first of many! When Amelia had been born it was a disappointment that had turned bitter when it was discovered Jessica could bear no more children. Yes, that's when things went wrong, when Seth no longer came to her bed. . . .

Jessica had been wildly in love with the larger-than-life, rawboned Seth Coleman. She always laughed when he told her she was just what he needed, a refined gentle lady to upgrade the Coleman bloodline. "Jess, you have class," he would tell her, sweeping her into his arms. He knew what he wanted and he wanted her. He made no secret of his desires, telling anyone who would listen. She couldn't resist the handsome, aggressive young man, though he had worked with his hands in the oil fields and still had the dirt under his fingernails two years after they were married. He shared his dreams of owning the biggest, grandest spread in all of Texas, and she had known that he would claw it out of the bare earth. Once she had thought he had wanted it for her. Now she knew better. He had wanted it for himself, just as he wanted her refinement and respectability. She had given it gladly, thinking she would receive love and tenderness in return.

She could have done so much better, her family had told her. Carl Bowdrie from the Austin bank had wanted her almost as much as Seth. But there hadn't been the challenge in Carl's eyes that there was in Seth's.

Living with her parents hadn't prepared her for a life with Seth Coleman. Her father had been a gentleman with a classical education and a small family fortune. Her mother had been a lady. They hadn't been rich, merely comfortable. Life had been pleasant—filled with affection, genuine affection and love—and simple: church suppers, quiet dinner parties with well-bred people carrying on intelligent conversations, good wine, delicately prepared food, discreet service.

She'd never gotten used to the shindigs Seth threw. Raw whiskey, beer by the keg, and the "wheeling-dealing," as Seth called it; that was the underlying reason. Things had changed recently, though. Instead of raw whiskey there was champagne and the wheeler-dealers had somewhere come by parlor manners. But underneath it was all the same, attended by the same people for the same reasons: money.

Just once she had asked Seth for something that had been important to her. She'd wanted to keep the house she'd inherited from her parents. She would have been able to go there, to escape to her girlhood home with her children and show them that not all of life was focused on one man's personality and wealth. But this had been denied her. Seth had refused her request, had taken it all away from her. Just as he'd taken her children.

She had been a young debutante when she'd met Seth. Now she was an old lady living in a monstrous house she detested, with a man who didn't care if she took the next breath.

Jessica reached out and took Billie's hand in her own, wishing she could impart the strength she herself had never possessed. "You have to be strong, Billie," she whispered. "Not tough, strong. There's a difference."

Just before they turned into the drive Jessica shook her

lightly. "Wake up, Billie. I thought you'd like to get your first glimpse of Moss's home—Sunbridge."

Billie rubbed the sleep from her eyes and looked through the split windshield of the Colemans' Packard. They passed under a high wooden arch that was emblazoned with the name "Sunbridge." Miles of white rail fencing stretched into the distance. Tall oak trees lined the winding drive and on either side were expanses of bright green lawn with sprinklers pulsing rhythmically.

Billie felt as though they were journeying through a tunnel of dappled green. Far up the drive, bright daylight shone, and when they achieved the final turn the house came into view.

Sitting upon a gently sloping rise, the great house basked beneath the blue Texas sky and was caressed by the sun. Billie thought, as they came out from under the dark of the trees, that only here, in this place called Sunbridge, could the sun seem so warm and golden.

The house was a three-story brick of the palest pink, flanked by two wings, which were also three-storied but set back several feet from the main body. This expanse of prairie rose was accented by white columns that supported the roof of the verandah sweeping the entire frontage. A multipaned fan light crested the huge double front door and the design was repeated again over each window on the top floor. Ornamental topiary trees and crepe myrtle hugged the foundation, and surrounding the house was a magnificent rose garden complete with trellises and statuary. Billie gasped with awe. "Moss never told me about Sunbridge. He just called it a spread!"

Jessica laughed. "How like Moss. Sunbridge is a spread; it spreads over two hundred and fifty thousand acres. We raise thoroughbreds and thousands of head of cattle. They're kept on the back acres, and other, smaller ranches are commissioned by Seth for breeding. But this is only a small part of the Coleman holdings and business interests. Seth built all of this himself." Jessica sounded proud but Billie noticed a sadness in her eyes.

"The name Sunbridge fits it so well," Billie said.

"Yes. When Seth first saw the land he says he felt as though he could almost reach up and touch the sun. He came from very dark beginnings, Billie, and building this place was a major achievement for him. He hoped that a great house upon this rise would bridge his past with what he wanted for the future. Seth's not a romantic, not by any means, but the name of Sunbridge was entirely his own conception." The sadness had remained in Jessica's eyes, and as though to break herself from her solemn thoughts she forced a smile in Billie's direction. "We'll get you inside, Billie, where it's much cooler. Then I'll have the housekeeper fix something for you. I know you're not feeling well, so I'll spare you a formal introduction to the servants."

At the front portico Carlo opened the door for them and tipped his hat. Jessica gave him instructions concerning the baggage. The ethereal grace of the rose garden and the feminine sweep of the clematis vine surrounding the heavy oak doors did nothing to prepare Billie for the inside of the house. Shining oaken floors, massive beams studding the ceilings, thick dark Oriental carpets, and man-sized leather furniture. As Jessica took her on a tour of the downstairs rooms, it was easy for Billie to imagine them filled with smoke and noisy with deep masculine voices and thudding high-heeled cowboy boots. Panoramic paintings filled the walls, all of them depicting burly, tanned men at some masculine endeavor: branding steers, breaking horses, riding the range. It seemed that Jessica's feminine influence stopped in the gardens. The great house of Sunbridge was Seth Coleman's domain and every detail of the furnishings stated that fact.

"Come upstairs, Billie," Jessica said. "We've opened the second floor of the east wing for you and Agnes, and of course for Moss when he comes home. I hope you'll like what I've done with your room."

Here Jessica had exerted her influence. Pastel-colored walls, vases of fresh flowers, lighter, feminine furnishings. Billie's own bedroom was larger than the entire downstairs of the house on Elm Street. Soft mint-green silk moiré covered the walls, while pinks and golds were used for the draperies and bedspread. A luxurious carpet in a soft green-and-beige pattern quieted footsteps.

"It's such a large house," Billie said with wonder. "Our house back in Philadelphia could fit in this one at least six times. You don't try to keep it up yourself, do you?"

"My, no! The rose garden alone would put me under." Jessica laughed lightly. "There's Carlo, whom you've met. He chauffeurs and acts as a general handyman about the house. He's married to Tita, our cook, and he does the shopping for her, as well as other errands. Besides Tita, there are two or three other young Mexicans who come in for general cleaning and laundry. Then there are the stablehands and of course Julio, our gardener. Sunbridge supports quite a few people, Billie. Ever since Amelia—that's Moss's sister, you know—left for England, I'm quite grateful for female companionship. And now that you and your mother are here, I couldn't be more delighted. I want us to be friends, Billie. More than that, I'd like it if you learned to think of me as a second mother, if it's possible."

Billie was so heart-touched that she found herself rising above her initial shyness and stepping into Jessica's outstretched arms. "Moss loves you very much," she whispered, "and I know I'm going to love you, too."

Jessica's eyes were bright with tears. "It's going to be so good to have you here, child. And a baby on the way! Sunbridge has been lonely without young people and children. Now off to bed with you. I can imagine how nice it will be to be in a bed that isn't rocking back and forth."

During her first days at Sunbridge, Billie kept very much to her room. A stationary bed did not work its prescribed miracle. Billie still teetered on the edge of nausea for most of the day, and when she didn't, she was so exhausted from retching that she confined herself to the bedroom. Jessica fussed and fretted over her. Billie had never felt more loved than by this gentle white-haired mother-in-law, who spent hours with her to keep her from being lonely. Everything about Moss's mother was kind, gentle, considerate. Billie saw very little of Agnes during this time except for morning and evening visits, when she regaled Billie with her observations of Sunbridge. Agnes was very busy these days, familiarizing herself with every detail of the Colemans' house and family history.

One morning when Agnes came to sit with Billie over a cup of tea, Billie mentioned how helpful and concerned Jessica was. "Well, she should be," Agnes stated flatly, fussing with her ever-present rope of pearls. "After all, you are going to bring her first grandchild into the world."

Billie blinked and stared at Agnes. This was going to be her mother's first grandchild, also.

"Oh, I know what you're thinking, Billie, and you're wrong. I'm delighted about the baby and I do worry about you. It's just that . . . well, I'm much younger than Jessica, you must realize. I haven't really adjusted to the thought of becoming a grandmother. I feel as though a whole new world has opened up for us and I'm determined to explore it. You understand, don't you, dear." It wasn't a question but a statement. "Besides, I mustn't be selfish. I've had a lovely daughter and Jessica hasn't been quite so lucky with Amelia. You've never given me a day's trouble, but, from what I understand, Moss's sister has been quite a hellcat, rebellious since the day she was born. Certainly not the kind of daughter that brings a mother gratification."

"But Jessica loves Amelia dearly!" Billie exclaimed.

"Of course she does—Amelia *is* her daughter. But from what I gather, Amelia's running off to England was more to get out of a rather nasty scrape here than from any display of patriotism. Besides," Agnes added, lowering her voice, "we all know what kind of girls join the military, don't we?"

"Amelia didn't 'run off' to England, Mother; she was assigned there," said Billie. "She joined the Women's Army Corp right here in Texas and the WACs are important to the war effort. I just hope you never hurt Jessica by insinuating anything else."

Agnes interrupted with a change of subject. "Has Seth come to see you this morning?"

"Yes, he did, but I don't think he likes me, Mother."

"Don't be silly, and don't you antagonize Seth, Billie. He's simply a very autocratic man and autocratic men find it very difficult to show affection."

At this, Billie raised her eyebrows. "And did you learn this from the same person who told you about Amelia? I find it strange that you'd defend Seth and at the same time be critical of Jessica."

"I wasn't being critical, just observant." Agnes placed her cup and saucer back on Billie's breakfast tray and then stood up, smoothing her russet silk dress.

"Isn't that a new dress, Mother?"

"Yes, and don't you think it's the perfect color for me? It's been so long since I've had anything as nice as this and there are several more on order. The sale of the house should go through anytime now, so I'm not afraid to dip into my savings, just a bit."

Billie, who had an eye for fabric and fashion, realized that it had taken more than a bit of dipping to buy this dress. She looked at her mother objectively. There were subtle changes about Agnes. . . . She seemed more polished and put together, somehow. Was it that she was wearing more makeup these days? Or was it just being here at Sunbridge that put color in her cheeks and a glow in her eyes? Billie sighed. She supposed she'd been selfish. She hadn't noticed the strain her mother had been under for so many years to provide for both of them. Now mundane worries like taxes and grocery bills were no longer her concern.

"You look wonderful, Mother," Billie said.

"I wish I could say the same for you, Billie. Why, you're positively haggard—no wonder Seth doesn't like to come up to visit! When are you going to get out of that bed and come downstairs? The Texas sun is wonderful and at least it would help you get rid of that sickroom pallor. Pregnancy isn't a disease, you know, Billie!"

"I *do* get out of bed." Tears came unbidden to Billie's eyes. She cried so easily these days. And she was always so sleepy when she wasn't sick.

"Oh, for goodness' sake, don't cry. I didn't mean to upset you." Agnes was halfway to the bed to embrace Billie when she remembered her silk dress. Even one tear would stain it beyond repair. "It's only that I worry about you. Perhaps you can go down and sit on the verandah. That wouldn't hurt, would it?"

"No, I suppose not." Billie lay back against her pillows. The tea she sipped was roiling through her stomach and she recognized the signal. Agnes also recognized the green tinge to Billie's complexion.

"I'll be downstairs, Billie. Call if you need me," Agnes said over her shoulder as she made a hasty exit.

During the second week at Sunbridge, when Billie was feeling no better, she resentfully surrendered to Seth's authority. He arranged a series of tests at the hospital in Austin. Dr. Adam Ward became Billie's physician on call. What this meant, Seth explained, was that he was available for the slightest problem. If even a headache lasted more than an hour or two, Adam was to be summoned. It was an order. Billie nodded her compliance. Later Agnes told Billie that the entire third floor wing of the hospital had been donated by the Colemans and it was there that the baby would be born. The Coleman heir.

Dr. Ward prescribed vitamins for Billie and a daily regimen of diet and exercise. There were to be twice-weekly vitamin B injections as well, which the doctor administered himself at Sunbridge. That a busy physician would drive the forty-plus miles from Austin was her first realization of Seth Coleman's clout. In Philadelphia, a doctor made house calls only if his patient was completely unable to make the trip to his office.

Aside from a telegram informing them that he'd arrived safely in San Diego, there had been no word from Moss. Billie wrote him care of an APO number, San Francisco. V-mail was notoriously slow, she'd been told when she'd fretted about Moss's not answering her letters. She wrote every night, using the onionskin paper commonly known as V-mail stationery that Jessica had brought her from the post office.

After the very first vitamin B injection Billie began to feel more like herself. But the days were still long and lonely for her. It was Jessica who kept Billie company on those afternoons when she was feeling better. Billie welcomed Jessica's attentions and company. She liked to hear stories about Moss when he was a child, and looking through the family photo album was one of her favorite pastimes. One day, Jessica asked Billie if she would like to see Moss's room.

Jessica opened the door to a room on the second floor, west wing. "This was Moss's room when he was a boy," Jessica explained. "When he was seventeen he moved to the room next to yours. And then, of course, he went off to college." Billie stepped inside and immediately felt herself immersed in Moss's life. School banners almost covered the walls by the narrow low bed. Books, hockey sticks, baseball bats, and other assorted sports equipment littered the corners. Dresser tops and bookshelves were studded with sports trophies, and from the ceiling, on fine, almost invisible wires, hung model planes, put together by Moss himself with painstaking attention to detail.

"Why don't I just leave you here, Billie? That's the first smile I've seen on your face in almost a week," Jessica said. "If you need me, I'll be in the kitchen with Tita, going over next week's shopping list. When you're through here, I've something else to show you."

Jessica closed the door quietly, a sympathetic smile touching her lips. Poor Billie, she missed Moss so. Such a quick courtship, so little time to get to know each other. And now there was a baby on the way. As she walked to the kitchen, she thought of Seth's disapproval of Billie—"not the stuff Colemans are made of." But there was one thing Seth and that lovely girl had in common: their love for Moss. The thought occurred to Jessica that perhaps Seth was so disagreeable to

Billie for just that reason—he saw the girl as a rival for Moss's affections. Well, Jessica sighed, hadn't that always been the case? Since the day of Moss's birth nothing and no one else had existed for Seth, and that included herself and poor Amelia, who had tried her whole life to gain her father's love. And when she'd failed, Amelia had opted for her father's attention instead. That was the reason for most of her scrapes and rebellion. It seemed that all of them, Moss included, thought nothing was as important as being worthy of Seth's love. A love so grudgingly given.

Billie hardly heard the door close, so enthralled was she at being surrounded by Moss's things. It wasn't difficult to imagine his young dark head bent over the scarred and battered desk as he studied his schoolwork or meticulously painted one of his model planes—and so many of them! It was easy to see that his love of flying had begun at an early age. Her eyes wandered over a cabinet filled with athletic trophies, the floor-to-ceiling shelves littered also with books, some of them read over and over again, judging by the tattered corners and dog-eared pages. Photographs hung on the walls—Moss playing baseball, football, one with his arm around a pretty girl at what must have been his senior prom. She was a slender girl with dark hair and angular features. Several photographs were of Moss with this girl. One, bent and dog-eared, as though it had been carried for a long time inside a wallet, was of the girl, stylishly dressed in ski togs, smiling up at Moss, who had his arm around her possessively. Across the bottom, Moss had scrawled, "Alice 'n' me."

Billie knew a pang of jealousy. Who was Alice?

Several photographs were of himself with his sister, Amelia, whom Billie recognized from pictures Jessica had shown her. Two sleek dark heads close together, Amelia's arm around a pony's neck, Moss grinning into the camera while he authoritatively held the animal's bridle.

Sinking down onto the foot of the narrow bed, Billie smoothed her hand over the green wool sweater that lay beside her. There was so much about Moss she didn't know, couldn't even imagine. He was still a stranger, she realized sadly, a man who had come into her life and taken her heart. There had never seemed to be time for questions, for delving into the past. All that had mattered was the present, the all-too-short present. And now here she sat among his things, in this room that seemed to be maintained as a shrine to his youth. She felt as though she'd been sent here to Texas to be stored among his possessions and to wait for his return, something more that belonged to Moss. Unthinkingly, her hand went protectively to her middle, where the life their love had created nestled warm and safe within her. This was Moss's also. And the baby would wait, just as she would, to be reclaimed.

The feelings of an echoing past stayed with Billie when Jessica took her later to the little workroom behind the stable. Here an older Moss had littered the small space with radio innards, electric motors, screwdrivers. Here, too, was the sense that Moss had only just left for a little while, that any instant he would appear at the door to finish a project or begin another.

"This should have been cleared out long ago," Jessica complained good-naturedly, "but Seth wouldn't hear of it. That man's as stubborn as a sore-toed mule. It's not as though Moss will ever use this place to tinker again, not when he's got factories and laboratories with all the latest equipment."

Billie's brows lifted in question. "That's right, dear. Didn't Moss tell you? Or was he too busy sweeping you off your feet?" Jessica laughed indulgently. "Seth's business isn't just cattle and oil. Heavens, no. The Colemans are involved in aeronautics and electronics. Moss always was bright when it came to new ideas or new uses for old ones. That's a direct quote from Seth, but I was always proud of Moss, too. Considering the way his father dotes on him—and certainly he never wanted for anything money could buy—Moss was never spoiled or lazy, never what you'd call a playboy. He gets more pleasure from his little inventions than he would from a new sports car." Jessica's pride in her son was evident in her glowing smile. "Moss always had good judgment, I'm glad to say, and he's shown extraordinary taste when it comes to choosing a wife."

Jessica threw her arms around Billie and hugged her. "You've become very dear to me, child. I won't pretend it doesn't have something to do with the baby, but I'm so glad you've come to Sunbridge."

"Moss's good judgment extends to his choice of mothers," Billie teased, returning the hug. "And thank you for showing me his room and his workshop. There's so much about my husband I don't know."

"The Coleman men are a hard lot to understand, Billie. There's a lot of Seth in Moss, and even being married for almost thirty years I still can't say I know my husband. But this is Moss's world, Billie, and it must become yours if you're ever to be happy. Your child will belong to Sunbridge. And while you're discovering Moss's world and his work, I hope it will bring him closer to you, ease some of the loneliness."

Together, Billie and Jessica stepped out of the workshop and into the bright Texas sun. When Billie looked over the expanse of lawn and the pastures beyond, she tried to see through Moss's eyes. Sunbridge. Moss's home. Would it ever be home to her?

Seth was taking unusually long to select his dinner clothes. Normally he reached into the closet and whatever his hand touched was what he wore. Tonight there were guests. Guests, he snorted. Moss's sickly-looking wife and her mother, who could double as a barracuda. He withdrew a five-hundred-dollar, custom-made suede jacket that was the color of tumbleweed. He had a shirt to match and he'd even wear a tie. Dress up, spruce up, show off a little. Agnes Ames would catalog his entire outfit complete with prices. He hadn't managed to get this far in life without knowing something about people, and Seth had seen Agnes before, in himself. There was a burning fever in her eyes that had once been in his own.

The pier glass threw back his reflection. He looked fine. Fitter than a tick on a brown dog, and the image of success. Not long ago *Texan* magazine had done a spread on him, noting his humble beginnings. Humble my ass, Seth snorted. Born to an abjectly poor tenant farmer, he had worked by day beside his five brothers and his father to eke out a living from the barren land. By night, he'd huddled on a bare mattress with only unwashed brothers for warmth. He would never forget the stink. He would never forget any of it. . . . His ma was always carrying a big belly or spewing another life into the already too crowded shack. The naked defeat in her eyes and the stench of moonshine on his father's breath convinced him at an early age that life on someone else's land would never bring a man a good meal or a clean bed.

He was twelve years old, scared of the big world but scareder still of what staying in that tenant shack would make of him, when he cut and ran with the rags on his back and sixty cents stolen from the cracked milk jug. He poked around some for a year or two, begging and finding odd jobs. But most men took him for older than he was because of his size and the curiously solemn expression in his eyes, and he talked himself into a job in the oil fields. He worked like a slave and was treated like one, but at the end of the first month he had fourteen dollars and eighty-five cents and that was all that mattered. He saved, spending only what was necessary to survive: a warm coat, sturdy boots, and a stupid old mule to carry him about. And at the end of each year the sock in his bedroll bulged fatter and fatter.

He was twenty when he met Skid Donovan, an old catter with a lease on a pumped-out well but no money. There was still oil in that old hole; Seth could smell it. All around them the black stuff was making men rich. It was a chance, a gamble, and he took it. They became partners.

Seth worked like a mule and sharpened his business savvy. That other companies wanted to take over Skid's lease confirmed Seth's opinion that there was more oil down there. He had to fight and develop eyes in the back of his head. Luck decided to ride with him and the well proved. But while he did all the work, Skid drank away his half of the profits. After two years Seth had enough and sold the partnership out from under Skid without guilt. Hell, Skid would guzzle himself to death in another six months anyway, so what difference did it make that he'd gotten his signature while the old man was blind with rotgut whiskey? The world was made of survivors. . . .

The mirror was showing Seth something he didn't want to see. He was aging just like his father. The grooves and trenches in his face were the same ones he'd despised in the old man. Without a second thought, he raised his booted foot and smashed the pier glass into thousands of sparkling shards.

He supposed that somewhere down the line he should have sent some money to the old man and those shiftless, sorry creatures who were his brothers. But hell, if they wanted to wallow in poverty, who was he to stop them? Sending money would have been like pissing in the ocean. They were all too stupid. He didn't owe them anything. He couldn't even remember if the old man had ever called him anything besides "boy." And when he'd left, he was sure, it had been a relief to his family that there was one less mouth to feed. They hadn't exactly sent out a search party for him.

Seth had never wanted Jessica to know the whole truth. Once he'd set his sights on her, he'd wanted nothing to stand in the way of making her his wife. She knew he came from modest beginnings, but he'd never told her how sorry it had all been—it never did for a woman to have something to hold over a man's head.

Yes, he'd wanted Jess. Good family, good bloodlines, a little short on money—but that was all right; he was going to have more than enough. Poor Jessica. Pretty as a picture and crazy in love with him. But weak, no grit, no starch, too emotional. He'd been expecting a passel of robust sons and what he'd gotten was a worthless daughter who had made it impossible for Jess to bear more children. Sometimes there was no justice. And of course, she'd given him Moss. For his one magnificent son, Seth did have to thank Jessica. He'd given her an easy life and she had no complaints.

Agnes Ames, now that was some woman. He admired her rigid posture and her capable hands. A strong woman, damned attractive, too. He wished he could say the same for the pitiful little gal Moss had married. Billie would have to toughen up if she was going to fit into the Coleman family. He hoped he was wrong, but he thought he saw many of Jessica's weaknesses in the girl. Too thin and narrow-hipped.

Yes sir, he'd come a long way by the shortest possible route. He made the rules. The legacy he would leave behind to his son and future grandsons had been worth it. His family, his legacy. No guilt, no remorse. When you won, you won all the way.

Seth Coleman presided over the cherrywood dining table in proper patriarchal form. His thick, freshly combed gray hair brought his healthy tanned features into relief beneath the glow of the Victorian globe chandelier. A russet-brown, western-cut jacket fit snugly about his broad shoulders and he wore a silk waistcoat that belonged to another age. Billie tried to see something of Moss in Seth's face but could recognize only the summer-blue eyes; they were older and wiser, of course, but they lacked the warmth and humor that were in her husband's. Those qualities, she decided, he'd inherited from Jessica.

"What's for supper?" Seth growled in his peculiarly graveled voice. "I don't mean to offend you ladies," he said with a smile toward Agnes, "but I hope to hell we've having something a man can sink his teeth into."

"Now, Seth, you know what the doctor said about your

diet." Jessica kept her words light but there was a loving chastisement in her tone. "As it happens, tonight we're having roast beef and potatoes. That should suit any man, Seth, even you."

"Damn the doctor. What I've been needing is a mess of ribs or maybe some chicken-fried steak. Now that's man food. Tita! Bring on that beast you've roasted and I hope to hell it's still bloody in the middle. If we've got any delicate appetites at this table, they can have the end slices."

Billie knew the "delicate appetite" Seth referred to was her own. She determined not to think about the blood-rare beef Seth preferred and hoped her stomach didn't begin to churn halfway through dinner. Her eyes went across the table to Agnes for encouragement, but her mother was already dipping her spoon into the thick corn soup, another of Seth's favorites. Billie glanced away from the lump of butter floating on its surface.

"I took Billie to Moss's old room today, Seth, and out to the workshop," Jessica said. She was optimistic; perhaps with more frequent exchanges between Seth and Billie their relationship would improve. Her technique had never helped reconcile Seth and Amelia, but with a father and daughter, emotions always ran too high.

Billie felt Seth's eyes on her. "What'd you think gal? Quite a little display, wasn't it?" Seth always brightened when the subject of Moss came up. "That boy's got a head on his shoulders. I can remember him taking a jolt or two from an electrical short in those little inventions of his, but that never stopped him from setting out to do what he intended."

"What was he trying to do?" Billie asked innocently. "I know he likes to tinker with things, but I didn't understand any of what I saw in the workshop."

Seth's expression was disdainful. "Of course you wouldn't. Before that boy was twelve years old he'd redesigned the pump station we use for irrigation," he said, pointing his fork at her for emphasis, "and it's still in use today. That boy can do anything he sets his mind to, and don't think otherwise. Through-and-through Coleman and the nut doesn't fall far from the tree. He's got a few things to learn and I'm here to teach him. If this war hadn't come along, my son never would've left Sunbridge—or Texas, either—to find himself a wife. The Colemans, and Jessica's family, too, for that matter, have been in Texas for damn near a century. Texas born and Texas bred. And that's the way it's going to be for Moss's sons, even if his wife is a Yankee from Pennsylvania." Seth's voice was thundering now, and his eyes pierced the distance between Billie and himself, leaving her dumbstruck.

Jessica's fingers frayed the edges of her linen napkin. Agnes sat silent and tall, her mouth pinched into a sour line as she stared across at Billie, willing her daughter to stand up to this cantankerous old man before he devoured her. When Billie's shoulders hunched forward in defeat, Agnes tossed her napkin onto the table like a fighter throwing his hat into the ring—Seth had not only insulted Billie's heritage but her own as well.

"The Colemans may have been in Texas for nearly a century, but long before any of them saw their first Indian *my* family fought in the Revolutionary War!" Agnes bristled. "I'm a member of the DAR, just like my mother before me and her mother before her! And since you've openly admitted that the bloodline has been stagnant for too long, it seems to me Moss showed good sense in looking elsewhere for a wife."

The room was still. Even chubby, dark-skinned Tita ceased rattling dishes in the adjoining kitchen. Jessica's gentle blue eyes went to her husband in a silent plea for domestic peace. Suddenly a great sound filled the room, booming from the rafters. Billie quickly lifted her eyes to see Seth with his head thrown back in laughter, shoulders shaking and belly bouncing. When he'd dried his eyes on the back of his hand, he smiled across at Agnes. "Good for you, Aggie! I guess I've been told, haven't I? Between you and me we're gonna have ourselves one hell of a grandson!"

Agnes accepted this as a compliment and retrieved her napkin. "Eat your soup, Seth, while you can still choke it down," she said, and went back to the business of eating. Jessica and Billie were bewildered, Jess because it was the closest she'd ever heard her husband come to complimenting a woman, Billie because it was the first time she'd known her mother to allow herself to be called Aggie.

When coffee was served, black and aromatic the way Seth liked it, he made his announcement. "Got an invite in the mail today" was his offhand remark to Jessica as he added a third lump of sugar to his cup. "We're flying over to Dallas sometime before Thanksgiving; the date's not set. The Barretts are having a shindig for Lyndon Johnson. A real down-home Texas barbecue. It's something we should have done, instead of letting the Barretts get the jump on us. Lyndon's decided he'll be more useful in the navy than in Washington. Leastwise, that's what he's saying. It's really only because he thinks it'll add to his political image."

"When did Lyndon decide this?" Jessica asked worriedly. "Poor Claudia, she must be beside herself!"

"Lady Bird will do all right," Seth said. "She always does all right. Luckiest day of Lyndon's life was when that woman agreed to marry him; otherwise he'd still be a no 'count teacher in the sticks somewhere. She told him he could do anything and he believed her. When she pointed him in the direction of politics he took to it natural as a newborn calf to its mother's teat."

"Now, Seth, that isn't saying much for Lyndon, and you know he's an able man. I've heard you say so yourself."

"Lots of men are able, Jess, and lots of men never get anywhere. That's because they've hooked up with the wrong woman. We leave Friday, just after lunch."

Jessica wrung her hands in her lap, clearly distressed. "Seth, couldn't I take the train and meet you? You know how I hate to fly."

"No, you cannot take the train. Who'd run the house from now till Friday? You'll fly with me."

Jessica paled. "What about Billie and Agnes?"

"What about them?" Seth dug his fork angrily into his lemon pie.

"It's just . . . it's just that I don't think it's a good idea for Billie to fly, do you? Considering the baby and the way she's been feeling? Billie and I could take the train together."

Seth swallowed another gulp of scalding coffee. "You ever been up in a plane, gal?" he said to Billie, who shrank back against her seat and nodded, remembering how she'd squeezed her eyes shut the entire time. Just the thought made her feel sick. "Well, Jess might be right. How about you, Aggie? You like to fly?"

"I love it," Agnes stated, ignoring Billie's amazement. "Or at least I know I'd love it. We usually drove to parties in Philadelphia, but I'm willing to try flying. According to Moss, it's an experience everyone should have."

"Believe him." Seth laughed. "Of course, I don't like that stunt-flying Moss is so crazy about. Just a nice safe, level trip. You'd better rest up, gal," he ordered Billie. "This family has got to be represented at this shindig and you're going, pukey or not. Lyndon Johnson has done a lot for this family with his connections in Washington, and we've got to show our appreciation."

"Billie will be just fine," Agnes assured him. "Billie, why don't you play a few piano pieces for us after dinner? You haven't been at the piano since before we left Philadelphia."

"I didn't know you played," Jessica interjected. "How nice it will be to hear that old piano again. Amelia had quite a bit of talent. Remember how Amelia used to play for our friends, Seth?"

When there was no answer, Jessica hastily went on to recall for Agnes and Billie some of the big parties that had been held at Sunbridge. But Agnes's attention was on Seth, who leaned back in his chair and lighted a thick brown cigar. She'd noticed that whenever Amelia's name was mentioned he withdrew from the conversation. Evidently, he didn't share Jessica's fondness for their daughter. Billie's child, she thought with satisfaction, would always hold a position of importance in the Coleman household, and without competition from Amelia or any of her future progeny.

Seth settled himself into a worn leather wing chair in the living room and frowned at his wife, who was busily uncovering the baby grand piano that stood in the bay of long-curtained windows. It wasn't until Agnes brought him a large snifter of cognac that his expression brightened.

"It's probably terribly out of tune," Jessica apologized. "I don't remember the last time it was played." Billie tried a few scales. The tone was acceptable but the instrument did need attention. Soon she broke into the beginning strains of Dvorak's "Humoresque," playing softly and haltingly at first until her fingers remembered their stretch and reach. Measure by measure her volume increased and the music filled the high-vaulted room with the lilting quality of her interpretation.

Jessica was impressed, smiling over at Agnes with pleased astonishment. "I never knew Billie was so accomplished," she whispered. She glanced over at Seth, who was clearly unmoved by his daughter-in-law's performance. Talent, unless it would enhance the power and property of Sunbridge, was unappreciated. When Billie broke into the waltz from Tchaikovsky's *Sleeping Beauty*, Seth was heard to growl, "Doesn't that gal know any saloon music? Some good old ricky-ticky tunes." Then, louder: "How about 'Red River Valley' or 'My Darlin' Clementine'? Why do women always like funeral marches?"

Jessica was embarrassed, Agnes annoyed. But Billie heard and immediately switched to a bouncing rendition of "Red River Valley," which brought a grudging smile of pleasure to Seth's face. He wanted saloon music, she'd give him saloon music—"Clementine," "The Cowboy's Lament," "Deep in the Heart of Texas." Soon Seth's feet were tapping with the rhythms and he was clapping his hands. Now Agnes's expression was bored, Jessica's hopeful. In time, she thought, and the Lord willing, Seth just might come to appreciate this new daughter of theirs.

It was then that the phone rang. After the third ring Tita picked up the receiver in the hall and quickly came to announce long distance, San Diego. "It's Señor Moss!"

Billie's hands froze in midair and she leaped to her feet. But she was no quicker than Seth, who struggled from his chair and then had to lean on his cane for balance. For one moment their eyes locked, and Billie was the first to look away. Seth would speak to his son before she could speak to her husband.

Agnes and Jessica followed Seth and Billie out to the hall, gathering close. "That you, son?" Seth barked into the receiver. "'Bout time we heard from you! Still in San Diego?"

"How you doing, Pap? Are you treating my girl right? Not pulling any of your tricks, are you, Pap?"

Seth's answer was a noncommittal growl. "When the hell are you coming home? Have you gotten those ideas about war and glory out of your thick head yet?"

"I'm calling to say I'm leaving for Hawaii at oh three hundred tomorrow, California time."

"Why the hell you want to go all the way over there? If you're fighting for this country, then that's where you should stay, right here in the States! You've got a wife here and a son on the way. This is where you should be. I can still fix it, you know. Why don't you let me?"

"Pap, this is what I want. I'm being assigned to the USS *Enterprise*. You take care of Billie and the baby for me. I'm counting on you. Where is Billie?"

"Right here. Listen, son, there's something I want to ask you. Remember that well we pulled in out over to Waco? They're telling me she's going dry and we should pull out before we lose money on her. My gut tells me there's still a lode down there and we just haven't tapped it. Christ, the whole area is pulling in oil and I can't see any reason why we shouldn't. What do you think about drilling another well along the same ridge? You were out there before you got that fool notion to enlist in the navy—what d'you think?"

Billie hovered near, with clenched fists, straining to hear the sound of Moss's voice. Frustration screamed through her. *Why* was Seth talking about oil wells and money. She thought she'd faint if she didn't speak to Moss this instant! She looked at Jessica, who signaled to her to be patient.

"That's not what those smart-assed geologists have been telling me," Seth complained. "They're saying those pumps south of ours are pulling and we're bottoming out. A slant rig, you say? Do you know where it's been tried?... Yeah, I've heard of him. He's a wildcatter out of Oklahoma, isn't he?" Another pause. "Hell, son, why don't you come on home? Turn in that leather jacket and come be where you'll do the most good. Those planes don't run on water, you know. This country needs all the fuel oil it can get."

Seth listened, the lines in his face deepening with discouragement. "Yes, your mother's right here and so's Aggie.... Yes, she's here, too." Without another word, Seth handed the phone to Jessica, who kept her loving remarks brief before turning the phone over to Billie.

"Moss? Darling, how are you?"

"Fine. How's my girl? Not letting the old man make you sorry you married into the Colemans, are you?"

"Never. Never ever. Are you still in San Diego? Have you written? I didn't receive any letters. Did you get mine?"

"Every single one of them, honey. I didn't write; they've been keeping me pretty busy. I'm being shipped to Hawaii along with my squadron. Thad Kingsley's here, too, and shipping out with me. You remember him, don't you? Tall guy from New England."

"How could I forget? I danced with him at our wedding. Will you write when you get to Hawaii? I miss you, Moss." Billie glanced over at Seth, who was standing beside Agnes and Jessica. There was so much she wanted to say to Moss, but how could she with everyone listening to her every word?

"I miss you, too, Billie. Take care of yourself and the baby. Do what your mother tells you and everything will be okay. Hear?"

She wanted to ask if he really missed her. She wanted him to say he loved her. "Moss, when do you think we'll be together again? Will you be home for Christmas?"

"Don't think so, honey. Hawaii's half a world away, don't

forget. Write to me, Billie. I love hearing from you. Write me all the news, okay?"

"Okay. And Moss?"

"Yeah, Billie?"

"Take care of yourself, won't you? I worry."

"Don't worry. I'm going to come home as good as I left. I've got to go now, honey. There's a hundred guys waiting to use the phone. Take care of yourself. I miss you."

Billie gulped, trying to ignore the three pairs of eyes that watched her. She wished for one instant of privacy. Turning her back, she whispered into the phone, "Moss, I love you."

"I know you do, Billie." Click.

Billie held the dead receiver in her hand, feeling it grow cold in her grip. "Well, what did he say?" Seth demanded.

"He . . . he said he missed me."

"No, I mean did he say anything important? When is he coming home? Will he be coming back to the States?"

Wordlessly, Billie turned and climbed the stairs to her room. She wanted to be alone with her thoughts of Moss, and more than anything she wanted to spare herself Seth's inquisition.

Moss pushed his cap back at a jaunty angle and crossed the hotel lobby to where Thad Kingsley waited. "Didn't I tell you," Thad said, "it'd be better coming into town to call Billie? At least you didn't have to compete with two hundred men for use of the phone. Besides, sometimes the lines from the base are so jammed it takes an hour for a call to go through."

Moss signaled the barman for another drink. "Pap's having trouble with a well in Waco. That old man thinks I've got the answer to every one of Sunbridge's problems. I told him to get hold of a wildcatter I know in Oklahoma. If anybody can find oil, that bastard can."

Thad's brow wrinkled as he balanced his long lean body on the high bar stool. "Wasn't Billie home? Didn't you get to talk to her?"

"Billie's fine, or so she says. She was having a little morning sickness last time I saw her, but I guess that's passed."

"Don't you know?"

"How should I know?" Moss asked honestly. "I'm here in San Diego and she's in Texas."

"Didn't you ask her?" Thad persisted.

"Hell, I just phoned to tell my wife I'm leaving for Hawaii

and I don't know when I'll see her again. Do you think I want to talk about vomit at a time like that?"

Thad considered himself properly chastened. Moss's relationship with Billie was really none of his concern. It was just that his impression of Billie was that she was fragile and too terribly vulnerable. And Moss Coleman could be such a bastard. "I suppose a phone call like that can get pretty heavy. It can't be easy to leave a girl like Billie, especially when she's carrying your first child."

"Pap'll take good care of her." Moss sipped his drink, oblivious to the frown creasing his friend's brow.

{{{{{{{{{ CHAPTER EIGHT *}}}}}}}}*

Billie was determined to make Moss's home her own. But so many things puzzled her; Texas was so different from Philadelphia. Seth entertained business friends and associates at Sunbridge, for instance, often completing financial transactions right on the front porch. Soft voices would discuss details over and over and then the deal would be formalized with a hearty handshake. Only later would contracts and agreements be put on paper; a man's hand on a promise held more weight than his legal signature.

And Billie's own life became internalized, as her focus turned more and more to the small life within her. The changes in her body came quickly and were always accompanied by a fresh bout of queasiness, if not sickness. Her breasts were swollen and painful, her balance seemed awkward, and she noticed in the mirror that her pelvis was tilting forward, which made the hem of her dresses hang unevenly. Agnes decided it was time for maternity smocks and skirts with tummy holes. Often, Billie yearned for the familiarity of Philadelphia. It would be nice to go shopping with a girlfriend or just walk into town and look in the windows. She had to remind herself that all her friends were at college and the only window-shopping available was nearly forty miles away in Austin.

When the subject of Billie's pregnancy came up at the supper table, Seth insisted on referring to his grandchild as a boy—and his tone said he'd accept nothing less. Jessica had told her kindly, "Billie, it doesn't do any good to argue with Seth. I've been married to him for nearly thirty years and you can believe me." She knew Jessica commiserated with her during these conversations and that was comforting. After all, once the baby was born, regardless of its sex, it couldn't be sent back. As long as it was healthy, what did it matter? Nevertheless, Billie wisely never mentioned the words *baby girl* or even hinted at a feminine name. But the pressure of Seth's possible disappointment was giving her headaches even Tita's potions or the doctor couldn't cure. She kept her miseries to herself and spent hours rereading Moss's sparse letters, which ran a half to a whole page, never more. At least she'd heard from him; for that she was grateful. If his letters were less than romantic, she would accept it. She spent long hours writing letters that she was certain he never read. It was something to do.

Billie found herself upset over Agnes's silent aversion to Jessica's company: her mother seemed to prefer accompanying Seth whenever she could on his rounds of the ranch, and she sat with him in his study listening to the radio news. While Billie and Jessica read Moss's letters, Agnes was reading prospectus reports on Seth's latest venture into the electronics industry. They got along well, these two, seeming to have a quiet understanding of one another. Cantankerous as Seth was, he had met his match in Agnes and he respected her for it.

Billie was seeing her mother as if for the first time. No longer did Agnes appear matronly and middle-aged. Now, with her new upswept hairdo, stylish dresses, and dainty shoes (instead of the durable, sensible ones she'd always bought in Philadelphia), Agnes was a very attractive woman. Even some of Seth's associates who came to the house seemed impressed with the Colemans' Yankee kin, and she'd been invited to dinner several times.

Agnes had set Seth straight almost from the beginning. She let him know that as Billie's mother she was in control of her daughter and of the child she carried. Sons left home. Daughters stayed and obeyed. Seth was to understand that if things didn't go well at Sunbridge, Agnes would pick up her daughter and return to Philadelphia. She should have been a man, Seth found himself thinking.

On the last day of September Billie and Jessica were sitting outdoors in the rose arbor drinking iced fruit punch when Tita wobbled out waving an airmail letter. Jessica's hand went to her throat in alarm; Billie rushed to her while snatching the letter from Tita's outstretched hand. "It's all right, Jessica. It's from England." She handed the letter to her mother-in-law and sat down opposite her, feeling the same relief that was evident on Jessica's face.

"It's from Amelia! I've been worried about her. I think the last I heard from her was just before you came to Sunbridge, Billie." Quickly, Jessica skimmed the contents, her face brightening and softening with maternal love. "Amelia has married! An RAF pilot, and she now has a small stepson. Isn't that wonderful?" There was a shadow lurking in Jessica's expression. "I would have liked to give her a wedding, but I suppose that's unreasonable, considering she's in England, and then there's the war, of course. But I'm very happy for her, nevertheless."

"A ready-made family," said Billie.

"Amelia deserves happiness," Jessica went on. "She has so much love to give. She'll be a wonderful mother. Both my children married, and we didn't get to attend either wedding."

Moss Coleman stood on the ramparts of Fort Kamehameha and looked down into Pearl Harbor at the lady he loved. She was 827 feet long, 114 feet wide, and displaced 20,000 tons empty and unarmed. His lady was both a warship and an airfield, the USS *Enterprise*. Four huge bronze propellers driven by steam turbines gave her more than thirty knots of speed, and behind the props a single rudder as big as the side of a barn swung at a touch from the bridge to provide an enviable maneuverability. In her breast she carried a new and secret device called "radar," which could find the enemy in the black of night or shrouding fog. Captain and mess cook, firemen and pilots, and more than two thousand men lived and fought on her. Her pilots, who romanced her from high above her decks, knew a special love for their lady. It was from her that they went to do battle, but it was always to her that they prayed to return. And no pilot's love was greater than Moss's own.

As Moss's eyes squinted lovingly over her, from the superstructure to the aft deck, he knew the reason for her existence was the flight deck that covered her from stem to stern. Her deck was broken only by the island amidships on the starboard side where the control centers of the ship were housed. On both bows were catapults to launch the planes, and forward, aft, and amidships heavy-duty elevators lifted the planes from the cavernous hangar deck below. Over eighty aircraft were stored below—stubby Grumman F4F Wildcats with squared-off wing tips.

Moss throbbed with anticipation. Today was October 16, 1942, and his lady had taken a new master, Captain Osborne B. Hardison. Preparations were being made to get under way. In the month since he'd arrived, he'd been engaged in practice flights and drills. He was ready, like the lady, to engage the enemy. The controls of his Wildcat—affectionately christened the Texas Ranger—felt right in his hand. His ear was tuned to the drone of the engine and the lift of her wings. In less than an hour he would report to duty, along with his team of eager pilots. In a few hours the lady's lines would be cast off and she would cruise out into the narrow channel toward the blue Pacific, past Hospital Point and Fort Kamehameha. And when Diamond Head was lost beyond the horizon, scuttlebutt had it that she would turn her bow toward the Solomon Islands. The Japanese troops on Guadalcanal were pressing hard against the marine lines that protected Henderson Field.

One week later, Moss and Thad Kingsley stood bareheaded on the *Enterprise*'s aft flight deck, their gazes turned to Rear Admiral Thomas Kinkaid as he inspected the decks of the floating airfield. That morning, at dawn, they'd met their supporting ships and the tanker *Sabine*. Hours ago the carrier class *Hornet* had joined the task force.

"Kinkaid's briefing was an eye-opener," Thad said, exhaling a cloud of smoke that was drawn away in a thin stream by the wind.

Moss agreed. "Let him handle the tactics and we'll do the rest. Some of the guys are worried he'll get so fancy with his moves that we'll never find the ship before we run out of fuel on our return scat. Not me, though. I'd find this beauty if she was six fathoms under."

Thad laughed guardedly. Moss's bravado sometimes worried him. It was too easy to be too cocky. "Just follow orders, Coleman, and the Big E will be waiting for us. Remember the objective."

Moss tossed his butt over the side. "We have to stop the

Japs from taking Henderson Field. It's an important link in the U.S.–Australian lifeline. And the Japs' strongest naval forces since Midway are at sea: four carriers, eight heavy cruisers, two light cruisers, and twenty-eight destroyers. That's a hell of a lot of targets and I'm going to get my shot at them!"

"We've got targets of our own to protect, don't forget. The *Saratoga*, the *Wasp*, now us and the *Hornet*. The battleship *Washington* will look mighty good to those zeros. Kinkaid's worried that we're undermanned and he may be right." Moss's seeming overconfidence was a trait Thad knew was keeping his friend from making full lieutenant. The command worried that he'd take unnecessary risks with men and machines.

An announcement came over the loudspeaker:

"All pilots to the wardroom. All pilots to the wardroom."

"That'll be for Crommelin's briefing," Moss said. There was admiration in his voice for their flight trainer. His combat record was impeccable and when training the *Enterprise* pilots under his command, he'd given them confidence in their F4Fs by showing them a slow roll at under a thousand feet: he required nothing of them he was not able to perform himself. Moss could still hear Crommelin's voice coming over the radio: ". . . over and over and over and over again."

Thad and Moss sat together among the other pilots. Everyone wore open-necked khaki. The green-covered tables held brimming coffee mugs, and cigarette smoke rose in blue clouds up to the cables overhead.

"You've all been thoroughly and carefully trained," Crommelin began. "You know how to drop a bomb and hit a target, and that's what I damn well expect you to do. Our marines have had a long, miserable struggle for Guadalcanal and now they're depending on us. There's no room for waste, no excuse for misses. If you can't do the job, it'd be better if you stayed back in the States and give men who could do it your bunks and your crack at the Japs." There was a long moment of silence. "Now I want you to get some rest, write a few letters, eat light, and lay off the coffee. Come morning, I expect you to knock those Jap sons of bitches right off the face of this earth!"

The sound of the men's uplifting cheer was still ringing in Moss's ears as he wrote to Billie.

Darling Billie,
    Things are happening quickly around here and I wanted

to write. I know I have been remiss in the letter department, honey, but it hasn't been because I don't think about you and our child. I left for San Diego so suddenly that we hadn't even had a chance for those little games parents-to-be like to play. We never even discussed a name for our son. Mam's family name was Riley and I'd like it if that's what he is named. Expect to get some objection from Pap but stand firm, won't you?

I miss you, honey. More than you know. But I know I'm doing what I have to do and there is consolation in that. You are so young, Billie darling, and I was so selfish to send you off to Sunbridge, especially at this time when you would probably like to be in familiar surroundings with friends you have known all your life. Sunbridge is my life, Billie, and it's a good one and one I want for you and our child.

I guess it is at times like these that a man takes stock of who he is and what he has done. Little wife, if I have anything to be proud of, anything to fight for, it is you. From the first, your trust and belief in me have made me a better man. I'll come home to you, Billie. I will.

Moss

Before dawn on October 26, while first-shift breakfast was being served to sailors still grumpy with sleep, a message was received from the headquarters of the commander, South Pacific Force. It was in the familiar style of Admiral Bill Halsey. Three words:

ATTACK. REPEAT. ATTACK.

The flight deck of the *Enterprise* was a confusion of efficiency as aircraft were raised from the hangar bay and rolled to the catapult mechanisms on the runway. Yellow-jacketed men wearing radio headsets listened for the order to signal takeoff amid the roaring whine of the engines and the thrum of the props.

Moss stood among the pilots, helmet and goggles in hand, waiting for his squadron to be signaled. His leather jacket was opened to the early-morning wind. Thad Kingsley pushed through the others and grasped Moss's hand in a firm shake. If there was a time for farewell, this was it. He knew without doubt that Moss held him in great affection and friendship but that it wasn't his style to initiate the gesture. "Hey, buddy, don't get too eager for those meatballs," he said, referring to the Japanese flags that were affixed to a pilot's plane to indicate a kill. He clapped Moss on the shoulder affectionately. "I'll meet you back in the wardroom for debriefing when this is over, you Texas bastard."

"I'll be there, you Yankee cracker. Make certain you are." Moss flashed a white smile. "There's my plane." As he loosened his grip on Thad's hand and moved forward, he turned suddenly and grinned, shouting above the roar. "Hey, Thad, did I tell you what my son's name is? Riley! Riley Moss Coleman!" Turning again, he sprinted for the Texas Ranger, his mind shifting gears from the elusive reality of his unborn child to the business at hand.

In the cockpit, eyes forward, expression grim, he adjusted his headset and tested the elevator flaps. Efficiently he performed his checklist, switching on controls and inspecting gauges. His parachute pressed into his back but he disregarded it. Mentally, he became one with his machine; if she went down, so did he.

The battlefield had been chosen; a thousand square miles of South Pacific lying just north of the Santa Cruz Islands. The sea was calm except for the long ground swells that never ceased. Above, at approximately 1,500 feet, drifted white-and-gold clouds. As the Big E probed ever westward, the scouting fighter squadrons would return by appointment for refueling. Again and again they would land and depart in their relentless search, until the enemy was met.

Watching from amidships, Thad saw the Texas Ranger catapult into the air, her wheels leaving the deck before she reached the edge. He'd been astounded and pleased at the mention of the baby. It was rare that Moss was sentimental, but hell, when a guy was about to fly his first mission, what else could be on his mind but what he'd be leaving behind? He prayed Moss would be around to meet little Riley Coleman. Thad pushed his fingers through his sandy hair and grinned. Moss even had him believing the baby would be a boy.

Navy Fighter Squadron 4 took to the air, circling wide of the mother ship and setting a northward course, eight pairs of glinting wings in the early sun. Moss flew starboard wingman for his squadron leader, Lieutenant Commander Jimmy McVey, holding slightly aft in the V formation. They settled into a hunt-and-search pattern, eyes scanning above and below for the enemy.

When only ten minutes of flying time remained, a voice rasped over the headset: "Zeros, up-sun, twelve o'clock!" Moss looked up, squinting, and had his first sight of the enemy. The bright sunlight at 14,000 feet beat into the cockpit, but it couldn't warm the cold at the pit of his stomach. His experienced eye read the fuel gauge. Bursts of speed and fuel-consuming maneuvers could mean a sudden point of no return. He felt his teeth bite-down on his lower lip.

The attack came from the rear, arrow straight and just as deadly. Curses were mumbled into headsets; grim and determined faces peered through cockpit windshields. Explosive firepower flew all about the American fighters and they were helpless to return it without coming about and taking the zeros head-on. McVey radioed their position back to headquarters. The return message was to pursue and attack—where there were zeros there would be Japanese carriers. Two were known to be in the area. Moss once again glanced at the fuel gauge.

"Break formation," came McVey's voice. "Spiral down and jump from the rear." It was a maneuver that didn't generate the squadron's faith. It was already known that zeros could outclimb and outmaneuver American fighters.

One by one, the squadron spiraled portside and dropped to 11,000 feet. The maneuver wasn't working—the zeros were still on their tails. Mooney, second port wingman, broke radio silence. "Squad four, two zeros hanging back. Repeat, two enemy hanging back. Total nine enemy."

"Coleman, MacGuire, drop back and take them. Squadron ready and ahead," McVey commanded.

Two machines, one order. Moss and MacGuire held back on the throttles, losing air speed, allowing the rest of the squad to shoot ahead. Accomplishing a forty-degree turn to port, they climbed to seek their zeros. The Japanese craft flew toward them at a thirty-degree angle, coming from above. Moss saw MacGuire veer eastward. The zeros went after him, increasing air speed and losing altitude. MacGuire was a sitting duck. A long burst and MacGuire's Wildcat was a burning pyre. Moss watched for signs of a bailout, ready to cover his partner, praying to see a cloud of silk. There was no sign except for vapor trail.

Moss clamped his teeth shut against the roiling in his gut.

He gripped the control stick as though it were a lifeline, his finger tickling the trigger. He could sense the zeros hot on his trail, hungry for the kill. A part of his mind wondered how the rest of the squad was doing. Would McVey send a craft to double back? Instinctively he led his pursuers north, away from American territory. His eye judged the fuel gauge. It had to be now or never.

The enemy dove down on him, closing the distance, coming within firing range. Moss throttled back, hoping they'd overshoot. As they flashed past, he poured on the coal, got on their tails, and fired. He felt the burst from his guns send vibrations through the cockpit, jiggling the needles on his instrument panel. He hadn't known he'd squeezed his eyes shut until he looked to see both of them falling, bursting into flames, paper lanterns crashing toward the sea.

Taking a wide circle that would set him on a course for the *Enterprise*, Moss headed home to refuel. It was only the beginning of a very long day.

Later, much later, after long hours of battle between ships and aircraft, after the Japanese navy retreated, leaving Guadalcanal and marine bases intact, Moss would acknowledge two enemy zeros destroyed, but he would take credit for only one. Lieutenant MacGuire would be credited for the other.

On the third of November, at the barbecue at the Barretts' ranch outside Dallas, Representative Lyndon Baines Johnson told Seth in confidence that the *Enterprise* had engaged in battle. She was now known to be anchored in the hill-rimmed tropical harbor of Nouméa, New Caledonia. She'd been hit and was under emergency repair. No list had yet been released of wounded and fatalities.

Seth kept the news to himself. It wouldn't do to have Jessica become anxious or for that fragile little gal from Philadelphia to get hysterical and jeopardize the only chance for the Coleman bloodline. It was Agnes who took up the relus after Seth finally confided in her. She saw that the gaiety of the party was gnawing on his nerves and that he'd rather await any news at Sunbridge. She resourcefully claimed to have received an important phone message; Seth was needed back home immediately. Grateful, and happy for her company, Seth asked Agnes to go with him and together they boarded his private plane and departed for Austin.

Jessica and Billie returned to Sunbridge the following Thursday. They knew something was deeply troubling Seth. He claimed it was a business problem and for Billie's sake Jessica did not challenge him, but she knew, somehow, that it had to do with Moss. When they were alone, Seth put her fears to rest, or tried to, by telling her it was that damn oil well that had tapped out. Again, she didn't believe him, but nearly thirty years of marriage had taught Jessica not to contradict her husband or test his patience. She watched as Seth paced the floor or rode old Nessie until the mare nearly dropped in her tracks. Day after day she suffered, silently, praying for her son and worrying over her husband. Migraine headaches kept Jessica to her room, and she reluctantly handed over the household management to an eager Agnes. It was all becoming too much. Moss at war, Amelia marrying, Billie's pregnancy, and Agnes's increasing closeness to Seth. And Jessica knew her health wasn't what it should be, but she kept it to herself. Seth disliked what he called "ailing females."

Relief came nearly three weeks later when two letters arrived from Moss. One was addressed to Billie. In it he said he'd like the baby to be named Riley, Jessica's family name. The other was sent after Guadalcanal. He was fine. Only a small note was enclosed for Billie, half a page. The other nine pages of bold scrawl were directed to Seth. Moss told of his first kill, but the bulk of the letter was devoted to describing how Thad Kingsley and his wingman had caught an unprotected Japanese light carrier. The two of them alone had sent her to the bottom of the South Pacific.

"Who the hell is this Kingsley fella?" Seth growled. "Seems like he's gotten himself pretty close to Moss, if you ask me. If Moss had found that Jap ship, he wouldn't have needed any help in sending her to the bottom. And what the hell is a meatball?"

The next week a truly grateful Thanksgiving was spent at Sunbridge.

{{{{{{{{{ CHAPTER NINE }}}}}}}}}

In the study, Agnes sat back in her chair across the massive desk from Seth. She had just completed taking down a letter he'd dictated and later she would type it. When he was at home, Agnes acted as his secretary. Today, she was marveling at Seth's expertise in manipulation. There were lessons to be learned here and learn them she would. For the first time in years she felt her talents were being put to use. First the house, which Jessica was relinquishing to her care, and now working beside Seth. She knew that Sunbridge was a family-held business, all of it. Any fool could see that Jessica was in failing health and that Seth was a prime candidate for a stroke if he didn't ease up a bit. With Moss off to war, that would leave only empty-headed Billie to handle things for the Colemans. Learning as much as she could about the business was not only a pleasure; it was a necessity.

Agnes nodded her approval as she typed up the letters Seth wanted sent to his contacts in Washington. Moss was building an honorable reputation for himself as a fighter pilot. Within the last few weeks he'd been promoted to squadron commander; lieutenant commander was only a step away. Surely the boy was entitled to leave. To have Moss home for Christmas was not, Seth felt, a request out of bounds. And he was offering a prime dressed beef to grease the gears.

Within two weeks Seth was notified that Moss would be sent to San Diego to assemble a group of replacement pilots and would be given a seven-day leave to join his family in Texas.

Billie's joy knew no bounds when she received the news. She didn't know or care how it had all come about; all she knew was that her husband was coming home and she would be in his arms again.

The news of her son's homecoming roused Jessica sufficiently to join the holiday preparations. Agnes prepared the menus and scrupulously oversaw the holiday cleaning, but it was Jessica who knew how to bring Christmas to Sunbridge. The house was bedecked with holly and evergreens and awash with the fragrances of Christmas. Gifts arrived by the carload, wrapped and beribboned and making Billie's eyes widen with disbelief.

Jessica took Billie into Austin to shop for presents. It was an experience to sit in a comfortable store lounge and have items paraded before them for their approval. Billie missed the frantic hustle and bustle of Philadelphia and the taste of snow in the air. But she resigned herself to Jessica's pace, knowing she wasn't capable of much activity herself. A few weeks of relief from morning sickness had come to an end and she was once again suffering the full range of pregnancy symptoms.

Three days before Moss was due to come home, Billie awakened early, crawled out of bed, and headed straight for the commode. She retched miserably and then sat on the edge of the bathtub while she bathed her face in cold water. Nothing was helping. Not Tita's home remedies or Dr. Ward's prescriptions and vitamin injections. Billie felt a mess and looked a mess. Her ankles were so swollen that she'd been reduced to scuffling around in a pair of Agnes's large house slippers. She needed a haircut and a permanent wave, but the thought of the smelly chemicals she'd have to endure made her queasy. A new dress was a must. Lord, what was Moss going to think when he saw her? When he'd left she still had a waistline! Her breasts had become fuller, but now they showed faint stretch-marks as they lay heavily against her burgeoning middle. It would have been all right if Moss had been with her day after day, accepting the changes in her body; but now, after so long an absence, he couldn't help being shocked, possibly even revolted. Billie tipped her face into her hands and cried. She was still dabbing at her tears when she sat down at the breakfast table.

Seth's eyes went to Agnes, who answered his silent question with a shrug. He stole another look at Billie. The little gal looked terrible. Moss was in for a shock when he got home. Seth disliked pregnancies. A woman changed and became an awkward, ungainly, puffy individual, a caricature of herself. Billie's appearance annoyed him, just the way Jessica's had annoyed him when she'd carried his children. But he was tolerant—or rather, he was forcing himself to be tolerant. After all, this young lady *was* carrying his future grandson.

"Three more days and your son will be home," Agnes said brightly as she cut into a succulent sausage. Billie's head went up and her eyes narrowed. His son? Moss was *her* husband. Agnes took note of Billie's look. "We have to do something about your appearance," she said. "Why don't we go into town and get your hair done and perhaps pick up a new dress? One that isn't so ... so ..."

"So like a tent, Mother? I need the room, or haven't you noticed how much weight I've put on? I'm afraid there aren't too many styles that will fit me."

"You can try," Seth said coolly. There it was. Agnes's backup. She was to go into town. Seth excused himself, and when he returned he laid a check next to Billie's plate. She looked down at it and winced. A thousand dollars to get her hair done and a new dress. "Buy yourself some pretties," Seth said. His tone clearly stated that he thought she needed *something*. Regardless of how she felt, she knew she had to go to town. Seth tolerated no excuses. Agnes smiled benignly. Seth was so good to them.

The entire day was just one long trial of misery for Billie. At the hairdresser's she'd sat with her shoeless feet propped up while lotions and the heat-wave machine were applied to her hair. Between bouts of nausea she kept reminding the beautician that she wanted a *soft* curl, no frizz! Twice she'd had to retch into a wastepaper basket while the clamps and wires were still attached to her head, making it impossible for her to bend over. In the end, her hair looked as though she'd stuck her finger into a live light socket and she nearly sobbed when she was told it would relax within a few weeks. It was cut too short, it was permed too curly, and she thought she resembled a bowling pin when she hazarded a look in a full-length mirror. Thankfully, after the setting and an eternity under the dryer, the effect was not quite so bad.

When Agnes saw Billie's haircut and permanent wave she had to refrain from gasping her shock. "Did you choose that particular style from a magazine, Billie?" she asked offhandedly. Suddenly, Agnes felt very old, hardly a strong-spirited active woman of forty-three. A forty-three-year-old woman couldn't possibly have a woman of forty for her child. And that was exactly how Billie looked, old and worn. Even her pink-and-gold complexion had faded into something resembling jaundice. For the first time Agnes was truly alarmed for her daughter's health. "Billie, what did Dr. Ward say the last time you saw him? I've tried not to be an interfering mother, but . . ."

"Lately, Mother, you've hardly been interfering. Not interested is closer to the truth. Dr. Ward said I should have my teeth checked. Pregnancies are hard on women's teeth. Lord." She managed a grudging laugh. "My teeth are the only part of me that don't hurt! Can we go back to Sunbridge now?"

"Absolutely not. First we're going to have lunch. Seth took me to the Paladian once and their food is wholesome and simple. Next we're going shopping for some new dresses for you. Now that I've finally gotten you away from the house, we're going to accomplish what we've set out to do. Honestly, Billie, you're getting to be a drudge, just like Jessica."

Billie shot Agnes a warning glance but was feeling too ill to pursue a defense of her mother-in-law. "Whatever we're going to do, let's do it quickly. My feet are swollen and my shoes are pinching and I just want to go home."

Back at Sunbridge, Billie immediately went to her room. All she wanted was to take her shoes off and have a nice warm bath. She sat on the edge of her bed looking down at her swollen feet with clinical interest. And to think she'd been a double-A narrow only months ago. Would things ever be the same again?

After her bath, Billie went to see how Jessica was feeling, and spent the time before dinner reading the daily paper to her mother-in-law. Jessica's headaches had been too severe to allow her to use her eyes for either reading or working on the baby sweater she was knitting.

"You'd better run along and dress for dinner, Billie. You look so tired. I think the day in town was too much for you. Tell me what you bought. Was Seth generous with his check?"

"More than generous," Billie assured her, remembering for the first time that she hadn't spent anywhere near the entire sum. The remainder must still be tucked away in Agnes's purse. Would she return it to Seth? "I bought a few dresses and tops. One I especially like is a soft sage color with long sleeves and a bias-cut bodice that buttons off to the side. I needed lingerie and a few nightgowns. But there was a dressing gown I simply couldn't resist. It's long and flowing and I thought I'd wear it when Moss arrives so he won't see how swollen my feet and legs are."

Jessica heard the anxiety in Billie's voice and sighed. "Dear child, I think you're making too much out of your appearance. Moss is not even going to notice how you look. You're going to be the mother of his child and that's what he's going to think of. I don't want you riling yourself up so that you can't enjoy your husband and the Christmas holidays."

"Are you sure, Jessica? I don't want him to have regrets." Her young voice was so full of hope and despair that Jessica found it hard to speak. "I'm sure, child. Run along now and dress for dinner."

Billie leaned over to hug the older woman. "I always feel so much better when I talk to you. I'll come back after dinner. I bought you two new mystery stories." She gave the older woman another light kiss and left the room.

There were tears in Jessica's eyes when she watched Billie leave the room. Billie was a Coleman now and she would have to accept the Colemans the way they were. They couldn't be changed—she had learned that hard and bitter lesson years ago. Billie was a fighter; she had that much going for her. How and when she was going to do her fighting would be what was important. Perhaps she was wrong not to confide in the young woman she had come to love. But how could she tell Billie that Seth hadn't come near her bed after the fourth month of pregnancy? How could she tell Billie about Seth's philandering over the years without making it sound like Moss would do the same thing? A wave of pity washed over her, not for Billie or herself, but for Seth and Moss. They were the losers. In the end, when it counted, she hoped that both men would realize that fact. She blessed herself quickly for her uncharitable thought. She *was* a Coleman after all.

Moss stepped off the train in Austin's depot, his duffel slung carelessly over his shoulder. "Pap!"

After the two men embraced, Moss pointed to his sleeve. "Take a look, Pap. Lieutenant commander."

"Good for you, boy. You might make admiral yet. You want admiral, I'll get you admiral!"

"Hell, no. Thad's the one who's going to make admiral the way he's going. No more string-pulling, Pap. I'm doing things on my own these days. Where's Mam and Billie? Anything wrong?" he asked as an afterthought.

"Your mother isn't feeling well, Moss. You need to know that."

"Pap, if that's another of your little tricks to get me stateside,

{ 135 }

forget it. Mam has you to look after her. Billie and Agnes can take up the slack. I've got a war to fight."

"Hrmmph! You're being overly dramatic, aren't you, son?"

"With you, Pap, everything has to be overstated before you get it through that head of yours."

"I knew you were going to say that," Seth grumbled good-naturedly. "What's important now is that you're home."

"Where's Billie?" Moss asked again.

"Back at Sunbridge. She's not up to par these days and you'll have to go easy on her. I hate to say it, but you didn't pick yourself a breeder when you picked that one. Pity we men can't try them out first. I had the same trouble with your mother. Seems like the finer bred they are, the harder time they have. Why, I've seen Mexican peasants give birth on the side of the road and go right back to work in the fields."

"What's wrong with Billie, Pap? Give it to me straight. Is the baby, okay?"

"Fine, fine, according to the doctor, anyway. But your little Yankee is having a hard time of it. Sick and pukey all the time. She tries to hide it but I can see it just as plain as the nose on your face. You got any fool ideas of picking up where you left off, just cancel them. You're not going to take chances with my grandson. You get my drift, boy?"

Moss stared at his father. "Is that your way of telling me I should take my biological needs to a cathouse, Pap?"

Seth grimaced. "The navy teach you to sass your pap, boy?"

"The nut doesn't fall far from the tree, Pap. You've got a strong way of talking yourself, if I remember."

"Damn well you remember. Just be nice to that little gal. She's carrying Riley Seth Coleman."

"I see you've accepted my preference for his name, with a little addition of your own." Moss laughed at the bright gleam in his father's eye. It was clear Seth couldn't wait for the baby to be born.

"C'mon, Carlo is waiting. Let's get the hell out of here. Once we're in the car I want you to tell me everything you've been doing. All of it. And who the hell's this Kingsley fella? Not letting him get the jump on you, are you?"

Moss felt as though he were swimming against the current as he talked to his father. What the hell was going on back at the house? Billie sounded fine in her letters, all seven of them each week. Jesus, he hadn't known there were so many ways to say the same thing over and over. Not that he didn't appreciate her daily letters. He did. He couldn't wait to see her. That's all he'd been thinking of for the past ten days. He had it all planned in his mind. He was going to rush her right off her feet and carry her up the wide circular stairway, and then, look out! A little bump in the middle wasn't going to make a bit of difference. There were ways to get around that.

"I've got it all planned, boy. We're going to ride the range like we used to do before you decided you wanted to fly planes. We'll roast a whole steer, have some people in so I can do a fair share of bragging, and then I'll tell you all about my new business ventures. Seven days, son, that's all we got this time around. I tried for a full two weeks but they balked. Seven was a gift."

Now. Tell him now, before he got up any more grand plans. "Pap, it isn't seven, it's four. I have to get back. I'm sorry as hell, but that's the way it is. Big things are in the wind and when they blow I want to be sure I'm there. If you're going to make a fuss, do it now. I don't want anything spoiling my leave with Billie."

"Boy, you haven't heard a word I said, have you? The little lady is in no condition to do much of anything. You're in drydock. Get it through your head. One of these days, that hot head of yours is going to get you into a lot of real trouble. Trust me. Tell me, I don't suppose you did any Christmas shopping for the ladies, did you?"

"Pap, Christmas shopping on an aircraft carrier?" Moss laughed.

"That's what I thought. Agnes did it all. I gave the lady a blank check and she bought out the stores. You're safe on that score."

"You two getting along?" Moss grinned.

"Like pigs take to the cornfield. We understand each other," Seth said generously. "You might say we have common objectives."

"I thought you would. How's Mam get along with her?"

"Now, son, you know your mother. If anything, she's too damn good, always looking for the best in people. How d'you think she's stood me all these years?"

A wry grin spread on Moss's face. "Sometimes, Pap, I've wondered. Hear anything from Amelia? I had a letter from her when I was in Hawaii but nothing since."

"Your sister has gotten herself married," Seth announced. "This time she's really gone and done it. Found herself an RAF pilot, a widower with a small son." He guffawed. "Imagine Amelia, harebrained and shiftless, being a mother. Glad it's not a Coleman she's raising. That little gal of yours has more sense in her little finger than your sister has in her whole head. And she marries a limey to boot."

Moss frowned. "Why're you so hard on her, Pap? Especially since you know she'd lay down her life for you if you asked her. What's her pilot like? How old is her stepson?"

Seth waved his hand through the air to cease all questions. "If there's something you want to know, you'll have to ask your mother. The details of your sister's life always either embarrass or bore me. If nothing else, your sister could have come home, given your mother the pleasure of planning the wedding and seeing her only daughter married. Selfish as she is, she does it half a world away."

"Pap, it isn't as though it's easy getting back and forth across the Atlantic. There is a war going on."

"Then she should have waited," Seth grumbled. "But your sister never waits for anything, as you well know." He sighed. "I suppose it's for the best, after all. Your mother isn't exactly up to planning weddings."

"What's ailing Mam?"

"Who knows? Doctors seem to think she just needs bed rest and there's something about her blood pressure. She's been in bed off and on. Mostly on, but it doesn't seem to be doing much good. Billie is good to her; I'll give her that. She spends a lot of time with your mother. They like each other."

That meant Seth didn't approve. Seth was likening Billie to Jessica and that was a definite fault in his eyes. The qualities Seth admired were strength and guts; Jessica had never had enough of those. Moss's eyes narrowed. "Why don't you like my wife, Pap? She's a wonderful girl and half the time I feel terrible about having married her. She deserves a lot better than the Colemans. We're too hard on our women. Jesus, Pap, if I find out you've made her unwelcome, I'll never forgive you."

"Calm down, son. You're going off half-cocked. It's nothing like that and you know it. It's just that she's always sick. She was sick the day she got off the train and she's been sickly ever since. She always looks like she's about to puke or faint or something. I never see her eat, but she must have put on ten pounds for every month she's been with us. Still pretty enough. But sickly, and you know I've got no patience with mewling females."

Sick. His Billie was sick and no one had told him. The car couldn't take him to the house quickly enough. He had to see for himself. From the beginning, Moss had had plaguing doubts about becoming involved with Billie. She was so young, so fresh and innocent. So trusting. And the two people she trusted most in the world—himself and Agnes—had betrayed her. Billie hadn't been ready for marriage, especially one where her husband preferred to be flying fighter planes. And he doubted she was ready to become a mother. It was like whelping a dog that hadn't come into her second season. The drain on her health and vitality could be devastating. Feeling guilty and worried, Moss sank into the plush seat of the limousine, only half listening to Seth as he explained in detail the new electronics division of Sunbridge. Who gave a damn if there was a radar installations contract pending with Washington when his own selfishness and Agnes's greed had caused Billie's suffering?

Billie stood beneath the front portico watching the long black Packard come up the tree-lined drive. She huddled in her thick sweater, her heart pounding so fiercely she thought it could be heard miles away. She was dizzy with anticipation. Tears burned her eyes when Moss leaped from the car before it came to a full stop. At that moment she would have given anything if she could have run to him, light and slim and girlish, just the way he'd left her.

Moss's shock beat at his brain. Lord, this couldn't be Billie! What had he done to her? The long dress she was wearing couldn't disguise her solid thickness. There would be no picking her up and carrying her up the long staircase. She looked puffy and ill. The old man hadn't been exaggerating.

Billie smiled and held out her arms. She had to trust that Jessica was right. Moss would swoop down on her and . . . and . . .

"Billie!" His arms were out but almost as if they were holding her at a distance. Her own outstretched arms dropped instantly to her side. He leaned over and kissed her full on the lips. A hurried public kiss. Billie kept smiling as she reached for his hand to walk indoors with him.

He'd been expecting so much. Wanted so much. Four days in the sack and then off into the wild blue yonder. Now it looked like he would get calluses on his ass from riding the range with Seth. Four days in the saddle could kill a man if he wasn't used to it. His eyes dropped down to Billie's hand clutching his. It seemed like a lot of flesh to him. The ring on her left hand was cutting into her finger. The long slender hands he remembered were now thick and swollen like over-stuffed sausages. Jesus! It was his fault. She looked like this because of him. He had to talk to the doctor; Seth said he came nearly every day. What if something went wrong? "How do you feel, Billie?" It was a goddamn stupid question, but he had to say something.

"Actually, I feel better than I look," Billie lied brightly. "The doctor is keeping his eye on me."

At a loss for words, Moss drew Billie to him. "I'm sorry, Billie, that you have to go through this while I'm not here to be with you." A waterfall of guilt poured over and through him.

"Let's not talk about that. We have seven whole days to be together. I want to hear everything and I have so much to tell you. But first, why don't you run up and see your mother? She's been waiting for days and days to see you."

Moss smiled at Billie. It was a meaningless, empty smile, she thought, but somewhere in his eyes had been relief. Relief that he could escape her? When Moss charged up the stairs to visit with Jessica, Billie turned to find Seth standing in the open doorway, the winter sun making a brilliant backdrop that threw him into shadow. She couldn't see his eyes but she felt them, hard and appraising. She was a disappointment, both to him and his son. And there was the mortal sin, being unworthy of his son.

Before Moss was home two hours he seemed to have fallen easily into his old routines at Sunbridge. He'd cast off his uniform for boots, plaid flannel shirt, and tight cord trousers. The few minutes he'd spent with Jessica had ended with her promise to come downstairs for supper. Billie waited for him downstairs in the cozy little den off the dining room. A fire had been lit and was hissing pleasantly. When he finally found her, he was wearing a rugged sheepskin jacket. Kissing her perfunctorily, he announced he was going out for a short ride with Pap and would be back after lunch.

"You'll be okay, won't you?" he asked politely.

Why shouldn't she be okay? She'd been okay all this time at Sunbridge without him, hadn't she? Why should now be any different? "You go on with your father. I'll have you all to myself after you get back." She tried for a brave and under-standing smile that wasn't quite up to par. Moss's blue eyes studied her seriously and she knew he was about to say that riding with Seth would wait. Then his father appeared in the doorway.

"There you are, son. Grease your tail; we want to get back before the sun goes down. These old bones don't take to the cold like they used to."

"You go along. I'll be here when you get back," Billie said with more enthusiasm than she felt. She wanted Moss here with her, sitting beside her, touching her. His homecoming was like a dream. She still could hardly believe he was really here.

He kissed her again, a lingering caress on her mouth. "I won't be long, Billie. And you could use the time to get yourself all gussied up for me." He was gone.

Gussied up! What did he think? That she'd just rolled out of bed this morning and lumbered out under the portico to meet him? She *was* gussied up! Hairdo, makeup, new dress . . . Tears flowed down her plump cheeks. Of course he couldn't know about the painful preparations she'd made. She looked like a baby whale and her hair was too short. He didn't like it or else he'd have mentioned it. The baby moved within her; she imagined she could feel one tiny foot land a solid kick. "Not you, too!" she cried miserably.

Jessica appeared for dinner as she'd promised. Although she looked a bit wan and her usual sleek hairdo was a bit askew, her joy at having her son home for Christmas had put a bloom in her cheeks. In honor of Moss's arrival (or so she said, but Billie thought it was more to keep her own hostess gown from looking out of place), Jessica was wearing a long, simply tailored dress with a delicate ruching of antique lace at the cuffs and a diamond brooch at the neck. It was violet, one of Billie's favorite shades, and although the style was a bit dated the velvet was still soft and lustrous.

Moss hovered near his mother's side, offering her a small glass of sherry. "Not for me, thank you, dear, but perhaps Billie could do with a drop."

Before Moss could ask Billie, Seth interjected, "Might improve her appetite! Little gal eats like a bird, mealtimes certainly can't account for . . ." His eyes flicked over Billie in embarrassment.

Billie flushed uneasily, feeling the color swim to the roots of her hair. Moss said, "Billie, what's this I hear about your finicky appetite? Don't you know you're supposed to be eating for two?"

At that moment, Agnes made her entrance in the doorway. "Like Seth says, she only nibbles at the table. Maybe she's got a hoard of chocolates under her bed." Her remark was softened by her presenting her cheek to Moss and welcoming him home. "I was in town when you arrived. Last-minute shopping. You look fit, Moss, but then you always do."

If Moss had been startled by the change in Billie's appearance, he was astounded by Agnes. The only term that came to his mind was *chic*. Very, very chic. Sunbridge certainly agreed with the old girl. Only Moss wasn't so sure "old girl" fit this new Agnes Ames. She'd done something with her hair—it was upswept to reveal a still youthful, graceful neck and over her forehead tumbled risqué little curls. And hadn't she lost a few pounds, or was it only the slim, obviously expensive, silk dress she was wearing, long enough to be tasteful but short enough to show an elegant curve of leg? And what had she done with those sensible shoes she'd always worn? These open-toed high heels didn't belong to the Agnes he'd known in Philadelphia.

"You're the one who's fit, Agnes. You're stunning!"

Billie lowered her eyes but not before Jessica saw the pain in them. Moss should be complimenting his wife, telling her how beautiful she was to him as she carried their child. "Shouldn't we go into dinner, dear?" she asked Seth. "Tita must have everything ready to serve."

"Billie hasn't had her sherry," Seth countered, preferring to remain here in the living room, enjoying the drama taking place. He avoided his wife's glance. Let Aggie have her moment of glory, he thought. Moss was right; she was a stunning woman. He couldn't wait for Christmas morning when she opened his gift.

Moss handed Billie a tiny cordial glass of sherry and sat down beside her, his arm on the back of the sofa behind her. "Having a rough time of it, honey? You never said in your letters."

"I'm exhibiting every classic symptom of pregnancy and then some." Billie tried for lightness. Moss would find self-pity unbearable. "I've missed you so much," she whispered when he leaned over to kiss her cheek. The baby suddenly fluttered and she quickly placed her hand over her middle. "This child has a kick like a mule!"

Tenderly, Moss's hand followed Billie's and a look of wonderment came into his eyes. "Riley Seth Coleman, you're giving your mommy a hard time. You're going to deserve that slap the doctor puts on your bottom." Heads together, Billie cuddled against her husband, craving this tender support and love.

"Hurry up with that sherry, Billie. You heard what Jessica said. Tita has everything ready and Moss could use a good meal under his ribs." Seth broke the moment. His expression was intense, as though he were silently trying to convey a message to Moss.

"There's no romance about you, Pap." Moss laughed uneasily, taking his arm from around Billie and helping her to her feet. "You're right about the meal, though. Sea rations and powdered eggs were never my favorites."

Billie could have wept (tears came so easily these days). Why did there have to be so many people about? Why couldn't she have a minute alone with her husband?

"Why don't you ladies go into the dining room?" Seth suggested, hanging back with Moss. "Did you forget what I told you this morning?" he hissed as the others exited. "I don't want anyone taking chances with my grandson, not even you! Don't think for a minute I didn't know you were trading yourself off when you had yourself reassigned. A bargain is a bargain, son, and a Coleman stands by his word."

"Moss, Seth, where are you two?" Jessica's voice carried through the hall. "Come in here and eat."

After dinner, when they had all congregated once again in the spacious living room, Seth tried to spirit Moss away into the study but Jessica wouldn't allow it. "Now, Seth, don't be greedy with Moss's company. We still haven't heard how he got his hamburger."

"Meatball, Mam, and I'm proud to say there are five of them on my fuselage. I don't know whether you know it, but the Big E saw action in the Solomon Islands after Guadalcanal." Moss sat beside Billie, taking her hand in his.

"Kingsley was the guy who made marks that day," Moss told them. "He was on a predawn strike force and was the first to sight a Japanese transport, but he was reaching the point of no return—that's when you've got just barely enough fuel to get back to mother, I mean the carrier. Anyway, he didn't get a chance to do any shooting. He was ordered back to the ship, but the positions he gave were good enough to blast the Japs to the bottom. Tough break for Thad."

"Hrmmph!" Seth punctuated. "Watch your step, son. This Yankee seems eager to me and likely to get ahead of you."

"So you said." Moss's tone was sour. "Pap, when I talk about Thad it's like I'm talking about myself. That's how proud I am of him. He's a good man, isn't he, Billie? Like Billie says, she danced with him at our wedding."

"Where's he from, this Yankee? Who's his family? What do they do?"

"Pap, I'm not Amelia out on her first date. You don't have to put my friends through the inquisition. Don't forget, I'm a big boy. Billie'll tell you, won't you, honey?"

Billie didn't like Moss putting her on the firing line with Seth. Besides, it was ridiculous to think that anything she could say would convince Seth of anything. After all, she was only "that little gal" to the patriarch. Agnes seemed to be the only woman whose opinion counted.

Jessica decided to retire early. The excitement of Moss's homecoming had proved to be a strain. "It's wonderful to have you home, Moss. I wish it were for good." There was a sadness in her eyes that went beyond worry for a soldier son at war.

Moss clasped Jessica's hand to his chest and leaned down to kiss her powdery cheek. "Someday soon it will be, Mam. Everything will be the way it used to be, only better. Have a good night and I'll come in to see you in the morning."

"I'll go up with you, Jessica," Billie offered, her gaze swinging to Moss. Surely after a few minutes he would follow.

After helping Jessica into her nightgown and tucking her into bed, Billie went to her room and gratefully removed her clothes. It was ironic that just months before she would have cheerfully died for a pair of silk stockings and now that they were a part of her daily wardrobe, she couldn't wait for evening to take them off. The garters cut into her thighs and her toes always felt squashed.

She ran a tub for a quick bath and donned one of the new nightgowns she'd purchased, topping it off with its matching peignoir of fine pale blue lace. Fondly she remembered sleeping nude with Moss or, at most, wearing one of his undershirts. The clinging cotton knit would never fit over her burgeoning belly now. She whipped a brush through her hair until it crackled and applied just a touch of cologne to her throat, wrists, and between her breasts. Then she waited for Moss. And waited. And waited.

The bedside clock read two-thirty—she must have fallen

asleep. She remembered putting her head down on her pillow for just a minute. The lights were still on and she was chilled from sleeping in the cool room uncovered. Where was Moss?

Going to the door, she opened it, peering into a darkened hallway. There were no lights coming from downstairs. The house had been locked and closed for the night. Everyone had gone to bed. Where was Moss? Why hadn't he come to bed? Her attention focused on the room next to hers. Moss had moved into it when he'd started college, abandoning his boyhood room in the far wing. Not believing that he could be there, Billie tiptoed to the door, tapped softly, and then turned the knob. A shaft of light came from within. Moss was asleep on the single bed, book in hand, bedside lamp still burning.

Billie sank back against the wall, her hand pressed against her mouth to keep the cries from escaping. A hunger welled in her breast, coming from so deep within her that it brought actual pain in her need for him. Didn't he care how lonely she was, had been all this time without him? Closing the door, she stumbled back to her bed and flung herself across it. Disappointment was a physical ache. She was cast off, ugly and undesirable. All she wanted was to be beside him, be held in his arms, feel close to him. She wanted to feel loved, feel his body beside her, touch him, have him press tender kisses to her lips. Desolate, abandoned, forgotten, Billie clutched her pillow and silenced her sobs.

{{{{{{{{{ CHAPTER TEN }}}}}}}}}

When Billie dragged herself downstairs the next morning she bore the badges of sleeplessness beneath her eyes. Moss had already left his room when she peeped in, so she hoped to find him waiting for her downstairs. Tonight was Christmas Eve, her first Christmas with her husband, but the disappointment of the night before had cast a pall over the occasion. Moss's rejection burned, but she was determined to face him as though nothing had happened. As though her heart weren't broken.

The dining room was empty except for Tita, who was fussing at the serving board with dishes and trays. "Good morning, Tita. Where is everyone this morning?"

Tita knew that "everyone" meant Moss. Poor Señora Billie. "Your mother is in Señor Coleman's study calling the florist about something and Señora Jessica will stay upstairs until the party this evening. Señor Moss left early this morning with his father. They took the plane over to Corpus Christi, but they say they will be back in time for dinner."

"I'd almost forgotten about the party," Billie said, struggling to keep her voice steady. "What time did my husband leave?"

"Very early—perhaps he didn't want to wake you, seño-ra. . . ." Tita avoided Billie's glance.

"Who'll be here tonight?" Billie asked, swallowing her vitamin capsules. She would have liked nothing more than to spend a quiet holiday with Moss, alone, with tender little touches and sweet caresses and whispers that promised more wonderful Christmases to come. Would she ever be alone with Moss again?

"Just the family for dinner and later a few friends drop in, nothing big, very simple," Tita said. "Everyone goes home early," she added reassuringly.

"Is there anything I can do to help? Back home, Mother and I used to bake cookies and—make . . ." Her words faltered. Those days seemed a lifetime ago.

"You can see if Señora Jessica has last-minute wrapping to do, and maybe you can have lunch with her. Then you make yourself pretty for the party, sí?"

Pretty. As though she'd ever be pretty again. "Sí," Billie answered listlessly.

Billie took a lunch tray up to Jessica's room and they ate together. Afterward, she took a long bath and lay down for a nap. Outside the window, the wild Texas wind howled, pushing against the house, finding cracks and chinks in the siding to whistle through. Twilight came so early this time of year, daylight deepening to a dark gray and then quickly to blackness. There were no streetlamps, of course, no uptown buzz of last-minute Christmas shoppers and endless holiday music. All that was forty miles away, in Austin. Billie's sense of abandonment and isolation increased as the day waned. She refused to think about the strong winds, which could affect Moss's flying home from Corpus Christi. She refused to think about anything at all as she lay on her bed and closed her eyes.

Moss followed Seth into the house, bringing with him a burst of frigid air. His wide-brimmed Stetson was glazed with frost, as was the sheepskin collar of his leather bombardier jacket, and there was a frown of frustration on his brow. Seth suggested a brandy in the study.

"Pap, that trip to Corpus Christi was unnecessary and you know it," he said, watching his father splash cognac into a snifter.

"Nonsense, no amount of attention to business is unnecessary. Can't let the men think I don't take an interest—they'd take advantage. Besides, with this dang war, it's hard to get help."

"The hell with the war," Moss muttered. "And you've still got the same old cowpokes driving that cattle as you always did. It's Christmas, Pap, a hell of a time to make an unexpected visit and take the men away from their families."

Seth's expression soured. "Don't go soft on me, boy. Those men have a job to do and I'm here to see they do it. Cattle still got to be fed and watered, don't they? If you hadn't run off to play soldier, you'd be here to help me."

The cognac slid down Moss's throat and warmed his belly. "I'm going up to change for dinner," he announced. His thoughts were on Billie. He wanted to see her. . . . There was an uneasy stirring in his loins.

"You've got plenty of time to change. I wanted to ask you what you thought of an idea I had. . . ."

"Not now, Pap. I'm tired and it was a hair-raising trip home. That wind must be blowing at thirty knots."

"We could've stayed in Corpus Christi," Seth muttered. "You were the one hot to get back here."

Moss drained his snifter and placed it on the table beside his chair. He was more than familiar with Seth's tug on his time and attention. But things had changed. Now it was more than a mother and sister he wanted to come home to, it was a young wife with a baby on the way. "You would've liked that, wouldn't you, Pap? Me and you staying over in Corpus."

"Damn right. Nothin goin' on here but a lot of women's foolishness. Parties, Christmas trees, bah!"

"Same old Scrooge." Moss laughed. "Remember the Christmas we were all supposed to go skiing and you sent Mam and Amelia on ahead of us and something came up so we never got there? I thought Mam's heart would break. They came rushing home here soon as they could, but by then the holidays were over and I was on my way back to school. For the life of me, Pap, I'll never understand how Mam put up with you all these years." Actually, Moss was thinking more about Amelia's disappointments than about his mother's. Amelia would've walked through fire for Seth if he'd just whistled. He never had. There were times when Moss felt guilty about the attention and affection their father showered on him. If Amelia wasn't such a good person, it would have created profound jealousy. But Moss knew her love for him was almost as great as her need for Seth's love.

"Jess puts up with me the same way that little Yankee gal will put up with you," Seth told him. "Have another drink."

"No more, Pap. I'm going upstairs to my wife. You just reminded me how hard we Colemans are on our women."

"Remember what I said, boy. Keep your pants zipped. I don't want anything going wrong for my grandson."

Wearily, Moss left the study and lifted himself up the long staircase, his boots noiseless on the thick carpeting. First he'd go see Jessica and then Billie. He worried about both of them—neither looked well. Jessica was tired and wan and Billie was bloated and sick. Poor Billie. She should be wearing pretty dresses and going to dances. Right now she should be enrolled in Penn State and looking forward to Christmas vacation instead of teetering around on swollen feet, balancing a pregnant belly. And then to be uprooted and sent all the way here to Texas, away from everything familiar . . . Christ! It was a wonder she didn't hate him.

Jessica was sleeping soundly when Moss peered in and he quietly closed the door so as not to disturb her. He worried about his mother but it was a concern that was somehow free of responsibility. With Billie, it was different.

When he opened Billie's door he saw that the curtains had been drawn and she was on the bed, lying on her side, a pillow propped between her knees to take the strain from her back. As he came nearer, he could see her face, full and round and still so pretty. Her mouth was soft and gentle but there was a pucker between her brows. Had he put it there? A stray blond curl rested against her cheek, accentuating the unhealthy flush. As his hand reached out to touch it, to smooth it away, his heart reached out for her.

Billie's eyes opened at his touch and he was gratified by

the slow, sleepy smile she bestowed on him. No, she didn't hate him, and somehow that wrenched his conscience. So young, so pretty, so very pregnant. And all for a debt, a payoff for his freedom.

Slipping out of his boots, he climbed onto the high bed beside her, taking her into his arms. She rested her head on his shoulder, throwing her arm over his chest. He could feel the heat from her body, the press of her breasts against his side, fuller and more womanly than he remembered. The intrusion of her rounded girth lay between them. He could smell the freshness of her hair, feel its softness against his lips. If he closed his eyes, he could almost believe this was the same Billie he'd met in Philadelphia—golden and pretty, fresh and unspoiled.

Billie lifted her chin, nuzzling his neck and kissing his jaw, her hands moving over him passionately, encouragingly. "I won't make love to you, Billie. I don't want to hurt you or the baby," he told her, softening his rejection with a kiss.

"*This* is loving," she whispered, hiding her disappointment. Pregnancy had changed her needs; physical lovemaking was no longer one of them. But it would have been nice to know he still wanted her. Perhaps he still did and it really was only his concern for her that held him back. Her hand slipped to his waist and then smoothed over his hip to his thighs. "Touch me, Moss. Touch my breast," she said, gratified by the signal of desire beneath her exploring hand.

"Billie," he murmured, his lips lost in her hair, "don't do this. Just let me hold you. That's all I want." Pap's warning was pounding in his brain.

"Your body is saying other things, Moss." She worked his belt and fumbled with the zipper. "There are so many ways to make love—you taught me yourself. Don't you remember?" His breath caught in his throat as her fingers made contact with his naked flesh. "You want me to, don't you, Moss? You want me to touch you like this. Don't you?" Her voice was deep and seductive and her lips were nuzzling his chin and intruding into the warmth beneath his collar. "Touch me. Touch me here." She leaned into him, disregarding the child who lay between them, sliding his hand down the firm globe of her belly to the place where her thighs met.

Moss's determinations and resolutions were fading quickly. She was right; there were many ways of making love and he

{ 149 }

would explore them all. Her body was exciting him; different, yet the same. She was fuller, warmer, strangely exotic. . . . Let Pap be damned!

Agnes, Jessica, and Seth waited around the Christmas tree for Moss and Billie. Agnes nervously fingered her strand of almost good pearls, and Jessica desperately attempted to keep a conversation going. Both women were all too aware of Seth's glowering anger. "What's keeping those two?" he asked impatiently. "That boy knows I like to sit down to dinner at exactly six o'clock. We'll hardly have time to eat before our friends start arriving!" He was drinking, not sipping, corn whiskey and he paced with agitation, leaning more heavily than usual on his cane.

"Seth, the children will be down. They just want to spend some time together, that's all," Jessica said soothingly. Despite her husband's annoyance she was happy for Billie. That's all the child needed, her husband's attention and comfort.

Agnes was not so charitable. Her fears ran along the same vein as Seth's. She should have said something to Billie, warned her of the possible danger to the baby, but she never thought that Moss would be romantically inclined in the face of Billie's full-blown pregnancy.

"Aggie," Seth growled, "you go upstairs and get that daughter of yours. Now!"

"That's not necessary, Pap," Moss said smoothly as he led Billie into the living room. "Here's our little mother-to-be, the hope of the Coleman clan." The sharpness of his glance covered the distance between himself and his father. Seth read it correctly. Moss was warning Pap that he'd better be careful how his wife was treated. Consideration and respect, and nothing less would do.

Billie was entirely unaware of the others' emotions. Her cheeks were flushed pink and there was a softness in her hazel eyes like that of a contented cat. A cat who'd spent the night on the back fence with her mate.

Seth turned away, slapping his glass down on an end table with an angry clatter. Moss wore the grin of a little boy.

Jessica sighed, rubbing her temples. Years of practice told her she must be the one to ease the situation if they were to have a pleasant dinner. "Moss, dear, we were waiting for you and Billie so we could each open one present from one another before we go in to eat. This is Christmas. Let's not be glum." Her last statement was for Seth.

"Holy bejesus, Jess! We'll hardly have time to swallow our beans before the Richardsons get here and you know I hate to rush when I eat. It sticks in a lump and takes me two days to get rid of it."

"Moss, why don't you give Billie her present?" Jessica said, ignoring her husband's complaints. "Billie, you go sit near the tree. I want Moss to use my camera to take pictures of us all." A disgruntled snort erupted from Seth. "You look so pretty tonight, Billie. Is that one of the new dresses you bought in Austin?"

Billie turned gracefully, modeling her long full dress. It was dark navy georgette with a square white sailor collar trimmed in red. "I was thinking if I had to be a navy wife, I should look the part," she told Jessica brightly.

"She looks terrific, doesn't she, Mam?" Moss said proudly, disregarding another snort from Seth.

For the next few minutes torn wrapping paper littered the living room. Billie squealed with pleasure when she opened Moss's present. A Chinese silk wrapper and tiny matching heeled slippers. Laughing, she slipped it over her shoulders and brought the front edges together. "I'll save it for after the baby," she announced, demonstrating how the protuberance of her belly prevented it from closing. Only last night she would have been overcome with self-consciousness and embarrassment about her size. But since this afternoon and Moss's ardent loving, she was accepting the changes in herself because he could. *That* was a gift more precious and valuable than any other.

For Jessica there was a carton from England, from Amelia, and inside was a delicate bone china tea service and a letter.

Seth received his usual box of cigars and bottle of bourbon and Moss had brought him an ornamental bridle for old Nessie. Seth presented Jessica with a $2,000 voucher in her name for her favorite charity, the March of Dimes. It was a tradition that had begun several years ago, after Seth had complained that buying a present for Jessica was harder than roping a wild steer in a blind canyon. Seth handed Agnes a long, slim box carefully wrapped in bright paper. He stood by while she fumbled with the ribbon. "For Christ's sake, Aggie, just rip it open. My beans are gettin' cold!"

It was a jeweler's box and inside was a twenty-four-inch

strand of perfectly matched pearls. Agnes's hands trembled when she lifted them out of their nest.

"Don't go saying you can't accept them, Aggie. Can't have the grandmother of my first grandchild going around wearing dimestore jewelry. And since you're so partial to pearls I thought you should have them."

Billie looked from the gleaming rope of her mother's gift to Jessica, who attempted a smile. The old bastard, thought Billie. She was very glad that she'd bought the antique silver picture frame to give to Jessica. It had a place for a portrait of herself and Moss, and one that waited to be filled with one of the baby. Certainly it could never compensate for Seth's thoughtlessness, but it was an acknowledgment that Jessica would be the baby's grandmother, too.

Agnes was overwhelmed by Seth's generosity, but her poise and polish made it appear that she was merely accepting what was due her. That seemed to rattle Seth. "Put them on, Aggie! I told you my beans are getting cold. What're you waiting for?"

A slow smile touched Agnes's lips. "I'm not so certain I like the idea of you thinking about my neck, Seth," she told him sharply.

"Take it easy, Aggie. If I ever want your neck on a chopping block, I'll give you fair notice. Put them on, dammit, and let's eat!"

The pearls slid over Agnes's head and rested on the cranberry velvet of her cocktail dress like twenty-four inches of smiling teeth.

That night, after the traditional Christmas Eve dinner, after the friends had gone home and all the presents had been opened, Moss slept in Billie's bed, holding her, caressing her, and allowing the drinks he'd consumed to overpower Seth's warning again. This was his wife and she was offering herself to him, consoling him for the time he'd gone without a woman, being the essence of womanhood when she welcomed his flesh into hers.

Christmas morning, when the first rays of daylight invaded the room, Moss awakened to the sound of Billie's pitiful retching in the adjoining bath. Hastily, he grabbed up his clothes and escaped to his room. Christ! What if he'd hurt her last night? What if it was all too much for her? He should have listened to Pap.

Two hours later, at the breakfast table, Billie was pale and weak, yet bravely making the best of it. But Moss was unable to look into her shadow-rimmed eyes any longer. He made the announcement that he had checked with San Diego, and he was ordered back at once. Billie's fork clattered onto her dish. Seth was appalled by Moss's statement, which he didn't believe for one second. He was leaving because of *her*! Billie glanced up at her father-in-law. His eyes hated her.

On February fourth, Billie began her labor. A private ambulance was dispatched on Seth's excited phone call. Billie was trundled into the back of the vehicle and a nurse held her hand. Agnes and Seth followed the ambulance in the chauffeur-driven Packard. Jessica watched the ambulance and Packard leave, her rosary clutched tightly in her hand. At that moment she didn't know whom she'd feel sorrier for, Billie or Seth. Billie, if the baby was a girl, Seth, if he should be disappointed.

Billie had fourteen hours of agony. Until the moment the mask came down over Billie's perspiring face she prayed for death, anything to take away the relentless pain. . . .

When Billie opened her eyes the first person she saw was Seth Coleman. He stared down at her accusingly. Her mother stood next to him with a judgmental look on her face. So, she had delivered a girl! Jessica would be pleased. Moss would be . . . Moss would be disappointed. She had failed. She wasn't a Coleman yet. Not yet, Seth's eyes told her. Should she apologize? They were waiting for her to say something, probably to ask about the baby. Instead she closed her eyes and slept. Deeply.

Later, on the ride back to Sunbridge, Agnes realized that she had never seen Seth so angry, so controlled. She understood perfectly. Perhaps too perfectly. Her own position—and Billie's too, of course—was in jeopardy until there was a Coleman heir. Good God, if something happened to Moss, Billie and she could be shipped back to Philadelphia without a moment's notice or a backward glance.

Striving for a light tone, Agnes said, "First pregnancies are usually hard on a young girl. Billie is young and healthy. Living at Sunbridge will put the bloom back in her cheeks. She'll be right as rain in a month. In three months she'll be ready to try again."

Seth hardly acknowledged Agnes's words. A damn baby girl, for God's sake! Moss was going to be fit to be tied. It should have been a boy; he'd depended on it being a boy. It was part of the bargain. Seth sank lower into the backseat of the Packard and gritted his teeth. That little gal Moss had taken for a wife had no more spunk and grit than Jessica. Sure, he'd hit pay dirt with Moss, but Jessica had failed him after that, first producing Amelia, then drying up completely and forever. Agnes had said something about three months and they could try again. That would be around the beginning of May. Three months to arrange for Billie and Moss to be together again.

When Jessica heard the news that her first grandchild was a girl, she stared down at the rosary in her hands. A girl, a little girl, just like her Amelia. Seth must be in a rage because this was something over which he had no control. She almost cried with relief that the child wasn't a boy. Seth's possessiveness could be a little boy's undoing. She threw her rosary beads angrily onto the bed. It was one of the few violent outbursts she'd ever experienced, and she was surprised at how good, how right it felt. Perhaps if she'd given vent to her anger all these years, she wouldn't have these terrible headaches and her heart wouldn't thump so madly in her breast.

Moss climbed from the cockpit of the Texas Ranger. As was his custom, he patted the plane fondly, the way a man might touch his woman. Less than a week before he'd fought in the battle of Rennell Island, the last of the Guadalcanal campaign. The heat of the victory still ran in his blood.

Two more meatballs would be added to the eight already on Moss's fuselage. He'd be asked to command his own squadron, to train his men, instill them with confidence. Well, he was ready. He'd had the best teachers, known the best men. He'd seen battle and smelled its hell, known victory and felt its elation.

The flight deck officer was running toward him. "Coleman, the chaplain wants to see you. Pronto!" It was in such contradiction to his train of thought that Moss's belly immediately constricted. Something was wrong, very wrong. Gut fear propelled his feet, his mind racing as fast as he ran. Seth? Billie? Jessica? But no way, no matter what it was, would he leave the Big E. He was being assigned to command his own squadron, things were turning up for him, things he wanted, needed. He wasn't going home until this was over, one way or the other, whether he walked through the door of Sunbridge under his own steam or was carried in in a box.

His salute was snappy, his words crisply spoken. "Lieutenant Moss Coleman reporting, sir."

"At ease, Lieutenant." The chaplain smiled. Freckled hands extended to give Moss the slip of paper from the radio room.

Moss read the message, a grin stretching across his face. A baby girl, Margaret Jessica Coleman. February fourth. Four pounds, three ounces. Mother and daughter both fine. Jesus, he was a father! Two months early! Billie was fine. His sigh of relief sounded loud in his ears.

A knock sounded on the office door and Captain Hardison stepped in, extending his hand to Moss. "Congratulations, Coleman. I was in the radio room when the message came through." He reached into his breast pocket and withdrew three cylinders, fondling them reverently before extending one to the chaplain and one to Moss. "I filched these from Admiral Halsey's private stock when we were in Pearl. If you tell anyone, I'll clip your wings, and as for you, Father, you will keep to the confidentiality of confession. Agreed? Pure Havana—I've been saving them for a special occasion. Think of me when you smoke it, Lieutenant."

Moss saluted. "I'll do that, sir." It wasn't until he was back in his own quarters with the cigar clamped between his teeth that he took a second look at the radio message. A girl! What the hell, a baby was a baby. There'd still be time for boys. Pap was probably belly up over the disappointment. He took a satisfying pull on the cigar, blue smoke ringing his head, then almost laughed. Agnes had been so certain that the baby would be a boy. "You were wrong, you old buzzard," he said aloud. He was the littlest bit disgruntled about it himself, but his delight over what he imagined was Agnes's chagrin was compensation. "Aggie, old girl, you've got to learn we Colemans are a slippery bunch. Very slippery indeed."

Billie returned to Sunbridge ten days after the birth of her daughter. Dr. Ward's dire warnings against another pregnancy too soon had darkened her day. She hadn't even considered having another child, suffering another nine months, swelling and vomiting and aching her way through another year. Seth was hell-bent on having a grandson. But boy or girl, it didn't matter to Moss, did it? Maggie was a beautiful baby, a little too small from being born prematurely, but she was healthy enough to be allowed to go home. Still, Billie hadn't liked the expression on the doctor's face or the technical language he'd used. Toxemia, low birth weight, breech presentation—it was all too much to understand but it left her with the feeling that whatever had gone wrong was her own fault. She still wasn't a Coleman woman, to have her children on the side of the road and run back to work, and perhaps she never would be. Dr. Ward's words made her afraid. At the same time, he had presented a challenge.

A private ambulance brought Billie and Maggie the forty miles out from Austin and she walked to the front door under her own power. When she reached out for Maggie, the nurse Seth had hired shook her head and cradled the baby protectively in her arms.

"I want to take Maggie upstairs and present her to her grandmother," Billie explained. If she spoke as though Maggie had only one grandmother, it was what she was feeling. Jessica's phone conversations twice a day to the hospital had been loving and her inquiries about Maggie sincere and enthusiastic. Now Billie wanted to proudly take Maggie up to Jessica's room and be gratified by grandmotherly croonings.

"I'll take the baby now," Billie said more forcefully, meeting the nurse's stare.

Agnes, who had followed the ambulance in the family automobile, came forward. "Don't be ridiculous, Billie. For all you know, Jessica is sound asleep. You're behaving like a child. The nurse has her instructions and you're not to interfere." For a moment, Agnes thought Billie would stand her ground. A warning bell went off in Agnes's head: Billie might very well become difficult and totally unlike the respectful, obedient daughter she'd always been. Until she'd met Moss, Agnes qualified. Before Billie could argue, Agnes touched her arm solicitously.

"There will be plenty of time to spend with the baby, Billie. You're still not completely recovered from the whole ordeal. Until you get your strength back, why don't you just rely upon me to know what's best."

Agnes's gentle caring penetrated Billie's reserve and she felt herself slipping back into the old rhythms of following her mother's directions. She was tired and still sore and cried easily. Dr. Ward said it was natural for a woman to feel depressed after the birth of a child. And it was just easier to have someone else make the decisions.

Settled back in her room, Billie rested in bed. She'd written Moss about the baby, describing Maggie's shock of nearly black hair and telling him that it was already obvious her eyes would be the same clear light blue as his. But what else could she tell Moss about their daughter when she hardly saw her? Little Margaret Jessica Coleman was at the other end of the house in her pretty little nursery with her own nurse in attendance. On Dr. Ward's suggestion, probably orders issued Seth, Maggie was to be bottle-fed. The doctor's words—"You're hardly strong enough, Mrs. Coleman"—echoed in her head. Something else in which she was lacking. She felt fine now, even if a little tired, and her breasts beneath the agonizing breast binder were heavy with milk.

Reaching into her bedside table, Billie withdrew the stationery she'd received from Agnes at Christmas. Her name was engraved at the top: Mrs. Moss Coleman. Tears threatened. Whatever had happened to Billie Ames? She felt as though she'd been swallowed whole and was being digested as permanently and efficiently as Seth's favorite beans.

The bedroom door opened and Agnes came into Billie's room. "Darling, are you writing to Moss? That's good. Seth and I were worried about your lackadaisical attitude these past few days. Now that you're on the mend your life is going to be just wonderful. Aren't you ever so grateful that there is a nurse for Maggie? Why, when I had you I would have cut off my right arm for just a *little* help. Babies are so draining and they do prevent one from regaining one's strength. I also think it was very wise of Dr. Ward to start Maggie on bottles. There's nothing more loathsome for a woman than pulling out her breast for a baby to guzzle. Seth agrees.

"Billie, you are so lucky. I do hope you appreciate all of the help the Colemans are giving you. If we were back in Philadelphia, we'd both be worn to a frazzle. Now, with all of these tedious chores taken off your hands, you can concentrate on regaining your strength and getting back to normal. You never know—Moss could get leave, just like that." With this she snapped her fingers and then, in a rare moment of affection, bent over and kissed Billie on the cheek.

"We're going to have such wonderful times, Billie. As soon as you're on your feet, I'll take you to all the clubs and organizations Seth feels we should belong to. I've made some lovely friends and everyone is dying to meet you. You have to do it, darling, for Jessica's sake. That's what the Coleman women do, you know. *We* do the social scene while the men harvest the money. It's such a wonderful tradition."

"Mother, have you seen Maggie?"

"Of course I have. Everyone has seen the . . . the little darling. Why, I peeked into the nursery just moments ago and she was sleeping soundly. The nurse is preparing her bottle right now. Canned milk and Karo syrup. Jessica is waiting in her room to be allowed to feed her. The nurse felt it would be better if you stayed here in your room. Just for a few more days. You have to take things slow at first. Trays will be sent up."

"Mother, I'm not an invalid. All I did was have a baby. Millions of women have babies. Why can't I go downstairs to dinner? Why do I have to have a tray? Is Seth so upset he can't look at me?" she said bitterly. "I know I spoiled his grand plans by having a girl instead of a boy."

Agnes stiffened. "Now that's enough of that kind of talk. I don't ever want to hear anything like that again. You're a Coleman now and it's time you were properly appreciative. It's the stairs, Billie. You can't keep going up and down. Not for a while yet. Those are Dr. Ward's orders. Seth had nothing to do with that, for heaven's sake. How could you think such a thing?"

Billie leaned back in the chair. She had forgotten the steps. They had been a chore to climb. So what if she had to stay up here for another week or so—at least she could walk down the hall to see Maggie. She could read to Jessica, and they could talk for hours about the baby and the delivery. She could write to Moss every day and tell him of Maggie's progress. As soon as possible she would have a picture taken and send it along. Moss could carry it in his wallet and show his friends. But would he? Seth would never brag about a daughter; of that she was sure. Would Moss? She had to admit she didn't know.

"I think I'll take a nap and then write to Moss. I'm rather tired, Mother." It was a dismissal and Agnes was grateful. They didn't have much to say to each other.

An hour later Billie realized she didn't need sleep. She settled herself in the chair by the window, her writing pad on her knee. It struck her suddenly how alone she was. Maggie was being taken care of. Agnes was off doing only God knew what—plowing the south forty, for all she knew. Her husband, dear, sweet, wonderful Moss, was off fighting a war to make the world safe for her and Maggie.

Billie sat for a long time, staring at the blank pad on her knees. In the end she wrote a trite, newsy little letter that told none of her true feelings. What would Moss think of her if she said she didn't care for his father? How could she tell him of the look in his father's eyes when she'd come out of the anesthetic? Moss didn't need or want to hear that sort of thing.

Little Maggie, as we call her, is doing fine. Nurse Jenkins seems to think she's a bit ahead of herself, gobbling down six bottles a day. She sleeps constantly, as do all babies. I rarely hear her cry because the nursery is down at the end of the hall, and anyway I think Nurse Jenkins picks her up as soon as she even whimpers. She does go through an exorbitant amount of didies. Tita is going to have her hands full with laundry. Mother said your father will get someone in to do Maggie's laundry. Isn't that generous of him?

I labored for almost fifteen hours, but I'm fine now, and pounds lighter. When you see me next I plan to look like the girl you left behind. The only difference will be that that girl is now a young mother. I hope you're pleased with the name we gave her.

The war news hasn't improved. I listen to it every chance I get, and I read the papers cover to cover every day. Please, Moss, take care of yourself, and when you have time, think of Maggie and me because we're here loving you.

How I treasure those few days we had at Christmas. If only it could have been longer. I'm not complaining; it's just that I miss you so.

Your mother sends her love. She's been talking about Amelia a lot of late. Before I went to the hospital we spent one entire afternoon looking at baby pictures of you and Amelia. She really does miss your sister. I wish I could meet her. Your mother seems to think that we would get on well together.

Darling Moss, I must close for now. I want to check on Maggie and it's almost time for dinner. I thought I would have mine with your mother this evening on my first night home. I guess it is my home now that Maggie's here, but in the beginning I rather felt like a visitor. Having Maggie seems to make me permanent, if you know what I mean.

All my love to you, Moss. Please write when you can.

Love, Billie

Billie sealed the letter and put an airmail stamp on the envelope. She wondered when Moss would get it. There had been no mail from him for over two weeks. Perhaps tomorrow. I'll say an extra prayer, she thought, and couldn't help wondering if Seth had heard from his son. She had shared her letters with him and Jessica, but Seth had not shown her the same courtesy. She hadn't wanted to make an issue of it and so had remained quiet, but it seemed so unfair. Didn't he know how worried and upset she was? And whom was she fooling about being permanent and belonging? At best she was merely tolerated. In a sense the baby did make a difference, but Maggie was a girl. Seth Coleman wanted a grandson.

Doctor's orders or not, she was going to take a shower and wash her hair. What harm could it do? And she would feel so much cleaner and better than with a sponge bath and talcum powder. She'd lock the bedroom door and the one to the bathroom. Who would know? Who would care, really?

The thick steak staring up at Billie made her gulp. Jessica's light salad and small dessert of Jello-O was more appealing. Billie picked guiltily, knowing she should be grateful for the meat. Back in Philadelphia her friends would have given anything for a steak like this one. Tita removed the heavy dinner almost intact. Jessica smiled as she poured the coffee from a handsome silver urn.

"Now tell me, child, how bad was it?"

"Bad. But it's over now."

"Billie, giving birth is the most wonderful experience in the world. We've been so fortunate. True, there is pain, but it's the most easily forgotten kind. Once you see that little pink or blue bundle, nothing else matters. Don't you agree?"

Billie knew what she was supposed to say. But to forget fourteen long hours of the most excruciating misery known to woman! And that pink bundle. Perhaps if she had been able to hold Maggie after the delivery, she might feel as Jessica did, but it had been three days before Maggie had been brought to her because of the baby's low birth weight. Still, pleasing Jessica and being agreeable was so much easier than telling the truth. Besides, Jessica didn't want to hear unpleasant facts. She was living her life within the four walls of this room, sheltered from unpleasantness and stress. Seth had said Jessica was to remain calm at all costs. So she forced herself to meet Jessica's eyes and took a deep breath.

"Yes," she lied.

"She's beautiful, Billie," Jessica went on enthusiastically. "So healthy-looking, despite how little she is, and all that hair! I'm sure Moss is delighted. Seth said he sent word to the *Enterprise*. I expect we'll be hearing from Moss any day now. I pray that we do every day. At least you'll never have to worry about Maggie going off to war. Good girls always stay near their mothers."

Billie sipped her coffee. Good girls? Did that mean she didn't consider Amelia to be a good girl?

"In England, Jessica, the women are doing their bit. I've been reading about it. They're so brave. The whole thing is just so terrible. While I was in the hospital I read—" Billie bit her tongue. What she had read would be considered upsetting to the frail Jessica. A young woman had been driving an ambulance with four wounded men inside and they'd been bombed right off the road. Only bits and pieces of the bodies were found. No, that surely would upset Jessica, with Amelia in England. Maggie was the only safe topic of conversation, or the weather. Mentioning Agnes always brought a tightening of Jessica's lips.

"I just wrote Moss a letter telling him all about Maggie," Billie said. "That reminds me. Can you recommend a good photographer to come and take her picture? I want to send it to Moss."

"Seth has already taken care of that, Billie. A photographer will come out when Maggie is christened next week."

"Christened? Next week? I suppose I'll be up to it, but I'm not sure about any of my clothes fitting me. My goodness, so soon?"

"Billie, there's nothing to fret about. Seth and Agnes will take care of everything. Besides, the mother doesn't go to the church. It's not going to be an event. A simple christening with some pictures taken. A sit-down dinner for a few of our closest friends. That's all there is to it. Maggie will of course wear the same christening dress that Moss and Amelia wore. I was very careful about preserving it when I packed it away. The laundress will see that it is cleaned and each tiny ruffle ironed to perfection. You don't have to concern yourself about these details."

But I want to! Billie almost screamed. She couldn't go to the church? It was unthinkable. She was going to miss her own baby's christening? Well, we'll just see about that!

"Billie, what is it? What's wrong?" Jessica asked anxiously.

With great effort, Billie forced herself to speak quietly. "I would like to do these things I want to go to the church to see Maggie christened. She's my first child. How can I write Moss about it if I'm not there?"

"Darling child, this is the way we do things here. You're going to have to get used to it. You're a Coleman now and you have to accept our ways. That's why Moss sent you to us. I think you're overly tired and it *is* your first day at home. Tomorrow you'll realize that Seth is more than capable of handling all these matters. Your mother is helping—or will help, if she's needed. Moss expects it."

And that was the last word.

Billie held her tears in check when she bent down to kiss Jessica good night. "I'll go by the nursery and check on Maggie before I turn in for the evening."

Jessica hated to do it and she practically bit her tongue to make the words come out right. "Why don't you wait for morning, Billie. I'm sure the nurse has settled Maggie for the night and you might wake her. Routine. Nurses always have such strict routines."

"Is that the same as telling me the nurse won't allow me in the nursery to see my own baby?" Billie asked in a trembling voice.

"I'm afraid so, Billie. If the door is closed, it stays closed."

Jessica ached to gather Billie close to her, to pat her head and tell her everything would be fine. Lately, though, she'd begun to have the feeling she wouldn't always be here to comfort Billie. Mollycoddling, as Seth called it. The sooner Billie learned and accepted that things were done the "Coleman way," the better it would be for her. There was little sense in spurring the child into rebellion. Jessica drew her rosary from her dressing gown pocket, leaned her head back against the chair, and closed her eyes. There were cruel lessons that Billie would learn, the same lessons she'd had to learn herself. And for what? To end up a woman old before her time, sitting alone in her room with every unfought and unfinished battle still tearing at her heart. No, it would be easier in the long run if Billie became a true Coleman: hard, greedy, and selfish. Otherwise she'd have to run away, just as Amelia did. Just as she was doing herself.

Billie fled the room. Her eyes went down the endless hallway to the nursery door. It was closed. Her shoulders slumped as she entered her own room and locked the door behind her. She wasn't used to closed doors; she hated them. Tears rolled down her cheeks as she picked up the letter to Moss and held it close to her heart. It didn't bring him any closer.

Maggie was three months old the day Seth entered Sunbridge by the kitchen door, his weathered face wreathed in smiles. He'd just come from the Cattlemen's Club.

"You look like someone just handed you their prize bull," Agnes said as she poured herself a cup of coffee. "Would you like a cup? I just sent Tita up with tea for Jessica."

"My news is a damn sight better than getting a prize bull. I just got a call from Washington: the *Enterprise* is coming into Pearl for repairs. My boy is safe and sound and we might be able to get some calls through and talk to him. They're due into Pearl on the eighth of May; that's four days away, Aggie. I'm going up to tell Jessica."

Agnes stared after Seth's retreating back. It was awesome how the Colemans got everything their way, but things had to be handled delicately, quietly. Billie was getting her back up these days about the smallest things. If she were to suspect for one minute that another pregnancy was being planned by her father-in-law and her mother, there was no telling what her reaction would be.

Billie would be delighted to go to Hawaii to see her husband, though. And when she returned, with any luck she'd be carrying the Coleman heir. And luck *would* be on their side. How could anything be simpler than letting nature take its course?

PART II

CHAPTER ELEVEN

Agnes stared out the multipaned window in her bedroom, sa-
voring the seemingly limitless expanse of Sunbridge. For months
now she'd considered the homestead, as Seth called it, her
own.

She had sailed into her duties with a capability that had
stunned Seth. At first she'd merely been efficient, making the
household revolve around him and his activities. She could tell
he liked the way she did things and she anticipated his every
need. Often, she wondered how close she'd come to spending
the rest of her life wasting away in Philadelphia, becoming
older and dowdier caring for a small house and boarders. The
thought made her shiver with revulsion.

Seth found Agnes amenable and smart and often invited her
along to luncheons at the Cattlemen's Club. The day he'd
leaned across the table and asked her opinion on a matter, in
full view and hearing of his friends and their wives, she'd
enjoyed their astonishment. Seth Coleman had never been known
to ask a woman the time of day, much less her opinion! That
day had marked Agnes's total acceptance into Austin society.
All she had to do now was sit back and reap the rewards. But
no matter how efficient she was or how dependent Seth had
become upon her, she accepted reality. She was dispensable.
At least until Billie produced a male heir. And what better
place to get the ball rolling than the paradise of Hawaii? Romance and baby making went hand in hand. Moss would be
more than agreeable, especially once he saw this new, ripe
Billie, more than a girl, just a shade less than a woman. How
appealing! The urge to smack her lips was overwhelming.

A rolling tumbleweed danced across the front lawn. Agnes
frowned. Now where had that come from? She pressed her
face against the window to see where the offensive weed had
landed and made a mental note to remind the gardener to search
it out in the morning. Her eyes strayed heavenward to the early

spring sky. Even the first stars of evening seemed bigger and brighter, the moon more silvery and round. Perhaps it was true that everything in Texas was bigger than life and better than anywhere else. She, for one, certainly believed it.

A muted cry filtered down the hall and was instantly hushed. The baby. Agnes's lips thinned to a hard line. Maggie Coleman. Thank the Lord for nurses and nannies. Billie would be able to go off to Hawaii and not have a care in the world. Money was such a marvelous thing.

A second, more piercing yowl shuddered down the hall. Agnes gave her head a little shake and left her room. Seth would be waiting for her in his study, and she'd be willing to bet that the man hadn't poured his own bourbon but was waiting for her to do the honors. It was now a ritual she rather enjoyed, feeling a certain little warm spurt of power in being the one to please him.

A smirk played around Seth's mouth as he watched Agnes walk toward him with his evening drink. The woman amazed him. Bourbon and branch water. He'd been dumbfounded the first time he'd seen her pour and swallow the beverage as if it were Coca-Cola. And she was probably the only woman in Texas who didn't mind his cigar smoke. Liked it, she'd said when he caught himself apologizing. A thick Havana cigar found its way to his mouth. He clipped the end and lit up. Old Aggie never gasped or sputtered or dabbed at her eyes. Once he'd tested her and had blown smoke directly at her. She'd sniffed and smiled and passed his test. And she knew it.

Right now, he sensed there was a bee buzzing around in Aggie's bonnet. He could almost hear the droning. He thought he knew what was on her mind, but so far, except for the day Maggie was born, it had remained unspoken. He decided to play her little game, hear her out, see how she'd handle him. He always enjoyed how Aggie went about things. Every day she learned something new, some new kind of maneuver, some devious little trick to get what she wanted. It pleased him that he was making her work for what he would have given her anyway. She was going to be rocked back on her hind end when she found out he had Billie's ticket to Hawaii in his desk drawer.

Seth downed his drink in one gulp and held out his glass for a refill. Agnes stared at it a moment and then shook her head. "That was a double I gave you. You know the doctor said one drink and one drink only. If you want another, you'll have to get it for yourself. I refuse to be a party to your destroying your health." Seth knew she meant it. He clamped his teeth down on his cigar and almost bit off the end. Women!

"There's tumbleweed in the front yard again."

"For Christ's sake, Aggie, this is Texas. Tumbleweeds are all over the place. If it bothers you that much, I'll speak to the gardener in the morning."

"I've already mentioned it to him," Agnes lied. She was in charge of the house and that included the front lawn as well.

"Did your daughter get a letter from my son today? Tita said she did. I waited all through lunch for Billie to mention it and when she didn't I thought maybe Tita was mistaken."

"I really don't know if Billie received a letter, Seth. I'll check with her when I go upstairs." Damn Billie. And damn that Tita, too. If she ever got the opportunity to fire her, she would. The woman knew too much about family business.

"Billie looks well," Agnes began, "don't you think? Dr. Ward has given her a clean bill of health and the go-ahead to resume all her activities." Agnes met Seth's speculative stare unblinkingly. "I was a little concerned for her during her pregnancy." She led into the question and let it lie there.

"Well?" Seth demanded impatiently. "Just how concerned are you for her now?" Damn woman, she liked to play games as much as he did.

"Oh, I'm not concerned at all. Why should I be? Nature takes care of itself, I always say. Why, just look how she's bloomed. She's not the young girl who first came to Sunbridge. There's something different. Perhaps it's maturity. She's more of a woman, if you know what I mean."

"Damn right I do," Seth said dryly. "I was thinking the same thing myself. 'Course, I never knew Billie when she wasn't feeling sick, but right now I'd say I could almost see why my son married her."

Agnes ignored the left-handed compliment. "The baby is gaining rapidly, especially for a premature birth. Now that she's on a rigid schedule she's eating and sleeping better. Nurse is very pleased. It's so nice to know that Billie doesn't have to tax her strength with middle-of-the-night feedings and all that goes with a new baby. And little Maggie is just remarkable."

"She's a Coleman, isn't she?" Seth said gruffly.

"Moss is going to be so pleased when he sees what motherhood has done for Billie. It would be so nice if they could get together. Christmas was almost a farce, you know. I'd hate to think that Moss could only remember what Billie looked like then. A pity he can't see her." Agnes drained the last of her bourbon. She might need another before this conversation was over.

"C'mon, Aggie, pour me another drink. What can it hurt? You're going to have another. How can you sit there and drink it in front of me?"

Aggie. It was said with affection. She could hear the tone, feel it. "All right, but if you tell that fool doctor, I'll deny it."

Seth winked conspiratorially and maneuvered the cigar from one side of his mouth to the other. He liked it when he had her on the run. So much for her worrying about destroying his health.

When she handed him the refill, Seth removed the soggy cigar from his lips. He swirled the amber liquid in his glass, staring at it as if mesmerized. Agnes watched him, hardly daring to breathe. She had his habits down pat, knew what he was going to say before he said it. In the end she always let him think it was his idea.

"Aggie, do you think the girl is up to a trip to Hawaii? It's barely three months, you know. Jessica never mended this quickly."

"Billie comes from hearty peasant stock. On her father's side," she added hastily. "I'm sure she's well enough. We can check with the doctor and Billie herself. Seth, how marvelous of you to think of this. Billie will be forever in your debt if you can arrange it. You can, can't you?" she asked anxiously.

"For my boy, anything. Billie, too," he added hastily. Agnes understood. She held up her glass and Seth did likewise.

"What shall we drink to?" Seth asked.

Agnes pretended to ponder the question. "What else but love?"

Seth almost choked on an inch of wet tobacco. "To love."

"To love," Agnes said, swallowing the remainder of her drink. For one wild, crazy moment she wondered if Seth were going to throw his glass into the fireplace and smash it to smithereens. She wished he would, so she could do the same. Instead she set her glass firmly on the little coaster on the table.

"How long do you think it will take you to make the arrangements?"

Seth thought about the airline ticket in his desk drawer. "Five days. Take the girl shopping. Get her the best. Get something spiffy, Aggie. Moss always liked spiffy things."

Agnes hated to ask but she forced the words from her mouth. "How much should we spend?"

"As much as it takes." Agnes nodded. Silk and satin. Sheer gossamer nighties, silk underwear. Frilly, lacy, frothy unmentionables. A daring low-cut gown for dancing. Surely the Officers' Club would have dancing on the weekend. Officers always had the best. Some French perfume for wickedness. Moss was a sniffer. Scent was important if worn discreetly. Billy was going to be ecstatic. "Don't stint, and I suggest you start out first thing in the morning. In case you need alterations."

"Right after breakfast," Agnes said briskly. "I think it's time for me to go up and say good night to Jessica and check on Maggie. I'll stop by Billie's room and tell her, unless you want to tell her yourself."

"You do it. You're the gal's mother. I think I'm going to turn in myself. I plan to ride the range tomorrow. Old Nessie's been missing me. Five days, Agnes. Make sure the gal is ready."

"She'll be ready," Agnes said firmly. "And Seth, no more liquor. We bent the rules a little tonight, but this is the last time. You really have to start taking care of yourself."

Seth mumbled something unintelligible as Agnes left the room. Later, when she thought about it, she thought he'd said, "Until you want something else." She snorted.

Agnes's idea of saying good night to Jessica was a light wave in her direction as she walked past her lighted room. When she passed the nursery she put her finger to her lips to show she understood little Maggie was sleeping. Seth didn't need to know everything. She rapped quietly on Billie's door and opened it at the same time. Her daughter was sitting at her little cherrywood desk, writing beneath a gooseneck lamp. "Billie, can I talk to you?"

"Of course, Mother. Is anything wrong?"

"On the contrary, everything is wonderful. I have a wonderful surprise for you. Seth just told me this very evening. Minutes ago, in fact, and I came right up to tell you. You're going to Hawaii to see Moss. Isn't that wonderful? Don't ask me how Seth did it, but he's arranging the entire thing. Five days, Billie, and you'll see Moss. Tomorrow we're going shopping!"

Billie leaped up from the desk. "Truly, Mother? I can't believe it. Does Moss know? How? When? Five days. Good

Lord, Mother, what about Maggie? I don't think I can be ready in five days. Oh, Mother, I'm so glad the doctor said I was fit. It will be all right, won't it?"

Agnes preened. "Darling child, it's all been taken care of. When Seth says he has friends in high places, he means high places. We just have to be thankful that he's able to do all this for you. Moss is going to be so surprised. Darling, you are not to worry about Maggie. She has a nurse. Remember, now, you're a Coleman. You can go off and not worry. I'll be here to look after things. Be sure, though, to take some pictures of little Maggie to show Moss. Start thinking of all the gorgeous things you can buy to dazzle your husband. We really have to buy some wickedly expensive perfume to drive him out of his mind. Men have to be driven to the brink every so often to keep them in line." Agnes was almost babbling. All she could think of was the shopping trip and what she could buy for herself—and the ultimate outcome of the Hawaiian visit.

"Mother, does Moss know I'm coming?" Billie asked excitedly.

"I'm not sure. I'm sure Seth will get word to him within the next day or so. He has to know you're coming so he can arrange his schedule. Seth and I want both of you to have a marvelous time to make up for the Christmas visit. Seth will take care of things. Finish your letter and then get ready for bed. I think we should leave right after breakfast. Ask Jessica if there's anything we can bring her. Good night, Billie." Agnes leaned over to plant a dry kiss on Billie's forehead.

When the door closed behind Agnes, Billie threw herself on the bed and curled into a ball with the pillow clutched against her chest. Tears of sheer happiness burned her eyes. How generous of Seth. How wonderful of Seth. For the first time in her young life she was beginning to understand what power and money could do. It was going to be so wonderful. A second honeymoon. In Hawaii. The excitement was almost more than she could bear. She hugged the pillow tighter. New clothes. If she had anything to say about it, she wouldn't be wearing much more than a towel while she was with Moss. How long? Her mother hadn't said how long her visit was to be. It didn't matter. She would make the most of the time. Wicked perfume and a towel. She smiled as she dabbed at her eyes with the corner of the pillowcase. She was going to see her husband. She had never been happier in her life.

When Billie tripped down the hall to the nursery she felt light-headed. She rapped softly and peeked in the door. The nurse in her starched white uniform put her finger to her lips. Billie nodded and advanced on tiptoe into the room. The tiny pink bundle lay peacefully in the cradle that had belonged first to Moss and then to Amelia. One tiny, plump fist was being sucked on. Billie smiled.

The desire to hold her daughter was so strong that Billie leaned over the cradle. "Now, Mrs. Coleman, you know the rules," the nurse said in a harsh whisper. "When baby is sleeping we do not disturb her. Gas, colic, diarrhea, any of those things can result. Sleeping babies need their sleep." The nurse's voice was stern yet not unkind. Secretly she often felt sorry for the young, wealthy mothers who missed so much when they had nurses take care of their babies.

"Could I speak with you outside for a minute, Miss Jenkins?" Billie whispered. The gray-haired woman followed Billie into the hallway, leaving the door ajar. She was a good nurse.

Quickly Billie explained the situation, and the nurse said, "Mrs. Coleman, go to your husband. He needs you more than Maggie does right now. All that bundle in there needs is warm, loving arms and competent care. I can see to that. But your husband needs *you*. Maggie will be fine. I've been nursing babies for thirty years. I nursed Amelia and your husband, you know. I know Moss would want you to come to him."

"It's just that I'm her mother, Miss Jenkins. I should be feeding her and changing her. I should be rocking her to sleep. Don't misunderstand; I want to go, but I'm torn. I feel I should stay here with my baby. I know everything you're saying is true. Maggie won't know whose arms are holding her as long as they're warm and loving. *But I'll know.*"

The nurse walked her back to her room and patted her comfortingly on the shoulder. "Trust me, Mrs. Coleman. I'll take care of Maggie as if she were my own child."

Billie nodded and watched the older woman walk back down the hallway. The woman had an ample bosom for Maggie to snuggle against. She hoped that the starchy stiffness of the white uniform didn't chafe the tiny face.

Before retiring for the night, Billie walked across the hall to Jessica's room. Her mother-in-law lay propped up in bed with her glasses perched on her nose, her head at an awkward angle, sound asleep. Billie removed the glasses and laid them on the night table, along with a new murder mystery. She turned off the bedside lamp and tiptoed from the room. She would bring Jessica a new book, perhaps two, from the city tomorrow. Maybe she would even buy her a small sack of licorice. Jessica loved candy. Billie was sorry that she couldn't share the news with Jessica. Living upstairs the way she did now, the former mistress of Sunbridge was the last to hear of any of the doings in the house.

But Jessica seemed happy in her little haven, thought Billie, where every need was met and she lacked for nothing. Her prayer beads, her endless supply of mystery novels, her small secret hoards of candy, and her writing implements were all she seemed to need these days. And, of course, her twice-daily visits to the nursery when she got to hold the new infant for a few minutes. Someday, Billie was going to try to figure out how her mother-in-law could be so happy shut up on the second floor. Someday, but not now. She purposely pushed away the worrisome thought that maybe she wouldn't like the answer.

Back to her room to finish the letter to Moss. Dear, wonderful Moss. He was going to be so surprised when he saw her. How ugly she had looked at Christmas! Now she'd knock his eyes right out of their sockets. It was going to be a honeymoon fit for a princess. Hawaii.

Billie finished the letter and crawled into bed. It would probably arrive after she did. She smiled to herself as she hugged her pillow to her cheeks, pretending it was Moss. The misgivings she'd felt about leaving Maggie and the ache in her chest when she'd stared down at her little daughter were gone now. She thought only of her husband and of the time they would have together.

Thad Kingsley bellowed into the buzzing wardroom: "Hey, Captain Marvel, you've got a call coming in. The radio room says it's your father and the captain has given you clearance for the call. Move it, Coleman!"

Moss looked up, startled. Thad never raised his voice. A call from home? Mam? Christ, they'd only docked in Hawaii that afternoon and he wasn't even officially detached from the ship. Something must have happened to Mam. He didn't need Captain Marvel's magic word to do a disappearing act. He skidded to a stop in the radio room and reached for the phone. "Pap? What's wrong?" Moss shouted into the receiver.

"Moss? That you, boy?"

Moss's stomach settled down. There was too much exhilaration in the old man's voice. "Christ, Pap, if you got through to me just to ask how the weather is, I'll shoot old Nessie when I get home."

"You touch that old nag and I'll turn the gun on you!" Seth's voice was jovial. "Everything is fine here, real fine. Listen, I found a way to send that little Yankee gal you married over to see you. She's leaving in a few days. I'll be getting back to you with more information, but I just wanted you to know your little wife is fit as a fiddle and hungry to see you. Take care of yourself, boy."

The wireless operator grinned up at Moss. Some guys had all the luck.

"Pap? Pap, you there?" He looked at the radio operator, who shrugged and tapped the instruments.

"Hope your call was finished, sir. The signal's been terminated."

Leave it to Pap to drop the bomb, Moss thought with annoyance. He wished the old man would quit manipulating his life. Fit as a fiddle. Billie coming here! The first charge of excitement plotted its course. Now how in the living hell had Pap pulled this one off? Memories flooded. Fit as a fiddle. But he already knew that from Billie's letters. Then the dawn began to creep over the horizon and he saw the light. If Mohammed couldn't come to the mountain, Pap had found a way to ship the mountain. And when Mohammed sent it home it had better be pregnant. This time with a son.

"The old bastard!"

"Did you say something, sir?" the radio man asked.

"No, nothing. It's just that there are some advantages to this war after all. My wife is coming to Hawaii!" Moss pushed his cap to the back of his head and returned to the wardroom. Billie was coming here; damn the reasons, she was coming. Despite it being Seth's idea, the thought pleased Moss immensely.

Moss returned to the wardroom, bellowed *"Shaazz-zaaammm!"* at the top of his lungs, made a lunging leap into the air, and spun into the bulkhead.

"This, gentlemen," Thad announced, "is the navy's secret weapon. The expression of pure euphoric bliss worn by Captain Marvel can only mean he's next in line for Halsey's job. Come on, Coleman, spit it out so we can all hit the chow line."

"Billie's coming . . . my wife," he explained to the others. Hoots of approval and boos of envy resounded.

Thad grinned and clapped Moss on the back. "You lucky devil! Someday I want you to tell me how your old man does it."

Moss grinned. "He says, 'Shazam!' Didn't you know I'm a chip off the old block?"

There was no envy in Thad Kingsley or the other officers. How could you resent a guy because his wife was coming to see him? Besides, there wasn't a harder worker or better pilot than Moss Coleman.

"That was fast work, even for your Pap," Kingsley told Moss. "When's Billie coming? Where will you stay?"

"I've no idea. I'm certain Pap will arrange everything, but I spoke with him only for a few minutes. He said he'd get back to me. Knowing Pap, Billie will arrive with a list of instructions a mile long. All I have to do is wait it out. Christ, Thad, Billie is coming here, all the way to Hawaii!" He laughed. "When I met her she'd never been out of Philadelphia and now she's traveling halfway around the world to be with me. And from the looks of things the Big E will be in dry dock for a month at least."

"Billie will love Hawaii. You'll put in your day at the airfield and the nights are your own. Don't screw up, Coleman."

"What the hell is that supposed to mean?" Moss demanded.

"It means whatever the hell you want it to mean. I was with you last time we laid over in Hawaii and I know where you spent your nights and weekends. Try to control your greedy appetites. And I wouldn't take Billie sight-seeing—she might get a look at that little cutey you found yourself on the other side of the island."

"If you saw me on the other side of the island, you were there for the same reason."

"With one slight difference, my friend. I'm not married," Thad drawled, imitating Moss's accent.

Moss squinted past his cigarette smoke. "When I'm in Texas I'm married. When I'm not with Billie, I'm just ole Moss Coleman. Period. Don't go preaching at me, Thad."

"I'm not preaching. I'm telling you a fact. Remember, I met that little girl you married and I always thought she was too young for you. Don't make her grow up the hard way."

"Enough, Kingsley," Moss snarled.

"You're right. It's none of my business. I'm hungry. See you later."

Moss watched his long-legged friend stride across the wardroom. For a few moments his anger roiled, but then better sense prevailed. Thad hardly ever offered advice. Or was it a warning? He couldn't think about that now. Billie was coming to Hawaii and he'd have her to himself for over a month. He felt himself stiffening inside his uniform. He didn't need food. What he needed was a cold shower to tide him over until he could beg a Jeep and drive to the other side of the island. It would be more than a week before Billie arrived.

The five days allotted Billie flew by on eagle's wings. Agnes and Seth both were at their wits' end with Billie's wide mood swings. She would be wildly exhilarated one minute and depressed the next that she was leaving Maggie in strange hands. Soothing words of comfort were offered by her mother, while Seth made no pretense about his displeasure, telling Billie over and over of the lengths to which he had gone to secure permission for her travel plans. In the end she left Sunbridge with a smile on her lips, an ache in her heart, and tears in her eyes.

The Coleman luggage consisted of a trunk and four heavy travel bags jammed full of costly dresses, frilly nightwear, and enticing underwear that was more lace than cloth. One bag was full of nothing but shoes. Another held her nighties and her underwear and stockings, all silk. She had almost choked when the matronly salesgirl had asked demurely if there would be anything else, as though a five-thousand-dollar purchase of clothing that couldn't be worn outside the house was an everyday occurrence. They had bought little dresses, as Agnes called them, by the dozen. Summery, demure, sometimes sultry little numbers that exposed even as they covered up. A must, Agnes had said with authority. Later, in the quiet of her room, Billie had tried to tally her purchases in her head and almost fainted. Who in their right mind paid $9,000 for clothing for a trip to Hawaii. Agnes knew that Seth wouldn't blink an eye. But then again, it was Agnes who was writing out the checks these days.

When the chauffeur-driven car drove out of Sunbridge's long, circular driveway, Billie turned to look back. Once before she had seen that smug look on her mother's face—on the night Agnes had come home early from her graduation party and found her and Moss in their compromising position. How odd that she should now remember that look on her mother's face. A year ago she had thought it was disapproval.

It was to Jessica, standing in the upstairs window, that Billie waved good-bye.

"I think this calls for a drink, don't you, Agnes? Fetch me a triple Scotch and don't mess it up with water or ice."

"Why don't I just bring the bottle," Agnes called over her shoulder as she made her way into the house. She couldn't recall a time when she'd felt more proud of herself. Maybe Seth thought he'd pulled off a coup, but she knew better. Without her help he wouldn't have gotten to step one. They understood each other so well.

"Moss, I don't believe what you're telling me," Thad said. "It will be unforgivable of you not to pick up Billie—there must be a way," he muttered, running his fingers through his sandy hair.

"Try telling that to Captain Davis," Moss snarled. "The good captain doesn't approve of what he calls asshole saddle jockeys who have friends in high places. You're going to have to fill in for me, Thad. Billie will understand once you explain it to her. I'm giving you the day off. Take care of my wife for me till I can get to wherever Pap has her staying. I'll bet you a month's salary it's a house up in the hills."

"When it comes to your old man, I'm not putting money down on any kind of a bet, but you owe me for this one," Thad said, and grinned. "Okay, I'll stand in for you."

Moss laughed. "See that's all you do. I'd appreciate it if you would take my gear with you. The captain is allowing me to be off base five evenings a week but I have to be here full-time on weekends. He's going out of his way to show me I'm not a favorite of the Navy Department. It's okay. I'm not sweating it. Billie will understand. You're a good friend, Thad."

There were a hundred other things he would rather be doing than standing in for Moss with his wife. Secretly, he agreed with Captain Davis. Favoritism at this time was not a good morale booster for the others. The other guys had sweethearts and wives behind in the States. But he realized that Moss had had nothing to do with his wife's coming to Hawaii. The guy did what was expected of him and then some, and he did it well. He was a damn good pilot and the Texas Ranger had seen more action than most of the others. Thad stowed Moss's gear in the back of the Jeep and headed out of the base.

An hour later he was shading his eyes from the golden

sunshine to get a better look at the pretty young woman standing at the top of the airline's portable stairway. One hand was holding on to a wide-brimmed picture hat and the other was trying to hold down the hem of her skirt. Good legs. Damn good legs. This wasn't the same Billie Coleman he had met months ago. Thad sucked in his breath and stared a little harder.

Billie crossed the tarmac, her hands still keeping her hat and skirt from the clutches of the playful breeze that was whipping about the airfield. Her eyes were anxious as they searched for Moss. The minute she spotted Thad she smiled. Wherever Thad Kingsley was, Moss would be close behind. But there was no sign of him. The smile stayed in place when Thad took her by the arm and escorted her toward the car. "It's nice to see you again, Billie. Moss had duty and couldn't be relieved. I'm to take you to wherever you're staying and he'll join you around six. I've got his gear in the Jeep. We'll have to wait a few minutes till your luggage gets here. Do you have much?"

Billie hid her disappointment well. "A trunk and four bags. I don't think you're going to get it all in the Jeep if you have Moss's things, too." She was a navy wife and had to get used to these wartime changes in plans. Six o'clock was only three hours away.

"We'll manage. There's no way I can commandeer another vehicle today. This one was wheeled and dealed, so don't ask questions." Thad grinned. "Where are you staying?"

Billie withdrew a slip of paper from her purse. "Mr. Coleman said it's high up in the hills," she said. "Supposedly there's a cook and a gardener and it's very private. I think Mr. Coleman said it was the main house on a macadamia plantation. Do you think you can find it?" she asked anxiously.

"Didn't Moss tell you? I have a trace of bloodhound in me. I'll find it, Billie, and have you all set by the time your husband gets off duty."

"How is it you're off duty and Moss isn't?" Billie asked as she settled herself in the Jeep. Thad stared at Billie's legs. He'd always been a leg man and an open admirer of Betty Grable. From now on the long-legged movie star was going to be relegated to the rumble seat.

Thad waited till one of the ground crew secured Billie's baggage in the back of the Jeep. "Because Moss is my superior and he gave me the day off. *His* superior is not as generous as your husband. Moss thought you would be more comfortable with me, since we've met before, and he trusted me to explain the situation. I know you're disappointed but it can't be helped. This is the navy."

Billie smiled, her whole face lighting up. "Six o'clock will give me time to unpack and take a bath. Perhaps it's best this way. When you get back to the base, tell Moss I'll be waiting."

"I'll be sure to do that. Now, let's have another look at that address." Thad scrutinized the tiny square of paper and then drew a crumpled map from his flight coverall. "Okay, I know where you're going. May I say, Mrs. Coleman, that your father-in-law has exquisite taste." He smiled to show there was no jealousy in his statement. Billie thought she had never seen a more spellbinding smile. She liked Thad Kingsley.

Thad whipped the Jeep through the gates and headed toward the north shore. He drove effortlessly, forsaking the Wahiawa turnoff for a route through Kunia. The road was narrow, running alongside the Waianae Mountains and through endless fields of pineapple and sugarcane.

Thad expertly guided the car through Haleiwa, but instead of using the bridge to the north he opted to go left, past the harbor, so Billie could see the surf. The Jeep came to a stop. "Take a good look, Mrs. Coleman."

Billie's gasp of pure pleasure was all that Thad needed to hear. He knew he had chosen the right route for Billie's first look at Hawaii's famous surf. The waves were breaking clean, eight to ten feet high. Native Hawaiians were scattered all along the shore stretching out nets for fish. Children were gathering shells to sell for a pittance to the military men

"It's unbelievable," Billie said breathlessly. "I've only read about Hawaii. Seeing it is something else entirely. It's gorgeous."

"Mrs. Coleman," Thad teased, "you ain't seen nothing yet. This is just a teaser."

"I didn't think there was water so blue. It's like a giant jewel."

"That it is. Come along now, I have to get you to your house."

Thad drove steadily for forty-five minutes. When he took a second quick look at his rumpled map he was relieved to see he hadn't missed the entrance. Lush hibiscus and a monstrous banyan tree, like a giant umbrella, shrouded the time-worn iron gates at the entrance to Ester Kamali's estate, where Billie was to stay. The snakelike drive eventually widened and became circular, edged on both sides by regal palms standing sentinel. Billie's eyes widened. The house was long, low, and sprawling, with the sparkling Pacific below as a backdrop. Thad felt his breath hiss between his teeth. It was probably the most beautiful house he had ever seen.

"Are we allowed to walk on the grass?" Billie whispered. "It looks like a velvet carpet. Doesn't it, Thad?"

"It looks like soft green fur to me," Thad whispered back.

"Why are we whispering?" Billie asked. Thad shrugged.

Banks and mounds of scarlet hibiscus blinded Billie as they tripped across the emerald meadow. "What's that smell?" Billie demanded, wrinkling her nose.

"Plumeria. That's what the island girls make the leis with. Sometimes they use orchids, but mainly plumeria because of its strong scent. It lasts forever, or so it seems. The maids in the local hotels hang strands of it in the bathroom showers for the guests."

"What a charming custom." Billie sighed. "This has got to be the closest thing to paradise I've ever seen. Of course," she said, laughing, "I'm not a world traveler. I only have Philadelphia and Texas to compare this with."

"I'm sure you and Moss are going to be very happy here. You have the Pacific at your back door and this gorgeous garden at your front. The house is a work of art. You go ahead and ring the bell. I'll bring the luggage and then I have to high-tail it back to the base."

A tiny woman attired in a bright red muumuu opened the door. Her smile was warm, welcoming. Her eyes sparkled like black stars in the small round face. "You dat same *wahine* Missy Kamali say is here?" At Billie's perplexed look the little woman frowned. "You *haole* lady from far, I t'ink." At a loss, Billie smiled and motioned behind her for Thad to hurry. The luggage should convince the housekeeper she had a right to be here. "No *pilikia*, no *pilikia*," the little woman muttered, her face wreathed in a wide smile.

Thad grinned. "She's saying there's no trouble. *Pilikia* means trouble. That's one of the first words you learn over here."

"Ass awri," the woman said, motioning them inside.

"She's telling us it's okay. In other words, she's been expecting you. I hate to leave you like this but you'll manage. I've got to get back to the base. You do want your husband here on time, right?" Billie nodded.

Thad pointed to the luggage and made a motion asking where it should be taken.

"Dat humbug question? What'sa matah you. Phillip carry for *wahine*."

"That settles it." Thad grinned and smacked his hands together. "I think you're in good care. Give my regards to Phillip, whoever he may be. Welcome to Hawaii, Billie," Thad said, and bent to kiss her cheek.

"Thanks for everything, Thad. Don't worry. I'll manage here. Hurry—I don't want you to be late or get in trouble because of me."

Thad's step was jaunty as he sprinted across the velvety lawn. At the last second before leaping into the Jeep, he picked a lush hibiscus bloom and stuck it between his teeth. He drove at breakneck speed down the winding road with the colorful flower in his mouth. A native trudging along the road turned to stare in amazement. Thad laid the red bloom on the seat and started to whistle. Billie Coleman was one hell of a looker. Moss might be wise to keep her here in this lush island hideaway.

{{{{{{{{ CHAPTER TWELVE }}}}}}}}

The hilltop house opened its arms to Billie. It was low, sprawling, yet not overlarge, and it gave her a cozy feeling of coolness and light, so different from Sunbridge, with its heavy leather furniture and somber colors. In this house, the first she would share alone with Moss, every room opened to the outside. The French doors leading to the patio were sheltered from sun and rain by the sloping overhang of the tiled roof. Beautiful gardens were part of every view and seemed to come indoors to blend with the light bamboo furniture and the vivid greens and whites of the walls. Graceful paddle fans were centered on every ceiling, creating a pleasant breeze. And the tang of the sea far below seemed to fill each room.

Shown to the larger of the two bedrooms, Billie was welcomed by the scented sea breeze that billowed the sheer curtains hanging in the patio doorway. The carpet underfoot was eggshell white, bringing into relief the dark tones of native mahogany furnishings. The bed, headboard, and upholstered chairs were covered with fabric of pale blue flowers scattered over a deeper blue background. Here, too, a paddle fan beat the air in a slow, hypnotic rhythm. The pudgy dark-skinned housekeeper moved unhurriedly as she unpacked Billie's bags, fingering the garments admiringly before hanging them in the louver-doored closet or laying them in sachet-scented drawers. Unwilling to break the spell this house was casting upon her, Billie silently crossed the room to find a tiled bath complete with tub, shower, and expanses of mirrors. Towels and accessories of palest blue complemented the eggshell fixtures and ceramic. This was indeed the loveliest house she'd ever seen and she was already wishing she could spend the rest of her life here with Moss.

After partaking of a light meal of fruit, cheese, coarse bread, and a cool, exotic fruit punch, Billie occupied herself by taking a shower and washing her hair. She primped for Moss's arrival, dabbing perfume between her breasts and behind her ears. From her closet she chose the intriguing Chinese dressing gown Moss had given her for Christmas. It was difficult to believe that the front edges once had barely met over her stomach. Now it fit perfectly and the tight sash accentuated her tiny waist. Nurse Jenkins's firming exercises had worked wonders.

Time was heavy on her hands. She walked the perimeter of the grounds surrounding the house. She arranged her toiletries in the bathroom and on the dressing table. She waited for Moss.

She explored the efficient and surprisingly modern kitchen and waited for Moss.

The minute hand on her slim gold watch hardly seemed to be moving. Again and again she shook her wrist, but she knew it was keeping perfect time. At last, weary from her trip, she fell across the bed and promised herself she would only close her eyes for a minute while she waited for Moss.

Driving up the steep hill road, Moss cursed the time. Captain Davis was a man without a heart. It was already almost nine o'clock and twilight was deepening to that purple shade peculiar to Hawaii. And half an hour ago he'd taken the wrong turn and had had to double back. Pulling into the drive, he was greeted by dim lights shining through the patio doors. Billie was in there, waiting. His pulses beat a rapid tattoo and his blood was heated in anticipation. When he'd asked Thad how she was, his friend had merely winked and smiled slyly. "Moss, you've got one hell of a surprise waiting for you!" Now what the hell did that mean? And was he going to like it?

Pulling the keys out of the ignition and stuffing them in his pocket, he carried his ditty bag to the front door. He decided to try the knob rather than clang the cowbells that hung from the eave. The door was open and the house was quiet. Not even a radio was playing. He followed the lights through the living room and into the bedroom. There, on the bed, lay Billie, one arm thrown over her head, knees bent, lovely face serene and composed in sleep. His eyes traveled the length of her from her slim ankles up her coltish legs to the width of her hips and the fullness of her breasts. Her waist was nipped, her belly flat. This was the Billie he'd married. Or was it? On closer examination, there was a new, angular quality to her face, the limbs seemed more elegant, slimmer, graceful. Had she done something to her hair? It was lighter, paler, sun-streaked, blonder than he remembered. And it had grown since Christmas, falling lustrously against her cheek. So this was the surprise Thad had hinted at. Billie was all grown up into a beautiful woman, riper, lusher. A slow smile grew on his face as he undid his tie and worked the buttons of his shirt.

Billie thought she was dreaming. She felt herself taken into strong, warm arms, felt herself nestled against a broad deep chest. She didn't want to awaken from this dream, so vivid, so languorously delicious. She felt his eyes upon her, heard him inhale her fragrance as he curled her beneath him. Her arms enfolded him, stroking his back, falling lower to his naked haunches where her palms smoothed over the curve of his buttocks. She heard her name.

"Moss!" she murmured, pulling herself from her dream and deeper into his embrace. "Oh, Moss! I've missed you so." She heard her voice, deep and throaty with desire. For months now she'd wanted him this way, dreaming about this moment every night, waking in a sheen of sweat, emptiness at her center. Now he was here, truly here, and she was in his arms and he was loving her.

The Chinese silk robe fell open under his commanding fingers and when he captured her breast, its pink nipple rose to greet him and bring him delight. Slowly he teased her ear with his tongue, following the pulse points to her neck and throat. He wanted her, urgently, but he would take her slowly, deepening their pleasure. His hands traced the contours of her body, following its curves, caressing its hollows. He explored the recesses of her mouth and the silkiness of her thighs. This was his Billie, his wife, as familiar to him as the back of his own hand and yet, somehow, new territory to be charted.

Her emotions were charged, more finely tuned than he remembered, and when she closed her hand over the proof of his desire she communicated her own demands.

She hurried him with her kisses, excited him with soft mewlings and murmurs, undulated beneath his caresses. She wanted him now, desperately. She felt she would erupt with a wildness too long contained. There would be time later for luxuriating in his arms, to have his hands soothe this fever, to have his lips take possession of her inch by inch. But now she needed completion.

Her thighs opened, her back arched, and he became a part of her. In the white heat of her passion she entrapped him, feeling him stroke within her, locking her legs behind his to take him deeply inside her where the warmth was building.

For the next week and a half, Billie thought she'd died and gone to heaven. Long evenings with Moss, lying in his arms. Midnight swims in the little cove at the bottom of the hill. Quiet dinners on the lanai, looking up at the stars. Two nights ago Moss had invited Thad for supper and she'd repressed her giggles when her enthusiastic husband had thrown broad hints that it was time for his friend to leave. Moss liked to be alone with her, to have her to himself. It seemed he couldn't get enough of her and this pleased her, because it was exactly how she felt about him. Hawaii was the the first time they'd been alone since their marriage. No Agnes, no Seth or Jessica, no one, just the two of them.

On the last morning before he had to leave for his weekend duty, she lay beside Moss, hearing his light breathing and feeling his warmth. Her lazy gaze drifted over to the miniature traveling clock stitched with Sunbridge cowhide. The time was five-ten. She had to wake Moss in another five minutes if he was to make the long drive back to the base. She stored the memory of how Moss looked the way a squirrel stores nuts for the winter. How dear, how beautiful, how wonderful he looked! There was a certain boyish charm in his dark tousled hair, but the rest of this exciting person was all man. Her man. She relished the peacefulness a moment longer before she rolled to his side of the bed. At the precise moment the minute hand on the clock reached three, Billie smacked Moss on the rump, let out a war whoop, and leaped from under the sheets.

"What the hell!" Moss bellowed as he fought with the covers. "A goddamn air raid at this time of the morning!" Seeing Billie laughing, he fell back against the covers. "If you ever do that again, I'll turn you over my knee."

"Is that a threat or a promise?"

"All you have to do is test me, Mrs. Coleman."

"Some other time, Mr. Coleman. Right now you have to hit the shower. You'd better hurry or you'll be late. Oh, Moss, I wish you didn't have to go. It's such a long time till you get back."

"Come here, Billie."

Billie practically ran to the bed and threw herself in Moss's arms. "Oh, Moss, I love you so. This is all so perfect. This place, this house, everything is just so wonderful. I want to share every minute with you. The hours we have together are so few. I'm not complaining. It sounds like I am but I'm not. I understand. There are so many couples who don't have what we do. I love you so. I guess that's the reason."

"I know you do, you little vixen. What do you think? Do we have time for a quickie?"

"Depends on what your definition of 'quick' is." Billie giggled and tugged on Moss's chest hairs. "Why don't we take a shower together? I'll wash your back and you wash mine. . . ."

"And I'll tickle your fancy and you'll tickle mine." Moss laughed, finding her suggestion exciting. He loved her skin when it was wet and slick with soap, yielding beneath the exploring press of his fingers, each curve and swell of her exquisite figure offering itself to him. He lifted the pale curtain of hair that fell across her face to kiss her. Her eyes shone with expectation and pleasure, her mouth was soft, her lips parted to allow him entrance. His arms closed around her, pulling her close, her nearness already affecting his desires. "Billie," he murmured, "if you don't go in and turn on the shower, we'll never get there at all."

Billie stood on the balcony, wrapped in a pale blue towel, her body still flushed and tingling from Moss's lovemaking. She shaded her eyes from the early-morning sun on the horizon. The military Jeep was a dot on the winding mountain road when she crept back into bed. Delicious memories of their total communion brought a smile to her lips as she drifted into a deep sleep.

Billie was walking along the private beach when she heard the Jeep coming up the road. She slipped into her beach sandals and raced around to the front of the house. "Thad!" she called in disappointment.

"Hey, I'm sorry I'm not the man, but he did send me. I can go back. I come bearing gifts, however, so think hard before you make any rash decisions." Thad grinned.

"Gifts! What kind of gifts? Why did Moss send you? Why didn't he wait till this evening to bring it? Not that I don't want to see you. I crave company that speaks the king's English. Tell me quick, before I explode."

Thad reached behind him in the Jeep and withdrew two cans filled with gasoline. "Moss said there was a Ford in the garage with no gas. Now you have gas. When you have gas you can drive. Drive, as in sightsee. Diamond Head. Waikiki. All kinds of great places."

"How wonderful of Moss. How did he get the gasoline?"

"You don't want to know," Thad said, reaching down to take his shoes off. I brought my bathing trunks for a quick swim before I head back. How much trouble would it be for you to get me a nice cold beer? Is it okay if I change in the cabana out back?"

"Of course. Go along and I'll fetch the beer. The water is crystal clear today. Hardly any whitecaps at all. I swear, Thad, I have never seen bluer water or bluer sky. It's as though they're married to each other. I'll never forget this vacation. Everything is so marvelous. I'm so glad Mr. Coleman knew Miss Kamali and arranged this for Moss and me. I don't know how I can ever hope to repay him."

"I don't think he wants payment of any kind. He wants both of you to be happy. Accept it, Billie, and enjoy the time you have," Thad said gently.

"Of course, you're right. Don't just stand there—move, sailor. This is the navy, and navy men do not stand around in their bare feet."

"Aye-aye, ma'am."

Billie uncapped a frosty bottle of beer from the icebox and placed it on a tray with some crackers and two wedges of cheese. Something was wrong. Thad was too up. His grin a little too wide. He was a shade too nervous. It had to do with Moss; of that she was sure.

"What do you think, Billie, could I pass for King Neptune?" Thad asked as he walked from the ocean brandishing a piece of driftwood.

Billie pretended to ponder the question. She took in his tall, lanky form and his dripping hair. He was thin, but not skinny. Muscular in the right places, denoting a whipcord strength. A honey-colored tan made him appear heavier than he really was. She liked the leanness of him. But more than anything she liked his dry, droll sense of humor and his ready smile.

"Okay, don't answer that. Ummm, this beer is good. You sure know how to treat a guest, Mrs. Coleman. Cheese and crackers, too."

"What's wrong?" Billie asked bluntly, the concern in her hazel eyes letting Thad know she was asking about Moss.

"Moss showed up late for training class this morning. He's been restricted to base for three days after this weekend," Thad replied just as bluntly.

"Oh, no!"

"Oh, yes. That's why I brought the gas. You're going to be pretty much on your own. I can come for you or meet you in Waikiki after hours and show you around a little if you want. It's the best we can do, Billie."

We. He had said "we." That meant Moss approved. Damn navy. Didn't they care that she was here and her husband couldn't see her? Then she remembered the early-morning hour in the hot, steamy shower. It would be a long time before she forgot this morning. A warm flush crept up her neck and settled on her cheeks. Thad pretended not to see and slugged away at his beer.

"Three days in addition to his weekend duty is a long time. He'll be here only one day and then he has to report back for the next weekend. It's awful, Thad."

"It's better than nothing. Learn to enjoy what you have, and you'll do fine."

"I never thought of it like that. Thank you, Thad. Of course you're right."

"I'm always right," Thad muttered under his breath. "What say, Mrs. Coleman, that I race you out to the first coral reef? First one back with a one-pound chunk wins."

"Wins what?" Billie laughed.

"Another beer, what else?"

The swim to the coral reef was effortless, with neither finding a pound chunk of coral. Then the lanky New Englander and the girl from Philadelphia frolicked like playful porpoises in the sparkling Pacific. There was no one to notice the darkening of Thad's eyes when he looked at Billie. And of course, the slight trembling of his hands could be blamed on the cool water. When he touched Billie's shoulder to tell her it was time to swim back he couldn't understand how his hand could feel so scorched. He shook his head to clear his thoughts and lashed out against the water. When he reached the shore he was gasping for breath. Billie was still some distance away, swimming slowly toward shore. He dried off with a thick towel. Anything to keep moving. A glass of lemonade and another beer for himself were held aloft as Billie swished into shore on a miniwave. He had to get out of there.

"Billie, I'm going to dress. I have to get back. Think about what you want to do."

"All right. But first I have to dry off. I can't think when I'm wet."

He would have cut off his right arm at the elbow, he thought, to be able to touch her. "The sun will dry you," he said gruffly.

Thad returned fully dressed. "I'm going to pour this gas in the tank of the Ford and start up the engine to make sure it's okay. What did you decide?"

Billie trotted after Thad. "I'd like to do some sight-seeing, if you have the time. Thad, really, I don't want you to give up any plans for me. I can just as easily settle in here with a good book. Miss Kamali has a fully stocked library. But if you can really manage it, I'd like a firsthand view of Diamond Head and perhaps make a trip to Hana Drive."

"Hana Drive is in Maui. I don't know if I can get you there or not. I'll have to work on that one and check it out with Moss. You can't do it in one day. We would have to stay overnight. Diamond Head and Waikiki will be more than enough for one day. I'll draw you a little map and show you where to meet me. I can get off duty tomorrow at three."

"I appreciate it, Thad. Tell Moss... tell him... tell him I said it was worth it. He'll understand."

"I'll tell him. You'd better put something on over your suit or you're going to get a sunburn. This sun is different from Texas and Philadelphia sun."

"I will. Thanks for driving out. I'll see you tomorrow."

Thad didn't look back, nor did he glance in his rearview mirror There was no point.

Moss caught up to Thad in the dining hall. "How did Billie take the news?"

"Like a trouper. She sent a message. Said to tell you it was worth it. She said you would understand."

A devilish grin split Moss's features. "At the time I thought so myself. Now, with three days' restriction, I'm not so sure. What did she say about the gas?"

"She's driving down tomorrow. I said I would meet her and show her around. I think you'll agree that you want her to start back before dark on that road."

"Absolutely. Thanks, Thad. Listen, I have an idea. I want to see if I can get a message to my old man. I want him to ship me two longhorn steers. I'm going to throw a Texas barbecue that will make a Hawaiian luau look like a grade school picnic. The Kamali pit is big enough. We might have to extend it a little or do up the second one on the beach, but it will be worth it. What do you think?"

Thad's mouth dropped open. Just like that he was going to have his father ship two steers for a barbecue. The damn fool would pull it off, too. "Listen, Coleman, if you can pull this one off, I'm right there with you. I could sink my teeth into some good Texas beef. How you going to explain it all to the captain? Two Texas longhorns turning on a spit aren't going to go unnoticed and they sure as hell can't pass for the traditional pig."

"Once it's a fact, who's going to say anything? If Pap can swing it, they'll be coming in from on high. So high, Captain Davis is only going to congratulate me. Talk to Billie about it tomorrow and if you have any spare time, work on the guest list. Hell, invite everyone. Tell Billie to buy herself something real colorful so she makes a big splash. I want Davis to eat his heart out."

He won't be the only one, Thad thought glumly. "I'll work on it. When are you planning this event?"

"Shindig. We call it a shindig in Texas. Just as soon as I get through to Pap. Hell, he might as well send all the fixings, too, as long a he's going to all this trouble. It will give him something to do. The man does like a challenge."

"Chip off the old block, or is it a nick in the old leather?"

Moss shrugged and grinned as he left the dining hall. He'd invite the brass, of course. Some of the enlisted men. Music and local girls doing the hula. Christ, Pap was going to go up in smoke. He told himself he was doing it for Billie so that she would have a wonderful memory of her visit to the island. Billie would love it. The perfect little hostess, and she'd sure impress the brass.

When the call came, Agnes picked up the phone. She quickly roused Seth from his desk. "It's Moss. Good Lord, you don't suppose something went wrong, do you?"

"Of course not. My son does not screw up. Moss? How are you, boy?" Seth said with forced heartiness. He listened for a moment and then laughed. "For a minute I thought you were going to ask for the impossible. Cleaned and dressed. I understand. Fixings? I'll take care of it. Three days, four at the most. You're right, boy. Billie won't ever forget this. Imagine, a Texas barbecue in Hawaii! Don't worry, boy. I'll take care of you. That's what fathers are for. I'll tell your mother. Leave it to me. Take care of yourself, son." He hung up and turned to Agnes.

"Now if that don't beat all. The boy wants two longhorns." There was pride in his voice. Agnes wrinkled her nose. Barbecues were so messy. Everyone ate with their fingers and wore checkered bibs and drank beer. "Fixings. He wants the works. Aggie, get out your pencil and let's get to work. We want to do the boy up proud."

"Seth, how are you going to get all . . . get it over there?"

"Don't you go worrying your head about things like that, Aggie. I got my ways. Moss must want it for a special reason and that's good enough for me. Hell, woman, I'd try moving the earth if the boy wanted it. Start writing."

"Seth, what is this going to cost?" Agnes gasped.

"Cost? You mean money? Not a cent. It's our beef. All the fixings come from the ranch, I might have to plunk out a little for the kegs." Seth favored Agnes with a heavy-lidded look. "I'll call in a few favors. You wash my hand and I wash yours, that kind of thing. Does your silence mean you don't approve?" For some reason Agnes's reply was important to Seth.

"On the contrary. I know you have friends in high places." Her voice was a shade short of being apologetic. She was going to have to get used to Seth and the way he did things.

Seth fiddled with a long fragrant cigar, rolling it back and forth between his fingers. "Aggie, who do you thinks supplies all the grade-A choice beef to the military? Not just here in the States, but all over the world?"

"I never thought much about it. Coleman beef, is that what you're saying?"

Seth nodded and clamped his teeth down hard on his cigar. "Now, if I was to get myself into a flap over something and shipped late or not at all, some five-star is going to get upset. You don't mess with the brass's dinner parties. You get my point?"

"Perfectly. I'll get on this right away. You said three days, possibly four. Which is it?"

"Make it four. We don't want to appear too eager. Coleman beef ships out on the first. That will give me three days of palavering."

Palavering. These Texans had a language all their own, just as they had a style all their own. More and more, she decided, she liked their flamboyance. She couldn't help wondering at what point she would consider herself a hundred percent Texan. Soon, she thought. Just as soon as Billie produced a male heir to the Coleman fortune.

The vintage Ford had its assorted shimmies and shakes. Billie drove carefully. Every so often she was forced to pull over to the side of the road till the engine quieted down. She would have to mention it to Thad.

The day was exquisitely beautiful, the sky so blue it made Billie gasp and long for at least one little cottonball cloud. The scarlet hibiscus along both sides of the road was so vibrant and colorful it made her eyes water. She wished she were an artist so she could capture the rich colors of the foliage and the cerulean ocean.

With several quick looks at the map Thad had made for her, Billie managed to arrive at their appointed meeting place without getting lost. She drove down Kalakau, the main street in Waikiki. She was conscious immediately of the smell of plumeria that scented the warm trade winds. Cottage after cottage was almost obscured by thick, lush foliage and red hibiscus. Billie parked the car and stepped outside to wait for Thad.

He arrived five minutes later, followed by a horde of children all demanding pennies. Dutifully he emptied his pockets. Billie combed through her change purse. How beautiful they were, these children of another culture. She thought of her little Maggie back home, who was so pale compared with these children. Their warm, molasses-colored skin enhanced pearly white teeth that shone in perpetual smiles.

Thad signaled the oldest and tallest boy. He brandished a silver quarter and told him to watch missy's car till they got back. He handed over the quarter and promised another on their return.

"I think it will be better if we go in the Jeep. How are you today, Billie?"

"I'm fine. How's Moss?" Surely he had sent a message. Thad was probably embarrassed to deliver it. Men!

"Cranky," Thad replied shortly. Billie waited. Thad steered the Jeep away from the curb and concentrated on retracing his route. "I'm taking you to Diamond Head first. Actually, you would have seen it if you were sitting on the right side of the plane when you came into Hawaii. But seeing it from the air and in person are two different things. Get prepared."

There was a pause and then he went on. "Moss asked me to talk to you about something." Quickly he explained about the Texas barbecue and the call to Seth. "It's all arranged. Moss picked the date and I'm to make up the guest list. He wants you to buy some colorful island wear to dazzle everyone with."

She couldn't help herself. "Was that all he said?"

Thad bit his tongue. "Yep."

"Did you give him my message?"

"Yep."

"Well, what did he say?"

"Nothing. He grinned." Billie smiled. Thad grimaced as he swung the Jeep onto Diamond Head Road. "Get ready now. I boned up on this last night just for your benefit. Diamond Head is seven hundred and sixty feet tall. The natives call it *Leahi*, because it looks like the sloping face and brow of an *ahi*, which is a yellowfin tuna. We're going to go inside the crater. I hope you're impressed, Billie."

"I am, I am. Tell me more." Billie giggled at the serious look on Thad's face. Imagine studying up so he could be sure she got all the facts!

"We could actually drive inside, but I think we'll leave the Jeep and walk. Supposedly we're going to get all kinds of breathtaking views once we climb to the top. I understand they have picnics and luaus on special occasions."

"Why do they call it Diamond Head?"

"I know the answer. Just let me think a minute. . . . Because," he drawled, "nineteenth-century sailors found crystals that resembled diamonds. They were actually calcite. But the nickname 'Diamond Head' stuck. Now that's all I know."

"I'm so impressed that you would do this for me, Thad. Truly, I appreciate it. I know Moss is grateful to you, too. If we're going to hike it, let's go before I change my mind. I am not at my best in high places." Billie looked at him and grinned. "Swear to me that I won't have to go near the edge of anything and that you'll protect me," she said teasingly.

With my life, Thad thought, but he merely nodded and cupped her elbow. He didn't like what he was feeling. Why in the hell had he agreed to Moss's request to show Billie around? Christ, what kind of man was he to lust—and by God, he was lusting—after his best friend's wife? There were plenty of women in his life. Why did this particular one have such a hold on him?

The view of Honolulu from the awesome crater was beautiful. She would treasure this sight forever. If only Moss were at her side drinking in the splendrous beauty, she thought, instead of Thad. Then, when they were old, sitting in their respective rocking chairs, they could reminisce about this moment. . . .

"I think I've had enough," she said. "Thank you for bringing me. I can't wait to tell the others back at the ranch how beautiful this is. Thad, you're awfully quiet. Is something wrong?"

Wrong? What could be wrong? I want to kiss you. I want to hold you. I want to share this moment with you. "I was thinking," he said, "about how much easier it's going to be going down than it was coming up. Would you like to take in the sights at Waikiki? I boned up on that, too. There isn't too much to see except for two big hotels. Quite grand, I understand. Or maybe you just want to go back to the house." He had to get away from her before he made a damn fool of himself. He could plead a headache, a stomachache. Anything. The only problem was, she would never believe it.

"Thad, if you don't mind, I think I'd like to go back. Could we do the hotel bit another day? I am rather tired from that climb and I still have the drive back to the house. Would you mind taking a look at the engine? The car shimmies and shakes something frightful. Twice I had to pull over, it was making so much noise."

That was something positive he could do. He hoped his relief didn't show too much. Damn Moss Coleman to hell. "Sure thing. Careful, now, that you don't trip."

Thirty minutes later, Thad raised his head from under the hood of the Ford. "I can't find a thing wrong. I'm no expert, but I'd say the knocking you hear is because the car hasn't been driven for a long time. It probably needs a complete overhaul, but it should get you back okay. Oil and water are all right. Just take it easy and don't speed. I don't think you'll have a problem."

"I'm sure I won't." Billie reached up on her tiptoes and planted a light kiss on Thad's cheek. "That's for being so nice and taking pity on a lonely lady. What a wonderful friend you are to Moss. Don't worry about me. I'll be fine." She waved airily as she turned the car around and headed back. It wasn't till she was halfway home that she realized Thad hadn't said anything about taking her out for the next two days. She shrugged. It was a lot to ask of anyone. Why would he want to spend his free time taking a married woman around the island?

She would have to make up her mind to amuse herself. Then when Moss did get back it would be twice as good.

The rusty Ford seemed to be working out its kinks as Billie drove along the mountain range. Jessica was going to be so enthralled when she sat down to tell her about her visit to Hawaii. Jess would want to know the "exact" of everything. The exact shade of the hibiscus, the exact feel of the velvety lawn, and how it could be so soft when it was so near the ocean. She made a mental note to find out. Jessica would want to know about Diamond Head and all about the climb and the breathtaking view. And she would certainly want specifics on Moss's friend, Thad. It would be the Pacific with its glorious colors that Billie was going to have difficulty describing. How did one describe one of God's greater perfections? The foaming curling whitewater and the fifteen-foot waves. "Breathtaking" was the best she could come up with at the moment.

Someday she would tell Maggie about this wondrous trip, too. She would save all her mementoes and bring them out to show the little girl, when she was old enough to understand.

The iron gates and the ancient banyan tree came into view.

Billie climbed from the car and opened the monstrous gates to the estate. She drove the car through and then secured the gates for the night. Again, as she walked around to the back of the house, she was assaulted with the scent of the ever-blooming plumeria. But she was getting used to it. It reminded her of honeysuckle, back in Philadelphia, but was sweeter, more heady somehow. And much more beautiful. Night-blooming cereus dotted the walkway down to the beach. Billie tossed her bag on the coral and slipped off her shoes. She walked carefully, not wanting to cut her feet. The warm trade winds were almost as gentle as her touch with little Maggie. Tears burned her eyes and she dabbed at them furiously, ashamed of herself. Maggie was being cared for by an expert nurse and didn't miss her. Jess showered her with love on the two short visits she was allotted each day. But she shouldn't be thinking of Maggie and Jess. Texas was practically half a world away. She could almost hear Seth's repeated reminder ringing in her ears that she wasn't to bother her head about such things.

Billie sat on the beach and stayed for a long time, her thoughts everywhere and nowhere. She stared out across the ocean and wondered if it met the Atlantic at some point. In her wildest dreams she never thought she would be sitting on a private beach in Hawaii. Alone.

The trade winds died down. She'd been hardly aware of the shift from the southwest. A niggling worm of thought attacked her mind. Pregnancy. The thought of Maggie had prompted it, she was sure. She was healthy, fit. On her last visit, the doctor had given her a clean bill of health and patted her on the back. However, he had also repeated that it would not be wise to contemplate pregnancy again. He had told her in his gentle manner that he had felt duty bound to inform Seth and her mother of her condition. Condition? she had queried. But stubbornly the doctor had only kept repeating his warning: she had a child now, why endanger her health again? She had listened solemnly, not overly concerned at the time. Moss was so far away. By the time she saw him again, whatever was wrong would certainly have mended. Women had babies every day of the week. She was young, healthy, and fit as a fiddle. Those were the doctor's exact words.

Moss had taken no precautions and she hadn't cared at the time. Did she care now? Moss had taken it for granted that things were all right. How could she tell him that she was less than perfect? Babies were a part of marriage. She couldn't tell him. Wouldn't tell him. In the whole world she wanted nothing more than to be perfect for her dashing young husband. She would take her chances.

Billie's teeth chattered with another abrupt change in the wind. Kona winds, bringing humidity and rain. It was late. She should be getting back to the house. She needed a shower to wash off the salt spray. Or maybe a long hot soak with some of the scandalous bath oil Agnes had insisted she buy. Then she might try out the piano in the living room. It had been so long since she'd played. It would soothe her so that she could fall asleep in quick order. She wondered what Moss was doing. She wondered if he ached for her the way she ached for him.

Billie contented herself over the next two and a half days by learning a few Hawaiian words, with Phillip's help. She learned that *kamaaina* meant "longtime island resident" and referred to Ester Kamali. *Mahalo* meant "thank you." *Ono* meant "tastes good!" (She said that over and over as she devoured twelve mangoes!) *Wahine* was "woman" and *wikiwiki* was "to do something quickly." Before the servant walked back to his quarters, he told her she was *nani*, which meant "beautiful." Billie smiled. The words weren't all that difficult to pronounce and sounded so lovely. When Moss arrived she would show him what she'd learned and practice on him.

Moss drove the Jeep carefully up the hill road, already anticipating the feel of Billie in his arms. She'd be there, waiting for him, ready for him. He smiled, biting down on the slim, ivory-tipped cigarillos he'd come to favor. He had deserved being restricted to base, he knew, but it had been rough duty when he'd tossed and turned all night long, waking to find himself alone instead of lying beside his wife. Damn, a man could get used to the nicer things in life.

Before he'd left the base, it had seemed as if Thad were avoiding him for some reason. He mentally shrugged. Maybe old Thad was more discreet and understanding than he'd thought and hadn't wanted to intrude on him and Billie. Still, it bothered him somewhat that when he'd suggested Thad keep Billie company, his friend had suddenly been busy with other obligations. Of course, though Billie certainly excited *him*, she was not exciting to be with. Perhaps that would come later, when she'd had more time to mature. But now, Billie posed no challenge; there was no aura of danger or mystery about her. He supposed most men felt that way about their wives and that was how it should be. A wife was steady and secure, predictable and safe. That was why men didn't marry girls like Lola, who worked at Holli Loki's on the other side of the island. Lola was never safe or predictable and she ran around with dangerous men, but Lola was exciting. And she showed him more interesting things than baby pictures of an infant he'd never seen.

Maggie. Now where the hell had Billie come up with that name? One of these days he'd have to ask her. Undoubtedly, she'd tell him it was after the author of *Gone with the Wind*, Billie's favorite book. Christ, there was no figuring women! Seth probably wouldn't have cared if Billie had named the baby Pepsi-Cola. Pap had no trouble keeping his priorities straight and the hoped-for grandson was most likely the only reason the old man had moved heaven and earth to send Billie to Hawaii. Pap had done his share and the rest was up to Moss. Making her pregnant with Riley Seth Coleman would be Moss's pleasure.

There couldn't be anything wrong with Billie, could there? She was the picture of health; she positively bloomed with it. Jessica's letter to Moss, arriving just about the same time as Billie herself, must have been written out of maternal concern. Still, his mother's words nagged at him. She had said that she'd talked with Dr. Ward one afternoon when he'd looked in on her for one of her headaches. He had warned against another pregnancy for Billie. Now what the hell was that supposed to mean? And if there was any truth to it, why wouldn't Billie have said something herself?

As he did with everything else that threatened his plans, Moss stowed this puzzle away on the back shelf of his mind. Billie was a big girl now—she was a mother herself—and it was nobody's damn business but Billie's and his! Moss began to whistle as the hilltop house came into view. Vaguely, he wondered if his son would have his dark hair.

CHAPTER THIRTEEN

Thad Kingsley stood just off the runway, smoking a cigarette.
It was forbidden, but there wasn't anyone around of importance
to report him. He took a deep drag and then crushed the butt
out with the heel of his flight boot. He bent over to pocket the
incriminating evidence and then looked overhead. A plane bearing the medical insignia of the Red Cross was about to land.
The pilot touched down with ease. Thad felt like clappng. The
guy, whoever he was, was loose as a goose.

Medical supplies? Usually they came by land in supply
trucks. Curiosity got the better of him and he stood around
until the bays opened. Two figures in army fatigues hopped
out. The taller of the two advanced to one of the ground crew
and held out his manifest. Thad watched as the sailor scratched
his head and then shook it. Thad inched a little closer, in time
to hear the big corporal say, "We got this delivery for some
guy named Coleman, stationed here. Look, don't give me any
of this crap that you don't know who the guy is. He's some
goddamn admiral, is who he is. If I told you where this stuff
came from, you'd know he was an admiral. What say we get
the lead out and tell Admiral Coleman his personal Red Cross
plane full of food is here." There was distaste on the man's
face.

"I'm telling you, I know every admiral on this base and we
ain't got no Coleman. We got a Coleman who's a second looey.
You want I should get him?"

"You better get somebody before this stuff goes bad. And
get more ice. My orders say a medical vehicle is to meet this
plane and take the contents to . . . an undisclosed destination.
This is all bullshit, sailor. Somebody's screwing around. I just
deliver. Go get this Coleman or get that truck, but do something."

"I don't have orders to do that," the sailor complained. "And
we don't have an Admiral Coleman. So, you do whatever the

hell you damn please. I go off duty in another three minutes."

"Where's this Coleman who's a second looey hang out? The one who ain't an admiral."

"In that building over there. He's a flight instructor. I'm officially off duty now. No more questions. Solve your own damn problems."

"Close those goddamn bays till I figure out what the hell to do with this stuff," the tall man shouted to his partner. "This heat will melt what ice is in there and whose ass do you think will be in a sling then?"

Thad stifled a laugh and turned his head.

"I need this. I really need this," the corporal grumbled as he loped toward the building. Thad could have told him that Moss had taken his class down to the far end of the airstrip, but he didn't. This was the best show he'd seen since joining the navy.

Two hours later, every admiral, captain, and commander on the base, it seemed, was on the airstrip to claim the contents of the Red Cross plane. "You got the password, you get the contents," the belligerent corporal said tartly. "No password, the stuff rots on the plane. You see who signed this manifest?" Thad felt a bubble of laughter rumble in his chest at the awed looks.

Moss Coleman led his weary band of students down the airstrip. His eyes took in the scene and the Red Cross plane. Next to it was a van with the same insignia. He took a deep breath and started to whistle "Deep in the Heart of Texas."

"That's good enough for me. Sign here," the corporal bellowed in Moss's direction. "If that guy's an admiral, I'll eat the entire contents of this plane," Thad heard him mutter.

Moss signed his name with a flourish. He turned and addressed the assembled brass. "Sirs, you're all invited to a Texas barbecue at my house in the hills. I've taken the liberty of posting a small map and directions on the flight bulletin board." He favored Thad with a heavy-lidded wink and ordered his flight group to about-face.

"Who the hell *is* that guy?" demanded a three-star with a forty-five-inch waist.

"Beats the hell out of me," a commander said shortly. "All I know is I saw the signature on the manifest and I am not about to ask one question. I'm going to the barbecue and that's all I know. Maybe we'll all be mentioned in *Stars and Stripes* if we play our cards right."

Thad had all he could do to keep a straight face. He walked over to the Red Cross truck, handed the driver a map, and bent through the window to give him Moss's instructions.

The burly corporal stared at Thad a minute. "You son of a bitch, you been standing here for three hours and you knew all along whose stuff this was and where it was supposed to go and you never said a word. You navy punks stink. Why didn't you say something?"

"I didn't know the password and I can't whistle. Would you have believed me?"

"Guess not. This stuff is like gold. Okay, sorry I blew up at you, but I still think you navy guys stink."

"Oh, yeah?" Thad growled. "Buzz off, buddy. And I out-rank you, so lets not bring it to a test. Move it! Corporal!"

"Yes sir!" the corporal said, smartly saluting. The minute Thad's back was turned the smart salute was minus four fingers.

Billie watched the hectic preparations for the barbecue. She could tell that Moss was irritated to the point where he was going to do or say something hurtful to the slow-moving Phillip. "Yes sir, Mr. Moss, sir, *wikiwiki*. Cow is big difference from pig. Pig is easy to roast. Cow much meat. Much more heavier. You have two cows. Much work. No help. You bring more help we move *wikiwiki*."

"Steer. It's a steer," Moss said in exasperation. "More help is on the way. Let's get this spit going and we can set up the other one on the beach. I don't see what the big problem is. Roasting a pig is the same principle as a steer. The only dif-ference is you put an apple in the pig's mouth. You want an apple in this steer's mouth, you have my permission."

"Apple too small. Maybe pineapple. Stupid you no want luau. In Hawaii you have luau. We not make"—he searched his mind for the words Moss had repeated over and over to him—"Tukas barkut."

"Texas barbecue." Moss grimaced. Billie giggled behind her hand. Secretly she had to agree with Phillip. A luau would have been so much simpler.

It was three o'clock in the morning and Billie was tired. All she wanted to do was go to bed and sleep in Moss's arms. But Moss, she knew, had no thoughts of sleep. He was going to supervise until it was time to leave for the base at five-thirty. How he could devote all his attention and energy to this ridic-ulous cookout was beyond her. Phillip was literally falling asleep on his feet, but Moss would show him no mercy. Once the pit was just right and the steer secure on the spit, Moss stood back to view his handiwork. "Pap would be proud of me," Moss said with a clap of his hands. "Now all we have to do is get the other pit ready and then sit back. Billie, you took care of all the other food, didn't you? Ice is coming first thing in the morning—I want that beer to be ice cold. Who's shucking the corn? What about the sauce? Are you sure that gal in the kitchen knows what to do with it?"

"Trust me, darling. Everything is under control," Billie said wearily.

"Did you get yourself a colorful muumuu?"

"I didn't have the time. Don't worry. I have something to wear."

"Billie, I told you to get a muumuu. Or rather I told Thad to tell you. I wanted you to wear something bright and colorful with a hibiscus behind your ear. You've been lying around the house for days. How much trouble would it have been for you to go down to one of the shops in Waikiki and get one? Goddamn it, Billie, was that too much to ask?"

Billie felt like a whipped dog. Moss had never, ever spoken to her like this before. "I'm ... I'm sorry, Moss. I didn't think it was all that important. I brought all these new clothes with me that I've never worn. They're so much prettier ... than a baggy muumuu." Her shoulders slumped. "I'm sorry, Moss. I'll get one this morning."

Moss swung around. "You can't go anywhere today. You have to stay here and keep your eye on things. I don't want you to even think of leaving."

"All right, Moss. I'm sorry. Please, don't be angry. I don't want us to argue. Our time is so short and I don't want anything to spoil it."

Moss's eyes softened. "I'm sorry, too. It's just that you've always tried to please me. I rarely, if ever, tell you to do anything. I thought you would understand that it was important to me to have you wear a muumuu. I plan on having some pictures taken to send on to Pap and Mam. All the guys from the squadron are wearing floral shirts. Most of the brass is coming in island dress. You're going to stick out like a sore thumb. The hostess standing out like a sore thumb is not something I wanted, Billie. Pap and Mam are going to be disappointed.

"Well, it's too late now, so let's forget it. Old Phillip here looks like he's about wrung out, so you're going to have to help me with the beach pit. You can do that, can't you?"

At that point, Billie would have done anything to bring a smile to her husband's face.

When Moss left the house at five-thirty, Billie was exhausted. Both longhorns were turning slowly on the spits. The tender beef would be ready for serving by ten o'clock that night. Wet sand and salt covered every inch of her skin. Her blond curls were matted and caked with salt spray. She sank to the sand and cried. Moss had only pecked her on the cheek. It was the kind of kiss, she thought, a man would give his mistress as he exited her apartment so no trace of perfume would stay with him. She felt wretched. Angry tears scalded her eyes. Moss hadn't even responded when she'd said she loved him and warned him to drive carefully. He'd nodded curtly and climbed into the Jeep. He was angry with her. How could she have been so stupid?

Angry and frustrated, Billie kicked off her sandals and ran into the ocean. She struck out, beating at the waves as though they were the enemy. By the time she swam back to shore she could feel the tension finally leaving her shoulders.

Imperceptibly the slim shoulders squared. Moss wanted her attired in a muumuu. Moss would find her attired in a muumuu. Somehow, some way, she would find one. She shivered in the cool early-morning air. A smile touched her lips when she saw Phillip dozing on the lanai side of the house. She dried off and went in search of the housekeeper. When there was no answer to her quiet knock, she opened the door and stepped in. Again she squared her shoulders. She needed a little Coleman guts to do what she had to do. Gently she shook the plump woman's shoulder. "Wake up, Rosa. I need your help. Big *pilikia*," she said. "I need your help. You have to get up. Come, please. I know it's early, but it's going to be a busy day." The plump woman glared at her and smiled at the same time. "Please, Rosa," Billie pleaded.

Rosa rolled over, the bed springs creaking with her weight. "You wake me when sun high," she muttered, pulling the sheet over her head.

"Rosa, you don't understand. You have to get up, *wikiwiki*. Now. I need a muumuu. It's so important to me. I'll have to try to make one somehow. Is there a sewing machine here someplace?" Billie was so frustrated she wanted to stomp her feet and wail like a banshee. How *could* this woman sleep like this? How could she lie there and refuse to help her? Her happiness depended on getting a muumuu.

Phillip, perhaps he could help. Billie raced back to the lanai to rouse Rosa's husband. She hated to wake the old man after he'd worked all night with Moss, but she had no other choice. She shook him awake, none too gently. A full fifteen minutes later Billie had Phillip's less-than-interested attention. At least his eyes were open, she told herself. Quickly she explained her problem. Phillip snorted. "You tell she look like Queen Kamamalu. She get up and do what you say. Is only way. But you no mention word tattoo. She want. You listen good."

"Yes, yes. I understand. Don't say anything about a tattoo. Tell her she looks like Queen Kamamalu. That's it? That's all I have to do?" But Phillip was already asleep.

Billie rolled the queen's name over and over on her tongue. She had to look up the famous lady in Miss Kamali's library. Queen Kamamalu, Queen Kamamalu, Queen Kamamalu, she repeated to herself as she sprinted down the right wing of the house where Rosa slept. "Rosa, I had to come back and tell you something." Billie's voice was a bare whisper. "I simply couldn't let another day go by without telling you that I think you look just like Queen . . . Queen Kamamalu. You really do." Childishly she crossed her fingers for the little white lie she was being forced to tell. Maybe it wasn't a lie at all. She uncrossed her fingers.

Rosa rolled over and sat upright. "You think so, Missy Billie? Nobody believe but Phillip. Need tattoo here and here and here," Rosa said, jabbing at herself. "Queen Kamamalu much tattoo. Phillip say no."

Billie grimaced. "Husbands, Phillip, loco." Billie pointed to her head. She would do anything, say anything to get the housekeeper moving.

"You smart *wahine*. Smart *haole wahine*." Rosa smiled as she struggled from the bed.

"Now this is my problem. I need a muumuu," Billie said, enunciating each word carefully. "I thought maybe we could make one, or at least try to put together something. Is there a sewing machine here?" At Rosa's perplexed look, Billie made motions with her fingers as though she were threading a needle and then weaving it in and out of the hem of her shorts. Rosa smiled and said, "No. No sew. No ricky-ticky sew."

Tears of frustration gathered in Billie's eyes. "I need a muumuu, Rosa. My *kane*, my *ipo* won't like me." She felt stupid when she made kissing motions with her lips to show Rosa how serious the situation was. Billie never knew if it was the words that meant man and sweetheart or her tears that finally moved the housekeeper from her bed.

"Come duh udder room." Billie followed Rosa down the hall to what must have been Ester Kamali's bedroom. Rosa stood at moment as though undecided. A second glance at Billie's tear-filled eyes seemed to convince her to open the door. Billie advanced and then backed up a step. She knew this had to be the most beautiful room she had ever seen. Everything was pearl white or a light moss green, even the wicker. Splashes of yellow as golden as sunshine added just the right touch. Billie drew in her breath. It was a woman's room. She didn't know why, but she had the feeling no man had ever set foot across the threshold. It was too perfect. It smelled new, never used. Billie raised her hands palms up to show she didn't understand.

"Missy Ester's *ipo* died. No marry udder man, ever."

Ester Kamali's sweetheart died. How sad. Billie felt as if she were trespassing. The feeling was so strong she turned to leave, the tears running down her cheeks. Here she was worried about a simple thing like a muumuu and her kind, unseen hostess had lost her sweetheart. Rosa moved quickly and drew Billie back into the room. "Missy Ester go way. Not come back many, many years. No udder man for missy. You come."

Dabbing at her tear-streaked face, Billie followed Rosa into a small dressing room off the bedroom, watching as she reached up to one of the shelves for a porcelain jar and withdrew a small brass key. "You see, *wikiwiki*." Rosa blessed herself and dropped to her knees before a large wicker chest beneath the last shelf. Honey-colored hands were gentle with the mounds of tissue paper that lay inside, then they probed the depths of the chest. Rosa seemed to know what she was searching for by touch rather than sight. When her plump hands found it, she withdrew and held up a rainbow of multicolored silk. "For you, Missy Billie. No udder *wahine* wear. Missy Ester say hokay."

Billie was speechless. She was selfish enough to want to reach out for the dress but woman enough to know what the beautiful silk had meant to Ester Kamali. Tears welled in her eyes again. She shook her head at Rosa and backed off a step.

"You take. You wear. Missy Ester want you *kane* see you in her dress. You take. Is hokay. Is much hokay. Take."

Almost without intending to, Billie reached out for the vibrant silk. It was just what Moss would have expected her to buy for herself. She held the flowing gown to her shoulders. Rosa's jet-black eyes glowed with pleasure. "Rosa, are you sure?" Billie wanted the dress more than anything in the world. She'd do anything to be able to wear it. Anything to erase Moss's displeasure. "I'll take care of it. I promise. I won't go near food. I won't even take a drink while I'm wearing it."

Rosa frowned. What *was* the *wahine* talking about? When Billie smiled, Rosa relaxed. "Missy Ester much happy that the dress make *wahine* happy."

Billie carried the silk gown back to her room and laid it on the bed. Moss was going to be pleased. She knew he wouldn't ask questions. He would simply accept the fact that she had somehow found a way to do as he wished.

Billie showered and washed and set her hair. She let the warm shower run, creating steam in the bathroom so that the silk, hung from a scented, padded hanger, would be free of wrinkles. There was no way she was going to lay an iron to this gorgeous creation.

When she made her way to the kitchen, Rosa and Phillip, along with assorted cousins, nephews, and nieces, were busily preparing food for the barbecue. The food that had arrived on the medical transport was off to one side. Rosa and a bubbly niece were making Hawaiian dishes that would be served separately. Already there were huge platters of *lau lau*, a mixture of fish, pork, and taro leaves wrapped and steamed in a Ti leaf. Billie selected one and popped it in her mouth. "Delicious." She laughed and took a second. Baking *ulu* and *opihi* were sending off delicious aromas. This would be the first time Billie would taste breadfruit and limpets. There were small pots of purple *poi*, made from crushed taro root. Billie wrinkled her nose. The young girls laughed as they dipped their fingers in the *poi* and licked them. Even if it was the traditional Hawaiian dish, Billie decided to pass on it. Instead her eyes were drawn to the containers of barbecue sauce and huge sacks of corn. She had a feeling she was going to be the one to shuck the yellow ears. Phillip made motions to her to indicate the beer kegs were on ice. That was good. The two cases of bourbon would go out on the terrace, where Moss was going to set up a bar. Two gunnysacks full of Idaho baking potatoes were being inspected by Phillip. He had his instructions as to baking them on the beach, next to the steers. "Much time left for totes."

"Potatoes," Billie corrected him.

"What I said, totes."

Butter was being iced and salt by the pound was being poured into heavy ceramic shakers. Cartons of heavy paper napkins were opened and a child of ten or so was busily folding them into intricate squares. From what she could see there were at least six red-and-white-checkered tablecloths. Seth did all this! she thought in amazement. Surely he'd forgotten something. Billie poked and pried into the cartons and sacks. Her eyes were wide when she extracted two full boxes of toothpicks and three one-pound cans of peppermint candies. For indigestion, she supposed. She rummaged more and found cabbage for coleslaw and six graters. God! Dressing was in the icebox in gallon jars. All this food, all the way from Texas. It was unbelievable. When her search was finished she had to admit that there was no fault to be found. Seth had thought of everything, right down to the huge cans of baked beans.

"Phillip, if you or one of the boys will carry the corn out to the monkeypod tree, I'll clean it. I'll need a basket or something to put it in." She had barely finished speaking when a tall youth hefted one of the sacks and slung a wicker basket over his shoulder. He favored her with a dazzling smile as he motioned for her to go ahead of him.

Billie crossed the terrace and smiled at a cherub brigade as they deftly ran thread through plumeria blossoms for welcome leis. Moss had thought of everything, too. It might be a Texas barbecue, but he was deferring in small ways to the beautiful Hawaiian customs.

As Billie sat under the tree shucking the corn she realized how far away from home she really was. The ripe yellow silk lay like a carpet at her feet and the lime-green leaves piled up. The lemony-colored corn was beautiful, the kernels in perfect rows. It was a pity she wouldn't be able to taste it. She was already regretting the promise she'd made not to eat while wearing Ester Kamali's dress. After the guests had gone she would take the dress off and eat some of the leftovers.

Two hours later, Billie massaged her neck and turned the balance of the shucking over to one of the boys. He wrinkled his nose at the pile of corn but fell to his task at a sharp command from his Uncle Phillip. Time to see how the sourdough bread was coming along.

Satisfied with the flour-strewn kitchen and dark mutterings from Rosa, Billie made a hasty retreat to the beach, where she went for a long solitary walk. At first her thoughts were lazy and dream-filled, but they intensified as the swells from the ocean whipped onto the sandy shore. All this commotion, all this fuss, all this trouble for a barbecue: what was Moss thinking of? And Seth, sending all the food from half a world away? She didn't think she would ever understand the Colemans. Moss's attitude and his sharp words to her this morning had hurt. Deeply. Secretly, Billie admitted to herself that she was jealous of the evening's plans. Why wasn't Moss satisfied just being with her? The two of them. The days were to be treasured now. She guessed the *Enterprise* was about ready to leave. Repairs were ahead of schedule. Who knew when they would see each other again? Learn to enjoy what you have, Thad had said. She must keep that in mind at all times.

This party was going to go into the early hours of the morning. Moss had to be back on base for his weekend restriction. That meant the cleaning-up chores after the party would fall to her and Rosa.

Billie sighed as she looked out across the waves. She should be delirious with happiness. Here she was in an island paradise with the man she loved with all her heart, a beautiful gown to wear for the evening, and she was feeling sorry for herself. Top brass, beautiful women . . . the party atmosphere should be intoxicating. Why did she feel so miserable, so let down? Was it fatigue from having worked through the night at Moss's side? No, she'd been up all night on many occasions and hadn't felt like this. Soul weary? Perhaps. Disappointed? More true than not. Was it too much to expect to spend every moment possible with her husband?

In just a few hours Moss would be home. At least they would have some time alone before their guests arrived. Unless of course Moss took it into his head to supervise every little detail. She would go to her room and take the bobby pins out of her hair. Maybe she could fix herself a glass of lemonade and sit in the sun on the balcony. A good book or magazine would help her wile away the time. But before she did anything she had to check both barbecue pits and make a second inspection of conditions in the kitchen. It was almost laughable. What did she know about roasting steers?

Phillip clucked his tongue and made clapping sounds with his hands to show his disapproval as Billie picked up the smoking banyan leaves. She fared no better when she peeked into the kitchen. It looked like utter chaos to her. There were pans and platters of food everywhere. Flour and something that looked like a pot of melting glue stood on the chrome kitchen table. Later, she must ask what it was.

The ornamental clock on the desk in the living room chimed six o'clock. Billie checked the gold circle on her wrist. Five minutes past. She was resetting her watch when she heard the Jeep coming up the road. She ran to the wide double doors and flung them open. Her excited welcome died in her throat. In the Jeep with Moss sat Thad Kingsley and three other friends. She forced a smile to her lips and walked out to the driveway. "Look, honey," said Moss. "I brought help. Come on in, guys, and Billie will fix you a drink. I want to check out the pits. Phillip is a grand old guy, but he isn't up on longhorn beef. Did you check on things during the day, Billie?"

How excited he was. How happy he looked. This was all so important to him. How could she even think of spoiling things? She was so glad now that she had accepted Miss Kamali's dress. "Yes, Moss, I did. Everything looked fine to me. Don't even consider going into the kitchen. Rosa will box your ears."

Thad and the others laughed. Moss loped toward the beach and Billie led the way to the outside terrace. She offered drinks and made small talk.

Twenty minutes later Moss was back and mixing his own drink. He settled down near his friends and conversation ran to the events of the day. Billie looked from one man to the other. Only Thad's eyes met hers in silent apology. She excused herself and knew no one was aware that she was leaving, except possibly Thad.

Billie filled the tub for a long, leisurely soak. She added a liberal dose of bath salts and watched the water foam. It was almost as frothy as the Pacific. She wouldn't cry, she just wouldn't. Sometimes this new married life stunned her. Moss probably didn't even remember that he had been sharp with her this morning. He was probably unaware how hurt she had been. It was time to shake this depression, time to get dressed and join Moss and his friends. Their guests would be arriving shortly.

When Billie made her entrance an hour later on the lanai all five officers jumped to their feet, but it was to Moss that Billie's eyes went. There was approval and pride in his glance and smile. The long sarong-like gown displayed her smooth tan shoulders and high rounded breasts, the side slit skirt allowing peek-a-boo glimpses of an elegant length of leg.

"You look lovely, Billie," Thad said sincerely. The other three pilots echoed Thad's approval. Moss kissed her lightly on the cheek and put his arm around her shoulder. Billie wanted to lean into him, to snuggle against him, but she held her emotions in check. She smiled warmly and settled herself on one of the wicker chairs. The silk crept up around her ankles, exposing a scandalously sexy high-heeled shoe that was nothing more than straps. Thad Kingsley swallowed hard. He had never seen anything so provocative as that gently swinging foot.

"I think I'll take a walk to the beach and check out your longhorns," he said. "If I were you, Coleman, I'd get the lead out and get dressed. You are the host and the brass should be arriving any minute now."

"Good thinking. I won't be long. Billie, refill the guys' drinks."

"We can do it, Moss. Let your wife rest. We enjoy sitting here looking at her."

"Suit yourself. I told you guys to bring dates."

"Surely you jest. When I party I party. All the way. You can't let go with the top brass milling about. Don't worry about us. We're here to eat all that beef you've been jawing about."

Moss shrugged. The guys were right. Jesus, Billie was going to knock the socks right off the brass. And their wives were going to do some double takes. He'd never seen her look so beautiful. The guys were impressed. Thad had looked like a fish out of water for a minute. The party was going to be a success. He could *feel* it.

By nine-thirty the last guest had arrived. Moss drew Billie aside as they surveyed the scene on the terraces and lanai. "Did you ever notice that all generals' and admirals' wives are old and wrinkled? Look at that one over there." Billie looked in the direction Moss was discreetly pointing. The woman's face was leathery and wrinkled, and the skin on her neck hung in unattractive folds. "So help me, if you ever get to looking like that, I'll divorce you."

"Are you going to be an admiral someday, Moss?" Billie teased, enjoying the few moments of intimacy.

"Not me, but Thad is. I'd bet Sunbridge on it."

Billie giggled. "Do you think he'll have a wife like one of these women?"

"God, I hope not. Thad's pretty selective. What kind of shoes is the general's wife wearing?" Moss asked curiously.

Billie peered straight ahead in the yellow lantern light. She giggled again. "Serviceable. Maybe she has a foot problem. But we're being unkind."

"The hell you say, Mrs. Coleman. That lady is a living, breathing bitch. She controls the officers' wives with an iron hand. The general doesn't make a move until he checks with her. It's common knowledge on the base. I'm glad you aren't staying there, Billie." Moss's arms tightened protectively around his wife's shoulders. This time, Billie leaned against him and whispered. He bent down to hear and grinned. "I'll take you up on that later. We better start to circulate, honey. Phillip is going to start carving soon and we have to head the line. I'll meet you on the lanai in, say, twenty minutes."

Billie maneuvered through the milling crowds, stopping to speak to one person and then another. The party was a success.

The moment Phillip's relatives struck the first chord of "Deep in the Heart of Texas" on their ukuleles, Billie made her way to the lanai to meet Moss.

Moss held up both hands as a signal for quiet. *"Hele mai ai!"* he shouted. "Come and eat!"

The small orchestra split up, half going to the area beneath the monkeypod tree and the other half to the beach. They strummed softly while native girls in their grass skirts swayed to the music. More than one man's eyes was on the girls instead of his beef. Billie felt smug. Moss had eyes for no one save herself.

"We'll have to do this again sometime, old buddy," Thad said with a slight slur to his words.

"The next time you can do it." Moss grinned. "What do you New Englanders do for a bash?"

"We have fish fries. And chowders. Stick-to-your-ribs chowder. Did I tell you you are the most beautiful woman here?" Thad said gallantly to Billie as he tried for a low, sweeping bow.

"Three times," Moss said, grinning. "You're getting crocked, Thad."

"Yeaaahhh. Billie, would you play the piano for me? That tinny music is getting to me. I have a yen for some good old U.S. of A. music. Old man, can your wife play me a couple of tunes?" Thad asked Moss.

"I don't see why not. It's up to Billie. Billie?"

"Of course. What would you like to hear?"

"Something with some beat. Something with heart. A little

honky-tonk, maybe some boogie-woogie. Is that a tall order?"

"Not too tall. I think I can manage. Come along, Lieutenant."

Billie settled herself at the keyboard. She flexed her fingers and tested out the keys. The baby grand was a magnificent instrument.

Billie was lost in the music, unaware of Thad's intent gaze as he leaned over the piano. She finished the last chord of "When the Lights Come On Again All Over the World" and swung into "The White Cliffs of Dover." "Harbor Lights" followed and then "Always."

"Slide over, Billie," Thad ordered. Billie obeyed and was stunned when Thad ran his long fingers the length of the keyboard. "Let's have a duet. Name your choice."

"I didn't know you played, Thad."

"There's a lot of things you don't know about me. Come on, let's tickle these ivories."

Billie laughed. "Name it, Lieutenant, and I'll keep up with you."

When the last guest had left, Moss took stock. "It was a roaring success, honey. We really did ourselves up proud. Mac took some great pictures. I'm not even going to try to get them developed over here. I'll send them straight on to Pap. Listen, honey, Thad, Mac, and Jack have to get back. If they take the Jeep, I won't have any way to get to the base in the morning, so I'm going along with them. I'll be back Monday night."

"Moss, it's only three A.M. You cold get a few hours' sleep and drive the Ford in the morning." If he left now, she wouldn't see him for another three days. "Moss, please."

"It's best this way, honey. By the time I get back, I can shower and change and write to Pap. He's going to want to know how things went. I'll see you Monday night. By the way, Mrs. Coleman, did I tell you how beautiful you looked this evening? Hey, are those tears? Billie, Coleman women don't cry over something as silly as this. Come on now, give me a smile." Billie's effort was hardly more than a grimace, but it seemed to satisfy Moss.

"Come on, you flight jockeys, move it! Who's almost sober?"

"I am," Thad said quietly. "Haven't had a drink in hours. I'll drive. Moss, if you don't want to drive the Ford down in the morning, I'll take it now and you can take the Jeep. You look done in. Why don't you catch a few hours' sleep?"

Moss shook his head. "We'll do it my way."

Billie's eyes thanked Thad for what he was trying to do for her. "Good night, gentlemen," she said quietly. "Thad, drive carefully. Moss, I'll see you on Monday." Without another word, she turned and headed for the bedroom, tears spilling down her cheeks. She'd been so sure Moss would stay.

Thad wanted to push his fist through Moss's smiling face. The ride back to the base was silent, heavy with emotions and confused loyalties. Moss was his friend, his best friend, Thad reminded himself. He would try never to forget it.

{{{{{{{{ CHAPTER FOURTEEN }}}}}}}}

Billie's Hawaiian honeymoon seemed to have ended. After the barbecue it was only rarely that she and Moss spent an evening alone together. They'd broken the ice; now it was their turn to accept social invitations, and Moss frequently entertained at the Officers' Club, just outside the base.

"It's important to me, Billie," he'd say when she complained. "It's not like I'm asking you to do anything but *be* there. All the arrangements are handled by the club."

"But I want to be *here*, alone with you, not with twenty other people. And I'm so much younger than the other wives, we've got very little in common."

"I don't like it when you whine, Billie. I don't like it at all. Promotions aren't handed out on merit alone. Not even in wartime. You're my wife and a Coleman. You've lived at Sunbridge long enough to see how things are done and I expect you to do them. Now get dressed."

"I could almost understand it if you were planning a career in the service, Moss, but you're not. Why is it so important to you?"

"Because I want to go as far as I can. I want to be up there where the decisions are made. There's no telling how long this war will last and I want to have some say in it. I've got some ideas of my own but no one will listen to them if I'm still just a flight jockey. Now do you understand?"

"Not quite. I really don't see why it should involve me. Thad doesn't have a wife to entertain for him and he's certainly not wanting for promotions."

It stuck in Moss's craw that Thad had been promoted to full lieutenant. His friend seemed to be fulfilling Pap's prophecy: "Watch out, boy, or that Yankee'll get ahead of you."

Billie was immediately sorry for what she'd said and meekly went to the bedroom to change. At least her expensive wardrobe was being put to good use. There was the Coleman image to preserve. Later, Moss would smooth her ruffled feathers with a gentle kiss and an approving whistle. And if there was one thing Billie desperately needed, it was her husband's approval.

Moss wasn't certain he liked the new assertiveness in his wife. In many ways he wanted her to be more independent, because it would mean greater freedom and fewer responsibilities for him. Yet he never really wanted her to change from that pleasant, acquiescent girl he'd met in Philadelphia. He rather liked being the one in control, and he considered Billie's occasional balkiness unattractive. Things were so much nicer when he could tell her not to bother her pretty little head about something and she would listen. This new Billie seemed to demand answers, and often he wasn't prepared to give them.

What Billie had said concerning Thad's promotion was niggling at him—perhaps she was closer to the truth of the matter than he was. It was possible that Billie's arrival in Hawaii had created jealousy among the other officers, reminding everyone he was a Coleman and had received special treatment. Then, too, perhaps the barbecue hadn't been that great an idea. Billie's instincts had been correct again. Settling back with his drink, Moss made a decision. Everyone had met the little wife . . . now it was time for her to go back stateside.

Billie stood under the shower spray wishing she had time for a bath instead. A nice long bath, fragrant with perfumed salts and a delicate powdering afterward. Then it would be so nice to crawl into bed beside Moss and make love to him. She wrinkled her nose in disappointment. Their social engagements usually ended late and Moss had to leave for the base so early; they had little time alone together. At least not for slow, luxurious arousals and falling asleep in each other's arms. Their lovemaking had become as hurried and demanding as everything else in their lives.

She lathered her arms, her neck, and her breasts, which were feeling heavier and more sensitive than usual, a sensation she remembered from her pregnancy with Maggie.

A little stab of remorse sent her thoughts to the baby she'd left back in Texas. It had been almost two months since she'd seen her daughter. Counting on her fingers, Billie realized that she'd left for Hawaii seven weeks ago. Seven weeks and no menstrual period. The thought was so devastating she felt light-headed, and suddenly Dr. Ward's warnings flashed through her brain. No, it wasn't possible. It was all the activity, all the swimming. Gingerly, she pressed her fingers into her breasts, feeling their tenderness. Missing a period didn't necessarily mean pregnancy and this was the way her breasts usually felt at the onset of her monthlies.

Hurriedly, she finished washing and rinsed off. Moss was waiting for her and she could practically feel his impatience. She wondered, not for the first time since arriving in Hawaii, if she should tell him what Dr. Ward had said about becoming pregnant again. Yet, as always before, it was something she couldn't bring herself to share with him. It would cause him worry and he had enough on his mind. Deep inside, she knew the real reason she wouldn't confide in Moss was that she didn't want him to think she was lacking in any way. She was ashamed of her inadequacies, even though this one was something over which she had no control. Besides, Agnes was well aware of the doctor's warnings and if there was anything to really be concerned about, her own mother would have said something. Wouldn't she?

By the time Billie stepped out of the bedroom, dressed in a white linen evening suit and high-heeled strapped slippers, Moss had come to the decision that his wife's return to the States was imperative, even if he had to fabricate the reasons for her leaving. "Billie," he said with a grin, eyeing the way the white linen skirt hugged her hips and thighs, "you're a knockout! Maybe you're right and we should stay home to-night "

Billie stepped into his arms, raking her fingers through the dark hair at the back of his neck. His thighs pressed enticingly against her own and his lips found the hollows of her throat. As her desires heightened, her questions subsided. This was her husband and he loved her and didn't want to share her with anyone tonight. When his mouth captured hers and she heard him emit a low groan of passion, tears of love and gratitude made crystalline paths down her cheeks.

* * *

Less than a week later, Moss arrived home early. Billie immediately knew something was terribly wrong. "What are you doing home?" she asked, dreading the answer.

"Billie, love, I can't stay. I've just come to pick up my things. I've got to get right back, but I wanted to see you before I left."

"Left? Where are you going?" There'd been so little time, so little time. Already she ached with missing him.

"I can't tell you that, Billie. You understand. I've already gotten through to Pap and he's making arrangements for you to go back stateside."

"Why can't I stay here and wait for you?"

"Now, Billie, love, don't look at me that way. Why would you want to stay here? I don't know when I'll be getting back and you do have our daughter to think about. I can't leave you all alone here in Hawaii. It just isn't possible. I'd never have a minute's rest!"

Billie sank into Moss's arms, too shocked for tears. "I've got to know where you're going. I've got to know when I'll see you again."

"Chin up, Billie. You knew this would happen. Pap knew it, too, when he sent you out here. It's out of my hands. Come here," he said softly. He tucked his chin on the top of her head so she wouldn't see the lies in his eyes. The Big E was still in dock.

Billie melted into his embrace. With her head against his chest, she could hear the wild thumping of his heart. She had to be brave; it was the least she could do for the man she loved, who was about to go off again to war.

Moss's hands trembled slightly as he caressed Billie's soft golden hair. She smelled so good, felt so good. He was a cad for what he was doing and he knew it. But hell, he was making a sacrifice, too! "Honey, I have to go. Take care of yourself and write to me. Every day, long letters. Tell me about Maggie and what's going on at Sunbridge. It makes me feel so close to you. Give my love to Pap and Mam. Tell them I'll write."

"Moss, I love you so much. I can't bear this."

He placed a finger against her quivering lips. "Shhh. Smile, Billie. Smile for me—it's how I want to remember you."

Billie felt beaten and bruised. . . . Would she ever be whole again? She helped him pack his ditty bag and saw him out to the Jeep. "I love you, Moss," she told him, leaning into his embrace.

"I know you do, honey. I know you do."

The following afternoon, Billie Coleman left Hawaii. She was pregnant with her second child.

Billie was welcomed back to Sunbridge by an aroused household in nightclothes. Too tired to respond in detail to questions, Billie issued a terse report on Moss and his well-being to her mother and Seth, then headed straight for her room. They were just going to have to wait until she felt up to the lengthy discussion they wanted. For now she wanted to see her daughter, to hold her and feel the soft downy head against her cheek. And then she wanted to sleep. For as long as possible.

"What the hell was *that* all about, Aggie?" Seth demanded. Agnes tried to hide her amusement at Seth's sleeping attire. She hadn't known they still made nightshirts these days. Red flannel, and with the seam split over his rump. She was going to have to speak to Tita about that. "Doesn't the girl know I've been waiting all day like a heifer in a mud slide for news of my son?"

"She gave you the highlights, Seth. She's tired. It's possible that our objective has been accomplished and Billie is feeling it even at this early stage. Patience. Tomorrow is another day. Moss is well and that's what is important. Go to bed now and we'll talk in the morning."

Dismissed. By God, Aggie was dismissing him like a kid. Seth bristled, but one look at Agnes's eyes told him he would get no further. Honey always worked better than vinegar, or so Agnes was fond of telling him.

Billie tiptoed down the long hallway to the nursery. The nurse was up from her narrow bed along the wall immediately. She brushed back her gray hair and sighed when she saw Billie. A weary smile crossed Billie's face when she peered down at the sleeping baby. She looked like Moss. At least she had his nose. Billie's chin, but Moss's nose.

A long arm shot out when Billie bent to pick up the sleeping baby. Billie straightened and locked eyes with the woman. "Go back to sleep, Nurse. I'm going to pick up my daughter and hold her. And then I'm going to sit in your rocking chair and rock her. If you don't like what I'm about to do, I suggest you pack your bags and leave now. The chauffeur is probably still awake because he just drove me here from the airport. Decide now. I'm very tired and I want to hold my baby."

"This is not good for the baby. She's colicky and needs her sleep. I never allow my charges to be awakened in the middle of the night." Her words were firmly said, but her eyes looked away first and her step was slow when she waddled back to the nursery bed. She had never been discharged from a position yet. This, she thought, was no time to start.

The downy head was soft against Billie's cheek. How sweet and clean Maggie smelled. How good she felt. It was almost as good as holding Moss next to her in a warm bed. Maggie squirmed and let out a large belch. "Just like your daddy." Billie smiled as she carried the sleeping baby to the rocking chair.

Billie rocked the old chair gently as she murmured an account of her trip to the islands to the sleeping baby. An hour later, when she could barely hold her eyes open, Billie nuzzled her face in the baby's neck, reveling in the scent and feel. Her own flesh and blood. Hers and Moss's.

Billie stood over the crib a good five minutes watching the sleeping child. Then she walked over to the nurse's bed. "Maggie is fine. She burped once, very loud, as a matter of fact. I didn't smother her. I didn't fall asleep while I rocked her. She's in a sound sleep and will no doubt sleep through the night. Good night."

"I'm going to have to speak to Mr. Coleman about this, Mrs. Coleman. He placed me in sole charge of Maggie."

Billie spun around and walked back to the bed. "I wouldn't do that if I were you, Miss Jenkins. Not if you want to continue to work here. The choice, however, is entirely up to you."

The nurse stared at Billie. Secretly she wanted to applaud the young mother. Hawaii must have been good for her. Maybe she'd give that old man a run for his money yet. She nodded.

Billie dragged herself back to her room and stripped off her clothes. Too tired to look for a nightgown, she slipped beneath the sheets naked. She was used to sleeping "in the buff," as Moss called it. In fact, she rather liked the satiny feel of the sheets against her skin. She was asleep as soon as her head touched the pillow.

The inquisition began over the dinner table the following evening.

"How did the boy look? Is he all right? Where is he now? You should have stayed longer. Don't tell me you came back because of Maggie."

Billie stared across the width of the table at her father-in-law. "Moss is fine. He looks wonderful. I don't know where he is. The navy didn't confide in me. Thad is with him. So are the others."

"What did you do while he was off duty? My God, girl, don't you understand I want to know everything about my son?"

Billie scooped out the soft mush of her baked potato, added a glob of sour cream, and then stirred it into a thick paste. Not because she wanted to eat it, but just to have something to do with her hands. "We talked about Maggie a lot. We took long walks on the beach. We went swimming early in the morning and late at night. When Moss was restricted, Thad Kingsley took me sight-seeing. I didn't have all that much time with Moss. In fact, if you want, I could total up the hours. I doubt that they would come to a full week."

Agnes broke a piece of bread and then crumbled it in her fingers. She had never heard such a resentful tone in her daughter's voice. She glanced at Seth.

Seth pierced his daughter-in-law with his bright gaze. "Why did Kingsley have to take you sight-seeing? Why didn't Moss take you? I know he doesn't like that piss-assed business, but it was your first visit. Just how thick are those two?"

"I told you, Seth, Moss was restricted. Thad was good enough to take me around to see the sights. Moss asked him to do it. He's very nice. He's Moss's best friend. They depend on each other."

"How was the barbecue?"

"The barbecue was a huge success. Practically everyone was there. Officers and their wives, some enlisted men, and a few Hawaiian civilians who worked on the base. Thad took pictures and Moss said he was going to send the film on to you to have developed. It lasted till three in the morning. A crew from the mess took the leftover beef back to the base. I think they made hash out of it. At least that's what Thad said."

"Did he send a letter? Did he give you a message for me?" Seth demanded. Billie stared into Seth's bright, hopeful gaze.

"He said to tell you he loved you and Mam very much and his next meatball was for you."

Agnes laid down her fork and reached for her water glass. Her eyes met Billie's. She recognized the lie and nodded approvingly. Billie's shoulders squared imperceptibly at the satisfied look on her father-in-law's face.

Billie excused herself and left the table. She wanted to spend some time with Jessica. The brief hour after luncheon hardly counted. She'd been appalled at the change in her mother-in-law on her return. *Feeble* was the only word she could come up with. Billie knew little or nothing about it, but she could sense that Jessica was dying. There was a lost look in the sunken, hollow eyes and a vagueness to her words that made Billie ache.

Jessica was napping, her rosary clutched in her hand. Prayer seemed to give her comfort even if she got the words mixed up. *He* knew what she was saying and thinking. *He* understood.

Billie stood at the window looking out at an arthritic-looking oak on the lawn. It was older than Jessica and would live many more years, dutifully giving shade in the summer and firewood when the limbs were trimmed. What more could a person ask of a tree? And what was expected from this frail creature in her high-necked dimity nightdress? Nothing. Her life was over. Dutiful fifteen-minute visits by Agnes and Seth. And the nurse, at Billie's firm-eyed insistence, would bring the baby every day.

Jessica woke just as Billie turned around. She smiled. "How are you, Billie? Did I fall asleep again? Lately I can't seem to stay awake. Forgive me, child. Please, sit down and tell me more about your trip. Would you mind terribly starting from the beginning? I fear I forgot most of what you told me earlier. But Billie, before you start, did you send off my letter to Amelia?"

"Yes, I did. I posted it right after lunch. Get comfortable and I'll tell you everything, right down to the beautiful monkeypod tree in the yard." Billie settled herself comfortably in a high wingback chair. An hour into her monologue Jessica's eyelids closed. Billie continued to speak for a few more minutes. Then, satisfied that Maggie's grandmother was soundly sleeping, Billie tiptoed about the room, turning off the lamps. She tilted the lamp shade on the night table so the light wouldn't bother Jessica and bent over to kiss the dry, wrinkled cheek.

Billie closed the door and went across the hall to her own room, thinking about the letter to Amelia she had included with Jessica's. After three pages of doings in Sunbridge and news of her father and Moss, Billie had thrown caution to the winds and written that, in her opinion, Jessica was dying. "If there's any way," Billie had written, "please try to come home. We all understand the war is making things impossible, but if need be I'm sure that your father will intervene and help you." She had signed it "Billie."

Billie woke slowly and knew there was something wrong. It was early in the morning, a month to the day after her return from Hawaii. It took barely two minutes for her sleep-filled brain to register that she was going to be sick. She bolted from the bed and raced for the bathroom. Her knuckles were as white as the rim of the basin she was gripping.

Agnes and Seth, on their way down the hall to a sunrise breakfast, heard the sounds from Billie's half-opened door. Their eyes locked, but neither missed a step.

Billie looked at her wretched reflection in the bathroom mirror. Her face was the color of a week-old mushroom. When she fell back against the pillows, she knew she didn't need a calendar to tell her what was wrong. She was pregnant. Somehow she had known. It must have happened the day Moss had been late back to the base.

Billie buried her face in the pillow and wept. Eight more months of misery. "Oh, Moss," she cried.

It was midmorning when Billie made her first attempt to get up. Her head reeled sickeningly. She swallowed hard and managed to get to her feet. By the time she had showered and dressed, she felt slightly better. Some tea and toast would help and then she would place a call to the doctor. He was going to be shocked that she'd ignored his advice. And right now she wished she had paid more attention.

When Billie's feet touched the bottom of the steps she looked up to see her mother walking across the wide central hallway. She was alone, which was odd because lately she and Seth were like each other's shadow. "Where's Seth?" she blurted.

"Out riding—why do you ask?" Agnes said sharply.

"No reason. Mother, join me for some tea. I want to talk to you. If you aren't too busy, that is."

"My, aren't we feisty this morning. Are you all right, Billie? Is there something bothering you? Can I help?"

Her mother's solicitousness prompted Billie to link arms with her. It had been a long time since there had been any closeness between the two of them. Since before she met Moss.

The tea was warm and spicy. Agnes stirred sugar into her cup and waited expectantly. "It's about Jessica, Mother. I'm sure you must know she doesn't have long. Will you ask Seth

{ 221 }

to see if he can get Amelia back home? I wrote to her but haven't heard anything. It could be months before she ever gets my letter and Jessica doesn't have months, Mother. Seth has powerful friends. It will be awful if Amelia doesn't get here in time."

Agnes felt confused. This wasn't what she'd expected to hear. This wasn't what she *wanted* to hear. Surely Jessica wasn't as bad off as Billie thought. Seth didn't seem overly concerned. "Darling," she said, "Jessica is ailing but she's nowhere near the end. The doctor's been most encouraging lately. I admit Jessica had a setback after you left for Hawaii, but she's on the mend now. If I do as you ask, Seth will think we're busybodies—he won't thank us; I can tell you that."

Billie's back stiffened. "Does that mean you won't speak to him?" Agnes nodded. "Then I'll speak to him myself."

"Billie, do you have any idea of what you're asking? We're at war. England is an exploding powderkeg. I doubt very much anyone can come home to the States now."

"We have to try. Mother, don't you care?"

"Of course I care. But you're asking the impossible. I don't think Seth's influential friends can help him in this."

"I don't see why not. Seth's influential friends helped him send a Red Cross plane full of food to Hawaii," Billie said bitterly. "This is a little more serious and a lot more important. It's a question of Jessica seeing her daughter before she dies."

"All right, Billie. I'll speak to Seth. But I can tell you right now that he's not going to be able to do anything. There's a war going on over there."

"There's going to be a war going on right here if someone doesn't do something," Billie snapped. "Excuse me, Mother. I have a phone call to make and then I want to read to Jessica for a while. You know, it wouldn't hurt you to really take some time when you visit with her. Now that you're the mistress of Sunbridge, I would have thought . . . well, never mind, Mother. I'll talk with you later."

Her little Billie was making demands! She never thought she would live to see the day. Agnes diddled with the spoon in her cup, clinking it against the edge. She would tactfully lead Seth into a conversation concerning his daughter and see what developed. Jessica wasn't dying. Or was she? Men had a way of not seeing what was right in front of their noses. This was something she was going to have to check out herself. Before she spoke to Seth.

Billie watched her mother's performance later in the day. Jessica made the effort and rallied for a short time for Agnes's benefit, appearing alert and aware of what was going on about her. It wasn't until Agnes left that the frail old woman collapsed against the pillows.

Billie ran to her. "Jess, are you all right? Should I call the doctor? Lie quiet and let me get your medicine. Why? Why did you exert yourself like that?"

Jessica lay quietly for a long time, the transparent eyelids closed. When she finally did speak it was with an effort. Billie had to strain to hear the words. "It's expected, Billie. Your mother has grit. I admire that. I never had grit. Seth admires that in women. I couldn't let your mother see me at less than my best. Yes, child, it has cost me but it was something I had to do. Give me my medicine and I'll sleep. Why don't you go in to Maggie now. Spend time with your daughter, Billie. Don't make the same mistakes I made. Love her, Billie."

"I will. Swallow this down and I'll be back later to check on you."

"Bless you, child. I think sometimes you're more like my own daughter than a daughter-in-law."

"No one can ever take a daughter's place," Billie said softly. Jessica was already asleep, an unhealthy blue tinge on her lips.

Dinner that evening was strained. Billie ate with her eyes lowered, volunteering nothing to the conversation. She was about to excuse herself to take her dessert and coffee with Jessica, when Seth fixed her with his steely gaze.

"Aggie here tells me *you* think Amelia should be brought home. She tells me you think Jess isn't long for this world. Now where would a slip of a girl like you get an idea like that?"

Billie swallowed past the lump in her throat. "From Jessica," she replied coolly.

Seth grimaced. "I'm the first to admit that Jess looks a mite peaked, but the Grim Reaper's a far piece down the road. I can't be asking my friends for favor upon favor. How is that going to look?"

Billie stood up. "I imagine it's going to look the same way it looked when you sent two longhorn steers to Hawaii for a barbecue to impress some top brass. Excuse me, Mother, Seth."

"You wanted backbone, you just saw backbone. I'd give this some real serious thought, Seth," Agnes said softly. "Some real serious thought."

"Spunk, Aggie. I wanted to see spunk. There's a world of difference between backbone and spunk. Like Rhode Island compared to Texas, if you get what I mean."

Agnes sat up a little straighter in her chair. "I'm afraid, Mr. Coleman, that you're going to have to settle for backbone. Personally, I wouldn't have it any other way." Agnes tossed down her napkin. Seth was reminded of another time when she had done exactly the same thing. He watched her ramrod-straight back exit the dining room.

Tita asked permission to remove his dinner plate. "Fetch me a coffee and a brandy and I'll drink it here at the table," he ordered.

Bring Amelia home, he thought speculatively. Go to the top and ask for another favor. Too soon. Much too soon. Go straight to the Red Cross. Possible. That damn fool doctor hadn't indicated that Jessica was seriously ailing, but the girl sounded so positive. Too damn positive. He felt guilty for a few seconds. He should have spent more time these past weeks with Jess. Up there all alone, of course she would feel badly. Make more of her illness than there was. When you didn't have anything to do with your time but pray for all the sinners of the world, your mind was sure to come up with all kinds of terrible thoughts. Death was so goddamn terrible. It was also inconvenient as hell. For those left behind.

He made a mental note to get a letter off to the Red Cross asking them to help grease the wheels for Amelia. He'd write the damn letter himself. His daughter probably wouldn't even want to come home. All this damn fuss because of that little Yankee gal. All he'd wanted was a little spunk, a little grit, some starch to the girl. Well, he wasn't giving in; he was compromising. It was important that everyone understand that. He'd make damn sure they all understood, and the first person he was going to inform was Moss. He'd write him a long letter this evening. Spell things out a little.

He was in a foul mood now. The girl could do that to him without even trying. Sometimes when he just looked at her he would get angry. He could literally feel his blood pressure shoot up. Times like now. Then he remembered the sounds he and Agnes had heard coming from her room this very morning. His mood lightened and he started to whistle. He called for a cigar and another shot of brandy.

* * *

The moment Billie stepped into the wide front hallway she knew something was different. An unnatural stillness seemed to permeate the very air. She found herself taking a long deep breath and holding it. What? Who? Maggie? Jessica? Never Seth or Agnes.

Billie released her indrawn breath with an explosive sound. *She knew.* She didn't need anyone to tell her Jessica was no longer a member of this earth. She knew.

She put her parcels and packages down on a cowhide-covered bench. There were two new mystery novels and a monstrous sack of licorice for Jessica. Jessica. Billie sat down with a thump on the cowhide seat, unmindful that the packages toppled to the floor. She didn't want to go upstairs. She didn't want to walk into that room where Jessica would be lying. Somebody should be about. Agnes, Seth, Tita... or were they all locked away in their rooms, telling themselves that Jessica just looked a little peaked?

Amelia! Amelia could never get here in time. Moss. Moss might not get the news for days, possibly weeks. The ground would be cold, the rains would come, and it would be all over.

The climb up the wide circular stairway was the longest she could remember. Her grip on the mahogany banister was like a vise that opened and closed. The empty bed, the coverlet and sheet tossed back as though Jessica had gone to the bathroom, brought a wild look to Billie's eyes.

Maggie! Billie's step quickened. But Maggie was lying in her crib gurgling happily. The nurse was knitting in the rocker. Her eyes met Billie's.

"I'm so sorry, Mrs. Coleman. I know how fond you were of the elder Mrs. Coleman. They called me right away but there was nothing anyone could do. It was peaceful and quick. It was Tita who found her. Mr. Coleman was out on the range. Your mother was at a meeting. The doctor has been and gone." Billie nodded miserably. "I don't know if this will give you any consolation, but when I took Maggie in after her noon feeding Mrs. Coleman asked if I would lay the baby in her arms. I was right there. She stared at Maggie for a long time and kept saying over and over that she reminded her of Amelia. Before I took her away, she was calling Maggie Amelia and saying she was sorry. I think she knew she was dying. When her daughter arrives, perhaps you'll want to tell her."

"Yes. Yes, I'll do that. Thank you for telling me. I know

it will mean a lot to Amelia."

Billie leaned over the crib, reached down for a colorful red rattle, and shook it gently. Maggie gurgled and kicked her feet. Billie reached out her arms. "Come to Mama." The nurse watched as Billie picked up her daughter and held her fiercely against her breast. "I'm going to try not to be like Jessica. . . . I don't want to die alone," Billie whispered against the baby's warm, soft head. When the baby started to whimper, Billie kissed her and laid her back in the crib.

"Where are the others, Nurse?"

"Your mother and Mr. Coleman are in the study. Tita and someone from her family are cleaning . . . what I mean is, they're getting . . ."

"I know."

Seth was standing next to the fireplace, in his hand a squat glass filled to the brim with bourbon. Her mother was sitting in Seth's chair. It didn't look right to Billie. She felt they should be doing something.

"Have you tried to reach Amelia?" was Billie's first question. When no one answered she tried again. "What about Moss?"

Seth turned to face Billie. There was a blank look on his face. "Not yet. I decided to wait until the *Enterprise* puts into port somewhere. I don't want him flying missions with . . . Later, he'll be told later. When the time is right."

"Amelia?"

"I wrote a letter to the Red Cross some time ago. I haven't heard."

Billie stiffened from head to toe. "That isn't good enough, Seth. You have to do something now."

"There's nothing to do. She could never get here in time for the funeral even if she left for home yesterday."

"I can't accept that. You have to try. If you won't, then I will."

"Billie, please. Can't you see that Seth . . ."

Billie clenched her hands into rock-hard fists. "Stay out of this, mother. Seth, I'm going to call the Red Cross myself. With or without your permission. You may be right about Moss, but Amelia is different."

"Billie, wait."

"Let her go, Aggie. She won't get very far. If she wants to strangle herself in red tape, let her," Seth said wearily.

"Shouldn't we be calling people, Seth?" Agnes asked hesitantly.

"No. We're going to have a private mass. It will be just us. She'll be buried here at Sunbridge. We'll put a notice in the paper next week."

"If you don't need me, Seth, I think I'll take a walk."

"You go along, Aggie. I'm fine. Tend to that daughter of yours."

It was two o'clock in the morning when the Red Cross returned her call. Billie picked up the receiver on the first ring.

"We found her. Now the problem is getting her on a plane. It's important but not top priority. I have to be honest and tell you I doubt that we can get her there in time, but we're going to do our very best."

"I'm so grateful. We all are. And if there's any other news, will you call me?"

"Of course. We're only too glad to help. I'm sorry we can't do more."

Should she wake Seth and tell him? Billie wondered. No. He wouldn't thank her for disturbing his sleep.

"Billie?" It was a soft whisper.

"Mother! What are you doing up at this hour?"

"I've been sitting in the kitchen waiting for you to get your call. I'm proud of you, Billie. I think it was wonderful of you to stand up to Seth and do what you did. I would like to think you would do the same for me. For the first time, perhaps, I have become aware of my own mortality. Now, why don't you join me in the kitchen for some hot chocolate? I've been keeping it on the back of the stove for you."

"I'd like that, Mother. There's something I want to talk to you about."

"Like back in Philadelphia. I miss those times, Billie."

"You're always so busy, Mother."

"Yes, I know. Sunbridge is so wonderful and heady. Perhaps I adapted too quickly. I'm sorry about Jessica, Billie. Really I am. I know how much you cared for her."

"How is Seth taking this?" Billie asked coolly.

"He was shocked. He is shocked," Agnes corrected herself. "He's had a long and loving life with Jessica and now it's come to an end. I'm sure, Billie, he would have tried to get through to Amelia once the initial shock wore off. He's very concerned about Moss, about not telling him. That's a terrible decision to carry around."

"And he's making me a party to it. How can I write to Moss and not let on? I think it's awful. I understand, but I still think it's awful. Moss *should* be told."

"It does place you in a rather awkward position. I'll speak to Seth later on. As I said, Billie, he's in shock now. He may look at things differently tomorrow."

"I hope so. I won't lie to Moss and I won't evade. My God, Jessica is his mother . . . was his mother. You know what I mean."

"Finish your chocolate and go to bed, Billie. It's late. Tomorrow is going to be very trying."

Agnes sat at the kitchen table for a long time. She drank cup after cup of coffee and it was bitter on her tongue. Billie hadn't yet mentioned a word about her pregnancy. How long did she intend to keep it a secret? By Agnes's best calculations it was already almost three months. The child would be born sometime in February. Agnes blanched. Maggie would celebrate her first birthday in February. This would be physically trying for a healthy woman, one who hadn't had complications during her first pregnancy. Agnes swallowed her coffee as though she were trying to push down her guilt. What was done was done. She hoped Billie would announce her news soon. Seth would feel so much better.

The small private service Seth had arranged for Jessica seemed to include half of Texas. And the other half sent flowers and telegrams and notes of condolence. Answering the door and the telephone kept Billie on the run.

Billie had never really dealt with the finality of death before. Her father and grandparents had died when she was too young to realize what was happening. Jessica had become a second mother to her, a more sympathetic and understanding one than Agnes, and Billie had come to love the woman dearly. She felt the need to creep off somewhere and grieve. Instead, she'd been asked to tend the door and the telephone.

Jessica was laid out in the front parlor in a huge bronze-and-oak casket, dressed in a pale blue lace gown and tiny satin bedroom slippers. Whoever had coiffed her hair had parted it on the wrong side. No one seemed to notice but Billie. Agnes thought the whole idea of having an open casket at home an archaic and heathenish practice. In Philadelphia things were done with a shade more taste. And wasn't that what funeral homes were for?

Jessica was buried on a sunny meadow hillock in the midst of a crowd of strangers. Billie had had no idea a funeral would be such an exhausting experience. The people here had come out of respect for Seth, business acquaintances and friends of his for the most part; the people who'd known and loved Jessica seemed very few. Billie shed her tears and placed a single white rose from Jessica's garden on the casket, whispering prayers through her grief. Poor Jessica. So alone. Moss and Amelia should have been here, Jessica's own children, her own flesh and blood. Even little Maggie should have been here, but the notion had been quickly vetoed by both Agnes and Seth.

Seth stepped forward, his thick gray hair waving aristocratically on his head, hat held respectfully in hand. He leaned on his silver-handled cane, his voice rumbling from deep in his chest. "Jessica Riley Coleman was a fine woman. We're burying her at Sunbridge because this was her home. It's where she belongs. Jess always knew what was expected of her. She was a good wife and a loving mother. She gave me a fine son, the best. And a daughter," he added as an afterthought. "We'll mourn her but we'll never forget her."

It was short, quickly said, and it summed up the total of Jessica's life. Seth put on his broad-brimmed Stetson and led the procession of mourners away from the grave. The Colemans never looked back. What was done was done.

{{{{{{{{{ CHAPTER FIFTEEN }}}}}}}}}

The day after the funeral everything was back on schedule. Jessica wasn't missed at breakfast, of course, because for months she'd been taking most of her meals in her room. Even the living room bore no trace of her last hours there; not a petal from the hundreds of flowers remained.

Agnes sat at the table opening the early mail. Her dark hair was upswept, its severity broken only by a few artistically placed curls over her brow. For the first time Billie noticed the slightest graying near the temples. "Please finish your breakfast, dear," Agnes said distractedly as she opened another letter. "There's so much to do today and I need the table cleared."

"Why do you open all of Seth's mail? Do you even open letters from Moss and see them before I do?"

"What a question, Billie! Of course I don't read Moss's letters. What are you thinking of?"

"Do I see every letter Moss writes Seth?" Billie persisted. "Or only the ones Seth thinks I should see? Why do you insist that I share my letters with him? Doesn't anyone around here think Moss and I are entitled to our privacy?"

Both Agnes and Billie were shocked to hear Seth's voice. "Colemans have no secrets from one another, little gal. Agnes, what's wrong with this youngster of yours? Ever since she's come back from Hawaii she acts like she's got a burr under her saddle."

Agnes's eyes went from Billie to Seth as though trying to communicate something. "Billie feels Jessica's death deeply, Seth. Emotions run high in young mothers."

Before Billie's very eyes Seth's anger abated and his pomposity seemed to deflate. "That's all right, gal," he said forgivingly.

Billie bristled. Why should *she* be forgiven? She'd done nothing except ask a few direct questions.

"What are your plans for the day, dear?" Agnes was asking, busy again with the mail, sorting business letters from notes of condolence.

"Oh, I thought I'd go into town. You won't be needing the car, will you, Mother? There're a few things I thought I'd look at in Balden's Department Store."

It was on the tip of Agnes's tongue to argue that it was improper to be seen window-shopping the very day after burying a family member, but her eyes slid to Billie and she held her tongue. Billie was lying or, at the least, not telling the complete truth. Agnes knew her daughter very well indeed. "How late do you think you'll be? Planning on having lunch in town? Perhaps you'd like me to come with you?"

"No, I'll probably be home for lunch. You've already said you've so much to do today, I don't want to bite into your time, Mother."

So, Agnes thought with satisfaction as she slit another envelope, Billie was going into town for nothing in particular.

She'd be home in time for lunch at one o'clock and she didn't want anyone with her. Agnes's heart was thumping. Billie was going to see Dr. Ward.

Less than an hour later, just after the car left the portico, Agnes whipped up the phone receiver and dialed Dr. Ward's number. "Hello, this is Mrs. Ames. Can you tell me what time my daughter's appointment is? I seem to have forgotten. . . . Yes, Mrs. Moss Coleman. I think she mentioned an appointment. . . . Ten o'clock? . . . No, that will be quite all right. I simply wanted to know if I should expect her home for lunch."

Dr. Ward's receptionist looked up and smiled when Billie entered the office. Mrs. Moss Coleman certainly dressed up the office in her crisp lemon-yellow dress and sparkling spectator pumps. Quite a difference from the young girl who had first visited the doctor in a loose-fitting cotton jumper and flat heels. Mrs. Coleman had developed her own style, one that would take thousands of dollars to imitate. The receptionist sighed. Some women had all the luck!

Billie was nervous and out of sorts. She knew she was pregnant. This trip would only confirm it.

After the examination she joined Dr. Ward in his office and faced his concern. "I'm disappointed, Billie. I really didn't want you to get pregnant again so quickly, if at all. I feel remiss in not emphasizing this sufficiently after Maggie was born. It isn't good, Billie, and I feel we should talk about a clinical abortion. You're endangering your health."

All of a sudden he was calling her Billie. Did all doctors assume a familiarity when they had bad news to deliver? "Are you trying to frighten me? Surely you aren't serious."

"I'm quite serious. Listen carefully. You didn't carry Maggie to full term because you became toxic. Toxemia. She was a breech birth and you had a very difficult time of it. The birth left you with a prolapsed uterus and it's quite likely you won't carry this child past the fifth month. Miscarriages are dangerous. Very dangerous. The possibilities for infection and childbirth fever are quite high and I don't think I would be serving your best interests if I didn't advise a clinical abortion."

"If I'm careful and don't gain too much weight and stay off my feet—would that help?" Her lower lip was quivering and her fingers played with a stray thread on her glove.

Adam Ward's heart went out to Billie. It was such a difficult decision. Her husband was fighting a war and her father-in-law was exerting tremendous pressure for a Coleman heir. She was playing out of her league. He himself was mighty sick of Seth Coleman's demands. If he weren't the head of gynecology and obstetrics at Memorial Hospital and more than aware that the Coleman patriarch could just as easily donate his money to other institutions, he never would have put himself under the old man's thumb. A single tear slipped down Billie's cheek and Adam Ward was tempted to lean over and wipe it away. She was so young and inexperienced, despite this new gloss of sophistication.

"Billie, you're facing a difficult decision. But it's against my best advice to continue this pregnancy. Don't let personal issues or religion enter. We're talking about your life. You have a husband and a daughter to consider. Let me call in a consulting doctor. You'll feel better and so will I."

"That's not necessary. I trust your opinion. But, as you say, in the end it's my decision only. I have to think—this isn't something I can answer right now."

"You can't wait too long, Billie. Another three weeks and that's it."

"I have to think! Don't push me! I can't think straight right now. I have Jessica on my mind, Maggie is cutting a tooth, and I haven't heard from Moss in almost a month. How could I keep something like this from Moss? I couldn't. I want to know how he feels. And Seth would never forgive me. I have to think! I have to think!"

"Billie, I want to remind you that this matter would be strictly between you and me. I won't discuss this with anyone, not even your father-in-law. *Especially* not your father-in-law."

"I understand, and I thank you. . . . I haven't mentioned this pregnancy myself." She looked up at him with gratitude and now it seemed perfectly acceptable that he call her Billie. He understood and right now it was so important to have someone in whom she could confide.

Settled in the back of the Coleman limousine, Billie watched the countryside flash past. Abortion. The word lay heavy on her mind . . . a vague, shadowy image of dark hallways and mortal sin gleaned from whispered conversations. Abortion. Hesitantly her hand went to her stomach, where another life grew. This little life that beat within her was not an unreal mystery, as Maggie had been before she was born. The same force that had created Maggie had created this little one, and Billie could already imagine the child in her arms and the

{ 232 }

sweetness she would find when she nuzzled its cheek. This unborn had a face very similar to that of the child she'd already birthed. To abort it, to kill this child, would be like killing Maggie.

She'd almost decided against the abortion when other arguments flooded her thoughts. According to the doctor there was every chance she would miscarry—and her own life would be at risk. Fear reached out with clutching fingers. She'd never considered her own death, never thought it a possibility. When death finally came it wouldn't be for *her*, but for the old woman she would become, a person so far removed from her that she could face that thought without fear and emotion. At least she always could before now. She wanted to *live*, for Moss, for Maggie, for herself. She wouldn't be robbed of what was rightfully hers! Years with Moss, years of watching Maggie grow. Yet as she thought again of abortion, she imagined she heard the cry of her unborn child.

Sunbridge was coming into view and Carlos stopped the Packard beneath the portico. Billie leaped out and ran for the door. She didn't stop until she'd climbed the stairs and burst through the nursery door. Even the stern Miss Jenkins didn't protest when Billie lifted the sleeping Maggie from her crib and cradled her to her breast.

"Seth, I'd like to talk to you," Billie said firmly.

"Talk away," Seth said gruffly as he pored over his open ledger. Billie knew it was a ploy. Agnes handled the books.

"Are you going to call the Red Cross so they can get word to Moss about his mother's death?" There, she couldn't be more blunt. It was out in the open.

"In good time. I don't want Moss endangered. When he gets into port."

"I'm sorry, Seth. I don't agree. I will not be a party to this deception. If Moss is man enough to fight a war, he's certainly man enough to handle his mother's death. And he will handle it. You cannot keep this from him. I doubt that he would forgive you. I can't write to him and not mention it—what will he think of me?"

"That's not important."

"Well, I think it's very important. You're asking me to lie to my husband. I won't do it."

Seth swiveled around in his leather chair. He wrapped his burly arms behind his head and fixed his gaze on his son's wife. "You don't know the boy the way I know him."

"Moss is no longer a boy. He's a man and my husband. I insist," Billie said coldly.

"Insist all you want, little gal, but my decision stands. Moss could do any damn fool thing. His timing could be off. Anything." His voice sounded desperate to Billie and she pressed her advantage.

"You're going to look rather foolish, then. I sent a telegram to the Red Cross an hour ago. I want you to trust me when I tell you Moss will handle this. I know my husband."

"You went ahead after I expressly told you not to do anything?" Seth bellowed.

Billie's heart pumped furiously. He wouldn't intimidate her. He would not. She owed Jessica that much. "Yes, damn it, I did. I'd do it again, too."

"By God, if you weren't Moss's wife, I'd boot your tail out of here."

"Don't let that stop you. I can be packed and out of here in less than an hour. Decide now, Seth."

"You had no right."

"I had every right. I'm his wife."

"I'm not going to forget this."

"I plan to forget it. It's done. It's past. We have to go on from here. How we do it is up to you."

"Where you getting all this grit lately, little gal?"

"From you," Billie said shortly. "It rubs off. I can't say that I like it entirely. How about you?"

Seth snorted. "Go on, leave me to my misery. See if you can't stir up some other trouble to torment me. I'm an old man. Leave me be." Seth sounded downright pitiful.

"A *cantankerous* old man," Billie said.

"Out!" Seth thundered.

Billie was achingly alert for any return word from Moss. Every time the phone rang her heart leaped. She believed she had been right to send news of Jessica's death, but Seth's fears had become her own. What if Moss's grief for his mother clouded his thinking, dimmed his reflexes? What if . . . What if . . .

At the dinner table Seth pointedly ignored Billie's presence, directing his conversation, if any, completely to Agnes. Watching from beneath lowered lids, Billie was amazed to notice how fidgety her mother was.

Over coffee and dessert, Agnes looped her precious rope of pearls around her thin fingers and blurted, "I received a telegram from New York this afternoon, Seth. It was from your daughter. She's arriving in Austin tomorrow morning and asked that the car be sent to the airport."

Seth's coffee cup clattered in its saucer and he threw his napkin onto the table. "Her mother's gone and buried! What the hell good does she think coming to Sunbridge will do? She ran off and left her mother and now she comes crawling back."

"Seth, please try to be reasonable," Agnes said. "What could I do? You weren't here. I couldn't take it upon myself to cable New York and discourage your daughter from coming to Sunbridge. You couldn't be reached. I didn't know what to do. . . ."

"I'm not blaming you, Aggie. It's that damn fool girl. She's been a thorn in my side since the day she was born and I sure as hell don't need her here now! I suppose she's coming with that husband of hers."

"There was no mention. But I don't imagine a British officer could have gotten enough leave during wartime to come to the States."

"Well, what the hell did she say, Aggie? Where's that telegram?"

"It was read to me over the phone, Seth. It simply said she was in New York, had managed to secure a flight to Austin, and asked for the car to meet her at the airport."

Seth stood up from the table, leaning heavily on his cane. "I can tell you this, Aggie. I never wanted to lay eyes on that girl again! She's been willful her entire life, getting herself into one scrape after another! When she lived at home I teetered on the edge of embarrassment because I never knew what she'd do next. Whatever it was she did, I knew I wasn't going to like it. And I don't like this! Why the hell can't she just stay away? I'm too old and too damn tired to put up with her pranks."

"Seth, she's a married woman with a young son—"

"That's not her son! That boy belongs to some limey! She didn't even have the sense to marry an American, for God's sake. That boy's not of my flesh and he's not of hers, either." With that closing statement, he left the dining room.

"I can't believe this," Billie gasped. "Amelia is his own daughter. And you, Mother, you defended yourself. Not Amelia! How could you be so cruel? Did you actually consider sending her a cable telling her to say away?"

Agnes's eyes glittered and her mouth formed a bitter line.

"I certainly did consider it and if I'd thought it wouldn't backfire on me, I would have. What you don't seem to understand, Billie, is that not *all* fathers love their children, at least not all of their children. Amelia has been a great disappointment to Seth and he can't find it in his heart to forgive her. And Seth's relationship with his daughter is none of our concern. Sometimes, Billie, you can be quite stupid, and you fail to remember where your bread is buttered."

"And just what does that mean?"

"Simply said, dear, I am concerned about Amelia coming home because Seth is quite vulnerable now since Jessica's death; a reconciliation between him and his daughter could have devastating results on your position here at Sunbridge, should anything happen to Moss. Never forget for one moment that blood is thicker than water. Even Maggie could quite easily be discarded if Amelia should ever have a son of her own. There's a lot at stake, Billie, and I wish you'd stop being so naive."

Billie sat back in her chair feeling as though the wind had been kicked out of her. "I never knew you to be so crafty and calculating, Mother. I never knew. . . ."

"What you never knew," Agnes said coldly, "was how I scraped and scratched to give you a good life, to put you on a level where a daughter of mine belonged. Just how far did you think your father's insurance policy and the little bit your grandmother left would go? And that house—you never knew there was a second mortgage on it, did you? And when you were about to go off to college, where did you think the tuition was coming from? From me, Billie, from me! I was prepared to go to work to pay for your education and you call me cruel? No, dear, you are the one who is cruel, taking all I ever had to give with never a thought for me. This is our one chance at security, Billie, and if you're too stupid to see it, I'm not!"

The next afternoon Billie watched for the limousine. Seth and Agnes had left the house, and Billie was determined that Amelia would receive the welcome to Sunbridge she deserved as Jessica's daughter.

The sound of tires on the cinder drive brought Billie once again to the window. Carlos brought the limo to a halt and sprinted around to the other side to open the back door. A tall, slim young woman with hair as dark as Moss's stepped out. She was wearing a travel-rumpled suit in somber grays and black. Amelia stood for a long moment staring at the double front door with a strange expression on her face, as if she expected it to fly open and reveal a fire-breathing dragon. A dragon, Billie thought, that would be carrying a silver-handled cane.

Amelia then looked up to Jessica's window. Her shoulders slumped beneath an invisible weight. It was only when a little boy hardly three years old came to her side that she smiled.

Billie opened the door and wrapped the trembling, fine-boned young woman in her arms, crooning words of sympathy, much as Jessica had embraced her that first morning at the Austin train station.

The child clung to Amelia's skirt, blond hair ruffling over his worried brow, coffee-bean eyes gleaming. "Rand, darling, this is your aunt Billie." Amelia dried her eyes and lifted the boy in her arms. "He's so tired, poor darling. It was such an exhausting trip, but I couldn't leave him in England with any peace of mind. Things are hell over there. It isn't even safe in the country outside London."

"Why don't we take Rand up to the nursery and settle him in? A nice warm bath, something to eat, and a nap is all he needs. He's a beautiful child, Amelia."

"Yes, he is. The image of Geoffrey."

Nurse Jenkins welcomed Amelia home. "Rand is my son, Miss Jenkins. There was an edge of defiance to Amelia's voice, as though she were well prepared to face opposition.

Rand tugged his mother's skirt until he was allowed to peek into the crib at little Maggie, who was sleeping peacefully and sucking her thumb.

"She's a beautiful baby, Billie," Amelia said. "With that dark hair there's no doubt she's a Coleman. She's the picture of Moss, isn't she?"

"That's one of the reasons I love her so much." Billie beamed. "Why don't we see if Rand will stay with me so you can go freshen up? Carlos is taking your luggage up to your old room and I suppose Rand can sleep in the nursery with Maggie."

Amelia's shoulders squared. "Rand will sleep in my room. There's been enough of separating the children from their parents in this house."

"Whatever you say, Amelia. Of course Rand will stay in with you," Billie said reassuringly. "After all, this is your home. You can do as you like."

Amelia took Billie's suggestion and left Rand with her while she went to freshen up. A tub was run while the little boy explored the nursery, investigating Maggie's collection of stuffed animals and issuing a cry of delight when he spied a jack-in-the-box on the shelf. "Mine! Mine!"

"No, that's not yours, young man," Miss Jenkins corrected. "That belongs to Margaret!"

"He must have one like it. Get it down for him, won't you? It reminds him of home."

"Mrs. Coleman, it isn't wise to spoil a child with everything he wants. If I'm to care for him, he must learn from the beginning what he may and may not have."

"You're not caring for him, Miss Jenkins. Rand will be staying with his mother during their visit. Now give him the jack-in-the-box and then get some fresh towels for his bath."

"Staying with his mother! Isn't that just like her to come and upset the household. I was nurse to both your husband and his sister. There was a selfish streak in her then and it's still there, I can see."

"Or is it you never quite gave Amelia the attention and care you gave Moss, because he, and not she, was the apple of Seth Coleman's eye? Now go get the towels."

Miss Jenkins sputtered away while Billie played with Rand as she got him ready for his bath. "You certainly know what you want, don't you?" Billie said, laughing as he reached for the toy, refusing to be separated from it.

"Listen," he said as he turned the crank to work the music box. Slowly, he worked toward the end of the song. "All around the mulberry bush . . . the monkey thought it all in fun—now watch, Aunt Billie," he said, holding up the box. "*Pop* goes the weasel!" Billie pretended to be surprised and laughed along with the child. He was a delight and his precise British accent, so like Amelia's—though she may have been born in Texas—pleased her. When Miss Jenkins returned with the towels, he splashed water at her and made a funny face. Amelia certainly had her hands full with young Master Nelson, but already he was like a ray of sunshine in the house.

An hour later little Rand Nelson had been fed and nestled down in Amelia's room for a nap. Billie sat with him until he closed his eyes and then she tiptoed quietly out of the room. She'd expected Amelia to come back and tend to her son. Where was she?

Billie found her sister-in-law sitting in Jessica's darkened bedroom. The draperies were drawn but a slim shaft of light slipped between their folds. "Amelia? What are you doing sitting in the dark? Rand is sound asleep."

"He's a wonder, isn't he, Billie? So like his father. Mother would have loved him—" Her voice broke off in a choked sob and she sank down on the edge of Jessica's bed.

"Oh, Amelia, I'm so sorry," Billie said, going to offer comfort. But Amelia's hands went up in immediate defense.

"No, no, don't touch me. I couldn't bear it. I'm afraid I'll fall apart at the first gesture of sympathy. I'm really a crybaby, you know."

"Anyone would cry. You've just lost your mother, your husband is still in England fighting a war. . . . You've got every right to cry," Billie said softly.

"Geoffrey was shot down over France last month," Amelia said through her sobs. "They saw his plane go down. It burst into flames. . . . He didn't have a chance."

Amelia's announcement was like a physical blow to Billie. She, too, was married to a pilot; she, too, had a husband fighting a war.

The women wept together, then Amelia stood up and moved across the room, taking Billie's now cold hand. "Don't worry about Moss. He's got the luck of the Colemans going for him. He'll come back to you safe and sound. You wait and see."

"You're a Coleman and you haven't been that lucky." Billie had thought about death, the danger of flying, the hell of fighting a war, but it had always seemed one step removed from her and Moss.

"I'm not *all* Coleman, not the way Moss is. Come downstairs with me. I think we both need a drink. At least I do. The hell with taking a bath. I'll do that later. Right now, I need to talk. What do you say?"

"Well have the study to ourselves; your father is out somewhere. He doesn't spend much time at home since your mother died. I think it's his way of dealing with his grief."

"You think so, do you?" Amelia led the way downstairs. "I would say you're being quite generous, Billie. I'm sure the old man won't mind if I tipple a little of his bourbon. At least not any more than he minds anything else I do." She forced a smile.

Amelia and Billie sat in the dim cool of Seth's study for almost three hours, talking and sipping highballs. Two young women with common loves, Jessica and Moss, became friends.

"I loved him so much, my Geoff," Amelia was saying. "He was everything to me . . . friend, lover, husband. In many ways he made up for my being separated from Moss. And in more ways than I care to admit, he gave me the love and attention I never had from my father. Now he's gone and there's only Rand and me. I think the day I fully realized how much Geoff loved me was when he asked if I would adopt his son. That boy meant the world to him."

"Did Geoff have family left in England?"

"Oh, yes, quite a tightly knit family, in fact. So naturally, I'm the outsider now, except for Rand. Geoff was the oldest son, and he inherited the title and land, a very healthy estate, even by Texas standards. Now it all belongs to Rand." She laughed bitterly. "Can you imagine, that little boy up there is officially known as Lord Randolph Jamison Nelson, Earl of Wickham. Rand's net worth would make even my father squint. Of course, and thankfully, the estate is entirely in the hands of the family solicitors. I unabashedly admit I've no head for figures. Further proof I'm not a true Coleman."

"Then you won't be able to stay on in America, will you? Not if Rand has a heritage and tradition to return to."

"Thank God, no. We'll return to England in a few weeks, if the war permits. It was hell getting over here in the first place. Lord only knows how or when we'll get back, but get there we will." Her blue eyes, so like Moss's, flashed with confidence.

"When I heard you were coming back to Sunbridge I thought you wanted to mourn for a while, where memories of your mother are the strongest."

"You are only partly right," Amelia said quietly before she drained her glass. "Actually, I came back to get an abortion."

Billie was uncertain that she'd heard correctly. "An . . . an abortion? I . . . I don't understand. Why, when you've just told me how much you loved Geoffrey? How could you think of destroying his child?"

"It's the only way. I have Rand to consider. Billie, the responsibility of raising Rand on my own is overwhelming. Rand is Geoff's child, the child he entrusted to me, and if I'm to keep him, I'll have to fight tooth and nail. Geoff's family is taking legal action for custody of Rand. I can't allow that to happen. Rand is my son, not legally yet, but where money and influence play a part, I won't stand a chance. That's a little lesson I learned at my father's knee. Those who have, get.

Those who don't, get the shaft.

"I can't be strong and take on the vultures if I'm burdened with a pregnancy and another child. I'd be too vulnerable, too weak. Geoff loved me, he entrusted Rand to me, and I won't betray that trust."

She lifted her gaze and looked directly at Billie. "You're not saying anything, Billie; I've shocked you, haven't I? Are you all right? You look a little pale."

"No, no, I'm fine—at least I think I am. Amelia," she blurted, "I'm pregnant, too, and the doctor wants me to have a clinical abortion." Quickly, Billie told of her last visit to Adam Ward.

"You haven't said anything to Pap, have you? You already know by now that the sun rises and sets on Moss as far as he's concerned. I hate to say it, Billie, but my father would gladly risk your health and life if it meant he would have a grandson. It's all he's talked about since Moss was old enough to marry."

"I know. Even little Maggie doesn't count for anything."

"How well I know. And I suppose he had quite a lot to say about my coming home with Rand." Billie's embarrassed flush told Amelia all she needed to know. "Have you decided what you're going to do?"

"No. I suppose I'm feeling guilty because I really don't want to go through another pregnancy—not now, anyway. Also, as the doctor said, I could lose this baby without doing anything at all. It's risky." Billie's anguish was evident. "If anything should ever happen to Moss and I had gone through with the abortion, I'd never forgive myself. I don't know what to do."

This time Amelia comforted Billie. She wrapped her arms around her. "You'll do what you have to do, Billie. You'll think it out and come to a decision and it'll be *your* decision. I'll be here for you, but I promise I won't try to sway you one way or the other."

Seth's angry voice suddenly filled the room. "You gals having a sorority meeting in my study? And helping yourselves to my best bourbon, I see. You've got a whole house to your-selves—this room is off limits!"

"Hello, Pap, it's nice to know you're glad to see me. Still your lovable old self, I see. It's delightful to be welcomed back to home and hearth."

"Don't you go getting snotty with me, daughter. You don't have your mother around to cover for you anymore," he growled.

"Pour me one of those. Just how long do you intend to stay?"

"As long as I have to, Pap," Amelia said, lifting the bourbon bottle. "Three fingers or four?"

"Three, for starters. Christ, you look like something the cat dragged in. Don't tell me that's the latest style in London."

"Oh, you mean my clothes. No, they're not the latest style, but then widow's weeds were made for utility, not fashion."

Seth took a drink, walked around to the chair behind his desk, and sat down heavily. "That fool pilot you married bought it, did he? How's he listed? Killed in action or only missing?"

"Killed. His wingman saw him go down. It was over France."

"I hope he left you well off. The day you married that limey my responsibility to you was over. Jess left you a tidy sum. If you ever get your hands on it, that is."

"I didn't come home for what Mam left me and you know it, Pap. Any lawyer can make sure I get what's coming to me."

"Only God himself can see you get what's coming to you, Amelia. I can't say I'm glad you've come back, because I'm not and I won't be a hypocrite. I can feel my stomach going sour already. What'd you do with that stepson of yours? Left him where he belongs, I hope."

"Rand is upstairs in my room taking a nap. Which reminds me, I should go up and look in on him.

"Poor little tyke, he's really done in," she said to Billie, who was watching this confrontation with amazement.

"Amelia!" Seth called just as she was about to step through the door. "It's just as well your husband was killed. He spared you the humiliation of having him walk out on you!"

For an instant Billie thought Amelia would crumple to the floor and fragment into a thousand pieces. But she caught at the door frame and steadied herself. "You should know, Pap. Didn't Mother do you the same favor?" And then she was gone, leaving Billie to stare in shock, her heart thumping madly in her breast. When she again dared to glance at Seth, she found him smiling and unruffled. He took a sip of his drink.

"What are you looking at, little gal? I can see you're shocked by this little scene you just witnessed. You shouldn't be. You knew there was no love lost between Amelia and me. Now that Jess is gone, so's the pretense. We don't even have to be nice to each other for her sake.

"Which reminds me, little gal, I can't help wondering what Amelia's limey was thinking about when he let himself get shot down. Problems at home? Responsibilities? Bad news?

I'm warning you, if anything happens to my boy because you sent word of Jessica's death, you'll be the sorriest person alive. You'll think what you just saw between my daughter and me was a family picnic. Understand? I don't cotton to being crossed. I don't care who it is. And you, little gal, would be nobody if anything happened to Moss."

{{{{{{{{{ CHAPTER SIXTEEN }}}}}}}}}

Agnes, taking her cue from Seth, practically ignored Amelia's presence, but Billie could see that her mother was impressed with the Nelson family title. "If your husband was a lord, doesn't that make you a lady?" Agnes asked innocently.

"Ask my father, Mrs. Ames; he'll tell you he doubts anything in this world could make me a lady."

Agnes pretended not to hear her and looked at young Rand just as he dropped a forkful of peas onto his lap. "Really, Amelia, must that child eat at the table with us? He's far too young to have proper manners."

"When Maggie is three years old I intend to bring her to the table for informal family dinners," Billie said. "Really, Mother, one would think we never lived in Philadelphia and ate at the kitchen table every night, except for Sundays if we had company. Would you really like to consign Rand to eating dinner every night with old sourpuss Jenkins?"

"Supper!" Seth corrected. "Here in Texas, dinner is served at noon and anytime you eat after that it's supper."

"Well, supper, then. Besides, the way people carry on here Rand is a welcome relief at the table."

"None of my doing," Seth protested. "Look here, gal, you're not picking up that tone of voice from Amelia, are you? Moss wouldn't like it. I can tell you that. My boy never liked an ox in a ditch."

At Billie's questioning glance, Amelia explained. "That's Texan for trouble, Billie."

Agnes fidgeted with her rope of pearls. She wished Amelia

{ 243 }

would go back to England, and quickly. She didn't like having Seth so upset and ornery all the time. It made him difficult and, worse, suspicious of everyone and everything. She had to watch her attitude toward his daughter. To be too friendly and accepting would turn Seth against her, but to be too indifferent might arouse his family loyalty. She wished she knew when Billie was going to announce her pregnancy. What was she waiting for? Did she want to tell Moss first and wait for his response?

"Billie, dear," asked Agnes, "could you give me Dr. Ward's phone number? I thought I'd make an appointment with him."

"It's in the phone book beside the phone, Mother," Billie answered, pushing food around on her plate. Instinctively, she knew it wasn't the response Agnes wanted.

"Yes, of course, how silly of me."

"Something wrong with you, Aggie?" Seth looked concerned.

"No, it's nothing. I just thought I'd have a checkup. Have you seen Dr. Ward lately, Billie? Isn't it time? Maggie is nearly six months old now and I know Dr. Ward takes a special interest in you."

"'Specially since the Colemans built him that fancy new wing at the hospital," Seth interjected.

"Yes, Seth, especially. Well, have you, Billie?" Agnes waited, watching her daughter, watching for the lie, praying for the truth.

"As a matter of fact, I have seen him. Everything is fine."

Agnes's hands nervously played with her pearls. Not a lie, but not the truth, either.

"Billie, I'm going into town tomorrow afternoon. Care to come with me?" Amelia stepped in. Agnes was like a vulture about to pick bones. The woman had taken Jessica's place, running the house at Sunbridge as though it were her own, as thought it were her right.

"Yes, I'd like that. I haven't been in since you came. We could go shopping. Will we take Rand with us?"

"No, not this time. I'll leave him with Miss Jenkins."

At the sound of the nurse's name, Rand dropped his fork onto his plate and roared.

"That's Rand's interpretation of Miss Jenkins—a real dragon," said Billie. "Right, Rand?"

"Sourpuss!" Rand said and laughed, tossing his bright blond head.

"You'll stay with Miss Jenkins when Aunt Billie and I go into town, won't you? That's a good boy. Mum'll bring you something nice."

Rand nodded his head. "Maggie, too. Maggie cries a lot, Mum. Bring Maggie a present."

Amelia and Billie laughed, but Agnes shook her head in disapproval. "That's hardly teaching the child proper manners. Sourpuss indeed! That's quite disrespectful. You should be careful, Billie, that it doesn't rub off on Maggie."

"Oh, Rand gets on with Miss Jenkins well enough, Mrs. Ames. It's just that he calls them the way he sees them. Even Pap would approve of that!" Amelia leaned over and kissed Rand's cheek, her sleek dark hair in dramatic contrast with his towhead curls. "Drink your milk, Rand darling, then Aunt Billie and I will take you upstairs so we can decide what we're going to do tomorrow and what kind of nice present we can bring for you and Maggie."

Upstairs in Billie's room, Amelia reclined on the chaise longue and sipped coffee from the cup she'd brought up. Rand was occupied in the nursery with Maggie. "I was serious about going into Austin tomorrow, Billie. I hope you will come with me."

"Love to. They should be showing some of the new fall clothes now and I thought I'd like to shop for some wools. It's been so long since I've sat at a sewing machine and I find I miss it. Your mother always told me I was welcome to use hers."

"I'm not going in to shop, Billie," Amelia said ominously. The gaze she directed at Billie was unflinchingly severe. "I've made contact with a few people I used to know and the arrangements have all been made for the abortion. We'll have Carlos take us into Austin and from there we'll use a taxi. My mind's made up and I'm going through with it. It's the only answer, for me and for Rand."

"Amelia, surely there are other considerations, other solutions. . . ."

"No, there are not! I received a cable from New York this afternoon. From a lawyer hired by Geoff's brothers. They're threatening legal action because I took Rand out of England."

"But he's your son! You have a right to take him anywhere you want!"

"Yes, he's my son in my heart, but the adoption hadn't gone through before Geoff was killed. I'm going to have a fight on my hands. I'd already contacted a lawyer in London. His best advice was to stay here at Sunbridge, or at least in Texas, for as long as I can. With the war in Europe and bad communication between here and there, it's the only way to delay action. I can't lose him, Billie, I just can't! I love him so much. Every time I look at him I see Geoff. And I promised, I swore before God and Geoff that I would always be here for Rand and I won't go back on that now.

"Geoff hadn't had the happiest of childhoods, despite the advantages of wealth and title." She laughed. "Geoff said I was Rand's hope of growing up happy and normal. Me! Amelia 'Never Does Anything Right' Coleman Nelson, a young boy's salvation. I'd sacrifice anything, Billie, to live up to the promise I made to Geoff. Please, help me."

The soft light from the lamp cast half of Amelia's face into shadow. Her shining cap of dark hair was sleekly molded to her head and knotted at the nape of her neck. The style lent her a severity that made her plea all the more poignant. Billie didn't want to help. It was contradictory to all her beliefs, and yet she herself was being forced to face the issue.

"You're backing off from me, Billie. I can see your principles are offended. Forget I asked. Forget I even told you anything about it. No hard feelings, just look after Rand while I'm gone tomorrow."

"Where are you going? Who's the doctor?"

Amelia's laughter was almost a shriek. "Billie, surely you can't be serious. Abortion is illegal, or did you forget? No doctor—no good doctor, anyway—would touch me. This is a connection I made through some not very respectable friends I used to have. Only clinical abortions, like the one Dr. Ward wants you to have, are performed in sterile hospitals."

Visions darker than creeping black cats walked through Billie's imagination. Stories of back alleys and butcher knives and knitting needles, stories whispered in the back of the girls' gym at school. "Amelia! You can't. It isn't safe!"

"I can and I will. Just you watch me." Her hand went to her middle, patting her stomach. "You know what's in here, Billie? A dream. That's all it is, a dream. But it's not for me and I want to forget it before it becomes a nightmare. Do you know how frightened I am? I'm scared to death of letting Geoff down. I've never done anything right in my entire life except love Geoff and Rand. I'm really quite selfish, you know. Very selfish. Ask anyone who knows me. Ask my father.

"I must do this. I want to do this!"

"I'll come with you," said Billie. "You need someone. I don't like it, I admit, but if you need me, I'm here. Moss wouldn't have it any other way. I won't sit in judgment of you, Amelia. I simply want to be your friend."

"Oh, Billie!" Amelia cried, clasping Billie's hands. "You are my friend. You're more. You're my sister!"

The next afternoon Billie and Amelia drove into Austin. They gave Carlos instructions to meet them at five o'clock in front of the Coleman Building, then waited until he pulled away before hailing a cab. Amelia sat stiff and silent in the backseat while Billie gave the address to the driver.

"You sure that's the address, miss?" the driver said, chewing on a cigar stub. "You don't look like the kind of ladies to go into that neighborhood."

"That's the address," Billie answered, her tone barring further comment. Amelia sat beside her, staring straight ahead, her cold pale hands clutched in her lap.

When the taxi came to a halt, Billie looked doubtfully out at the sleazy honky-tonks and littered sidewalks. "This is the place," Amelia said tonelessly. They paid the fare and stepped out.

"You want I should wait for you?"

"No, driver, thank you," Billie said, glancing around nervously. Men loitered on street corners; loud music with a Mexican flavor blared from the Loco Saloon; ragged children and hollow-eyed women walked aimlessly down the street. "Amelia, are you sure you have the right address?"

"This is it," she said, looking at a ramshackle doorway. "Let's get this the hell over with. Come on."

Billie had never been in such a place. The dark hallway smelled of burned garlic, mustiness, and garbage. Radios, each tuned to a different station, created a muffled cacophony. On the third floor, Amelia rapped sharply on a scarred door.

The door opened a crack and a pair of snapping dark eyes peered out suspiciously. When Amelia extended a crisp hundred-dollar bill, the door opened to admit them. A man in a dirty white shirt that strained across his vast belly called out in Spanish. A woman stepped into the room. Billie heard the locks being snapped behind her and knew a sense of panic.

"This is my friend," Amelia was explaining. "She's here to see I get home."

The woman shook her head and grumbled something to the man. "You were to come alone," he growled.

"No one said anything about coming alone. I need my friend with me."

The woman began sputtering and the man shouted at her. "You have all the money?" he said to Amelia. "Two hundred dollars?"

"Yes. My friend will give you the other hundred when everything is over."

"Your friend will wait here."

"No. She comes with me. Or I go somewhere else."

Again the woman began chattering. "*Silencio!*" the man raged. Billie was feeling weak-kneed and her hands were icy, despite the warm day.

"Okay. Go in there with Maria. She take care of everything. First I see the money."

"Show him the money," Amelia instructed. "Dammit, Billie, do what I say! Show him the money!"

Billie fumbled with her purse, extracting the bill and showing it to the man, who appeared satisfied. She replaced it in the zippered compartment quickly, as though it were burning her fingers.

Maria stepped aside to allow them into the adjoining room. It was empty except for a kitchen table and a single chair. Just beyond, Billie could see a filthy toilet. Newspapers covered the long windows that faced the back of the building. Voices shouted at one another from the other side of the wall. Maria was wearing an apron made of oilcloth. It was the same pattern that had once covered the Ameses' kitchen table in Philadelphia. A jumble of impressions penetrated her awareness like short punches to the brain.

She could feel Amelia's cold trembling hand in her own as she stood beside the table on which Amelia was lying, legs spread, teeth biting into her lips to keep from crying out. Maria was working between her legs. The pattern of her oilcloth apron swam before Billie's eyes, making her stomach heave. Suddenly there was the smell of blood and the sound of something dropping and spattering into the chipped enamel dishpan on the floor near Maria's feet. Billie's eyes reluctantly lowered to the floor. Dark red clots of blood and tissue swam in the pan. It was done. The small nebulous life Amelia had carried had been scraped and torn from her womb.

The cracked and filthy floor threatened to rise up and engulf

Billie. It had been so quick, so callously done. She felt as though her own insides had been ripped. There was a burning at her center, demanding she turn her focus inward. The small life that clung there could not survive without her. It could be torn from its haven and discarded just as easily as the contents of Maria's dishpan. That it would occur in a sterile operating room and she would be anesthetized made no difference. She was a mother and it was her child, and without her it would never breathe or cry or be hungry.

Billie had come to her decision. Her unborn child's life would depend on God, not the surgeon's knife.

Amelia's hands gripped hers, her teeth were chattering, and tears rivered down her cheeks. "Billie! Billie! God, what have I done!"

Later that night, after Billie had visited to the nursery to kiss Maggie good night, she stopped by Amelia's room.

"Amelia?" Billie whispered into the darkened room. "Are you sleeping?" She moved quietly across the carpet to the bed, careful not to disturb Rand, who was asleep in the little trundle bed on the far side of the room. "Amelia!"

"Billie. Billie, I'm so sick."

She touched Amelia's forehead. "You're burning up!"

"And I'm bleeding. Badly."

Billie clicked on the bedside lamp. Amelia was pale and white-lipped. "I'm calling Dr. Ward—"

"Billie, no! You can't. . . ."

"What will we do? You're sick!"

"It'll pass, I promise, it'll pass."

"No. No, it won't. Something went wrong this afternoon." She lifted the bedcovers and pulled at Amelia's nightgown. A spreading red stain darkened the pink cotton. "You are bleeding, worse than you probably know. I'm calling the doctor. . . ."

Amelia's hand gripped her wrist. "You can't. You can't! I can't let anyone know. I can't take that chance! I've got Rand to think of. . . . Geoff's family would use this against me if they knew. And Pap is just mean enough to tell them if he thought it would hurt me."

"Seth's a mean old codger, but he'd never . . ."

"Look at me, Billie. Look at me and never say never. No, you can't, and I can't let you call Dr. Ward."

"All right, then, let me call someone else. Anyone. What if I drove you into Austin myself? You could go to the emergency room. No one would have to know."

Amelia's head sank into her pillow, rocking back and forth in denial.

"Amelia, you said you have Rand to think of. You could die from loss of blood, from infection. Think of Rand!"

"All right. You take me into the hospital. Not Memorial. Clinton General, on the other side of town."

Billie struggled with the Coleman family Packard through the dead of night. The ribbon of highway stretched out before the headlights like a long, narrow tongue. Amelia sat beside her, head thrown back against the seat, beads of perspiration glistening on her brow. The clock on the dash read twelve-thirty. As far as she knew, no one realized they'd left the house. But in the morning there would be explanations to be made, lies to be told, guilt to be hidden. She wouldn't think about that now. She had to keep her mind on the driving. This limousine was too long, too wide, and she was having difficulty judging distances. Her eyes kept going to the odometer. Twenty miles, thirty, thirty-five. Nearly an hour had passed. Amelia was quiet now, too quiet and too pale.

The lights of the city glimmered before her and traffic increased. The main avenue leading to the hospital was blocked by street lights, all of them red. "Hold on, Amelia, just a few more minutes," she promised, praying fervently all the while.

Things happened quickly when she pulled up to the emergency entrance of Clinton General. Amelia was placed on a stretcher and wheeled away. Then a nurse in a crisply starched uniform came to interview Billie.

"Patient's name?"

"Am . . . Amy Nelson."

"How long has the patient been bleeding and do you know the reason?"

"I don't know. . . . I don't know. . . . Where's the doctor? I want to see the doctor," Billie demanded.

"The doctor is with her now, but the patient is too ill to answer his questions."

Billie's eyes swiveled around the sterile waiting room. She didn't know what to say: how much should she tell?

"And your name?" the nurse was asking.

"Willa. Willa Ames." The misinformation came easily to her lips. "I'm a friend."

"Miss Ames." The nurse's eyes darted to Billie's wedding

ring. "*Mrs*. Ames, we already know that there's vaginal bleeding. We need to know if Miss Nelson is pregnant. Is she?"

Billie shook her head.

"Has she miscarried, do you know? Has she had an abortion? You must tell me. It could mean your friend's life."

"No, she hasn't miscarried" was all Billie would say. The other was just too horrible to admit. Visions of that chipped enamel dishpan turned revoltingly in her head.

"Then she's had an abortion. Correct? Do you know her family? Someone we can contact?"

"No! She has no one. Only me."

The nurse stood, her white uniform rustling stiffly. "Wait here, Mrs. Ames. I'll speak to the doctor."

Billie waited and waited and waited, each moment bringing new doubts and anguish. The minutes ticked by and then the hours. Seven o'clock. Daylight was streaming in through the wide glass doors. People milled about, white uniforms rushed from room to room, and there was still no word of Amelia.

At seven-thirty, Billie knew Sunbridge would be stirring. Rand would awaken and look for his mother. Agnes would soon go down to breakfast and wonder where her daughter was. Carlos would go out to the garage and find the car missing. Resolutely, Billie went to the pay phone and dialed the number. Thankfully, it was Agnes who answered. "Billie? Where are you? Aren't you upstairs?"

"No, Mother, I'm not. Don't ask any questions. Have Miss Jenkins look after Rand. Tell Carlos that Amelia and I took the car last night and I'll have it back soon."

"Amelia? Is Amelia with you? What do you mean you'll have the car back soon? Isn't Amelia coming with you? Billie, I demand to know what this is all about!" Something was wrong, terribly wrong; she could hear it in Billie's voice. "Billie, are you all right? Where are you?"

Billie sighed. There was no avoiding an explanation. "Mother, I'm at the hospital with Amelia. That migrane headache she had last night became worse during the night and she passed out."

"I don't believe you. Not for an instant. Billie, have you done something foolish? I know you're pregnant, Billie. Tell me, are you all right?"

"I'm fine. And so is my baby. Don't ask questions, Mother." There was an unmistakable threat in her tone. "As long as you know I'm pregnant then you should also know that Dr. Ward

{ 251 }

doesn't think I should go through with this pregnancy."

"Billy! What are you saying?" There was real fear in Agnes's voice now.

"What I'm saying, Mother, is that you are to cover for Amelia and me. You're not to let Seth know where we are or why. Take care of the children. I'll be back with the car as soon as I can. Don't let me down, Mother, and I won't let you down. Do we understand each other?"

Agnes's mouth gaped open. Could this really be her daughter talking to her this way? Issuing thinly veiled threats? Billie would never do anything to harm her child, would she? Yet something told Agnes this was a new and different Billie.

"Come home as soon as you can, Billie," she said softly. "I'll take care of everything here."

"Good for you, Mother. Good for you."

At a quarter to nine Billie was pacing the small waiting room on the second floor. Her eyes kept flying to the clock every thirty seconds. What were they *doing* to Amelia? Why wasn't anyone telling her anything?

"Mrs. Ames?" a woman's voice called. "Mrs. Ames?"

"Yes, here." Billie stood anxiously.

"The doctor would like to speak to you about Miss Nelson. Come this way, please."

Billie fell into step behind the nurse, her heels clicking on the tiled floor. She was shown into a cubicle. A young man in a white coat spoke. "Are you Mrs. Ames? I'm Dr. Garvey. I'm afraid we've had to perform an emergency surgery on your friend." At Billie's look of alarm he added quickly, "She's fine now. Her uterus was perforated, rather badly, and we had to perform a hysterectomy. Do you know what that is, Mrs. Ames? We've had to remove her uterus. Whoever performed the abortion was a butcher. You got her here just in time. She was hemorrhaging. Now we've got to be on the lookout for infection."

Billie's face had whitened during his recital and her lips were pale blue. "Mrs. Ames—here, sit down. I know this has been a shock."

"Will she be all right?" Billie managed to murmur.

"We expect so. Shame, though, in so young a woman. It would have been her first child, correct?"

"When can I see her?"

"She's in recovery now. Fortunately, she was conscious and able to sign the permission form; otherwise we'd have lost time attempting to get in touch with a blood relation."

"She has no one, anyway, only me. When can I see her?"

Dr. Garvey checked his watch. "About forty-five minutes. Why don't you go up to the third floor and I'll have someone get you when she wakes up.... Mrs. Ames, is there anything I can do for you?"

Billie raised her hand defensively, staving off the doctor's attentions. "No, I'm fine. Really. Third floor, you say?"

When Billie was finally admitted to see Amelia she had difficulty swallowing past the lump in her throat. Amelia was whiter than the pillow on which she lay, her lips dry and parched, her eyes lusterless and hollow.

"Billie." She could speak only in a kind of croaking whisper. "I know what you're thinking. It's no less than I deserve. Rand... please, take care of Rand for me." Her outstretched hand was cold and pale in Billie's.

"My God, what have they done to you?" The sympathy and compassion in her overflowed in salty rivulets down her cheeks.

"Don't cry for me, Billie, please don't...."

Amelia turned her head away, her bloodless lips moving. "Go home, now," she said in a choked voice. "Take care of Rand. What's done is done.... There's no crying over spilt milk. Didn't I tell you I never do anything right? Go home."

There was nothing more Billie could do or say. She would go home and make excuses for Amelia's absence and look after the children. The children. Her hand went protectively to her stomach and she imagined she could feel the nebulous life of her unborn child beating there. It was safe, secure, and, most important now, wanted. Amelia's child would have been its crib mate....

Billie's feet tapped a rapid tattoo on the tiled floor as she headed straight for the pay phone near the elevator. She fished in her pocket for a nickel to call Dr. Ward and tell him her decision.

Back at Sunbridge, Billie was numb to everything, including Seth's rage. "What does this gal of yours mean, Aggie?" he bellowed. "Where is that daughter of mine? And why did she leave that youngster here with us?" Agnes had no answer for him. "Damn fool troublemaker," he grumbled. "Never could trust her and never will. Goes off with friends and leaves that boy here. Friends! Miscreants is more the truth!" He glared at Billie. "When the hell is she coming back? I want to know when to wear my boots so I can kick her the hell out of my life!"

Agnes looked worriedly at Billie, who stayed silent. "Seth, Amelia needs a little time to herself right now. The boy is no problem—Billie is looking after him. Amelia won't be gone more than a week." She glanced at Billie for confirmation.

"And let me tell you one thing, little gal," Seth said, moving heavily on his cane toward Billie, "the next time you help yourself to the car without my say-so you'll hear it from me. What's gotten into you since Amelia's come home? I used to credit you with a *little sense!*"

"I suppose pregnant women do silly things," Billie said, hardly able to keep from sneering.

"What's this? Aggie, what's she saying?"

"I think she's telling you she's pregnant," Agnes cooed. "Billie, when can we expect our new arrival?"

"Maggie should have a little sister or brother for her birthday present."

"You mean a brother, don't you, little gal?" Seth countered sharply, yet he could not suppress a smile. "*This* one will be a son!"

The days trickled into weeks, the weeks into months. Billie and Amelia's friendship strengthened. Amelia's deft fingers crocheted and knitted little sweaters and baby blankets as she eagerly anticipated the birth of Billie's child. Her belief that nothing would go amiss, despite Dr. Ward's warning, was a comfort and pleasure to Billie. Amelia's concern was almost parental and, in Moss's absence, even husbandly. When Billie began to hemorrhage in her sixth month and she was confined to bed, it was Amelia who cared for her. She did it with such loving willingness that it brought tears to Billie's eyes. She was doing it for Billie, but for Moss, too, her adored brother. Little Rand was installed in the nursery with a nanny who catered to his every whim. Maggie thrived and grew like a healthy weed.

Moss's letters were infrequent and sparse. He was alive; that was about all they knew. Each of them lived in fear of the day a delivery would come by way of Western Union.

Billie lay in her half doze, her drowsy thoughts on her husband. Where was he now? What was he doing? Was he thinking of her?

"Being half-awake is better than being asleep," Amelia said

cheerfully as she poked her head in the doorway to check on her charge. "Time for tea, if you'd like. Rand and Maggie are napping, so it's just you and me, kid," she teased, doing her best impression of Humphrey Bogart.

Billie laughed, delighted. "Sounds good to me. I was dozing and thinking of Moss. It helps me to think of him and sometimes I have beautiful dreams! Do you think I'm sleeping too much?"

"As a matter of fact, I do. I know it's boring for you all alone in this big bed. Three months of complete bedrest is enough to drive anyone nuts. But I think I have a solution for keeping you happy, sane, and busy. Let me get the tea and we'll talk."

Tea trays were a creative process with Amelia. She always fixed them so prettily, delighting in the British custom. This afternoon the tray held a slim vase with two budding yellow roses, a white linen napkin embroidered with spring flowers, a simple white plate holding tiny sandwiches of melted cheese, and Jessica's best English bone china teapot. Fragile porcelain cups and saucers and tiny silver spoons nestled beside blueberry muffins.

As soon as they were settled Amelia came right to the point. "I've been thinking, Billie. I'm going to have to go to court when I get back to England and as you know, court appearances are just that: an appearance, almost like being on stage. Judgments are made on the weight of appearances. We've talked so much about your design studies and how much you loved them. I've seen what you've done with some of your maternity clothes and I've seen the things you've made for Maggie. They're gorgeous, Billie. Would you consider designing some clothes for me? Proper things, stylish but sedate. Something that conveys my responsibility and worthiness to be Rand's mother. This is important to me, Billie, very important."

"Amelia, I'm not a professional. I'm overwhelmed that you should ask. And I admit to being suspicious! Are you just looking for ways to keep me busy so I don't languish here alone in this room?"

"Hell no, gal!" Amelia did her best impression of Seth and made Billie laugh. "Seriously, I'd like you to do it."

"Don't forget I'm fresh out of school and what little I learned from Mrs. Evans back in Philadelphia I've probably forgotten. Why me? You could go to the best designers in New York or even have someone come here."

"I know all about those designers, but you see, Billie, I

want something that's perfectly me, Amelia Coleman Nelson. You know the real me, Billie. You really wouldn't have to do the actual sewing; there are seamstresses right here in Austin. You thought about pursuing a career in design, didn't you?"

"Yes, but Mother wanted me to become a teacher. Instead I married Moss and here I am. I can't even begin to think of a career—I want to be a wife and mother. Maybe later."

"Billie, later never comes. Something always gets in the way. This is the ideal time for you, while you're confined to bed. I'll help. Let's go back to the time when you hadn't met Moss. What were you going to do? What did you *want* to do?"

"I wanted to design fabrics, explore colors and shapes. Mrs. Evans, my home economics teacher, said she saw potential in me and worked with me after class. Before she married and had a family she worked for Oleg Cassini and she promised to head me in the right direction. I was even accepted to the Fashion Institute in New York, but when Mother got wind of it those plans changed. Perhaps Mrs. Evans was just being kind."

"Kind my foot. Don't forget, I've seen what you can do and from what I hear, acceptance into the Fashion Institute is no mean feat. Why was someone like your Mrs. Evans teaching school?"

"Mr. Evans thought life in New York too glamorous, so they moved to Philadelphia. She wanted her marriage more than a career. I do, too."

"Billie, it wouldn't hurt to lay some groundwork. Let me type up a letter to your teacher asking for the names and contacts she promised. You don't have to use them now, but we'll start a portfolio for you. When and if the time comes, you'll have everything at your fingertips. It won't hurt, Billie. I don't want to see you end up the way my mother did, wasting away here at Sunbridge, dying for lack of attention."

Billie didn't have the heart to tell Amelia those people could very well be dead by the time she got around to thinking about a career. But Amelia was right; it couldn't hurt, and if it would please her: "Okay."

"Oh, Billie, I'm so excited! I think it's wonderful. Moss will be so proud of you."

Billie's eyes widened. "Do you think so?"

"I know so. Moss likes interesting, exciting people. Billie, you're a Coleman now and Colemans always amount to something, or haven't you heard?" This last was said with an edge of bitterness. "Do you want to spend your life doing charity work and going to club meetings? Just remember my mother and her empty life once we children were gone."

Billie grinned. "You're making more sense all the time. Let's do it!"

Satisfied, Amelia leaned back in the chair and propped her feet on Billie's bed. "Talk to me. Tell me what you want to do when the time is right," she encouraged in the big sister voice Billie loved.

"Someday I want to work with silks and satins and brocades, but there's too much for me to learn before I can go into that. I'd start off with cotton. It's such a wonderful fabric, simple and clean and comfortable. No other fabric has those qualities. You always have to be aware of texture and weight if you want to combine it with another fabric for contrast. If I were designing something right now in cotton, I'd begin with the natural colors, wheat and ivory and oatmeal, and I'd add white for a catalyst.

"Later, I'll show you a design I did on cotton in high school. It's impressionistic bouquets of flowers in lines of black, white, and purple . . . sort of like a floating island. That was my first thought when I finished it and when I showed it to Mrs. Evans she said the same thing. She wanted me to do some work with batik, calico, and foulard, but they all seemed to call for stripes and I'm really not that fond of them so I went on to something else. There's so much more I need to learn."

"Tell me where to get the books, whatever it is you need. I'll ask Mrs. Evans to send me a list when I write her. You'll read them, won't you?"

"Of course! You're right, Amelia. It'll give me something to do and it's something that interests me."

"And you'll design some things for me?"

"I'll try. Designing a dress isn't as simple as it sounds. For you, I think it has to be soft yet have the body and substance of good construction and fabric. Nothing heavy, nothing stiff."

"I love it already."

"A kind of casual elegance." Billie narrowed her eyes as she measured Amelia's slim frame. "Maybe a suit skirt with asymmetrical pleating. A jacket in cotton or twill. Something you can wear with a hat. A dress with pure clean lines, maybe in a wool crepe. What would you think of a full tunic . . . ease and width, but we can control it with a belt. It would be different and you could carry it off with your height. I'll know more when I see and study some of the clothes you have. We can do a few mix-and-match outfits so it will look as though you have more. I like doing that; it's a challenge. What are your favorite colors?"

"All of them." Amelia laughed.

"Me too. Someday I want to create my own palette of colors as well as fabric designs. I have them all in my head. I've even given them names—the colors, I mean. I want to use them in silk, when I've learned more."

"What kind of colors? What sort of names?"

Billie laughed aloud. "Promise you won't laugh?"

"Cross my heart and hope to die."

"Blink Pink, Choke Cherry, Sherry Flip, Cocktail Fuchsia, Turquoise Icing. I could go on. If I ever do work in silk, I plan to use those names."

"Billie, I'm so impressed. It seems the Colemans got themselves a heifer with brains. Someday you'll put them to good use. My prediction, Mrs. Coleman, is that one day you'll be right up there at the top of the heap and not because you're Mrs. Moss Coleman but because your Billie Ames Coleman."

Billie wanted to cry. It had been so long since anyone paid her a sincere compliment. For the first time since coming to Sunbridge, she felt worthy of being a Coleman. The feeling was fragile and tenuous and she would treasure it and hold it close. Almost like a secret that only she and Amelia knew.

"I have an idea," said Amelia one Sunday after breakfast. "Why don't I read you the funny papers? What would you like, the Katzenjammer Kids or Tillie the Toiler?"

Billie sighed. "Neither. I'm too distracted over the patterns and construction for the wool suit I designed for you. I keep wondering if, when Mrs. Parker finishes the basting, it will live up to the design. The proof will be in the pudding."

"Don't worry, Billie. Mrs. Parker comes tomorrow for the first fitting and you'll see for yourself. Let's talk about something else. I don't like to see you this agitated."

"All right," Billie agreed, her mind refusing to leave her anxieties behind, struggling for something else to talk about. "How are things going downstairs with your father? Did you two make peace yet?"

"Surely you jest. No, we've not made peace and we won't, not in this lifetime, anyway. My father doesn't like me. He's never liked me and he'll never like me. As for love, the only thing Seth ever loved or will love is Moss and his horse, Nessie. You have to accept that. I have. Now if you don't want the funnies, how about one of Mam's mysteries? I saw one that looked like it would curdle our blood. Okay?" She scrambled out of her chair and went in search of the book.

Billie leaned back against the pillows and sighed. After the baby was born, Amelia and Rand would be leaving for England. Billie knew she was staying on at Sunbridge only out of concern for her; soon Amelia would need to return to face the inevitable lawsuit and her fight to legally adopt Rand. Billie would miss her, miss her terribly. Amelia cheered her up, bolstered her worries with a strength that seemed to know no bounds. She'd even fought with Seth for her—and won.

After the doctor had ordered Billie to bed for the balance of her pregnancy, Seth had stormed about Sunbridge like a rooster with no hens in sight. One disappointment was enough: no way was he going to lose a second chance at a grandson. A white-clad, stiffly starched replica of Miss Jenkins showed up in Billie's room.

Amelia took command. "Don't move," she said to the nurse. "Don't unpack and don't do a thing for Billie until this is straightened out." She turned to Billie. "I'm going to settle that old man, once and for all. He's not going to get away with this—unless of course you want the nurse." Amelia waited, holding her breath for Billie's answer. It was a negative shake of the head. Billie would feel so helpless and smothered by routine. The nurse pursed her lips and Billie could almost read her mind. These rich people never knew what they wanted. . . .

Sounds of the verbal go-round wafted up the circular staircase. Billie tried to distract herself by working a crossword puzzle, not very successfully.

"Don't speak to me like I'm one of your riffraff friends," Seth thundered at his daughter.

"Friend? Friend! You've never been a father to me, so how could you be a friend, riffraff or otherwise? And don't think you're going to throw me off the subject. If you want to talk about the relationship we never had, fine, but some other time. I want to talk about Billie. The doctor himself said she didn't need a nurse, that I could take care of her. I intend to do just that—did you hear me, Pap? I'm taking care of her. I already wrote Moss about it and so did Billie. Don't interfere. Because if you do, I'll snatch Billie right out of here. Chew on that one for a while. Now you get that goddamn nurse out of here and don't you ever pull something like that again. Not while I'm here. And just for the record, I'm staying until Billie delivers and is on her feet. Do we understand each another, Pap?"

"You always were a cantankerous little bitch," Seth snarled. "Your mam coddled you too much. I knew it would come to no good. Why couldn't you turn out like Moss? Jesus God, the things I've had to live with!"

"That's not the way I remember it, Pap. Every time Mam tried to coddle me, you slapped her away. You never approved of anything I did—my school work, my athletic ability, my friends, my driving, my music. You didn't approve of me at birth, so why I ever expected more is beyond me. But I kept hoping, trying to be what you wanted. Mam tried in her own way to tell me, but I never understood. I'm a female, and with you that counts for nothing. Not Mam, not me, not Billie, either. That little baby lying upstairs— is *she* going to have to pay the price the way I did? And this new baby, what will you do if it's a girl? Ignore it, too? And your son, the one who is so perfect, is he going to learn from you? Is he going to do to Billie what you did to Mam? God help us all."

"That's enough, Amelia."

"It's not nearly enough. It will never be enough. I won't let you take over Billie's life. Not while I'm here I won't."

Amelia's voice had risen to a high-pitched shriek. Billie imagined Seth backing off a step and Amelia advancing on him. "I'm young, I'm healthy," Amelia went on. "I've got guts and I have grit, not to mention spunk. You're an old man. You lost your wife, the only friend you ever had. You're going to dodder soon. Moss is gone. All you have left is your horse and Billie. The odds are a little more even now, Pap. Stacked in my favor, if you will."

"Get out of my sight! I couldn't stand looking at you the day you were born and I still can't stand the sight of you. If there's anything to be thankful for, it's that your mother isn't here to see how you turned out. She's probably turning over in her grave right now."

"You don't know and you never knew a thing about Mam. Don't bring her into this." There was a second's pause and then Amelia said, "If you think Mam didn't know about your carousing and those tramps you picked up in the city, you're wrong. She knew. She knew and she didn't care. I heard her praying one day. She actually prayed you would continue so you would leave her alone. What do you think of that, Pap?"

"You should have been drowned the day you were born. Get out of my sight."

The hatred in Seth's voice stayed in the air, drifted through the house. Then, Amelia's voice finally broke the silence, cool but threatening.

"Tell the nurse to leave. Now."

"If that's what it takes for you to leave my sight, all right. Send her down."

"Fetch her yourself. You hired her, now you can fire her."

"No-good tramp," Seth muttered as he made his way up the stairway.

Amelia told Billie what had happened next. The minute Seth was out of sight, she'd run to the kitchen and into Tita's arms. "My God, did you hear the things I just said? Was I wrong, Tita? Would Mam have been angry?"

"Your mother loved you very much. At the end, you were all she talked about." Tita had patted Amelia reassuringly. "You take this tea up to Miss Billie. The two of you can have a tea party, like you used to do when you were little. See how nice I fixed the tray? The cinnamon rolls are fresh, look."

It was a wonderful tea party. Their guests were Maggie, in her high chair, Rand, and Rand's little toy cat, Sally Dearest. No one paid any attention when he fed half his roll to Sally. As if by mutual consent, both women had pretended the sharp words with Amelia's father had never happened. But Billie would be a long time forgetting the murderous look in Seth's eyes when he'd arrived in her room to escort the nurse downstairs and back to town. And whenever she thought of that awful scene, she ached for Amelia. Moss had never told her those things. Did he understand how deeply Amelia had been hurt all the time they were growing up together? He loved his sister—that much she knew—and Amelia adored Moss.

Susan Amelia Coleman was born on a rainy day in February, almost exactly one year after Maggie's birth. Things happened suddenly, too quickly for Billie to be transported to Memorial Hospital in Austin. Tita and Amelia acted as midwives. Agnes sat near the head of the bed holding Billie's hand and wiping her brow, waiting for the arrival of the child who would secure their place at Sunbridge. When the child presented herself and her sex was declared, Agnes quietly left the room to solemnly announce the birth to Seth, who paced the upstairs hall. The instant he knew he had a second granddaughter, he stomped downstairs, threw on a cracked yellow poncho, and left the house, his face more thunderous than the storm outside.

Amelia was the first to hold the tiny infant. Exhausted, Billie lay back on the bed and watched the woman she'd come to love as a sister gaze down at her newborn daughter. The softness of Amelia's touch as she fingered the light damp curls brought tears to Billie's eyes. Amelia should be holding her own child, a child that could never be.

Dr. Ward arrived thirty-five minutes after the birth, examined mother and baby, and pronounced both healthy. Billie beamed. Doctors didn't know everything after all.

Amelia wept with joy when Billie asked her to be Susan's godmother. "I already love her as though she were my own," Amelia sobbed. "Thank you, Billie."

Seth managed to absent himself from Susan's christening, saying he had business in Corpus Christi.

When Moss received the news of Susan's birth he let out a whoop and threw his arms around Thad. "Son of a gun, it's another girl! Billie named her after my sister. What do you think of that?"

"I think it's great. What do you think?" Thad said quietly.

Moss frowned. "For sure I thought it would be a boy. I think everyone did. But as long as Susy is healthy, that's what counts. My sister is going to be the godmother—I like that. Did I tell you the doctor put Billie in bed for the last three months? Amelia took care of her all by herself. Billie says she was waited on hand and foot, and doesn't know what she would have done without her. That's my sister. We Colemans always come through in the end. Amelia's a great person."

"You didn't tell me Billie was having trouble." Thad's tone was accusing. "Three months is a long time to spend in bed. Billie isn't the invalid type."

"I know. It must have been rough on her. I could have sworn I told you, but I guess I had other things on my mind. Billie is okay and that's all that matters. Maggie is crawling around. Christ, I can hardly believe it!"

"It went all right with Billie this time, but if it happens again, she might not be so lucky. Just remember that you're responsible for Billie. You, Coleman, no one else."

Moss watched his friend walk away. Jesus, what was *that* all about? Well, with Thad in a snit over something there would be no gin rummy tonight. Good time to write to Billie.

In his quarters, Moss got out paper and pen. He hated writing letters. Except to Pap, but that was different. Pap was a man and they had things in common. Things that interested them both.

Darling Billie,

    I just received the news about our newest daughter. Congratulations, honey! I'm pleased as punch that both you and Susan are fine. I was a little worried when you said you had to stay in bed. It's a good thing Amelia was there to care for you. Thank her for me. I knew you would like my sister. She's aces with me. Don't tell her I said that—her head is big enough.

    I think of Mam often. It's wonderful of you to have Amelia take fresh flowers to the cemetery every day. I'll do it myself when I get back.

    Tell Pap I have four more meatballs to my credit. He'll like knowing that.

    Thad was just here and I told him about Susan. He said to congratulate you. He's such a hell of a nice guy. He sure was impressed with you. He thinks you're the most beautiful girl he's ever seen. He told that to one of the other guys, not to me. But I knew it.

    I miss you, Billie. I think of our time in Hawaii. It was memorable. When you write to me again, send pictures of the girls.

Love, Moss

Billie's strength returned only slowly, much to her dismay. Frequent naps, good food, plenty of fresh air and sunshine, were the cure-alls, Amelia said. Billie obeyed and spent her recuperation waiting for the mailman and writing long, detailed letters to Moss.

When Susan was four months old, Amelia announced that is was time for her to leave. Her solicitor had prepared the case and she had to take Rand back home. Both young women clung to each other and cried. "I understand, Amelia. I'll always be grateful to you for what you've done for me."

"I'm going to miss you, you damn Yankee. And I'm going

{ 263 }

to miss that little tyke in the nursery. Promise that you'll send pictures every month. I want to see her grow. Don't miss even one month. Promise now."

"I promise. Oh, Amelia, what will I do without you? I've come to depend on you too much."

"It's time you took over the reins. The doctor says you're back to normal—I wouldn't leave if I had a moment's doubt. It's time, Billie. Pap is going to heave a sigh of relief when I'm gone. I really think I've outstayed my welcome, if you could call it that! Be sure to write Moss and tell him I love him and to take care of himself. You're a wonderful person, Billie, and don't you ever let anyone say different."

Two days later Amelia was gone. Billie and Tita saw her off in the huge Packard. Rand clutched Sally Dearest in one chubby hand and waved good-bye with the other, his face full of smiles.

"I don't know why your father isn't here, Amelia," said Billie. "Something must have happened."

Amelia's eyes were bright with unshed tears. "Darling Billie, the eternal optimist. If you ever discover the *real* reason, let me know. Meantime, I won't hold my breath. Kiss Susan again for me. I miss her already and I'm not even out of the drive."

"I'll do that. Take care, Amelia, and be certain to write. I hope things work out with Geoff's family. Keep your chin up—after all, your lawyers seem quite optimistic."

"Yes, I know. But oh, if only Rand hadn't inherited his father's title, we'd be able to stay here."

"I wish they'd agreed to wait until it's safe to return there. I'm so frightened when I hear of the bombings. Those damn Germans . . ."

"Shhh. We'll be all right, Billie, I promise you. After all, I've got little Susan to come back to, and that's exactly what I intend to do. Take care of her, Billie, and take care of yourself." She gave Billie one last hug.

"And you take care of yourself and Rand. You're going to have one hell of a time getting back to England. Keep in touch."

"Don't worry, really. The Nelsons want Rand back. With them pulling the strings, getting back into England will be a piece of cake. I promise."

"Good-bye, Rand, be sure to take good care of Mommy for me, won't you?" Billie said. "Good-bye, Sally Dearest." She gave the cat a pat on the head.

The little boy nodded solemnly. "I'm almost four, Aunt Billie. I'll take care of us both."

Blinded with tears, Billie raced back to the house as soon as the Packard rounded the curve of the drive. She picked Susan up from her crib and kissed the downy head, as she'd promised Amelia. Tears of loneliness and loss streamed down her cheeks. The infant in her arms brought no comfort. Amelia, in the few months since Susan's birth, had been more of a mother than she. Billie hugged Susan closer and waited for the rush of maternal warmth to seize her. Susan's protests shrilled through the nursery.

{{{{{{{{{ CHAPTER SEVENTEEN }}}}}}}}}

Thad Kingsley leaned into the Enterprise *sick bay. Moss was* sleeping quietly in the right-hand bunk. The shelf over his bed held the portrait of Billie holding Maggie and little Susan. It was a familiar sight, yet it always came as a shock to Thad that Billie was the mother of two children. She was hardly past girlhood herself. It was November; soon Maggie would be two years old and blond-haired Susan would have passed her first birthday. It was unbelievable that a year and a half had passed since he'd seen Billie in Hawaii. Unbelievable that he'd never stopped thinking about her since.

The *Enterprise* fighter squadrons had been involved in night raids on the Philippines. It was after one of those raids that Moss had not returned to the carrier with his group. Radio contact with the "Texas Ranger" had been lost. Thad had stood with the warrant officer on the captain's lookout, peering through binoculars in the murky early-morning sky. He'd thought about the letter he might have to write to Billie and felt physically sick.

Scanning, watching, listening for one of the Big E's own. Finally: "Aircraft sighted, sir," the warrant officer had relayed to the captain. "Thirty degrees off bow, one o'clock. Stand by for identification." After a moment: "Identification positive, sir. Wildcat, listing to starboard. She's ours, sir. She's ours!"

Then a shout from Moss's squadron—the Texas Ranger was in sight! Flying like a wounded bird, it had made a less than perfect landing, but no man had faulted him for that. Moss has been rushed to sick bay and emergency surgery. He had taken shrapnel deep into the flesh and bone of his shoulder. Lacerations of face and neck, chipped collarbone and tissue damage. There was suspected nerve damage, which would be evaluated in San Diego.

Later, word was that when Moss had come to from the anesthesia, the first thing he'd said was "How's the Texas Ranger?"

Thad laughed to himself over his friend's concern for his plane. He loved this guy like a brother. Not that he approved of everything Moss did, but the pluses far outnumbered the minuses. With everything Moss had, with Billie and two beautiful daughters, with the backdrop of Sunbridge and all the wealth, it still wasn't enough for Moss. He was a bastard, bigger than life in all he did and all he was; so big that nothing less than a war was enough for him.

Thad decided against waking him and was just turning to leave when he heard a hoarse croak. "Thad?"

"Hey, buddy, you're awake. I've been here a couple of times but you looked like Sleeping Beauty. How do you feel?"

"Like mushrooms should be growing on the back of my throat. What happened?"

"Don't you remember?"

Moss nodded. "I remember. But I don't remember how I got back to the ship."

"On your own. And twenty minutes late at that, Coleman. I wouldn't be surprised if they put you on report!"

"How bad's the plane?"

"It's not being pushed over the side, if that's what you mean. I hear you're leaving us."

Moss shifted, or tried to, and scowled at Thad. "Like hell! This is just temporary; all I need is a week or so and I'll be good as new!"

"Afraid not, Moss. It's San Diego for you. Just think, San Diego and Billie. You both deserve the rest. You'll see your daughters for the first time. What more could a guy want?"

"How long? Did they say?"

"Jesus, Moss, I'm no doctor. All I know is they suspect some kind of nerve damage and they want San Diego to check you out. They don't have the facilities in Pearl. You don't want to take chances with that arm, do you? Sometimes, Coleman, you have to bend with the wind."

"I didn't even see that bastard come at me. He came out of nowhere. I had a bad feeling about that cloud cover. I could smell that slant-eyed son of a bitch."

"It *was* a little busy up there."

"The others get back okay?"

"Everyone's okay. Listen, fella, I've gotta get back to the wardroom. Try to sleep. You leave the Big E tomorrow at oh five hundred. Go to sleep and dream about them." Thad pointed to the photo over the bunk.

"Who put that there?"

"Your buddy, John Cuomo. He's always flying your wing tip, isn't he? He'd thought it'd cheer you up."

"Sure," Moss said tonelessly. He closed his eyes dutifully, but it wasn't Billie's pretty face he saw. It was the zero, coming out of the clouds at him. Over and over he played the scene in his head. He couldn't have handled it any other way. Now he was going to be in dry dock for a while. But not for the duration, by God. His bunk on the Big E would be waiting for him.

Seth Coleman hung up the phone, hands shaking, face drawn. Agnes waited, knowing that the message was about Moss. Her mind spun as she looked around the living room. She couldn't give all this up. There was no way she was going to give all this up! She forced herself to a calmness she didn't feel. Her voice was pitched low and full of concern. "What's wrong?"

"Those yellow sons of bitches got Moss." Agnes's heart thumped painfully in her chest. "They busted up his shoulder. Moss is being transferred to a San Diego hospital. We're going, Aggie. All of us. Tell Billie. Even the babies. The nurse and nanny, too."

Agnes heaved a silent sigh of relief. Alive. The man was too damn arrogant to die. Thank the good Lord.

"Do you know what I wish, Aggie?"

"What?"

"I'd like to blast the lily-livered yellow weasels right off the face of this earth. One of these days some smartass in Washington is finally going to say enough is enough and blow them to smithereens. They could have killed my boy, Agnes. He came *that* close."

"It's not going to last forever, Seth. Try looking on the bright side of things. You're going to see Moss soon. I think it's wonderful that we can all go to welcome him back to the States. Billie will be so pleased."

"How's her health?" Seth asked bluntly.

"Good. Why do you ask?"

"Because I have a feeling if the girl doesn't get herself pregnant now, she might not get another chance. It's that simple, Aggie. I want a grandson. And it damn well better be a boy this time around. You're the girl's mother. If I were you, I'd make sure she understands she might not get another chance to give Moss a son. Plain and clear, Aggie. Don't talk around it. If you aren't up to it, I'll do it."

"Seth! I'll handle it. This is woman talk. I know you're upset right now. Let things be. I take it you're going to make all the arrangements."

"I always do. We'll rent a big house with lots of bedrooms and lots of privacy. Why the hell did it have to be Moss? Why couldn't it have been one of the others, like that Kingsley?" Seth said viciously.

"Seth! You should be ashamed of yourself. How would you like it if one of their parents said the same thing about your son?"

"I'd expect it. I'm no hypocrite, Aggie. If it has to be them or Moss, I want it to be them. Not Moss. Never my son."

Billie dialed the operator and rattled off Amelia's number. Her anger rose to volcanic proportions when she thought of how Seth had insisted Amelia didn't need to know about Moss being wounded. "Save your time, little gal, and my money and forget it," he'd said in his usual voice, as loud as a freight train pulling into the Philadelphia yard. His unruly gray eyebrows had shot up when she'd picked up the receiver in defiance and then he'd stomped back into his study and slammed the door shut. But this was one time she couldn't care less about Seth's disapproval. Amelia had a right to know and a furtive phone call from the upstairs hall would not do, not this time.

"We'll ring you back, ma'am, when we get your call through. Will the wire be free? It may be a while."

"I'll be here and the wire will be kept free." Billie replaced the heavy black receiver and stood looking at it for a moment.

Billie settled herself in the living room, trying to focus on the fashion magazines she had carried down from her room for just this purpose. The minutes hung in the air; the quiet of the house accented the ticking of the clock on the mantel.

Four hours later the call came through. Billie picked up the receiver on the second ring. The operator's voice was clear, but Amelia's sounded scratchy and very far away. Billie pressed the phone tightly to her ear and spoke directly into the mouthpiece in a loud voice.

"I can barely hear you, Billie. What's wrong? Did something happen to Pap?"

Billie heard the anxiety in Amelia's voice, the concern for Seth. Her eyes went to the study door and then slid away. "No. He's fine! It's Moss, Amelia. He's got himself a shoulder wound. I thought you should know. We have every reason to believe he'll be fine. I wanted you to know."

"Is there anything I can do? Do you need me? Tell me the truth."

"It's just as I said. A wound. I'm fine, Amelia. Everyone is fine. How are you?"

"As good as can be expected. Have you gotten any mail from me?"

"Not recently."

"I wrote you a letter about the court case. It was a killer, Billie. A night didn't go by that I didn't cry myself to sleep. In the end, I had to flash the Coleman name and money. I hated to do it, but when it looked like I might lose, I brought it out. I had to prove to the courts I didn't need Rand's inheritance. Fortunately, his uncles couldn't prove the same. And of course they sliced me to pieces when they attacked my past and reputation. Whoever said the past is forever a part of the future must have been involved in a custody battle."

"Did you win, Amelia? That's what I want to know."

"Yes, thank the Lord, but it was a fight every step of the way. You'd be proud, Billie. I didn't lose my temper once, not in front of the judges, anyway. I behaved like the lady my mother brought me up to be. In the clothes you designed for me I was the picture of confidence even though inside I was dying. I did everything you said; I followed every shred of advice you gave me. I'll never be able to thank you, Billie. Left to my own devices, I would have gone off half-cocked and blown the whole thing."

"I'm so happy for you, Amelia. I prayed it would work out for you."

"It was your positive attitude and confidence that helped

me, Billie. When I think of that awful abortion and all I went through, I couldn't let those greedy vermin get Rand. I just couldn't. As Moss would say, it's a whole new ball game. I have to be a mother now and that means I must behave like one. A *good* one, do you know what I mean, Billie?"

"You can do it, Amelia. How's Rand?"

"Poor little tyke, he doesn't know half of what was going on, thank goodness. He's well. Really fine. That child loves me, Billie. Really loves me. When I think how close I came to losing him . . . Rand's uncles would have stopped at nothing and that would have included creating a doubt that my pregnancy was a direct result of my promiscuousness. Not that I ever was. At least not since I met Rand's father. It's been a hard thing to carry, Billie; you know what I'm talking about. But I couldn't have saved Rand if I hadn't done what I did. That boy means all to me, Billie, and he just thinks I'm his whole world."

There was such awe and emotion in the tinny voice coming over the wire that Billie was moved to tears. "Of course he loves you, Amelia. You're his mother!"

"I think we're about to be cut off, Billie," Amelia said hastily after a series of sharp clicks and static. "Give my love to Moss when you write. Take care of yourself and give Susan a squeeze for me. A letter is on the way. Write back."

The connection was broken before Billie could say good-bye.

Billie was pouring herself a glass of sherry to celebrate Amelia's victory when Seth came up behind her. "I heard the phone ring. What did the tramp have to say?"

"Tramp?"

"Amelia."

"Oh, you mean your daughter. Not much, Seth."

"You talked for a long time."

"Actually, Seth, I was doing more listening than talking."

"What did she tell you to tell me? What'd she say about Moss?"

"She told me to give Moss her love. Excuse me, Seth. I want to check the children."

Billie climbed the stairs, holding her back stiff and erect to hide the trembling she was feeling. She'd held her own there for a few minutes, anyway, and she owed Amelia that brief defense. Thank God things had gone well for her. Always it had been in the back of Billie's mind that Amelia might have sacrificed her own child for nothing. Now she would enjoy waiting for Amelia's letter, knowing it would have only good news. Good for you, Amelia. Good for you.

Amelia's letter arrived three days later, just before the Coleman entourage left Sunbridge for the Austin train station to begin their trip to San Diego and Moss. Seth and Agnes rode in the limousine while Billie, the children and the nurse rode in a separate car.

Billie carried the letter in her purse to read during the trip. It felt thick, a lot of news, Billie thought happily. The postmark was dated more than two months before. With the war, she realized, she was lucky to have received it at all.

Leaning back into the comfort of her seat, the children quieted by the motion of the moving car, Billie slit open the envelope. She had already heard the news about the trial, but there was more:

I've moved from London to a little village in the northeast. Billingford. London is torn to hell, thanks to Hitler, and each day we were forced to stay in the city filled me with dread. The nightly air raids and sirens frightened Rand. Fresh milk and eggs and all the other things young children need were difficult to get. Now there's fresh milk. I actually milk our one and only cow each day. Rand hasn't quite gotten the knack of pulling her teats, but he tries. We have a few chickens and fresh eggs daily. Meat is scarce. Rand, bless his little heart, will eat anything as long as we sit down together to eat. We take long walks, play ball, and I'm teaching him his letters and numbers. He seems to excel in arithmetic. Billie, can you believe I'm doing all this? I never knew how to cook and I never paid any attention in school, yet here I am, solely responsible for this child. I am taking it very seriously because I came so close to losing him. I can't ever allow that to happen again. Those dastardly uncles of his are not about to give up. I know they fell back to regroup and will have another go at me as soon as they can. My adoption of Rand won't be final for at least a year and with this damn war, it could take longer.

How are things in Texas? Is Pap still riding you hard?

You're going to have to learn to speak up and say what you mean. Don't worry about offending him; the ignorant can't be insulted.

Write and tell me about the children. They must be growing like weeds. I know Rand is. Children are wonderful. They blossom before our eyes and thrive on love and affection. We must be certain our children know how much we care for them. We must never stop telling them how we love them. If you're laughing at me, Billie, I can't help myself. I'm so overcome with all these new emotions.

I want to hear the latest news of Moss. He hardly ever writes me. How is he? Where is he? Do you know? Send him all my love when you write and tell him of my victory. Moss was always my champion and I love him dearly. How lucky the big galoot was to have found you. Tell him I said so.

I must sign off for now. I promised to play croquet with Rand and he's standing here with the clubs waiting so patiently with Sally Dearest under his arm. Take care, dear Billie.

All our love,
Amelia and Rand

Billie wanted to weep. Instead, she pressed the letter to her heart. Amelia was happy. Only one indirect mention of Seth. . . . Billie sighed. Some things in life simply could not be changed.

The entourage arrived in San Diego on a bright, blustery day. Moss was going to be confined to the hospital for at least two more weeks. Then he would spend his thirty-day recuperation in the rented house that stood high above the bay.

In its own way, the rambling, Spanish-style house was almost as luxurious as the one Seth had rented for Billie in Hawaii. The manicured lawns were magnificent, she thought. There was a tennis court and a heated pool, certainly a plus for anyone interested in swimming and tennis. She wasn't. Moss wouldn't be, either. There were servants, of course. Billie marveled at how easily she'd accepted having her needs catered to.

After settling the children and Agnes in the big house, Seth and Billie paid a first visit to the hospital. For the first time

Billie didn't hang back, but ran ahead of Seth to Moss's room and to his arms. His eyes met Seth's stormy gaze in silent apology.

"Billie, Pap," Moss said, "this is so wonderful! A visit from the two most important people in my life. It's so good to see you." And then he whispered against Billie's soft hair, "You feel wonderful, Mrs. Coleman."

It was what Billie needed to hear. Confident that Moss was all right and wanted her, she relinquished her position to Seth. Her eyes glowed brightly as she watched Seth's clumsy efforts to embrace his son, cumbersome cast and all.

"I hope you gave those yellow bastards what for for doing this to you," Seth growled, his grip on Moss's good shoulder fiercely tight. Moss didn't flinch.

"He came at me from my blind side from out of cloud cover. He got me before I could do a thing. They got him—my wingman saw to that. He took over when he saw I was hit. He's one hell of a guy, Pap. They don't make them any better."

Seth bridled. Of course they did. *His son* was the best. There would never be anyone even as good as Moss, much less better. Why did Moss always make light of his accomplishments? By God, he'd taught him better than that!

"They tell me you're okay, boy. Lucky, they said. Time to make another donation to the church."

Billie bit the inside of her cheek. It would be better if the old man *went* to church. She prayed constantly. Jessica had, too. Living proof of the power of their prayers was her husband smiling up at her right now. He winked and grinned. There were some things money couldn't buy.

"You'd better make it sizable, Pap. I still have a war to fight. I'm going back just as soon as they say I'm fit. No tricks. I mean it, Pap. I didn't come this far to quit now because of this little scratch."

"Little scratch! Little scratch!"

"They rebuilt it good as new, Pap. I might not be able to swing a pitchfork for a while, but I sure as hell can fly a plane. And I intend to fly, Pap."

"I know, boy. I know. You'll be able to come home with us soon. We're all settled in, the lot of us. Agnes, the nanny, the nurse, your children."

Billie noticed her father-in-law had difficulty saying the word *children*.

"I can't wait to see the girls. Some of those pictures were

terrific. Thad has two of them in his plane. Hell, all the guys do. I passed them around. None of the guys are married but me. I wanted to share my family a little. I hope you don't mind, Billie."

"Of course not. I think it's wonderful of you."

Seth snorted.

Trouble. Trouble between Billie and Pap. Moss knew the old man well enough to know that there was trouble, and then there was *big* trouble. He felt removed from the situation. Billie and Pap would handle it. He wasn't going to get involved. There was too much going on in his world to think about some petty domestic problem. After all, wasn't that why he insisted Agnes make her home with them? She was supposed to be handling all of this. And where the hell was Agnes?

"How's your mother, Billie?"

"She's fine. She wanted to give your father and me some time alone with you. She'll come tomorrow or the next day. Oh, Moss, I can't wait for you to see the girls. They've gotten so big. Maggie is talking already."

Another snort from Seth. He helped himself to a plug of tobacco. So, Moss thought, it was *big* trouble. Seth only chawed when things were out of hand. Okay, but he still wasn't going to worry about it. "They aren't even going to know who I am," he grumbled.

"Darling, they will! Every day I hold class and show them pictures of you. I talk about you and read them your letters over and over. Maggie will know. She actually asks questions. Can you believe it? She's a little confused between a bird and an airplane. I thought you would be able to explain that to her."

"Have you heard from Amelia?"

"I had a letter the day before we left. I brought it along so you could read it."

"Amelia's okay . . . a bit feisty at times, right, Pap?" Moss said, hoping to draw his father into the conversation. He didn't fail to notice that the smile left Billie's face at the question. So Amelia was the big trouble. He should have known. Pap was like a bronc with a burr under his saddle.

"So, Pap, how's things at the ranch? Any new colts? How many head of cattle did you ship this month?"

Seth shifted his chaw. He looked like he wanted to spit but didn't know where. He spoke out of the corner of his mouth. "I could have used you this past month, boy. Heaviest month yet. The army is after me for more, more, and then some more. Six new colts in the past three months. Nessie is ailing. Breaks my heart. That old gal has carried me a lot of miles. The vet is telling me I'd be doing her a favor if I put her down. Can't do it. She's gonna have to die of old age, same as the rest of us."

Billie listened to the tenderness in Seth's voice as he spoke of his horse. She'd never heard him speak like that about his wife. And Billie doubted he ever had in all their life together. Her features hardened. So, Moss thought, Amelia was at the center of the trouble, but there was more. Much more.

"You look tired, boy. I think we'll go along and come back tomorrow. We don't want you overdoing. Take a nap. Get your strength back. Come on, girl, let's let the boy sleep."

Billie stiffened. "No, Seth, I think I'll stay. If Moss wants to sleep, I'll read a novel. I brought one with me." Billie refused to meet Seth's eyes as she rummaged in her bag for the book she'd thought to bring at the last minute.

Seth glowered and shifted his chaw a second time. "How will you get home? Do you even know the address?"

"Of course I know the address . . . and the phone number. You go along. I'll find my way back. Taxis looked plentiful outside."

"What about the girls?"

"What about them?" Billie asked quietly. "You've seen to their every need. There isn't a thing I can do for them that Miss Jenkins can't. Mother is there to take up the slack. Don't wait dinner for me, Seth. I'll catch something here or filch something from Moss's dinner tray."

Seth all but snarled. "Dinner? That's hours away. How long are you planning on staying here?"

Billie laughed, to Moss's delight. "Until the nurse or my husband throws me out. Don't worry about me, Seth."

"I'm not worried. I think it's a damn fool thing to be doing. Using valuable gasoline for a second trip when I'm going now. Damn foolishness!" Billie smiled again but said nothing. She settled herself in the only chair by Moss's bed.

"I believe I will sleep," Moss said, feigning tiredness. He appeared to be asleep in seconds.

"Women!" Seth snorted. He shifted from one foot to the other. When he saw that his son was asleep, he turned and left without another word.

Moss cracked open one eye and grinned at Billie. She giggled. "Is the old boy gone?" She nodded. "Then come here, Mrs. Coleman, and welcome me home properly."

He didn't have to ask twice. Billie was on the side of the bed in a second, her arms around her husband, offering her lips, making up for all the months of longing. Her fingers raked through his thick dark hair; her breasts swelled beneath his caresses. He was home, here in her arms. Once he saw how much she needed him, once he held his daughters for the first time, war, hell, or heaven could never separate them again. Now that she had him, she would keep him.

His family was lined up on the verandah when Moss climbed from the ambulance with the aid of a corpsman: his father, Agnes, Billie, and his two children.

He saw it all in a flash but it was to Maggie and Susan that his eyes went. A lump rose in his throat as he climbed the dozen steps to the porch. How beautiful they were! His own flesh-and-blood family. Remarkable. "Hello, everybody, I'm home," he said spiritedly.

Billie watched the kaleidoscope of emotions on her husband's face and decided that the months of agony and misery and the difficult births had all been worth it. The love on Moss's face touched her soul. She bent low and whispered to Maggie. The child tugged harder on her mother's dress and then stepped forward. She lowered her dark head and peered at her father from beneath incredibly long lashes. Billie held her breath.

"Hello, Pap."

Moss stared at his daughter. He could feel something burn his eyelids. He was about to reach out to Maggie when Seth finally maneuvered his way between Billie and the little girl. He slapped his son on his back and drew him forward.

The precious moment was shattered. Billie wanted to cry. Instead, she hugged Susan closer. Agnes looked away. Moss turned and looked down at Maggie, who was once again sucking on her fist. The burning sensation behind his eyelids was gone. He knew he'd lost something in that moment, and still his eyes lingered on the little girl.

"We waited lunch, Moss," Agnes said cheerfully. "Sirloin tips with fresh mushrooms. I seem to recall it's one of your favorites. And the cook made a lemon meringue pie just for you."

"Sounds great. I'd like a nice cold beer, if possible. It's

been so long since I've had a beer I've forgotten what it tastes like."

"I'll get it for you, Moss," said Billie, "but you'll have to hold Susan. Would you mind? She doesn't wiggle and I don't think she'll hurt your shoulder."

"The boy doesn't want to hold a squealing baby," Seth said sourly.

"Sure I do, Pap. I want to hold both my girls. Come here, Maggie, and sit next to me. Let me get settled, Billie, and then hand me Susan."

Billie's eyes were so grateful—and full of something Moss didn't want to think about. He looked away. It was goddamn sinful the way his wife looked at him. And he loved it.

Susan let out an ear-splitting shriek when Billie tried to transfer her to her father. She grabbed at her mother and kicked out with her foot.

Seth's bellow of outrage could be heard all over the house. He stepped forward, yanked the shrieking Susan from Billie's arms, and thundered for the nurse. "Children belong in their rooms with their nannies. I told you this wasn't a good idea, but did you listen to me? Jess would never have pulled a damn fool stunt like this. The boy needs peace and quiet, not screaming, yelling brats."

"Pap, it's okay. Susan has never seen me. What do you expect? I don't mind. How do you expect me to get to know my children if you keep them penned up in a nursery?"

"You have plenty of time. You just got home," Seth said gruffly.

Billie stood staring from her husband to her father-in-law. What to do? Moss looked tired and he wanted a beer. He wanted *her* to get the beer. In the end she took Maggie's hand and led her from the room. She handed both children over to the nurse, raced to the kitchen, uncapped the beer, and reached for a glass. She double-timed back to the living room and just caught Seth handing his son a beer and a glass. She stood foolishly in the doorway. When Moss looked up, she smiled tightly. "I thought I would join you."

The girl was learning, Agnes thought as she excused herself to see about lunch.

"Good girl. Come sit here by me and rub my back. Remember that massage you gave me on the beach in Hawaii? I want one just like that."

{ 277 }

"The atmosphere isn't quite right," Billie said, laughing as she filled her glass.

"I thought you didn't like beer. When did this start?"

"When your father beat me to the refrigerator. Waste not, want not. You'll probably have to finish it."

Seth glowered at Billie and settled himself directly across from Moss. "I want to hear everything you've been doing. Don't leave a thing out. Billie, why don't you help your mother in the kitchen?"

Billie locked eyes with her father-in-law. "What could I possibly do? There's a cook, a maid, and a young girl to serve. Mother herself is probably in the way. She's merely checking on things. You go ahead and talk. I'll just sit here."

Moss's hand tightened imperceptibly on hers. Billie glowed.

After Moss had climbed the stairs for a nap, Agnes suggested she and Billie go for a walk. "It's such a beautiful day and the girls are napping. Neither of us is needed here."

"Moss might wake and want something."

"That's why we have servants, Billie. We won't be gone long. I would like to talk to you."

"All right, Mother, but no more than thirty minutes. I want to be with Moss when he wakes."

"Thirty minutes will be fine. People tell me this is the best time of year to be in San Diego. It's beautiful, don't you think?"

"Yes, Mother, it is. What did you want to talk about?"

Agnes frowned and then decided on bluntness. "Billie, child, I know you've had a harrowing time with your last two pregnancies, but I think you had best give some serious thought to having another child as soon as possible. I know this is none of my affair, but you are my daughter. The next time Moss might not be so lucky. If . . . if he . . . What I mean is, if something happens, you won't have that piece of Moss that can only be yours with a son. The girls . . . well, they're girls. I'm sure you know what I'm talking about. You have to give it serious thought, my dear. A son, Billie. You need a son. Moss needs a son. We both know how disappointed he was when the girls were born."

"No, Mother, I didn't know he was disappointed. He never said any such thing to me." Billie stopped walking. She faced her mother.

"Darling, a husband doesn't say something like that to his wife. Think how inferior you would have felt. . . . But, darling, surely you knew, felt his disappointment."

"No, Mother, I never knew or felt anything like that. Did Moss say something to you?"

"Not to *me*, Billie."

Agnes looked away at the stricken look on her daughter's face. "Darling, don't you think Moss looks remarkably well for what he went through? If that shell had been a little higher or more to the left, you would be a widow, Billie. That's what the navy doctors told Seth. I'm sure Moss didn't want to worry you and that's why he's making light of his injury."

Billie felt as if her knees were going to buckle under her. They were coming at her from all sides. Seth with his deviousness, Agnes with her blunt information, Moss with his omissions. Didn't any of them care about her? Her jaw tightened. "I think this is far enough, Mother. I want to go back and wait for Moss to wake up. The girls will be awake soon. He might enjoy seeing Susan get her bath."

"I think you're absolutely right, Billie. It will do Moss a world of good to see his daughters and get to know them. They're so dainty and wispy. If you had had a boy, he would want to rough and tumble on the floor with him and he wouldn't be able to do that with his shoulder injury."

Billie was tight-lipped all the way back to the house. Her mother had the finesse of a buzz saw. It must have something to do with her spending so much time with Seth. She was beginning to sound like him, act like him. God forbid, she was even swaggering like him!

Billie settled herself in a comfortable chaise longue across the room from where Moss was sleeping peacefully, his good arm flung back on the pillow. It must be hard for him to sleep like that, Billie thought. He had always liked to sleep scrunched up into a ball on his side. The same side as his bad shoulder.

Her thoughts were chaotic. Her mother had voiced aloud what she herself had been thinking. In fact, it was all she had been able to think of from the moment Seth had told her her husband had been wounded. She *needed* a son. She wanted a son. For Moss, yes. But for herself, too. She wanted that piece of Moss that would only come with a son. It was a shame that girl babies couldn't give that same feeling. It wasn't fair, but it was a fact. Good Lord, whatever would she do without Moss? Would she be able to survive? Physically, yes. Emotionally . . . she had her doubts. But if she had that small bundle that was part of Moss, she would make it.

Marriage certainly hadn't changed much in her life, she thought with a grimace. Agnes had controlled everything she did up until the day she'd married Moss—and she hadn't relinquished that hold yet. If anything, her mother had even more control because of her alliance with Seth. Her very existence was in their hands. Moss, dear, sweet Moss, trusted them to take care of her and that was exactly what they were doing.

A horrible realization dawned. If anything happened to Moss and Seth died, Agnes would be in total control—unless Billie had a son. The son would inherit, but she, Billie, would be the dowager queen. She would be in control of her son and safeguard everything until he came of age. She could see to it that Maggie and Susan received their rightful share. Gamblers had a phrase for it—an ace in the hole. The ticket to everything. She *needed* a son. It was that simple.

Perhaps it was time to become a little selfish. Or, to put it another way, perhaps it was time to grow up and face reality, with the rest of the Colemans.

Moss woke, feeling vaguely disoriented. He gazed about the strange room. So many rooms lately, places where he'd slept, none of them secure and familiar. He suddenly yearned for his old room at Sunbridge, for old, familiar things, for things that he could hold and feel, that would give him a sense of his past and offer a promise for his future. A muted sound from down the hall brought a grin to his face. He had something better: he had two little girls, his own flesh and blood!

He noticed Billie sleeping on the chaise. She was beautiful. He lay quietly and watched her for a long time. She was so young to be the mother of two children. Twenty years old, not even old enough to graduate college or to vote, and here she was a wife and a mother. She hadn't fooled him with her letters that made light of what she'd endured with the pregnancies. He'd seen her that Christmas when she'd been carrying Maggie, swollen and worn and frightened. He decided he wouldn't put Billie through that again, no matter what Pap said or wanted. Two little girls were enough for him and if it didn't suit Pap, too damn bad.

It was time for Billie to enjoy life. Time for her to enjoy the girls and watch them grow. Maybe later, when the war was over, they'd take time out of their lives to try for a son. He was confident his luck would hold—the war hadn't gotten him so far and it would never get him. He was too smart, too quick.

He was a Coleman. Death was nowhere on his horizon. There would be time for a son. He would think of Billie now. Two children in two years was more than enough to ask of any woman.

Billie wasn't the same girl he'd met in Philadelphia and married. He could see it and feel it. He recognized she was growing up. She wasn't a girl any longer, but a beautiful, desirable woman. She was learning every day. She'd stood up to Seth. And, when she really became Billie Coleman, a woman in her own right, she would be formidable. He smiled. Billie. Dear, loving Billie.

Carefully, Moss inched himself from the bed. First stop, the nursery. He stood in the doorway for a few minutes watching the girls. Maggie was building a stack of blocks and he held his breath while one chubby hand added another and another. His eyes were drawn to Susan, playing quietly with a stuffed teddy, mangling its ear with her two bottom teeth. She looked up curiously from her playpen and Moss watched her apprehensively. Would she scream again? But evidently she felt safe behind the bars. Moss grinned because she looked so much like a fat little monkey in a cage.

Miss Jenkins was not present, and the grandmotherly nanny followed Moss's suggestion that she leave him alone with his daughters.

Maggie's brightly colored tower of blocks toppled to the floor. Maneuvering her plump little bottom and getting up on her haunches, the rosy-cheeked, dark-haired toddler looked around for nanny. But there was only Moss. She pointed a pudgy little finger at him and said seriously, "You did that, Pap."

Moss threw back his dark head that was so like Maggie's and laughed. By God, if someone had to be blamed, why not him? "I'll tell you what," he said, hunkering down, "I'll build you a castle. Would you like that, Maggie?"

The toddler jabbered like a magpie as Moss added block upon block. "Susy wants out. Get Susy, Pap!"

"Is that allowed? Would nanny like that?"

Maggie hung her head, her cheeks flushing just like her mother's. "No."

"Good. Then let's do it."

"Nurse will holler," Maggie warned precociously.

"Pap will take care of things. I think Susy wants to build with blocks, too. We can pretend she's the princess."

"Who am I, Pap?"

"You're the queen, Maggie darling."

Maggie pondered her father's words. "The queen is bigger!" She stretched her pink arms upward. "So big!"

"I think you mean better, don't you? Yes, the queen is bigger and better." Moss was grinning. Sibling rivalry already. "But just a shade better. Princesses are important, too."

"Yes! Get Susy!"

"I thought you'd see it my way." Moss took it slow and easy bending over his youngest daughter. He hesitated before touching her, afraid she'd begin to cry and upset Maggie, too. When his little girl wrapped her sweet arms around his neck and squealed not with fright but with delightful anticipation, Moss felt his heart melt.

Billie woke an hour later to laughter. She listened for a moment. The booming laugh came again, unmistakably Moss's. He must be with the children, she thought, and tiptoed down the hall. At the door to the nursery she clapped her hand to her mouth to prevent her own laughter from shattering the moment. Moss was sitting on the floor with Susan between his legs. She was busy peeling the paper from Maggie's crayons, and Maggie was drawing squiggly lines on his shoulder cast, telling him it was her name, Mommy's name, and Grandmam's name.

"Where's my name?" Moss complained. "Don't you know how to spell Pap?"

Maggie considered the question for a moment. Then she brightened. Her eyes flashed with mischief and a sudden girlish giggle erupted from her pouting mouth as she grabbed a deep purple crayon and drew a long bold line. Sitting back on her heels, she added another flourish and proudly announced, "Pap!"

It was Billie who insisted, despite Seth's objection, that Moss retire early. Her husband's face was ashen when he climbed the stairs to their rooms. He didn't object when Billie helped him undress, and he was asleep almost before his head touched the pillow.

Billie was satisfied just to have Moss here, in their bed. As long as he was near, within touching distance, she could be happy.

There would be other days, other nights. Clearly, her indestructible husband had overdone it today. It was the strain of coming home, dealing with the pain, playing with the girls—

and of being torn between his loyalties to his wife and to his father. But she would always remember this afternoon when her husband and their babies had shared wonderful hours together. If a son had been there, would it have been different?

She leaned over and brushed her lips across his brow. Quietly she undressed and climbed into bed beside him. How good it felt—and how lonely and empty her bed had been without him all these months.

It worried her that Moss was so eager to get himself back into the action. If only, just once, Moss would want her more than he wanted anything else. Why couldn't she and the girls be enough? As she turned toward him and slipped her arm around his waist to nestle close, she knew her decision was a good one. If his wife and daughters weren't quite enough, a son would be. A son.

{{{{{{{{{ CHAPTER EIGHTEEN }}}}}}}}}

The days in San Diego passed swiftly and smoothly. They were busy—Billie saw to that. Overnight, she had seemed to take charge. Family breakfast on the terrace included the girls. Then some time for play in the nursery, with Billie watching from the sidelines. After that, an hour or so for Moss to read the papers and maybe for a casual talk over a second cup of coffee. Lunch was on the terrace, too, and then the girls went down for their naps and Moss left for his physical therapy session at the naval hospital. When he came home from the hospital he was always exhausted and she made sure he had at least an hour of rest. Billie generously shared Moss with Seth at dinner and for an hour afterward. Then he was hers. If Seth didn't like the arrangements, he kept his opinions to himself.

One warm evening, as a gentle breeze stirred the lace curtains at the French doors and Billie and Moss lay quietly together listening to soft music on the radio, Billie said, "I want another baby, Moss."

She felt him tense. "Just like that? No. No more. Not now."

"Just like that," Billie repeated. She traced a long, delicate line down his chest and stopped just short of the rough patch of hair at the base of his stomach. "Look at me, Moss. Do I look sick? I'm young; I'm healthy. I take care of myself. And I'll do what the doctors say—I always do. Susan arrived safely and almost exactly on time. This baby will, too."

"You make it sound like it's already a fact." Moss pretended to glower. He was a man after all, and flattered that this beautiful young woman wanted to bear him yet another child.

"Isn't it?"

"No, Billie, it isn't. I don't want you taking chances. You've got to be strong for the two children we already have. When the war is over and I'm here with you, that's the time to think of another child. Unless, of course, you've got your doubts about my coming out of this one in one piece." His gaze was sharp, keen, piercing Billie.

"I don't think that at all. I know nothing will happen to you. That's another reason—I want to have a son for you when you return. Please, Moss. Darling?"

"Billie, I never willingly refuse you anything, but I think we should wait. The girls are wonderful, they're beautiful and charming, and they are more than I ever imagined daughters could be. I don't need a son."

Lie. Lie through your teeth, Coleman. Make it sound like the truth. Need. Want. There was a difference. He had said he didn't need a son. Change it, Coleman, before it's too late.

"I don't want a son right now, Billie," he said. "I'm content with Maggie and Susy."

Diversion. That's how some battles were won. "Billie, have you written Thad lately?"

It took Billie a moment to adjust to the sudden change in the conversation. "No, I haven't. Do you want me to write to him?"

"I think it might be a good idea. He only gets mail from his mother. He likes you, Billie, and I know he'd appreciate it. You could give him all the lowdown about how the girls are growing. When I tell it, it sounds like bragging."

Well, if he could do an about-face in the conversation, so could she. "Lieutenant, how would you like me to make love to you, Billie Coleman style?" The finger that traced the length of his torso insidiously invaded private property.

"Is there a difference from the Moss Coleman style?" he

asked, shifting to present himself to her hands and lips.

"Considerable . . . however, I'm not certain you're up to it," Billie teased as she nibbled his ear.

"I'm up to it and you know it!" He seized her hand and pressed it against him.

"Darned if you aren't!" She laughed, a soft, womanly sound, deep and husky with the knowledge of the pleasure to come. It was a sound that ripened his interest, that made him ache to caress her body and to lose himself in her. "If you promise me you won't go away, I'll be right back."

"In this condition? Where would I go? Billie, don't forget to—"

"Use the diaphragm," she finished for him. After Moss had been released from the naval hospital, he'd talked intimately with her about taking measures to prevent another pregnancy and made her promise to see a doctor in San Diego. He'd been so concerned, so sincere, that she could not deny him. She would use the diaphragm tonight, but she would also remove it whenever she felt like, even too early. She didn't think of herself as devious; she was just giving the odds a little boost. If it was meant to be, she would conceive another child. Her conscience didn't prick her, but her image in the bathroom mirror was bitter.

When Billie slipped beneath the silken sheets against Moss's warm, vital body, her face was warm and glowing. "Are you ready, Lieutenant Coleman?"

"Mrs. Coleman, when I see you like this, I'm always ready." The timbre of his voice sent a tingling ripple down her spine.

"No more talking, Lieutenant. I want you to just lie there. You're not to do a thing, understand?"

"Aye-aye, ma'am." His hands reached for the ashen fall of silky hair that fell about her face. He held it to one side and found her mouth with his own.

Billie let all thoughts evaporate. She was a woman, receptive only to loving sensations—the way her thighs felt between his hard, muscular ones; the way the tips of her breasts brushed against his furred chest. Her fingers found the planes and hollows of his body, knowing them more intimately than she knew her own. And as she traced moist patterns with her lips from the base of his throat to the flatness of his belly, she was attuned to his intake of breath, the little gasp of desire that quickened her pulses with a sense of her female power. She seduced him with her hands, her lips, the motions of her body upon him. And when she straddled him and took him into herself, there was victory in her cries of pleasure.

Billie lived in a dream world, surrounded by her children and her husband. It was an idyll, something she'd craved and needed and had never had. Even Seth smiled at her these days, and Agnes was complimentary about everything Billie did. Billie's sense of security grew, and she looked forward to Christmas. This year there would be two perfect little girls under the Christmas tree and Moss would be there, with that look of love and admiration in his eyes.

On the afternoon of December 31 Moss came bounding into the house on La Cienega Boulevard. His face was beaming with excitement. His summer-blue eyes twinkled.

"Look!" he told Billie, opening his jacket. She saw that the last of the bandages and the brace had been removed. "Good as new, fit as a fiddle. I leave to rejoin my squadron on the fifth!"

Before she could say a word, Moss took her into his arms and buried his lips in her smoke-blond hair. "Be happy for me, Billie. It's what I want. What I need."

And what of her needs? she thought. What of them? And the children? She was beginning to understand that if she forced Moss to make a choice, he wouldn't choose her.

"I'm going to tell Pap. Better batten down the hatches. He's not going to like this." He left her as quickly as he'd embraced her and hurried away to face Seth.

Agnes found Billie in the hallway on the bottom step of the stairs, elbows on knees, head in hands. "Billie? What's wrong?"

"Moss. He's going back to his squadron. He's telling Seth now."

Billie heard the hiss of her indrawn breath. "And what about you, Billie?" she asked. "What about us? All of us, including the children?" There was a desperate edge to Agnes's voice that she didn't try to disguise. Her long, brightly painted fingers played with her rope of pearls. The taffeta slip beneath her light woolen suit rustled pleasantly as she sat beside her daughter. "Do you remember our little talk? And do your remember how Seth treated Amelia, his own flesh and blood?..."

"That's enough, Mother! I don't want to hear any more. And as for our little talk, I'm doing the best I can. And this time it's for *me*, Mother, for me! Because *I* want a son. Everyone else be damned!"

Billie stood, leaving Agnes sitting alone on the stairs, and went into the living room. When she returned she carried a decanter of cognac and two snifters. Back straight, expression solemn, she climbed the stairs without a glance or a word to her watchful mother.

Outside her bedroom door, Billie shook back her hair and lifted the corners of her mouth into a smile, then burst into the room. "Hi, darling. I battened down the hatches but I didn't hear a sound. How's your father taking the news?"

"How else?" Moss said bitterly. "He's never understood what was important to me. He's furious and refuses to go out with us tonight. What've you got there?"

"Oh, I thought you needed someone to celebrate with. And I couldn't think of anyone better than myself. I want you to be happy, darling, and I'm happy for you."

Moss's expression softened. "You're quite a woman, Mrs. Coleman. Did I ever tell you that?"

"Not in those words. I didn't bring any ice—do you need ice?"

Moss laughed. "And ruin twenty-year-old cognac? C'mon, let's pour us a drink and celebrate a new year." He never noticed Billie locking the door behind her.

Billie lay beside Moss, her head fuzzy from the cognac, and felt his hands trail lazily over her body. "My wife, my beautiful wife," he was murmuring against her ear as his fingers worked the front buttons of her blouse. He'd drunk too much, taken two glasses to one of hers, and she knew that his judgment had evaporated in his excitement over being allowed to rejoin his squadron. It was exactly as she wanted it. Men had their war machines for battle; women had their own bodies. Hard stool or soft flesh, strength or passion. In the end it was the same, and always for the same selfish reasons.

Slowly, almost lazily, they undressed each other, lips kissing and moistening newly bared skin. It was late afternoon and dusky shadows hovered outside the lace-covered windows. Rosy light invaded the room, warming the color of their bodies and splashing intriguing designs on the walls and bedclothes. Billie curled toward him, one hand exploring his rock-hard chest, one leg resting lightly against his. Moss hovered over her, his liquor-scented breath pleasantly fanning her cheek. One bold finger charted her face, stroking her golden brow, following the slender turn of her nose, the downy prominence of her cheekbone and the yielding softness of her rosy mouth. He nibbled her lower lip, smiling when her mouth trembled. Her hazel eyes were sultry and alive, open to welcome him into their silvery depths.

He caressed her tenderly, tracing the tender hollow of her shoulder, the globes of her firm, coral-crested breasts. The nipples hardened and rose beneath his palms. His hands moved lower, to her narrow waist, the round curve of her hip, the soft flesh of her belly, the enticing golden down, and the warm valley.

Her eyes closed then, and she moved against his fingers, whispering in delighted encouragement when his mouth followed where his hands had been, finding her satiny contours. It was her murmur of delight that heightened his passion and left him trembling. The tide of his emotions was sweeping him into a sea of sensation. He was exhilarated by the cognac, by the power of bringing this woman such pleasure, and by the knowledge that he would soon be returning to his squadron. All of life was his and it pounded through his veins in a rhythmic rush that made all things sweeter. Life. Love. Passion.

He covered her body with his own, his mouth finding hers as he pressed into her and felt himself enveloped in warm, pulsing flesh that welcomed him.

Billie offered her mouth to his, tasting herself mingled with the cognac. Deeper and deeper he penetrated, slowly, languorously, until she completely surrounded him, taking him inside her, tasting, kissing, until there was no sensation beyond him. Moss, only Moss, within her, surrounding her, becoming her. Moss, filling her life, touching her heart, becoming her world and her universe. She did not exist outside of this moment. She needed, she wanted, she took. And gave. What had begun as a calculation was ending as a glorious gift, shared between them.

They fit each other. Her rhythms perfectly matched his own, her flesh and bones supported him, melted into him, comfortable, yielding in ever-deepening, ever-quickening undulations. Flesh swallowed flesh and became one, again and again, deeper and deeper, caressing with each stroke, possessing with rippling waves until there was nothing except those two parts of themselves that merged and joined and bonded, lifting them together in a path to the sun.

The Texas Ranger soared into the endless sky, away from Moss's squadron and back to the Big E. Something had jimmied in his instrument panel and his Wildcat was having difficulty maintaining altitude. The mechanics would have the Ranger right in no time. Moss banked to port and read his compass heading, exhilarated by the unhampered freedom of flight, by the satisfaction of a job well done. In late January, he'd been involved in strikes on Formosa and Okinawa. February had seen the first air strikes on Tokyo, and now it was March and the Big E and her men and machines were supporting the occupation of Iwo Jima.

There was a vibration in the fuselage, a shudder beneath his feet. He was steadily losing altitude! He attempted to make voice contact with his squadron, but the frequencies in his headset seemed jammed. Again he tried. Nothing.

Swallowing panic, Moss pulled back on the stick, feeling the Ranger attempt a response yet continue on her downward course. Her engine spit, then coughed. Emergency procedure drilled through his brain, but he wouldn't admit he needed to use it. Like death, it had always seemed only a remote possibility. The Ranger was spiraling down, about to roll into a tailspin. Moss tried to regain mastery of the fighter plane, all the while attempting to make radio contact with either the *Enterprise* or his squadron. The panel lights dimmed and then failed altogether. The prop was slowing before his eyes. If the Ranger went into a tailspin, a safe bailout would be impossible. The prop was making lazy windmills. Desperately he worked the rubber pedals, feeling them stiff, unresponsive. Useless. He'd heard an old flight chief talk about setting a Wildcat down on her ailerons and elevator, but the Ranger had gone dead in the air and was plunging from seven thousand feet to the hungry sea below.

Never bail out below a thousand feet! It was a precaution he reiterated several times a day in training. Yet he knew he must be below that when in a single explosive motion he hurled back the canopy, climbed to his feet, jammed the stick full forward, and pulled the ripcord of his chute. The dead Ranger dropped from under him; the parachute fluttered and opened and snatched him upward.

The sea felt like a concrete wall when he hit, but he managed to release the snap hooks that held his chute. The sea engulfed him and he went deep into its blackness. But when he struggled upward and broke the surface, he was free of the entangling silk.

He took huge gulps of air and pulled the toggles on his Mae West. One side filled at once; the other hung limp. Treading water, Moss laboriously blew up the lifesaving jacket. It was then that he noticed blood ribboning into the water beneath him. He must have torn his leg when the chute yanked him from the cockpit. Blood drew sharks, which were numerous in these waters. He must get himself out of the sea!

Reaching around, he zipped the pararaft out of its envelope and pulled the inflation toggle. It responded, whuffing into shape. Encumbered by the Mae West, he struggled aboard, lifting his torn leg into the raft. He could feel panic closing in on him, but he recognized it for what it was and held himself in rigid control.

Bobbing along on the waves with nauseating regularity, Moss watched the sky and waited. The long night descended. He prayed for morning and waited.

When the sun finally broke the horizon it was a hot, angry, crimson ball that rouged the cumulus puffs. His salt-caked face and the exposed skin at wrists and ankles began to burn. And still he watched the sky. He concentrated on guarding against despair.

He checked his watch and gratefully found it still working. He noted the time. If he fell asleep, it would seem only minutes but in reality it would be hours. He took a position fix on the sun. The wind seemed constant and he was drifting in a northwesterly direction, away from the last-known position of the *Enterprise*. Moss's equipment consisted of a sturdy bladed knife sewn into a sheath on the leg of his flight suit and a .45-caliber automatic pistol in a holster on the web belt around his waist. He worried that the pistol would be useless, but when he test-fired it the satisfying recoil sprang up his arm to the elbow. At least he wasn't completely defenseless.

He was parched and ravenously hungry. Before shielding his face from the sun by hunkering down into the protective shadow of his life vest, he checked his leg wound. A satisfactory clot of blood had created a scab. At least he wouldn't bleed to death.

The sun was only thirty degrees above the level of the sea when Moss awakened. Late afternoon. He cursed himself for having fallen asleep. Precious hours had been wasted; he should have been on the lookout for a passing ship. He squinted into the distance, blinked, and squinted again. Was it his imagination or was that a ship coming out of due west? The sun was blinding him and he was light-headed with hunger, panic, and thirst, but he would swear on his life it was a ship. As the sun sank behind it, its silhouette began to appear. A superstructure, a smokestack, a gun mount. It was a destroyer and it was heading straight for him.

Throwing himself onto his belly and reaching into the water, Moss paddled himself forward, attempting to close the distance between him and the ship. Rescue was imminent. He stood in the raft, balancing himself on widespread legs, waving his white cotton undershirt. With a whoop of excitement he saw the white water boil behind the stern, saw the bow make a course correction. It was coming for him! A sheer solid wall of steel rising and falling with the ocean's swell. Moss resumed paddling. A rope ladder was flung down to him. He grabbed it solidly with both hands and hoisted himself to safety. The prayer in his heart had been answered. A wide grin split his face—there was no beating the Coleman luck! He looked up, ready to shout howdy to his rescuers. His grin froze. The deck rail was lined with faces. All of them Japanese!

{{{{{{{{{ CHAPTER NINETEEN }}}}}}}}}

March had arrived at Sunbridge like the proverbial lion and was leaving like a lamb. Seth watched Billie's advancing pregnancy with a knowledgeable eye. This time it would be a boy, a grandson; he could feel it in his bones. Billie herself seemed pleased with the pregnancy. She was more confident, healthier. There was no nausea and sickness with this child as there had been with Maggie and Susan. Seth thought there was a peacefulness about Billie that had never been there before.

Agnes also watched her daughter. Although Billie was only beginning her fourth month, Agnes satisfied herself that the signs were there. Billie was carrying high and straight, instead of round and hippy as with the girls. It was definitely a boy this time. Seth would grunt whenever she mentioned it to him, but he believed every word.

Billie smiled. Neither of them could be one hundred percent certain. Only her. Billie Coleman would have her son.

Billie had announced her pregnancy only two weeks before, on the same day she'd written Moss telling him about their "little accident." She'd hugged the letter to her breast before she'd mailed it. By now, Moss would know another child was on the way and that she was certain it would be a boy.

As Billie settled down to write to Moss, she looked at the calendar as she did every day and crossed off the date. It was six weeks and three days since she'd heard from Moss. Even Seth hadn't had word. It worried her but it wasn't unusual. Often a pack of letters would arrive at once. Moss was fine; she felt it. If something had happened to him, she would know.

The bedside clock read 11:20 when Billie decided to go downstairs for a glass of warm milk. As she was crossing the wide, central hall the doorbell shrilled, startling her.

"Telegram for Mrs. Moss Coleman. Sign here." Billie's trembling hands reached for the yellow envelope. The delivery boy's face was a study in sympathy and pity. The return address was the War Department.

"Mother!" she screamed.

She experienced everything after that through waves of blackness, in slow motion. Agnes coming down the stairs. Seth stepping out of his study. She knew that in reality Agnes had flown down the stairs and Seth had exploded from his study.

Seth sat down on the cowhide-covered bench and stared at the rectangle of yellow paper. He seemed unable to move.

"Would you like me to open it, Seth?" Agnes asked quietly. He suddenly looked old and beaten. Two pairs of eyes watched as Agnes deftly slit the envelope. The words jumped off the page:

WE REGRET TO INFORM YOU LT. MOSS COLEMAN HAS BEEN LISTED AS MISSING IN ACTION.

Missing, not killed. Missing. Missing. It was all Billie had to hold on to.

"That's all it says." Agnes relinquished the telegram to Seth's shaking hands. She straightened and belted her blue chenille robe more tightly about her. "I'll make coffee. Follow me to the kitchen, both of you. We will not have hysteria. Moss is missing. It did not say he was wounded or dead, only missing. Until we know something definite we will carry on as before. Billie! Get hold of yourself! You have a baby to think of. We're going to have coffee and even some cake and we'll talk, all of us together. And then we'll all go to bed because that's all we can do."

"Those Jap bastards have him. They torture, they—"

"Not another word, Seth," Agnes said sharply. "I don't want you upsetting Billie. She's pregnant, or have you forgotten? We'll have no more of that kind of talk. And you, Billie, you have to believe that Moss is well and will come back. He promised he would come back and we must believe he will. Now, that's good enough for me and it has to be good enough for both of you." Billie nodded miserably as she dabbed at her eyes with the cuff of her dressing gown.

"All right, Aggie. Where the hell is that coffee you said you were making?"

"It's right here. What did I tell you about swearing in front of me? I know you're upset now but don't let it happen again. It has to perk. Five more minutes. Tita had the pot all ready for morning. I can't seem to find any cake, so we're having cornbread with butter. And some blackberry jam would be good."

Billie noticed the slight tremble in her mother's hands as she set the table. Busy. Always keep busy so you don't have to think. Agnes would keep busy and she and Seth would eat. They would chew and swallow. Then when Agnes dismissed them they would go to their respective rooms and cry like babies. Seth for his son, she for her husband, and Agnes for the good life.

They carried on; it was all they could do. Agnes prodded and poked at them to busy themselves. Her tongue was sharp and they obeyed.

Billie managed to fill her days with the girls and writing letters to Moss which she hid away in her lingerie drawer. It made no difference if she could mail them or not. It was something to do. She didn't cry; she didn't know why exactly. It had nothing to do with her mother, more with Moss's conviction that he would return. She hung on to that thought. It was the letters that arrived from Thad Kingsley that bolstered her sagging spirits. They arrived weekly and were full of nonsensical news that made her smile. He always mentioned Moss at the end, expressed certainty that he was safe somewhere and would manage to make it back home.

It never occurred to Billie to question how Thad's letters managed to be delivered weekly, with no in-between skips. He was fighting the same war as Moss, flying in the same squadron, serving on the same ship. It was enough that he wrote.

In a month's time Billie knew every member of the squadron and all about their personal lives. She knew about the girls they'd left behind and the pets they had grown up with. She learned about the inside of the planes and what made them fly. She learned Thad's middle name and what New England looked like in autumn. Her mouth watered for some Vermont maple syrup. The letters were long, written in a close, cramped style with many, many words to the page. Billie treasured the man's thoughtfulness. Someday, she would find a way to make it up to him. The comfort his letters gave her, the hope, could never be measured.

Seth stomped into the house late one afternoon, his shoulders bent and his face filled with misery. Billie's heart almost stopped. "What is it, Seth? Have you had word about Moss?" she asked anxiously.

Seth shook his head and wiped at his eyes with the back of his hand. "Nessie died."

"Your horse?" Billie said stupidly.

"Yes, my horse, Nessie. She died. Just now. I have to call the vet."

"If the horse is dead, why do you have to call the vet?"

"Because I do," Seth snarled. "Because I do."

It was as if the horse had been a flesh-and-blood person. It was almost more than Billie could bear.

Agnes's summary of the situation was simple: She and Billie didn't understand because they weren't born-and-bred Texans.

But Billie did understand. Nessie had been more important in Seth's life than his wife. There had been no tears for Jessica. She watched him make daily pilgrimages to the place where the horse was buried, and he always returned with red-rimmed eyes and a surly tongue. This, too, shall pass, Billie told herself. And it did. Seth, though, hovered over Billie after that. This child was his last hope—nothing must go wrong. It was all he had left. God help me, Billie thought, if this baby fools us all.

* * *

Moss was flung against the cold, damp bulkhead. The sea was rough tonight. He'd been blindfolded when they'd thrown him down here, but he could tell from the sounds of the engines and the slick sliding behind the steel wall that he was below the waterline in the hold of the Japanese transport ship. The hold was blacker than a cave and twice as cold. For mates he had several other Americans, a few Australians, and a rat.

Shortly after being rescued from the sea he'd been questioned mercilessly and then hoisted over to this passing transport. The poop had it that they were on their way to Japan. That had been eight days ago—he'd kept count by moving the end of his bootlace into successive holes and knotting the end. Once a day the forward hatch would open and uniformed soldiers, armed and at attention, would bring in a pail of water and rice balls for each of them, eight in all.

While Moss had been flying the Ranger, he'd thought of the Japanese as faceless robots of a corrupt government, enemies to the American way and all it stood for. Now the enemy had a face, yellow and flat and menacing, and he hated them, not just their government, not as a nation, but each and every one of them individually.

The prisoners' lives had become an eternity of blackness, of sensations of cold and filth. One marine, wounded on Iwo Jima, had died two days before. His body lay somewhere in the dark. One of the Aussies knew a bit of Japanese and had told the soldiers of the marine's death. Instead of removing the body, they'd merely withheld a rice portion, and tossed a dipper of precious water onto the metal plate floor. When an Australian infantryman had hauled himself to his feet and begun shouting at the Japs, he'd received a solid blow from a billy club as his reward. No one had spoken after that for a very long time.

Hours were endless, time meaningless; yet each day, after their one poor meal was served, Moss moved his bootlace into another eyelet. Now he was working on the holes in his left boot. He wondered if he would still be alive by the time he reached the top. He wondered if he wanted to be.

One cold gray dawn the transport ship's engines were cut and the ship rolled with the tide. The eight beaten, sick, half-starved prisoners came out on deck, into the fresh offshore wind, and saw that they were part of a larger group than they'd realized. There were sixty other prisoners. Word spread that they were all going ashore to a place named Muishi. Moss tried to remember his geography but he couldn't place it. Muishi, as it turned out, was a coal-mining camp deep in the hills of northern Japan.

Life became a living hell. Each dawn, shirtless, shoeless, the prisoners were herded into Muishi's coal mine, half walking, half crawling for almost two miles underground where the air was stale and noxious and the temperature dropped nearly thirty degrees. Each night they were herded out again, more dead than alive.

Nearly four hundred men slaved in the mines, working to their last breaths to dig and haul the coal from the earth for their Japanese masters. . . .

Food became an obsession in Muishi. The hard rice balls and an occasional watery stew and hard biscuits were hardly enough to keep the men alive.

The Japanese were ruthless and cruel taskmasters, but they respected religious ceremonies. So when the prisoners told their captors that it was the custom when a man died to leave food by the body and that the living smoked cigarettes and prayed and spoke praise of the dead, they were believed. And from then on, whenever a man died, the guards would provide bowls of rice, which they placed at his head, and a basket of fruit, which they rested by his feet. And cigarettes were given to the mourners.

In time, the prisoners' appetites faded; the mindless work anesthetized them; hope became a dim memory. But *home* was something shared by all, remembered by all, even though to each it was a different place and different people.

The desire to live strengthened in Moss. He wanted to see his children again, to hold his wife in his arms. Each day became a battle to hold on to his mental agility and to his toughness. And the only way he could do this was to hate, hate the enemy, hate the Japs. Hate.

Those who gave in to hopelessness soon died, believing the Japanese braggarts who insisted the war would last a hundred years. There was so little information coming from the outside that there were moments when Moss almost believed them, too. Those were the moments he nearly broke, nearly gave up. But he would remind himself he was a Coleman. Colemans never stopped fighting. Colemans were tougher than beef jerky and more stubborn than mules. He clung to his heritage and dreamed of his children. Maggie. Susan. The son that would never be if he gave in to despair. . . .

Early during the heat of August, Moss and the others noted that something was happening. Food became more plentiful, drinking water more available. No one was punished or beaten for being too sick to go down in the mine. Something was happening.

President Harry Truman had given the go-ahead. The ultimate weapon was dropped on Japan. On August 14, 1945, the Japanese government agreed to an unconditional surrender. Muishi was so far north that word didn't reach them until two weeks later.

On September 2, 1945, Japan surrendered formally aboard the USS *Missouri*. V-J Day. Victory over Japan. Moss and his fellow prisoners were brought aboard an Australian troop transport and into the arms of the victors.

Early that same day, as his missing father was being welcomed by the jaunty Australians, Riley Seth Coleman was delivered into his mother's arms. Billie had finally achieved her victory.

PART THREE

The land and the place known as Sunbridge had changed little in the fourteen years since Billie had first arrived from Philadelphia. The grazing lands were lush this year, thanks to plentiful rain, and the winter's tumbleweeds rolled silently along the miles of white rail fencing. The shrubbery surrounding the house was taller, but the rose garden was still perfectly tended, a living memorial to Jessica, now more than twelve years buried on the little hill behind the house. The house itself had mellowed to a softer hue, bleached by its years in the sun, now paler than the prairie rose.

But the seemingly unchangeable stability of Sunbridge halted at the front door. Inside, time had made its mark. Seth Coleman, righteous monarch, leaned more heavily on his cane and his shaggy mane of hair was more grizzled. But his tongue was just as sharp as ever, his watery blue eyes just as piercing. His only interest in life was his ten-year-old grandson, Riley. When Moss's look-alike wasn't flying, strapped to the seat beside his father, he was riding the hills with his grandfather. Riley had just given up his pony for a mare, a descendant of old Nessie, which Seth had given him.

Riley had been made a part of Sunbridge since the day he was born. As heir apparent to the Coleman throne, he was taught to love his heritage and was schooled with one aim: to someday take the reins of the Sunbridge empire. Riley was a lanky boy with soft, shining blue eyes and gently rounded cheeks. Despite the attention lavished upon him, he was unspoiled, a loving child who never demanded anything. Not that he had to demand anything; whatever he asked for was promptly given, whatever seemed to interest him was his—within the hour. But young Riley Coleman was a sensitive, responsible boy and his growing surplus of possessions alarmed him; he was beginning to learn to disguise his interests, to force his glance away from a new attraction. With his every wish anticipated, his every dream fulfilled, there was too much to see to, too much to care for. It overwhelmed him.

To Riley, it just wasn't right to own a complicated German-made camera and not know how to use it (he would have been more than satisfied with a Brownie Hawkeye, anyway), so he spent long, tiresome hours poring over the directions and studying books on photography, and what should have been fun became a chore.

Riley was just as conscientious in his personal relationships. He loved his sisters and took his role as brother to Maggie and Susan seriously. He knew just when to stop teasing and he could be counted on to keep secrets, any secret, especially Maggie's. With Billie, Riley was both boy and baby, warm and loving, seeking an extra little smile or a tender kiss at bedtime. With Grandmother Agnes, Riley was polite and always gentlemanly—although conversation was mostly limited to "Yes, ma'am," "No, ma'am," and "Thank you, ma'am." Agnes was satisfied.

But it was with Moss that Riley was all boy, all noise and vitality, whooping and hollering, rambunctious. It was with his father, too, that he shared his hopes and dreams, his hurts and wounds. He never cried, this Coleman child, because it was unmanly. The girls, though, who seemed more their mother's children than their father's, were permitted to wail or whimper at will.

Riley tried not to show favoritism, but Susan was his favorite sister. She didn't shriek and yell and call him names. She was soft and gentle, like Mam, and played beautiful music on the piano. Susan always did as she was told and no one ever needed to punish her.

Maggie, on the other hand, was willful and rebellious, and found more ways to get into trouble than he could ever dream. Sometimes he lay in bed at night and tried to figure out why Maggie was the way she was. There were times when he actually believed she hated him, hated everyone. She drank beer in the barn with the cowboys, and when Pap and Grandpap were off on the range or in town on business, she drove their cars around the ranch. She had ugly friends, friends who only wanted to be with her because she had money to spend and could steal wine and beer and cigarettes. Riley always included Maggie in his prayers. He should tell on her—he knew he should—but he didn't. He couldn't. He'd come upon Maggie one day in the new barn, where his horse was stabled. She was snuggled down in the sweet-smelling straw crying great, hard sobs. He'd never seen anyone cry that way and it bit at him, making him run away. Maggie would have felt terrible if she knew he'd seen her—she felt bad enough already. That was why he didn't tell her, or anyone. He'd seen her take boys into the barn, but so far he'd never said anything about that, either. The boys would come out smiling and furtive, but Maggie always looked surly and miserable. Someday, though, he was going to talk to Pap about Maggie. Pap would know what to do. Pap knew everything about everything, so the troubles of a thirteen-going-on-fourteen-year-old girl wouldn't stump him. Not Pap . . .

Tita and Carlos had been pensioned off with a generous monthly allotment and three acres of good Coleman land. Seth never ceased to be amazed at how generous Agnes was with his money. The elderly couple had been replaced with a spiffy buxom girl named Charlotte and her pockmarked brother, Miguel. They wore made-to-order uniforms, which Agnes ordered by the dozen. Trained by her, they were the perfect servants and, the most valuable of their attributes in Agnes's opinion, they recognized her position in the household and honored it. Sunbridge worked like a well-oiled clock. Things were in hand.

If anything could be said of Agnes Ames, it was that she had aged beautifully, thanks to the finest hairdressers, an expensive wardrobe, a weekly massage, manicure, pedicure, and facial, a careful diet, and exercises done secretly in her bedroom. A quiet little trip back east ("to visit with old friends") had taken her no nearer Philadelphia than New York City, where a plastic surgeon had removed the fatty pads around her eyes and tightened her jawline. Now nearer sixty than fifty, Agnes had achieved just the life she wanted. She was about to accept her second term as president of the prestigious Canterbury Club and had been sitting on the board of directors of Sunbridge Enterprises for the past six years. Agnes had come into her own and she ruled with a steel scepter. No one, not even Seth, questioned her. Agnes Ames always smiled right before she fell asleep.

Since returning from the Japanese prisoner-of-war camp, Moss's zest for living had never flagged. Acceding to Seth's demands, Moss had thrown himself into Sunbirdge activities: ranching, beef, corn, and oil. But always his greatest efforts were reserved for electronics, where his curiosity and firsthand knowledge of airplanes were put to best use. He and his personal team of researchers had patented a number of inventions that were adopted by the aircraft industry, including a high-range radio antenna and a method for pressurizing commercial aircraft cabins. His dream of building the biggest and most efficient aircraft factories would soon become a reality.

Moss worked and he played. He also drank more than was good for him, but he was still handsome and trim. And there were women. Billie was his wife, the mother of his children, and he loved her. But he had faced death many times during the war, then had endured a living death in the Japanese camp, and now he was going to savor and taste everything life had to offer. Life had so much to offer a man like him and he saw no reason whatever to deny himself.

The love of Moss's life was Riley. His son. His own chance for immortality. Maggie and Susan could never become as important a part of his life as Riley. Daughters were pretty, sweet, and they could flatter and charm their fathers. But a son was a projection of the man himself, both a whisper of the past and a statement for the future. Daughters grew up and married; other men became the focus of their lives. A man's son was his own forever, as much his own as a broken-in pair of boots or the money he earned.

Somewhere along the way—Moss wasn't exactly certain when—he had converted his childhood room into an office and shop that was kept strictly for his own private endeavors. He'd installed a couch in place of the single bed and more often than not, he worked long into the night and fell asleep there. It hadn't been his intention to abandon the bedroom he shared with Billie, but more and more of his clothes were finding their way downstairs and he had less and less occasion to climb the stairs to the room where his wife slept. It hadn't been planned; it had just happened, and Billie had voiced no objection.

It was to his business, his ambitions, and his friends that Moss was attentive. A week never passed that he didn't speak to Thad Kingsley on the phone. The bills had been enormous during the progression of Thad's career in the navy and his travels all over the world. Thad was a buddy, and whenever possible they got together. Now Thad was a rear admiral and commandant of Naval Air Operations, based in Corpus Christi, just a hop-skip-jump in the Sunbridge plane.

{ 304 }

Moss confided in Thad, drank with him till the early-morning hours. It was Thad who made certain Moss was bedded down for the night. It was Thad who called Moss's private number the following day to check on his hangover. It was not unusual for the tall, lanky New Englander in his immaculate uniform to step from his own Piper Cub onto the dusty airstrip that ran two miles south of Sunbridge and come to the house for lunch or an afternoon drink that lasted through dinner. Then Thad and Moss would relive old times, hash over Moss's deep hatred for the Japanese, make plans for their futures.

Thad liked visiting Sunbridge, he liked seeing Billie, watching her from across the table, hearing the soft lyrical voice that had never really surrenderd the rounded sounds of the northeast to the flat drawl of Texas. He enjoyed Susan's gentle blondness—so like Billie's—marveled at Riley's charismatic charm, and watched Maggie's brunette beauty bloom like the darkest rose in Billie's garden.

Often lately, Billie hadn't been at home when Thad made his impromptu visits. Busy, Moss would say, Billie was always busy. Then, at Thad's inquiring glance, Moss would clarify. "Billie seems to have picked up where Mam left off. She belongs to all the little women's groups and she's active in the PTA, and, of course, there's Memorial Hospital in Austin. Pap expects it and she complies. Also, she's developed an interest in painting at this little studio. She's damn good, too, Thad. You should see the picture she did of Sunbridge for Pap this past Christmas. Pap said she finally did something worthwhile with her dabbling."

Billie added a delicious dab of perfume behind each ear. It was wickedly expensive and it always made her feel good. This morning she needed it. Perfume was hardly a substitute for her husband, but it would have to do.

She couldn't help letting her eyes stray to the mound of gifts piled on the chaise longue. Birthday gifts from her family and friends, presented to her the night before at a celebration at the Canterbury Club. Conspicuously absent was a gift from her husband. Unless, of course, you counted the bunch of wilted daisies lying on her dressing table. Charlotte had brought them up before the party and said Mr. Coleman had picked them himself. Picked them himself but couldn't be bothered to climb the stairs to present them. Angrily, Billie swept them off the glass-topped vanity.

Moss had danced with her once. He had even brought her a drink—the wrong kind. Then he had gone off to the bar to sit with Seth and the other ranchers.

When the party was over, Susan had helped her mother with her coat and Maggie had sneered when she'd seen tears in Billie's eyes.

"What did you expect, Mother? Did you really think Pap was going to sit here and pay attention to *us*?"

Yes, that was exactly what she'd thought. It was what she'd wanted. She had lain awake, alone, in the huge bed, waiting. Until dawn. She wanted her husband. She needed to have him beside her, needed to feel his touch and hear him whisper the old words. Even if they no longer held the same passion, she needed to hear them. She could always separate the lies from the truth later. . . .

Why *hadn't* he climbed the steps to their room? Her room now. Why hadn't he wanted her? Couldn't he see how she ached for him?

Where had it gone wrong? When had his clothes disappeared from the huge double closet? She couldn't remember exactly. Little by little, until one day only her clothes and shoes were behind the louvered doors. Why hadn't she seen it coming and done something? Was it too late now? Could marriages be mended the way ranch fences were? Was it worth it to try?

She had her own life now. A busy life, filled with busy things. Her clubs, shopping, the hairdresser, her classes at the studio. Billie sniffed.

Billie knew she was going to be late for breakfast. Lately it seemed she was always late. What did it matter? Moss only had coffee and it was usually on the run or in the backseat of the car. Agnes ate with Seth around sunrise, a habit she had begun on her arrival fourteen years before. Riley, Maggie, and Susan, in exclusive private schools in the city, returned only on weekends to Sunbridge and sometimes not even then.

The table was monstrously long. It was also empty. Billie sat down and pressed the little bell at her plate. "Coffee and toast. A three-minute egg," Billie said as an afterthought. "Where is everyone?"

"I don't know, madam. Would you like me to call your mother? I'm sure she knows where everyone is."

"No, Charlotte. And don't make the egg. I'm not in the mood for an egg."

"Very well, madam."

"And another day begins at Sunbridge." Billie sighed.

"I thought I'd find you here, Mother. I need some money. Fifty dollars." Maggie stood in the doorway, shoulders straight, back rigid. But her expression was sweet, her blue eyes mild and trusting, her gleaming cap of dark hair smoothed into place. Billie tried to deny the thought that whenever Maggie wanted something she donned the good-and-grateful-daughter pose like a cloak. Gone was the sullen rebellion, the tightness around the soft girlish mouth, the challenge in the eyes. Standing before her was a defenseless child with a need.

"I know it seems like a lot, Mother, but it's for books and there's this angora sweater in Kaplan's—" Maggie's words halted when Billie's face closed.

"I don't want to hear how I spend too much money!" Maggie said suddenly, her voice harsh. "Either say yes or no. I'm not in the mood for a lecture."

"I'm not in the mood to give you one," Billie said wearily.

Maggie's expression became a sneer. "Still smarting over Pap's ignoring you last night? I'd make him pay for that if I were you. I saw the pitying glances people gave you." When Billie turned her head, unable to defend herself, Maggie attacked again. "Well, are you going to give it to me or not?"

"You say you need it for books? And a sweater?" Billie knew it was a lie but was reluctant to delve for the truth. She knew she wouldn't like it. Anything was possible with Maggie, her poor hurting little girl. Her little girl who, more than anyone, missed Moss's attention. She was so like Amelia. The same hurt was there in Maggie, the same defiant rebellion. Billie forced her voice to express loving attention. "What color is the sweater, dear? Will it go with that new navy skirt I brought home for you last week? Why don't you sit with me while I have my coffee?"

Maggie knew there was no need to respond to the invitation—nor did she want to. She recognized this tender affection in her mother as surrender. The fifty dollars was as good as in her hand. "Can't. I'm meeting some of my friends. Well, are you going to give it to me?"

Billie was miffed and her hostility surfaced, but she overcame it. She wasn't up to an out-and-out fight with Maggie this morning.

Maggie accepted the money and stuffed it into her pocket. "I'm going to Galveston this weekend with Carol and her family. Tell me now if you're going to make a stink about it."

"And if I did decide to make a 'stink,' as you call it?"

"Then when I leave today I'll just go over to Carol's house and won't come home."

The challenge was there. Billie felt defeated but her motherly concern prompted her to try reasoning with Maggie. "Maggie, we have to talk. These friends of yours, I don't—"

"Forget it, Mother. You don't like anyone except that man you married, but the question is, does Pap like you? I think after last night the answer should be clear to you. You don't count, Mother. I don't count. Susan doesn't count. Only Riley matters. Riley and Grandpap. Go ahead and tell me it isn't true."

"Maggie . . ."

"Spare me, Mother. No more lectures. I'm up to here with words that don't mean a damn thing."

"Maggie, watch your language. You sound like a ranch hand. Why can't you—"

"Behave and act like a Coleman? Do you want to know something? I'm sick of the Colemans. I'm just plain sick to death of the whole lot of us. I didn't ask to be born into this stinking family. I can't wait till I can leave home and breathe some other kind of air. Air that Colemans don't own. God! They even own the damn air!"

"That's stupid," Billie said harshly. "Maggie, get control of yourself."

"Sure, everything I say is stupid. When did you ever hear me say anything that wasn't stupid? I'm no good. I'm ugly. I'm stupid. But I *am* a Coleman, so that makes me something, doesn't it, Mother?"

Billie's mouth opened and then closed, her brows drew together over the bridge of her nose, but her expression didn't begin to convey the hurt she was feeling for her child. "Maggie, how did all this begin? All I asked was what color sweater you were going to buy."

"And don't think I don't know why you handed over the money so easily. It's because you're afraid you'll have to come down to the police station again because I was caught shoplifting. I told you, that was all a mistake, but I don't care if you go ahead and tell Pap about it or not. So don't threaten me, Mother. You won't tell on me anyway, because you're like all the other parents—guilty. So don't ever help me again. See if I care!"

Maggie's arrow pierced the tender spot of Billie's confidence in herself as a mother. "Maggie, I mean it. I *want* that talk...."

"All right, Mother, let's talk now." Maggie flopped down on one of the dining room chairs.

Almost fourteen years old and all that brightness wasted... so much hatred, so much hostility. Billie recognized that talking with Maggie now would only intensify her anger and would be more destructive than helpful. Would they ever reach an understanding? Why wasn't her love and attention enough for Maggie? Why was it Moss who should matter so much to the girl? "Not now, Maggie. I said this evening; it will give us time to cool down. We're both too angry and overwrought."

"It figures. It's never now. Always later. Funny thing is, later never comes. Did you ever notice that? Yes, I guess you have. Last night was your later, if you get my drift."

Billie glanced at her watch and looked at Maggie again, who was watching her knowingly. She could miss her art class today—she was already late—but she didn't want to miss it, didn't want to be here with a rebellious daughter who was beyond reason. And she didn't want to see Moss if he came in for lunch, either. Class was a refuge and she needed to be there. "Tonight, Maggie. Be here," she said firmly.

"You see, Mother, you didn't hear a word I said. I'm staying with the Lamberts and going to Galveston for the weekend. We can talk some other night. *If* you don't forget."

"Maggie! I didn't give you permission...." But what was the use? Without another word, Billie picked up her purse and left the house.

Maggie ran to the window and watched her mother until she was out of sight. Her eyes ran and she didn't care. Maggie wasn't allowed at the Lamberts' house anymore. She'd been deemed unfit company for their precious daughter Carol since the two girls had been caught drunk with an empty six-pack of beer and the dregs of a bottle of Jack Daniel's. Maggie would never go to Galveston with them again. Carol was sorry but she was afraid to disobey her parents. And the only reasons the Lamberts hadn't told Moss and Billie was that Mr. Lambert had several real estate deals riding with Grandpap. They were intimidated by the Coleman power and money, too, of course. Still, word had spread among the parents of Maggie's other friends and invitations were few now and grudgingly given. No more Galveston, no more friends. But there were other ways of passing the weekend. A motel out on the highway with whoever picked her up. Two days spent with total strangers, men who weren't afraid of the Colemans. No questions. No answers. Then a two-hour soak in the bathtub to rid herself of the dirt. . . .

Riley skidded to a stop at the foot of the stairs. "Where to, Maggs?" he said, glancing at her overnight case.

"Galveston. Want to come along?"

"No. I'm going up in the new Piper Cub with Pap. How far is Galveston? Does Mam know you're going? Is it a secret?" Riley always asked what was or wasn't a secret.

"I told Mam. She doesn't care. I don't care if you don't come along. I didn't want you, anyway. Go on up in the new plane with Pap. I don't care. You stink, Riley. You and Susan both."

"What'd I do? All I did was ask if it was a secret. I think you're the one who stinks!" Seeing the dangerous glint in his sister's eye, Riley took off at a sprint.

Maggie stopped long enough to poke her head into the sunroom, where her sister was playing the piano. Everyone could do something. Riley could fly. Susan was terrific at the piano. Mother could paint *and* play the piano. No wonder Pap loved everybody except her. She was a nothing, a nobody. Susan's golden head was limned by the sunlight coming through the windows. So delicate, so pretty, so unlike her own harsh, dark looks. "You stink, too, you little snot!" Maggie yelled above the music.

Susan kept on playing, her long slender fingers racing over the scales. She'd heard this all before. Maggie hated everyone.

CHAPTER
{{{{{{{{ TWENTY-ONE }}}}}}}}

As Billie parked her little Italian sports car in the studio lot she could feel the tension in her shoulders. The scene with Maggie this morning had been a replay of many before, but she was still shaken. She had had to face the realization, one more time, of her ineffectiveness as a parent to her daughter.

Maggie needed Moss. They *all* needed Moss. But only Riley, bless his heart, could claim the prize of his father's attention.

Crossing the small dusty lot, Billie could already smell the turpentine and oil paints wafting through the open door. She loved coming here, facing the challenge of an empty canvas. Here among the paints and the easy camaraderie of the other students she could forget Sunbridge and her troubled marriage and family. Two hundred and fifty thousand acres and a twenty-room house, and she had to come here to find privacy and comfort.

The studio itself consisted of one large room with two sky-lights, a northern and southern. It was comfortable and it was beautiful, with canvases lined up against one long wall. Brilliant colors lived in this room. Comforting colors, exciting colors, somber colors, even dreary colors. The splendor of life, Billie thought as she hung up her short jacket and took her place. Today, only two other students were working. A third figure looked up at her approach and smiled, a great heart-warming smile whose intimacy seemed to encircle her. Jordan. Jordan Marsh was her teacher and her friend, tall and thin, with sandy hair—more brown than sand, really, with streaks of gray at the temples. When he smiled—and he was smiling now—he was almost handsome, showing off perfect teeth. She felt some of the tension leave her as she returned his smile. At least someone was glad to see her.

More tension dropped from her as she set about mixing pigments. Today she was going to finish a still life she had started earlier in the week. A single daisy in a small vase that resembled a child's pudgy hand. Riley's hand.

An hour into her work, Jordan came to stand behind her, watching her bold, sure strokes. "What's wrong, Billie?" he asked softly.

Billie turned on her stool and looked up at him. It had been so long since anyone had used that soft tone with her. She couldn't even remember the last time anyone had asked if she was all right. Asked as though they cared. Tears brimmed in her eyes. "I'm not sure, Jordan. Probably everything."

"Can I help? Do you want to talk? There's no point in continuing with this. Your colors are all wrong. The stem on that daisy looks like a dead snake."

"You're right, Jordan. I shouldn't be working today. I could use a cup of coffee, if you have one."

"I have a whole pot. Made it right before you arrived. Come

on, let's go back to my apartment. We can talk in private."

Billie had only been in Jordan's apartment once before, when he'd held a surprise luncheon to celebrate a private showing of his work. It was so nice, so private, and the best thing was he could simply walk into his studio at any time of the day or night, whenever he felt like working. He didn't have to go off somewhere like she did.

Jordan took her on a brief tour of his quarters. The rooms reflected his personality. Bold and bright living room, kitchen alive with hand-painted designs on all the cabinet doors. Natural hopsacking hung at the windows and were tied back with vivid scarlet sashing. It was just enough. The assortment of green plants and copper utensils completed the comforting, inviting atmosphere.

But it was the bedroom that Billie liked best. Jordan had done it all in earth tones. It was probably the most restful room she had ever seen. She wondered what it would be like to make love in that comfortable room . . . and promptly flushed.

"Hold that wicked thought, whatever it is!" Jordan said, smiling. Billie laughed, but the crimson stain stayed as they went back to the kitchen and talked over steaming cups filled to the brim with Louisiana coffee.

They chatted about an upcoming show for one of the other students. Then Jordan asked, "Now tell me, beautiful lady, what's wrong?"

"I'm sure I'm making more out of all of this than is necessary. I got up on the wrong side of the bed this morning," said Billie. "My father-in-law hosted a birthday party for me last night. It didn't turn out the way I wanted it to. I was disappointed, Jordan. The reasons aren't important."

"Yes, they are, Billie. They're important to you. Talking about it will bring it into perspective. Look at me, Billie. Where would I be today if I hadn't had someone to talk to, to help me when the bottle was killing me? I'd be in the gutter somewhere, trying to panhandle more money to buy more cheap wine. Someone cared enough to help me. Open up, girl. Share your problems. I know I don't come from your social circle, but I've knocked around, seen life, and I care enough to help you."

"What you are or where you came from has nothing to do with it, Jordan. I find it difficult to even admit there is a problem. Coleman's don't *have* problems. We aren't permitted. So we tend to ignore unpleasant things. We know that sooner or later they will go away." She took a deep breath. "But this is not going to go away."

Jordan was persistent. "Billie, you have to tell me what you're talking about—what isn't going to go away? Friends help one another. Don't shut me out now."

"I can't unload my problems on you just because I'm not strong enough to handle them."

"Have you tried? Or have you been coasting?"

"That's exactly what I've been doing," Billie said miserably. "I failed all the way down the line. I don't know where or how things went wrong. I can't give you a date or a time. Things more or less crept up on me. I feel as though there's a black cloud hovering over me and every day it gets lower and lower." Billie shook her head as though to clear her thoughts. "I think I might just be feeling sorry for myself," she said with forced cheerfulness.

"I don't believe you think that at all. You'd never've come back to my apartment if you weren't upset. How many times have I asked you back here? At least a hundred. You would never come, because it wasn't proper for a married lady to enter a man's apartment."

Billie laughed. He was so good for her. If she could still laugh, there must be hope.

Jordan leaned back on the wooden kitchen chair and watched Billie carefully. Didn't she know how he ached to fold her into his arms? Couldn't she feel the heat that emanated from him at the mere sight of her? Was he forever to be her teacher and no more?

"I don't think you can help me," she said, "but if you want to listen, I would like to talk."

Jordan rummaged in his smock pocket for his pipe—which he never smoked—and stuck it between his teeth. He nodded. He was ready to listen. Billie laughed again. "Someday you aren't going to be able to find that pipe and then where will you be?"

"Up the creek without a paddle." Jordan grinned. "It helps me concentrate. My security blanket, if you will. We all need one, you know."

"No, I didn't know that. I don't think I ever had something like that to comfort me. That is what you're talking about, isn't it, comfort?"

"In a manner of speaking. Start, Billie."

It poured out. Like a waterfall. Jordan sat without moving,

the pipe clenched between his teeth. He made no sudden moves, not wanting to break or disrupt Billie's flow. He didn't even nod.

And then she wound down, slowly, like a locomotive running out of steam. The flush was back on her cheeks. She had opened up, talked about things she hadn't known she remembered. . . . She didn't know if she felt better or worse.

Finally Jordan spoke. "That's a mighty heavy load you've been carrying around for years. But don't you feel a certain amount of relief now that you've opened up?"

Billie pondered. "Yes," she said quietly, "I do. But I still don't have the answers. What do you think, Jordan?"

"I think you have problems that only you can solve. I can't tell you what to do, Billie. You have to come to terms with things, make decisions and stick to them. You can't permit other people to control your life. Both of us know that.

"I will tell you one thing—and it's something I learned from experience, so I can share it with you. My problem was alcohol. It was destroying me. I had a love and it was, and is, art. I had to decide which was more important to me. There are days when I want a drink so bad I think I could kill for it. Then I look at one of my students and I know I can't even touch that bottle again. I was put on this earth for a reason. It's corny, but . . . Billie, I love you, you know."

"I rather thought you did." Billie smiled. Jordan looked a little surprised, and happy.

"Did it help to talk?" he said.

"I think so. I have a lot of thinking to do. I have to do something about Maggie before it's too late."

"Maybe. But wouldn't it be better to get to the root of things and work from there? I'm not saying Maggie isn't important, but until you resolve other things, I don't see how you can do much for her. And she'll recognize the desperation, anyway."

"I'm a coward, Jordan."

"Aren't we all."

"I could botch it all up."

"Then you'll have to live with that. But what's better, trying or doing nothing?"

"I have to think."

"Of course you do."

"I have strange feelings where you're concerned." She was

amazed at her calm, the feeling of easy candor she had with him.

"I rather thought you did." Jordan grinned.

"Time."

"Yes."

"The coffee was great. The talk was even better. I enjoyed sitting back here with you, but I think I should be out there painting. This might be a good time to work on my angry seascape."

"I'd say this is a perfect time."

"Time, Jordan. Give me time."

"All the time in the world. I'm not going anywhere."

On the return ride to Sunbridge Billie could feel her cheeks grow warm as she thought about her conversation. She'd handled his confession very well. Jordan was in love with her. Was that the same as loving? Still, it pleased her to know that an attractive, talented man like Jordan could feel something about her. Her self-esteem was pretty well trampled these days.

An affair with Jordan. It was something to think about. She wondered what it would be like to make love with him in his beautiful bedroom. Jordan was nothing like Moss. Jordan the man, the artist. Jordan the lover. And when it was over, because affairs were always over at some point, what would be left? Bitterness? Disappointment? Were the ashes of an affair as cold and hostile as the ashes of a neglected marriage?

As the miles spun on beneath the wheels of her car so did her thoughts. Before she reached home she knew without doubt that a woman didn't just fall into a man's arms, innocent and unaware. Not a married woman. It was a deliberate act, with eyes open, admissions made. Billie faced the fact that she needed a man to want her. She needed to be held, to hear the soft, wonderful promises of early love. She hungered for a kind word, a loving hand. But she also knew that in the end, she would be the one to break it off. Never again would she give herself as completely to a man as she had to Moss.

Billie parked her soldier-blue car beside Moss's racy Porsche. He was home. Before she made the decision to allow herself to fall into Jordan's arms, she'd try once more to talk to Moss. To get closer to him, to look for that little glimmer that would let her know he still wanted her and their marriage. Her steps faltered. It was really Moss she wanted; it was Moss she would always want. She still loved him beyond reason. How much of herself did that leave for Jordan? Would she lie in his arms and pretend he was Moss? Her heels tapped across the tiles in the front hall. Suddenly she wanted to see Moss, have him smile at her. After all these years, how could he still have this effect on her? Still make her pulses race and her arms ache to hold him? She must be a fool.

"Make me a gin and tonic, please, Charlotte, and bring it out on the terrace," Billie murmured distractedly. She wanted a little more time to think before approaching Moss. Get her lines down.

She had first discovered his unfaithfulness years before, but the pain was as fresh as if it had been yesterday. She'd been so wounded, so humiliated, she'd wanted to die. What was she lacking that had made him look elsewhere? The anger, when it came, had been brutal, eating at her like a cancer. She'd never really recovered.

It had been her decision, made in the solitary darkness of her bedroom, not to confront Moss. His infidelity was a passing thing, she promised herself. He would come back to her and their marriage would be as strong as ever. Sometimes affairs strengthened marriages. She would forgive...but she would never forget. That would be her punishment; she had to be at fault somewhere.

After the first time, Billie was aware of every one of her husband's indiscretions. Each time, he would return to her, as loving and kind as in the early days of their marriage. He would bring her expensive gifts, share her bed three times a week, whisper beautiful words in her ear. She endured because she loved her husband.

The gin and tonic was finished, and Billie set the glass down firmly. It was time to seek out her husband. She shoved trembling hands into the pockets of her jacket. It was all so ridiculous she wanted to cry.

"Mam? Look, Pap, Mam is here!" Riley exclaimed.

"Billie, what brings you down here? Is something wrong?" Moss asked.

"What could possibly be wrong in this paradise called Sunbridge?" Billie responded with forced cheerfulness. "Riley, I want to talk to your father for a few minutes. Why don't you go to the kitchen and ask Charlotte to make us some coffee."

Billie was alone with Moss. She looked at him through what she hoped were objective eyes. Still tall and rangy, more rugged-looking now, still so damned handsome. Hair thick, dark, a frosting of silver at the temples, and those blue eyes that could reach into her heart. But most remarkable about her husband was the power he exuded. Little wonder women found him so attractive. Even in this little room, amid a mess of papers and school pennants and trophies that he'd never removed, Moss was a powerful man. It was in the set of his shoulders beneath his finely knit sweater, in the tone of his voice and the light in his eyes.

She took a breath, knowing she must speak now before the moment and the will were gone. "Moss, what did you think of the party last night?"

"It was nice. Did you enjoy yourself? Pap went all out for you. I hope you thanked the old boy."

"Yes, it was nice. And yes, I thanked Seth. But it would've been nicer if you'd spent some time with me. After all, it was my birthday."

"Are you complaining?" Moss asked coolly, turning to face her.

"No— Yes, yes I am. I was embarrassed and I could see people were whispering. Why were they whispering, Moss?"

"How the hell should I know, Billie? You know I've never been much good at playing the attentive husband. I just don't know how."

"Perhaps you don't, but you're not stupid. I asked you why people were whispering."

"You're just imagining things." He turned back to his desk. At this point in any other conversation with him, Billie would have considered herself dismissed. Not this time.

"I asked you a question, Moss."

Moss's hairs prickled on the back of his neck. There was something going on here. This interrogation was unlike Billie. He turned to face her once again, all his attention focused on her now. The light from the window behind him fell on her face, making it golden and radiant, illuminating her hair and the clear sweep of her brow. She was beautiful, this wife of his, his Billie. She was also upset.

Warmth crept up from her neck to bloom on her cheeks. "I waited for you, Moss," she whispered. "I waited all night. I wanted you. Something's wrong, Moss. We seem to be losing each other and I don't know why and it frightens me."

Billie heard herself choke. Lord, she hadn't meant it to

sound as though she were begging. But wasn't that exactly what she was doing? Begging Moss to save her from falling into Jordan Marsh's arms?

"Billie, we're old married folks now. The honeymoon doesn't last forever. We're settled in. You know, old shoes."

"Moss, I don't want an old shoe. I didn't ever want to lose what we had. It's like dying. When was the last time you came to the room we used to share? Do you even remember? We need to talk, to communicate. We have children who need us, together. We were happy once. Tell me what's wrong. Tell me what I've done that you don't want me anymore."

She hadn't wanted it to pour out like this; she hadn't wanted to sound so lost, so desperate. Yet it had to be said and now was the time. Perhaps he didn't know how he'd hurt her.

"Billie, what's all this talk about communicating? You sound like one of those beatniks."

"And you sound like a man with something to hide. Is there someone else, Moss? Do you love her?"

"You're never here, Billie. You're always busy with your classes, the children, or whatever it is you women do. I have pressures, commitments. The ranch, the business. They're all taking their toll. Do you see this mess here?" he said, indicating the shelves and desk filled to overflowing with ledgers, charts, and blueprints. "I'm only one man. Pap is depending on me."

"I understand all that, but you could get someone to help you. Yes, I've been busy. It's the only way I can get through the days. What about the nights, Moss? I'm not busy at night, but you are. You haven't answered my question. Have you found someone else? If you have, tell me. We have to talk."

"We are talking. You just don't like what I'm saying." She knew. Christ, she knew and she had never said a word. That was like Billie. Ignore it and it would go away. He wondered if Agnes knew. "No, I haven't found anyone else. We're married, Billie. We'll always be married. You should know that. We have a commitment."

"If that's true, why don't we make love? You're a very virile man. We last made love two months ago and I had to hogtie you even then. I don't like this position you've placed me in. I don't like it at all." Some of the resolve had come back into Billie's voice. She spoke more firmly. "The fact that you aren't interested in making love with me can only mean one thing. You're involved somewhere else. We should be adult enough to discuss it."

"All the little nitty-gritty details, is that what you want to know? What color was the lace on her underwear? Was she exciting? Is that what you want to know?"

"Moss!" Billie said, shocked. "No. No, I don't want to know. All I want us to do is talk. About the children. Us. Our lives. Something's wrong. Can't you feel it? Can't you see that we've drifted so far apart that if we don't do something soon, it will be too late?"

"Billie, Billie." Moss sighed. "Where in the world do you get these notions? Nothing has changed. We've gotten older; the children are growing up. You have your interests and I have mine. That's the way marriage is. That's the way it was for my parents. I know you lost your father when you were young so you have nothing to compare to. Trust me, Billie. We're fine. Nothing is wrong. You're a romantic. You thought the honeymoon would last forever. Mam was sort of like that until Pap told her the way it was."

Billie suddenly felt smothered by self-doubt. The words stuck, hard and cutting, in her throat. "I'm afraid, Moss, that that isn't good enough for me. I want more. I want us to be a family, a united family. Maggie needs you. Don't you see what you're doing to her, have done to her? You're just like Seth and the way he treated Amelia. All you think about or care about is Riley—you should remember you have two other children. Maggie especially needs—"

"To be left alone," Moss finished for her. "You're right. She is like Amelia. She's a little wild and willful, but she'll settle down. The more we hound her, the worse she'll be. Believe me, I know what I'm talking about. Your problem is you worry too much, Billie. Relax, enjoy life a little."

"Like you do, Moss?" Her tone was bitter, accusing.

His gaze locked with hers. "Yes, like I do."

"All right, Moss, that's exactly what I'll do." Scalding tears of humiliation and frustration were about to escape down her cheeks. He was daring her to follow in his footsteps and have an affair! Only he didn't believe she had the guts to do it. Didn't believe in his heart that he could ever lose her. He was so certain that her emotional world began and ended with him, and the occasional crumbs he threw her.

Where had she gone wrong? Hadn't she loved enough? Hadn't she given enough? Billie shrank into herself. None of it made sense.

Moss went to Billie and lifted her chin with a tender hand.

"Billie, darling, don't look so defeated. We're all right, and we'll always be all right. You're my wife and you'll always belong to me. Don't you know that?"

Before she could shame herself by falling into his arms and begging for his love, his touch, Billie stepped back and turned away from Moss, her shoulders square, her head high, leaving the room that had become her husband's haven.

He sighed with weariness, just the way she sighed over Maggie. "Where are you going, Billie? I thought you said you wanted to talk. Come back here."

"I'm going to enjoy life, Moss, exactly as you suggested. I'm going to be just like you." She closed the door quietly behind her.

Moss sat silently, fighting the impulse to run after her. He always felt this way when he couldn't maintain complete control over the things and people that were his. But something told him that running after Billie would be useless, that she was too hurt, too wounded, and that it was his fault. He realized what it had cost her to come down here and to practically beg him to pay more attention to her, to the family. He was sorry for it but he hated to have demands placed on him. Billie had always given him enough room to spread his wings, to pursue his own interests. What had changed?

She sounded desperate. He guessed he *should* pay more attention to her, be more loving. Hell, he did love her, in his own way. Billie was probably the best thing that had ever happened to him. Because of Billie he had Riley, and God only knew how much he loved that boy.

Moss turned to face the clutter of his desk. As soon as he finished up here he'd go upstairs. A long, loving time with Billie would be just the ticket to get things back on an even keel. He would apologize. Billie was very forgiving. Maybe afterward they'd have dinner brought up to their room and have that long talk about Maggie. That would be good; that would clinch things with Billie and she'd be happy again.

There was a tap at the door and Riley peeked in, several books in his hand. "What've you got there, son?"

"Schoolwork. I thought you'd help me with this science project. The one who comes in with the best poster on how a pump works will get a prize. Will you help me, Pap?"

"A prize?" Moss said thoughtfully. "Have you got any ideas of what kind of pump you want to do?" He smiled, remembering the pump he'd designed when he was about Riley's age. The boy was a chip off the old block and Moss puffed with pride.

"I thought I'd show a windmill and how it takes energy from the wind to pump water for the cattle. How's that sound, Pap?"

Moss was already making room on his desk for Riley's books. "Sounds okay to me. But you're a Coleman, Riley. Why don't we show how oil is pumped from the ground?"

Riley dumped his books on the desk in the space Moss had cleared. He had wanted to do a windmill pumping water for cattle. Cows were nice and he loved animals. "Sounds good to me, Pap. We'll show an oil well."

"That's good, son. Whenever you do anything it should be something important. Oil is important. We use it for fuel and it heats our houses and flies our planes. . . ."

In her room, Billie kicked off her shoes and looked around at the result of the Coleman money. None of it made her happy. Not the satin drapes, the matching bedspread, the antique furniture, the closets filled with clothes. She'd be happy in a cozy two-room apartment if it meant she could lie in Moss's arms each night. That was the dream she'd concocted when she'd first met him, before she knew about the Colemans and their money and their power. Moss had made her think he was just a ranch hand, a dirt farmer, anything but what he really was. And damn her soul, she had loved him. She still loved him. Nothing would make her happier than to have him come to her now, this minute, to take her into his arms and love her.

The phone jingled musically on the bedstand. Once, twice, three times. Charlotte must be out of earshot. Billie picked it up and held the receiver to her ear. "Hello."

"Mrs. Coleman, please. This is Hester Eastland, from the Perret School."

"Yes, Mrs. Eastland, this is Mrs. Coleman. Is anything wrong?"

"We were wondering about Margaret, Mrs. Coleman. Is she feeling better? She hasn't been to school today."

"I should have called you, Mrs. Eastland. Maggie went away with Carol Lambert and her family to Galveston for the weekend. I'm terribly sorry I didn't notify you." Billie's temper rose. Damn Maggie! She hadn't said a word about not going to school. Billie had just assumed the Lamberts wouldn't be leaving until the end of the day. And that was another thing.

She'd intended to call Dottie Lambert and thank her for inviting Maggie along. Everything seemed to be getting out of hand; she was losing her grip on things because she was so wrapped up in her own misery.

"I don't understand, Mrs. Coleman. Carol Lambert is in school today. She brought some papers down to my office just a few minutes ago. Mrs. Coleman, don't you know where your daughter is?"

"I guess I don't. I thought she was going to school today, but she also said something about going shopping. I'm certain there's nothing to be alarmed about."

"Mrs. Coleman, as you know, Margaret has been a disciplinary problem in the past. I assure you, our only concern is for your daughter. However, if you're certain there's no problem . . ."

"There's no problem, Mrs. Eastland." She replaced the receiver, a sour grimace on her face. It was no good calling Susan at her school to see if she knew where Maggie was. And Riley would clamp his mouth shut out of loyalty, the way he always did. There was nothing she could do but wait. Then a thought occurred to her. She lifted the receiver again and dialed the Lamberts' phone number.

"Hello, Dottie? Billie Coleman." Something cautioned Billie to tread easily. It would never do to embarrass the woman. "I was wondering if when you're in Galveston you'd be doing any shopping. Moss is so fond of those homemade chocolates from that little shop in town."

"Why, I'd be glad to pick some up for you next time we get down there, but I don't know when it'll be. Zachary has been recovering from a nasty case of chicken pox. Lands alive! I can't remember when I last left this house! And all the poor boy is doing is scratching—I'm afraid he'll scar himself for life."

Billie listened impatiently to Dottie Lambert's dissertation, her mind racing. The Lamberts hadn't made any last-minute change in plans if Zachary had been down with the pox for more than a week. There had been no plans. Where *was* Maggie? Had she gone shopping? Why had she lied?

When Billie at last was able to extricate herself, she dropped onto the chaise to still the quaking of her knees. She was worried about her child, but it hadn't yet bloomed into fright. There were still several hours until dinner. Maggie would come home then. She would. She must.

A headache was building and would soon be a full-blown migraine. Then she'd be unable to cope with anything. Billie leaned back, yearning for sleep. Maggie would come home for dinner. . . .

CHAPTER
{{{{{{{{ **TWENTY-TWO** }}}}}}}}

Rear Admiral Thaddeus Kingsley arrived Saturday morning for one of his impromptu visits just as the Colemans were finishing breakfast. Even Seth and Agnes were sitting down for a late cup of coffee. Maggie's chair was conspicuously vacant. Moss's family, all together breakfasting on the terrace on a warm June morning. The oldest child was missing and everyone behaved as though it didn't matter. Billie's head pounded fiercely. The huge Texas meal of steak and eggs and grits was congealing on her plate; the sight of it almost made her gag. She sipped her weak tea and lit a cigarette, not because she wanted to smoke but because it was something to do, a way to calm her fury.

Last night, when Maggie still hadn't returned home, Billie had told Moss after dinner about Mrs. Eastland's call from the school and the made-up Galveston story.

"What should we do?" Billie asked.

"What should we do? We wait. We simply wait. Perhaps you got it wrong, Billie. Perhaps you didn't understand Maggie and she was going over to some other friend's house."

"No, Moss, I didn't misunderstand. Maggie said she was going with the Lamberts to Galveston. She even threatened to go whether she had my approval or not. I called Dottie Lambert—Zachary has the chicken pox. There never were any plans for Galveston this weekend."

"What's goin' on in here?" Seth's voice demanded from the doorway of the living room, arriving, as usual, at the least opportune moment. "Moss, what's the matter with your wife? She's shaking like a dog shitting peach pits."

Billie turned on her father-in-law. "You may address your questions directly to me when I'm present, Seth. I do know how to speak for myself." Then, turning back to Moss: "I think we should call the police. I want to know where my daughter is!"

"Which daughter?" Seth growled. "Don't tell me. It's that Maggie. Just like Amelia, a thorn in a man's side. What's she done this time?"

Quickly, Moss outlined the situation for his father.

"And you say you called the Lamberts? What kind of fool are you, little gal? There's no call to go around making fools of us all. Calling the Lamberts and letting them know Maggie can't be trusted! That was a damn fool thing you did!" Seth pounded his cane onto the parquet floor. "And we won't be calling in the sheriff. Why, our name'd be spread through the county inside of twenty minutes. You're her mother. Why don't you know where she is?"

And so it had been settled. They would all wait until Maggie came home under her own steam. The evening had been endless for Billie and when Moss had come to her bedroom, suggesting he join her, she'd been so furious at his lack of concern for Maggie and for what she herself was feeling that she'd slammed the door in his face.

A picture of Maggie lying in a roadside ditch with her face battered was so vivid that Billie nearly choked on her cigarette. A savage burst of hatred for the Colemans turned her face crimson. She shouldn't be sitting here calmly at the breakfast table, knowing nothing. Where was Maggie? Where?

Moss was excited over Thad's arrival, and the two men embraced each other unashamedly. Thad was tanned and lean, with the same strong-featured good looks and the same quiet ways. It had been almost a year since Billie had seen him. Seth glowered sullenly but shook hands. Thad Kingsley, rear admiral. A power. And the talk was he would be vice admiral before long. Moss's long-range prediction that his friend would someday be head of the Pacific fleet was coming true and it was more than Seth could bear. He'd roared like an angry lion at each of Thad's promotions. He'd always compared his son with every other man he knew, and there were times when Thad had scored higher on Seth's invisible chalkboard. Billie took a certain pleasure in her father-in-law's dislike of Thad.

"Billie, it's impossible!" Thad exclaimed, bending over to kiss her cheek.

"What is?" she said.

"That you're more beautiful than when I saw you last. I'd

keep a tight rein on this little filly, if I were you, Moss. You know what they say—'Never older, only better.' Billie is living proof."

"Why do you think I keep her penned up at Sunbridge?" Moss joked. The merriment didn't reach his eyes. Billie noticed and so did Thad.

He turned his attention to the children. "Lord, Susan, you're growing prettier every time I see you. Have they booked you for Carnegie Hall yet?"

Susan blushed prettily and bit her lip. She liked Pap's friend. He was always nice and didn't demand kisses, like some of the other people who came to the house. She secretly believed he looked almost exactly like Gary Cooper.

"Where's Maggie?" Thad said.

"Maggie is off with friends this weekend," Seth said coolly.

Thad recognized the lie and his gaze locked with Billie's for an instant before he reached out his hand to Riley. "It's nice to see you again, Riley. How are things? Still going up with your father and taking over the controls?"

"Yes sir! Pap's got a new Piper Cub and she's a beauty. She's equipped with the new autopilot Pap designed and I'd like to show her to you, if you'd like."

"I'd like that very much, Riley." Thad smiled, then turned to Moss. "I take it you've brought that autopilot into production, Moss. Have any of the airlines picked up on it yet? Or do you save your best achievements for the navy?"

"What do you think? I worked long and hard on that project and only finished the designs the first of the year. The Pentagon is interested, but they think the price is too high. They'll come around, though, as long as Sunbridge Enterprises holds the patent."

Billie looked blankly from one man to the other, and her glance included her son. Autopilot? Is that what Moss had been working so furiously on all last year? And when it had been completed and declared a success, why hadn't he told her? Resentfully, she realized how little she knew about her husband—and how much of himself he shared with others.

The heir to Sunbridge and his sister were excused and Seth and Agnes made their apologies: "pressing business." Sunbridge operated on a seven-day-a-week schedule. Thad was left alone with Moss and Billie. Charlotte brought half a scallop-edged melon for Thad and fresh coffee for everyone.

Thad thought he had never felt such tension in his life. Not even on the Big E before a strike. Billie looked beautiful but brittle, as if she were about to disintegrate into a million pieces any second. Moss was strung as tight as bailing wire on the south forty. Trouble in paradise. Big trouble. "So, what's new?" he asked casually.

"Nothing," Moss grunted.

"What could be new at Sunbridge?" Billie said brightly. Too brightly.

"Why do I have the feeling I stepped into the middle of something?" Thad asked bluntly.

"I'm worred about Maggie," Billie said defiantly. There, it was out. Let Moss defend it now, in front of Thad. Let his good friend see what a fine, wonderful father he was to his oldest daughter.

Moss's features froze and then he laughed. "Mothers! Mam was just like Billie."

"Not quite," Billie said fiercely. "Not quite, Moss. Don't think for one minute that I'm going to end up like Jessica. I'm going inside and I'm calling all of Maggie's friends. I should have done it yesterday. I don't care if you and Seth like it or not. I want to know." Without another word, Billie rose from the table and entered the house through the French doors.

Thad stared after her for a second. "What was that all about?" he asked. "I thought your father said the girl was with friends."

"She is. Billie got it into her head the girl is off hanky-pankying or something. She's a mother, Thad. All women are like that with their kids."

"Isn't that what motherhood is all about? It's the way you are with your son and the way your father was with you. Why aren't you concerned?"

"Maggie is just like Amelia was. Nothing any of us could do or say could tame my sister. She was willful and determined to do what she wanted when she wanted. In the end, everything turned out fine. Maggie is just like her and it's nothing to get excited about."

When Billie returned to the terrace, her face was ashen. Thad jumped to his feet. "None of her friends know where she is. I've called half of Austin looking for her. Moss, we must call the police."

"Billie, get hold of yourself. If Maggie said she'd be back on Monday, she'll be back—and then you'll be standing there looking foolish. You're getting excited over nothing."

"Nothing! God only knows where she is or what she's doing.

My God, Moss, she's not even fourteen! I never told you this, Moss, but Maggie's been in trouble before. Last April I had to go to the police station in Austin to get her. She'd been caught shoplifting. Fortunately, I was able to smooth things over by paying for what she took. Before that, she was riding around with some boys and drinking. *That* time she got off with a reprimand from the juvenile officer. I didn't say anything to you because I couldn't bear to see the hateful looks on your face. And your father's."

Moss laughed. "Maggie must have been reading Amelia's diary. She did exactly the same thing. Wait till Pap hears this."

"I know I can depend on you to tell him," Billie said frigidly.

"What do you want to do, Billie?" Thad asked quietly. "Do you want to go look for her?"

"That's exactly what I want to do. I just can't sit here and do nothing."

"Moss? You going?" Thad said.

"And let that little snippet make an ass out of me, too? No, thanks."

"I'll go with you."

Billie looked at Thad with grateful eyes, seeming not to hear Moss. "Let me get my purse and address book. My car is out front. I'll meet you there."

"This wasn't what I had in mind for the weekend," Moss grumbled.

"No, I don't suppose it was," said Thad. "What will you be doing while we're out looking for *your* daughter?"

"I'm going riding with Riley. I'll take him out and show him your plane. That kid's going to be an aviator. You mark my words. He's a great kid, Thad. Chip off the old block."

"Just what the world needs, another Moss Coleman," Thad said coldly. He picked up his seabag and went into the house.

Ten minutes later his navy whites were hanging in good order in the guest room and he was dressed in Sunbridge's official uniform: Levi's jeans and a shirt.

Billie was waiting by her car, her slender fingers playing with the key ring. She held them out to him and then quickly slipped into the passenger seat. Thad slid behind the wheel, gunned the powerful engine, and guided the sports car out of the drive and onto the main highway. "Direct me."

"Head toward Austin. I'm so grateful, Thad. I've been worried out of my mind and had no one to turn to. As much as I hate to do it, I think we should go to the sheriff's office first."

"I agree. Have you been having trouble with Maggie for very long?"

"I don't know if it's exactly trouble. Yes, I do know. She's always been a rebellious child. She's resentful of Riley and Susan and even of me. Perhaps resentful isn't the right word. Jealous. Jealous of anyone who has a claim on her father besides herself. She wants and needs Moss's attention so badly she'll do anything to get it. Moss, of course, is oblivious to it all. It breaks my heart . . . but I'm not entirely free of blame, either." She stopped a moment and her mouth tightened. "I let the Colemans dictate to me what kind of mother I should be to Maggie," she said bitterly. "They were wrong, Thad, and I was wrong."

"It's never too late, Billie," Thad murmured comfortingly. "Take things in hand now. Do the best you can. Caring is half the battle."

Billie turned sideways in her seat and looked at this quiet, solid man. It meant so much to her that he was her friend. "You've always been so good to me, Thad. Your caring means a lot. That's another thing I should have done, told you long before this."

"Friends don't have to be told, Billie." His eyes left the road for a moment, taking in the sight of her, a sight that warmed his heart. Even now, amid all her worry for Maggie, Billie was a beautiful, sensual woman. The slight breeze coming in through the cracked window stirred the spun-gold strands of her hair. Her face, once softly round with youth, had molded itself around her striking bone structure. There was a womanly warmth about her, but within still lived the innocence he'd seen when they'd first met in Philadelphia all those years ago. Clear hazel eyes faced him with unblinking sincerity.

"I'm so ashamed, Thad. I can't seem to get control of my own life, so I suppose it's not surprising that I've failed my children. The Colemans are like charged rockets aiming for the sky, but I fizzle out on the launch pad. The girls, too. I resent it bitterly, but I don't know what to do about it. Maybe there is nothing I can do."

"Yes, there is. When it's time for you to take action, you'll do it, like you are now. Don't be so hard on yourself, Billie. I won't allow it."

In the police station parking lot, Thad reached for Billie's hand. The silence in the small car thundered in Billie's ears. "I'm here with you," Thad said quietly.

Billie squeezed the strong fingers. "I know, and I'm glad."

Thad wanted to bring her close and whisper comforting words. He wanted to tell her that he'd always be there for her. . . .

"C'mon, Mrs. Coleman. Let's get our tails in there and do what has to be done."

Billie smiled. "I know you're just teasing, but please don't call me Mrs. Coleman. 'Billie' reminds me that we're friends just for ourselves, not because of Moss."

"Aye-aye, ma'am. C'mon, Billie."

Thad and Billie exited the police station an hour later. She hung her head in shame at all the questions, questions for which she had no answers. She leaned heavily on Thad's arm.

"They're right, Billie. It's really too soon to file a missing persons report. Maggie said she would be back Monday. She knows she has school, so it's very likely she'll be back tomorrow night. We'll both hold on to that thought. In the meantime we'll ride around and go to all the places where you think she might be. At least we'll be doing something and you'll feel better."

"Thank you, Thad."

"For what?"

"For being my friend. I really don't have any friends. Did you know that? I mean real friends. Acquaintances are different. I have loads of those. But not one friend that I can confide in." Jordan didn't count, she told herself.

Thad's eyes were soft in the early-morning sun. She could feel the pull of the man as they walked back to the car. She wanted to fall into his arms and sob her heart out. But she couldn't subject him to herself and her problems. Thad deserved so much more.

It was late in the evening when Billie called a halt. "It's useless, Thad."

"At this point, I have to agree. Tomorrow is another day. We can start out early and hit every place you can think of that we didn't cover today. It might be a good idea to make a list."

Thad drove back to Sunbridge and parked the car facing out on the concrete apron. They sat quietly, each with his own thoughts. It was Thad who broke the silence. "Have you thought about what you're going to do or say once Maggie comes home? I think it's important that you have something concrete in your mind." He could see Billie shudder. It took all his reserve not to reach out to her.

{ 329 }

"I think I can handle it, Thad. I'm all Maggie has. I'll be there, I'll do what I can. Maybe, when the time comes, I'll have some of the right words."

"I wouldn't be a mother for anything in the world," Thad said lightly.

But it wasn't his words that caught Billie's attention; it was the expression in his eyes as he looked at her. And as though a veil were being lifted, she saw behind the humor and the friendship to the tenderness and yearning hidden deep within him. It was a sudden revelation and she was moved to caress his cheek. What she had seen in his eyes made her heart leap. She felt like bursting into song. "When?" was all she could manage.

"That day on top of Diamond Head. Back in Philadelphia. When isn't important."

"It's important to me."

"Then you'll have to settle for forever." She held his hand and they sat for long minutes in silence. "It's late," Thad said finally. "We'd better go inside and report our progress."

"To whom? Do you really think there's one person inside that monstrous house who even cares?" Billie said bitterly.

"Look at me, Billie. You *can* handle this. You do have choices, options, whether you realize it or not. You're the only one who can decide what to do and when to do it. Tuck that thought away in your mental file cabinet. Now, I think I could use a drink. I deserve a drink. Move it, woman. I've had a hard day."

"When did you become such a tyrant?" Billie teased as they got out of the car.

"On the Big E, when I had to keep your old man in line." The moment the words were out, Thad regretted them. Billie smiled, but her eyes filled with pain and tears. It was more than Thad could bear. He turned abruptly and ran to the house.

The house was empty and silent, the way a house is when the inhabitants lead separate lives. Thad understood. Finally.

"It's goddamn pitiful," he muttered through clenched teeth.

"Did you say something, Thad?"

"I said I was thirsty."

"I'm fixing it as fast as I can. Sit down. Take your shoes off. I'll get us some sandwiches."

"A girl after my own heart." Billie smiled such a dazzling smile Thad felt like a kid on Christmas morning. Billie Coleman smiling, for him. What more could a man ask for or want? All of Billie Coleman.

The jukebox glowed eerily in the dark of Eddie & Arnie's Bar and seemed to throb with the rhythm of the country song whining through its speakers. A male tenor crooned a lonely lament from the spinning black disc. "Take a little time with me. . . ." Several couples swayed in each other's arms in a sensuous imitation of dancing.

Sipping his bourbon and branch water, the man glanced again at the girl sitting beside him at the bar. Thinking of her as a woman would have been ludicrous—he never considered a female a woman until she reached the age of thirty. Yet it was hard to place this one's age. She could have been anywhere between nine and twenty-nine. The revealing roundness to her chin and jaw and the smooth flesh of her upper arms could have belonged to a little girl. Yet there was a world of knowledge in those thickly mascaraed eyes and in the full lipsticked pout of her mouth.

When she'd come and sat down beside him, he'd been surprised. Even more surprised when the bartender had served her a drink. She hadn't spoken yet, but every move of her body told him she was very much aware of him. This, too, was surprising, considering there were other, much younger men in Eddie and Arnie's tonight. He wondered if she was waiting for someone. It was still early; the bar hadn't begun to fill with the usual Saturday-night crowd. Suddenly she drained her glass and asked him if he'd like to buy her another. For an instant he almost looked over his shoulder to be certain she was talking to him. Hell! He was forty-six years old and the father of three, and his waistline had disappeared a decade ago. It had been so long since something this young and vital had given him a "come hither" that he'd almost forgotten how to react. Almost.

Maggie perched on the barstool, her slim legs crossed in what she believed was an irresistible pose. The bracelets on her wrists jingled against one another as she reached for her pack of Pall Malls. The sleeveless black dress hugged her hips pleasantly and rode upward on her stockinged thighs, showing a long length of leg down to her high-heeled pumps. He liked her, she could tell. Just as she knew he was a traveling salesman. They were *all* traveling salesmen.

Someone dropped another nickel into the jukebox and a nice

slow song came on. She wished he'd ask her to dance. "I just love this song, don't you?" she said. She tamped her cigarette and put it between her lips, inviting him to light it for her

He struck a match and held it. Maggie gazed above the little flare directly into his eyes, the way she'd seen Joan Crawford do in the movies. Yes, there it was, the slight tremble of his hand, the sudden intake of breath. This was going to be easier than she thought.

"Huh?" he asked, clearly puzzled. "Oh, the song. I don't get to listen to music much."

"You come from around here?"

"No, this is just part of my route. I live in Oklahoma. But Austin is a nice city, little rough around the edges compared to New York or Los Angeles, but nice." He'd meant to impress her by mentioning how widely traveled he was, but she seemed more interested in her rum and Coke. "Are you waiting for someone? A boyfriend?" He wasn't springing another seventy-five cents for a drink just to prime her for some other joker.

"No. I just stumbled in for a quickie before heading home." Another line from a movie, Barbara Stanwyck, this time. She fixed her eyes on his face, willing him to ask the next question.

"You live alone?"

There it was. From here on in, things were going to be easy. As they conversed, Maggie leaned closer, intimately closer. Soon his arm would automatically go around her. She knew the younger men sitting at the other end of the bar were watching her. When she'd first come in they'd tried to strike up an acquaintance but she would have none of them. They were too young, too crass, and they frightened her a little. But a nice man like Fred, here, was somehow safe, reassuring. And besides, older men were so grateful to have a pretty young girl make a fuss over them. They knew how to be nice and attentive, and affectionate. Younger guy's only pawed and prodded and they didn't want to talk or anything; they only wanted to get down to business.

"You didn't tell me, Ruthie. Do you live alone?" Fred asked again.

"Not exactly, but my roommate's out of town this weekend. That's why I'm down here, 'cause it's so lonely in my apartment."

"I thought you said you came in before going home."

"I did. What I mean is, I didn't want to go home to a lonely apartment. Do you like to dance, Fred?"

He seemed undecided for a moment, but then he stood and led her onto the small space in front of the jukebox. She walked into his arms and fit pleasantly into his embrace. He felt a little guilty about what he was contemplating. She felt even smaller in his arms than his sixteen-year-old daughter back home. Just how old was she, anyway?

Maggie laid her head against Fred's broad shoulder. His arms around her made her feel so safe and protected. And she liked the way he talked to her, as if he were really interested in what she had to say. As they danced, she told him lies about the kind of work she did. Tonight she was a shopgirl in Kaplan's Department Store. He told her about his work, selling hardware for boilers. It wouldn't have mattered to Maggie if he'd said he was Jack the Ripper; he was nice. Nice to talk to her, to dance with her. Nice.

Pap never talked business with her, not the way Fred was doing. Pap thought she was too young to know or to care, but she wasn't. She would have sat and listened for days if it meant that she could just have Pap smile down at her, like Fred was doing, or have him let her rest her head against his shoulder and make her feel safe.

The music stopped and Fred gave her a handful of change to select her favorite songs. Maggie chose indiscriminately. She didn't want to lose the moment, lose his rapt attention. Later, when he asked if he could take her home, she'd suggest a motel just down the road, saying she had a fussy landlady. That would be the part Maggie would like least, she felt sure—being with Fred with both of them naked and him rolling on top of her. But one or two more rum and Cokes and she'd hardly mind at all.

The neon sign outside the Morningside Motel glared in the darkness. "Hey, Ruthie, you know what motel spells backwards? Letom!" Fred seemed to think his joke very funny and he laughed uproariously as he walked her from his car to the room. He was drunk but not too drunk; Maggie knew by the way he kept pressing her hand against his crotch.

The room was like a thousand others: dark, dingy, and foul, but the bathroom was passably clean. Maybe someone had actually changed the sheets since last week. Maggie was feeling the effect of her four drinks and was beyond caring about the condition of the room anyway. All that mattered was that Fred was a nice man and he liked her.

Someone in the next room had a radio playing. Perry Como

was singing "Prisoner of Love." The song was melancholy, one of Maggie's least favorites, but Fred seemed to know it, because he hummed along while he urinated into the toilet. "You gotta use the john, Ruthie?" he called, peeking out into the room. Seeing she was already undressed and in bed, he muttered, "Guess not. You're a real nice girl, Ruthie. Real nice. I haven't met a nice girl like you in a long, long time."

Maggie squeezed her eyes shut, hoping he'd put out the light. She didn't want to see him naked, see his penis rigid and erect, ready to pierce her flesh. She didn't want to know if his stomach was flabby and his legs skinny. She wanted to pretend he was tall and handsome and wonderful.

Fred took her into his arms, feeling the delicacy of her bones, the youthful slimness of her hips. Again he found himself wondering just how old she was. Not old enough to have her backside spread a little or her hips widen. For a moment doubt crept into his mind, but her hands were playing over his chest and sliding down under the covers and there was no time to think.

His weight was pressing on her, making her legs spread wider than she thought possible. He was grinding himself into her, plunging deep inside her, hurting her, making her afraid. She hated this part. Hated being pressed into the smelly mattress. But she was afraid to protest, afraid to cry out as she'd done once before when she was with a man she'd thought was nice. That man had hit her, punched her, and then used her anyway, leaving her alone in the scary darkness where she'd cried and cried and cried. And the name that had always come to her lips was Pap.

Maggie bit into her lower lip to keep from crying out. From somewhere outside there were noises, men's voices. Fred didn't seem to hear until suddenly there was a sudden loud knocking at the door. She felt him stiffen, utter a low curse.

"Police! Open up!" came the command.

Fred padded to the door, a sheet wrapped around his midsection. "Hold your horses, I'm coming."

The door swung open and one of Austin's finest stood in the doorway looking beyond Fred's bulk into the dim room. "Identification, please, sir. Is this your wife?"

Fred was already turning back to dig through his pants pockets for his wallet. The pallor of his complexion spoke his embarrassment and fear. He wouldn't want anything like this to get back to his wife.

"Is this your wife, sir?" the officer repeated. "Can you present identification, ma'am?"

Maggie was dumbfounded. She clutched the sheet to her chin and held on to it like a lifeline.

"Mind if I turn on the light, sir?" the policeman said in mock affability. Maggie saw his eyes go to her again, studying her, taking in the smeared makeup, the black stains under her frightened eyes.

"What's this all about?" Fred demanded, fishing through his wallet for his driver's license.

"It's a crackdown, sir, on prostitution. It's a known fact that this place is frequented for illegal purposes. Is this your wife, sir?"

Fred's eyes swung to Maggie, his mouth agape. He'd never considered that she might have been a prostitute. There'd never been any question about an exchange of money. "No, no, she's just someone I met tonight," he stammered.

"Identification, miss?"

"I . . . I don't have any."

"No driver's license? Social Security card? Identification from your place of employment? Just how old are you, miss? What's your name and address?" Now, with the light fully illuminating Maggie's face, the officer could see the tears swimming in her eyes. He was becoming more suspicious about her age.

"No, nothing," she whispered, "unless you'll take my student membership card."

"Student membership!" Fred choked. "Listen here, officer, I just met her tonight. I didn't know how old she was. Not with that dress she was wearing and all that crap on her face. I didn't know!"

"Did she solicit you?" the officer asked. "Think carefully, sir. You could be facing charges for corrupting the morals of a minor."

Frod took a second to think, his face going paler by the moment. The effect of the alcohol was wearing off, leaving him to face reality. He had himself and his family to consider. "Damn right she solicited. Twenty bucks and I was fool enough to go along with it. Hey, you're not going to hold me or anything, are you?"

"Not if what you say is true. It's only the whores we haul in, not their customers."

Maggie wanted to die. She was ordered to get dressed. She

{ 335 }

was going for a ride downtown. They were going to take her to jail!

"Just for the record, miss, your name, please."

"Maggie. Margaret Coleman. You can reach my father at the Sunbridge ranch. His name is Moss Coleman."

The officer looked blankly at Maggie. There was going to be hell to pay.

When the phone rang at 3:10 in the morning, Billie reached for it instantly. She'd been expecting the call. She felt calm and in control. It was about Maggie—she could feel it.

"Billie Coleman speaking."

"Mrs. Coleman, this is Sergeant Daley at police headquarters. We picked your daughter up a short while ago. I'd appreciate it if you would come down immediately."

"Is Maggie all right?"

"She's not hurt, Mrs. Coleman. We'll look after her until you get here."

"I'll be right there. Thank you, Sergeant."

Billie knocked quietly on Thad's door. She wasn't surprised to see that he, too was fully clothed. "I heard the phone ring. It's Maggie, isn't it?" Billie nodded. "I'm ready. Shouldn't we wake Moss and have him go with us?" Billie shrugged and shook her head.

The urge to throttle Moss was strong enough to make Thad clench his fists. The two went back a long way and God knows he'd been angry at his friend before, but this was different, because at the root of it was a thorough dislike of the man. Thad felt a flush of guilt and pain mix with his anger, but even more painful were the shadows of disappointment and futility he saw in Billie's eyes.

"Shouldn't you at least leave a note?" he asked.

"Why? I suppose this is how Maggie feels. The only family feeling you'll find at Sunbridge is family pride, and that's not quite the same thing." They were outside now, in the cool, fading darkness. Billie tossed Thad her car keys. "Take me to my daughter, please, Thad."

After a briefing by Sergeant Daley Billie and Thad were directed to a holding room. Before they even opened the door they could hear Maggie's sobs. Inside, at the far end of a long table, she sat, head in her arms, shoulders shaking.

"Maggie," Billie said, hands already reaching for her daughter. She still could not believe what Sgt. Daley had told her . . . her little girl picked up for prostitution. The man she'd been with hadn't been held, once he'd answered a few questions. When Maggie had identified herself, it was decided that the incident would be treated as a family matter and no charges were being brought.

Slowly, Maggie lifted her head. Her face was ravaged with tears and smeared makeup. The dress she was wearing was one Billie had never seen before, cheap, slinky tight, revealing. Her dark hair hung in her eyes. Billie gasped when she saw the pain in those eyes.

"Maggie, darling . . ." It was a cry from the heart. A sound torn from her throat. A mother's lament.

"Mother, I . . . I didn't want you to see me this way. I asked them to let me clean up, but they wouldn't. . . ." Maggie's voice choked off. Her eyes went to Thad, standing behind Billie.

"What's *he* doing here? Where's Pap? Why didn't you bring my father?" It was both an accusation and a plea. "Is Pap outside?"

"No, he's not. Thad drove me down here. . . ."

"Oh, I get it—Pap's not home or else he couldn't be bothered," Maggie said bitterly. "Can I go home now?"

"Yes. Maggie . . . is it true what the police officer said that you . . . you . . ."

"That I was in bed with a man old enough to be my father? It's true all right. But I never asked him for money. I never do!"

Billie swayed backward against Thad. Her hand itched to slap Maggie's rebellious face and at the same time her arms ached to hold her, to take away the pain. Where had her little girl gone? How had she come to this?

"Are you taking me home or aren't you?" Maggie demanded. "Or are you kicking me out?"

"Of course you're coming with us. Sunbridge is your home, Maggie. Poor Maggie." Billie almost wept. She took a step closer to her daughter, her arms extended, wanting to pull the child into her embrace, offer her safety, security.

"And I suppose you'll tell Pap all the tawdry details," Maggie said accusingly.

"No one is going to tell your father if you don't want them to," Billie whispered. She believed that was what Maggie needed to hear, that she didn't want Moss to know.

But Maggie's head sank down again on her arms and she

heaved great, shuddering sounds. Thad touched Billie's shoulder, prompting her to go to Maggie, and then he stood silently, his heart breaking for both, as he watched them embrace. Moss should be here, seeing this, hearing this. But he wasn't. The job had been left to a friend of the family. A friend who needed to be so much more.

CHAPTER TWENTY-THREE

Billie watched the raging storm outside her sitting room window. It was only ten o'clock in the morning, but the sky was midnight black. It was what Seth referred to as a real Texas storm, coming down from the Panhandle. Billie shivered and crossed her arms over her chest. She wasn't going to be able to go to the studio today. Rain and wind slammed against the window pane. Billie edged back a little, fearful that the glass would shatter. She could do a little reading, work on some needlepoint. Or she could go back to bed and try to sleep through the day. None of the ideas appealed to her. She could write to Thad, but what about? She wasn't in a chatty mood and there was no news.

Maybe she should make the bed. No, because then the timid little maid would think she'd done wrong and run to Agnes to plead her case. The rumpled bed would stay as it was.

She could reread some of Thad's letters. They arrived weekly and were just the right length, two and a half pages. He always asked about everyone and shared news he'd received of his hometown from his subscription to its weekly newspaper. She always went to the last paragraph first because it was about her. Sometimes it was whimsical, and at other times she could feel his heartache. Lately, he had been encouraging her to try her hand at textile design. He hadn't laughed like the rest of her family when she'd confided that for as long as she could remember that was what she'd wanted to do. Thad was special.

Tears burned at her eyes. She squeezed them shut to allay the stinging pain. When she opened them again her mother was standing in the room, looking as if she'd just stepped off a magazine cover. Billie hardly knew her anymore and that was just as well. Their views on things were so far apart they might have been living in different states.

"I brought us some coffee. With that wicked storm raging out there we're all housebound. I thought it would be nice if we had a little talk, the way we used to. We've all been so busy lately that we hardly see one another. We can't let that happen, Billie. We're a family."

Billie grimaced. Her mother was talking as if it were Billie's fault. She remembered one of Thad's letters about a visit to his hometown and family. He had made it sound so wonderful—the closeness of the family, the shared laughter. She had felt so envious. No wonder his face always wore a puzzled look when he saw the way things were at Sunbridge. "Thank you for the coffee, Mother. I can certainly use it," Billie said in a neutral tone. "I thought that last storm was bad, but this is horrendous. What are your plans for the day?"

"About the same as yours, I imagine. Seth says this storm will last well into midafternoon. By then all the roads will be flooded, so there's no point in thinking about anything but staying home. I have plenty to occupy me."

"Is there anything in particular you want to discuss, Mother? The children, Moss, Seth? My going to the studio every day?"

Agnes ignored Billie's tart tone. "As a matter of fact, now that you bring up the children, I couldn't help noticing how quiet Maggie was this past weekend when she came home from school."

A frown puckered Billie's brow. She didn't need anyone to tell her about Maggie's withdrawal. Maggie had been a different girl since she and Thad had had to pick her up from the police station: quiet, withdrawn, her usual sullenness turned to something deeper, more obscure. Billie didn't like to think about that night at the police station; it was something she wanted to bury. It was all part of the past now, she kept telling herself. Once she had taken Maggie to Dr. Ward for an examination and blood tests for venereal disease, from which Maggie had been found free, her sense of relief had been so overwhelming it was as if that night were part of an awful nightmare.

All through the summer and since school had started again, Maggie had spent inordinate amounts of time alone in her room, claiming to be working on a school project. But it didn't feel right to Billie and she had her doubts. She'd written to Thad about it; his advice had been simply to love her, to be there for her, and Billie had tried. But Maggie had not been receptive.

"I think it's high time you took that child in hand, Billie," Agnes was saying now. Heaven only knows when the tongues will cease to wag. Seth says we have to ignore the gossip, but I, for one, find it very difficult to do. You *are* her mother, Billie. You should do something!"

"Maggie also has a father and a grandfather, who ignore her."

"If you weren't so busy defending and protecting that child all the time, things wouldn't be this way. I found it reprehensible that you tried to keep it a secret, Maggie's being with that man in that sleazy motel. If you'd gone to Moss or Seth when it happened, the gossip could have been squelched there and then." Of course, that had been Seth's reaction, too. Moss had turned from Maggie in disgust and shot accusations at Billie.

Billie felt a tightness in her chest. "Funny how you're always quick to point out where I've been wrong, Mother. Seth and Moss are innocent in your eyes. But you're right. I am her mother and I'm going to do the best I can for her. I'll always be here for her, just the way you were for me," she finished bitterly.

"Feisty this morning, aren't we?" Agnes said blandly. "It must be this wretched storm. We're all out of kilter. Were you writing a letter? Did I come at an inopportune time? Thad, is it? You do correspond regularly, don't you? How does Moss feel about that?"

"Full of questions this morning, aren't we?" Billie mimicked. "Since when must I ask Moss's permission to write an old friend?"

"Feisty and testy." Agnes's eyebrows shot up. "Why are you so defensive?"

"Because I don't like the drift of your questions. I really don't owe you any explanations. Thad's always been a good friend and I plan to keep it that way."

"Yes, well, I suppose you could use a friend along about now," Agnes said offhandedly as she prowled Billie's room, touching objects and sniffing perfume bottles.

"If you've got something to say, Mother, come out with it."

"I didn't want to say anything, dear, but I think I should. You should have taken more interest in your husband. You never should have allowed him to move downstairs to that stuffy little room. I wonder if you know that Moss has been having...uh...I don't know quite how to say this, Billie."

"You mean am I aware that Moss has had affairs? Is that the word you're looking for, Mother?"

Agnes's face was pure shock. "You knew?"

"Contrary to what you may believe or have heard, Mother, the wife is not always the last to know. Yes, I knew."

"Does Moss know that?"

"Yes," Billie said shortly.

"And?"

"And what, Mother?"

"That's the beginning and the end of it? Did you talk it out? Did he promise to stop his..."

"Philandering? Now there, Mother, I *am* the last to know. My husband doesn't care to take me into his confidence when he makes decisions."

"His...past infidelities are one thing. All men go through that phase at some time or other. But I understand his current affair has been going on for close to three years. It could be serious, Billie."

Billie felt as if one of the packhorses in the barn had kicked her in the stomach. But she'd be damned if she'd let her mother know of her ignorance. "What do you propose I do, Mother?" Billie asked coolly.

"I must admit you've taken all of this rather well—I expected hysterics. Now, we have to map out a strategy. We cannot allow this to go on. The longer an affair goes on, the worse the marriage is. Now that's a pure, hard fact, Billie."

"Mother, strategy? Really! We're talking about my marriage. If Moss isn't interested in preserving it, why should I torture myself? I've come to terms with it."

Agnes reeled a little but recovered herself. "Surely you aren't thinking of divorce? What about the children, Billie? Moss would never let you have Riley. The girls, yes, but not Riley. He's your baby, your only son." Your only bargaining point, she wanted to add, but she held her tongue. "What *are* you going to do?"

"Not *do*, Mother, *did*," Billie lied. "Sauce for the goose is sauce for the gander."

{ 341 }

"Billie Coleman!" Agnes said. "Are you telling me that you . . . that you . . . my very own daughter . . . No, I refuse to believe it Not *you*!"

"Believe what you want, Mother."

"It's Thad Kingsley, isn't it?"

Billie looked her mother straight in the eye. "No, Mother, it isn't Thad Kingsley. Thad is too noble to take advantage of his friend's wife. I would have thought you'd realize that."

"Then who is it—I demand to know."

"Demand all you want, Mother. My privacy is my own."

"How ever do you keep a straight face when you see Alice Forbes at the club?" Agnes asked savagely. "Knowing she's been sleeping with your husband, doing the same things you did with him? . . . How can you bear it?"

"That's enough, Mother. I don't want to discuss this any further."

Alice Forbes, the girl in the photograph hanging in Moss's boyhood room. Billie felt sick to her stomach. Alice Forbes, playwright. Broadway playwright. Backed by Forbes money. Forbes money was right up there next to Coleman money. A real threat. Three years was a long time, almost an eternity. Did Thad know? It was suddenly important for her to know. As soon as her mother left she would call Thad and ask him. He would tell her the truth. Thad would never lie to her. Three years! A wife could possibly forgive, never forget, a one-night stand, a chance encounter where two people were caught up in a moment of passion. But three years? All the planning, all the lies, all the covering up.

Her sense of betrayal was so strong that she ordered her mother out of her room, actually pushed her through the doorway. She only felt safe and calm when she heard the tiny click of the lock shooting home.

A planned affair was when you slept in each other's arms. Overnight. An entire weekend. Vacations. Moss had gone to Europe not too long ago. Now that she thought about it, Alice had been absent from the last two club meetings. Alice and Moss in Europe. Tasting and exploring all the newness. Laughing and sharing as they made their way around the countryside.

Billie paced the room like a nervous filly. Angry tears rolled down her cheeks. Three hundred and sixty-five days a year for three years. What had she been doing on some of those days while her husband was making love to another woman? How many times during all those hours had they made love? You bastard, you miserable rotten bastard! she thought. How could you do this to me?

What did Alice have that she lacked? Was it Alice's money? Her profession? Was it their similar backgrounds? The shared childhood memories? Was her body better? Of course it was—Alice Forbes had no children. But she had given her husband a son. Alice Forbes could never say that, but she didn't need to. Alice Forbes wasn't insecure, plagued with a Seth or an Agnes. She was her own person. She had a career. She was interesting. A stunning-looking woman, more sophisticated than Billie, recognized in the entertainment world, a pleasing personality. She liked to ride horses. And she could pilot her own plane.

Billie cried till she was spent. She blew her nose lustily and then washed her face. The little address book that Riley had given her for Christmas last year was in her hand. This would be the first time she had ever called Thad at his office. Thad wouldn't lie.

"CO's office, secure line," a voice said briskly.

"I'd like to speak to Admiral Kingsley, please. This is Mrs.—this is Billie Coleman."

"Just a minute, ma'am, the admiral is on another line. Will you hold?"

"Yes."

Two minutes later Thad came on. "Billie, to what do I owe this pleasure?"

Billie cleared her throat and then apologized. "Thad, I have to ask you something. Are you aware of Moss's affair with Alice Forbes? The affair that's been going on for three years?"

Thad didn't know what he had expected, but this question was like a thunderbolt. How in the name of God could he answer? "Billie, that's not a fair question to ask me."

"I apologize, Thad. You just gave me your answer. You shouldn't always be so kind. People take advantage of you when you do that. Good-bye, Thad."

Billie dragged herself into the pretty bathroom that only she used. She looked at the floor-to-ceiling mirror without really seeing her reflection. The sight of the thick plum-colored towels hanging against the powder-blue tile was comforting, in a way. Moss had always rolled up his towel and tossed it either on the floor or in the tub. The toilet seat was down. He had been notorious for leaving it up all the time. The one bright yellow toothbrush in the holder looked particularly lonely. Without thinking, Billie opened the medicine cabinet and took out a new red toothbrush. She slipped it through one of the small openings. Two. As in couple. A small jar of Pond's Cold Cream, a bottle of Seconal, and some toothpaste were all that was in the cabinet. Billie's eyes lingered for a long time on the bottle of sleeping pills. She reached for it. It would be so easy. All she had to do was take a glass of water and swallow the pills. Lie down and go to sleep. No one would miss her until dinnertime. How many pills were in the bottle? She shook it and tried to count. Fourteen, she decided.

A vision of Seth at Jessica's funeral swam before her weary eyes. If she knew for certain that Moss would truly mourn her, it might be worth it to die. But the thought of him attending her funeral the way Seth had Jessica's made her dump the contents of the bottle into the toilet bowl. The sound of the flush was loud in the quiet, pretty room. She wouldn't end up like Jessica. The glass vial made a loud thump when she tossed it into the white wicker basket.

Billie's step was firm when she walked from the bathroom. The storm was still raging but it didn't seem as bad. The inky blackness was now a sooty gray. The rain was still coming down in great splashes against the window, but the wipers on her car were powerful. If she took the main highway to the studio, she might make it before serious flooding occurred. She threw on a bright yellow slicker with matching hat.

She wasn't going to Jordan Marsh's studio. She was going to Jordan Marsh.

{{{{{{{{{ **CHAPTER TWENTY-FOUR** }}}}}}}}}

Billie maneuvered her car along the rain-slicked highway, her mood and thoughts as threatening and oppressive as the thick gray clouds scudding above. Rain pelted the windshield. Matching the beat of her heart, the wipers beat a furious rhythm. "Shavers," Maggie called them when she was young. God, wasn't a girl of thirteen young? Or was it that since that June night in the police station she'd ceased thinking of Maggie as a child? The dreadful experience she'd seen on her daughter's face that night was that of an older, jaded woman. A woman who knew men's ways, as Agnes would have put it.

Billie drove the curves of the highway automatically, as though her car knew the way. Automatically. Autopilot. That's what Moss had been working on for this past year and he'd never mentioned it to her. Why? Did he think she was too stupid to comprehend? When they were first married he'd tell her not to worry her pretty little head about this or that. Then she'd found security in leaving the worrying to him, or so she'd thought.

Billie's foot pressed down on the accelerator, sending a sudden surge of power through the Italian-made engine. Even this damn car was one of Moss's choosing. *He* was the one who understood engineering and machines; *this* was the car she was to have. Billie regretted that she hadn't insisted on the Chevrolet she so admired. Italian sports cars were for women like Alice Forbes. Chevys were for the Billie Ameses of Philadelphia. Moss made every decision on every aspect of her life, even the aesthetic ones like choosing cars and travel plans, and even the vital ones concerning the children, like where they should go to school. She'd followed Moss's "suggestions" for so long that she hadn't even realized how long it had been since she'd made a choice of her own, a decision of her own, for herself.

Billie bit down on her lower lip and veered her car around the bend. Well, she was making one today in going to Jordan. And this was her own choice and it was entirely for herself.

When she pulled into the small parking lot adjacent to Jordan's studio, she was gratified to see his Oldsmobile parked near the door. No other cars were present; the storm had probably kept the other students away. For a long moment Billie sat in the shelter of the car, her hand gripping the steering wheel. It would be so easy to just restart the engine and leave. He'd never even know she'd come. She could forget it herself. Before she had time to reconsider, Billie swung open the door and stepped out into the rain, skipping across puddles as she made her way to his door.

"Jordan! It's me, Billie! Jordan?" She rapped on the glass pane.

"Billie? Billie, come in! You're drenched! I wasn't planning on holding class today; I thought the storm would keep my students away. At least the less devoted of them." He smiled, the warmth in his eyes chasing away the gloom of the day.

Billie stepped inside and let him help her off with her slicker; small puddles formed on the floor around her. "I didn't come for lessons, Jordan. I came to be with you." The words were out, but she was afraid to look into his face. Her hands groped for him blindly. She was in his arms. He felt so good. Smelled so good. The soft, well-worn shirt and faded jeans followed the lines of his body, making him accessible to her touch. His shoulder was against her cheek, his lips in her hair, and when he spoke her name with a sense of awe and wonder, she knew she'd been right in coming here. She was a wounded soul, pushing away thoughts of Moss's betrayals. Jordan could heal her.

Jordan tipped her face up to his with a gentle touch of his long, artistic fingers. When his lips met hers, his kiss was gentle, moving across her mouth slowly, meltingly. Then he pulled away, looking deeply into her eyes, and whispered, "Are you certain?"

Her answer was to step back into his embrace, holding to him tightly, offering her mouth again to the tenderness of his. She needed this, needed him. A great wrenching of her heart brought a sob to her lips. It had been so long since she'd been held this way, wanted this way. Even when Moss did come to their room, their lovemaking had become mechanical, a greedy self-serving act to satisfy themselves. An act. Gone was the spontaneity, the great yearning desire to give and share.

"Billie? What's wrong?" Jordan asked, searching her eyes for the answer.

"Only that I need you. So much," she told him truthfully. "I need to be loved, to be wanted."

"That's what I have to give you, Billie. Love. I want to make you feel my love."

Their clothes fell from their bodies like the petals of summer's first rose. His body felt strange and unfamiliar against her own. The stubble of beard on his chin was softer than Moss's. His touch was searching, tender. Moss's was sure and possessive, out of long years of charting her body and knowing it as well as he knew his own. Billie felt herself inwardly backing away from the intimacy Jordan offered. The very thing she so desperately wanted, this close loving affection, seemed unattainable and out of her reach. Memories intruded of that other man she had loved more than she loved herself. Moss.

Jordan's lips traced lazy patterns along the sweep of her shoulders and down to her breasts. His effect on her was hypnotic, sensuous, and Billie willed herself to surrender to the moment and the man. She accepted his nearness, his touch, his kiss on the most intimate parts of herself. She accepted these things the way she would have taken food or warmth or air to breathe, because she needed them. And she did need them, to reaffirm herself as a woman.

Billie lay quietly in Jordan's arms, listening to the beat of his heart and to the lovely words he spoke. She was beautiful, desirable, loving, and warm. She was a beautiful lover. And yet it was Jordan himself who was all these things. They'd shared the most intimate act possible between two people. He'd brought her body to life beneath his hands and his lips. But it was her soul that was dying and however he tried he could not touch it.

Her body was satisfied, her ego fed, and yet misery lived in her core. There was no future with Jordan and she knew it. She had taken all he could give and she'd given nothing in return. With Moss, her greatest ecstasy had been losing herself in him, giving totally of herself and knowing that the offering was pleasing to the man she loved. She didn't love Jordan. She had nothing to give and taking wasn't enough.

"Will you come back to me, Billie?" Jordan whispered against her ear. "Was it good for you? As good as it was for me?"

"It was good," Billie murmured, wrapping her arms around him and nuzzling his jaw. "I'll come back."

Billie could never make up her mind about Sunday dinner at Sunbridge. With Agnes at the helm it resembled a Cecil B. DeMille production with Mickey Mouse overtones. The array of crystal, china, and silver was blinding. The maids were attired in bright pink uniforms with frilly white aprons and little starched caps. The children were always in attendance on Sunday night and then, after the large heavy meal, were driven by the chauffeur back to their respective schools. While the setting and the accoutrements were Hollywood style, the dinner participants and their moods were strictly Coleman. Seth ate like a ranch hand, talking with his mouth full, mostly about the ranch. Agnes did her best to look regal from her position at the foot of the table. She ate daintily, taking small bites of food and chewing each mouthful thirteen times. Moss and Riley jabbered and babbled nonstop. Maggie and Susan were quiet, depending on Billie to keep up their end of the conversation concerning school and their various activities.

Billie always took two aspirins at the end of the meal.

Something was off center this evening. Maggie was answering when she was spoken to but otherwise there was a blank vagueness about her that alarmed Billie. Was the child sick? Or was she getting ready to pull what Seth referred to as one of her aunt's stunts?

"Maggie, do you feel all right?" All conversation at the table stopped as the family listened to see what kind of story Maggie would come up with this time.

"I feel fine, Mother. Why do you ask?"

"You look a little flushed to me. Let me take your temperature after dinner."

"I don't have a fever, Mother. I feel fine. It's warm in here."

"We'll take the temperature anyway. I can't send you to school tomorrow if there's a chance you're coming down with something. The whole class could get it."

"Why aren't you eating your dinner?" Moss queried.

Maggie's head shot up. It had been a very long time since her father had asked her a direct question. Billie's throat constricted at the naked adoration on her daughter's face. She started eating immediately. "I guess my mind was on school and a test tomorrow," Maggie said between mouthfuls of food.

"Don't stuff your mouth. You're old enough to eat properly. And don't ever talk with your mouth full."

Billie's eyes narrowed and her left hand clenched into a tightly balled fist in her lap.

"I can't eat any more. Mother, may I be excused?" Maggie's tears were close to the surface, and Billie didn't dare take a chance on the girl's erupting into one of her screaming outbursts.

"Of course. Come along. I want to take your temperature anyway." Billie laid her napkin on the table. The glance she shot Moss was stormy.

"There's nothing wrong with the girl," Seth growled.

Billie stopped in midstride and turned. "I'll be the judge of what is or isn't wrong with my daughter. Don't interfere between my daughter and me, now or ever."

"Billie!" Agnes was aghast. "Now that wretched child has spoiled another dinner. You really are going to have to do something."

Billie's back stiffened. "The next time you feel compelled to blame someone for a spoiled dinner, try to blame the right person. My husband!" With a venomous look at Moss, Billie marched from the room with her head held high.

"That wife of yours is getting out of hand, Moss."

"That's enough, Pap. Billie's a mother. Mam was the same way." Agnes cringed inwardly at the accusing glance he directed at her.

Upstairs, Billie shook the thermometer. "You don't have a fever, but you don't look right, Maggie. You know your marks are good enough for you to take a day or so off. Maybe a bug is going around and we can nip it at the onset so you don't lose more time later. I really am worried, Maggie. Have you been sleeping?"

"Off and on. I have a lot on my mind. Mother...I..."

"Yes, Maggie? Whatever it is, do you want to talk about it?"

"Oh, never mind. Not tonight. Why don't you and I go shopping next weekend? I think I gained some weight. Too many late-night snacks with the girls after lights out."

The wan smile bothered Billie. "I'd like that, Maggie. Just the two of us. We'll go to all the big stores and get a whole new wardrobe. I think it's time you had some new clothes. You didn't want to go the last time, when I took Susan."

"I didn't need anything then. Why waste Pap's money? I told him he didn't have to give me such a generous allowance and that I was saving, but he didn't listen. I'm trying, Mam, but he—"

"Shhh, I know, honey. We're going to work it out. You let me worry about your father. If you feel all right, you'd better get your things together and get downstairs. I want you back at school before curfew."

Maggie picked up her weekend bag and a pile of books. "I'll see you on the weekend. I'm sorry about dinner. I never seem to do or say the right thing. I don't know why. I think there must be a devil in me somewhere. Grandpap says there is, anyway."

Billie could feel her temper rising again. "He said *that* to you?"

"It doesn't matter. Pap says it, too. I'm just like Aunt Amelia. Pap likes Aunt Amelia but he doesn't like me. You figure it out, Mam. I have to get going."

"If you don't feel well, call me. Promise, Maggie."

"I promise," Maggie called over her shoulder.

Susan and Riley ran in, kissed Billie quickly, and then ran out and down the stairs. Their clattering made Billie smile, but then the front door slammed behind them. Sunbridge was like a tomb again.

Billie sat down with a thump on her velvet-covered slipper chair. She kicked off her high heels and propped her feet on a hassock. Out of habit she reached for the packet of letters on the round cherrywood table. Reading Thad Kingsley's letters always made her feel better. Someday she was going to tell him how much they meant to her. She knew them by heart, but she still searched for the letter she wanted. The naval stationery was as crisp as fresh celery.

I can only try to imagine the heartache you are suffering over Maggie. You have to try to be strong, my dear. She's still a little girl in so many ways. She's not quite a young lady and yet she's not a baby. She's caught in that in-between time. I have to side with you when you say money, and by that I mean having too much, is not Maggie's problem. We both know what her problem is and until you can get Moss to see the light, both of you are going to be miserable. There are times when Moss needs to be hit over the head. His stubbornness can be overwhelming. In that respect Maggie does take after him. I feel that the constant comparisons to Amelia do not help matters. You asked for my opinion; otherwise I wouldn't comment or foist my thoughts on you. I have every faith that you will manage to pull things together. You have strength you haven't tapped yet. Trust me when I tell you it's there and to draw from it.

I would love to come to Sunbridge for a visit, but I don't think it would be wise under the circumstances. Moss drew the line on that last visit and I would feel very uncomfortable. He feels I betrayed him by going with you to look for Maggie. Moss doesn't take betrayal well. Our friendship is in jeopardy, as I'm sure you know. I also know that that's the main reason for your invitation, but I'm afraid, dear Billie, that it will have to come from Moss.

I would like to invite you and the girls to Corpus Christi for a weekend anytime you're free. I have a wonderful housekeeper and cook, and plenty of room. I have a monstrous fireplace. It's a nice place to sit and pretend. Fireplaces with blazing logs, the funny papers, and a cup of grog are for families. Oops, I almost forgot the dog! I have this mutt that wandered by one day and never left. I call him Solomon because he was wise enough to know that if he didn't do his business outside, he couldn't stay. We get along fine. He greets me when I get home and lies by my side all evening. Put him in the picture when you visualize my fireplace.

It's almost time for Solomon's nightly walk, so I'll close for now. Take care, Billie, and remember, if there's anything you need, anything at all, call. I'll always be here for you.

Warm regards,
Thad

Billie folded the letter and replaced it in the worn envelope. She must have read the letter three dozen times at the very least.

She was busily sketching in charcoal at her easel when Moss appeared in the doorway. Billie's eyes hardened. Let him see what she was doing. What did she care? She steeled herself for what he was going to say. He seemed ill at ease, which was strange for Moss. Always-in-control Moss. "Did you want something, Moss?"

"I can't seem to find—"

"Whatever it is, it isn't here. There's not one thing in this room that belongs to you. You saw to that. You're blocking the light."

"Billie . . . goddamn it, I want to talk to you."

Billie clenched her teeth so hard a shooting pain ran down the side of her neck and into her arm. "Why don't we make an appointment for later in the week. I think I might be able to squeeze you in then."

"I won't be here later in the week. I have to go up north for a week or so. I think we should talk now."

Alice Forbes was in New York. Everyone at the club assumed that rehearsals for her new play were getting under way.

Billie looked at the charcoal sketch. It had been giving her so much pleasure until Moss appeared. It was a sketch of Thad sitting in a deep armchair in front of his blazing fire with a sleeping Solomon at his side. She turned away and continued sketching, ignoring Moss completely.

"When I get back, we'll talk."

"If you happen to find yourself on Broadway, make sure you bring home a program for Susan. She saves them."

"I'll do that," Moss said harshly. "Good night, Billie." He waited in the hallway for a second to see if she would call out to him or run after him. She didn't. The pain he felt was like a knife slicing into his gizzard.

Billie continued sketching. This picture was therapy and it was giving her pleasure. It would bring a smile to Thad's face when he saw it.

It was midnight when Billie made the last touches on her drawing. The likeness of Thad was perfect. She hoped she had Solomon right. By two o'clock she had the drawing framed and packed in cardboard. Tomorrow, right after breakfast, she would put some of the Coleman money to good use. She would have the carton taken to the airport and put on the first flight to Corpus Christi. From there a private messenger service would deliver it personally to Thad at the naval air station.

For the first time in months, Billie slept soundly for the remainder of the night.

Ensign Calvin James accepted the package and signed for it. He marched smartly to the admiral's office and waited for clearance to enter. "Special delivery, sir."

"Anything special?" Thad asked curiously.

"It's from a Billie Coleman in Austin, Texas, sir."

"Don't stand there, James. Fetch it here."

He felt like a kid as he ripped at the cardboard carton and the heavy inner paper. When he drew out the framed charcoal drawing he didn't know whether to laugh or to cry. But Ensign James was standing at attention.

"Sir, you have a meeting in five minutes."

"When I get back I want this picture hanging right there where I can see it." Thad pointed to a wall across from his desk. He would have direct eye contact with the picture anytime he sat at his desk. By God, who would have thought Billie would do such a wonderful thing? He was going to call her. The hell with what Moss thought. Such thoughtfulness deserved a personal thank-you.

"Aye-aye, sir. I'll see to it right away." Ten minutes later everyone on the admiral's staff was admiring Billie Coleman's handiwork. "It does look like the old man, doesn't it?" James asked the staff. "But when did the old man get a dog?"

"Who the hell is Billie Coleman?"

"Some guy the admiral flew with during the war, probably," James answered. "Looks nifty. The old man will be pleased."

Billie Coleman's world was already teetering on its axis. It turned over and crashed around her the morning she went to wake Maggie for their promised shopping trip to Austin.

Maggie's bedclothes were tossed and rumpled, most of them at the foot of the girlishly draped canopy bed. Maggie herself was in her powder-pink bathroom leaning over the bowl, gagging and retching. An alarm, too poignantly familiar, sounded in Billie's head. All the signals were there. The sleepiness, the change from rebelliousness to quiet introspection, the thickening of Maggie's waistline despite her loss of appetite. Maggie didn't need a shopping trip into the city. She needed a doctor to confirm what Billie already knew: her daughter was pregnant.

Billie groped for the edge of Maggie's bed before she collapsed. How could this be? She'd taken Maggie to see Dr. Ward only days after discovering what Maggie had been doing. But then, of course, it would have been too soon to diagnose a pregnancy. That had been nearly four months earlier, back in June. Just when she was overcoming visions of her little girl in strange motel rooms with strange men, this had to come along. Just when it seemed she was making headway with Maggie, getting closer to her, rekindling lost feelings of trust and love. Poor Maggie! Her life would never be the same. None of them would ever be the same. Forcing the numbness out of her legs, Billie stood in the doorway to the bathroom. "Why didn't you tell me, Maggie?"

"Mam . . ." Maggie tried to lift her head, her face a ghastly shade of green, her eyes sunken and miserable.

Billie dropped to her knees, cradling her child's head against her breast. "Why didn't you come to me? Why, Maggie?" Billie cried brokenly.

"Because you'd tell Pap and he already hates me!"

"He doesn't hate you, Maggie. But he has to know. Now, later? Does it really make a difference when he knows?"

"Send me away, Mam. Send me somewhere. There are

places. He doesn't have to know. Please, Mam. Help me!"

"Oh, Maggie, I wish it were that simple, but it isn't. How many periods have you missed?"

"Three."

"Oh, my God!"

"Mammmm!"

They sat on the cold bathroom floor, mother and daughter, two women. Billie brushed back Maggie's dark hair from her white brow and crooned soft words as her daughter retched.

"Don't fight it, darling. It only makes it worse."

God, what was she going to do with this child of hers? At that moment she felt as sick as her daughter. What would be best for Maggie? Her brain clicked and raced as she tried to second-guess the family's reaction. The word *abortion* loomed frighteningly in front of her. Never! Amelia was still too fresh in her mind. Moss had to be told. What would he say; what would he do? Tears filled her eyes. She had failed so miserably at everything. But to fail with one's own firstborn, that was unforgivable. Billie sighed wearily, knowing she was in for a storm of emotion from everyone in the house. Maggie herself would give her the most problems once she was on her feet.

"I feel a little better, Mother. I think I should go back to bed. I don't want to go shopping."

Billie had to shake her head to clear her thoughts. One minute the child was so close to her and now she had withdrawn again and was talking about shopping. Surely she realized the predicament she was in. Her whole life was at stake here. "I think that's a good idea. You get into bed and I'll ring for Charlotte to fetch some tea. Perhaps some dry toast and crackers. It's about the only thing that will stay in your stomach."

Billie waited till Maggie finished her tea before speaking. "What are we going to do, Maggie?"

"This is my problem. I'll take care of it."

"How will you do that, Maggie? Please, I want to know. I don't even know what to do at this point."

"That's your problem, Mother. You never seem to know what to do. You coast. I'll go away. I have some money I've been saving. If you know the right people, you can get an abortion. It's simple."

"No it isn't, Maggie. It's a terrible, horrible ordeal. That's not an easy answer. I need time to adjust and think."

Suddenly the little girl in Maggie came out as she clung to

her mother. For the moment all the girl's angry hostility and insecurity were shelved in her fear. "What's Pap going to say?" Billie ached at the tremble in her daughter's voice. Maggie didn't mind her knowing. She didn't mind her mother seeing her misery. Mothers accepted. That's what made them mothers. Maggie didn't care what she thought. In the end she was confident Billie could make it right.

"Maggie, I have no idea what he'll say. He's in New York. It does give us some breathing room to decide what we're going to do. Who's the father of this baby, Maggie?"

Maggie looked blank. "Father?"

"Yes, Maggie, father. Who is the father of your child?" Please, God, let her come up with a name. Don't let her . . .

Maggie sank back into the pillows. The old defiant look was back on her face. "I haven't the faintest idea, Mother."

"Maggie, I don't find that statement humorous at all."

"I wasn't trying to be humorous. All right, Mother, some guy I picked up. Steve something. I really don't remember. Maybe it was Earl. On the other hand it might have been Harry. Or Dick or John. Take your pick. What does it matter?"

"It matters a great deal."

"Face it, Mother. I'm a T.I.T."

"What's that?"

Maggie laughed, a short brittle sound. "For shame, Mother. Surely Grandpap or Pap told you."

Billie clenched her teeth. "What does it mean, Maggie? And how do you know your father and grandfather refer to you in that way?"

"Because Susan and Riley heard them talking and came and told me. That's how I know, Mother. Your precious Riley and Susan would never tell a lie. You really don't know, do you? Tramp in training, Mother. That's what it means. At least they won't be disappointed."

The blood drained from Billie's face. "Maggie, I swear to you, I didn't know. If I had . . ." She reached out and Maggie slapped her hand away.

"What would you have done, Mother? Let me tell you. You'd look away like you always do. Grandpap calls the shots around here and Pap backs him up. Would you have gone up against either of them for me? I don't think so, Mother. Your safe little world would have been disturbed. You know Pap is out there messing around. Grandpap did it, too."

The crack of Billie's hand on Maggie's face thundered in the quiet room.

"Do it again, Mother, on the other side. Maybe it will make you feel better. You can't hurt me. None of you can hurt me anymore. What did I say? The truth? Keep looking the other way, Mother. When Pap leaves you, what are you going to have left? Oh, I forgot, the Coleman money."

The pounding in Billie's head was no match for the pounding of her heart. She was going to be sick. Billie drew the heavy draperies and left the room. Maggie's eyes glared at her from the semidarkness.

The phone rang in the VIP suite of the Astor Hotel, and Moss reached out a reluctant arm as though to quiet an alarm. The shower was running as a background to a woman's sultry voice humming a tune from last night's Broadway musical. Awareness descended. It was 10:10 in New York; 8:10 at Sunbridge. He looked down at the messy bed and frowned. He hated wadded and twisted bedsheets. The phone continued to shrill. Moss came to terms with the fact that he'd have to answer it. Partying with Alice's friends until the wee hours of the morning and then two hours of bedroom calisthenics were not conducive to morning calls.

Moss heard Billie's tight, anxious voice just as Alice Forbes walked into the bedroom stark naked. Her body was always a shock to Moss. While her face was beautifully structured and feminine, her body was slim and lean to the point of boyishness. He was so accustomed to Billie's rounded body and soft, full breasts that he'd almost had difficulty achieving an erection the first time he'd taken Alice to bed. Almost. Now he appreciated those small, girlish breasts with their large brown areolas and those rack-thin hips that could undulate with such a greedy appetite.

"Darling, I know you're awake," Alice called out. "I have to leave for the theater. The second act still isn't right. Say you forgive me." Her hand flew to her mouth when she realized her lover was on the phone.

Moss's stomach lurched. Billie would have to be deaf not to have heard Alice. Jesus Christ! If Maggie was pregnant, why did she have to tell him at this hour of the morning? He couldn't change anything. "I can't come home now," he said, more coldly than he'd intended. "My business isn't finished yet. A few more days. You can handle things, can't you? Have a talk with Seth and your mother."

Trouble. He'd known the call was trouble the minute the phone had rung. It was Amelia all over again. Seth was going to go up in smoke.

Alice was dressed in minutes. She mouthed, "Billie?" When Moss nodded, her eyebrows shot up. She favored him with a conspiratorial grimace. Moss ignored her.

"I'll be home by the end of the week," he said. "We can discuss all of this then. It goes without saying the girl will have to have an abortion."

His daughter pregnant. At thirteen. Jesus! Where in the hell had Billie been all this time? How had she let this happen? He didn't need these problems right now. The girl was an alleycat. Seth had said it time and time again.

"That's enough, Billie! This is not something to discuss over the phone. The girl is pregnant and a few more days isn't going to make a difference. When I get back I'll have the name of a doctor *you* can take her to. I'll be home Friday night. Take a drink, Billie. You sound as though you need it. It isn't the end of the world. After all, the same thing happened to us."

Billie's gasp shrilled in his ears. "That was different," she said icily. "Your daughter doesn't know who the father is. What do you have to say to that?"

Moss stared at the phone in his hand. It took him a minute to realize Billie had hung up on him.

Moss didn't return on Friday as promised. "Unfinished business," he told Seth on the phone. He did, however, have the name of a doctor for Billie.

Sunbridge was as quiet as a mausoleum when Moss let himself in late Sunday afternoon. Thoughts and memories had haunted him since Billie's phone call: Maggie as a baby, growing up, her first real party. How in the hell had his lovely little girl gotten herself into this mess? Where had Billie been while it was happening? Where had he been?

Moss knew what a man's return to his castle should be like: his pretty wife running lightly to the front door to welcome and embrace him, children gathering around, clamoring for his attention. Daddy's home, he thought dourly, and there's no one here who gives a damn except Riley.

Billie heard Moss's step in the hallway. Her shoulders tensed but she continued sketching on the pad in her lap. The sun coming through the living room window had felt warm and good a moment ago.

Moss loomed in the doorway. "I'm here," he announced bluntly. "I don't suppose you can stop to make me a drink?"

"I suppose." Billie attempted to keep her voice level. Laying aside her charcoals, she crossed the room to the bar, stopping to dutifully kiss Moss's cheek. Moss's senses reeled unexpectedly at the familiar scent of her perfume.

Billie felt the charge leap between them. Would she never conquer these feelings she had for him? Even after all these years and so many disappointments, she still wanted him as a man. It had little to do with her need of him as a husband; this was something more instinctive.

Moss accepted his drink, waiting for Billie to speak. Instead she seemed about to go back to her sketchbook. This irritated him, though he realized he was being unreasonable. Unreasonable to expect her to pretend she'd never heard Alice's voice in his hotel room. Unreasonable to wish she'd come to him in this silent house and welcome him into her arms and her bed. Groping for words, he asked, "Did you call that doctor for Maggie?"

Billie turned and stared at him levelly, her soft hazel eyes sharpening. "No, I did not. And I won't."

Moss sighed. "All right, if you're going to be stubborn about it, I'll call him myself."

"No, you won't. There won't be any doctor. Except one who will deliver our grandchild safely. I've had time to think, more time than I need." Her gaze accused him. "Maggie is a child in years but certainly not in experience. She'll have to live with the consequences of her actions. She's pregnant and she'll have this baby. Abortion is against the law and she knows it. To have us condone it, help her get one, wouldn't be good for Maggie. God only knows what she'd get herself into next time. Where will it all stop? I won't have any part of it, Moss. She's not even fourteen years old, and she'll have to live with it the rest of her life. I'd rather she live with having the baby than destroying it. In other words, Moss, two wrongs don't make a right."

"You shouldn't foist something on her just because your own principles will be affronted."

"And whose principles will you foist on her, Moss? She's

only a child and someone must give her the direction she's seeking." Billie knew she was right. Her code of ethics, her principles, might be right only for herself, but they were the only ones she had to offer Maggie.

"She is too young to be saddled with a kid, Billie. I am thinking of Maggie, whether you believe it or not."

"Things go wrong with abortions. I . . . I know someone . . ." Billie stopped, remembering her promise to Amelia. "Maggie won't be saddled with anything if she doesn't want to be. There's time enough to decide what to do with the baby. There are perfectly respectable adoption agencies."

"Just get that out of your head, Billie. This baby is part Coleman, and we don't put Colemans out like unwanted kittens. Stick by this decision and you'll be the one to live with the consequences. If you'd been more of a mother to Maggie, this never would have happened."

Billie's face was frozen and passive, her shoulders square and back stiff. He'd done and said his worst, and she was still standing. There was no glistening of tears. Moss experienced a sudden rush of admiration for her.

"*I* am not stuck with anything. We are. Maggie is a product of us and our failing marriage." There, she'd said the words she could barely admit to herself. "It's only a matter of time before the situation between us ruins Susan and finally Riley. If we fail now, Moss, it's all been for nothing. We'll count for nothing. I won't allow that to happen. Somehow, some-where, we lost our lives. I want it back, Moss. All of it."

Moss seemed to deflate. He'd been expecting a confron-tation, but not this. "What exactly are you saying, Billie? You know I'll give you anything in my power."

"I want a commitment from you, to your children and our marriage. I want us to be a family. I demand it."

"You do, don't you?" There was wonder in his voice.

"Yes, I do. And I believe that somewhere down deep, you want it, too."

"And what do the children want? Maggie, for instance. What does she say about the abortion?"

"At first she wanted to be rid of it, pretend it never happened. She's so young, Moss, she has no conception of the child she carries. But when I told her you wanted her to have an abortion, she became hostile and changed her mind. Now she wants to keep the baby. Moss, I don't know what's right or wrong. All that matters to me is Maggie and her future. Your daughter says she wants to have this child. What do you think, Moss? How do you read it?"

Moss shrugged. "She's almost a woman and I suppose she's changeable. . . ."

"Don't you ever look beneath the surface? Don't you see that she will go against anything you suggest? And why? Because it's the only damn way she knows to get your attention. Go against Pap and he'll always notice. Agree and he can forget you even exist. But this is too serious to play games with."

Moss gulped the last of his drink. "Billie, I'm tired. I have to think. Can't we talk about this after dinner? I'll come up to your room and we'll talk, just like the old days." He sent her a charming grin.

"We never talked in the old days. You talked and I listened. This time it's going to be different."

"C'mon, Billie, let me off the hook for a few hours, won't you?"

"No, Moss. We'll finish this conversation. I've never made demands on you, and perhaps I was wrong. But I'm telling you now, if you don't go along with me on this, on making us a family, I'll leave you. I'll take the children and leave. I want you to be a father. I want you to be a husband. I want a family, Moss, and I want it now."

"Just like that? No looking back? No accusations and recriminations? Forget everything and start over?"

Billie's eyes locked with his. "Just like that."

"All right, Billie, you've got it."

"Your sworn word, Moss."

"My sworn word. Billie . . . I . . ."

"Please, Moss, let's just leave it at that. . . ."

She'd won, and yet her victory seemed hollow. Was this really what she wanted? This bargain, like a business deal?

"No, Billie, you've had your say and I want mine. You're my wife and I know I've let you down. I've been a heel but you've let me get away with it. I thought it didn't matter to you, that you didn't care. Do you know how much it means to me to know you care?" His voice was soft; his summer-blue eyes softened. She saw his arms open to her and felt herself move into them. But just for an instant, she imagined it was Thad's mouth seeking hers and the beating of his heart she felt against her breast. Billie hurled the image away. *This* was her husband, the father of her children, the man she'd promised to love for a lifetime, and God help her, there was a part of her that loved him still—a very old and tired part.

Moss's arms held his wife; his mouth touched hers tenderly, making unspoken promises. He felt her tremble for an instant before she lifted her face to his and he realized the old power he still had over her. It was a good feeling, this sense of possessiveness, a celebration of his prowess. A recommitment to his family wouldn't be so bad. He liked the idea of a family.

{{{{{{{{{{ CHAPTER TWENTY-FIVE }}}}}}}}}

At times Billie felt as though she'd created her own hell. Moss was living up to his promise to commit himself as a husband and a father, but somehow it wasn't working. He was loving, attentive, and seemed to have foresaken his extramarital activities, but still there was an unrest within Billie. At night, lying in his arms, listening to his soft breathing, feeling the afterglow of his expert lovemaking, she fought against the growing restlessness and bitterness. This was what she wanted, wasn't it? To have Moss as her husband again? To have his love and his attention? She should be sitting on top of the world. But she wasn't; she was dissatisfied. Only this time she was dissatisfied with herself.

Moss had his work and had thrown himself into it with renewed fervor, as though to compensate for the quiet domestic life he was living. He talked about his plans for building a new enterprise that he called Coleman Aviation and the difficulties of procuring the proper licensing from the federal government. Billie made every attempt to listen, to appear interested, but it never came from her heart. She was envious of Moss's energy and ability to get a job done, to have meaningful work. She herself had no such outlet.

Billie had given up her art classes when she'd told Jordan Marsh it was over between them. He had accepted her decision with humiliating calm and she had had to wonder when he himself would have called an end to the affair. It had been difficult to pursue her craft on her own, without a teacher to criticize her work. Billie began to create a workshop out of one of the outbuildings behind the house, but it seemed to her that she was directing more effort to the project than to her art itself. Day after day she struggled with her decision to commit herself to home and family.

Maggie didn't make things any easier. As her pregnancy progressed she became more sullen and withdrawn, seeming to resent her mother and father's new, delicate relationship. It never mattered whom or what Maggie hated; she just did. She hated green beans. She hated the soft yellow they'd decided upon for the nursery. She hated babies.

Susan suffered gossip at school, where Maggie's pregnancy was common knowledge. Riley fell prey to Maggie's jealous scorn when at home on the weekends. When Amelia arranged for her talented goddaughter to study at the London Conservatory of Music, the family decided that Susan would be better off in England. Riley would just have to keep out of Maggie's way.

Seth and Agnes, who had become as much a team as peanut butter and jelly, Abbott and Costello, went about with sour expressions. They had completely disapproved of Billie's decision to continue with the pregnancy. They had been forced to face down the disgrace of one of their clan and had been made vulnerable to the many enemies of their power, real and imagined.

Billie juggled all these delicate and uneasy relationships and pretended to believe it would all work out in the end. She refused to admit, most of all to herself, that perhaps she'd been wrong. As Maggie's belly grew so did Billie's discontent.

Maggie's daughter was born during an early spring storm just a few minutes after midnight in the nursery at Sunbridge. Billie, cloaked in a sterile gown, was the first to hold the new infant. A surge of love and protectiveness rushed through her as she cradled the small bundle of life next to her heart. Sawyer Amelia Coleman looked up into the clear hazel eyes of her grandmother and perfected a bonding that would last a lifetime. Billie's finger trailed along the baby's delicate cheek. It had all been worth it. All the indecision, the pain, the pretending. Any price was worth this tiny infant's life.

Hours later, when Maggie lay in an exhausted sleep, Moss quietly tapped on the nursery door and entered. His eyes were full of something Billie couldn't identify. He walked over to the cradle to stare down at his first grandchild. Carefully, Billie lifted the infant and placed her in Moss's arms. His hands were trembling as he accepted the offering.

"She's beautiful." His voice was husky.

"Yes, she is," Billie murmured. "You're holding part of us, Moss. Us. This little girl was birthed by Maggie but she's ours, too. She'll always be ours. Another Coleman for Sunbridge."

"Billie, so much has happened to us. I don't know why or how and I'm more than willing to take the blame. Seeing you here like this, holding the baby, makes me realize how much of our lives I've missed. I should have been here with you when Maggie was born. And Susan and Riley. I should have been—I even wanted to be—but I had this crazy idea in my head that other things were more important. I was a fool, Billie, a damned fool."

Moss had uttered the words she had so longed for. His emotions were genuine—of that she was certain—but she felt no triumph, only sorrow. Sorrow for all the time lost, for the wasted passion, for the loosening of their bond. So many years she'd lived her own life just on the perimeter of his. They were married, they shared three children and now this precious, precious first grandchild, and this was the first and only time he truly mourned all that had been lost between them.

His eyes were moist and glowing, a silent pleading in their depths, and Billie's heart opened to him, to this man whom she'd sworn to love forever, this man of so many complexities. He leaned over the baby's head, his mouth finding hers in a tender kiss. Overwhelming emotions were released from Billie's soul as she allowed her lips to cling to his. "I love you, Moss. I love you," she whispered. And it was true. Or was it only the dream she loved, the home, the family, the unity and belonging? Whatever it was, Moss was an intrinsic part of that dream.

She'd learned many new things since those halcyon days when she was a girl and madly in love with her navy flyer, and she'd changed her opinions hundreds of times. But one fact was undeniable: she never wanted to be without him. She did love him and knew she always would. She'd learned that love had many faces, both beautiful and ugly, but one truth always remained. She loved him.

He tenderly touched his lips to the baby's downy brow before settling her down in her cradle. His fingers, warm and large, found Billie's hand and drew her to him. Arms about each other, they quietly let themselves out of the nursery and moved as one down the long wide hallway of Sunbridge to the silence and dimness of their room.

Billie's heart was tripping beneath her breast. Every sense was attuned to him, to his every touch and action. Some of her girlhood passion and excitement was stirring, blending with the patience and maturity of a woman. When he closed the door behind them she stepped easily into his arms, holding him close, the full length of her body pressed against him, her lips finding the opening at the neck of his shirt and nuzzling in the crisp dark hairs of his chest. She reveled in the scent of him, clean and faintly spicy, but was sharply aware of the deeper male scent beneath. His hands were in her hair, stroking. His lips were tracing concentric little circles near her temples. It felt so good to be held this way, close against him, almost a part of him. And his tenderness was unhurried. He would woo her, court her, and only when she wished it would he take her. Somewhere in her mind's eye she saw again the little kiss he'd placed on the baby's head. Sweet, loving. That was the way he was kissing her now. She was aware of his protectiveness and possession and it awakened long-dormant memories of the first time they'd made love in her girlhood bedroom back in Philadelphia. He'd been the master then, her teacher and guide, and his concern for her pleasure and regard for her inexperience had endeared him to her forever. That was how he was touching her now, as though she were a delicate flower that would bruise and wither with an indiscriminate touch.

The kisses that he was tracing along her neck sent delicious little quivers down her spine. The hunger in his voice when she touched the tip of her tongue to the base of his throat echoed within her. Expectation plucked at her nerve endings and heated her blood.

It was a familiar ritual, yet there was much to discover as well. As her hands caressed the smooth of his back, those muscles and planes to which she'd become accustomed were no less intriguing than they'd been the first time. Her pelvis undulated in a dance, pressing against his stomach and loins with a hungry need of its own. He was her husband and his body was even more familiar to her than her own, but there was an exhilaration in this knowledge. Although the room was dimmed, curtained and shaded against the approaching dawn, her mind's eye saw him clearly, knowing the hair patterns of his body, where the skin was smooth and white, delicately sensitive to her touch. There was assurance in this familiarity, certainty and comfort. The time for newness and timid exploration was behind her. There was no bashful experimentation to bring pleasure as there'd been with Jordan; this was the security of a well-traveled path, the route finely drawn on the chart of their lovemaking, and the reward was well known and joyfully anticipated. This was Moss; this was her husband, the man who shared her life.

His possession of her was tender, loving, making the exchange of pleasure between them sweet and unhurried, while beneath the surface ran a current of dizzying sexuality. As her garments fell away beneath his hands so did her defenses. Was this the way it was to be, then? A new beginning? Starting with the birth of their first grandchild? How fitting, Billie thought. She felt her hostility peel away, leaving her clean and pink and fresh. She *could* love again, she *could* give of herself; and with that thought she turned in his arms as he eased her down upon the bed, placing herself above him.

He wanted her, there was the physical evidence between them, pressing against her thigh. She caressed him with soft, loving fingers, thinking how through the years his male organ had been expressly shared by both of them, almost becoming a third party in their lovemaking. It never ceased to fascinate her, tempt her touch and invoke her kiss. It was her barometer of herself as a woman together with the glow in Moss's eyes and the sounds from his lips.

He helped her mount, holding her firmly by the hips, directing her movements. He fit into her smoothly, snugly, as she slowly descended the length of him, bringing herself tightly against him. His hands were on her breasts, teasing and enticing, drifting upward to caress her lovely face and trace the line of her jaw. She turned her face into the palm of his hand, breathing the scent of herself mingled with his own, feeling the tips of his fingers softly touch her lips.

"Come here to me, Billie, my Billie," he whispered, pulling her downward to meet his kiss. It was then, when she felt the moistness on his cheeks, that she realized she was crying. Her tears mingled with his and the hungry fulfillment of their bodies was secondary to the needs of their hearts. Overwhelming emotions engulfed her, drawing her body closer to his in an effort to touch his soul. Was it to be? This dream against which she'd hardened her heart? Was this love rediscovered? Was she at long last a part of Moss, the most precious part?

{ 365 }

She heard her name upon his lips, saw the expression of love in his eyes. Her inner being reached out with long tender fingers, groping through the years of disappointment and darkness, to find him. Her soul seemed to feel him close, so close, closer than a breath away. But before she could reach him he was gone and only loneliness and emptiness were there to greet her. Before she could cry her grief her body commanded her back to an awareness of the here and now, driving to climax.

When it was over she lay weeping in his arms, hiding herself from him, curving her back and drawing herself inward.

Moss kissed her tear-wet cheeks and cradled her, sighing deeply with satisfaction. He was sated, she knew, and so should she be. Her body had demanded and received. But what of her soul? What was wrong with her? She choked upon her own sobs. Why wasn't it enough that he was her husband, that he cared for her, even loved her? Why must she demand something that perhaps he could never give? What part of her must demand that he also understand her?

"Billie, my own Billie," he was saying as he turned her in his embrace. She saw the tears that still glittered in his eyes as dawn streaked through the curtains. "Don't cry, sweetheart," he soothed. "It was wonderful for me, too. No one could ever love me the way you do."

But do I, Moss? she wondered. Do I really love you? And if I do, what becomes of me?

Maggie would have nothing at all to do with the baby. As soon as the doctor gave his permission, she was out riding at every opportunity and Seth complained that she would ruin the best mounts on the ranch with her carelessness. Her surliness and talent for mischief seemed inexhaustible.

Billie's gentle prompting was met with a stubborn denial. "I never wanted that baby. *You* wanted me to have it. You take care of it! I don't even want to know it breathes the same air I do!"

The entire Coleman family was at its wits' end and looked to Billie for a solution. They'd already faced down the worst of the gossip and the baby presented no problem. The problem was Maggie.

The solution of how best to help Maggie came about in a conversation with Thad. There was, he said, a very private, very good school in Vermont that operated with a limited enrollment, and although it wasn't mentioned in their brochures, they were known to help emotionally disturbed children.

Billie balked at the term Thad used but had to admit that he was being charitable. Seth and Agnes had far more dire adjectives to describe their granddaughter. Besides, she had to admit Maggie had problems, and she couldn't allow words and labels to stand in the way of what was best for her child. Still . . . Vermont?

"I can't just send her so far away, Thad! Certainly she needs schooling and, I'll admit, psychological help, but surely a family is important, too!"

"Contact the school, Billie. I'm certain they'll take her. And as far as a family goes, she can board there and on free weekends she can go to the country to my cousins. They've raised four kids of their own, and hell, it's worth a try, isn't it? What other ideas do you have?"

Billie had to admit she was at a loss. She wanted what was best for Maggie and there was the baby to consider. Maggie needed help.

Before mentioning the plan to Moss, Billie checked it out with the school and waited to hear whether or not Thad's cousins would agree. When she was met with approval from all sides, Billie breathed a sigh of relief and went to Moss with the proposal. He heard only "very exclusive, very private, and very expensive." Emotionally disturbed children were something other people had. Maggie was going north for the best education money could buy.

"I'll never forget this and I'll never forgive you, either of you!" Maggie shouted as the car taking her to the airport pulled away from Sunbridge. Billie's heart ached. Her last sight of Maggie, with red-rimmed eyes and teeth bared, was what she took to bed each night. To her lonely bed. Moss's promise, it seemed, had departed with Maggie. Once again he threw himself into his work, spending long hours away from home. Often, when he crept into their room in the wee hours of the morning, Billie could detect a faint aura of very feminine, very sophisticated perfume. With Maggie gone, Moss obviously considered the family problems solved.

Billie tried to tell herself it really didn't matter. But it did, terribly, and she seemed to spend her days swallowing a dry, hard lump that had become lodged in her throat. What was it she did want? Since the night of Sawyer's birth when she and Moss had made love, she had come to the realization that sexual gratification wasn't enough. Loving wasn't enough. There was supposed to be more—there *had* to be more—but for the life of her she couldn't put a name to it. Even her anger was gone; only a sense of bleakness remained.

Billie's invitation list to the opening of her studio—which was to take place today—was small and select. Two of Jordan Marsh's students with whom she'd kept in touch, Thad, and the family.

For weeks carpenters, painters, and delivery men had thrown Sunbridge into chaos, and the old carriage house was now ready for occupancy. Huge windows and skylights let in blinding amounts of light. Canvases and easels were set up to take advantage of the light at different times of the day. Boxes of paint, brushes, and pallettes were stacked neatly on sweet-smelling cedar shelves. A soft, downy sofa that opened to a bed took up one wall; a small refrigerator, an equally small stove, and a thickly padded rocking chair lined the other. Green plants in tubs stood in all the corners. And Billie had told the carpenters to section off a small room, right next to the sparkling new bathroom, for Sawyer's nursery. That way, any sound the infant might make would carry to Billie no matter where she was working.

Now Billie held Sawyer up on her shoulder. She was a round, cuddly baby, big for six months, the doctor said. She was bright-eyed and alert, gurgling constantly, to Billie's delight. Soft music played in the background as Billie walked about her new domain. She was excited about her new venture—she was reaching out for something.

Seth and Moss were the first to arrive. Billie handed the baby over to Moss, who reached for her unwillingly. Agnes arrived a few minutes later with Riley and the servants from the kitchen. Billie smiled when she overheard Agnes discussing their cleaning schedule. Never would one of her mother's servants take a cloth or broom to this private place. She would clean it herself. This was hers and she wasn't about to share it with anyone but Sawyer.

The coffee was gone, the Danish finished, and Riley had been driven back to the school. The two students lingered a moment or two longer and then departed behind Agnes. Seth limped off and Moss waited a moment longer. "I think this is wonderful for you, Billie. You should have done it sooner," he said. "I don't know much about art, but I can tell that you've improved since you went into the city to that commercial studio. I'm proud of you, Billie."

Billie scrutinized Moss's features for some sign that he was mocking her for doing something on her own. When she read the sincerity she had to smile. A year ago, even six months ago, she would have wept in sheer rapture at her husband's approving words. She felt pleased, but she felt more ecstatic at taking Sawyer from her husband's arms.

"I've got to get back to the office. I'm sorry Thad didn't make it. He must have gotten caught up in something. The navy isn't all that concerned about personal lives. I'd really like to see the old boy again. We've kind of lost touch. I'm glad that you've kept up your correspondence with him. Thad is one in a million."

Billie nuzzled Sawyer's neck. "One in a million," she repeated.

Moss looked around. Suddenly he didn't want to leave. He didn't belong in this place that was his wife's, yet he didn't want to leave. His eyes swept around the room, settling on the sofa bed. He'd be damned if he would depart this place without leaving his mark. The studio would become *theirs* instead of hers. "Billie, I want to make love to you," he said huskily, his hand reaching to touch the soft blond fluff of curls that fell against her neck.

Billie raised her head and at the same time gave Sawyer a slight pinch. The infant wailed on cue. "I'm sorry, darling. Sawyer needs to be fed and changed. Later, in our room. I'll wait for you."

Billie loved her new studio. It was the one place at Sunbridge that was hers alone. She wouldn't share it with anyone, not even Moss. She wanted no memories of him here.

"How long can it take to feed a baby? Can't you prop up the bottle?"

"I wish it were that simple, darling," Billie said sweetly. "However, Sawyer is now eating food that has to be warmed and then she takes a bottle that also has to be warmed. Then she needs to be changed from the skin out. The little love is a messy eater. At least an hour. If you want to wait." She made it sound like the question it wasn't.

"I can't wait. I have a board meeting. Good-bye, Billie. I'll be late this evening."

"All right," Billie called over her shoulder.

Moss stormed out to the garage.

Billie cooed to the baby. "It was necessary, sweetie. Forgive your grandmother." Sawyer gurgled as Billie placed her in the new crib. She wound up a colorful musical toy and within minutes the baby was sleeping soundly.

Now she was alone in her own place, organized and decorated by herself. It was what she wanted, the way she wanted it. It was hers. All hers!

The cigarette she lighted gave her something to do with her hands as she walked around the studio. Today was for looking and enjoying. Tomorrow she would get down to work. She was standing by the huge north window when she saw the plane flying low overhead. She knew who it was instantly. Thad would never forget. Now her perfect little place was complete. She watched the plane circle and then come in low, landing perfectly. She quickly checked Sawyer and then changed her shoes. If she ran like the wind, she could get to Thad before he took off in search of a ride to the main house.

As she ran across the field, her hair billowing out behind her, she kept saying over and over to herself, Oh, God, what am I doing? She didn't care.

At first he didn't see her and then the sound of his name circled around him like an exaltation of larks. He turned and watched Billie run to him. Then he was running toward her. "Billie!"

Billie skidded to a stop two feet from Thad. He pulled up short and both of them burst out laughing.

"Thad! I'm so glad to see you. I thought you weren't going to make it. I waited and waited. Now the day is complete. They're all gone. All except Sawyer and she's sleeping. Where were you? Why are you late? I'm so glad to see you. I've missed you." She was babbling but was unable to stop herself. How wonderful he looked. So fit and . . . and so . . . ready.

"Billie! I'm sorry I'm late. Last-minute check of the plane turned up a small defect. I was out on the field and couldn't get to a phone. I'm sorry. You know I wouldn't have missed your unveiling for anything. How are you? You look beautiful. You always look beautiful. How's the baby? How do you like being a grandmother?" Jesus, he was babbling just the way she was. He wanted to reach out, to take her in his arms. But it wasn't the time and it sure as hell wasn't the place.

"I'm so glad to see you. So damn glad." Billie laughed as she linked her arm in his. "Hurry, I want you to see Sawyer. She's sleeping. I left her alone for these few minutes. I shouldn't have done that. Run, Thad." Laughing like two children, they raced back to the studio.

"Billie, this is wonderful! It's so sunny with all the windows. Now I can picture you here working. I'm glad you invited me."

"You ain't seen nothing yet, Admiral," Billie said, drawing him into the little mininursery. She stood back proudly as Thad stared down at the pink-cheeked baby. "Well, what do you think?"

"What do I think? I think she's the most gorgeous thing I've ever seen, next to her grandmother, that is. Is she as perfect as she looks?"

"Admiral! Surely you jest. Would a Coleman be anything but perfect?" Billie teased. "Yes, she's a good baby. She's gaining weight rapidly and sleeps through the night. I just love her, Thad."

"I wouldn't have known if you hadn't told me," Thad teased back. "Have you heard from Maggie?"

"No. But I write and I send pictures of Sawyer almost every week. I tell her everything. I called a week ago. She sounded fine. She hasn't forgiven me or her father, but we're living with it. The school mails out a progress report at the end of every week. It's not exactly glowing, but her teachers seem to have a positive outlook. Now, tell me about you. I'll make some coffee. I saved some Danish in case."

"In case of what?"

"In case you made it after all. Did I tell you how happy I am that you made it?"

"Yes. But tell me again."

Billie laughed as she measured coffee into the percolator. "I'm so glad you could come. I've missed you, Thad. I think of you more often than is good for me. How's Solomon?"

"Ask a man about his dog and you have his heart. He's fine. His owner isn't all that well. I think of *you* more often than is good for me. I have to be honest with you, Billie. I wasn't going to come today. I was going to call you and say good-bye. Then I realized how cowardly that would be, so I hopped in the plane. I have new orders. I'm leaving tomorrow."

The cup Billie was holding fell and shattered on the new tile. "You're leaving? Where? Why? No, I'm sorry. I have no right to ask that. For how long?"

"I don't know for how long. It's the Pacific. My guess is at least three years."

"Three years! That sounds like forever. Oh, Thad!"

She cared. Jesus, she sounded as though she really cared. There were tears in her eyes. "It's only thirty-six months, or one thousand ninety-five days if you're counting. Who's counting?" He couldn't stand the stricken look on her face. He had to get things back on an even keel. "How are things with Moss?"

Billie drew in a deep breath. "Things are . . . things are . . . what they are. What I mean is, I try too hard. Moss doesn't try hard enough. It's what it is . . . for now. Moss will be sorry he missed you. He was saying this morning that it's been too long since you've seen each another. He's so busy, Thad. Really he is. He's home at night but he works in his office."

"And what about you, Billie?" Thad hoped his voice didn't sound as anxious as he felt.

"I think I'm content. I have my painting and Sawyer. Did I tell you? Of course I did—I'm working on some textile designs."

"I think it's wonderful, Billie. Would you like me to send you some silks when I get to the Orient? I'm to be stationed in Japan."

"Would you do that?"

"It would be my pleasure. As long as you're happy, that's all that matters."

Billie didn't respond right away. "Happy, Thad? I feel as though I'm on hold for the moment. I don't know if that makes sense to you or not, but it's as though I'm marking time, waiting for something or . . . you understand."

Or someone, Thad thought.

Why couldn't they say what was on both their minds? Why wasn't he telling her how he felt about her? Because, he answered himself, Billie was another man's wife—his best friend's wife.

"You'll keep in touch?" Billie asked. It was a plea.

"Of course. The Colemans are part of my life." That was a safe statement.

"What are you thinking now, this very second?" Billie's eyes were bright.

"About that time we were standing in the cavern at Diamond Head. What made you ask me that question?"

"I was thinking that one thousand ninety-five days is a very long time for two . . . for two friends to be separated. I've never been to the Orient. I'd like to see Hong Kong, Japan, the Philippines."

Thad tensed. "When?"

Billie's clear hazel eyes met his gaze honestly. "When?" she whispered. "When I need you most."

{{{{{{{{{{ CHAPTER TWENTY-SIX }}}}}}}}}}

When Sawyer was eighteen months old, Moss came to the realization that Billie no longer lived and breathed solely for him. Days went by when she didn't enter Sunbridge at all but ate and slept in her studio. Once, unable to comprehend what was happening, he had tiptoed out of the house and gone down to the studio. He had stood in the dark and drizzling rain watching his wife play with his granddaughter. He could have gone in. He could have stormed in. Billie's rich laugher as she tussled with Sawyer on the thick carpeting brought a lump to his throat. He was losing her in so many little ways. He knew he had no one to blame but himself. A blanket of self-pity covered him as he stood watching. He didn't belong in the studio. He knew if he knocked on the door or simply walked in, Billie would smile but it wouldn't reach her eyes. The laughter would stop and a tenseness would take over. Billie's eyes would send silent questions: What do you want? Why are you here? She would say, "Moss, how nice to see you." She would be polite. They would be like two strangers.

His children were settled now and gave him no anxiety. It was Billie who was the thorn in his rose garden. This new Billie, who had ideas and opinions of her own and didn't hesitate to speak them. She had to be the youngest, the most beautiful, most caring grandmother he had ever seen. The love and devotion she showered on Sawyer should be his.

They should be doing things, going places, sharing. Instead, they were leading separate lives. Maybe Thad had the right idea after all. Bachelorhood couldn't be all that bad.

Back in his office, Moss delved into his paperwork. Two hours later he knew another trip to Europe was necessary. The sooner the better, and it was business that had to be handled personally.

Suddenly, Moss sat up straight. Maybe, just maybe he could work it so that his business trip coincided with Billie's tour of the Orient, make all the arrangements in advance for her to accompany him, then persuade her to drop her plans in favor of his. She'd discussed her trip with him and he had agreed she could go, although he'd known she would go regardless of what he said. Billie had been writing and making calls halfway across the world, setting up appointments and meetings that, she said, would add to her knowledge and further her career; whatever the hell *that* was! Now he could head her crazy ambitions off at the pass and offer her something far more suitable: togetherness.

A few calls produced two confirmed reservations on a flight to England, with return passage on an Italian ocean liner. A cruise home was just the ticket. What could be more romantic? Billie would love it. It would be a second honeymoon. Or was it their third? A month. A month for the two of them to see Europe. Billie would be ecstatic. He would tell her at dinner tomorrow night in front of Agnes and Seth. Riley would be there, too, since it was Friday and he'd be home from school for the weekend. Three allies.

Moss got up and poured himself a drink. Life had certainly changed since his marriage. Time was slipping through his fingers. He couldn't let Billie drift further away from him. He had to do something to bring things back to the way they were. The trip abroad could do it. He just had to stand firm.

Why? Why was he putting himself through this hassle? Things weren't uncomfortable. Billie shared his bed willingly. She never complained. What really bothered him? The studio? The baby? She still loved him; he could feel it. Sense it in the way she looked at him. He could hear it when they made love. It was all there, all the right things. There just wasn't enough of it. Billie was holding back, not giving one hundred percent to him anymore. A wife was supposed to give her *all* to the marriage, like Mom had. Blame? Fault? His? Every married couple had differences. Every married couple had trouble with their children.

Moss poured himself another drink and walked over to the French doors. He threw them open and squinted to look down across the back lawn to Billie's studio. There were lights blazing through the expanse of glass. Sawyer's bedroom was lit. It was almost the child's bedtime. Would Billie come back to the house or would she sleep in the studio? He'd been keeping track. Four nights out of seven she slept at the studio.

He could walk out, cross the lawn, knock on the door, and say he'd come down to watch Sawyer get ready for bed. It would be acceptable. Or he could carry down two drinks and offer to share a nightcap. Or he could go down there and kick the damn door in. Excuses. He needed an excuse to go there. He was an intruder, an interloper. His money was paying for it. He had rights.

The light went out in the nursery. His eyes narrowed. "The hell with it." He closed the French doors and locked them for the night. His eyes fell on the phone. Why the hell not? He dialed a number from his memory. "Alice? If you aren't busy, I'd like to come over. Yes, too long. Business, the children. I read the reviews. You must be very pleased. I can be there in thirty minutes." He listened for a second and then laughed. He hadn't laughed like that since the last time he'd been with Alice Forbes. "You got yourself a deal." There was a grimace on his face as he drew the drapes across the French doors, shutting out the blazing lights in Billie's studio.

Billie kissed Riley and then hugged him. The boy grinned and suffered the motherly embrace. How tall he was, Billie thought. He was a handsome youth. He looked so much like Moss, it was uncanny.

"How are things at school?" Billie asked.

"Great, Mam. Got an A this morning in my English test. I left my folder on the hall table, if you want to take a look at it. Pap has to sign some papers. How's everyone?"

"We're all fine. Sawyer had a big day and she's asleep already. Tomorrow you can play with her. But I have to warn you, she's got a wicked left hook." Riley laughed.

"I had a letter from Maggie and one from Susan this week. They seem to be doing all right. I'm going to answer both of them over the weekend."

"See that you do." She was so pleased that this son of hers thought enough of his sisters to write them. What was even more surprising was that Maggie kept up a steady correspondence with him. Susan, too, but her letters took longer to arrive. Her children did love one another. Neither Susan nor Riley judged Maggie. They accepted. Why couldn't adults do the same? Oh, no, they had to hang labels, make judgments, dole out punishments. She hated conditional love. Children were wise in so many ways.

"What's for dinner? I'm starved."

"I don't think I've ever seen you when you aren't starved," Billie teased.

"Mam, I missed lunch and only had oatmeal for breakfast. I could eat a side of beef myself right now."

"I think we're having prime rib. Your grandfather insisted. Blackberry pie for dessert. What do you think of that?"

"I can't wait. Where's Pap?"

"Someone call me?" Moss wrapped his son in both arms.

Dinner on Friday nights was always pleasant. Everyone, it seemed, put more effort into being pleasant. Early on, Billie had realized it was for Riley's benefit. Seth talked nonstop about the ranch and the business. Riley devoured every word and ate steadily. Moss never took his eyes off the boy. Agnes presided at the foot of the table with a little bell at her plate to summon the maid.

The atmosphere was a little different today, more electric somehow. Something was brewing; Billie could tell. Moss was moving his fork around on his plate, but he wasn't eating. He, like all the Coleman men, adored prime rib. The others were acting normally. It was Moss who was going to drop a bombshell. How well she knew this husband of hers. There was nothing to do but wait. He would bring it up over dessert or coffee.

Just as the new dark-eyed maid started to pour the coffee, Moss leaned back in his chair and reached inside his jacket pocket. He withdrew a folder and handed it across the table to Billie. "What do you think of that, honey?"

Billie frowned. She reached for the thick packet and opened it. Her eyes widened. She could feel her back start to stiffen. She was trapped; it was a familiar feeling. She slid the papers back into the packet.

"Well, what is it? Don't keep us in suspense, little gal!" Seth bellowed.

"Mam, what is it? Pap looks as though he just won a prize. Tell us!" Riley shouted. For a moment he forgot his second piece of blackberry pie.

"It appears to be two tickets to Europe." Billie said in tight, clipped tones.

"Moss! How wonderful!" Agnes trilled excitedly.

"Mam, you'll get to see Susan and Aunt Amelia. Aren't you excited?" Riley demanded.

{ 376 }

"You don't look very pleased, gal," Seth growled. "Your husband went to a lot of trouble to do this. The least you could do is show you're happy."

Billie ignored everyone at the table. "Moss, you should have asked me before you did this. The thought is wonderful, but I can't go to Europe now and you know it. I've made plans to go to the Orient. We spoke about this several times and you said it was all right with you. Now you go ahead and arrange all this without consulting me. I'm sorry."

Seth scowled. "Sorry about what? You cancel your plans and go with your husband, the way a wife should. That's what you're going to do. Moss, settle this wife of yours."

Moss seethed. It was happening again. It was slipping out of his grasp. His plan wasn't going to work.

"It would be wonderful, Billie," he said. "We could tour Europe, get to see Susan and Amelia. You could go to the woolen mills over there. A second honeymoon, Billie."

Billie could feel herself begin to cringe as everyone at the table waited for her reply. Second honeymoon indeed. She'd been the one to hang up Moss's suit this morning and she'd been the one to take his shirt and underwear to the hamper. The faint scent of Alice Forbes's perfume still clung to his clothes. A second honeymoon. It was too ludicrous for words.

"I'm sorry, Moss. I've already made my reservations. You know I'm not interested in the woolen mills. My interest, if you paid attention to what I've been talking about, is in Oriental art. I'm sorry, Moss, but I can't make it. Perhaps when I get back from the Orient we can make plans to go sometime again in the future. Now, if you'll excuse me, I want to check on Sawyer."

"I'll be a son of a bitch!" Seth shouted as he struggled up from the table. "She's got you by the short hairs, boy. Reel her in and take hold. What's going on here? What's this garbage about going to the Orient? This is the first I've heard about it. Cut her off at the pass. Take away her money and she'll step into line. You only have to do it once and then they know who's boss."

"I can't do that," Moss said stiffly.

"And why the hell not?" Seth thundered.

"Because she told you the truth. She did talk to me about the trip to the Orient. *I* said she could go." This had to be an all-time low for him. Christ, he was eating crow in front of the old man, his mother-in-law, and his son. His eyes went to Agnes, who was twirling her pearls nervously. What the hell was *she* worried about?

Agnes excused herself with a remark to Riley to be sure to finish his milk. Moss headed for his office. Riley looked around the empty table. Sometimes Sunbridge could be so lonely. Maybe next week he would bring a friend home with him. His pal David would like the ranch. But first he would explain that his grandfather was a cranky man. And his grandmother wasn't the cookie-baking kind of grandmother the other kids talked about. He gulped down the remainder of his milk and left the table.

Billie lay quietly in the narrow bed, aware of Sawyer's light breathing in the next room. She wasn't fooling herself for a minute. She had choices and she had options. She was capable of making a decision. She had reinforced her commitment to Moss and she would honor it. She loved Moss. She would always love him. But now it was a different kind of love. The breathtaking grand passion was gone. The closeness and the intimacy of early marriage were gone. All that remained were biological needs that required exercising from time to time. And the commitment to each other. To do what? To live in the same house. To unite when the need arose in regard to the children. The name of the game was pretend. Pretend she didn't know about Alice Forbes. Pretend she never smelled perfume or saw lipstick on her husband's shirt. Pretend she didn't mind if he went off to Europe. Pretend that he cared about her work.

Billie stared into the darkness. How could she be so wide awake so late at night? She tried to make out the objects on the dresser across the room. For some reason it seemed important that she know exactly what was on the dresser. Over and over she told herself Moss was the father of her children. Over and over she told herself she loved him. It wasn't supposed to be like this. Her marriage was supposed to be the ultimate fairy tale with the ultimate fairy tale ending where both the prince and princess lived happily ever after. But reality didn't hold with fairy tales.

All the words had been said. All the tears had been shed. Reality was being wise enough to know when something was finished.

{ 378 }

The churchlike silence in the house the following morning grated on Billie's nerves. If it wasn't for Sawyer's gurgles and cries of delight, she knew she would have screamed.

The young girl who helped out with Sawyer was waiting patiently by the front door for her charge. She enjoyed the pony cart ride in the morning almost as much as Sawyer did.

"Be sure to strap Sawyer in tightly and only keep her out for an hour," Billie said. "It looks as though it might rain. When you bring her back, give her a cookie and some milk and then fetch her over to my studio. Now, Sawyer, you be a good girl for Nancy, and later you and I will build a big castle with the blocks Grandma Agnes gave you." Sawyer reached out chubby hands and arms for a hug and a kiss.

"Solly good girl."

Billie laughed. "Yes, darling, you are. You're the best girl in the whole world. Now say Sawyer. Saw-yur."

"Solly." The little girl giggled.

Billie laughed, which had been Sawyer's intention. "Go along, then, Solly, and have a good time."

"'Bye, Grandma." Sawyer waved.

As soon as the door closed behind her, Billie headed down the hall to Moss's workroom. She made excuses to herself as she started to rummage through his desk. In the early hours of the morning she had awakened and made a pact with herself. If Moss was being truthful when he'd said this was to be a honeymoon trip, she would cancel her plans for the Orient. If, on the other hand, the trip was for business and he was taking her along for his own reasons, it was another story. She felt like a thief and looked over her shoulder constantly to see if Seth or Agnes was watching her from the doorway. Damn, she should have locked the door. What if one of the maids came to clean? A second look told her Moss's workroom was like her studio. No one from the house staff touched it. When she found the packet of papers, she smiled to herself. Under the blotter of course. Her hands trembled slightly as she withdrew the airline and cruise tickets. She laid them aside as she flipped through the other papers looking for Moss's itinerary. It only took one quick glance to tell her all she needed to know. The second honeymoon was a farce. With all Moss had outlined for himself in the way of business meetings, she would be lucky to meet up with him at dockside for the return trip home.

Perhaps the honeymoon was to take place aboard ship? But

she was making excuses again. She was settling for less than she wanted. Moss had specifically said they would "tour Europe." Those had been his exact words. Billie looked again at the typed itinerary. Every hour of every day seemed to be accounted for. Nowhere did it mention her or Susan and Amelia.

Billie sat down with a thump. Moss's chair swiveled slightly with her abrupt move. As long as she was snooping, she might as well see what else she could find. In the bottom drawer behind a box of cigars and a bottle of Kentucky bourbon she found a packet of letters addressed to Moss at a post office box number, all bearing a New York postmark.

Billie shifted the packet from one hand to the other. The letters represented a part of Moss's life. She knew she had no right to read them, regardless of what was going on between Moss and her. She was afraid to read them. Her thoughts were confused. They were married, and yet they weren't married. Not if Moss could do the things he had been doing. What about you? a niggling voice demanded. What about Jordan Marsh, and what about all those feelings you have for Thad? Shame rushed through her. Her eyes lingered on the top of the pile. The date burned her eyes. The letter was only a week old.

Billie replaced the letters and closed the drawer. The packet containing the tickets went back beneath the blotter. She felt dirty. Guilt and shame made her clamp her hands to her burning cheeks.

The walk back to her bedroom was slow, torturous. How could she have snooped and pried like that? Because, the niggling voice said, you were willing to give up your career plans, you were willing to sacrifice again, as you always do. You were willing to put your husband first. Now you see what his priorities are.

He's the father of my children. I married him for better or worse, Billie reminded herself over and over. What about you? the pesky inner voice questioned. What about what you want? What about your feelings? What about your life? Martyrs finish last in this life.

In her room Billie paced the floor to an unheard drum. Her hands were clenched into tight fists in the pockets of her paint smock. The hands unclenched and her stiff spine relaxed. "No more!" she said coldly to her reflection in the mirror. "No more!"

She twirled around and shouted to the empty room, "No more!" She would survive because she was a survivor. That much the Colemans had taught her.

A week later Moss left for Europe by way of Dallas and New York. Seth clawed at him with bony arms and hands, thumping him on the back and warning him to take care of himself. Agnes smiled and accepted the dutiful peck on the cheek that Moss never failed to give. Billie grimaced. Some things never changed. She was always last. This time she found it amusing.

"Billie, I'm sorry you aren't coming with me. We could have done Europe up in style. Susan will be disappointed. So will Amelia."

Moss was trying to lay guilt on her shoulders. She forced a smile and turned slightly to offer her cheek the way her mother had. "Give them both my love. Tell them I wrote a long letter and mailed it yesterday," she said. "Enjoy yourself, Moss."

"Enjoy myself? How can I do that without you there?" Moss waited. She could still change her mind at the last second and say she would go. He hadn't turned in her ticket. How still and unnatural she looked. Christ, she was starting to act like her mother. Giving him her cheek to kiss. Saying inane words that meant nothing. And that smile on her face was as false as the masks he used to wear on Halloween.

It was on the tip of Billie's tongue to say he'd never had trouble enjoying himself before without her along, but she held her tongue. Go already, go! her mind screeched. I don't want to hear the lies anymore. Just go!

"I'll see you when I get back, Billie. Pap, take care of my girl," Moss said. He wrapped his muscular arms about his father a second time. Seth growled something unintelligible and then Moss climbed into the car. Then he was gone. Billie sighed with relief.

Two weeks later Billie left for Hong Kong. Except that she had to leave Riley and Sawyer, she was ecstatic.

Going through customs in Hong Kong, showing her passport, and having her luggage searched pleased Billie. She was handling it all by herself. She had studied up on the currency and felt confident enough to transact some simple shopping. Red, green, and blue bills that reminded her of Monopoly money were tucked into the zippered compartment of her handbag. Her letter of credit from the Coleman's bank in Austin gave her a sense of security.

There were hordes of people and no smiles in the airport. But Billie's smile didn't diminish as she motioned for a porter to take her bags. He nodded and bowed somewhat stiffly. Billie realized he was quite old and was appalled as he lifted her heavy luggage onto a cart to take to the taxi area. She'd have to give him a generous tip. When she was safely inside the taxi she handed the porter a five-dollar Hong Kong coin and watched his face for some kind of expression. When his features remained inscrutable, she hurriedly dug out another coin and offered it. The man nodded but still he didn't smile. How tired he looked, how weary. Billie knew it would take many five-dollar coins to make this man smile. Impulsively, she reached out to grab his arm. "Here," she said, handing him a fistful of coins. The man bowed again and stepped back from the taxi. She knew that she had been foolish, even that she had probably insulted him, but when she thought of the smile on his wife's face that evening, she felt justified.

"Peninsula Hotel on the Kowloon side," Billie told the driver.

The driver shook his head. "You want red-and-silver taxi for Kowloon side. I only drive Hong Kong side. You get out."

"What?"

"You get out and take red-and-silver taxi. They go Kowloon side."

"Will you help me with my bags?"

"I just drive taxi Hong Kong side."

"I'll pay you," Billie said in a panicky voice. Her first problem. She searched the milling crowds for some sign of her porter.

"For five dollars American I will help you."

Fifteen minutes later Billie was installed in a new cab that was indeed silver and red. Her luggage was stowed in the trunk and the driver leaned in the window. "How you pay, Hong Kong dollars or American?"

"What would you prefer?" Billie asked in her best businesslike voice.

"Twenty American dollars to drive you to Kowloon side. You pay toll in Hong Kong dollars."

"All right. Tell me something. How much do you charge to drive one of your countrymen to the Kowloon side?"

"Four dollars Hong Kong," the driver said as he pulled away

from the curb. He narrowly missed a tourist bus. Billie shuddered at the near mishap and decided to forget that she had been taken. Tomorrow she would practice up on the art of haggling. Now she was too tired. All she wanted was a warm bath and a nice clean bed.

Rolls Royces lined the circular drive to the hotel and two boy pages in crease-free white uniforms flanked the entrance to the opulent lobby. Tomorrow, Billie decided, she would admire it all.

Billie woke instantly, completely aware of where she was. Kowloon. Her first full day in Hong Kong. She was alone to do as she pleased. She could get up or she could stay in bed. She could bathe and dress and go to the dining room, or she could have room service. Brunch. That's what she would have. She would dillydally now, take a long luxurious bath, work out the kinks from all the sitting on the airplane. Then a long, leisurely brunch before business.

Billie clapped her hands childishly and bounced on the bed. She was truly in Hong Kong!

Billie stood uncertainly in the wide central lobby of the hotel. Should she go outside to order the taxi or ask at the desk?

The majordomo looked at her from top to bottom, she thought. "May I help you, madam?" he said.

"I'd like to go to the central district."

"Would you like to take a taxi, or would you rather take the Star Ferry?"

Billie looked at her watch. "I think I'd like the ferry."

"Then may I suggest a taxi to the ferry?"

Outside, Billie watched in amazement as a taxi rolled to the foot of the steps. As far as she could tell, the man hadn't made a signal, had uttered no word. One of the white-uniformed pages took Billie's arm, escorted her down the steps, and held open the taxi door. Billie smiled at the boy and was rewarded with a solemn dark-eyed stare. He nodded slightly as he shut the door.

"Star Ferry, please," Billie said, leaning back on the seat.

Once there, Billie paid the fare and followed throngs of people down the wooden ramp to the ferry. She slid to the end of a long slatted bench so she could have a view of the harbor. She was busily snapping pictures of the colorful sampans before the ferry left the pier. She snapped an entire roll of film and was changing the camera when the ferry came to a stop. For a brief moment Billie panicked. She was alone, half a world away from Texas. Then excitement took over. Up the ramp she went like all the other ferry travelers. She tried to blend in with her black suit and white blouse. No one, she noticed, paid her the least bit of attention.

A wizened man held out his hand and smiled a wide, toothless grin. "Missie want rickshaw ride? One dollar American!" Billie stared at the old man and then brought up her camera. She laughed when the man brought his hand up to cover his face. "Picture is two dollars American."

"All right." Billie laughed. "But only because you're the first person in this land who has smiled at me." She aimed the camera and took three shots of the man. First he smiled, then he tipped his raggedy straw hat. Lastly, he propped his foot up on the rickshaw and threw out his arms. "A ham, too," she said. "You'd be a hit on Broadway."

"You take rickshaw ride wherever. Wiggly wiggly."

"What does that mean?"

"That means I go where you want to go. Roads go wiggly wiggly. Taxis not go wiggly wiggly."

"Cloth Lane. Will you take me there?"

"I take for one dollar American. Pay now. Pay picture now."

Billie handed over the money. The man pocketed the bills in baggy black trousers that were the Chinese uniform. He wore only thin black slippers that looked like ballet shoes on his bony feet. How in the world, Billie wondered, could this old man who weighed no more than eighty pounds drag the heavy rickshaw with her sitting in it? He trotted off, his head bent and his back bowed.

The ride was pleasant, but Billy felt guilty that the little man was pulling her on foot. Once she got her bearings, she would walk the crowded, congested streets and drink in the sights on her own. In spite of herself she laughed. She knew, just knew, he made more money having his picture taken than he did hauling people around.

"Cloth Lane," the old man called over his shoulder. "You get out now."

Billie reached into her bag and handed the man two bills. She was amazed to see him snort and look at her with disgust. Her brain whirled as she tried to compute the currency. A two-dollar tip seemed more than fair.

"Money for nothing is not good. You not do again. You lose face if you do this."

"You don't accept tips?" Billie asked incredulously.

"No money for nothing. Smart lady not do this again." Billie debated whether she should hold her hand out for her money, but then he stuffed the currency into his baggy pants.

She laughed. "I won't do it again."

The rickshaw driver waved his hands to show he was finished with her and all women. He muttered to himself as he turned his cart around to look for another fare back to his stand.

Billie was on Cloth Lane. All manner of fabric shops lined the narrow street. Hundreds of colorful banners and metal signs, all lettered in Chinese, hung overhead. They blocked the sunlight. In the end she was forced to work her way down one side of the street and up the other until she found the specific shops she wanted.

When Billie returned to the hotel from her day's outing, she lay down across the bed. She missed dinner and slept through the night. The succeeding days were jammed full of shopping, appointments, and sight-seeing. She stored her treasures in a large trunk she bought to ship everything home. She sent out postcards and wrote letters to Maggie, Susan, and Riley.

On her fifth day Billie felt confident enough to haggle over prices, to the shopkeepers' delight. She set prices in her mind and wouldn't budge a penny. Twice she walked out of a shop only to have the owner come after her and give her the object she wanted at what she considered a fair price. She bought a camera for Thad that the shopkeeper said was idiot-proof. For some reason Thad always had his thumb or finger in every picture he took. For Moss she bought a pure silk robe and one almost identical, except for the color of the dragon on the back, for Seth. For Agnes a string of lavender jade whose price made Billie's eyes boggle. For the children, toys and trinkets of every size and shape filled the trunk to overflowing. She had to buy another one just for her silks and brocades. Hong Kong was marvelous. The only thing she regretted was that she had no one to share her experiences. The urge to turn to someone and say "Look at that!" or "What do you think of this?" was overwhelming. Instead, she talked to the shopkeepers, asked questions, and smiled.

By the eighth day she had eaten in six of the finest restaurants in Asia, taken the Kowloon-Canton Railway, and ridden the

Peak-Tram 30 kilometers to a height of 397 meters above sea level. By the eleventh day, she had explored every shop on Nathan Road, learned to drink Lushan Yun Wu Tea with gusto, and seen a Dragon Boat Festival with a yellow Dragon Boat that belched fire. Truly she was making it on her own.

Billie's time was almost up—only five days remained to her visit—and she still hadn't received permission from the government house to travel to Zhejiang on the east coast of China. The silks coming out of the famous Silk City were described as clear as water, beautiful as poetry, like clouds in the sky and flowers on earth. After she had come so far, it would be a shame to miss the mulberry trees and silk experts of Zhejiang Province.

A long, leisurely soak in the tub, with room service for dinner, was a must, Billie decided wearily. Her busy schedule was finally catching up with her. As she slid down into the steamy water, she wondered how Moss was faring on his trip to Europe and if he had gotten to see Amelia and Susan. She rather doubted it.

CHAPTER
{{{{{{{{{ TWENTY-SEVEN }}}}}}}}}

Billie was sitting down to her exquisitely appointed room ser-vice dinner in her new crimson silk robe when the phone buzzed to life.

"Thad! Is that you? Where are you?"

Thad laughed. "I'm here at the Peninsula. Where else does a person stay when he comes to Hong Kong? You're traveling in high places, lady. This is the home away from home for kings, queens, divas, grand dukes, heads of states, captains of industry, and C.I.A. agents."

"How wonderful. When did you get here? How long are you staying? Why are you here?"

"Your last letter reached me in Japan. That's just a hop, skip, and a jump from here when one has a government plane at his disposal. I'm here for two days. I came to see you. It's that simple. How are you, Billie?"

"Oh, Thad, this is all so marvelous. I can't believe I'm here. I have managed to get around on my own. I missed having someone to share it with, though. I'm so glad you're here."

"Have you had dinner?"

Billie looked at the table with its array of fine china, silver, exquisite crystal. "No," she lied.

"Good. We'll have dinner here in the hotel, at Gaddi's. I'm sure you've tried it out by now, but I happen to think it's the finest restaurant in all of Asia."

"I'd like that very much. How much time do I have?"

"Ten minutes." Thad laughed. God, he felt good.

"I'll meet you in the lobby in ten minutes." Billie giggled. The new green silk off-the-shoulder gown with the slit on the side would be perfect. The jade earrings she'd bought on Nathan Road just this morning would set it off to perfection. Makeup and perfume would only take a minute. Her nails were freshly manicured. She could make it. Ten minutes to meet Thad. Billie never moved so fast in her life. Stockings, bra. The gown slithered down over her body. The feeling was so luxurious Billie gasped. Her heart leaped and fluttered at the thought of seeing Thad and spending the evening with him. Dear Thad. She had so much to tell him. Thad's being here was the consolation prize if the government wouldn't allow her to make the trip to the east coast of China.

Billie brushed her hair into place and picked up the seeded pearl bag that completed her outfit. The mirror told her she looked great. She felt wonderful. She hadn't felt this good since the day Thad had come to her studio. A year was so long. And the years kept slipping by.

When Billie stepped from the lift, Thad drew in his breath. Someone must have written a song about the way he felt. Billie had grown more beautiful over the years. His throat was dry. Christ, he hoped he'd be able to talk. This shouldn't be happening to him. He was no kid.

Their eyes locked across the wide golden room. The smile Billie gave him was radiant and spoke eloquently of many things. Thad was seeing Billie Coleman on her own in one of the most glamorous cities in the world. Hong Kong and Billie Coleman. The other guests were staring at her, too. There was a ring of heat around Thad's neck that was bent on choking him. Did she notice? Was she aware of how he felt? How could she look at him and not see what was mirrored in his face and eyes? Billie was no fool. Billie was a woman and he was a man. Adults. And it didn't mean a damn thing. She wasn't free. She was Moss's wife. He had to remember that. They were two old friends meeting for dinner. It was all he would allow.

Navy whites, tall and lean. Billie was aware of the man coming toward her. Lord, she was going to turn her ankle in the scandalous high-heeled shoes and make a fool of herself. What would he think? Who cared? How wonderful he looked. How dashingly handsome. Every woman there was eyeing him as he held out his arms. How right he looked. How good it felt to be taken into his arms in public this way. A kiss on the cheek was acceptable in this hotel lobby, where everyone waited for romance and wonderful things to happen. He smelled the same. Dear God, he was Thad.

"You look beautiful," Thad said, smiling down at her.

"I was going to say you're the handsomest man in this room, Admiral Kingsley. How are you, Thad?"

"You don't really want to know, do you?" Thad asked in a low tone."

"Yes, I want to know," Billie whispered.

"Why don't we just say I'm fine for the moment and let it go at that. How are you, Billie?"

"You don't really want to know, do you?"

"There are some things a man needs to know and some he doesn't. I seriously doubt that I could handle your answer right now. Let's go to dinner. I reserved a table."

Billie had no time or desire to appreciate the exquisite setting of the restaurant. She had eyes only for Thad. They talked of inane things while they sipped the finest wine the hotel had to offer. She hardly heard Thad order her for: *Emince de vilaille* in a sauce of *beurre maître d'hotel*, which, Thad told her, translated as sliced chicken in a lemony butter sauce. Later she could barely remember if she ate it, much less how it tasted. She was also unaware of the five waiters it took to serve their one table. It was only when Thad inquired after Moss that Billie forced herself to awareness.

"He's in Europe." She resented her husband's intrusion into this wonderful evening. "He flew over and is sailing back. I haven't heard anything from anyone, so I imagine those are still his plans. I hope he managed to see Susan and Amelia. It was a business trip. What about you, Thad? When are you going to tell me about your promotion?"

Thad dogged the question with one of his own. "How long will you be staying here?"

"I have a few more days and then it's back to Sunbridge. I miss Sawyer."

Not Moss, not her husband. Billie would have said if she missed him. No, it was the baby she missed. Thad smiled. "What do you think I could get for these four gold stars over here?"

Billie laughed. "Not much. If they were jade, you might come out with a few dollars—if you haggled first. I'm an expert. Tell me what you want. I can get it at a fair price and no one loses face."

It was midnight when Billie and Thad left the restaurant. "Would you like to go for a walk?"

Not wanting the night to end, Billie agreed. What did she care if she had to trip five miles in spike-heeled shoes? She could get twenty blisters and never be able to wear shoes again and she wouldn't care. She was with Thad.

"I've missed you, Billie. I can't tell you how I look forward to your letters. I told you, didn't I, that I managed to bring Solomon with me to Japan."

"Yes, you did. How does he like it?" Why were they talking about his dog? Why couldn't they talk about themselves? The two of them. If only she could look ahead into the future. Was Thad in her future anywhere?

Thad walked Billie to her door, kissed her again on the cheek, cautioned her to lock the door. They made arrangements to meet in the lobby for breakfast at eight and spend the day together.

When Thad heard the snick of the lock, he leaned against the wall outside Billie's room, fighting with himself not to knock on the door. When he finally forced his feet to take him to the lift, he started back down the hallway twice, only to return to the lift. Inside his room his hand went to the telephone four times in as many minutes.

He was brushing his teeth when his phone rang. He swallowed the glob of toothpaste and dropped his toothbrush in the bathtub on his sprint to catch the phone before it could ring a second time. "Hullo" was the best he could do with the minty toothpaste stuck to his teeth and tongue.

"Thad, did I wake you? I'm sorry. I just called to say good night and to thank you for a marvelous evening."

"I wasn't asleep." Christ, as though he would ever sleep again. "It was my pleasure, Billie. I enjoyed it as much as you did. I hope we can do it again tomorrow evening."

"I'd like that. I'll see you at breakfast, then. Sleep well."

Billie's hand was trembling so badly when she replaced the receiver that she had to clench both hands together. He should have said something. Made some overture. She'd certainly given him every opportunity. Short of throwing herself at him, what could she have done? Now she would never be able to sleep. True to her thought, she lay awake all night staring up at the high ceiling and listening to the bedside radio play the same songs over and over. She watched the sun come up through her window.

Thad dressed in casual civilian clothes the following morning. All night long he'd planned his day with Billie. He was more than familiar with Hong Kong, having spent a month of R&R at the famous hotel nicknamed the Pen, after the war. He'd enjoyed every incredible minute. Now he could share some of his memories with Billie. An entire day and evening with her.

After a light breakfast of tea and croissants he asked her to help him pick up gifts for his relatives back in Vermont. Billie was better at selecting gifts than he was, and she was indeed an expert negotiator.

Then they took a light picnic lunch to do some sightseeing in the New Territories. Thad showed her the Ching Chung Koon and Miu Fat Monastery, two of the most photogenic stops in the New Territories. From there they visited the market towns of Tai Po, Faning, and Yuen Long. The Amah Rock, Thad said, was a must and he proceeded to tell Billie the story.

"Legend has it that a fisherman's wife, with a baby strapped to her back, always went to that particular spot to watch for her husband's return. When she was told that her husband had perished during a certain trip, she refused to believe it. After a year of waiting and watching, the gods took pity on her and, with a lightning bolt, transported her and the child to her husband, leaving a stone monument to her fidelity."

"What a beautiful story. It really does look like a madonna and child." Not for all the tea in China would Billie tell Thad she had been here just a week ago and read up on the legend. Seeing it with him was like seeing it for the first time. Now she could share; now she could talk about what she liked and didn't like. Thad made all the difference in the world.

"I wonder if a man could be capable of being so faithful," Billie said sadly.

Thad turned and looked down at Billie. He reached for her hand. "Some men are," he said softly. Billie squeezed his hand slightly.

"Next stop, the Ten Thousand Buddha Monastery. This will be a first for me. They built this around 1950," Thad said, reading the brochure.

It was a beautiful, warm, close day for Billie. She couldn't ever remember feeling so good or so comfortable with another human being. If only...if...if... From time to time she found Thad watching her with a peculiar glint in his eye. She would smile and he would smile back. Once he put his arm around her and pointed out something. Billie found herself leaning into his hold.

"Today reminds me of the day we spent in Hawaii," she said. "Remember Diamond Head?"

"I remember," Thad said quietly. "I've often wondered if you ever thought about it."

Billie let her gaze meet Thad's. "It was a long time ago. So much has happened to both of us. That day and several others are memories I treasure. Thad...I think...I think we should talk."

"Not here. Not now." God, it was what he had been hoping for all these years. But not in this foreign land, where their lives weren't real. The pulse hammered in his temple.

It had been a mistake to say anything, Billie thought. What must he think of her? "I'm sorry, Thad. Forget I said anything. The worst thing we can do is talk about it. Please, forgive me. I didn't mean to put you on the spot."

"Billie...I..."

"Thad, please. Why don't we leave now. I think I've had enough of monasteries to last me for a long time. Why don't we go back and have some tea. I could really use some tea, couldn't you? Yes, that's exactly what we should do."

Thad turned to reach for Billie's arm, but she was too fast. She had swiveled and was all but running for the tour bus. When he caught up to her she smiled brilliantly and started to chatter about what they had seen so far. He'd fouled up and the moment was gone.

He took his cue from Billie and they chattered all the way back to the Peninsula Hotel. They parted at the elevator, promising to meet for dinner at eight o'clock.

Thad paced his room for over an hour. He had never felt so hopeless in his entire life. Why couldn't he say what he felt? Why couldn't he take what he wanted? What Billie wanted, too? "Right? Wrong? Who gives a good goddamn," he snarled as he smacked one fist into the other. Pain shot up his arm. It was so simple: you reached out and, if you were lucky, there was a hand reaching for yours. He knew Billie would meet him halfway, at least halfway. Nothing and no one seemed to matter except Billie and being free to tell her of his love.

His career had been, after all, a poor substitute for the one woman he could love. After all those wasted years, nothing mattered. The chance to become fleet commander of the Pacific loomed within his reach. It was something he'd worked toward, something to take the place of Billie. Honor, reputation, dedication—empty, empty, empty words. Right, wrong, Billie, Moss. It was all so confusing, so painful. It was a sad state of affairs when all a man had was a dog to call his own. A dog and a career. It wasn't enough and it had never been enough. It was all so meaningless without Billie.

The knowledge of what he was prepared to do was making him light-headed. He sat down on the edge of the bed with a thump. The hell with everything, with everyone. The years were precious now. Reach out!

Billie picked through the gowns and dresses, some still wrapped in the stiff rice paper in which the shops had delivered them. She wanted to wear something bright and mood-lifting, and finally chose a muted tangerine silk with slim sleeves and a mandarin collar. Gold earrings and a wide gold bracelet heightened the effect, and at the last minute she added a large topaz ring that almost obscured her wedding band.

Billie paced her room, feeling nervous and edgy, her thoughts filled with Thad. She realized how much she had shared with him over the years, how much of her time had been spent thinking of him, how important he had become to her emotionally. But now, she had to confront the knowledge that she wanted him physically as well as emotionally. It was something she had long denied.

Thad was already in the lobby when she stepped from the lift. He joined her immediately and Billie noticed a determined set to his jaw. His eyes held hers. A warm flush crept over her when he eyed her approvingly and tucked her hand into the crook of his arm.

Dinner was at the Chesa, a delightful Swiss restaurant that was a reproduction of an Alpine inn. Billie admired the hand-painted fabric used for the curtains and tablecloths and immediately recognized a painted bride's hope chest as being like one she'd seen as a young girl in Philadelphia.

"The cuisine is authentic," Thad assured her. "I've been to Switzerland for skiing and always come home with a few extra pounds around my middle."

"It's comforting somehow to think of you with a paunch," Billie teased lightly. "I never knew you had to be careful about your weight."

"There's lots of things you don't know about me, Billie," he said flatly, without any attempt to return her light banter. Something was different about Thad tonight, she thought. Something brooding.

They were shown to an intimate table that was quietly lit by a candle surrounded with freshly cut flowers. Billie would have liked something nearer the center of the room, where their conversation would be more guarded and the long looks he was giving her would be impossible. It didn't matter, she told herself. Nothing mattered except that there was tension between them and she was the cause of it. She struggled with the conversation, determined to say the right things in exactly the right tone. Thad, she noticed, was on his third drink, which was rare. He was about to signal the waiter again when Billie reached across the table and took his hand. "Don't, Thad. This isn't like you. We'd better talk."

Thad shook his head. "Not here, Billie. Later. I'm sorry I'm acting like such a boor. Forgive me."

"There's nothing to forgive. We'll talk later." Throughout dinner Thad seemed more himself, but neither of them really enjoyed the meal. They were both thinking about "later."

He watched her all through dinner, vacillating. But he had to take a chance, he had to reach out. She was so beautiful, this woman he had watched grow from a girl into this soft loving creature. She seemed to turn her face toward him the way a flower followed the sun. There was a new sharpness to her chin and jaw, the soft round contours of girlhood gone. All those years were gone, all those years of knowing she belonged to another man. But the real betrayal was knowing that she craved tenderness and love and was denied. That was killing him. He had so much to give, endless abounding love.

Billie was aware of Thad watching her. At times there seemed to be a hard glint in those dark, watchful eyes, and at others there was that golden light she'd seen when he'd seen Sawyer for the first time. Sawyer! Good Lord, here she was a grandmother, contemplating . . . contemplating what? Having an affair with Thad? Yearning for that gentle attention and tenderness she knew he had to give? What was it she wanted exactly?

Dinner over, Thad took her walking through the ornamental gardens across from their hotel. To suggest a quiet drink in his hotel room would be like putting out a fire with gasoline. Billie walked beside him, their shoulders touching, their fingertips brushing against one another. Suddenly Billie stopped and turned to Thad. "If you take me in your arms and hold me, I think I'll explode into a million pieces. And if you don't, I think my heart will break. Which shall it be?"

"I've always been good at putting the pieces together," he whispered hoarsely.

She slipped easily into his arms and rested her head against his shoulder. She felt so good, so right. This was not the first time he'd held her in his arms, but it was the first time he could feel her heart beating a staccato rhythm in tune with his own.

"Billie, Billie," he murmured, liking the feel of her name on his lips, the name he spoke only in his dreams.

She lifted her face to find his eyes, looking for answers to the questions her heart was asking. The moonlight caught that lovely oval and reflected the yearnings Thad found in his own heart. She was so appealing, this woman he loved. If he could never have another moment with her, he would remember this one—a moment out of all eternity and she was all that was appealing, this woman he loved. If he could never have another moment with her, he would remember this one—a moment out of all eternity that was theirs alone.

He found his voice, felt it rumble and tremble in his chest. "Darling, how long can we go on this way? I know you care for me—it's there in your eyes, in your voice when you speak my name. What's keeping us apart when we need each other so desperately?" Suddenly he panicked. Had he said too much? Would she reject him? Had he ruined what little they shared?

Billie lifted her hand and pressed tender fingers against his lips, stilling his words, fobidding any further declarations. Gently, sweetly, she rested her head against his chest and her words were spoken so softly that for a moment he thought he'd only imagined them. "Love me, Thad. Take me. I want to belong to you."

They found their way back to the hotel, clinging together like two children afraid to be lost to each other, fingers touching, hands holding, never losing contact with each other.

In Billie's room, surrounded by the dim glow from the little lamp on the bedside table, Thad's touch became more intimate, more demanding, hungrier, as he helped her out of her dress and smoothed the gentle planes of her shoulders and back. His breath was warm on her skin, his lips tender as they tasted each hollow and curve beneath his fingers. He lifted her face to his, kissing her eyelids, the curve of her mouth, lingering there and taking possession as he had only dared to do in his dreams.

Her hands were suddenly urgent on his clothing; she wanted to be closer to his flesh, wanted him totally. This was right, she knew; the rightness of it was singing through her veins. Thad knew it, too; she could feel it in his response, hear it in his voice as he whispered her name.

Lying beside him on the bed, close, so close she could feel each beat of his heart. Billie offered herself with love. It seemed as though she had been waiting her entire life for this moment, to hear him declare his love for her.

"I love you, Billie. I love you," he cried again and again, the words echoing from the chambers of his soul.

She needed to hear those words. She wanted Thad body and soul, complete with every kind of love he could express. And always, always, she gave all that she could in response. Her love was in the touch of her hand and in the softness of her kiss; it was there in the tremblings of her flesh and the yielding of her body. She welcomed him, this man who was so much a part of her life—more, a part of her being. Thad had shared with her, knew her joys and sorrows, her hidden thoughts and secret longings. But this was a new Thad, a different Thad; he was her lover, exciting her passions, lifting her desires, making their love everything she could ever want it to be. She knew she could spend the rest of her life exploring the wonders of this man who could love so softly, so unselfishly.

"I love you." They breathed the words together and moved in unison, each striving to give, to share, to make the other complete.

Thad poised himself above her, gazing down; her lovely

face seemed to hold an illumination of its own from the love-light within her. He kissed her mouth, the pink roses of her breasts, then began to move in command of her passions, still watching her until he became unaware of anything except the driving demands of his body and the welcoming heat of hers.

When he lay beside her, holding her tightly in his embrace, tears were burning his cheeks and he didn't know whether they were Billie's or his own.

It was late, almost midnight, when the telephone rang and brought the world back. Billie reached for the receiver. "Yes?"

Thad watched her face turn ashen and saw her white-knuckled grip on the phone. He waited, painfully aware that something terrible must have happened. Her body, which only a few moments ago had been warm and yielding, was now rigid and tense. "What is it, Billie? What's wrong?" he asked when she'd hung up. He had to ask twice before she turned to him.

"That was my mother. There was an air crash in Spain. There's every reason to believe Moss was on that plane, but he's not listed among the survivors. Seth suffered a stroke at the news. I have to leave."

Thad sprang into action. There was no time now to speculate on the cruelty of fate that this should happen now, when they were together, sated with their lovemaking and unburdened of their need to share and know each other's love. "Pack. I can fly you to Japan and from there you can get a commercial flight to the states. By this time tomorrow you'll be home. I've got to call the airport and have them ready my plane. Billie, will you be all right until I get back?"

"Yes. Do what you have to do. I'll call the desk and have them take charge of my trunks and ship them on later. Go along, darling, hurry, the children are going to need me. Especially Riley. Dear God, Riley!"

There were no trumpets to herald Billie's return to Sunbridge. Numb legs carried her through the massive oak doors and into the ominously silent house.

All the long journey home questions had pounded at her. Was Moss alive? Did the children know? Should she fly directly to Spain? How was Seth? God forbid, had anyone been callous enough to tell Riley before she could be with him?

The taxi driver who'd brought her from the airport placed

her carry-on luggage near the foot of the stairs and Billie quickly stuffed several large bills into his hand. She had been lucky to have found a cab to bring her all the way from the airport. After he'd tipped his hat and let himself out of the house, Billie's heels clicked impatiently on the hard tiles of the foyer and she shouted, "Motherrr!"

It was several moments before Agnes appeared from the back of the house. "Billie! I'm so glad you're home. Why didn't you call to have the car meet you?"

"That's not important. The plane was early. Has there been any word?"

"No news since I spoke to you. I have everyone working on it. Moss's name appears on the passenger list, but aside from that, we don't know anything. If the Spaniards are as haphazard as the Mexicans who work for us," Agnes said disapprovingly, "I imagine it's mass confusion over there. Perhaps later today . . ." Her voice trailed off and Billie looked at her sharply.

"How is Seth?"

"Resting comfortably. There's not much to be done, according to the doctors. He refuses to go to the hospital. I think you should go up and see him. Now."

"Later, Mother. The children?" She held her breath.

"They know nothing. It seemed senseless until we have confirmation."

Billie breathed a sigh of relief. At least she could be grateful for that. "Mother, had Seth heard from Moss while he was in Europe? How do we even know he was on that flight?"

"We don't! Moss called Seth several times and supposedly his last stop was Spain and from there he was flying home. I'm afraid we have to brace ourselves for the worst, Billie."

"Mother, exactly what did Moss say to Seth when he called? Did he give an outline of his itinerary?"

"Only that he was flying home via Spain and that he expected to stay over in New York for a few days before coming home." Agnes's eyes glittered with speculation. "I think you should go up and see Seth right now. He's very weak, Billie. The will seems to have gone out of him, and the doctor refuses to give us a prognosis. What's wrong with you? What happened in Hong Kong? You're different, somehow," Agnes accused. "It's as if you don't care about what's become of Moss."

"Don't be ridiculous. Of course I care. But this is no time

for me to fall apart. You go and see Seth. Tell him I'm home and I'll take care of things. Tell him I'll be up when I . . . when I do what I have to do."

Agnes stared at her daughter but obeyed her. It was something to do. Much as she disliked the sickroom and Seth's frail dependence upon her, it was better than being here with this strange Billie.

When Agnes was out of sight, Billie headed straight for Moss's study. She swallowed hard and opened Moss's private drawer where he kept his address book. Her hands fumbled with bourbon flasks and the box of cigars. The packet of letters was still there. Without hesitation, she read the top envelope and noted the postmark. A few days before Moss had left for Europe. She settled herself, opened the letter, and read it. Her face showed no emotion when she folded the perfumed stationery and replaced it in the pretty envelope. She slid the drawer shut with her knee, picked up the phone, and dialed.

The voice at the other end of the line was warm with sleep— or was it lax with drink? Billie didn't know and she didn't care. Her words were cold and full of venom. "You son of a bitch! Couldn't you at least call your father when you returned to the States? Or when you changed your travel plans? The plane you were supposed to be on has crashed. You are not listed among the survivors. Haven't you heard it on the news? Or have you been too busy? Seth's had a stroke, Moss; he's desperately ill!"

Billie listened a minute, then said, "Personally, I don't care much what you do. Your father might, however. Good-bye, Moss."

Billie's breath exploded in a loud *swoosh*. Something deep inside her had told her that Moss couldn't be dead. She would have known, would have felt something. Billie leaned back in Moss's chair, hands pressed to her temples. She loved Thad; she knew she did. It was a mature love, a woman's love. But would the girl in her ever stop loving Moss? Even now, there was a part of her that mourned this betrayal and grieved for her broken dreams.

Slowly, Billie reached for the phone. A migraine was hitting like a lightning bolt. She rang for the overseas operator. "Thad? I'm home. . . . I'm fine. Really I am. I just have a headache. I haven't seen Seth yet; Mother says he's resting but that his condition is serious. Moss is alive. I've just spoken to him.

He flew back to New York early. Fortunately, Mother was less than her usual take-charge self and didn't tell the children. Thank God for that. All the way home I was terribly worried about Riley. You know the way he adores Moss.... You're not to worry about me. We'll all be fine and I'll write in a few days. Thank you again for getting me to Tokyo. And Thad? Thank you for Hong Kong; I'll never forget it. Never."

At the silence from the other end of the line, Billie squeezed her eyes shut against the engulfing pain. She felt Thad reaching for her across the thousands of miles that separated them, tender fingers of love stretching over the distance. She knew he was waiting for her to say something more, but she also knew this was a luxury she must deny herself. She loved Thad deeply, but all the long way home on the plane she had grieved for Moss, the man who was her husband and the father of her children. Regardless of everything, even her love for Thad, Billie knew without a doubt that Moss was still a part of her life and always would be.

Thad's voice was a deep rumble of choked emotions that tore at Billie's heart. "Good-bye, Billie," he murmured. "I'll see you when I get back to the States."

"Yes, Thad. I'm counting on it. Good-bye." When she heard the connection break, Billie added with a tear in her voice, "Good-bye, darling Thad."

Billie climbed the stairs to Seth's room with difficulty. In the end she was forced to plant both feet on each step as she pulled herself to the top. The adrenaline that had raged through her, making her shake with unexpended energy, was gone. She was exhausted.

How fitting, Billie thought, that Seth should be confined to the same bed that had held Jessica prisoner for so long. It was almost divine justice. She walked into the room and stood near the bed, waiting for Seth to recognize her. Suddenly, Seth had become a very old, very frail man, a pathetic invalid. Agnes, who had been sitting with Seth, eyed Billie as if to agree with her daughter's observations. Then she quickly retreated, glad to be gone from the sickroom. Agnes poised outside the door, listening to Billie speak, marveling at her cool tone. There was authority there.

"Seth? It's Billie. I've just arrived home."

"Why'd you bother to come back?" he slurred. He was

difficult to understand, but there was no mistaking the resentment in those glittering hard eyes. "You should've been with your husband!"

Billie understood. What Seth really meant was that she should have been the one to die. "I didn't come to argue with you. I came to tell you that Moss is alive. He's in New York."

Seth shook his head in disbelief, his lower lip began to tremble, and a tear formed in his eyes. "You're lyin' to me, gal."

"Someday, Seth, you're going to call me by my given name and speak to me with the respect I deserve." She snapped up the phone from the bedstand and dialed the operator, giving her the New York number. "Your father would like to hear your voice," she said coolly when Moss answered.

Seth clenched the receiver in his hand with surprising strength. Billie helped him position it close to his ear. The raw emotion on Seth's face and the disbelief in his trembling voice was terrible in a man to whom emotion meant weakness.

"Son?" she heard him choke through his tears.

Billie stumbled from the room. Hearing Moss's voice again had knocked the wind out of her sails. She nearly bumped into Agnes, who asked, "Is it true? Really?"

"It's true. Believe it."

"Was he with that woman? Again?" Agnes persisted.

"Yes, he was with 'that woman.' Don't start on me, Mother. I don't want to hear how if I was a better wife, Moss wouldn't be the bastard he is. I'm not responsible for his actions, and hard as it is to believe, I am not accountable for his infidelities. Now I want to see Sawyer. Is she in the nursery?"

"Poor Seth." Agnes wrung her hands.

"That's right, Mother, poor Seth. All you've ever worried about was that I'd somehow fall out of favor and deprive you of the Coleman dynasty with all its prestige and power. Well, save your pity for yourself, Mother. Seth is not going to recover from this stroke and I know exactly who is going to take care of him from sunrise to sunset. You've bought yourself that honor, Mother, with all your little betrayals of me and the children and your self-serving alliance with Seth. Before long, Mother, you'll be looking for a little pity for yourself."

Billie turned and headed toward the nursery.

Rain drove against the Cadillac limousine windows and beat upon the roof. The distant crack of thunder reminded Moss of rifle fire. He was glad not to be driving today; it would have been impossible to keep his mind on the road. A jagged streak of lightning zipped overhead, making him shudder. A good old Texas rainstorm, bigger than life, punishing the open plains. Pap hated storms. The old man complained that they made the cattle skittish, but Moss knew storms were one of Pap's secret vulnerabilities. The other was himself.

Pap was getting old. He used to be tough and able to take anything in his stride. Oh, Billie had told him how Seth had grieved when his plane had gone down during the war and they hadn't known if he was alive or dead. But this time the old man had caved in. A stroke. Good God, a stroke! And it was all his fault. One lousy phone call and all this could have been averted. All of it. But he'd canceled the last of his plans because Alice had had some free time between plays and hadn't wanted to spend it alone. He'd whipped through Amelia's London house yelling good-bye to his sister and Susan. Susan had smiled limply and walked away as though to say she'd expected him to miss the recital she was giving at the London Conservatory of Music. Damn it, how could he have been so selfish? Alice Forbes would have waited; she always had. Just like Billie always waited. Billie. In a way, it was all Billie's fault. Her and her selfishness. If she'd traveled with him as he'd planned, there would have been no rush to get back to the States.

It suddenly occurred to him, for the very first time, that he could have been on that plane, that he and Billie could have been killed. The thought was horrible. But then he amended it. No, they wouldn't have been on that plane, because Billie would have insisted on staying in London for Susan's recital. Yes, he nodded, it was all Billie's fault. Her selfishness, her sudden attempt at independence, had driven him straight into Alice Forbes's arms.

It seemed a lifetime since Billie had called him in New York. How had she known he was there in Alice's apartment? Or had she just been doing a kindness by calling Alice to tell her about the plane crash in Spain? Would they have cried together? Tried to give solace to each other? The thought cheered him.

Before Moss climbed from the limousine he whispered a prayer. He didn't know exactly what to expect or how serious Seth's condition was. He knew in that instant he would gladly have gone down in that plane if Seth could have been spared.

Pap had to know he'd give his life for him. By God, he'd make Pap know and understand. They were father and son, and that counted. By God, it counted!

"Pap!" Riley called excitedly. The boy threw his arms around Moss and smothered him with a hug. As always, Moss was amazed at how tall and muscular the boy was. Chip off the old block.

"How's your grandfather?"

"Cranky." Riley grinned. "He doesn't like being kept in bed, but he can't move his left arm or leg. Grandmam says he's coming along. You'll make him feel better, Pap. He's been waiting for you ever since Mam told you weren't on that plane."

Moss studied his son, looking for a judgment in his clear blue eyes. How much did he know? Would Billie be so cruel?

Riley seemed to read the questions in his father's eyes. "I'm glad you weren't on that plane, Pap. Real glad. Grandmam told me that was why Grandpap had his stroke, 'cause he was so worried about you. He loves you a lot, Pap, and so do I," Riley said shyly. He was unused to professing his feelings toward his father. It was something both of them understood and accepted.

"What else did your grandmother tell you?" Moss asked casually. "How's your mother?" If either one of them had told Riley more than was necessary, there'd be hell to pay. He would not allow them to deprecate him in his son's eyes.

"That's all Grandmam said, that it was all a big mistake and that I should just forget about it and try to help Mam as much as I could. Mam doesn't need me, Pap. She's taking care of everything. But Pap, Mam's different. She's not the same anymore. I can tell. I think she got real scared hearing about the plane and thinking you were on it. She's different."

Moss's heart pounded. "How's that Riley?"

"She . . . she's keeping herself busy, answering the telephone and taking care of Grandpap. She lets the nanny take care of Sawyer all the time, and she hasn't even been out to her studio since I came home yesterday afternoon. That's not like her, Pap. She smiles but she isn't really smiling. Do you know what I mean?"

"I think so. Where is she now?"

"I think she's reading the paper to Grandpap. I was up there, too, but I got hungry. Do you want something?"

"I could use a sandwich and a cold beer, if you think you can make it."

"Pap, I'm not a little kid anymore. D'you want me to bring it up or will you eat in the kitchen with me? Grandmam gets upset if we carry food about the house. Bugs."

"I'll be down to join you. You go along. Don't open the beer or it'll go flat."

Moss climbed the stairs slowly. Normally he took them two at a time, but today it seemed he could barely make one foot follow the other. He dreaded this first meeting with his father. Billie, too. Riley had said she was reading the paper to Seth. That meant the old man wasn't too badly off, didn't it? Drawing a deep breath, Moss strode into his father's bedroom.

Billie lifted her eyes from the newspaper she'd been reading Seth and turned to face Moss, her voice trailing off in mid-sentence. Sensing another presence in the room, Seth opened his eyes. A lopsided grin stretched across his face; his right arm reached to the prodigal son. In an instant, Moss had grasped his father's hand and was huddled over the bed.

Billie turned her head so as not to witness Moss weeping in Seth's arms. Her lip curled with disgust, as much for herself as for Seth's blind acceptance. What right had she now to hurl accusations, when she was just as guilty as Moss in betraying their marriage and the commitment to their family? She glanced at her husband kneeling at his father's side. For all his tears and grief she knew he would never change. He would continue living his life exactly as he wanted, as it pleased him. And if she herself were to do the same, where would that leave all of them; the children, the family?

Quietly, she laid the newspaper at the foot of the bed and walked from the room on lifeless limbs, knowing she was embarking on a lonely voyage. Her life was here at Sunbridge and she was doomed to it.

CHAPTER
{{{{{{{{{ TWENTY-EIGHT }}}}}}}}}

Things at Sunbridge changed quickly after Seth's stroke. With the doctor's permission, Seth was moved downstairs and the study was converted to a hospital-workroom. File cabinets, a desk, a high bed with removable sides, and a tray of medicines were the new and prominent furnishings. All the leather furniture and heavy draperies were removed to the cavernous attic to gather dust. In the far corner of the room stood a gleaming wheelchair with a dustcover. Seth refused to use it.

Agnes reveled in her new responsibilities. While she "checked" with Seth and Moss pretended to oversee her activities and decisions, they all knew it was barely more than a courtesy. Agnes Ames was now totally in control of Sunbridge and loved every minute of it. She loved hearing the respect and admiration in people's voices when they proclaimed that they didn't know what Seth would ever do without her. She loved attending board meetings and issuing Seth's orders as though they were hers alone, or altering Seth's instructions to suit herself. Agnes loved power and for the first time in her life she held it—and guarded it closely. What she didn't love were Seth's demands on her and her time. When Seth demanded a cup of coffee, he wanted Agnes to bring it to him. A servant would not do. He liked having the paper read to him, and this she did resentfully. She was at his beck and call twenty-four hours a day, whenever he banged on the wall with his cane, and she hated it. But this was the price for her new position—so with a smile plastered on her face, she tended his bidding and tried to focus on the rewards her efforts brought her.

But it wasn't enough.... Late at night in the privacy of her room, in total darkness, she wished for the old man's death and for the guts to change her name to Coleman. If only she could have those two things, she would be the happiest woman on earth. Power and money. That's what it always came down to.

Six weeks after Seth's stroke, Agnes was sitting in his room, her well-coiffed head bent over a stack of papers. Her shoulders were tense, her writing small and cramped, not her usual flowing style. She could feel Seth's eyes on her back and knew he was trying to figure out something for her to do—some nasty errand to take her away from the things she loved doing, like balancing the ledgers for Sunbridge Enterprises. The total at the end of the columns always brought a smile to her face. She did love totals. Her own bank books, she reflected, were so full and round that she sometimes had trouble grasping the number of zeros. Once it had actually made her dizzy—dizzy with delight. One day she would pack her bags and take off for a trip around the world. The whole world with no clocks, no time schedules.

At the sound of her name, Agnes pressed harder on the pencil she was using and broke the point. The tiny piece of lead skittered across the table. Ulcers. She could feel them beginning to form in the pit of her stomach. That cantankerous old man lying there with his damnable silver-handled cane was giving her ulcers. She turned, a pleasant smile on her face. "Yes, Seth, what can I do for you?"

"You can talk to me, is what you can do. I'm sick of looking at your back. I'm damn sick of this radio, and I'm even sicker of this bed. What's going on? Is Riley coming home today? When was the last time you saw that son of mine and what was he doing? Where's your daughter? Locked up in that piss-ass place she calls a studio? Why hasn't anyone brought Sawyer in to see me? For God's sake, Aggie, I thought you had things in hand. This is all too much for you, I can see." Seth fixed his watery gaze on Agnes and defied her to answer him.

Too much? She hated it when he made statements like that. He could still cut her out, change things right out from under her. He still had the power. As the days wore on it was getting harder and harder to be pleasant to this cranky old man. "I could move the desk around so you wouldn't be looking at my back. Would you like that?" Agnes asked agreeably.

"No, damn it. Why don't you get me a drink?"

"Because you are forbidden to have alcohol. And don't think for one minute that if a nurse is brought in she would give it to you. It's for your own good. Blame your doctor, not me.

Riley will be home this evening, to answer your question. I have not seen Moss for three days. I think he went to Arizona. At least that's what the cook said. Your son doesn't see fit to confide in me these days. My daughter is in the studio, as you well know. Sawyer is with her companion. If you like, I'll have her brought down, but she's about as cranky as you are today. Her nanny said she had an earache. She whines and cries when her ears hurt. Now, what else can we talk about? Would you like some tea or coffee?"

Seth snorted. He should have known better than to ask Agnes anything. She always had an answer. "How're thing going? How was our profit on that last shipment of beef?"

Agnes beamed. "Splendid!" Seth believed her. Few things could make Aggie smile, but money was at the top of the list.

It took more than a year of intensive physical therapy for Seth's speech to return almost to normal. Now, when he was tired or cross, his mouth would droop and he had difficulty swallowing his saliva. Agnes considered this distasteful and made every effort not to be in his presence when it occurred. But by the end of the second year the cranky old man had made enough progress to slide in and out of his wheelchair. "Get goin', Aggie," he'd demand. "I want to see my spread!"

Agnes hated it. She would push Seth around the grounds, detesting her old ally, detesting what had become of her life. The damnable chair was motorized, but the old man refused to utilize it, preferring Agnes's "devotion" to duty.

Nine long years passed. At first, Agnes didn't really notice Moss taking control of some bookkeeping chores, discussing certain business decisions. She was even relieved to have some of the burden lifted. Gradually, though, she realized that Moss had taken almost complete control, and that she was spending more and more time at Seth's beck and call. She didn't like it. Not one bit! She had given her all for the Coleman family. When was it going to be *her* turn to reap her reward—to travel?

It was September 2, 1966, Riley's twenty-first birthday. Hard to believe, Agnes thought, that almost a quarter of a century had passed since she'd first come to Sunbridge. She prepared to leave early for the country club to check on the decorations and the menu. Seth had instructed her to make this evening as perfect as possible—as if she would do anything less. Riley Seth Coleman was her insurance policy against a cold, bleak, unfriendly world...and she never forgot it.

Moss and Riley were to take Seth and his wheelchair in the big car; Billie and Sawyer were to go alone in Billie's car. Maggie, if she got off in time from New York, would arrive at the club straight from the airport. Agnes sniffed. *If* she arrived, she would no doubt spoil the party altogether. Maggie hadn't changed, not really. Although a woman now and working in the historical art department of some minor New York museum, she still had that bitter, childish pout about her mouth, and those same hostilities glowered from the back of her eyes. Agnes didn't like Maggie; she never had. Maggie was a threat, stirring up old feuds and buried feelings. As far as her grandmother was concerned, she had absolutely nothing to recommend her.

It was Agnes's responsibility to carry all of Riley's birthday presents to the country club. The young man was certainly going to be surprised when he opened the little box from his grandfather, which contained the keys to a new Porsche sports car. Moss's gift was the title to a Piper Cub single-engine airplane. Agnes couldn't help wondering what Billie was giving her son. How could she possibly outdo a car and an airplane? Agnes herself hadn't even tried; she'd gotten him a subscription to an aeronautical magazine. Then, at the last minute, she'd bought him a leather billfold and stuck a crisp one-hundred-dollar bill inside.

Another week and Billie's last chick would leave the nest to return to college. Now only Sawyer remained. Agnes made a promise to herself, as she checked the flower arrangements on each table, to try to repair her relationship with Billie. Now that the family was dwindling, there was no reason for them to lead such separate lives.

This little shindig, as Seth called it, was setting him back close to twenty-five thousand dollars. She secretly thought it was rather cheap, considering that two bands and a cocktail hour were part of the flat package the club offered. Shrimp flown in from the Gulf of Mexico, lobsters delivered from Maine just hours ago, and Coleman beef would serve the five hundred or so guests. A real Texas shindig.

Just thinking about it made Agnes wince. What would she be able to eat? she wondered. Her ulcers were spoiling her life. She practically lived on gruel these days. And all because of that damnable, cranky, demanding old man called Seth

Coleman. Once Riley went back to college, she was going to do some serious thinking. She still had a lot of years left, and it looked as though Seth did, too. She knew in her gut that ten more years of waiting on Seth would drive her into the grave. She wasn't getting any younger, while he was the same miserable, cantankerous old man he'd always been.

Susan Coleman hung her dress in the closet exactly one inch from the garments hanging on either side. The neat closet always pleased her. Everything should be neat and tidy. Her life was like that in many ways, she reflected. It seemed to make things easier when everything was in its proper place and well ordered.

Auntie Amelia and Rand were forever taking her to task about it. "Let up once in a while, Suse," Rand teased. "You're becoming so . . . so sterile." She'd been offended by his choice of words, but she hadn't argued. What was the point? It was her life and she would do as she pleased. Then Auntie Amelia had told her that the lack of passion in her life was affecting her work. That had hurt; any criticism of her music hurt. But she had smiled and placated her much-loved Aunt with promises to relax a little.

Susan glanced at the little clock on her beside table. It was nearly time to call Riley and wish him a happy birthday. She was almost sorry now that she hadn't attended his party, but it would have cut several weeks out of her life, weeks away from her music and from Peter—and Jerome, too, of course. Besides, she disliked traveling.

Susan tied the belt of her dressing gown with precision. This particular shade of ice blue flattered her fair complexion and cool blond prettiness. She preened before the pier glass, straightening the belt so that the knot was correctly centered and the ends were the same length.

A steady hand with short-clipped nails reached for the phone to place the call. Thirty minutes, she was told—not enough time to go downstairs and brew a pot of coffee and not enough time for a leisurely soak in the tub.

Susan frowned, resenting this loss of precious time; she didn't like it when things did not go according to plan. But she should have realized that it was still a part of the business day in Texas and that transatlantic calls would take time. Thank goodness she'd placed the call person to person. If Riley wasn't home, there'd be no danger of having to speak to anyone else in the family. Except for Mam none of the others would really want to talk to her anyway, but she would do what was expected, regardless.

Her eyes were drawn to the telephone again, this time her thoughts on Peter Gillette. She'd left the handsome assistant conductor of the London Symphony Orchestra only two hours ago. He was probably home by now. Home, with his wife and two children. A familiar throb of misery touched her at the thought. Only when she was with him, held fast in his embrace, lying beside him, was she able to forget he was a married man.

She'd never known that passion could be so wild and uncontrolled. Peter had shown her and Susan had been a willing pupil. She loved him, desperately, but his wife would never agree to a divorce and his celebrity would thrust the affair into the spotlight. The thought of a public scandal frightened her.

Everything about Peter was wild and exciting and cluttered. He was cluttered with a wife and children and disorganization. He lived for nothing but his music and love, he had told her. Of this Susan had no doubt, but surely there was more to life. Without her, he would forget to have his hair cut and would appear before an audience of thousands in shirts with frayed cuffs. These were the obligations of a wife, and while she took a certain small pleasure in looking after him, she hardly wanted to elect herself as Peter Gillette's caretaker.

They had so much in common; if only he wasn't so... She grappled for the word. Used. Yes, that was it, he was used, shopworn. Love—at least the love in her life—should be fresh and shining, untarnished. She'd suffered enough messiness during her early years at Sunbridge to last her a lifetime: Pap's infidelities, Maggie's pregnancy.... How could she consider getting involved with Peter, who would have to fight for a divorce, even endanger his career, in order to marry her? How much better, how much tidier, it would be if she had fallen in love with Jerome de Moray instead.

Jerome, concert violinist of genius talent. She'd met him last year during a tour of Italy and Austria, and he'd recently come to London to further his studies. Young, inexperienced, and terribly in love with her. Jerome was exactly the kind of man she wished Peter could be. Peter claimed Jerome's talent was adequate, but Susan knew he was jealous. Jerome was a classical virtuoso, and her talent combined with his could lead them to paths of glory in the music world. It seem like a storybook marriage, glamorous and romantic. No loss of reputation, no newspaper scandal; everything would be tidy and neat. If only she loved him.

Shy, beautiful Jerome, cloistered by his wealthy family and his love of music. She didn't think he'd ever been to bed with a woman; his violin was his mistress.

If love took courage, Susan thought wearily, she didn't have it. Loving a man like Peter took courage; loving a man like Jerome took compassion. One would cause tumult and disorder; the other would fit into her life as though he'd always been there. She sighed. One of these days she would have to make a decision, and she knew she would choose safety.

The telephone near her elbow shrilled. Quickly she snapped it up. "Riley! Happy Birthday!"

Billie laid aside her escritoire and began to reread what she had written to Thad. Time was growing short and she still had to apply her makeup. She would finish the letter after Riley's party. Thad would want to know how it went. She'd have some news of Maggie, too.

Billie met her gaze in the bathroom mirror. She didn't look all that different, only older. Thankfully, her figure was still slim, and her skin was clear—although she was using more makeup these days. Lord, where had all the years gone?

Billie rummaged in her work cabinet for Riley's going-away present. She hoped he would like the gift: she'd toiled over it for months. Her special present for her son, a painting of Sunbridge with portraits of all the family members looming over the spacious spread. It had been painstakingly rendered on blocked silk, and she'd spent hours selecting just the right frame. Riley would have a reminder of home to take with him. It had been painted with love and it would be given with love. It was small, no larger than an eight-by-ten photograph. The package was flat and easy to carry. Doubt assailed her as she walked back to the main house to see if Sawyer was ready to leave. What if he didn't like it? What if Moss and Seth deprecated her efforts? Her shoulders straightened. She would live with it, the way she lived with everything lately.

Secretly, Billie was glad that Riley was leaving. She had little to say about any decision that had to do with him. The young man lived a charmed life. Approval and admiration came easily to him, as did friendships and distinction. Inwardly, she believed that Moss's obsessive love could be Riley's undoing. She could see the burden her son carried trying to live up to the Coleman ideal.

In some respects the boy was different from the two powerful elder Coleman men. Riley had always returned love and affection. He'd been a wonderful brother to Maggie and Susan, never letting a week go by without writing them even when they didn't respond.

Once, late in the afternoon, Riley had come into the studio to talk with her. When he'd seen what she was doing, he'd appeared stunned and said quite openly that he'd had no idea she was so talented. His praise and approval had made her feel wonderful. Then he'd told her he feared he would disappoint his father and confided that he had terrible nightmares about it. She'd offered to intervene with Moss, but Riley had been adamant and confessed that he knew things would be different when he went off to school. He'd grinned and put his arms around her. "Thanks for not telling on me," he'd said softly. On that day, for those few minutes, Billie and her son had been close.

Sawyer was waiting by the front door, her gift for Riley in her hand. She hugged her grandmother and turned about to show off her first long dress.

Billie beamed down at the child and tousled her glossy chestnut curls. "You look so pretty, I'm going to have to keep my eye on you or some young man will steal you away. Right from under my nose!" She laughed. "I'm ready. Are you?"

"Grand, do you think Maggie will come? You said she promised." Billie saw the unspoken questions in Sawyer's hazel eyes, eyes that were so like her own.

"Do you want her to be there?" Billie asked.

Sawyer shrugged, pretending indifference. "It's just that I wish I knew her better. Maggie is such a mystery, just like my Nancy Drew books—you never know what's going to happen next with her."

"And Maggie is a book you'd like to read, is that it? Sawyer, darling, I've tried to explain Maggie to you and there are no more words left. I'm counting on her being there. She and Riley have a good relationship, and I don't think she'll miss his twenty-first birthday. I know she cares for you, darling, and of course she'll want to see you, but don't go getting your hopes up and expecting grand things from her."

"Am I like her?" Sawyer asked shyly.

No, darling, Billie wanted to say, you're nothing like Maggie. You're the sunshine and Maggie is the shadow. But Billie knew instinctively that Sawyer needed to connect, to belong, even in the most intangible way. "Yes," she lied, "you're very much like your mother. You have her curly hair and her talents for riding and swimming. And I think you'll be as tall as she is when you're full-grown.

"Now we'd best hurry, darling, or we'll be late."

As Billie drove along the highway with the fidgety but silent Sawyer beside her, she struggled with her ambiguous feelings toward Maggie. She remembered how she'd felt when Maggie had finished school in Vermont and returned to Sunbridge. Sawyer was almost four years old and Billie had feared the mother-daughter reunion. But her fears had proved groundless. To Maggie, Sawyer was just another insignificance of Sunbridge, a long-forgotten cry from a cradle in the nursery. At the time, Sawyer's love for Billie was so total that it made no difference to her how she'd come into this wide, beautiful world; the open-hearted, smiling girl won friends on her own merit, and her personality was so pleasing, her character so far above reproach, that everyone welcomed her eagerly into their midsts. But Sawyer was older now, and more susceptible to rejection. If Maggie ever built her hopes and then dashed them mercilessly, it would create a wound from which the child might never recover. Billie knew what rejection could do to a grown woman, much less a child. Moss had seen to that.

Moss. Her husband. She should have ended it all years ago. Why had she persisted in the fight to hold on to something that couldn't be saved? She had come to hate the word *commitment*. *Her* commitment, *her* sacrifices. Living as they did was a farce—she in her studio and Moss in the house or off somewhere near Alice Forbes or someone like her for weeks or months at a time. At least there was some sort of comfort in knowing that Moss couldn't be any more faithful to Alice than he was to his wife.

It seemed the only thing they had in common was the growth of their respective careers and interests. Moss's aviation company had grown to huge proportions; because of the growing conflict in Southeast Asia, fighter and transport planes were needed, and Coleman Aviation was being underwritten by government contracts to provide them. Once again Moss was sitting in the catbird seat, raking in the profits. The Colemans had the Midas touch; their timing was impeccable.

To Billie's surprise, the balance sheets showed her to be quite successful in her own right. Nearly four years ago, her small studio had been no more than a haven; it had provided solitude and a place to work. Then one day, quite by chance, one of the abstracts she'd given to a local art gallery on commission had interested a leading textile manufacturer. That interest had inspired Billie to forge ahead and establish herself as a designer. She'd unearthed the folio Amelia had compiled for her so very long ago, then made countless long-distance calls, to initiate the contacts and set up appointments prior to taking her first business trip back to New York.

That first trip had been an education. Gradually Billie had learned how to sell herself. Each item of her wardrobe—all "Billie" originals—had been tailored to complement the image projected by each of the companies with which she'd had appointments.

Those had been terrible days, Billie reflected, filled with self-doubt and anxiety. Pounding the pavement, braving rejection, waiting for hours at times in reception areas, only to discover that her appointments had been forgotten or would not be honored.

At her fifth interview with a leading textile manufacturer, Billie's vibrant designs had been enthusiastically received, and she had returned to Texas with orders for one-of-a-kind "Billie" designs. The contract had been small, but it had been a start, all she'd really needed to validate herself as a designer. Now nearly four years later, her work could no longer be considered a hobby; it was a business with deadlines and decisions. Table linens and bedcovers bloomed with her original designs, as did wall coverings and even her latest venture—silk scarves and needlework kits. Her signature was a bold, black *Billie* and was even a registered trademark. It gave her enormous pleasure to see that copies of her imagination and handiwork were carried by the prestigious Neiman Marcus and other leading department stores. Her original oils were in demand for gallery showings. The art and textile design world seemed to be at her feet. Billie still wondered what she had done to justify this success. How much was luck and how much was talent? Once she'd become established, it had been revealed that she was one of *the* Colemans of Texas. How much had that added to the interest she generated from leading manufacturers and designers?

In the end, she reminded herself of the early days—how

hard she'd worked, how persistently she had pounded the pavement. She was a word-of-mouth success and it had been hard-earned. Now she was Billie. Plain and simple. In her circle of work and interests no last name was needed. To the outside world she was an artist, a success. To the family, she was merely eccentric, holing herself away in her studio, preferring her own company to theirs—the original sin.

This was the part of the flight to Sunbridge Thad liked best—the last ten minutes before his descent. Looking down on the Coleman empire from on high gave a man a sharper perspective. Things looked smaller, less intimidating.

It was difficult to believe nine years had passed since his trip to Hong Kong. Nine years since he had held Billie in his arms. It felt as though he had put himself on hold, only to pick up right where he'd left off.

He was free now, unencumbered by his seven-year marriage, a marriage that Billie had encouraged him to consider. "Make a life for yourself, Thad. Don't wait for me. Love and be loved," she had told him. Somehow he had allowed her to convince him.

It hadn't been easy to find someone who could ease the hurt, but eventually Kate Harrington had entered his life. They'd been buddies, playing golf, competing at tennis, taking Solomon for long walks, in an easy, comfortable relationship that made no demands on either of them. He smiled to himself when he remembered his less-than-romantic proposal of marriage, her easygoing, laughing acceptance.

But the marriage had failed. He'd underestimated Kate's love for him, thinking she felt as he did, comfortable and easy, more companions than lovers, more steady and caring than passionate. He'd been stunned by her sexual demands and had obligingly tried to satisfy her, but he'd been unable to give her the love—the desire and the passion—that he still felt for Billie. It had been two years since Kate had divorced him.

The divorce had hurt, and even though he had come to terms with it, put it into perspective, the hurt would always be there, more distant and less poignant, but still there.

The sound of the Cessna's landing gear being released sounded like thunder in Thad's ears. A few more minutes and he'd be there. Sunbridge. Suddenly his shoulders felt lighter. Billie. Riley's twenty-first birthday. Billie.

Sawyer's eyes sparkled when she saw the decorations and the number of people attending Riley's party. The club was closed for all other activities, but it appeared all the members were in attendance anyway. Billie foced a smile onto her face and began to lead Sawyer through the crowd toward the family table. Should she put her present on the long table with all the others and hope it wasn't lost in the shuffle, she wondered, or should she keep it with her? In the end Sawyer made the decision. She bounded up to Riley and dragged him back with her to Billie. "Will you promise to open Grand's and my present last? They're the best. You'll see. Will you, Riley?"

"You bet I will, cricket. Let's see, yours has the purple bow and Mam's has purple paper. I'll remember. What's in it, Mam?" He grinned, shaking the box with curiosity.

"It's a secret," Sawyer chirped. "This is better than Christmas, isn't it, Riley? Did you ever get this many presents at Christmas?"

"No, squirt, I never did." Riley smiled brilliantly, the smile that warmed Billie's heart and reminded her so much of Moss when she'd first met him—when she'd first loved him. "I'm going to need help getting all these to the car when it's time to go home. Will you help me?"

"You bet!" Sawyer quickly agreed, looking up at him adoringly. Billie realized that Sawyer had the same warmth and charm that drew people to Riley. Charisma, they now called it. She knew that she herself had never possessed such magnetism, and she was proud of these two offspring of hers.

"Have you seen your grandmother?" Billie asked Riley.

"Yes. I believe she's over there somewhere with Pap." He indicated a crowd of people near the bandstand. "Mam, I want the first dance. Promise?"

"Promise. Sawyer, you don't have to stay here with the old folks. I see Arlene, Susy, and Patty over there with Cynthia. They're probably waiting for you. Don't get stains on your dress or get into any trouble."

"Grand!" Sawyer protested, embarrassed by her grandmother's admonition in front of Riley.

Riley laughed and put his arm about his mother, escorting her to the family table. "I think half of Texas is here," he said. "Pap does know how to throw a shindig."

"That he does. You should have seen the one he threw in

Hawaii. It would have curled your hair."

Riley grinned. "Mam, I've heard that story so many times I could give it to you verbatim."

Billie found herself grimacing. "I think you should start playing the guest of honor and begin to circulate. Mother is here and we can talk for a bit. It's your party, Riley. Enjoy it."

Riley kissed her on the cheek and disappeared into the crowd as Billie took a seat next to Agnes.

"You outdid yourself, Mother," she said tartly.

"Do you think so? I've had so many compliments and Seth is more than pleased. Moss said it's the most colorful affair the club has had in a long time. Riley is delighted."

"You can feel proud, Mother. This party will be a smash. Riley will have something to remember."

And then she saw him, on the other side of the room. How could she not have known he was here? How could she not have felt his presence? No one had told her. She should have been warned. Of course he would come for something so important. He'd always been fond of Riley.

Agnes's eyes narrowed as she watched her daughter, and she tried to focus on the person Billie was staring at across the room. Something was going on—she could feel the tremor that was building in her daughter. "Billie, are you all right? What's the matter? What's wrong?"

Without taking her eyes from the far end of the room, Billie answered her mother. "On the contrary, Mother, everything is fine. Wonderful, as a matter of fact. Excuse me, Mother. I see someone I know."

Thad Kingsley, dressed in impeccable navy blues, was searching the crowded room for some sign of Billie when he saw her coming toward him. Her eyes were as bright as stars and her smile was warm and welcoming. Billie. His Billie.

"Thad! How wonderful of you to come. No one told me. I'm so glad to see you."

Thad could feel the trembling in her body when he bent down to kiss her cheek. His hands were gentle on her shoulders and he was stunned when he felt the trembling subside beneath his touch.

"Billie, you're the loveliest woman here. Do you realize I haven't seen you for almost ten years? I should have written I was coming, but I wasn't sure I could make it. I didn't want to disappoint you. Besides, I love surprises. Do you?"

"You know I do. Have you spoken to Riley and Moss?"

"I've spoken to everyone in this damn room. I think the only person I missed is Agnes. Sawyer gave me a hug and called me Uncle Thad. I liked that. Is Maggie here?"

Why were they talking about family? Surely he had other things to say. "We'll clear the decks and then I can have you all to myself," Billie said boldly as she led him over to the family table, where Agnes was sitting with one of her numerous club friends.

"Mother, you remember Thad."

"Mrs. Ames, how nice to see you again," Thad said, holding out his hand. "It's been a long time."

Agnes froze in her chair. She wanted to tell Billie to wipe that silly smile off her face. When in the name of God had she last smiled like that? When had her eyes been this bright? Somebody should be handling this. She couldn't do everything.

"Admiral, how nice to see you. Yes, it has been a long time. Moss didn't tell me you were coming."

"Don't blame Moss, Mrs. Ames. I let it hang in the air. I wasn't certain I could make it, but I did."

"So I see," Agnes said tartly. "Moss is over there." She pointed to a knot of club members.

"I've already spoken to Moss and Seth. Riley and Sawyer, too. Now I'm going to steal Billie away for a while and take her for a walk. All these civilians make me nervous."

"I'll see you later, Mother," Billie trilled as she tightened her grip on Thad's arm.

Agnes watched them leave, then moved jerkily across the room to Moss and whispered in his ear. She was rewarded with a dark look as he excused himself from the cluster of people with whom he'd been talking.

"Why are you so upset, Agnes?"

"Don't you realize how this looks? Moss, I've never pried, but the fact that you and Billie aren't exactly lovebirds is no secret. I wouldn't be a bit surprised if she wasn't trying to give you a dose of your own medicine, if you know what I mean." She glanced meaningfully at Alice Forbes. "I told you it was a mistake to invite that woman."

"Agnes, I could hardly *not* invite her; she is a member of the club and everyone else was asked to come." Moss sighed. "Where did they go?" he asked.

"Outside, I believe."

Moss weaved his way through the throng of guests to the

verandah. There was no sign of Billie or a navy uniform.

"So this is where you are. Too many people inside for you, darling?" Alice Forbes asked playfully as she came up behind him. "My, my, aren't we glowering this evening? Looking for the little woman? I saw her going down toward the tennis courts with a tall, handsome admiral. . . . Darling, are you upset? I can't believe it! How long did you think the little lady was going to sit and wait for you to play husband?" She linked her arm through his and smiled up at him seductively. "Now come back inside and enjoy your son's party."

Moss looked at her as if he'd never seen her before, then slowly took his arm away. "You go in. I'll be in in a minute." Alice bit down hard on her lower lip. Surely he didn't still love that little snippet? No, Moss didn't love anyone but his father, his son, and himself. Immediately she felt better. She and Moss were two of a kind—in fact, the only difference between them was biological.

Moss sat down on one of the verandah chairs and lit a cigar. Thad Kingsley and Billie! His mind raced back over the years. . . . Why in the goddamn hell hadn't he seen it? All those letters, all those visits, all those phone calls. His gut churned and the smoke from the Havana made his eyes water.

Something—an instinct, perhaps—told him nothing had gone awry. Thad was too honorable; Billie was too honest. She would never betray her husband, certainly not with his best friend. They were old friends enjoying each other's company, nothing more.

He stubbed out the cigar in a tall urn and went back indoors. This was Riley's party and no one was going to spoil it.

CHAPTER TWENTY-NINE

{{{{{{{{{ *}}}}}}}}*

The moon was full and shining brightly as Thad and Billie strolled arm in arm. Thad was intensely aware of her; her presence filled her senses. She was a heartbeat away, just beside him, beneath his touch. He felt like he was home again.

"It's so good to be with you again, Thad," Billie said, breaking the silence. "I was so sorry to hear about your divorce. I didn't quite know what to do, so I did nothing."

Thad flinched. "It's over now and we're each making new lives for ourselves. So many times I wanted to come here, to see you, to touch you, but I couldn't. I've missed you, Billie. Do you realize how long it's been since we've seen each other?" Thad groped for the words. "I tried to make a new life for myself with Kate, but it didn't work. It wasn't her fault. She's the one who told me I was a one-woman man and she's right. Do you know how long it's been?" he asked intently.

"Almost to the hour," she whispered, not daring to test her voice.

He laughed, a self-mocking, scornful sound. "We're so good, we two. We haven't seen each other for ten years, yet it seems like yesterday. Nothing's changed for me. I took your advice and it didn't work. So, here I am. Can we pick up where we left off?"

"We can work at it, Thad. We have been good people, and for too long. I was writing to you when it was time to leave for the party to tell you I'd come to a decision: I'm going to tell Moss I want a divorce. I can take care of Sawyer and myself. My business is coming along fine; we don't need the Colemans for anything."

Thad's heart leaped in his chest. Divorce. After all this time. "Are you certain, Billie? It's what you want?"

"It's what I want. The way things stand now in my life I'm just going through the motions. It's for me, Thad. What I want for me." She saw the love and relief in his face. He still loved her, wanted her, but he didn't want her to suffer the pain of a divorce merely on his account. If Billie reached out for what she wanted herself, she'd find him waiting.

"I really shouldn't be telling you this, since I haven't mentioned anything to Moss. With Riley's birthday and going back to college, it didn't seem right to spoil things. But I think it's time I started thinking of myself and what I want."

"Good for you, Billie. If I can help, if there's anything I can . . ."

"You'll be the first I call on." Billie laughed. "Wish me luck, won't you?" She reached out to touch his lapel, and his hand covered hers in a warm clasp. This was exactly the way it should be, she thought. He was there and he loved her, and he didn't need words to tell her. But she knew, without doubt, that when the time came to hear it, to know it, to have it said, he would speak his heart.

Thad's eyes misted. He was thankful for the darkness. "I want what's best for you, Billie. What makes you happy. Be sure in your heart, Billie. Be sure it's what you want."

Billie's eyes lifted, meeting his. There was a world of tenderness there, bridging the distance between them, waiting to be called upon, needing to be given freely and without reproach. "You're always kind to me, Thad. It's time for me to do this. And once I do, I'll be free and open to all life has to offer." She drew her eyes away from his, careful not to say too much, to promise too much. But there was joy in her heart and she could feel it emanating from Thad.

"Now that I've unburdened myself I think it's time to get back to the party before we're missed. Thad...I'm so happy you're here. I feel whole again."

"I love being here," he murmured in return. It was the closest they dared speak of love.

Four pairs of eyes were glued to the doorway as Thad and Billie walked back into the room. Seth glowered at them, angry and suspicious. Moss looked almost benign; his smile welcomed them, his best friend and wife, loyal to him and to all the Colemans. Agnes was worried. Did everyone see what she was seeing? Riley saw his mother enter the room with the man he called Uncle Thad. There was kindness and acceptance in Riley's smile. Mam deserved to be happy, and if Uncle Thad was the guy who could do it, more power to the both of them. "Go for it, Mam," he muttered. When they smiled at him from across the room, he gestured for them to join him. He felt no disloyalty to his father, only admiration for Billie. Moss had it all. Why shouldn't Mam have what she wanted?

They had just joined him when Riley noticed that Sawyer was staring at the front entrance. Maggie had arrived.

She looked wonderful; her sleek black silk suit was perfectly tailored to her neat shapely figure, her dark hair was stylishly pouffed à la Jacqueline Kennedy, and she even sported the tiniest of evening hats—barely more than a circlet of fabric to match her suit. Her eyes found him, centering on him as she drifted across the room. Beside him, Sawyer fidgeted expectantly. Please, Maggie, Riley implored silently, just smile at Sawyer; even a smile will make her day.

"Happy birthday, Riley." She kissed his cheek. "You're finally getting out from under the Colemans. Good for you!

This is a night I wouldn't have missed for the world." Then, turning, she looked at Sawyer. "You're taller," she said.

Unable to hide her joy that Maggie had noticed she'd grown, Sawyer pressed further. "Do you like my dress, Maggie? It's special for Riley's birthday."

Maggie's eyes flicked quickly over Sawyer's first long dress. "You don't even have to tell me who picked it out for you," she said, glancing at Billie. "It shows in each little ribbon and bow. When I get back to New York, I'll send you something *really* nice." Smoothly, with barely a breath between statements, she turned to Thad. "Is that a new stripe I see on your sleeve? Congratulations," she said brightly, offering him her cheek for his kiss.

Billie's joy at seeing Maggie again was spoiled by the sudden expression of hurt on Sawyer's face; she put her arm around the child's shoulder. "Hello, Maggie," she said quietly.

"Mother," Maggie greeted, almost as an afterthought, leaning to kiss the air near Billie's cheek. It wasn't until Moss turned and saw her that Maggie's eyes came to life. It was always like this, Billie thought. Maggie standing as though poised for flight, cheeks flushed, eyes hopeful, waiting for Moss's attention. She watched as Moss merely nodded and then turned back to his conversation. There it was—the sudden deadening of the eyes, the tiny bitter line around the mouth that so many mistook for sullenness. Now, Billie knew from experience, Maggie would snap at the first person who dared speak to her. Unfortunately, Agnes put herself on the firing line.

"Maggie! I wondered if you'd make it! It was getting so late."

"I told you I'd be here," Maggie snapped. "Not getting senile in your old age, are you, Grandmother?"

Agnes deflated like a punctured balloon. But she was at least partly responsible for some of Maggie's genes and quickly retorted, "I see you're still an admirer of Jackie Kennedy. They say imitation is the sincerest form of flattery. But really, Maggie, for someone who professes such sophistication, can't you develop a style of your own? Lucky for us that it wasn't Bess Truman you'd met at the White House!"

"Very good, Grandmother." Maggie barely smiled. "Now let's see, who was first lady when you were my age? Dolly Madison, wasn't it?"

"That's enough, Maggie," Billie interrupted. "I think you

look lovely. You always do. When next I come to New York, will you take me shopping?"

"Sure. Next time. Riley, why don't you go get me a drink? Scotch," she said pointedly, aware that all the others were drinking wine. "Make it a double, won't you?" When she noticed Billie's disapproval, she attacked. "You'll never guess who I ran into as I came in the door. Alice Forbes. I had no idea she was down from New York, did you, Mother?"

Thad broke in before Billie could answer. "That's a terrific band Agnes hired and I haven't danced in years. What do you say, Billie? Are your feet insured?"

Billie glanced at Sawyer, unwilling to leave her, but the child was already looking around for her friends. As though Sawyer were on the same wavelength, she said, "You go and dance with Uncle Thad, Grand. I see Arlene waving to me. Can I go?"

"I've got a better idea," Maggie trilled. "You stay here with Grand and *I'll* dance with Uncle Thad."

"It will be my pleasure, Maggie," Thad said uncertainly.

Maggie's eyes gleamed, challenging Billie. See, Maggie seemed to be saying, anyone can take your men away from you. Alice Forbes, your own daughter, anyone!

The party was in full swing when Riley looked around in awe at the turnout of people for his birthday. He would have preferred a simple family dinner with everyone in attendance. But that was being foolish; Pap would never allow his only son's twenty-first birthday to pass unnoticed. All this—the people, the food, the free-flowing drinks, a full orchestra— was an indication that society considered him a man today. Well, he wasn't certain he was comfortable with the role; he liked being a son, grandson, and brother.

Where was Maggie? He'd seen her a moment ago. Summer-blue eyes so like his father's scanned the room and he saw his sister at the bar. He began to weave his way to her side, stopping just long enough to smile, shake hands, thank people for coming. He was nearly there when Moss appeared from a knot of people and tried to draw him into the little crowd.

"In a minute, Pap. I just spotted Maggie and I don't want to lose her."

"C'mon, boy, this bash is for you. You can always find Maggie later if she doesn't get skunked and take off. And if she does, it's no loss."

Riley met his father's burning gaze, knowing he would

embarrass Moss if he didn't obey. Moss's friends were standing and waiting to see what the "chip off the old block" would do. But before the guest of honor could make a move one way or the other, Maggie was in his arms. "Congratulations, brother! Twenty-one . . . it's a landmark."

Relieved, Riley returned her embrace, murmuring, "Thanks, sis. Things were about to get sticky."

"Yeah," Maggie said softly. Poor Riley. She'd seen Moss deliberately put Riley in the position of having to choose up sides. It wasn't fair. She looked over her shoulder and saw her father glowering at her. Well, he wasn't talking to anyone now, and sooner or later he was going to have to acknowledge her.

"Pap, it's nice to see you," she said, and reached out to touch his arm.

Deftly, he reached up to straighten a tie that didn't need straightening. "Glad you could come," he said indifferently.

You bastard, Maggie thought angrily. She turned back to her brother. "I'll see you later, Riley. I want to talk to Mam and Uncle Thad. Doesn't Uncle Thad look terrific? He *always* looks terrific."

Riley gave Maggie a bone-crushing hug and another kiss. "I'll catch up with you later. Don't you dare leave until this is all over. I want your promise, Maggie."

"You have it," she said with false gaiety. "Enjoy yourself. This is your party." She waved once and was gone.

Riley was aware that Moss had hurt Maggie deeply. His eyes locked with his father's, and Moss could sense the disapproval. For a brief moment he was ashamed of himself. Then the liquor in his bloodsteam took over and with a wide smile he proudly displayed his son to his circle of friends.

Billie Ames Coleman filed for divorce on the first day of October, twenty-four years after marrying Moss. She joined Seth and Agnes at dinner to inform them of her action. Moss was out of town on business, but Billie decided to make the announcement anyway. Seth picked up his cane and swiped at the flower arrangement in the center of the table, scattering bits of crystal, flower petals, and emerald leaves. "Over my dead body!" he bellowed.

"If you want to drop dead over a divorce, that's your affair," Billie said coolly. "Personally, I think it's a little foolish. Why should you care? You never liked me from the moment I arrived here. You can no longer control my life. I'm forty-two years old and I want what's left of my life for myself. Accept it, Seth, because in the end that's all you can do. Sawyer will go with me. You'll finally have your son to yourself. He's always been yours anyway. I never for one moment felt as though he were mine. You did that to me. You made me feel like that. Now you can have him."

"There will be no divorce in this family!" Seth thundered.

"There will be a divorce. Count on it, Seth. I filed for it this very morning."

"Then you'll damn well unfile it."

"No!"

"Yes!"

"You can't intimidate me anymore, Seth. I've had enough!"

"Billie!" Agnes's voice came out in a tired squeak. "What are you saying?"

"Mother, my mind is made up. I wanted to tell Moss first, in private, but he's never here, and I can't defer my plans for his convenience any longer. Save your breath. You can't talk me out of it. As far as I'm concerned the subject is closed."

"Little gal," Seth bellowed, "I'm telling you for the last time, there will be *no divorce in this family*."

"Mother, the dinner was excellent. Enjoy your coffee, both of you. I'll be in my studio if you need me."

Outside in the cool, brisk air, Billie drew a deep breath. Seth had reacted exactly as she'd thought he would.

Inside the house Seth continued to rave at Agnes. "I'll boot her tail right out of here if you don't put a stop to all of this nonsense, Aggie!"

"Frankly, Seth, I don't think she cares. Perhaps you didn't listen, but Billie is prepared to leave Sunbridge. She's not a young girl anymore. I think we may have to accept it and go on from there. If you want me to leave . . ." Agnes let her words hang.

"Now don't go off half-cocked, Aggie. No one is going anywhere. Moss will smooth things over. So he hasn't paid too much attention to her lately and the little gal is miffed. Men are like that. I'll see to it that he does what's expected. You get that daughter of yours back in line, Aggie, and I'll make it worth your while."

"In what way?" Agnes asked lazily. It always paid to know these things in advance.

Seth pretended not to hear. "I will not tolerate a divorce in this family. I might be an old man, but I still control things around here. Moss will do what's expected. How does ten thousand sound?"

"It sounds fine, but I don't think there's anything I can do. I'm prepared to leave, if that's what you want. With my daughter gone I doubt that you would want me around."

"Stop talking drivel, Aggie. We both know I need you. You belong here at Sunbridge, just like that little gal. Riley is going to be mighty torn up about this."

"I don't think so. I rather think he's been expecting it. I know I have. Moss, too, when you get right down to it. You're the only one who is surprised. Things haven't been right for a long time."

"Since when are things ever right between two married people? You were married once. Was it ever right for you?"

"There were moments," Agnes hedged. "You can't make a life on moments, Seth."

"The hell you say! Moss will make it right or I'll know the reason why. Well, do we have a deal or not?"

"What if I fail to convince Billie?"

"You want it up front—is that what you're trying to say?"

"In a manner of speaking."

"Write yourself out a check. If the little gal doesn't step back into line, you give half of it back. Agreed? . . . Now what's wrong? You don't look as if you cotton to all of this."

"I don't, but money is money. It's agreed."

"What will make you perk up? A bonus? I know you love bonuses. Tack on another five if you convince her to drop this foolishness." This time Agnes did smile. Three more zeroes. No matter what the outcome, she couldn't lose.

Billie waited for Moss to come to the studio. The letter she'd left on his desk would surely let him know the situation was urgent. He was due back sometime around seven o'clock. Unless, of course . . .

No, she refused to worry. She would let nothing dim this wonderful excitement—she felt like a child on Christmas. Thad was her Christmas. She'd been so empty without him in her life these past years. It was fate that he should come to Riley's party. How was it possible he could still look the same, feel the same? He had tried to establish a little for himself by marrying and she was proud of him for that, but she was glad— oh, so glad—that he still loved her, had never stopped loving her. It was selfish, she knew, but she didn't care. The bond between them was stronger than ever. Soon, soon all those years of waiting and longing would come to an end. Whatever life might bring, they would face it together.

Moss tossed his briefcase on his desk and flopped down on his swivel chair. Christ he was tired. He hated Washington and all those damn officials who thought they knew what they were talking about. He goddamn well knew how to build planes—why couldn't those smartasses let him do what he did best? Why did they forever have to stick their noses in? He was going to have to talk to Pap about this.

Moss took his briefcase off the desk and noticed the square white envelope underneath. He opened it and read the short note from Billie.

Two minutes later, Billie let him into her cozy studio. She got right to the point. "I'd like a divorce, Moss. I was going to tell you earlier, but you were out of town. I told your father and my mother at dinner this evening. I filed this morning."

He'd known in his gut it was something bad. Somehow, though, he'd never thought of this. "Is it Thad Kingsley?"

"No, it isn't. Moss, we have nothing between us anymore. I don't want either of us to blame the other. It's over."

Over. She was saying it was over. She'd also said it wasn't because of Thad Kingsley. Billie never lied. God, a divorce. Pap must have taken the roof off with that one. "Why a divorce if you have no plans or there isn't anyone else?" How casual his tone was—almost as though he didn't care. But he did care; the threat of losing her made him want her more.

"I want to be free to do what I want. I want to be on my own. I want to see who Billie Coleman is. Can you understand that, Moss?"

"No. I know who you are. So do you. This is rather stupid, isn't it, Billie?"

"I was hoping you wouldn't take that attitude, Moss. I don't want to dredge up old hurts, old wounds. This is what I want and it's what I intend to have."

"I don't want a divorce," Moss said harshly.

"But I do. I mean to go through with it, Moss. I'm not going to back down."

"Are you trying to get back at me for all the hurt—"

"No! God, Moss, it's been so long since you've seen me for the person I am that you don't know me at all. I want this for me."

"What did my father say?"

"What you would expect. He said there would be no divorce in this family. I stood up to him . . . and I can stand up to you, too."

"Why don't we think about this for a while? I have to admit I wasn't expecting it. I need time to adjust to come to terms with it."

"Take all the time in the world. As I said, I already filed. I just wanted you to hear it from me and not your father."

"Billie, Billie . . . where did we go wrong? We had so much. How did it come to this?" Moss sighed wearily. He needed this. He really needed this along with everything else going wrong right now. Jesus, he was gong to have Pap on his neck, too.

"I don't know, Moss. I know I tried. But I'm too weary to keep batting my head against a stone wall."

"You are blaming me. I can hear it in your voice. You said *you* tried. You didn't say *we* tried. I did, too, damn it!"

"Not hard enough. We wouldn't be a divided family if *you'd* tried hard as *I* did. None of us has anything. Can't you see that?"

"Yes, I do blame you. I wanted this family united. I wanted you to feel as I did. You promised and you broke that promise. The one thing, the only thing I ever wanted you didn't give me. My family. Now, I don't need it anymore. I don't need you, either, Moss."

Moss stared at her. "Did you hear what you just said?" he said slowly. "Did you hear yourself?"

Billie walked over to the door and opened it. "I heard it; I also lived it. It's late, Moss. You'd better get back to the house. I'm tired."

Moss hated the sound of the bolt shooting home. He stood outside, a cigarette dangling from his lips. He stood there for a long time after the lights went off. How could it be over? It would be over when he said it was over. And he wasn't ready. He knew how to fight—and fight he would, for what was his.

Riley was glad the Thanksgiving holiday was over; he'd missed being at home with the family for the traditional dinner. But he'd had work to do, important work. He stared out his dormitory window at the effects of last night's snowstorm. It was going to be tough protest-marching against the military draft in weather like this. He hoped the media would still turn out to cover the event. Anne Marie Wolosky had said they would, and she always seemed to know how something was going down.

"It must be twenty degrees below zero out there," Riley muttered to his roommate, Mike O'Neil. "We're going to freeze out butts off out there."

"I know. I've got my long johns and two pairs of socks. Relax, Coleman, it's only for a couple of hours. We'll survive. This snowstorm is old hat to the news media and we'll give them something else to write about. It's worth the frostbite."

Vietnam, that unholy altercation on the other side of the world. Not many called it a war, but they would, Riley knew. It was still being called a "police action," Riley thought as he put the finishing touches to the placard he would carry: BRING 'EM HOME!!!

"It has its message." Mike grinned. "What d'you think of mine?"

Riley craned his neck to see the sign Mike was waving: I'M NOT GOING!!! "Is that your final word, O'Neil?"

"Damn right."

"Let's get going. The others are waiting and I don't want to have to hoof it over to the administration building. Creature of comfort that I am, I prefer to be warm until we get there."

The demonstration on the campus of Kent State University promised to be one of the largest launched yet; the media would have to carry it.

The march began peacefully enough and would have remained so if some rookie cop hadn't swung his billy club in frustration at the "rich asshole kids who had nothing better to do." Mike O'Neil took the blow on his left shoulder. The sound of his buddy's shoulder cracking drove Riley into a frenzy. He whipped about in the swirling snow and brought his sign down on the cop's right hand, knocking the club to the snow. Sara Fitz picked it up and brandished it in the air at the cop's partner. Riley shoved Sara out of the way and leaped on the cop, swinging wildly. A cameraman zoomed in on Riley's angry face as he pummeled the cop for all the world to see. All hell broke loose.

Mike O'Neil, his face contorted in pain, was handcuffed and shoved into a police car next to Riley.

"His shoulder's broken. Take his cuffs off," Riley pleaded. "We aren't going anywhere. Give him a break. Can't you see he's in agony?"

"Shut up and don't let me hear another word out of you. You're all scum. Draft dodgers are all scum."

"Think whatever you like, but please take the cuffs off him. Look at his shoulder if you don't believe me." For an answer, the officer laughed derisively.

"Save your breath, Riley," Mike muttered. "Look, if I pass out, don't hold it against me."

Riley stared at his friend. There was a bluish tinge around his lips and his face was ashen. The police wagon was warm.

"I'm not going to ask you again. Take these cuffs off my friend. Please."

"Shut up!"

Riley's brain whirled. Sometimes there just wasn't any other way. "My grandfather isn't going to like this," he murmured. The officer had to strain to hear him. "Neither is my father. When they get upset, a lot of other people get upset. Like police commissioners."

"I'm real scared." The officer grinned maliciously. These punks were all alike.

"You should be. My name's Coleman"—Riley paused—"just like the mayor's."

"Bellamy, check that kid's wallet," the driver said over his shoulder. Bellamy yanked Riley's wallet out of his back pocket.

"That's what it says. Riley Coleman." The police wagon ground to a halt and slid fifteen feet in the snow. "Should I take off the kid's cuffs?"

"Hell, yes, take them off. We don't need the department coming down on our necks. I've got a wife and kids to support."

"Take it easy," Riley warned. "Watch out for that shoulder. Jesus, can't you see it's broken?"

"Kid gloves, Bellamy. Wipe his nose, too."

"Good for you, officer," Riley snarled. "You okay, Mike?"

"Better . . ." There was a slight pause, then Mike slumped back against the seat, unconscious.

"He's passed out. You happy now?" Riley cried. "Let's get him to a hospital. Move it!"

"Get his cuffs off, too, Bellamy. Christ! I wish I were in Florida!"

"Oh, no, you don't. My cuffs stay on. You already read me my rights and arrested me. You're stuck with me. My buddy is something else. You get him to a hospital, and then you can book me. That's what you do, isn't it?"

"Then your grandpappy and your old daddy are going to

spring you. Get the hell out of this car. We'll take your buddy to the hospital."

"You pitch me out of this car and it's the last thing you'll ever do. . . . You're wasting time."

"He's right. This guy is still out. He don't look too good," Bellamy said coldly. "We can worry about this punk later."

An hour later, with the aid of a snow truck leading the way, the police wagon pulled into the emergency entrance of the hospital. Riley was pulled out of the wagon and a gurney with two white-clad figures rushed to help Mike.

"Riley!" It was Sara. Riley noticed she had a knot the size of a lemon over her left eye. "What happened?"

"Mike's got a busted shoulder. Anyone else hurt?"

"Devon has a fractured windpipe. Some cop caught him smack in the throat. He's in surgery. Betsy is having her arm set; it's broken in two places. Calvin is getting sewed up right now. He got a big gash in his cheek; his nose got tipped up a little, too. Those cops really came out swinging. We didn't start it—remember that."

"Hey, I was there, remember? Jeez, I hope Mike is all right. He didn't look good to me. These nerds handcuffed him."

Sara shifted the ice pack she was holding and sidled closer to Riley. "There must be a hundred reporters in the lobby. They're waiting for one of us to talk to them. Beats me what they're all doing out in this storm. I can't believe this happened. It was supposed to be peaceful. We all agreed that there was to be no violence, no matter what."

"It's hard not to fight back when someone is cracking your bones," Riley said bitterly. "Peaceful—bullshit! Who's going to do the talking?"

"I think you should. It will go a long way for our cause. Riley Seth Coleman of *the* Colemans. You game?"

A vision of Seth and Moss watching the evening news flashed before his eyes. And then another vision of his buddy's blue lips and ashen face swam before him. Sara was waiting. But it was the picture of his mother that decided him. "Okay, I'll do it. Give me a rundown on what happened after they shoved us in the police wagon." Riley listened intently as Sarah ran through the course of events. His agile brain sifted, collated, and filed the events in chronological order. He was prepared.

"The cops aren't going to want you to talk to the press. We might have to create a scene for you. All the reporters are at the front of the hospital. We're in emergency and that's at the

{ 430 }

back. They're going to want to take you straight to the police station."

"Hell, they wanted to boot me out of the car when I told them the mayor was my grandfather. When the press gets hold of the fact that I'm one of the Colemans of Texas, it's really gonna hit the fan. I had to do it," Riley said defensively. "They cuffed Mike and he couldn't stand the pain. They can't hold me for too long. Let me know as soon as possible how the others are. Deal?"

"You got it. I think Saul is our best bet. He's a charmer with the ladies. He's got a broken hand no one is paying attention to. Look at him—he's making a date with that student nurse. I'll have him get her to pass the word to the press. You stand tight and don't let them take you out of here till the press comes around back. Fight if you have to."

"Make it snappy. Here come those two cops now. How long do you think I can stall? I'm under arrest, in case you forgot." He watched as Sara hurried away to speak with Saul.

"Okay, Coleman, let's go, so your daddy can get some nice lawyer out of his nice warm bed to spring you."

"I'm not going anywhere till I know how my buddy is." Out of the corner of his eye he noticed the blond student nurse sprint down the hallway. All he needed was a few more minutes. Sara was sauntering over with Saul.

Riley held his one-man press conference in handcuffs on the steps of the emergency entrance. It was aired on the six o'clock news. The eleven o'clock news made it nationwide.

It was five o'clock when Agnes finally relented and allowed the servants to leave (now that the children were gone the live-in help had been replaced with dailies who left after dinner). However, Agnes had no intention of slaving away in the kitchen: she'd ordered all manner of food prepared when the snow had started to fall heavily.

"I think we'll all have trays in front of the fire," she said brightly. "The cook make a monstrous pot of black bean soup and we can have ham sandwiches. It's only fair, Seth. The help want to get home to their own families and the roads will close in another hour. Moss doesn't mind, and I called down to the studio to ask Billie to join us. Good hot soup is the best thing to eat on a day like this."

"The girl won't be able to find her way," Seth growled.

"For heaven's sake, Seth, the studio is only at the back end of the yard. I assume what you mean is you don't want her here since she filed for divorce. If that's the case, say so. I'll call her and tell her not to come."

"Tell who not to come where?" Moss demanded as he walked into the room, heading straight for the bar.

"I asked Billie to join us for soup and sandwiches." Her tone was defensive, something she hated.

"You letting this divorce throw you, Pap?" Moss asked sardonically. Agnes watched through narrowed eyes as Moss drained his double bourbon and poured another. If he kept this up, there would be an unholy row sooner or later. Better to call Billie and tell her to stay in the studio.

"You're damn right it's going to throw me. Colemans don't divorce. You slipped up, boy. I'm disappointed. Who ever heard of such a thing? Divorcing and socializing at the same time. How come she didn't up and leave like she said she was gonna do? How come our hospitality is good enough for her, but you aren't? Tell me that, boy."

"Leave it, Pap. Billie and I will handle our own affairs. That studio is hers. Sawyer is more comfortable here than in some apartment in town."

"The girl's in school all week. And when she is home on the weekends, she's off with her friends. Some logic," the old man snorted.

Hoping to divert the showdown she felt was coming, Agnes offered to turn on the television for the evening news. As she settled herself in her own soft, down-cushioned chair, Billie walked into the room, her head held high. There were two bright spots of color in her cheeks. "Billie!"

"Can I get you a drink, Billie?"

"Thank you, Moss. I'd love a glass of sherry."

"Seth says it's wicked out there. He was afraid you would get lost trying to find your way to the house," Agnes said nervously.

"Don't you mean Seth was hoping I *would* get lost? This house is lit up like a Christmas tree—all I had to do was walk a straight line. My feet are wet, though. You won't mind if I sit by the fire, will you?" She looked directly at Seth, who nodded curtly, not bothering to answer.

"Darling, I'll just run upstairs, and get you a pair of slippers. I don't want you catching cold. Pneumonia is nothing to sneeze at. Sorry about the pun," Agnes said, forcing a smile to her lips.

{ 432 }

The fire hissed and crackled. Billie moved from the hearth and settled herself next to the snack table Agnes had set up by her chair. Soup and crackers and a cup of coffee would do it for her. She was dipping her spoon into the soup when her son's image flashed on the screen.

"What the hell is Riley doing on television?" Seth bellowed.

"That is Riley!" Moss said with his sandwich halfway to his mouth.

"For heaven's sake, it is Riley," Agnes murmured nervously.

Billie watched as the scene was played out on the small screen.

Five minutes later they all knew what Riley was doing on television. In a fit of anger Seth tossed his soup, the bowl, and his sandwich into the roaring fire. Moss's face was as stormy as the weather outside. Agnes sat slumped in her chair. Billie calmly finished her soup, then excused herself and went back to the studio, silently applauding her son. If he truly believed in what he was doing—and she felt he did—then more power to him.

She wasn't out the door when the phone started to ring. The Colemans were going to have their hands full. Poor Moss. What a blow to his pride.

When the eleven o'clock news went off the air, Agnes called Billie on the studio phone. "Seth was furious, absolutely livid. Moss called Riley a draft dodger and said he was shirking his duty. Seth and Moss went at it tooth and nail. I wish you could have heard them, Billie. I was so appalled I had to leave the room. What's come over everyone? I simply can't understand all of this. My grandson in handcuffs! He's free now. Seth called the family lawyer, but Riley wouldn't leave unless the others were freed, too. Wasn't that nice of him? He's at the hospital now, waiting to see how his friend Mike is."

Billie sighed. That was so like Riley. "Mother, what do you think?"

"I don't know what to think. I guess I have to admire Riley, standing up for what he believes in. But national television! We had to take the phone off the hook. Moss is downstairs as drunk as the proverbial skunk. Why did you leave, Billie? You're Riley's mother."

"I'm only Riley's mother when it's convenient for the others. What good could I have done? I'm on Riley's side. You don't think for one minute either Seth or Moss wanted to hear that, do you? Mother, I don't want Riley going to Vietnam. I couldn't go through all that again. I almost lost a husband to the other war. I don't want to lose a son. I don't care what they call him as long as he's safe. Why was Seth so angry? He doesn't want him to go, either."

"For embarrassing all of us by being interviewed in handcuffs. At least that's what I got out of it. When Seth gets in a rage like that it's difficult to tell what he's really angry at. He was raving at Moss when I came upstairs. Why do these things have to happen to us?" Agnes lamented.

Billie couldn't help herself. "Because, Mother, we're Colemans. We're news."

"If that's the best answer you can come up with, Billie, I'll ring off. Good night, dear."

"Good night, Mother."

Riley Coleman didn't go home that weekend or the next. He didn't leave the campus until he was certain Mike was well enough to fly east for a special operation. He managed with the aid of his friends to successfully avoid phone calls from his father and grandfather. He just didn't want to hear all the words, all the harangues he knew would be forthcoming. His mother was a different story; she understood. When he'd called her at the studio she'd told him to take it easy, not to worry about his father and grandfather. He sighed. At least she hadn't thought it necessary for him to leave school and rush home to defend his actions. Christmas would be time enough. By then everyone would have a cool head. He was counting on it.

{{{{{{{{{ CHAPTER THIRTY }}}}}}}}}

The Christmas season at Sunbridge that year was dismal. The house was beautifully decorated, but it was Billie's studio that held the spirit of Christmas. Sawyer and Billie made handsome homemade decorations and hung them on a fragrant tree. They popped corn and hung stockings. Colorful gift-wrapped packages were everywhere. Pine cones burned merrily in the fireplace and gave off a tantalizing aroma as Billie and Sawyer drank hot chocolate in front of the fire. This place, this converted carriage house, was more of a home to Billie than Sunbridge ever was.

Lately, Billie knew, Sunbridge was divided. Agnes was finding one excuse after another to visit the studio. Seth was harder to get along with than ever. Moss acted the part of an outraged father—how dare his son associate with radicals... act less than a Coleman?

Billie could almost feel sorry for all of them. Seth, Agnes, and Moss were all unhappy. Riley was unhappy, too. Only she seemed to be moving in a straight line, taking things as they came.

It was three days before Christmas. Sawyer had finished her decorations by ten o'clock and was now in bed. When the doorbell shrilled, Billie ran to answer it before Sawyer awakened.

"Riley!" She embraced him in a warm hug. How good he felt. How good he smelled. Billie shivered as she pulled him into the studio and closed the door. "Take off your jacket and sit by the fire. Would you like some hot chocolate? With marshmallows?"

"Do you have some?"

"It's the only way Sawyer will drink it. Me too, for that matter. I'll just be a minute. Add another log."

Billie's hands trembled as she set the tray with cups and a plate of cookies from the big house. This was an unheard-of event. Riley never came to the studio first. He was evidently dreading the confrontation with his father as much as she was.

She waited until Riley had almost finished his chocolate before she asked about Mike.

"He's going to be okay. They're thinking of a bone transplant. He's back east now. I'm going to call him on Christmas Day to see how things are progressing. Mam, I had to do what I did. I'd do it again."

"I know that, Riley."

"Pap isn't going to understand. I've been avoiding him. I wasn't going to come home for Christmas, but I couldn't do that to you and Sawyer. I really wanted to go to New York to see how Mike is doing."

"It's time you stood up to both your father and grandfather. We can only hope they listen."

"Call Pap, Mam. Ask him to come down here now and talk. I sort of feel that this is neutral ground."

"Are you sure, Riley?"

"I'm sure."

"Do you want to talk to him on the phone?"

"No," Riley said shortly.

Moss picked up the phone on the second ring. "Moss, it's Billie. Riley is here. He'd like you to come down. . . . I can't do that. Riley wants you to come here. . . . I can't believe you're saying that, Moss. I didn't even know he was here till he rang the bell." Billie listened a moment, then hung up.

"He's angry. With both of us. He's not taking the divorce well, and I believe he's regarding this visit of yours here as betrayal. We'll wait awhile to see if he comes down. How about some more chocolate?"

"I'd like that, thanks. Mam . . . tell me—how do *you* feel about having a draft dodger for a son?"

Billie thought for a moment. "I think there are worse things in life. I think Vietnam is a senseless war, and the mother in me wants you safe."

"Mam, it has nothing to do with my personal safety. I don't believe in Vietnam. Our guys are being slaughtered over there. For what?"

The doorbell pealed, and both Billie and Riley jumped. Billie drew a deep breath and went to open the door.

There was no joyful reunion between Moss and Riley. Both looked to Billie as if they were squaring off to do battle. Billie's eyes were drawn to her son. The moment she saw the anguish in him, she realized that Riley would do whatever his father wanted.

"I'm disappointed, Riley," Moss said bluntly. "Let's not talk around and up and down this thing. What you did was wrong. It was sinful. I never shirked my duty. I never turned my back on my country. This country has been damn good to the Colemans and don't you ever forget it!"

"Pap, will you at least try to understand? Will you listen?"

"Not if you're going to give me that same old crap you gave those newspaper people. That hurt, boy. Your granddaddy almost had another stroke over that little performance."

"It wasn't a performance. It was the way I felt and the way the others feel. I still feel that way. We don't belong in Vietnam. And if you tell me we do, I'll tell you you just want to sell more planes to the government."

"That's enough, Riley."

"No, it isn't. I'm not afraid, if that's what you're thinking. I'm not a coward."

"That's the way it looks from where I'm sitting. That's the way other decent folks are looking at it. Jesus, in handcuffs yet. I had to do some fancy talking to get around that one. You *are* going to stop this, aren't you?"

Riley stared at his father. What had he expected? Love, understanding? Just like that his father expected him to stop— to restructure his thinking to the Coleman point of view. Out of the corner of his eye, he could see his mother wringing her hands as she followed the one-sided conversation.

Instead of answering his father directly, Riley turned to gather up his jacket. "Do you know what I wish, Pap? I wish I'd never been born a Coleman." Without another word, he left the studio.

Moss sat down in Billie's chair and dropped his head into hands. Billie wanted to go to him, but she stood firm.

"You were hard on him. Too hard, Moss. Why can't you try to understand?"

"Is that what you think, that I don't understand? I understand. He's afraid. Don't tell me you didn't think it for a minute or two yourself."

"Riley isn't a liar. If he says he isn't afraid, then he isn't afraid. He simply doesn't believe in Vietnam."

"Billie, he burned his draft card! Do you know what that means? Stop thinking like a mother for a minute."

"Moss, I *am* his mother and I'm simply trying to understand our son."

"You're condoning all of this, aren't you?" Moss exploded.

"I'm trying to understand! If you take that to mean I'm condoning it, then, yes, I am."

"Well, I'll never understand it, not in a million years. My son!" Moss said bitterly.

"Our son," Billie corrected Moss. "Why don't you go up to the house and talk to him? Talk to him like a father, not like the head of Coleman Enterprises. Don't spoil what you have with your son."

"Like I spoiled everything else. Isn't that what you were going to say next?"

Billie sighed. "Leave it, Moss. This isn't the time to air grievances."

But Moss wasn't to be deterred. "You remind me of Riley

now. Both of you; the girls, too. All you've ever done was bitch and gripe about the Colemans and the money. But not one of you ever turned your back on it."

"That's unfair, Moss. I never wanted the money. All I wanted was you."

"You had me."

"I never had you, Moss. You always belonged to someone else— Look, I'm very tired, Moss. It's late, and I would like you to leave."

"We'll talk again, Billic."

"It won't do any good."

"Nevertheless, I'll be back. I want us to have a nice Christmas."

"What makes this Christmas different from all the others? You never seemed concerned before. It's too late. Don't you understand? I'm going through with the divorce. Please, go to Riley—he needs to talk to you. You need to talk to him."

When the door closed, Billie wanted to cry. She sat in front of the fire, watching the flames shoot up the chimney. So many years had gone by. So much had happened. Her youth was gone; her children were grown. Her marriage was over—*by her choice*.

Perhaps this divorce action she'd initiated was a mistake. She shook her head, trying to clear her thoughts. What did she really want? What would make her happy? Moss's undying love? A bitter laugh escaped her. She bent over and tossed another log into the fire, then shifted her position on the comfortable sofa and curled her legs under her.

Love . . . that beautiful, intangible, fragile emotion. Where had it gone? It was still within her, she knew, but so deeply buried that resurrecting it would only cause more heartbreak and pain. No. Her marriage was over. Part of her would always love Moss. Part of her would forever cherish the dream. That's what she would mourn and grieve for—the loss of the dream. But it was her turn now.

Billie stirred and woke. For a moment she felt disoriented, then she remembered turning off the lamp next to the sofa where she'd been resting and realized she'd fallen asleep. The fire had become smoldering ashes. She shivered and wrapped her colorful afghan more tightly around her.

It was an hour or so till dawn, she surmised without looking at her watch—officially Christmas Eve. Thad always called on Christmas Eve or Christmas Day. This year it would be such a relief to talk to him. She had so much to tell him.

Christmas. A day to rejoice. If only there was something to rejoice about. Sawyer, of course. But little else. Billie sighed. Soon, after the first of the year, all of this would be behind her. She would move into the city and start her new life.

Shivering in the early-morning dawn, Billie tossed the afghan aside and added several birch logs to the fire. She sprinkled the fire with fragrant pine cones and then crept back to her nest on the couch.

Yes, one more week and she would be on her own for the first time in her entire life. Better make that two weeks, she amended, or even a month—apartments might not be all that easy to find. One more month. That sounded about right.

Moss raked his fingers through his hair as he stared at his son. "I can't believe all this nonsense you've been spouting to me for the past two hours. I send you off to school hoping to give you the best education possible and what the hell do you do? You turn into a goddamn radical.... I expected more, Riley, a hell of a lot more," Moss said, taking a deep breath. Jesus, was he getting through to this kid? Was he absorbing what he was hearing, or was he being polite? "Well, Riley, what do you have to say for yourself? Are you going to force me to yank you out of that college and send you someplace where you can't get into trouble? Someplace like Notre Dame?"

Riley could feel his gaze drift. He'd heard it all before, perhaps not in those exact words, but he'd played and replayed his father's response over and over in his mind for weeks now, and he was tired. Tired of fighting, tired of making excuses, and damn sick and tired of being a Coleman, whatever the hell that meant.

"Riley, I'm talking to you. Are you going to answer me?... I want you to stop this foolishness and start acting like a man. We're all going to put this behind us and start fresh. You are not to ever shame us this way again. Do we understand each other, Riley?"

"Yes, Pap. Can I go to sleep now? It's almost morning."

"All right, Riley, go to sleep. We're going to have to go through this one more time with your grandfather and then we're going to lay it to rest. Are we in agreement?"

Riley's gut churned, but he nodded and tried to respond when his father put his arms around him. Something was missing. He wondered if it was Moss's love. By day's end he would know.

It was shortly after two in the morning when Riley crept downstairs and placed his presents beneath the huge spruce tree in the living room. He laid Maggie's and Susan's gifts on the side for Mam to take care of, propped up the notes he had written to everyone on the mantel, and then left Sunbridge. He walked to the main road and hitched a ride for Dallas. No sense going into Austin. The old man would only alert the airlines and have him yanked off and returned to the bosom of the family. He managed, with the aid of a friendly trucker, to get within a mile of the Dallas airport and from there he took a flight to New York under an assumed name.

Riley did two things that day. He visited his friend Mike and offered him all the encouragement he could. Then he called Thad Kingsley and talked for two hours.

Riley stood on the corner of Thirty-fourth Street and Seventh Avenue, his eyes searching the deserted streets for a taxi. He huddled into his sheepskin jacket and jammed his hands into his pockets, wishing he had thought to bring gloves. This was probably the first time in his life he was somewhere other than Sunbridge on Christmas morning. But that was another life, a long time ago.

A cab snaked to the curb. "Merry Christmas," the driver greeted him. "You're in luck—this is my last trip before signing off duty. If you're going uptown, that is."

"That's where I'm going." Riley rattled off Maggie's address and settled back on the cracked leather seat. He was grateful for the steamy warmth of the cab. "Merry Christmas," he said as an afterthought.

The cabbie made good time, gauging each successive traffic light perfectly. The streets were nearly deserted, only a few pedestrians coming from or going to church. The desolation was contagious and Riley slumped down in the seat.

Ten minutes later he was admitted into Maggie's apartment building by the doorman, and after a quick call to the penthouse apartment, he was permitted to take the elevator. She was waiting for him and as he stepped off the elevator he was in her arms. He could feel the trembling in her slim body . . . or was it his own?

"Come in. You must be freezing. Coffee's brewing. We'll

go into the den. I made a fire. When you called earlier I couldn't believe you were here, actually here in New York. Here, give me your jacket. What's wrong, Riley? Why aren't you at Sunbridge? Would you rather coffee or a drink? You look awful and I'm talking too much and asking too many questions. Sit. I'll be right back."

Riley slumped into the oversized sofa and looked around at the spacious apartment. In the far corner stood a Christmas tree, a giant evergreen trimmed from top to bottom with sparkling ornaments. Presents were stacked beneath the tree, and even from here he would tell which ones were from Sawyer. His throat tightened at the sight. Maggie alone, opening her presents by herself. How many years, when he'd been happy and involved with the family on Christmas mornings, had Maggie been alone?

"Here we are—coffee, juice, muffins, and bottle of brandy to go with the eggnog. I think we should toast the holiday. Whatever the reason, I'm glad you're here, Riley. I can't tell you how I've been dreading this day."

"Why don't you turn on the lights so I can see how that creation of yours looks.... My God, it's beautiful," he said as the giant tree came to life.

"Just like home, huh?" Maggie said proudly. "Let me tell you, it was no mean feat getting that tree up here. I don't even want to think about taking it down."

"What are you doing here in the city on Christmas? I always thought you went to Saint Moritz for the holidays. I called you before I remembered that."

"I don't think I actually ever said I went there. I alluded to it. So now you know my secret. I hole up for the holidays and cry my eyes out. I make myself a turkey dinner and I open my presents and then I cry some more. Then I make a few drinks, get blitzed, and go to bed. What do you think of that?"

"Not a whole hell of a lot. You could have come home, been with us. Mam always said something was missing when you weren't there. She missed Susan, too, but at least Suse always called on Christmas Day. You never did." There was no accusation in Riley's tone, only sadness.

"Could I, Riley? Could I really have gone home? I never belonged there and I don't belong there now. I'd be a guest. This is okay for me; it's the way I handle things. Listen, can you stay for the day? Have dinner with me? We can open my presents and I can tell you what I sent you and the others at

Sunbridge. We can have our own family day."

Riley nodded. He wouldn't spoil this day for Maggie for anything in the world. Later, he would talk to her about his decision. For now, he had to find the strength he needed to deal with sad Maggie and this particular Christmas. "That's a sweet offer, Maggie. You've got yourself a deal. With one stipulation. We don't talk about the Colemans or Sunbridge or Texas. . . ."

Maggie laughed, a sound of pure delight. "Or Mam or Pap or Sawyer or Suse or Seth and Agnes. Doesn't leave much, little brother. They're our lives."

"Not right now," Riley said firmly. "This is our time. Can you really cook?"

"Damn right I can cook. Come with me. I want to show you something." Riley followed Maggie to a large kitchen containing every modern appliance. On a butcher-block cutting table stood a monstrous turkey with its legs trussed together. "Fully stuffed, little brother. Wild rice and chestnuts. These," she said, pointing to a bowl, "are fresh cranberries. These are yams and will end up with marshmallow, butter, and brown sugar. This is fresh asparagus, greenhouse variety. We're having mince, pumpkin, and apple pie; take your choice. I baked them last night. Candy canes are on the tree, one for each of us. Did I forget anything?"

Riley's face showed his awe . . . and something else besides. "Damn you, Riley," Maggie cried, "don't you dare pity me! This is the only way I know to get through the holidays."

Riley took his sister into his arms. "Hey, this is me. I don't think I've ever judged you. I'm not judging you now. In fact, I think I'm one hell of a lucky guy to be here right now. Just think—I could be back at Sunbridge listening to Seth squawk about how he doesn't need another flannel shirt and hearing Agnes squeal over her latest piece of jewelry. . . . Sorry, I broke my stipulation.

"Listen, let's go sit in front of the fire. I want to hear all about what you do. This is some fancy pad, must cost a fortune in rent."

"The price is right."

"Maggie, where are your friends?"

"Here, there, yonder. Who knows? I usually start talking about going away around Thanksgiving. They all think I'm in Saint Moritz, too. This is what I want and it's my choice."

"We Colemans make strange choices, I'm discovering. By

any chance did you happen to catch my television debut? Don't tell me you didn't see it. The whole world saw it, according to Grandpap."

"God, Riley, I couldn't believe it was you! Handcuffs. That must have set Pap back a pace or two."

"Yeah, he thought I was crazy."

"Not me. I was rooting for you all the way. That took guts. I don't know if I could have done it."

"Are you telling me this doesn't take guts?" Riley waved his arm to indicate the empty apartment. "You've got more guts than me, Maggie, than all of us."

They drank coffee while Maggie finished preparing the turkey. They talked about everything and anything, each careful not to say anything that would wound the other.

"You can set the table and I'll get dressed, okay?"

"Just tell me where everything is and I'll pitch in and do my share."

"Right there in that cabinet. That holiday tablecloth is a 'Billie' original, by the way," she called over her shoulder.

When she returned a few minutes later, Riley gave an appreciative whistle.

"What do you call those things you're wearing?" he demanded.

"Hostess pajamas. It's for entertaining at home. Mam sent it to me for my birthday. It's probably the most beautiful thing I own."

"Mam's talented, isn't she?"

"Yes, she is. I don't think she knows just how talented herself. I couldn't touch this outfit for less than five hundred dollars even if I could find it in a store."

"Are you serious?"

"Yup. Mam has it. This is what she calls Blink Pink. It makes me feel good to wear it.

"C'mon, let's guess what's in all these presents. I counted them. There's twenty-six altogether. There isn't one from you," Maggie said pointedly.

"Yes, there is, but it's back at Sunbridge. Mam'll send it on. When I left I didn't . . ." Riley flushed.

"You didn't know you were coming here. I don't care, Riley. I'm just glad you did come. You go first. Guess what I sent you."

Riley kicked off his boots and squatted down beside Maggie. "A shirt. A tie. A new wallet."

"Wrong. It's my turn. This is from Sawyer. I'll bet it's a new hairbrush. She told me she had twenty-seven dollars to do her Christmas shopping and she had to buy seven presents."

"What did you send Sawyer?"

"I have a friend who's an art dealer. I had him get me a set of lithographs of planes from the *Kitty Hawk* to modern jets. I had them framed and sent. You know how crazy Sawyer is about flying and planes. Just like you and Pap. I hope she likes them. And I sent her a couple of books on aviation. And there's a sweater and new slippers and a few other odds and ends. She's growing up, she's not interested in dolls any longer."

"The Cricket will go up in smoke when she opens them. But then she'd love a lump of coal if you sent it to her, Maggie."

Maggie avoided Riley's eyes. "This package is from Sawyer too. It's probably a picture of her standing next to one of Pap's planes. She told me about it in her last letter. She was tickled when Pap took her to the factory one day. This one is from Mam and Pap. I think it's some kind of fur. It's your turn to guess about my present."

"Pajamas, socks, sweater."

"Wrong. My turn again. This is from Susan. She always sends me a wool sweater." The bell timer in the kitchen rang, interrupting Maggie's guessing game.

The hours flew by as Maggie and Riley talked and played, trying to guess what each gaily wrapped gift contained. Occasionally Maggie would take time out to check on the turkey. Finally, she returned from the kitchen in triumph.

"It's time. Get your appetite ready. You can pour the wine and I'll carry everything into the dining room. You carve. Do you think we should have some pictures of this event?"

"Sure. Get one of me carving. I never did it before."

"Well, you're the only man in the house, so you won't have any competition." In the kitchen, with the door closed, Maggie's shoulders slumped. All this forced gaiety on both their parts. It was wrong, all of it. Riley belonged at Sunbridge with the rest of the family. Something was on his mind—this was no casual visit. There was a kind of desperation in his eyes, as though he were clinging to her. For Riley, she would play the game, say the right things, act the way he wanted her to act. It was the one thing in life she had learned to do well.

An hour later Riley loosened his belt. "I'm stuffed. I don't think I ever ate this much. Keep talking, Maggie, or I'll fall asleep."

"You won't have the chance. We have to clean up and do dishes."

"That's women's work."

"Tough. You eat, you work."

Maggie cleared the table and Riley wrapped the leftovers and put them in the mammoth refrigerator. Maggie washed and dried the exquisite china and crystal, not trusting it to the dishwasher. He was enjoying himself; he was glad he'd decided to come here, not just for himself, but for Maggie, too.

"Riley, would you like to take a walk down Fifth Avenue to look at the Christmas decorations?" Maggie asked as she hung up her apron.

"No, I want to see you open your presents. That's the best part of Christmas. You and I are probably the oldest two kids I know." Maggie laughed and settled down by the tree. She was so pretty, this sister of his. So troubled. How often, he wondered, did anyone but himself see the vulnerability in her eyes.

"I'll open and you clean up the paper, okay?"

"Deal."

"Ah, I told you. A hairbrush!"

Riley watched as Maggie carefully stacked Sawyer's presents in a neat pile. The lynx coat from Mam and Pap was left in the box and carelessly pushed aside as well as Susan's blue wool sweater. He showed no surprise when Seth's emerald bracelet and Agnes's satin robe weren't removed from the tissue paper. A sparkling cocktail ring with more diamonds than he could count was placed beside Sawyer's gifts. He did not question the giver.

"Give up?"

"Yep."

"I sent you a liftime supply of Tootsie Rolls."

Riley burst into laughter. "I also sent you a lifetime subscription to *Reader's Digest*."

"Maggie, you didn't!"

"Yes, and I also sent the required tie, socks, shirt, sweater, and pajamas. Now, what'd you get me?"

Riley was laughing so hard the tears rolled down his cheeks. "A fifty pound box of M&M candies and lifetime membership in *National Geographic*."

Maggie began to giggle and then joined Riley on the floor laughing, rolling into each other's arms at the ridiculousness of their gifts. When the joy ebbed out of them the laughter became tears of poignant sadness. So many Christmases they'd missed sharing with each other. So many years distance between them. Thank God they hadn't lost each other, especially not now, when everything else seemed to be changing or gone. "Let me get some wine. We both need a little fortification," Maggie said softly, wiping the tears from her eyes.

"Yes, it's time we talked about why I'm really here," Riley said hoarsely, clearing his throat, choking past the lump of raw emotion that seemed to be stuck there.

Maggie curled herself into a ball in the corner of the sofa and listened intently as Riley talked.

"That's it. I just picked up and left. No one knows I'm here. What do you think, Maggie?"

"The sister in me says don't do it. I'm scared, Riley. But part of me says go ahead." That's the part that wants revenge on Pap, she thought, hating herself. The ultimate revenge for years without loving and sharing. Anything to spite Pap. "Do it, Riley," she said, hardly believing the words she heard coming from her mouth. "Do it."

Riley's enormous faith in human nature shone in his eyes. Because he himself was so good-hearted, so trustworthy, he could never see any meanness in others. Maggie was his sister and she loved him as he loved her. It was what he'd wanted to hear. "I'll do it. Quick, before anyone or anything can change my mind."

At that moment, a little piece of Maggie Coleman shriveled up and died. Then Riley grinned and her heart turned over. She felt as though she were saying good-bye, and it scared her. "Riley, dear heart, are you certain you want to do this?"

"Now you sound like Mam." Riley frowned. "You can't have it both ways, Maggie. Either you think I'm doing the right thing or you don't."

Maggie took a swallow of her wine. "Let's not bring Mam into this, okay? It's better to leave all of that alone."

"No, Maggie, we can't leave it alone. I never understood why you always give Mam a hard time. My God, Maggie, she loves you heart and soul."

"Well, she shouldn't," Maggie snapped. "She has no right. We were never close, Riley. She was never a mother to me. Someone else always did for me." There was bitterness in Maggie's voice. "When I got pregnant with Sawyer, that's when Mam decided to become a mother, but then it was too late. I was the only one never to have anyone. Mam had her art and she thought she had Pap. Pap had his work, his father, and his son. And you, Riley—you got it all, and there wasn't anything left for Susan or me."

"And you don't hate me?" Riley asked, tormented.

"I love you, Riley. I know I'm filled with resentment. I tried to fight the only way I knew how. I became pregnant and had a child and I was sent away. Now that child lives at Sunbridge getting everything I never had. She belongs there and I never did. What's the use? . . . Why are we talking about this?"

"You have to talk, Maggie. I want to leave here knowing you're all right."

"I'm all right. I can live with it. Suse is the lucky one. Everything falls into place for her."

"No, Maggie, you're wrong. Susan missed out, too."

At least she never had to worry about rejection. She has what she wants, her music and Aunt Amelia, who dotes on her the way Pap dotes on you."

"Maggie, I'm younger than you and Suse, but I could see that Susan was just as scared as you, only her fears took a different turn. Suse never had the guts to be a Coleman, to stand there with egg on her face and stare the world down. She doesn't want to be sullied . . . and we Colemans are certainly mucked up, aren't we?"

"We certainly are, brother mine, we certainly are."

"What say we drink this wine and get a buzz on? Let's forget about Sunbridge, Pap, and the whole damn state of Texas."

"I'll drink to that," Maggie said, clinking her glass against Riley's.

At eight o'clock in the morning on the day after Christmas, Riley Coleman enlisted in the United States Navy.

Billie heard the news from Thad two days after Christmas. "Thad, why didn't you stop him?" she cried. Not waiting for an answer, she rushed on. "Why? Why did he do it? He didn't even spend Christmas with us!"

Billie's sobs tore at Thad's heart. "The boy did it because his father expected it of him. He's not a coward, Billie. Don't ever, for one minute, think that about your son. I know that boy. I'm sorry he felt he had to enlist this way, but I'm not sorry he chose the navy. Only the navy would have satisfied his father. I'll do my best to look after him. He's a man now, Billie. We have to let him act like one."

"Did you speak to Moss yet?"

"No. I called you first. I knew you would be in the studio. I'm going to call him now when I hang up. Riley wanted it this way. You first and then his father. He told me to break it to you easy and to tell you he loved you and not to be angry."

"I am angry. Not with him, but with Moss. Oh, Thad, what's going to happen now?"

"Riley is going to distinguish himself like his father did. At least that would be my guess. It's done, Billie. I'm sorry I didn't call you as soon as I knew, he specifically wanted me to call today. You understand, don't you?"

"I'm not blaming you, Thad. I'm sorry Riley had to place you in this position."

"I'm not sorry. I'm glad he came to me instead of some stranger. I'll call you over the weekend. Take care, Billie."

Billie threw herself on the couch in front of the fire and wept. Riley, Riley, how could you do this? Dear God, keep him safe. Don't let anything happen to my son. Thad would watch over him. Thad would keep him safe, if it was at all possible.

Billie sat up and wiped her eyes. Crying wasn't going to help. Things had to be done.

The trek to the main house in the deep snow left her exhausted. She stormed through the front door, not bothering to remove her snow-caked boots, and strode into the library where Moss, Seth, and Agnes were talking excitedly. "It's your fault, the two of you!" she cried. A long, trembling finger shot out and jabbed at Moss's chest. "It's your fault, and you know it. I'll never forgive you, Moss. Why couldn't you just leave it alone? The boy would have come to his senses sooner or later. Damn you!"

"Hold on there, missy," Seth bellowed. "None of us like what the boy did, but we're gonna live with it. I have a call in to Washington right now."

Billie turned and caught the glittering look in Moss's eyes. Surely he didn't approve of what Seth was doing? Or did he? "Moss, don't allow this. Riley did what he thought you wanted. You must let him go through with it."

"Stateside, we'll keep him stateside. That's all Pap is going to do, Billie," Moss said in a resigned tone.

"It won't work! Riley is going to do what you did. He feels he has to prove himself to you. Forget your call, Seth, and leave the boy alone."

"Don't interfere, little gal. You don't belong to this family anymore. That divorce action you started ended any rights you have here at Sunbridge," Seth said harshly.

"How dare you! Riley is my son, too!"

"Go back to the studio, Billie," Moss said wearily. "We'll handle this. We'll do what's best for the boy."

"Will you, now. Well, we'll just see about that. I'm calling Thad. I won't have either of you interfering in Riley's life. You've already done enough harm."

"Pap is right, Billie. You have no say anymore. Go play with your paints and brushes."

"I always knew you were a bastard, but I didn't know you were cruel, too. God forgive you, Moss, because I won't!"

CHAPTER
{{{{{{{{{ THIRTY-ONE }}}}}}}}}

"It's settled, Moss."

It was a week after Billie's confrontation with her husband, and Seth had sent Agnes to fetch Moss to the sunroom. Alone with his father, Moss knew there was no need for pretense. "How? Where?"

"The day the boy leaves the Oceanic Naval Air Station in Virginia he'll be on his way to that speck in the Pacific."

Moss's eyes widened. "Guam?"

"What better place? There's no way the boy will ever find out either of us had a thing to do with this."

"And Thad?" How bitter his friend's name sounded these days.

"Your friend will do as he's told. He's a military man. He's used to obeying orders."

Moss frowned as he paced the spacious sunroom. "Riley isn't going to like this."

"Trust me, Moss. The boy will be flying, but he'll be piloting weather planes...or an occasional search and rescue flight—he'll like that. The thing is, he'll be safe, and as long as he's flying he'll accept his orders. The Naval Air Station in Agana is just the place for our boy."

"For some reason, Pap, I'm not reassured," Moss muttered. "I can feel a snafu coming up somewhere."

"Where's Kingsley now?" Seth barked.

Caught off guard, Moss had to admit he didn't know.

"It could be important. Agnes will know." Seth banged his cane on the floor and bellowed Agnes's name until she came hurrying into the sunroom.

"Seth, must you shout? I placed a bell right near your chair. All you have to do is ring it."

"I told you I feel like a cow when I use that damn bell. You're supposed to anticipate my needs," the old man said sourly.

"I do. You're just too cantankerous to realize it. What is it you want?"

"Do you have an address for that Yankee admiral?"

"He's on Sunbridge's Christmas card list. Do you want it?"

"Why do you think I asked you about it? Yes, I want it. Right now."

Agnes was back in five minutes with a leather address book. "Would you like me to write it down?"

"It would help, Agnes," Seth drawled.

"Hmmmn, Commander Fleet Air Western Pacific. Atsugi, Japan."

"Jesus," Moss said in awe. "The old boy is right up there, isn't he? Japan is a stone's throw from Guam in case you didn't know it, Pap."

"Moss, you're worse than a pregnant widow. Relax. Kingsley isn't going to interfere. Now let's just roll with this till the boy is on his way."

"And Billie?"

"As far as I'm concerned that little gal is no longer a Coleman. I don't owe her any explanations. If you're wise, you'll take the same attitude. In fact, I'd suggest you close in, Moss, or I might just yank the rug from under you."

Moss lit a cigarette to avoid looking into his father's eyes. Even though the blue-gray cloud of smoke made Seth's eyes water, he had to smile. He recognized the ploy—and knew he was still in control.

Back in his workroom Moss lit another cigarette. What did he know about Guam? Not much, really. He'd spent a day and a half in Guam once. It was green—that much he remembered—and humid, like Florida in midsummer. He recalled that the people were pleasant, always smiling. Riley could do worse. In the end he wasn't going to have much choice but to go along with things. At least the boy would be safe. He wouldn't be going to Vietnam.

At the thought of Billie Moss groaned aloud. Jesus, where was it all going to end? He ached for the old days, his younger days, when he didn't have to account to anyone or anyplace. Of late, the feeling that his world was coming down around him was getting stronger. He felt helpless, and he hated it.

His feelings were so mixed with regard to Billie. Should he try to palaver, to negotiate—risk making a fool of himself? They'd been apart for so long. This new Billie with her emancipated thinking was someone he no longer knew. Did he want to put forth the effort to try to make things work again? He didn't know. He didn't want to know, not now, not when his mind was full of Riley.

Three weeks later, Billie Coleman moved out of Sunbridge to take an overly large apartment in downtown Austin. It was a penthouse with two skylights and an outdoor balcony, and it was just what Billie had wanted. She'd signed a three-year lease and made arrangements to move her work materials and her personal belongings into the apartment within the week. Everything would be new, right down to Sawyer's bedroom furniture. Moss had been very generous with what he'd called her "going-away check." Whatever she wants, he'd told his lawyer; give her whatever she wants. Keep her happy, but drag out the divorce. Maybe, just maybe, she would come to her senses.

Work was going well. She had two orders for her designs and the promise of a third if she could fulfill her first commitments on time. She hadn't been this self-confident since the day she'd married Moss, and she reveled in the feeling. She was Billie Coleman, textile designer; she was also solely responsible for her granddaughter, a responsibility she had every intention of fulfilling. She was in charge of her life and would see to it that only good things came her way.

It was a new beginning.

Lieutenant Riley Seth Coleman left Oceanic Naval Air Station in Virginia on the same day his mother moved out of Sunbridge. For Riley it was a new beginning, too. Guam! The

{ 451 }

old man would have a bird when he found out. Unless of course he was behind the written orders. Riley didn't think that was likely, though, and in the end he'd let it go. He and Adam Noble were going to Guam to fly P-3 weather planes and a few search and rescue flights. At least these planes had Coleman instrumentation in them—some of them were no doubt Coleman planes. That would give both his grandfather and father a kick.

He admitted to Adam Noble on the long flight to Guam that it wasn't what he wanted. The folks would be happy, though. What could go wrong flying a weather plane?

"I want to know what we're going to do with our free time," Adam said. "I hear they roll up the roads at five P.M. I don't think Guam is in the social book of records."

Riley grimaced. "We might like it. We aren't going to be all that far from Tokyo. Hawaii will only be five hours away. We have to look at the bright side of things. I brought plenty of books for the long hot nights."

"Good for you, Coleman. While you're reading I plan to explore and meet some of the locals. I've heard the girls are beautiful."

"And well protected." Riley laughed. "You're liable to have a duenna after you. Give it some thought. Besides, we're not supposed to mess around. You know that."

Adam's blue eyes sparkled. "I never forced a girl to do anything she didn't want to do. I think I can handle these sloe-eyed beauties."

"And their mamas," Riley reminded him. "You're a long way from the San Fernando Valley, Adam, and they play by their rules over there."

Ten days after setting foot on Guam Riley realized he disliked the humid island. The verdant foliage and lush tropical blooms made him homesick for sagebrush and rolling farmland. The rain depressed him. It seemed as though the skies opened hourly and warm, wet waterfalls cascaded down from the heavens. The roads steamed and the vapor rose to make him sweat like a Trojan. He itched. He perspired. He hated.

"C'mon, Coleman," Adam said one Sunday afternoon. "You're coming with me. I got you a date with a sweet thing, and if I have to boot your tail all the way to Barragada, I'll do it."

"Dust off, Adam. I'm staying here. I have some letters to

write. It would do you good to write home, too—the CO had a letter from your mama last week wanting to know if you were alive or dead."

"I'll write her tonight if you come with me this afternoon."

"Adam, I don't want to go. Tell the girl I got sick unexpectedly."

"Aren't you interested that I'm in love? This girl is different. I mean it, Riley, I'm in love. She loves me, too. I'm going to talk to the CO tomorrow about marriage."

"I don't believe it," Riley said in awe.

"I'm serious. Her parents aren't crazy about me, though. They're Chomorra, and I don't think they like Americans. I'm trying to win them over. Nita—that's her name—got you a date with a friend of hers, Otami. But that's not the main reason I want you to come along; I really want you to meet Nita. Will you do it?"

Riley sighed heavily. "All right, let me just slick down my hair and get some clean clothes."

An hour later, Adam swung the borrowed car into a rutted driveway that was overgrown with weeds.

A quonset hut was off to the left. Everywhere there were pots of flowers, some in bloom, others getting ready to bud. It was so colorful, so rich, Riley wanted to reach out and pluck one of the blossoms. His first thought was that the unseen Nita came from a poor family. Clean, neat, but poor. A dog barked and circled his feet. He bent down to scratch the animal behind his ears.

"If you say 'Good girl, Bo,' she'll be your friend for life," Adam said knowingly. "Here come the girls. Mine is the one on the left. Isn't she beautiful? That's Otami on the right."

Riley's cap was off in an instant. The vision walking toward him had to be the most beautiful creature he'd ever seen. Even her name was beautiful. Introductions were made. Riley shifted from one foot to the other, trying not to take deep breaths. Adam and Nita had already forgotten about him, intent on each other.

"*Hafa-adai*, Lieutenant," Otami said shyly. She was welcoming him to Guam, where the day begins. "Would you like to go for a walk?"

Walk? She wanted to walk with him. "Yes, I'd like that." He felt suddenly tongue-tied in her presence, too warm under the collar. Every word, every thought, had to be monitored so he didn't babble like an idiot.

"Come along then, Lieutenant. Nita can't leave the house until her parents return from a Christening, but we can go for a short walk, and by the time we return, her parents will be home. I can show you a little of the village. You're in Ordat, by the way."

As she spoke, he listened to her voice, wishing she'd go on forever. Her musical, lyrical way of speaking intrigued him. Her accent was soft—at times the way she strung her words together seemed awkward to his ear—but the effect was foreign and exotic, and he loved it.

She was small and slim, the top of her head barely reaching his shoulder, but her figure was womanly; all the curves were in the right places. She wore a simple cotton dress, fashionably short above the knees, and on her narrow feet were flat-heeled black shoes. Her long straight black hair was knotted at the top of her head, and long feathery tendrils escaped here and there. In the sunlight the mass of ebony glinted with shimmering blue lights, and it looked incredibly soft.

"Do you live with Nita and her family?" Riley asked.

"No. We attend university together. I live down the road with my uncle. He was quite, ill for a time and my parents wanted someone from the family to stay with him. At the same time they didn't want my studies interrupted, so I attend university part-time. I'll be going back to Tokyo when the term ends."

Riley missed her already. "That's not too far away."

"To me it is." She smiled. "I miss my parents and my friends. Where do you live, Lieutenant?"

"Texas. Near Austin."

"Do you miss Texas?"

Riley nodded. "Very much. I can understand your missing your home, but we have to make the most of it. We can always go home. Home will always be there. Please, call me Riley."

"Only if you call me Otami. You haven't said my name even once."

"Otami." He said the name almost to himself, liking the way it felt on his tongue, liking the sound of it in his ears. "What are you studying at the university?"

"Advanced English courses. I've done some translating for a publisher in Japan, but I'm mostly interested in journalism. My father owns a newspaper in Tokyo and I am hoping to work with him someday." She smiled. "Japanese fathers are very protective of their children. I think he would rather have

{ 454 }

me sheltered from the world. Naturally, he believes that one day I will marry and bless him with grandchildren."

"Will you?" He was panicked at the thought that there might already be someone who had spoken for her.

"Will I what? Marry or have children? Yes, I suppose I will." She turned up her chin to face him, her gaze almost a tangible touch to his face.

"Is there anyone special right now?"

Her smile was sunny and more than a little mysterious. "There may be, Riley. There just may be. Tell me about your family. Is your father the typical indulgent American father?"

Riley threw back his head and laughed. "If you ever met him, you'd eat your words. My grandfather would make you swallow them. There are some who'd say I've been indulged, but I've paid a hefty price." He thought of how hard he'd tried to please Moss and be worthy of all that love. "My mother is different, though. She loves just for the sake of loving, expecting little in return."

"As a mother should be," Otami agreed. "As my own mother is. It's wonderful to have two such people to care for you."

"Remarkable. Your hair is beautiful and your eyes are like black coffee." He half expected her to turn away or even to giggle. But Otami lifted her chin and stared up at him, pleasure coloring her cheeks and glowing in her eyes.

"And yours are like the skies of summer," she told him simply, truthfully. "My favorite time of the year."

"You didn't tell me if there was someone special," Riley said bluntly. He had to know.

"No. Do you have a special girl?"

"No." Until now, he thought. This girl was special from the top of her shiny head to the tip of her toes. There was a certain stillness about her—it was a trait he coveted. He himself always seemed to be churning and stewing about something.

"How do you like Ordat?" Otami smiled.

"Not as much as I like you," he said brazenly, wondering if he'd spoken too soon. Would she turn and run from him? Had he been too impetuous? She made a movement; he tensed. Suddenly she slipped her hand into his. It was small and soft and cool.

"Will you see me again? After today?"

"If it is what you would like."

"When?"

"Whenever you would like. My uncle is doing nicely now

and I don't have to spend as much time with him. You must come to our house, though. I cannot meet you here again; it is not really proper. My uncle would be displeased. He is a nice man, a fair man, but I must be honest. He does not like Americans, for what they did to Hiroshima."

"My father doesn't like the Japanese, for what they did to Pearl Harbor. During the war he was a prisoner and he's never forgotten."

"It is regretful, is it not? We must all live with one another in a world that seems at times too small. My father believes old wounds and old hurts must be put aside. Life goes on and we all endure, doing the best we can."

"Your father is a wise man," Riley said sincerely. "And he has a very beautiful daughter."

Riley lay awake for a long time that night. Was there such a thing as love at first sight? Was it in fact love? Or was it that this beautiful girl with the beautiful name was different from the other girls he knew? She was shy, but yet she wasn't shy, at least not when it counted. She was sweet and natural. She listened, she smiled, and she interjected her thoughts and opinions in a soft, melodious voice. And she wanted to see him again! He was in love. But if his father found out, he could ruin everything—get him sent home, away from this beautiful creature.

Well, I'm not going to allow that to happen, Riley thought. Not this time.

He'd have to keep this part of his life secret. Riley lay staring at the ceiling, his hands under his head.

Secrecy. He was good at that.

In the months that followed, Billie sensed a change in her son. A new kind of maturity, an empathy, came through his letters. Perhaps what he had needed was to get away from Sunbridge, away from Moss and Seth, even from her. It was as though he'd found himself, was seeing himself through someone else's eyes. She wondered about those eyes. Did they belong to a woman? Perhaps. Riley never said. She satisfied herself with being glad for him.

Her textile designs were in demand and she had licensed them through a very prestigious agency. Billie was happy in her work, happy with her quiet life. The only fly in the ointment was the divorce. The Coleman lawyers were doing everything, pulling every trick in their books, to delay a court action. Billie didn't think that Moss even cared any longer, although he called her once a week. He'd even taken her to dinner once or twice—to discuss the problems Coleman Aviation was having with the government.

She remembered her horror when he'd explained how they had demanded he step up production or lose the contracts altogether.

"And you're letting them do that to you?" she had cried. "Moss, our son flies planes manufactured in *your* company, and you're telling me they're not safe!"

"Take it easy, Billie. That's not what I said at all. The planes are safe enough; it's the instrumentation I'm worried about. There're some bugs that still have to be worked out, but the government won't allow the time for it. If I force their hand, they may give those contracts to someone who's not as conscientious as we are."

Billie had seen the pain in Moss's face, and she'd had to respect his judgment. Still, every time she thought of Riley and other men like him, her blood ran cold.

She'd thought of writing all this to Thad but felt it would be disloyal somehow. Besides, contact between them had dwindled. They still wrote, but there were longer and longer periods between letters. The last time she'd written had been to tell him that Susan and Amelia had come to the States for a concert tour, which had been very successful. Susan was a lovely young woman—blond and shining with serious eyes. Billie had been hopeful that they would stay in Texas for a time, wanting a chance to become reunited with her daughter. But Susan had been eager to return to Europe, where, it seemed, there was a particular young violinist who had put the glow in her eyes. Also, Susan hadn't wanted to stay at Sunbridge any longer than absolutely necessary; she'd been quick to perceive Seth's disapproval of her beloved Aunt Amelia and would have no one, absolutely no one, mistreat her.

Billie had conveyed their parting scene at the airport to Thad, since he was the only person besides herself who knew of Amelia's tragedy. At the last moment Amelia had thrown her arms around Billie, thanking her over and over again for allowing Susan to stay in England with her....

"You'll never know how much she means to me," Amelia wept, "or how much I love you for sharing your daughter with me. Now, it seems, we're both about to lose her. This affair with her violinist seems serious. Our little Susan is a woman grown."

"You were better for her than I could ever have been," Billie found herself confessing. "Here in Texas it would have been second-rate music teachers and living down Maggie's reputation. I heard someone say once that our children are only loaned to us, that they're not ours to keep. I just relinquished her a little early, Amelia, and into the most loving arms she could ever know."

"I do love her, you know," Amelia said, brushing a tear from her eye. "In most ways I've been a lucky woman. I've had Susan and a loving stepson. I've told Moss he should write to Rand and invite him over for a tour of Coleman Aviation. They'd like each other and they have so much in common. Rand loves anything that flies and he's quite a genius with computers and physics and all that rubbish. He asks for you often, Billie. He's never forgotten your kindness to him when we came to Sunbridge for Mam's funeral." Amelia's eyes told Billie she would never forget it, either. "Oh, look at me, gushing and crying like an old woman! I suppose I'm not looking forward to the prospect of being alone once Susan flies the nest. I should have listened to you years ago and married again, but it seemed so pointless, since I could never bear another child. My wanton ways have caught up with me. I envy you, having Sawyer. I've always suspected you refused to allow Maggie to have an abortion because of what happened to me. You were right. I can't bear to think of this world being denied our bright-eyed little Sawyer. How is it you always make the right decisions?"

"I don't, Amelia. Don't ever think that. I've hardly ever been in control of my own life. But that's all changing now, and I'm glad for it. You don't suppose Susan will run off with her young man, do you? Moss and I would like to meet him."

"No, I don't think our daughter will deprive herself of a wonderful wedding with all the trimmings. Don't worry about her, Billie. She's making all the right choices. I suppose when next I see you it will be at the wedding."

"At the wedding, then," Billie agreed, and hugged Amelia tightly. "It will be nice for Sawyer to visit London. She's never been abroad."

The flight announcement came over the loudspeaker and Amelia reached for her carry-on luggage and turned toward the gate. "San Francisco, here we come!" she said gaily. "Send Riley my love; next time you see my brother give him a good swift kick with my compliments, won't you?"

"I'll do just that." Billie laughed and waved to Susan, who turned and blew a kiss to her.

"After San Francisco we're headed for New York," Amelia called. "Why don't you think about coming up and joining us?"

"I'll do just that!" Another wave, another kiss on the wind, and they were gone.

Riley Seth Coleman was in love. When he looked into Otami's beautiful eyes, he saw himself as he wanted to be: tender, gentle, manly. Otami's love for him was quite different from any he'd ever known, unselfish and undemanding. Theirs was a sharing, two faces shining toward the future, certain of endless happiness and togetherness.

Wonderful days and nights raced into weeks and months. They had committed to each other and wanted to spend the rest of their lives together. Riley proposed marriage to Otami four months after meeting her.

Dark eyes sparkled with tears. "I thought you would never ask me."

"Will you? Marry me?" Riley held his breath, waiting for her answer.

"We will have to face many problems, my love and I," Otami whispered. "The military will frown upon our marrying and may not give us permission."

Riley gathered her into his arms and buried his lips in the soft wealth of her hair. They sat entwined in each other's arms and watched the moonlight on the rolling surf.

He knew what she said about the military was true, but he had already determined that nothing, no one, would stand in their way if she would have him. "Don't worry about a thing," he reassured her. "I think I've got that base covered. I have this friend—I call him uncle—and he'll go to bat for me. It's your uncle that concerns me."

"He will not give his permission. I will have to go against him and my family."

Riley took another deep breath. He couldn't make her marry him; either she wanted him more than anything or anyone else, or she didn't. He waited, willing her to give him the answer he needed.

"I love you, Riley, with all my heart, for all my life. How

{ 459 }

could I say anything but yes? Yes, I will marry you."

Riley touched Otami's chin and tilted her face upward to his. He kissed her deeply, little shock waves tripping through his veins at the thought that such happiness could be his. Otami was like an Oriental work of art, finely turned and created with beauty. So many times he had thought he'd be unable to control himself, that he must take her and make her his own. But always he remembered her words. "Lovers with true hearts," she had said, "bring honor to each other and their love. My body aches for you, Riley; my soul reaches for yours. But to claim a right that is not ours would dishonor us both. Please, try to understand." Now she would be his wife and welcome him into the garden of her desires, where they would find each other as lovers with true hearts.

"Otami," he whispered huskily against her cheek, "my heart has been yours from the moment I first saw you. You're my life. Remember that always. It may not be easy for you in the days to come. What will your uncle do?"

"He will cease speaking to me and then banish me from his house. I will no longer be his niece. My parents will be told and they, too, will lose face. If I marry you, I will bring disgrace upon them. It does not matter, Riley. I must live my own life and know my own heart. I can live with anything as long as I have you. In time, perhaps, my family will come to understand and approve. It has been known to happen." She smiled.

"I don't plan on informing my family—not right away, at least. Unlike your family, I'm afraid, they would insist on being involved. I can't see them disowning me, but I can guarantee a lot of grief. I'd rather do without their interference; there's time for that later. We'll have enough to contend with. I love you, Otami. There are no words . . ."

"No words are needed. Don't you understand, Riley? I know how you feel because it is how I feel. I will be whatever you want. I will do whatever you want me to do. We will have children and they will be raised in their father's way, in their father's religion."

Otami saw the frown on Riley's face. "Have I said something wrong?" she asked, touching his mouth with her long, cool fingers.

"Wrong? Never wrong," Riley reassured her. "I've never had anyone love me as you do, Otami. All my life people, my family, have given me things. Ponies, cars . . . airplanes, for God's sake! The only person who gave of herself to me was my mother, and then it was only what they permitted her to give. When I think back, I realize that for all their talk about family and closeness we were never a family in the true sense of the word. Everyone had a separate life, solitary ambitions. I don't know why and I suppose there were times when I wondered about it, but I don't do that anymore. You're my life now, Otami, and I want to keep it that way."

Riley gathered Otami close to him, resting his cheek on the glossy curve of her head, and looked out over the water. This was enough for him, he told himself, being here with the woman he loved and knowing she loved him in return. It had to be enough.

(((((((((CHAPTER)))))))))
THIRTY-TWO

Maggie Coleman heaved a sigh of relief when she affixed the last stamp of approval to the pile of paperwork littering her desk in Sandor Locke's prestigious art gallery. The remainder of the work requiring her attention would just have to wait. She needed a few minutes' break from sorting out the multitude of applications from artists, both well known and obscure, seeking a showing at the gallery. Each day it seemed she was busier and busier, with barely enough time to snatch a quick cup of coffee for lunch. She liked being busy; it gave her less time to think. Lately, however, she was beginning to wonder if she'd made the right choice in leaving her position at the museum to become the personal assistant to Sandor Locke. Working in this Fifth Avenue gallery was a plum of a job, and she knew she was envied by everyone on the staff. Sandor himself was the biggest, juiciest plum of all, and she had him right where she wanted him. The question she postponed facing was, What was it she wanted to do with him? It was the same old question that had plagued her entire life. Fight for what you want—kick, scratch, connive, manipulate, and do anything necessary to reach your goal—and then, when it was in your hand, you looked at it and realized it wasn't the goal you wanted but the challenge of reaching it. Maggie supposed it had something to do with being a Coleman. She didn't like living like this, but it was the only way she knew. "Go where the money is" was Seth's philosophy. Another of his ditties was "It's not *what* you know, it's *who* you know." How right he was. She'd dropped a few words here, a thought there, and Sandor Locke had come to her offering her the position at twice the salary she'd earned at the museum. She wished now that someone had told her ten-hour work days were part of the job.

Maggie leaned back in her chair and stretched her arms over her head, appreciating her newly decorated office, one of her first demands of Sandor. It was the perfect backdrop for her own striking brunette looks. The soft, plush earth tones were selected with care to show off the vibrant jewel colors she wore. The eggshell chair set off her glossy dark hair and honey-colored skin. If she owed anything to Billie it was her flair for fashion and her sense of color and balance; from Moss, his summer-blue eyes and ambition. Damn, why was it every time she tried to relax and enjoy her success thoughts of Sunbridge and the family would crop up? She should be over that hurtful stage of life. She was a woman now, with her own sense of worth. Sunbridge was behind her. She didn't live there anymore and hadn't lived there for years and years. Whenever she did go back, which was rare, she was a visitor.

It was a damn good thing she'd escaped, Maggie assured herself. Or had she been driven out? She felt the familiar dampness on her eyelashes. A visitor. She had to use the doorbell. She possessed no keys to the house. If only she had a key, perhaps she would feel as though she belonged there. Riley belonged there. Was that why she'd encouraged him to join the service? Because she was jealous that he belonged to Sunbridge and she didn't? Even though the letters she received from Riley expressed contentment it still niggles the back of Maggie's brain that she'd advised him to join the Navy more out of her own purposes than for her brother's welfare.

Regardless of how successful she became, no matter how high she climbed, it still wasn't enough. Something was missing. The sense of belonging, the sense of sharing in the closeness of a family. When was she going to accept that it was never there for her and put it all behind her? "The day I die," she muttered as she dabbed at misty eyes.

Deciding work was preferable to dwelling on memories, Maggie attacked the pile of applications with a vengeance. She sorted, appraised, and considered the stack of rejections grow-ing compared to the number of acceptances. Opening a folder of photographs of an artist's work, she was faced with an electric geometric design. Exactly what Sandor wanted to bal-ance the primitives he intended to display in early spring. It would be the height of the art season, and from these examples of geometrics and linears the showing would propel the artist's career into importance. She flipped through the photographs, appreciating the artist's sense of color and scale. But it was when several examples of textiles fell under her view that she turned back to the name on the application. Billie Coleman. Mam's agent had sent the folio and application without any idea that she was now employed by Sandor Locke and that a showing would rest on her own decision. A sense of power coursed through Maggie. She realized all too well that she could lift her mother out of the designer class and move her into the front-running category of accepted artists. "Well, Mam, paybacks are a bitch." The brilliant-hued designs were tossed onto the rejection pile. Maggie stared at it for a moment, the colors rioting in her head, her conscience pricking. Then, be-fore she could entertain reconsideration, she grabbed the folio and shoved it to the bottom of the stack. No, she couldn't allow Mam's work to hang for weeks in Sandor's gallery. Having to be faced each day with Billie's exhibition would create too strong a flow of memories. Maggie knew she was just not that strong emotionally.

She was raw enough now and she had to fall back and regroup and think things through again. Just last week she'd been lunching with Sandor when Moss walked into the restau-rant with Alice Forbes on his arm. Her initial response had been shock, and then the hatred settled in and she had glowered across the room at Alice Forbes with such intensity it was a small wonder the woman hadn't felt it as though it were a tangible thing and turned to face her.

It was then, when she'd looked back across the table at the slim, fastidious Sandor, that she realized he was actually her father in disguise. Charming, distinguished, and sophisticated, Seth would have called Sandor "slick." Even Agnes would have seen through to the cruelty beneath his layer of cosmo-politan charm. Sandor Locke, patron of the arts, wealthy, knowledgeable, and married. She herself was the Alice Forbes in Sandor's life and she didn't like it.

"Seen a ghost, Maggie?" Sandor asked perceptively.

"My father, Moss Coleman." She indicated the table where Moss and Alice were sitting.

"And the lady?" he persisted, clearly amused by Maggie's discomfort.

"Alice Forbes, the playwright. My father and she were childhood friends back in Texas."

"She is also an embarrassment I take it." Sandor refused to allow the subject to drop. There seemed to be more here than met the eye.

"Not to me, she isn't. She's just one in a long line of many. Only she's lasted longer. It's my mother who should be embarrassed."

"Do I detect an edge of bitterness, Maggie darling?" he said smoothly.

"Damn right I'm bitter. If my mother hadn't been so lilylivered she would have put an end to my father's philandering years ago and he would have been home where he belonged, being the kind of father he should have been."

"Why, Maggie, do you realize that in those few words you've told me more about yourself than you have in our entire relationship? This has been quite revealing."

Maggie's eyes glowed with fury. "Has it, Sandor? I didn't think there was much you didn't know about philandering husbands—being one yourself, I mean." She allowed her statement to settle on him, enjoying the fact that for once the suave, sophisticated Sandor Locke seemed to be at a loss for words. It was more than apparent he wasn't used to candor, especially where it concerned himself. "Thank you for lunch, Sandor. Can we leave now? I've an enormous amount of work waiting for me at the gallery."

"Certainly." Sandor peeled greenery from beneath a gold money clip, his brain whirring like a computer, sifting and storing facts. Maggie has said Texas. Coleman. Moss Coleman. Beef, oil, land, aviation, electronics, wealth, and power. Maggie was one of *the* Colemans. How interesting. He stored the information in his brain, knowing someday he might have to pull it out and look at it all again.

Leaning his elegant form against the frame of Maggie's office door, Sandor Locke quietly observed her as she rifled through the paperwork on her desk. She was going through an emotional turmoil; he could see it on her face. He knew she was so caught up in her thoughts she wouldn't have noticed him if he'd perched on the end of her desk. The yearning and regret in the summer-blue eyes startled him. He'd never quite seen that expression before now. Poor little lost black sheep. He was puzzled when he watched her shuffle a particular folio. Three times now she'd tossed it into a stack of others only to remove it. The sadness, the deep yearning, was replaced with bitter coldness when the particular folio was finally pushed to the bottom and covered with others. His eyebrows rose. This was Maggie's department, and she was very good at what she did. He wasn't about to ask questions and interfere.

Maggie Colman, and her flair and style, was a definite asset for the Locke Gallery. It was a lucky day when he'd heard she was interested in coming to work for him. He'd become quite fond of Maggie. She was an exciting woman and very attractive, with her honey skin and night-black hair, and more, she possessed a wit and natural charm that made her welcome into exclusive social circles. When she'd casually mentioned over cocktails one day that she was looking for a new apartment, he had come back with the offer to let her use the penthouse of the Locke Building while the owner was in Europe. At least that was the story he had told her. It was really his own apartment, which he reserved for private moments away from his wife and children. It was a wise man who didn't tell Maggie Coleman everything. It wasn't at all difficult for him to recognize certain traits in her that he possessed himself. She was sly, calculating, and manipulative. It wouldn't surprise him in the least if she'd known all along that the apartment was his. They had been enjoying their affair for almost a month when she had asked for a two-year lease. He had laughed. "Your rent is free. Why do you need a lease?"

"Because, Sandor, you're just like me. One day you'll wake up and say, 'This is the day I have to unload Maggie.' I'm not saying you'll do it; I'm saying you could. I need a little edge, that's all. And that doesn't mean you move in with me, either. You can visit."

He visited her on a regular basis and gave her an open lease. She could stay for as long as she liked.

"Maggie, darling, take a break. I want to talk to you for a moment," he said from the doorway.

Maggie lifted her head, and immediately the pain and longing disappeared from her lovely face and she welcomed him with a bright smile. "I'd love a break, Sandor, but really, I'm swamped." She indicated the work on her desk.

{ 465 }

"Dinner?" Sandor prompted.

"I was sort of planning an evening at home." Maggie continued sorting through papers. "Wash my hair and all that, you know."

"Maggie, I want to see you." There was not a plea in his tone but rather a command.

"All right, Sandor," Maggie complied. "Tell you what. You bring dinner and I'll cook it. We can lounge all evening with some wine and good music. Would you like that?"

Sandor's eyes narrowed in annoyance. He didn't like Maggie's knack for turning his demands into something she condescended, waiving the privileges of his rank and assuming a superior air. Back Maggie Coleman into a corner and she'd have you believe being there had been her intention all along. "I didn't know you could cook, Maggie."

She laughed. "I can broil or boil. Take your choice."

"Steaks?"

"You're talking to a Texas girl, so make sure you bring all the fixings. Shoo now. I want to finish this."

Sandor felt his pressure rise. She had dismissed him. He was no longer in her thoughts or worthy of her consideration; it was as though he didn't exist. No woman had ever treated him the way Maggie did, and by God, he was putting out for her. Anything she wanted he gave. Money, an apartment, a penthouse apartment, travel, gifts; hell, he even pleased her in bed, satisfying her hungry appetites each time she clamored for more. He was the perfect friend, boss, and lover. What more did she want? Something he couldn't give her. Whatever it was Maggie yearned for, it wasn't in his power to give. Poor little black sheep.

It was two weeks later when Maggie shuffled through her mail. A letter from Sawyer. The childish handwriting reminded her of her own years ago. She squinted at the sprawling letters with the exaggerated loops. Just like her own. They should have been sisters; Sawyer was much more Billie's daughter than she would ever be her own. Sawyer was at Sunbridge enjoying all the things she herself could never have again. Maggie knew she shouldn't be jealous, but she was. It was more than jealousy, it went deeper than that. It was all mingled with shame and disappointment and rejection.

Dear Maggie,
     Grandmam told me to write you. We are coming to

New York City next month. Grandmam is doing business. Do you think we could have lunch or go to the movies together? I would like that and so would Grand.

I love the Barbie doll you sent me. Grand has made me so many outfits for her that the other kids don't have. It was nice of you to send me the doll. How did you know I wanted one?

My friend Marjorie is so jealous that I'm going to New York. I wasn't jealous when she went to California. It's not good to be jealous because you cry at night. I like to go to sleep thinking about nice things.

My pencil needs a new point so I have to end this letter.

I love you, Maggie, with all my heart. I hope you love me a little bit, too. Grand says you do. Will you tell me that someday?

Love,
Sawyer

Maggie scrunched the letter into a ball. She opened it, reread it, and felt the tears begin. Dammit! Every time she was getting herself together she had another blow below the belt. The tears came then, great, ugly, choking sobs. When at last she lay on the sofa, spent of emotion, she folded the letter into a neat little square and slipped it into the pocket of her robe.

She reached for the phone. "Sandor, Maggie here. I'm glad I caught you in. Listen, I've some vacation coming. If the invitation is still open do you still want me to go to Europe with you?" She listened a moment. "I was hoping you'd say that. You will take care of the tickets and all those nasty little details? It's only a month away, but already I can see Paris and feel the excitement."

{{{{{{{{{ CHAPTER }}}}}}}}}
THIRTY-THREE

Bittersweet memories attacked Thad as he settled back in the taxi on his way to the airport. He supposed he was getting old to have weddings affect him this way. Or was it that he felt guilty for betraying Billie and Moss this way by being a party to Riley's secret marriage? Secret to everyone in Texas, that was. He'd done his best to discourage Riley, but the young man would have none of it. So Thad had done some checking on Otami. Family background, reputation, everything was impeccable. If anything, Otami and her family were as wealthy— and even more respectable—than the Colemans. One way or another, Thad knew, Riley would have found some way to marry the girl he loved.

Inwardly he felt he'd done the right thing in securing permission for Riley and Otami to marry. One only had to look at them to know they were made for each other. Only once before had he seen the kind of love that shone in Riley's eyes. It had been in Billie's eyes the day she'd married Moss.

And it had been in Otami's eyes today, as she'd married Riley in an entirely different kind of ceremony—two of them, in fact. First the Catholic service, where Otami had been the picture of innocent loveliness in her white dress; and then, later, a traditional Buddhist ceremony, where she had worn a kimono of bright red silk to denote her joy. Thad shook his head as he recalled those two beautiful faces bearing their undisguised love. That's what it was all about, he knew— finding that kind of love. He had found it years ago with Billie, and despite all odds that love had survived.

"I think our wedding is over, Mrs. Coleman." Riley grinned as the last of his friends piled into the car that was returning to NAS. "We have to thank the Santos again and tell them how wonderful everything was. It was wonderful, wasn't it?"

"It wasn't just wonderful, Riley. It was perfect. I hope you have no regrets about your family. Your uncle Thad is an amazing person. He's very fond of you," Otami said quietly.

Riley looked down at his new bride and noted the sparkle in her eyes. He knew he would kill to protect this fragile young woman. His wife. Jesus! Was she having regrets? Was she worried about the old uncle and her parents back in Japan? Maybe Thad could do something there. He'd have to give that some thought. "No regrets. Never regrets. You're my life now. Uncle Thad is one in a million. When the time comes, if I can't make it right back home, he will. It's you I'm worried about. I hope the day never comes when you have second thoughts about marrying me. Families are important. Very im-

{ 468 }

portant. One day you and I will have our own family."

"Riley, from this day on, I don't want either of us to talk about having regrets. If we're to discuss family, let us do it in loving ways. One day they will see how right this is and then they will be happy for us. Perhaps not for a long time, but it will be all right as long as we have each other. Can we agree to that?"

"Anything you want. By the way, now that the car is gone, how are we going to get to the farmhouse you rented?"

"We could walk. It's not far." Otami giggled.

"Are you sure you want to stay there? It's not too late to make arrangements for Hawaii," Riley said anxiously.

"Darling, this farmhouse is perfect. Wait until you see the way I fixed it up. Nita helped me. When you see it you'll know Hawaii cannot compare to it. On our first anniversary you can take me to Hawaii. I don't want to stay in an impersonal hotel and I don't want the long plane ride. I want to spend every hour of every day of your leave with you. I want to make breakfast for you with my dishes. I want you to dry them when I wash them. I want you to sleep in my bed, under the sheets that I embroidered. I want to hear you say what a marvel I am. I painted, hung drapes, scoured, and cleaned. I hung my painting from Hong Kong, and Nita's brother drilled holes and we hung ferns all over the place. We did such a fantastic job you aren't going to recognize the place. It's where we belong for now," Otami said shyly.

Riley was overwhelmed. She had done all this for him. All she wanted was him. Hawaii with all the glitz and glitter didn't appeal to this precious person who was his wife. Ten days of togetherness. Paradise.

It was Nita's youngest brother who finally found a truck in running order to transport the newlyweds to the farmhouse. Riley and Otami took one look at it and burst out laughing.

"It runs," Carlos smirked. "I lease it for a dollar a year. The springs are gone and the brakes are so-so."

Riley stood back to get a better look at the truck. Once it had been white. It wasn't the rust, nicks, or scratches that concerned him. In the bed of the truck there were two metal chairs with what looked like thirty-three coats of paint on them. Each was tied to the metal sides with stout rope. "I'm game if you are." Otami nodded as she gathered up the skirt of her long white gown and, with the help of her new husband and Carlos, settled herself on one of the chairs. Riley, in his crisp navy whites, settled himself on the other chair. "I think this is where we hold on for dear life and pray that we get to the farm. You'd think the owner would provide seat belts."

"Carlos, you will take our picture, please," Otami said seriously as she sat primly with her hands folded in her lap. "For our children one day." She grinned at Riley.

"Absolutely."

The truck backed out of the rutted driveway and careened down the road. Riley shouted to be heard over the rattling. "Always remember that I love you!"

"I will remember!" Otami shouted back as the truck screeched around the corner.

Eight houses up from the San Juan deBautiste Church, Carlos swung into a long driveway. A wooden sign tacked to a banyan tree read RILEY AND OTAMI COLEMAN.

"What happened to the jungle?" Riley asked in awe.

"You are pleased. Then it was worth it. Carlos and his brothers cut it back, and now the house can be seen from the road. It was important that our friends be able to find us. We have a lawn now. See, over there, that's a fern patch. Farther down in the back is a bamboo bed. I will show it to you tomorrow. There is a wonderful place there, a glade of sorts that would be perfect for lovemaking."

Riley laughed. "I thought you were shy."

"I wanted you to think that. I am really bold and brazen and I plan to devour you one hour from now."

Carlos handed over the key to Riley with a flourish. "You might need transportation," he said briskly. "It's only a short walk back to my house. Call on the padre if you need anything; he's at the bottom of the hill."

Trying desperately to keep a straight face, Otami thanked Carlos for the use of the truck. If she had anything to do with it, the truck would remain in the same position for the entire ten-day honeymoon. Riley winked at her. So, they thought alike. Good. But then, she had known that almost from the first day.

"What do you think, Mr. Coleman?" Otami said with her hands on her hips. "Carlos and Frank painted the house. See how it gleams. We were unsure of the maroon trim, but it makes the house noticeable from the road now that it's been cleared."

It was a small concrete house with a flat roof. Riley considered it trim and neat. By Texas standards it would have accommodated little more than a tractor or a horse and one groom. It suited him perfectly. It looked right and it felt right. Otami had known, bless her heart.

Riley reached down for Otami's hand and together they walked to the carport with its concrete overhead roof. Colorful blooms in bright clay pots hung from the beams. "We will eat breakfast here. And lunch and dinner, if you like. You will be in charge of carrying in the cushions if it rains."

"Ordering me about already, are you?"

"Yes. It is to be a fifty-fifty relationship. You will do what I tell you." Otami giggled. "You said your favorite colors were yellow and green, and I paid attention when it was time to stitch the pillows. Can you smell the new paint on the table and chairs?"

"I can hardly notice. You are the marvel in marvelous, Mrs. Coleman. It's time for me to carry you over the threshold. We want this to be right from the beginning."

"It is right. Can't you feel it?" Otami asked as she snuggled against Riley's chest.

"This is going to be tricky." Riley grinned. "If I'm holding you, how can I open the door?" Otami squirmed in his arms and leaned down to open the door. "It's stuck."

"Aha, so you aren't perfect after all," Riley chortled. "You should have had the presence of mind to rub soap on the sides of the door. Or oil. Or better yet, installed a screen door. Now I have to set you down and try to open this door. Is it locked?"

"No one locks doors here. It must be the humidity that makes it stick. I am so sorry. I spoiled the moment."

"Shhh," Riley said, laying a finger on her lips. "I was teasing. You haven't spoiled anything. I'll have this door opened in a second and we can get back on track."

Twenty minutes later the door was still stuck. Riley was huffing and puffing and sweat was running down his face. "It looks like you're going to have to climb through the bathroom window. You're tiny enough. I'll remove the louvers and push you through."

"And what happens if I can't get the door open from the inside," Otami asked anxiously.

"Then I'll blow a hole in the damn house. Or drive that ridiculous truck through the front window. Don't worry. I'll get in."

An hour later, Otami, with her gown tied in a knot about her waist, was standing on the kitchen counter removing the glass louvers. She poked and jabbed at the screen until it fell out. Riley climbed in the kitchen window and they both collapsed on the counter laughing and giggling. "I can't believe that Carlos varnished the door and then closed it. This is going to be the only way in and out until I can pry it open."

"We aren't going anywhere."

"That's true. The hell with the door. When we're old and gray we can tell our children and grandchildren that instead of me carrying you over the threshold I was forced to push you through a tiny bathroom window. Two more pounds, Mrs. Coleman, and you wouldn't have made it. But we're alone. We're finally alone."

"I know. Isn't it wonderful?"

"It's beautiful, Otami," Riley said, looking around his new home.

"It is beautiful," Otami agreed. "Nita and her brothers helped with the painting and scraping. I did the decorating. It wasn't all that difficult, since there are only four rooms. Cleaning the dirt and mildew was the worst. The house had been vacant for too long. Can you imagine, Riley, it only costs one hundred and twenty-five dollars a month. We must pay the electric bill. I looked and looked until I found what you could afford to pay on your salary. I know how to be economical."

Riley grinned. "That's exactly what I need, an economical wife. Why do you keep looking out the window? Surely you aren't expecting company, or are you?"

Otami frowned. "Something must be wrong. It always happens at this time of day. It was my last surprise for you."

"You mean there's more?"

"Yes, one more thing." Otami leaned over the kitchen sink to look through the window. "Ahhh, here it is. Come quick!"

Riley leaned over the sink and stared out into the twilight. "I'll be damned," he said. "Don't tell me you have something to do with this?"

Otami laughed helplessly. "His name is Pete and every morning he brings that bull he's leading to the field behind our house. Then he comes back in the evening to take it somewhere else. I couldn't wait for you to see it. I thought it would remind you of Texas and your steers. It's an old bull and it can barely walk, as you can see. But it is the same color as the pictures you showed me of your cows. Some days, it wanders down onto our lawn; that is why the grass is cropped so close. This will be another memory for us to hold close."

"You are a piece of work, Mrs. Coleman. How could you keep that a secret?"

"It was easy. Don't you see, Riley? This was all meant to be. Everything fell into place; everything worked out for us. It was not wrong for us to marry. This place is perfect for us. This will be our beginning roots, the start of our memories. Tell me I did right. Tell me this was meant to be. I need you to tell me, Riley."

There was a lump in Riley's throat. "It's right. It was right from the minute we met. We both know that. I'll be telling you that every hour of the day. You'll get tired of hearing it."

"Never!" Otami cried.

"Are there any more surprises you haven't told me about?"

"The bull was the last one."

Riley grinned and looked around him. It was time to explore his new home.

He was standing at one end of a long room divided by a bar that separated the living room from the kitchen. The appliances were old but sparkling clean. Chrisp white curtains fluttered in the warm breeze at the louvered windows. White wicker furniture boasted colorful yellow-and-lime-colored padding that complemented green-and-gold flecks in the new tile floor. Otami's Hong Kong picture set off one stark white wall to perfection.

"I put that up there for you by myself," Otami said, pointing to a brass butterfly near the front door. "The hook is for your navy cap. I bought it at the Ginger Jar—it is my wedding present to you."

Riley drew her close to him, overcome. "Thank you," he whispered against her sweet-smelling hair.

Silvery moonlight penetrated the lacy curtains, illuminating the farmhouse bedroom, chasing away the deepest shadows. Otami lay with her head nestled in the hollow of Riley's shoulder, her face, like his, betraying a sublime satisfaction. They had made love, shared love, brought to each other the best they had to give; it had been like opening a doorway to heaven.

Otami moved against him, her dark almond eyes opening slowly as she reached up to caress his cheek. She felt the tremor that rippled through him. "My Riley, my husband, did I please you?"

"Your husband is pleased." Riley sighed, drawing her closer, pressing his lips against her brow. His fingers slid through her long black hair. This woman, with her small high breasts and soft yielding thighs, fit him like a glove, as though she had been made for him. And he knew beyond doubt that it would always be this way between them, a sweet offering of love and amazement, because what they brought to each other was more than physical; it was the touching of souls.

Blissful, euphoric days followed. The communion between Riley and Otami was so complete neither felt the need for anything or anyone. Their lovemaking was wondrous and spontaneous. Shared, enjoyed . . . perfect.

On the third day of their honeymoon, Riley armed himself with a screwdriver, a spatula, and a hammer and finally managed to pry open the front door of the farmhouse. "I think, Mrs. Coleman, that it is time we explored this beautiful little island. What do you say? Why don't we take a picnic lunch and start out after breakfast and explore till we're tired."

"Where would you like to go? Guam is only thirty miles in length, twelve miles in width, and four miles wide at its narrowest point. I learned that on the second day of my arrival," Otami said proudly.

"I can do better than that. I," he said loftily, "have a brochure on the island. I also have all the poop from fellow officers. While you're making the pancakes I'll tell you exactly what we're going to do. While you pack our lunch I'll take a shower. Is that fair?"

"No. But I am a good, obedient, Japanese housewife and will do as I'm told. Until such time as I don't like your orders and then I will resign. How do you like that, Mr. Coleman?"

"As long as you warm the syrup and melt the butter for the pancakes, you can do whatever you want. You can even walk on my back."

"No, thank you. I am a modern Japanese. I will just cook and clean and make love to you."

"Well said," Riley beamed. "Now, let's see. We can take a drive through the Nimitz Hill area and get a panoramic view of the natural harbor. He'll be able to see the Glass Breakwater. My C.D. tables told me it was named after Captain Henry Glass, who claimed Guam as a possession of the United States. I think that's a must. I'd like to see it, wouldn't you?"

"Absolutely," Otami cooed in his ear as she set his plate of pancakes in front of him along with the melted butter and warm syrup.

"Do that again." Riley grinned.

"Do what?"

"Nuzzle my ear." Riley groaned as Otami willingly obeyed.

"What are you crossing out?" she asked a moment later.

Riley was flustered. "I—I didn't think you'd want to go to Nimitz Beach Park. I'm not sure I want to go there, either. It was the battle site of the American invasion in 1944. Why don't we leave it for last."

"All right, Riley. But I think you should see it. It will be something for you to talk about with your father later on."

"You're serious, aren't you."

"Yes. You aren't going to be able to hide from your father forever. Sooner or later you will talk. This will be common ground, something he can relate to."

"You always know just what to say and when to say it. In a way, I am hiding out. Why couldn't I say the words? Why did you have to say it for me?"

"Because I'm me and you're you." Otami smiled and the tricky moment passed. "Would you like a slice of mango?"

"Nope, I'm full."

Otami set about clearing the table. "Where else are we going?"

"To Fort Soledad Vista Point. According to this guide we'll be able to see Umatac—the place Magellan is said to have visited in 1521. We might want to tell our kids about it someday. History, you know."

"If we do all that you've said so far, it will be time for lunch. Where will we picnic?"

"Another cup of coffee, Otami. Quick, you aren't anticipating my needs. Two sugars."

"Two sugars, is it? I think I might like a second cup myself. I'll sit here till you fix it."

"I get the point." Riley laughed, jumping up to pour the coffee. "How about this place?" Riley asked, pointing to a map. "It's called Yigo. The CO was telling me there's talk about building a memorial park on the spot to commemorate the half a million Japanese and American soldiers—and civilians as well as Pacific Islanders—who lost their lives during World War Two in the Pacific conflict. They plan to erect a monument on the sight that will symbolize the determination of the United States and Japan to promote friendship and world harmony. Supposedly it will be a figure praying for eternal peace."

Otami's expression was as solemn as Riley's. "I think that you and I are the two perfect people to visit that sight. I will pray that it comes to pass and is built."

"Something else to talk to Pap about someday. I think that will be enough for one day. Provided that truck will get us back and forth. Wear good shoes, Otami, in case we have to hoof it. I wonder if there's gas in the tank."

"Of course there's gas. Who's going to do the dishes?"

"Not me, I have to take a shower and shave. Guess it's your turn."

"I have a better idea. I'll wait until you're finished and then you can dry as I wash. This marriage is fifty-fifty, remember."

"Okay, okay."

"When we come back from exploring, would you like to make love down in the glade where all the wild ferns grow? We can make a bed of them. We can even bathe in the pond."

"It's a puddle, not a pond. If you do the dishes, I'll meet you there."

The rickety truck proved to be a horror. Otami prayed and constantly blessed herself, to Riley's delight. The day flew by. The picnic lunch was quickly devoured, and before they knew it, it was time to head back to the farmhouse.

"There's a bottle of champagne in the refrigerator for us." Otami smiled. "My uncle sent it. While he could not participate in our wedding or give his blessing, he did what he could. He is a fine old gentleman and he loves me dearly. It is his way of wishing us well without losing face. We must drink the toast he wanted. I will prepare it for us."

Riley waited until Otami returned with a tray and two glasses. He took his glass from the tray and handed Otami hers. "I think we should have a flowery toast, something meaningful and different, but I can't for the life of me think of a thing. Why don't we drink to our new life, yours and mine? To love and understanding. May our new life be filled with humor, beautiful music, and wondrous words. To us."

"To us," Otami said softly. "Always us."

The *fanuchanan*, or rainy season, came and went. The *fanumnangan*, or dry season, set in, and Riley's two years in Guam were almost up. He'd come to love his new island home and dreaded the day he'd be ordered to leave. Otami had settled into the little farmhouse as though she'd been born there. She continued with her studies at the university and often, late at night, Riley would find her bent over the long, narrow kitchen table with its butterfly cloth, studying. The moment she spotted him, however, she'd run to his arms. Riley had never been happier in his life. This was paradise. This was home. He hoped he'd never have to leave.

But as always, with something so fragile as perfection, snafus are bound to happen.

When Riley's tour of duty in Guam was up, new orders sent him to Atsugi, Japan, and from there to Vietnam. Immediately, he was flying night missions over the Mai Cong Delta in Coleman aircraft.

When Thad Kingsley looked at the postmark on Riley's letter, he paled. Jesus, how had the kid ended up in Vietnam? He was supposed to remain in Guam—forever and ever, if necessary. What had gone wrong? He read the letter.

Dear Uncle Thad,

I know this letter is going to come as a surprise to you. I'm here! God, I hate it. I know that I'm capable of killing to get out of here. I am killing. Every day I kill. I try not to think about it, but sooner or later I have to take count and it makes me sick. I didn't know it was possible to be so piss-assed scared, but I am. I don't mind telling you I have had to fight with myself to keep from writing to Pap to get me out of here.

Otami went back to Japan. I haven't heard from her for a long time. She was going to see if her parents would welcome her back. She was worried about it; I could tell from the sound of her letter. The main reason she went back instead of staying in Guam to wait for me is she's pregnant. Jesus, Uncle Thad, she's going to have my baby all by herself. She needs her family. You have their address. Will you check on things and see how it's all going? If Otami's parents refuse to accept her back into the family, see what you can do for her. You might have to intervene and do some business with my bank back in Texas. Otami has all the papers. Do what you can.

I hate this place. I don't know why I'm here. No one else seems to know, either. How did this happen? Who's responsible? The only thing that makes it all bearable is that I'm flying Coleman planes. I feel safe in them.

{ 477 }

Give Otami a kiss for me if you see her soon and tell her how much I love her. Take care of her for me, Uncle Thad.

All my best,
Riley

Thad felt out of his depth. He hated Vietnam almost as much as Riley did. His gut churned and he knew his new ulcer was going to start acting up.

Maybe it was time to put in a call to Moss. He'd call Billie later; right now Riley needed his father's reassurance. He could be tactful, casually mention the boy, and see what developed in the conversation. He also had to get in touch with Otami and see what was going on. He'd have to go to Tokyo—this was too important to trust to a phone call. For Riley Coleman—for Billie's son—he would do anything he could.

Thad didn't sleep that night at all. At first light, he called Sunbridge and was told that Mr. Moss Coleman was away on a business trip and would be back in three days. By midafternoon he was in Tokyo and at the address Riley had sent him. He rang the bell and a trim maid in a silk kimono opened the gate for him. "Yes?"

"I'd like to see Otami. Tell her Admiral Kingsley is here."

"You come inside house, sir. Missy Otami is in garden. I fetch her."

Thad stood with his hat in his hands. He didn't know much about Japanese furniture or houses, but this place looked fit for a king. Wealth, the kind the Colemans were used to, was right here. Perhaps more.

The naked fear in Otami's eyes was more than Thad could bear. He quickly rushed to assure her that nothing was wrong, then kissed her. "That was from Riley."

"You have heard from him? Tell me. Is he well? How is he? I have had no word for many weeks now."

Thad handed her Riley's letter and watched as her hungry eyes devoured each word once and then again. She folded the letter carefully and handed it back to Thad. "Thank you so much for coming here. I know Riley was very worried about my family. They opened their arms to me. I am most fortunate that they love me as they do. You are to tell Riley that I do not need Coleman money. My family would be dishonored if they could not take care of me, their daughter. Riley will understand. I must accept, for the misery I caused them in the beginning."

"I'm happy that everything has worked out for you. Riley will be relieved."

"I've written him many letters explaining things to him. Soon he should receive them. Perhaps all at one time."

Or not at all, Thad felt like saying. The Vietnamese had a knack for knocking out mail planes. "If you want to write a letter, I'll take it back with me to Atsugi and put it on the next flight. Riley will have it by tomorrow night. Would you care to have dinner with me?"

"Admiral Kingsley!" Otami said, clearly shocked. "You must dine with my family. My father would be most upset if he found out you were here and did not honor us for dinner. My mother has a passion for American film stars and will want to . . . how do you say . . . pump you for inside information. Say you will dine with us."

"I'd like that very much. I want to meet your family."

"Good. I have met Riley's family. By that I mean you. Now it is your turn to meet my family. I would be very honored."

"Otami, when is the baby due?"

Otami laughed. "Any day now. My mother is much concerned. My father is also concerned, but he pretends that he isn't. Men are strong and brave. This is women's business. It will be the first grandchild for my parents. We are all nervous. Me especially. I wish Riley were here. My mother says it will be a boy. My father wishes for a girl that will look like me." Otami shrugged to show she couldn't fathom this kind of thinking. "I am praying for a son for Riley. But a daughter will be nice, too." She smiled impishly.

"Twins," Thad said inanely. Otami giggled.

Dinner was served Western style for Thad's benefit. He appreciated it and said so.

"We wish to make our daughter's uncle welcome. We could do no less for you, Admiral. I must admit that Yankee bean soup is not something I would want to eat every day." Shadaharu Hasegawa said with a twinkle in his eye.

"It's not a favorite of mine, either." Thad grinned. Both men laughed. Thad sucked in his stomach, waiting for what he knew was coming next.

"Come, we will have a cigar. In the garden. The women will have tea and then we can talk some more. My daughter will pester me if I keep you to myself. Go, go," he said, making shooing motions with his hands to his tiny wife and daughter. He rolled his eyes and said in an indulgent tone, "I promise you, my wife, that you can discuss film stars with Admiral Kingsley later if he is amenable." Thad nodded and the tiny woman squealed with pleasure. Otami put her arms around her mother and left the room. "Women, they are fond of films."

Uncertain of what his response should be, Thad merely agreed.

When the cigars had been lighted, Mr. Hasegawa spoke. "Now that we are out of earshot of the women we must talk of the young man, Riley, and his family."

"Mr. Hasegawa, I am not a blood relation to Riley. I am a family friend, but I love the boy as though he were my own son. I'm not sure I should be discussing his family with you. Not that I don't want to, but I did promise Riley and must honor that promise. I hope you understand."

Shadaharu Hasegawa nodded wearily. He contemplated the tip of his glowing cigar. "There is so much these days that I do not understand. I am not progressive, my wife says. My daughter says I must learn modern Western ways if I am to survive. The old ways, our culture, suddenly is not enough for the young people. I have many more daughters. Eight in all." He grimaced. "Do you know what nine women can do to one man who treasures the old ways?"

Thad grinned. How pitiful this rolypoly man looked. How woebegone—until you looked at his shrewd eyes. "I think I have some idea of what you are talking about. I'm very relieved that you welcomed Otami back into the family. I came here today to be sure she was well taken care of. On Riley's request, of course."

"Tell me of this young man. My daughter goes on for hours, but she is a young woman in love. I must know of the family this young man comes from."

"The Colemans are a fine old family. Very well respected. They're good people, Mr. Hasegawa. Your daughter married into a fine old family. They're wealthy, if that's important. Riley has a trust fund that will keep him and his family well off for all his life. You need have no worry on that score."

"I am well off, too. I can provide for my daughter and the baby." Mr. Hasegawa bristled.

"I'm sure you can. You will recall I said 'if it's important.' I don't think that Riley or Otami has given much thought to money. I mentioned it in case you were . . . were wondering."

"I was. There is no use pretending I wasn't. Why doesn't the young man want his family to know about his marriage to my daughter?"

He'd dreaded the question and searched his mind for just the right words. "I think—now understand, Mr. Hasegawa, it is merely my opinion—I think Riley was afraid that his father would spoil things for him. I must tell you that I agree—I think his father would have spoiled things. It is to your credit that you were wise enough to welcome back your daughter rather than lose her."

Mr. Hasegawa snorted and then puffed on his cigar. "My wife, that tiny porcelain doll, told me, as did my other daughters, that if I did not welcome Otami back, they were all going to America to seek careers in the films. What could I do? I, too, learn from the young. I know I must be progressive to survive. Also, I cannot, I simply cannot, stand all the chirping and chattering when I do not go along with their plans and ideas."

"You're a remarkable man, Mr. Hasegawa. You have a fine family. It is a wise man who knows when to . . ."

"Buckle under to the pressure of his womenfolk. I believe it is an ancient Chinese proverb, is it not?"

Thad laughed and puffed on his cigar.

"It would not be a wise idea, then, to get in touch with the Coleman family?"

"No, Mr. Hasegawa, it would not be a good idea. Not at this time. In the end it must be Riley and Otami's decision. Not yours. I'm sorry if that offends you, but that is the way I see it."

"My daughter tells me her husband has great respect for you. I can see why. You have told me what you wanted to tell me, what you think I needed to know. No more. I respect that, Admiral Kingsley. I will go along with their wishes. My daughter will always have a home with her family. It would dishonor us all if I left her to fend for herself—particularly now. The Colemans are not to be notified of the birth?"

"Only if Riley gives his permission. Otherwise, you must honor his wishes. You will have one consolation, though. You will have this child all to yourselves."

"It doesn't seem fair. To deprive one's family of a child. There is a grandfather, Otami tells me."

"No, it isn't fair. But it isn't up to either of us to judge or make decisions. All we can do is be here for them if needed."

"You are a wise man, Admiral. You must come to my house again so that we can get to know each other better. You will want to see the infant when it is born."

"I'd like that very much. I would be honored."

"My house is yours. You will come and go as you see fit. Anytime you wish. Now, I'm afraid we must return and you will tell my girls stories of the film stars. I beg of you, do not make them too glamorous."

Thad laughed. "I think I can handle that."

"Admiral, do you think you could tell them that Clark Gable is not as handsome in real life as he is on the screen?"

"I think I can tell them he has a wart on his nose that is covered with makeup. Is that all right?"

Shadaharu Hasegawa puffed contentedly on his cigar. "That would be quite wonderful, if you don't mind the little white lie."

"Who said it was a lie? Every man in the world believes it." Thad laughed as he followed his host back into the house.

Four days later Thad received a phone call from the *Tokyo Sun Times*. He was told it was a person-to-person call from Shadaharu Hasegawa. The excitement in Otami's father's voice could only mean good news. "A boy child!"

"Congratulations, Mr. Hasegawa. Give Otami my love. I'll get word to Riley."

"Thank you, Admiral. You will come to my house next week. Please."

"Thank you. Will Sunday be all right?"

"We will all look forward to your visit. Good-bye, Admiral Kingsley."

Thad ached with the feelings he had to suppress. This was the kind of news a person liked to deliver. Billie would be so delighted. Moss would be ecstatic—until he found out the mother of his grandchild was Japanese. This was news he would have to keep to himself.

Riley landed his plane and headed straight for his quarters. Sleep was what he needed. Sleep and dreams of Otami. He was halfway across the compound when his CO handed him a slip of paper. A boy! "Mother and son doing fine. Everything under control." The message was signed by Fleet Admiral

Thaddeus Kingsley. He'd known he could count on Uncle Thad.

A son. A boy to carouse with. To just look at, not smother. It was all so right.

His conscience pricked him for a moment. He should write to Sunbridge. Someday. Someday far away. For now he was going to sleep off his all-night air strike and dream of his wife and new son.

A month later the first picture of his new son arrived. Riley Shadaharu Coleman. Seven and one-half pounds. Twenty inches long.

It was two o'clock in the morning when Riley met his flight buddies on the makeshift runway for their nightly strikes. He lovingly touched the wingtip and offered up his daily prayer. "Let me come back to my wife and son," he whispered softly. "Coleman Aviation, don't fail me now."

An hour into the air strike Riley's plane started to lose altitude. Fear rose in his throat, threatening to choke off his air supply. Jesus, not here, not over this godforsaken country no one's ever heard about. Not for something no one understood. God, not now! Riley screamed. The plane banked and Riley's feet danced on the pedals. He was too low; he could never bail out. Red lights glowed, reminding him of eerie Halloween eyes. His last conscious thought before he crashed into the mountain ridge was that Riley Shadaharu had his grandfather Coleman's nose.

The Navy Department was only too willing to have Thad travel to Texas to break the news of Riley's death. He personally got on the phone and begged Washington to hold up notifying Otami until he could notify the Colemans. Irregular, they said, but because of their own snafus they were willing to make any and all concessions.

The moment Billie opened the door to her Austin apartment and saw Thad in full dress uniform she knew. She took a deep breath. Thad poured her a drink, which she declined. "Tell me everything you know." It was a while later when she finally asked, "Why can't I cry?"

"You're in shock, Billie. Come with me. I can't leave you here. I have to go to Sunbridge. Moss is going to need you. So is Seth."

"Yes, yes, you're right. Let me get a sweater. You're right.

{ 483 }

They're going to need me. Did I thank you, Thad, for coming?
I did, didn't I?"

"Several times. I thought you would rather hear it from me
than the War Department."

"Do you know what happened?"

"They were flying low strikes. Riley's plane started to lose
altitude. He crashed into a ridge. That's all we know."

"Moss won't be able to accept this. Neither will Seth. Was
it a Coleman plane?" she asked in a hushed whisper.

"They were all Coleman planes," Thad said softly.

CHAPTER
{{{{{{{{{ THIRTY-FOUR *}}}}}}}}}*

*The scene at Sunbridge set Thad's teeth on edge. Threats,
insults, and recriminations flew thick and fast.* Seth bellowed
and snorted like a frostbitten dragon. Moss downed half a bottle
of brandy in two gulps. Agnes flopped down on a chair and
fingered her strand of pearls, her eyes never leaving the raging
Seth.

"Don't interfere, you said. That's what you said, gal. Your
exact words, don't interfere. Now he's dead. Riley is dead.
My only grandson. It's your fault!" he shouted, pointing a
clawlike hand at Billie.

"But you did interfere. You had him sent to Guam to fly
weather missions. You can't blame me for my own son's death.
What kind of man are you? If you had left things alone, he
might still be alive. Oh, no, you and Moss, the pair of you,
you had to get right in there and do what you always do. Pull
strings, make threats, bribe people, to get what you want. Now
look what's happened. My son is gone. I have no son. Why
couldn't you leave him alone?" Billie cried brokenly.

"You don't even belong here. What are you doing here,
anyway? Who asked you to come here? Get her out of here,
Moss. I can't stand to look at her face."

"That's enough, Pap," Moss thundered. "Thad, what happened? I want it straight."

"Riley was flying in low, one of his nightly strikes. The

plane started to lose altitude and he couldn't bail out. He went into a ridge and the plane exploded. It's all we know, Moss."

"It was a Coleman plane?"

Thad had to strain to hear the question. "Yes, Moss, the whole squadron flies Coleman planes. You know that as well as I do."

"There was some kind of foul-up!" Moss cried. "Riley was supposed to stay in Guam for the rest of his tour. He was already in Vietnam when we found out. He was supposed to be rotated back day after tomorrow. Jesus. Two days! I can't believe it."

Billie stood up. "Moss, you've had enough to drink. Why don't we all go into the kitchen and have some coffee."

"Coffee! Get this stupid woman out of here," Seth roared. "I mean it, Moss. My grandson is dead and she wants to make coffee. Agnes, you raised one hell of a woman here. I never heard anything so stupid in my life."

"Shut up, Seth," Agnes said angrily. "One more word out of you and I swear I'll gag you personally. Coffee is something we all need. You will either keep a civil tongue in your head or you'll be wheeled to your room. Do we understand each other, Seth?"

"Don't tell me to shut up, Aggie. This is my house."

Thad, Moss, and Billie followed Agnes into the kitchen. Seth wiped at his eyes with the sleeve of his flannel shirt and spun his chair about. He'd be goddamned if he'd go out there and have coffee. In the end he wheeled his chair closer to the door so that he could hear the low voices coming from the kitchen. Billie was weeping, but Agnes seemed to be in control. As always. It was time to rid himself of both of them. Who needed them now? He certainly didn't. Everything was over. What was the point in going on?

Billie held herself in rigid control. Things had to be done, calls had to be made. Maggio, Susan, Sawyer. She had to do it, break the news. It took several tries before she could dial Maggie's New York number correctly. Her daughter's breathless voice came over the receiver on the fourth ring. "Maggie . . ." Now that she was actually hearing her voice, Billie was unable to continue. Some part of her was denying Riley's death, some part of her believed if she did not say the words, it would not become reality. "Maggie, oh, Maggie!"

A bolt of alarm electrified Maggie as she clenched the phone to her ear. "Mam? What's wrong? Did something happen to

Pap? Mam, are you there? Answer me!"

Moss took the phone from Billie's shaking hand and, with all the control he could muster, spoke. "Maggie. Riley was killed. We've only just got word. Mam can't talk, but we wanted you to know."

Maggie bit down so hard on her lip she could taste the blood. The pain, the rage, couldn't be stifled. Dear God in heaven, Riley couldn't be dead. He couldn't! She needed to lash out, to hurt in return. "He was flying one of your planes, wasn't he, Pap?" She broke the connection.

Helplessly, Maggie looked around her apartment, the place where she had encouraged her brother to enlist in the service in order to spite Moss, remembering that awful lonely Christmas they'd spent together. Now there would never be another Christmas.

Madness spurred her forward, to the desk, where she searched frantically for the packet of photographs she and Riley had taken that night. When she couldn't lay her hands on them immediately, she upended the desk. The pictures slid from their envelope onto the carpet. Maggie dropped to her knees and scrambled for them, tears streaming down her cheeks as she clutched them to her chest.

"No, no, no!" she cried aloud. "Not Riley, never Riley! Me! It should have been me! Dear God, I wish it had been me!"

Thad felt emotionally bruised and battered as he climbed into the cockpit of his plane for the return flight to California. He hated leaving Billie, but there was nothing he could do. How wrong they had been to think that Seth and Moss would need her. Feeling like an outcast, she had crept from the house with him like a thief in the night. When they'd said their good-byes there had been no tears. The tears would come later.

Otami stared at Thad, containing her grief. "He never saw his son," she whispered brokenly. "He never got to do all the things a father wants to do with his son. Do you think, Admiral Kingsley, that he thought of them, the things he would do when little Riley grew up?"

"I'm sure he did, Otami. I notified the Colemans. I didn't mention you or the baby."

"It is . . . was Riley's wish that they not know. We must honor that wish. My parents are away. My mother went with my father on a business trip. They will not return for another month."

"I can notify them. You shouldn't be alone now. They would want to be here with you."

"Admiral Kingsley, I am not alone. I will never be alone. You forget, I have Riley's son. I will be fine. You are not to worry about me. I knew that this might happen someday. I am not prepared, but I must accept it."

Thad gathered the girl close to him. "Cry. It will make you feel better."

"I cannot do that. Perhaps someday. I must go to the baby now. It is time for him to nurse. Thank you for coming. Would you like to stay for dinner?" At Thad's negative nod, Otami turned and left the room.

When Thad left, he knew he wouldn't be back—not for a long time. The Hasegawas would do all that was necessary. He would only be a grim reminder of Riley and that was the one thing they didn't need. Life had to go on....

Billie handled her grief in several ways. She painted and worked obsessively. She spent time with Sawyer, sometimes talking for hours, and Sawyer told her little things she had never known about her son. What gave her the greatest comfort were her long letters to Thad and his equally long replies. There had even been one hour-long phone call from Tokyo that she would always treasure. Thad's concern was almost more than she could bear. In the end, however, she had been the one to comfort him. She never knew where her strength came from, but she was coping, handling things to the best of her ability. She was going to survive.

Moss Coleman cradled the phone on his shoulder as he waited for his party to come on the line. His voice, when he identified himself, was cold and harsh. "I think it's a hell of a note when a father has to beg the United States Navy to return his dead son's belongings. I've written six letters, sent three telegrams, and I've had no word. There must be some paper shuffler or pencil pusher who knows what's going on. I'm not getting off this phone till I get the answers I want."

"One moment, sir. I think Major Henry is the person you want to speak with. He's on another line. Will you hold?"

"I'm holding. I've been holding for two months now," Moss snarled. "Of course I'll wait."

Five minutes later the phone crackled to life. "Major Henry here."

Moss ran through his speech a second time.

"Mr. Coleman, your son's effects were sent to his wife. Those are the rules. I can't change them, even for you."

"Wife! What wife? My son wasn't married. You idiots must have Riley mixed up with someone else. Just like his orders were mixed up. My son would be alive today except for that screw-up. What do you have to say to that, Major Henry?"

"I don't know anything about your son's orders, but I do know that the lieutenant was married for almost two years to a Japanese girl while he was stationed in Guam. His personal belongings and his military insurance were forwarded to his wife. There is also a minor dependent, a son. This information came to us after your son's death. It was included in his record. . . . Mr. Coleman, are you still there? . . . Mr. Coleman?"

Moss stared down at his desk. "Yes, I'm here, Major. I didn't know about the marriage. Even his mother didn't know."

"I'm sorry about that, Mr. Coleman. Sometimes these young men get antsy when they're so far from home. Everything was in order."

"Yes, Major, I'm sure it was. My son never did anything halfway. Could you tell me who this girl is and where she lives?"

The major gave him the address of Otami's parents. "I'm sorry for any inconvenience that this may have caused you, Mr. Coleman. And you have my deepest sympathy, sir."

Moss's vision blurred as he stared at Riley's picture on his desk. How could the boy have done such a despicable thing . . . married a Japanese, when he knew how his father felt about them? His fist banged the desk so hard that Riley's picture fell and glass shattered all over the polished floor. What the hell had happened to "like father like son"? Where had he gone wrong? A Jap! A goddamn Jap!

Major Henry had said there was a son living in Japan. Well, by God, no grandson of his was going to grow up in that hellhole, living on rice and picking in garbage cans! He'd go there and bring back the boy. Raise him here at Sunbridge. This was Riley's flesh and blood. He could learn to live with the rest of it. And a new baby in the house might be just what Billie needed. Moss smiled grimly. For Riley's baby son she would come back. He'd make book on it.

Moss left the following morning for San Francisco. From

San Francisco he caught a Pan Am flight to Guam, and from there he flew to Tokyo.

After checking into a hotel, Moss headed straight for a bar and downed three stiff drinks in quick succession. The liquor didn't help to steady his nerves. He hated this land and he hated every Japanese that walked the earth.

The doorman at the hotel flagged down a cab for him. Moss showed him the address and the driver's eyebrows shot up. "Yes, sir," he said in polite, stilted English.

"You understand English?" Moss barked.

"Yes, sir, I studied at UCLA for four years. Is there something you wish to know about Japan?" he asked politely.

"I know all there is to know about Japan. I don't want to know any more. How far is that address from here?"

"Not too far. Perhaps fifteen minutes, depending on traffic."

In spite of himself Moss couldn't help but ask, "If you studied at UCLA, what are you doing driving a taxi?"

"Japan is a poor country. It is difficult to make ends meet when you have a family to support. I have three sons to educate and that takes much money. It is not a dishonorable profession. Is this your first visit to Japan?"

"No. I was here once before. This will be my last visit," Moss replied harshly.

From time to time the driver looked into the rearview mirror at the brooding American face. He'd never seen such misery in a human being before. He concentrated on his driving, leaving Moss to his dark thoughts.

"Why are you stopping?"

"This is the address you wanted. See, the numbers are on the gate. You must ring the bell and someone will admit you. I bring many customers here."

"Customers? Is it a brothel? It looks like a goddamn palace."

"I beg your pardon, sir. I understand your words, but what makes you think that this is a brothel? It is the home of Mr. Shadaharu Hasegawa. Mr. Hasegawa owns three newspapers in Tokyo. This is his city home. Did you make a mistake in the address?"

"No, this is the address." Moss paid the man in American currency and knew the tip was outrageous, but he had no desire to quibble over price. He felt uncertain now as he stood outside the palatial house. Hasegawa was the right name. He jabbed at the bell with a blunt finger. The gate swung open and Moss walked through. He turned at the sound of the well-oiled hinges

{ 489 }

closing the gate: he was locked in. His forehead was beaded with perspiration as he waited in one of the most luxurious houses he had ever seen. This was no ricky-ticky rice paper shack. There was money here.

It was like a parade. First came a rolypoly man followed by a miniature little woman who must be the rolypoly man's wife. Behind them were eight young women.

Once they were all lined up, they bowed on a cue from the round man. "Welcome to my home, Mr. Coleman. Please, you will follow me and I will introduce you to my family." There was nothing for Moss to do but obey. This was not what he'd expected.

Mr. Hasegawa motioned for Otami to step forward. "This is my oldest daughter, your son's wife."

"Under what law?" Moss demanded cruelly.

"American law," Mr. Hasegawa said, enunciating carefully. "A legal marriage. There are certificates, if you wish to view them."

"I wish."

The Japanese man clapped his hands and a young servant appeared. He spoke quietly and the girl minced her way from the room, her head bowed, her hands clasped in front of her. She returned minutes later with a number of papers in a manila folder, and Moss scrutinized each of them.

It was all real.

"You wish to see your grandson?"

Moss nodded. He hated himself for staring at the girl, Otami, who was trying hard not to stare herself. Again, Mr. Hasegawa clapped his hands and this time merely nodded. The little maid returned minutes later with a fat cherub of a baby. Mr. Hasegawa indicated that Moss could step forward to view the infant. "I believe, as does my daughter, that the child has your nose. It is most remarkable."

Moss felt his throat constrict. Riley's son. He could see the resemblance in this placid, sleeping baby. It was enough. "I want to take the child back to Texas," he said coolly.

In the blink of an eye Otami stepped between her child and Moss. She said nothing, but her eyes implored her father.

"That is impossible, Mr. Coleman. The child belongs here with his mother and family. It was your son's wish."

"What do you know of my son's wishes? Don't think for one minute I'm going to buy that hogwash. That child is a Coleman. He belongs in Texas. Not here! Never here!"

"That is impossible. The child needs his mother. He will lack for nothing here. I believe I can match your income, if that is what's worrying you. Please, you will not insult us by offering to buy the child. That was your next move, was it not?"

Moss blustered, "You don't buy humans." But in his heart he knew that that was exactly what he had been going to say. "I'll go to court," he threatened.

"Your American courts have no jurisdiction here in Japan..... Please, it is not our desire to have trouble with Riley's family. We can all contribute to the child. You and your wife will be welcome in my house at any time. My daughter will be your daughter. It is fair and just."

"I don't want your damn daughter. I want my grandson. I won't leave here without him."

Otami stepped forward. "Mr. Coleman, Riley and I spoke of this many times. It was his wish that the child remain with me. When his time was up in the navy, he had planned to make his home here in Japan. I am speaking the truth to you. It is what Riley wanted."

"What you made him want. How did you do it? What tricks did you use to snare my son? Riley would never agree to any of this!"

"If what you say is true, then why am I here with my son, and why didn't you know of our marriage and our son? I assume the navy informed you. Riley himself did not want anyone in Texas to know. It is true, Mr. Coleman. And I did not trick your son. I fell in love with him and he fell in love with me. And our baby—Riley and I discussed this— our baby is named after Riley and my father. He is Riley Shadaharu Coleman."

It was the last bitter straw for Moss. Not to have his grandchild named after him. A damn Japanese name that he couldn't even pronounce.

Mr. Hasegawa stepped closer to Moss. "Please, Mr. Coleman, do not bring dishonor on yourself in front of my family. In my newspapers every day we have one reporter or another writing about ugly Americans. For all our sakes, do not act in this manner. You must accept the situation. Our home is yours whenever you wish."

"Go to hell," Moss barked, then he turned on his heel and left the house. There had to be a way. If necessary, he could kidnap the kid. Then he looked at the iron gates and knew it for the idle threat it was. He was beaten. He'd lost not only the battle, but the war as well.

He had nothing to do but think for eighteen hours on the long flight home. In the end he decided to keep the news of Riley Shadaharu to himself. No one would ever know of his humiliation. Not as long as he was alive, anyway.

When Moss returned to the United States he was a man driven by grief and rage. Besieged by the loss of his beloved son, he turned to the bourbon as though it were an old friend. Beset with rage over the humiliation he had suffered at the hands of the Hasegawas, he immersed himself in his work. He knew that he could have his grandson if he was willing to compromise; a basic kindness and acceptance would reward him with the only piece of Riley that was left in this world. But he hated and feared the Japanese; and he would not have anything to do with the child unless all ties to his mother's heritage had been severed.

Billie was aware of Moss's turmoil and tried to comfort him; she believed he was blaming himself and his aircraft for Riley's death. Moss never bothered to enlighten her. His reasoning was simple, at least in his opinion: he knew that if he told her, Billie would rush to Japan to embrace that child. And he did not want her to have what he denied himself—the comfort of loving Riley's son. He knew he was selfish. It was something he'd always known. It was something he could live with.

Seth watched what was left of his world crumble about him. A week after his son's return from Japan, he suffered two small strokes back to back that left him virtually incapacitated and entirely dependent upon Agnes. His speech was now slurred, but the timbre of his voice hadn't changed—he ranted and raved, cursed and cajoled her. He thought nothing of waking her in the middle of the night for a drink of water. He resented her because she was alive and well and could function on her own. He hated his deformity and made her pay for it by tormenting and ridiculing her in any way he could.

In the privacy of her room, Agnes broke down and cried. A victim of her own making, she could do no more than look after his health by day and plot his death by night.

That spring, Agnes made up her mind that she was going to get out from under one way or another. On the first truly warm day when the windows could be opened, she put her plan into action. "We're going for a ride today, Seth. It's time you got some fresh air. You're absolutely shriveling up to nothing. I insist."

"Insist all you please. I ain't going nowhere. Get it through your head, Aggie, that I'm confined to this room and that's where you and I are going to stay. Fetch me some coffee and read me a paper."

"Not today. Today the doctor said you were to go outdoors. It's an order, Seth. He said if you don't do as he says, he's discharging you as his patient."

"I'd like to see him try. I'll cut off all endowments to his fancy hospital and where will that leave him? No ride."

Seth watched Agnes out of the corner of his eye. She was taking his refusal just a little too well. She must be up to something. He'd have to pay close attention to see what it was.

With Agnes's diligent care and the doctor's daily visits, Seth began gradually to show signs of improvement. Each day, Agnes offered to take Seth for a ride in the country. The day he finally accepted, she stared at him with a stupid look on her face. "Well, don't stand there—get someone to come and help me into the car."

Agnes shifted from one foot to the other, her hands twisting at the pearls at her neck. "Are you sure? Why do you want to go today? What made you change your mind?"

"That damn fool doctor, that's who. He wants me in his office to give me some kind of newfangled test. That's where we're going. Don't get any ideas about stopping off at department stores. We're going to his office and then we're coming home. You got that, Agnes?"

"Yes, Seth, I have it. . . . You could have given me some notice, you know. The chauffeur isn't here this morning. Moss forgot some papers and wanted them brought into the office. And don't think for a minute that I'll drive you."

"That's exactly what I think, old woman," Seth demanded contrarily. "Now go get yourself ready. I don't want to be ashamed of you. How a woman can let herself go the way you have is beyond me. Have you no pride?"

"I have pride, Seth. Make no mistake about it. I'll just be a few minutes." Agnes turned and left the room, her back taller and straighter than Seth had seen it in a long time.

Up in her room, Agnes picked up the house phone and called the garage. "I want you to go into town and pick up Mr.

Coleman's prescription at the pharmacy," she told the voice at the other end. "Take the ranch truck and leave the limousine." Her eyes darted to the clock. "I'll need that prescription before noon, so you'll have to hurry."

When she replaced the receiver in the cradle she sank onto the edge of her bed, facing the window where she could observe the driveway. Within a few moments she saw the dark blue ranch truck churning up the dust. Quieting her pounding heart, Agnes picked up her coat and walked down the stairs.

As she helped Seth into his coat and wheeled him down the ramp they'd erected over the front stairs, Agnes felt the perspiration break out on her upper lip. Hearing her quick shallow gasps, Seth tormented, "Gettin' old, hey, Aggie? You can be replaced. Yes, indeed, that's what I'm thinkin' of doin', Aggie. Put you out to pasture, is what I'll do. Or maybe I'll just put you out!" He cackled gleefully, spitefully. Agnes's hands tightened on the wheelchair grips. She pushed him as far as the garage, then steered him toward the side door.

"Whatcha doin', you crazy old woman? You can't get this contraption through there. Go inside and open the big door and get me in that way."

Silently, deliberately, Agnes squeezed the chair through the side door, struggling with it between the fleet of automobiles. "Damn fool woman, it's easier to heft me in the backseat from out there!" He jabbed a finger toward the outside.

"Shut up, Seth. We'll do this my way or not at all. Now are you going to complain the day away, or are you going to help me?" She swung his arm over her shoulder and lifted; Seth obliged by swinging himself into the Cadillac.

"Fold that contraption and put it back here with me," he snarled. "Damn fool woman does everything ass-backward." Scowling, Seth reached into his breast pocket for his cigars, bit off the tip, and proceeded to light up. "C'mon, hurry up. We ain't got all day!" he scolded between puffs.

Agnes pretended not to hear. Her movements were slow and deliberate as she closed the door and sat behind the wheel to start the engine. The Cadillac roared to life. "You just sit tight, Seth. There's something I have to get from the house. I'll be right back."

"For crissake, Aggie, turn off the engine while you're gone, or at least open the big door!" His gaze narrowed when he saw her remove the automatic garage door opener from over the sun visor. "Aggie, I said shut the damn engine off!"

"I'll be right back, Seth. Sit tight. You're in no position to give orders."

"The hell you say!" Seth roared. "Shut that damn engine off! Open the door, either one! What the hell are you tryin' to do?" With surprising strength and agility, Seth lumbered forward and reached over the seat, grabbing Agnes by the back of her head, his clawlike fingers digging into her scalp before locking on her hair.

She struggled, trying to pull herself free. His strength was terrible, so unexpected. Agnes gasped for breath; Seth's voice roared in her ears. Her feet shifted, searching for purchase to brace herself against his assault. He was shaking her by the hairs of her head, pushing her backward and forward. Agnes's elbow accidentally struck the gearshift, tripping the transmission into drive. The Cadillac shot forward, crashing into the back wall, destroying the shelves mounted there and sending their contents shattering to the concrete floor. A spare container of gasoline puddled out of its bent and cracked container.

"Look what you've done, you stupid bitch!" Seth yelled. "What are you trying to do, kill us both?"

The words sent a chill up Agnes's spine. The gasoline, Seth's lit cigar. Quickly she turned off the ignition, and the engine died. "Your cigar! Where's your cigar?" she cried. She scrambled from the car and fell to her knees, searching.

"For crissake, Aggie, find that damn thing. It must have rolled out when you started your hysterics."

The oily smell of gasoline stung her nostrils as it puddled and rivered under the front end of the car. There it was! She reached for the smoldering object—a second too late.

"You've done it this time, Aggie!" Seth bellowed. It was the very last thing she would ever hear.

The funeral was small and private. Neither Billie nor Moss could face a large, curious crowd. Amelia could not come home for the funeral and neither could Susan. Concert bookings. Maggie had other plans. Only Billie, Moss, and Sawyer attended. Agnes was laid to rest in the family cemetery beside Jessica. Seth, as he had requested, was buried in an unmarked grave beside his old horse, Nessie. In the small cemetery stood a marker in memory of Riley Seth Coleman. They had never found enough of her son to bring him home. It was the first time Billie had seen the white marble plaque, and she gave in to her grief. Moss stood dry-eyed, staring off into the distance.

PART IV

All the partings, all the eternal separations, and all of them without a single good-bye. Riley, Seth, Agnes. Even a grandson, a poor substitute for Riley and one that Moss doubted he could have ever come to love and proudly show off to the world, was lost to him because of uncompromising prejudice and ignorant pride. Maggie and Susan counted among the losses, their lives twisting and turning them away from Sunbridge. Amelia, her life in Europe—time and change had separated sister from brother. And second only to Riley was the loss of Billie. Even though the divorce had not been finalized at the time of Seth's funeral, he had lost her.

Moss and Billie had been drawn together in mutual grief. He had pleaded with her to move back to Sunbridge, to give their marriage another chance. Recognizing her own need for continuity in her life and wanting to share these black times with someone who was also touched with the same grief, Billie had complied. The divorce had been put on hold. Resuming a marriage whose ashes were long cold was difficult at best, if not impossible, but loyalty to the past and what they had shared prompted Billie's return.

At first it seemed it might work. Moss was making every attempt to mold himself into the husband she'd always wished he would be. In a very carefully worded letter to Thad, she stated her reasons for abandoning the divorce. Only one phrase had leaped out at Thad from the pages. "We need each other." Thad had written to wish them well. Billie knew there was little else he could have said. There was nothing he could do.

Before the first anniversary of Riley's death, Billie realized her move back to Sunbridge wasn't going to work. She wasn't enough for Moss, who ghosted about the house shrouded in grief for his son. He thwarted her every attempt at closeness, preferring to lock himself in his workroom with his aeronautics schematics, his memories, and a bottle. He had already dissolved Coleman Aviation; he wanted no part of building government-contracted planes and instrumentation. Moss claimed that it was their fault Riley had died; but he knew that it was his fault for not standing up to them. And that was what tore him apart. He emerged from his workroom with haunted eyes, and an aged weariness slumped his shoulders.

Billie ached for him, but there was nothing she could do to help. Sharing his bed provided only a momentary respite. Billie realized that Moss was punishing himself and everyone else. But he needed her, and even if her own wants and desires went unfulfilled, she remained at Sunbridge, working by day in her studio and sleeping by night in the lonely bedroom on the second floor of the great empty house.

There were days when the loneliness was so intense that she believed it was insane to stay. Yet she realized that she had a commitment to Moss . . . and to the past. And yes, it was a kind of loving, too, but it was not *love*.

Air-mailed letters, phone conversations, unspoken wishes and devotions: these were her love; Thad was her love. She knew she had only to whisper the words and he would come flying into her arms. It was the one thing she would never ask.

Before two years had passed, Billie was convinced that Moss no longer wanted her at Sunbridge. He had set up a New York office, and he had not been back to Texas in over six weeks. Sawyer was away at school most of the time. The house was lonely, empty.

She decided to return to Austin, hungry for the stimulation of city life, for the sound of another voice. When she called Moss in New York to tell him she was moving back to her old apartment, his only reaction was surprise that she'd kept the lease for two years. His final words were "I'll miss you, Billie, but I suppose it's for the best."

Work was Billie's salvation. Designs spilled from her canvas, and most of them were accepted by textile manufacturers. Her sense of self grew along with her business, but Billie never pushed herself: she wanted to enjoy her accomplishments.

Billie's social sphere was expanding and she wondered how she had managed by herself for so many years. The university art department had pleaded with her to teach several classes each week, and in order to lecture on textile design, Billie was forced to learn more about it herself.

When a major manufacturer of bed linens and tableware seduced Billie into copyrighting designs especially for them,

{ 500 }

she had to hire an assistant. Judy Wood, a very capable young artist, was put in charge of this new endeavor. Designs by *Billie* was a runaway success; Billie Coleman had arrived.

She and Moss were now legally separated—on the advice of Moss's old family lawyer. Billie no longer thought in terms of legally divorcing herself from Moss. There seemed little point to it—she was already free, in body and in spirit. Perhaps deep inside her she may have harbored the secret hope that things might someday be mended between herself and Moss. For whatever reason, she couldn't take the action that would untie that final knot. Moss was a part of her—and always would be.

CHAPTER THIRTY-SIX

Billie hung the last of the Christmas cards on the narrow garland she'd strung near the fireplace. One of them caught her eye. MERRY CHRISTMAS AND A HAPPY 1979! The sight made her knees want to buckle when it suddenly struck her that soon it would be ten years since her son had lost his life somewhere in Vietnam. Where had that time gone? What had filled her days? The ache in her heart was still as raw as it had been the day she'd been told Riley was dead. How had she lived through it? Ten years of missing his face, his sudden smile, his love.

Often, more often than she liked to admit, she believed Riley had only been loaned to her and Moss. Conceiving her son had been a contrivance, a deliberate, desperate move to preserve her marriage, to secure Moss's love, and, shamefully, even to secure her own and Agnes's position at Sunbridge. Perhaps Riley was never meant to be; perhaps she had somehow forced the heavens into giving her a son.

"Billie? Darling? What is it?" Thad's voice, filled with concern, reached out for her. This was the first Christmas they were spending together in Austin, flying in the face of convention. Usually, especially during the holidays, Billie would meet him somewhere.

"I just happened to notice this card and realized it will soon be ten years since Riley was killed. Sometimes it just reaches up and smashes me in the face. It's funny, isn't it? I mean, I don't mark the day Maggie left home, or Susan. And I have to think to remember the day Seth and my mother were killed. Only Riley."

Thad moved across the room to take her into his arms. She nestled her head familiarly against his shoulder.

"It's only natural, Billie," he soothed. "Riley was your son and he's lost to you. Seth and Agnes were old. You know your daughters live in this world with you. You can hear their voices, reach out and touch them. The heart always yearns for what it can never have. Don't you know that?"

"I know in my head," she told him. "Knowing it here"—she thumped her breast—"is something else entirely. . . .Why don't you make us that toddy now? I get maudlin when I start thinking like this and I don't want to spoil Christmas for you."

He kissed her lightly on the cheek and released her. As he prepared their drinks, Thad recalled how often over the past ten years he'd ached to tell Billie that Riley had left the legacy of a son, a piece of himself to hold and to love; he knew it would bring her such joy. But Otami would not release him from his promise of secrecy. Thad had explained that Billie didn't know she had a grandchild, that Moss had never told her of his trip to Japan. For years he'd begged her to reconsider her decision. But Otami believed it was her duty to uphold her dead husband's wishes in the matter and had refused to give her consent.

And if Thad broke that promise and told Billie now, after so many years, would she hate him for having kept the knowledge to himself? Would she ever understand his allegiance to Riley and Otami? Thad shook his head. He couldn't take the risk; losing Billie now, after all these years, was unthinkable.

Billie curled against Thad as they stretched out before the fire, silently watching the flames flicker, burning away the darkness in the room. Her head rested against his chest; she could hear his heart beating beneath her cheek. They were so comfortable with each other, she thought, yet there was passion, too. His hands played in her hair, brushing the sensitive skin at the back of her neck. Emotions were building within her and she knew that soon he would kiss her lovingly, tenderly, and together they would reach out for each other and share their love.

As though reading her thoughts, she felt him move beside her, pressing his lips close to her ear. "I like being your lover, Billie Coleman," he whispered seductively.

"Lover," she answered. "I like that word. I like what it means. Somehow, though, I never think of myself as that. It always seemed to fit other people, other women." He knew she was thinking about Alice Forbes.

"You are my lover, Billie. We share so much, even though we're apart for so much of the year."

Billie sighed. "Yes, I know. I wonder sometimes how you can be so understanding, so patient."

"I love you, Billie. I've always loved you; it's that simple."

Billie's eyes filled with tears. "Hearing those words means so much to me, even at my age." She struggled for a laugh. "Moss never said them, you know. I would tell him I loved him and Moss would always reply, 'I know,' as though my loving him were inevitable and deserved. Such simple words and yet they mean so much." She turned in his arms, embracing him, pressing herself against him. "I love you, Thad. And I want you. I always want you."

Thad's mouth lowered to hers, drawing a deep, loving kiss. Her admissions of love never ceased to touch him; her whispered invitation to make love to her excited him. He captured her mouth with his own, entering to feel the velvet of it. He began the ritual of their lovemaking, feeling and knowing the freshness she brought each time they were together this way. He would never have enough of her; he would never tire of this woman who gave herself so willingly, so gently. Theirs was a finely tuned passion, giving and receiving, enjoying and delighting. He could almost feel her body vibrate with expectancy when he caressed her breasts and possessed them with his lips. When his hand strayed between her thighs she moved against him and he could hear the response to his own passion in the catch of her breath and the deep sound that came from her throat.

"I love the way you touch me," she confessed huskily, her own hands reaching for him, drawing him closer, wanting to share this pleasure with him.

Her body was delicious, her responses exquisite, but it was the gleam of love pouring from her eyes and the pleasure he saw there that evoked his own climax. Billie, his beautiful, loving Billie.

They lay together, legs entwined, basking in the afterglow

of their lovemaking, warmed by the heat of the fire that bronzed their skin and reflected in their eyes. He soothed and stroked her, enjoying the fullness of her breasts and the smoothness of her skin. In his eyes she was every bit as beautiful as she'd been that day in Hawaii on Diamond Head. Even more beautiful now, he amended, because now the light in her eyes was for him and she brought with her love all the sensitivity and maturity of a woman. "You're a beautiful lover, Billie," he breathed. "I never want to be away from you. I want to spend the rest of my life enjoying what we have now, this minute."

Billie turned in his arms and kissed him fully, sweetly. If only all of life could be this way, she thought, if only everything were so simple. I love you and you love me and all's right with the world. But the scars on her heart reminded her it wasn't so. Life could be bitter and jealous, taking happiness and joy and obliterating them. Perhaps it was maturity—or experience—but Billie had long ago learned not to take even the smallest joy for granted.

Billie stood at the kitchen sink rinsing the last of the breakfast dishes, a smile playing about her mouth. Thad had made feeble excuses to leave the apartment early, murmuring something about finding authentic plum pudding for Christmas dinner. Billie knew that when he returned, his arms would be full of gaily wrapped packages, which he would unsuccessfully attempt to sneak under the tree.

When the phone rang, she quickly wiped her hands and ran into the living room to answer it. It was her office manager, Judy Wood, wishing her a merry Christmas and assuring her that things were battened down at the office until after the holiday.

Billie sank down at her desk, smiling back at a photograph of Sawyer in riding clothes atop her stallion, Menghis. How she loved this bright granddaughter who was so like herself. Sawyer was to arrive in time for dinner tonight, and Billie had to admit that she could hardly wait to see her and hear all about what Sawyer was doing in college.

"Give the family my love" had been Judy's parting words. Sawyer and Thad were her family. Her daughters had been invited for the holidays, but they'd declined. She knew that the trip from Europe would be impossible for Susan and her husband, Jerome—who were to appear together in concert during the holidays—but she was disappointed that even after all these years Maggie still refused to share even the smallest part of her life with her parents. Billie knew that Maggie resented Moss's attitude both to her husband, Cranston Tanner, and to her son, Coleman Tanner. Even Billie was surprised when Moss had accepted the news of his first grandson so blandly, refusing to acknowledge the boy beyond a cash gift for his birthday and at Christmas. It was cruel to Maggie and Billie couldn't blame her daughter for being offended. And for some reason Moss and Cranston, who was a successful attorney and wealthy in his own right, were constantly at each other's throat whenever they chanced to be together. This was the first real Christmas Billie would be spending with Thad, here in Austin, and she was glad there would be no tension, no frustration.

The downstairs buzzer shattered Billie's reverie. Thinking it was Thad, she ran to the panel beside the front door and pushed the button to allow him into the building. Two minutes later she threw open the front door, ready to rush into his arms. But it wasn't Thad.

"Paul McDermott! How nice of you to stop by."

"Hello, Billie...."

"Come in. Can I get you a cup of coffee? You look frozen."

"Sounds nice.... Have I come at an inconvenient time?"

Billie was gracious but bewildered. She and the Coleman family doctor had hardly ever been on social terms. "Not at all.... I can hardly remember the last time I saw you, Paul. Wasn't it just before the accident in the garage?" Paul had been Seth's doctor.

"About then. I didn't have office hours today and I thought I'd come over. There's something I want to talk to you about." He accepted the proffered mug of steaming coffee, sipped it, then placed it on the table near his elbow. "Billie, there's something I thought you'd want to know. I'm aware that you and Moss no longer live together, but I also know that my coming here was required. I don't feel as though I'm breaking Moss's confidence by telling you this, since he didn't specifically ask me not to...." His jowly face seemed clouded and his words were halting. "Billie, this will be Moss's last Christmas. He's dying, Billie. Leukemia. And he refuses treatment. I stopped by Sunbridge today to check on him. He belongs in a hospital, but he won't hear of it. Is there a chance that the two of you can put aside your differences?... He needs someone, Billie. He needs you!"

Billie's mouth dropped open. The coffee mug trembled in her hand and the world seemed to sway under her feet. She'd heard the words, they'd registered, and now every fiber in her being was denying them. It was a long moment, a very long moment. Something inside her was railing against this betrayal. Ridiculous that she should feel this way, but she knew it was what she was feeling: betrayed. It was something she had become accustomed to dealing with in her life. Agnes, Seth, Moss, Maggie, and even Riley in his own way. "How . . . how long has Moss known?" she managed to ask. "You said he refuses treatment. Surely he knows how serious this is." Again the drum was beating inside her head. Moss knew something like this about himself, something so critical, and he had not told her.

Paul McDermott marveled at Billie's control. He'd always admired this shy, unassuming woman. "Moss has known for about six months. He came to me with complaints about his health and the tests have confirmed my suspicions. I've only recently learned that he's kept this from you. He's been alone for too long and he's been throwing himself into his work. He always has, I know, but this time it's almost with a vengeance. I don't think he ever recovered from Riley's death. He claims he has work to finish and it's quite important to him. Hospitals, tubes, medication, would prevent him from completing it, or so he says. Somehow, Billie, I believe him. I've seen men afraid of death and doctors, but that's not the case with Moss. It's as though he's resigned to it and simply must go on with his work."

"Yes, that would be typical of Moss. Do you think he'll finish it? His work, I mean."

Paul McDermott shrugged. "I have no knowledge of what he's working on, and if you're asking me how long he has . . ." The words trailed off. "Three months, six, a year? I have no way of knowing, Billie. No one does, really."

"Paul, how do I let Moss know you've told me?" Her voice sounded dry and raspy.

"I can't say for sure. I've had a long talk with him and at times I had the impression that he might tell you himself. And then again, maybe not. That's why I took it upon myself. At this point I don't know what he's feeling. I thought you'd be the best one to handle it. Can you, Billie?"

She nodded. "I'm trying." Then she said with more confidence, "Yes, I can handle it. It must have been terrible for Moss. He must have felt so alone."

"He is alone, Billie, but I knew he could count on you." McDermott was relieved. He'd known Moss for a very long time, and as a rule he didn't like to become emotionally involved with his patients.

Billie could only sit there dumbstruck. If only the doctor's voice weren't so kind. If only he would say something else, other words that didn't knife through her this way. "You should be getting home, Paul. It's the holiday season and you should be with your family." Family. A mother and a father. A husband and a wife. Children. Grandchildren. Family.

When Thad arrived back at Billie's apartment from his impromptu shopping spree, he found her sitting quietly in front of a long-dead fire, staring into the cold, blackened hearth. She was so still that for a moment he thought she'd fallen asleep, but there was something about the rigid set of her shoulders and the pallor of her skin that alarmed him. "Billie?" he said softly, dumping his armful of presents onto the sofa. "Billie, what's happened?" Alarms began blaring in his skull, and a dull, creeping sensation was prickling the back of his neck.

Billie kept her eyes averted. She didn't want to look into that beloved face and see the touches of gray near his temples, reminders of how much time had passed since she'd first known she loved him, evidence of how much time she had wasted. Most of all, she didn't think she could bear the expression in his eyes when she told him about Moss and the decision she'd come to during the past few hours, a decision that would break his heart.

He sat down beside her, immediately taking her into his arms. "Thinking about Riley?" he asked quietly, sympathy for her grief making his voice husky.

Billie shook her head. "No, I'm thinking about Moss." Suddenly she turned, wrapping him in her embrace. "Darling, I must tell you something, but first I want to tell you that I love you. I'll always love you. I need for you to know that, without a doubt. I need for you to believe in me."

Thad's apprehensions intensified. He accepted her embrace, feeling as though it would be the last time he would ever hold her in his arms, and listened while she told him of Paul

McDermott's visit and his news about Moss. With each word, Thad's heart sank lower and lower. He wished he didn't love her so much, so that he could argue with her, fight her, beat her if necessary, to make her see what she was doing to the both of them, to their love.

"I don't know if he'll have me," Billie was saying, "but I know I have to try. Can you understand, Thad?"

He buried his lips in her hair, inhaling the fragrance of her shampoo. "I can only try to understand. Yes, dammit, I *do* understand, but I don't want to! I don't want to share you again! I want you for myself, Billie. Dammit, I've waited too long as it is and I don't want to wait any longer!" In anger and frustration, he tore himself from her arms and paced the room in his long-legged stride, running his long fingers through his hair. "Don't look at me that way, Billie. Yes, I'm angry— hell, I'm mad! I think I could almost hate you right this minute. You're asking me to be noble again and I don't want to be. I wish I didn't care about Moss or the years I've known and loved him. I wish he were dead already and this was over and done with." Thad's face crumpled with anguish. "I love you, damn you, and you're taking yourself away from me!"

Billie ran to him, forcing her arms around him, giving him what comfort she could. He hadn't said anything she hadn't already told herself. All the hateful things; all the things she didn't mean. She felt Thad relent, felt his arms opening to her, and he held her for a long time. Then he left her arms and moved toward the door. She choked back a sob. He was leaving, then, leaving her with a broken heart. She wanted to cry out that he shouldn't leave her, not ever.

Thad stopped short of the door, standing before the desk, his eyes, like her own, immediately drawn to Sawyer's picture. He picked up the phone and dialed, waiting a long moment before someone answered.

"Hello! Moss? Thad here. Listen, I found I was able to make it to this great state of Texas for a good old-fashioned Christmas. I stopped by to see Billie and we were just thinking how good Sunbridge would look to us right now. Have you got your tree up? . . . Then we'll just have to come and decorate it for you!"

Billie sank down onto the sofa, burying her face in her hands, tears streaming from her eyes. Thad. Dear Thad.

"Yes, Sawyer is coming to spend Christmas with Billie;

she's coming in later this afternoon. . . . Just a minute, I'll ask her." Covering the receiver with his hand, Thad spoke to her. "Moss said his chauffeur is already in town and if we'd like, he can stay to pick Sawyer up at the airport. He sounds as though he's glad to have us come, Billie. We can leave now or we can wait for Sawyer."

Unable to meet his glance, Billie said simply, "Tell him to have Ephraim meet Sawyer. We can be at Sunbridge in a little over an hour, if he'd like. Ask him to have the heat turned on in my old studio."

There. It was so simple. Who ever said you can't go home again?

Sawyer Coleman, with the aid of the chauffeur, slid and skidded down the incline to Billie's studio. Laughing and giggling, she scooped up snow and tossed it at the stern man carrying her baggage. Her own shopping bags, filled with brightly wrapped packages, were scattered all about the lawn. "It's Christmas, Ephraim. Smile," she teased, then set about gathering up her damp packages and shoving them helter-skelter into her shopping bags. She could tell Ephraim felt that at twenty-one one should be more grown-up. Ha! Well, her grandmother loved a good snowball fight; she wouldn't have to coax her too hard.

"Grand! I'm home! Merry Christmas!"

"Sawyer! I was so worried. Was the plane late?"

"There's a storm out there." Young arms reached out and the embrace was warm, tender, and full of love. "You look wonderful, Grand. I bet you got some new accounts. But what's that sad look in your eyes? You always said a smile had to reach the eyes to count. I want to hear all about it."

Billie laughed. "And so you shall. All in good time. You are as gorgeous as ever. It must be all those carrots and string beans I made you eat when you were little."

Sawyer turned. "Thank you, Ephraim. I'm sorry about the snow. I'm just happy to be home. Being here at Sunbridge is such a surprise and it's something I always used to do when I was little. It wasn't fair to you. Forgive me."

Billie watched the stern chauffeur melt and smile at her granddaughter. Even the staunchest diehard responded to Sawyer's beautiful smile. When the door closed behind him, Billie questioned her. "What was that all about?"

"I felt like a snowball fight," Sawyer gurgled. "What do you say, Grand?"

"Sounds good to me. Let me get my boots and parka." How wonderful this child could make her feel. She could almost forget. . . . Almost.

Billie stopped in the hallway to take a long look at her granddaughter. Tall and slim, with honey-colored hair that fell to her shoulders in soft waves. For a minute Billie saw her as a little girl again, tucking her hair into a powder-blue parka with white lamb's wool around the edges. Those years, would they always haunt her? "I don't know which is bluer," Billie said affectionately, "your eyes or the parka. You should wear blue more often."

Sawyer preened for her grandmother. "Got my first semester marks ahead of schedule. Fourth in my class. I'm almost a certified aeronautical engineer. What do you think of that?"

"I think it's wonderful. . . . Sawyer, I want you to find the time to make your grandfather talk to you. I want him to know what you've done and how well you've done. It's important."

Sawyer sobered instantly. So, that was the reason for the sadness in her grandmother's eyes. She should have known. "I'll try. We have so much in common, but he simply isn't interested."

"He will be now. I think he's looking forward to your visit. You have to make him talk. Use every trick you know."

"I will, I will. Why are you so tense? Unwind. Come on, this snowball fight is just what we both need to get rid of all of our hostilities for a little while."

They rolled and tumbled in the carpet of white for what seemed like hours. They threw snowballs and pelted each other with great handfuls of the soft flakes. They laughed and shrieked until they were breathless.

Standing at the top of the hill with his cap pushed back on his head, Thad Kingsley watched the women with a wide grin on his face. "Hey," he called, "can you use another body?"

"Thad!" The cry of pure delight was almost more than Thad could bear, especially after the difficult hours he'd just spent with Moss.

"Uncle Thad!" How wonderful the young voice sounded, so much like Billie's had years ago.

"Well?"

{ 510 }

"If you think you can handle us, come on," Sawyer cried happily.

Thirty minutes later Thad's impeccable navy blues were covered with snow. His shiny black shoes were crusted with ice, and he complained that his feet were frozen and his ears were frostbitten.

"Let's hear it for womanhood!" Sawyer shouted.

"Yaaah!" Thad croaked hoarsely. "Now can we go in?"

"I was just getting warmed up," Billie teased. "I know I could last out here at least another two minutes. Had enough, Sawyer?"

"Yeah. I'm hungry. Why don't we call Grandpap to come down for something to eat?"

"Call him," Billie said, trying to shake the snow from her parka. "Better yet, since you love the cold, why don't you go up to the house and invite him in person?" She glanced at Thad for confirmation.

"Do that, Sawyer," he agreed. "I just left him a little while ago and I know he was going back into his workroom. Tear the old boy away, if you can."

Billie linked her arm in Thad's and they headed for the studio. "It's going to be a wonderful Christmas. I don't know if Moss will cooperate, but I sure as hell am going to try. *We're* going to try."

Thad frowned. "I just spent two hours with him and he didn't say a word to me, just wanted to talk about old times. If he knows about us, Billie, he didn't say anything. Something tells me he'll be glad for the company this Christmas."

Billie stood for a moment, looking up into Thad's face. "Have I ever told you I think you're wonderful?" she asked softly, watching the love flow into his eyes.

"You're pretty wonderful yourself, darling, and I love you, very much." Billie was aware of Thad's trembling hands and the moistness in his eyes. She pretended not to see. "You never took your suitcase up to the big house; it's still in the car. You'd better get out of that wet uniform. You can use the bathroom and I'll change in my room."

Billie and Thad were just getting the fireplace going when Sawyer bounded into the studio. "Hot toddies coming up!" she called gaily, heading directly for the kitchen to heat the water. "Grandpap said he already had something to eat but that he'd come down later for a drink. We'll all be together. Won't that be nice?"

"Yes, it will be very nice."

"Almost like a family again." Sawyer smiled brightly.

If there was one word in the English language Billie hated, it was "almost." In many ways, it summed up her life. Everything was almost. Almost married. Almost divorced. Almost loved. Moss was almost dead. God, she hated that word.

"I want to unpack and see if I can dry off my Christmas presents," Sawyer said. "You don't mind, do you, Grand?"

"Of course not. You go along. Thad and I will sit here before the fire and pretend that that little bit of snow invigorated us."

"Speak for yourself, woman," Thad teased. "If you could have gone on for another two minutes, I could have topped you at three."

"I have news for you both." Sawyer laughed. "I couldn't have stood that cold air for one more minute."

"What can I do?" Thad asked the minute Sawyer's door closed.

"Be there if he needs you. Be the friend you've always been."

"Moss was supposed to live forever," Thad said in a choked voice.

"I know. That's what we all thought. I don't think Moss was ever aware of his own mortality. Even now I don't know if he comprehends what's going on. Why?" Billie cried in a strangled voice.

"It's his time. It's going to happen to all of us."

"To us, yes. To Moss, never. I'm having trouble accepting it. I hope and pray that I'll do the right things, say the right words."

Billie's brokenhearted words tore at Thad. He should be comforting her. "Look at us. We're acting as though it's over. Moss would never want a wake. We have to accept it because there is nothing else we can do."

"He never came out of it after Riley died. Not even the death of his father affected him as intensely. That's when he sold Coleman Aviation and devoted himself to what I call his dream plane. It's all he's done for the past years. He blames himself for Riley's death.

"I remember when he returned from Japan after Riley had been killed. It was as if he'd simply caved in. I've often wondered what happened. I thought he went to see you. I never asked because I thought it was a private matter between the two of you. Can you tell me now what he spoke of and why he felt the need to go all the way to Japan to see you?"

Thad thought he was going to swallow his tongue. He knew someday this was going to come up. Still, he wasn't prepared for it. Should he lie? Should he tell the truth? Which was worse? He didn't know. She was looking at him so strangely, waiting for his answer. "He needed comforting. The kind of comforting one man can give another." Would she hear the lie in his voice?

Billie stared at Thad for a long time. The words didn't ring true, but this wasn't the time to press the issue. Let it lie. Don't raise old ghosts. Someday . . .

After a sketchy meal of canned soup and grilled cheese sandwiches, Sawyer, Billie, and Thad settled down in front of the fire, Christmas carols playing softly on the radio. At the sound of a light tapping on the door, Billie opened it to admit Moss. He looked much the same, thinner perhaps, a little more gray in the dark hair. The awkwardness of the moment was saved by Sawyer, who leaped up from her position on the floor and hid her hands behind her back. "Now don't look, Grandpap. I'm making you something for Christmas and it isn't finished yet. Close your eyes until I can hide it in my room."

Thad and Billie laughed aloud. "What's so funny?" Moss asked.

"We've seen what she's making. I hope you remember it's the thought that counts. Sawyer is definitely not a needle-woman."

"I heard that!" the girl protested. "But I do make extremely good toddies. Would you like one, Grandpap?"

"I could use one after that cold walk from the big house. . . . Say, Sawyer, would you come up to the house in the morning? There's something on my drawing board I'd like to show you."

"I'll be there at first light, Grandpap. I've been itching to get into that workroom of yours for years now."

Sawyer's statement seemed to please him; a broad grin struck his face. "Your grandmother has told me about your grade point averages in college. I'm proud of you, Sawyer. I have to be honest and say I never thought you'd stick it through. Aeronautics is hardly a profession for a woman."

"I'm not just any woman, Grandpap. I'm a Coleman woman."

"Yes, you are. And I'm proud."

Unable to contain herself, Sawyer spontaneously hugged

her grandfather. "I've waited a long time to hear you say that. I did what you always said and gave it my best shot."

"Well, it was a hell of a shot. We'll talk in the morning. Now I want your grandmother to tell me how her business is going." He turned to Billie. What was that she saw in his eyes? Was it regret? "That damn housekeeper of mine went out and bought bedsheets, all of them with your signature on them. Christ, all those flowers and Chinese pagodas. When I complained, she asked me if I'd prefer Mickey Mouse or Snoopy."

After a pleasant evening filled with laughter and reverie, Moss said he had to be getting back to the house if he was to get up in time for Sawyer's break-of-dawn visit.

"I'll go easy on you, Grandpap. How's ten o'clock?"

"Perfect. We'll rap in the morning. Isn't that what you youngsters say when you want to talk?"

"Right on, Grandpap." Sawyer laughed.

"You picked up some savvy along the way, too, I see."

"Along with my grit and spunk. Grand said I had to have those qualities or I couldn't be a Coleman."

"Well, you got them. Now if you'll excuse me, Billie, I have some work I want to finish before retiring. Thad, there's something I'd like to show you, if you have the time."

"My time is yours."

When the door closed behind them, Sawyer rushed to her grandmother and hugged her. "Did you hear what he said? I can hardly believe my ears. He wasn't putting me on, was he?"

Billie swallowed hard. "Yes . . . yes, I heard. Isn't it wonderful?"

"He's going to show me his dream plane, isn't he?"

"It doesn't pay to second-guess your grandfather. Just when you think you have him figured out, he does something completely out of character."

"What you mean is he throws you a curve and then you're back at square one. . . . You still love him, don't you, Grand?" It was said so casually, so softly, that Billie was taken off guard.

"I'll always love Moss." It was true, she realized. A part of her would always love the dynamic man she married. But that didn't mean she could never love anyone else, experience the kind of mutual giving and sharing that came later in life, when one was old enough to understand and appreciate it. Enduring love.

"I always loved Grandpap," Sawyer said quietly. "He was

all things to me. I know he had no use for girls. Riley was his life. Riley tried to explain him to me one day. I didn't understand what he was saying then, but I do now. It wasn't that Grandpap didn't love me or my mother, Aunt Susan, too. He never let his thinking go beyond a male heir. He couldn't conceive that any of us could contribute. That's what it's all about, Grand, contributing. Grandpap Seth used to say that women belonged in the house taking care of their men. There's something beautiful about that. I, for one, would never dispute the fact that men are stronger—physically, I mean. When it counts, though, we're the stronger ones. Look at the way you handled Riley's death. Grandmam's, too. You grieved, but you didn't fall to pieces. You grew and made a life for yourself despite everything that went on here. I used to hear you cry at night, Grand, when Grandpap had socked it to you in one way or another. Uncle Thad loves you, you know."

How like Sawyer to talk about one thing and then get to the heart of the real matter without a break in the conversation. "Yes, I know," Billie replied. "He's a wonderful person. He's been a magnificent friend, and I don't know what I would have done without his support at times. I'll always be grateful."

"Grateful is all right. Love is something else. It's there. If you want it, don't be afraid to reach out for it."

"If the time is ever right, I just might do that. . . . Isn't all of this a bit heavy for this time of night?"

"Okay, now tell me what you want me to do. I'm all yours till the end of January."

"Christmas has to be as special as we can make it. Christmas Eve dinner and Christmas brunch are all yours. Someone has to fetch a tree and it has to be set up and decorated. There's still shopping to do. . . . Look, I don't think either of us wants to go to bed, so why don't we make some lists?"

The two women were on their second pot of hot chocolate when the phone rang. They looked at each other. "Answer it," Billie said nervously. Who would be calling the studio at a quarter to six in the morning?

"Of course I'm awake. Isn't everyone?" Sawyer said cheerfully into the phone. "I'll be there in two minutes.

"Grandpap. He's waiting for me," Sawyer called over her shoulder. Billie smiled at the blue streak zipping up the parka, catapulting through the doorway.

Outside her grandfather's workroom, Sawyer wet her lips, pinched her cheeks, and brushed impatiently at her long hair.

Here we go, she thought. Taking a deep breath, she crossed her fingers and tapped softly on the door.

"Come in. You said two minutes. It's—"

"Three. I lost a boot coming up the hill in the snow." Sawyer held her foot aloft to show the soaking-wet sock.

Moss nodded. "Don't ever let little things stand in your way. Take your socks off and sit over there by the heater."

Sawyer obeyed. Her eyes were hungry, devouring the room that had been forbidden for so long. She loved it, loved every drawing, every scrap of paper, and every pencil in the room. "Can I look around?" Moss nodded.

He watched keenly as Sawyer walked from one wall to the other, finally standing next to him at his drawing board. "Is it done?" she asked in awe.

"Almost."

"When?"

"Things are slowing me down. I've been working day and night for some time now. I just don't know."

"Do you have a deadline?"

"A personal one," Moss replied wryly.

"What can I do?"

"I'm not sure yet. Let's sit down and talk."

CHAPTER THIRTY-SEVEN

It was noon when Thad sauntered downstairs and quietly turned the knob on the door of Moss's workroom. He smiled. Moss was leaning back in a deep chair and Sawyer was sitting at his feet with one boot on and one foot bare. They were deep in conversation. Thad closed the door softly and dressed for outdoors. Billie would want to know about this. He couldn't wait to tell her.

"It's something I've prayed for for a long time," she said, smiling. "But it does leave me with a problem." Quickly she showed Thad the lists they'd each made. "Sawyer was going to fetch a tree this morning—get it up and decorated."

Thad took the lists from Billie's hands. "Well, why don't

the two of us take care of all of this together?" he asked. "We could go out now to chop down a tree and drag it back to the house and trim it."

"Oh, Thad, that'd be wonderful! ... Would you like to take the sleigh? There's one in the big barn. Seth always kept it for the big storms. I imagine it's rusty, but if we oiled it, we could get it to slide. What do you think?"

"I think that's a marvelous idea. The big barn, you say?" Billie nodded. "I'll get a saw and rope and meet you there. Dress warmly. It looks like it's going to snow again."

There was something festive, something inspiring, about choosing and cutting down a Christmas tree, and Billie enjoyed the outing in the horse-drawn sleigh. Snuggled with Thad beneath a thick lap robe, she was aware of his body warmth and his powerful presence. Dear Thad. What would she do without him in her life—her one-man emotional support system? She needed him so, especially now. She felt so confused, so ... vulnerable.

"How about that one over there?" Thad asked. "The blue spruce? It's an eight-footer easy."

"You're the man with the saw. The ceilings at Sunbridge are twelve feet high. It's perfectly shaped," Billie said, climbing from the sleigh.

"I'll loop this rope around the middle of the tree, and when I say pull, you pull. But stand clear. I'm going to tie this end of the rope to the back of the sleigh, so you're going to be pulling slack. Can you do it?"

"Certainly," Billie bristled. "I've helped cut down trees for years. I'm no novice at this. It's you Yankees that can't get your act together."

"I'll remember you said that. Hold fast now. I'm going to start sawing."

It was totally unexpected. The minute the monstrous tree hit the ground, Billie herself slid down the side of the sleigh and collapsed in tears. Thad stood by helplessly as sobs racked her body. Then he dropped to his knees and pulled her close to his chest. "Go ahead and cry, Billie. Get it all out."

"Oh, Thad, what am I to do? I don't know if I can see this through. If I had gone ahead and divorced Moss, I wouldn't have to ... I wouldn't ..."

"Yes, you would. You'd be the first one on the scene and we both know it."

"I'm so mixed up. I was beginning to get my life in order

and thinking about starting the divorce proceedings again. Moss didn't need me. Months went by when we didn't see or speak to each other. When I think about it, I get so sick—all those years, Thad! My God, all those years."

Thad stroked her hair and listened. He felt helpless, out of his depth.

"All these years you've been there when I needed you," Billie said, weeping quietly now. "You never took advantage of my situation. You never made demands. How has your love for me endured all these years?"

"I don't know. I just know that my feelings have never wavered, never faltered. They have endured and will continue to endure. . . . In a way it seems heartless to be talking about love now when Moss . . . what I mean is, I feel so disloyal."

"I want you to understand about my commitment to Moss."

"Shhh," Thad said, laying his finger on her lips. "I understand. You don't have to explain anything to me. It isn't necessary. . . . Did anyone ever tell you you're a mess when you cry?"

"I seem to recall you saying that to me at one time or another. Forgive me for breaking down like this. I'm glad it happened here, away from the house. Isn't it funny . . . I don't mind you seeing me like this, but I don't want anyone else to see how vulnerable I am."

"I don't know if this has anything to do with anything, but I once read somewhere that Freud agonized all his life over the meaning of the word love. When he lay dying, someone asked him for his definition of love, and his answer was 'Love is letting the other person see your vulnerability.' I think I have to go along with his answer."

Billie smiled through her tears. "How like you to have the right words. Someday I'll let you know if it was the right answer."

"If you're done bawling, let's get this tree home," Thad said hoarsely.

It was going to be all right.

It was a very special Christmas. Moss closed the door to his workroom and joined them all in the great living room with the huge sparkling tree. He made every effort to join in the holiday spirit. Thad watched as his friend's eyes traveled from Billie to Sawyer and back to Billie. In the end, these two women, whom he had neglected, had discounted all his life,

{ 518 }

were going to help him fulfill his dream. How ironic that it had come to this. When he shook hands with Moss the day after Christmas, he knew he would never see him again. At the last moment Moss reached out both arms and drew his friend close. "Hey, you damn Yankee, I don't think I ever thanked you for being my friend. A guy couldn't ask for a better friend. We go back a long time. Look, if . . . ahh, what I mean . . ."

"I'll take care of her," Thad said in a choked voice.

Moss's eyes were full of unasked questions. Thad nodded. Moss sighed wearily. "Does Billie know?" Thad nodded a second time, unable to trust his voice. "Take care of yourself, Thad."

Thad could feel his throat constrict. Tears trickled down his cheeks. He made no move to wipe them away. Neither man seemed willing to let go of the other. "You too. If there's anything I can do . . . if there's anything you want . . . an arm, a leg, a kidney, send out a call."

"How about your heart? That was always special. You always had heart, Thad."

"It's yours."

"Get out of here before you have me blubbering like baby." One last bone-crushing hug and the door was closed behind Thad. Tears streaming down his cheeks as he stood outside in the freezing cold. He fished for a handkerchief to wipe his eyes and blow his nose. Then turned smartly, eyes dry, and gave a stiff salute to the closed door.

From his position behind the lace curtain on the door, Moss's salute was just as snappy.

Sawyer closed herself in Moss's workroom, allowing her grandfather and grandmother the time they needed to be alone. The blueprints in front of her blurred. How was it all going to end? She wished she knew. For now, she had to make a pretense of working until it was time to leave for the airport. Aunt Amelia and Rand were coming for a post-Christmas visit. Sawyer was excited; it had been ages since she'd seen them. Rand had to be a handsome devil. His pictures in his RAF uniform made her mouth water. Maybe it was time to start thinking about a man in her life. . . .

Minutes later, Sawyer slipped quietly out the side door of the workroom and left the house.

* * *

Billie sat on the sofa with Moss. Neither seemed sure of what to say. Moss took the initiative. "I would have told you. I'm sorry that Paul got to you first. I suppose I was trying to find the right time and the right words. I know now there is no right time and no right words. I need you, Billie. You and Sawyer. I can't do it alone. Maybe if I had more time, more strength, I could pull it off, but I'm no fool. This is one dream you're going to have to finish for me. There's not another soul in this world I'd trust to do this for me."

Billie reached for Moss's hand. She nodded. "Tell me what to do, what you want of me."

"I explained the intricacies of it all to Sawyer. She understands. The girl has a head on her shoulders. I never knew that. There's a lot of things I never knew. A lot of regrets, Billie. If I had done this . . . if I had said that . . . this is where I am now. There's so little time."

"Treatment?"

"No. It's too late for that. I need a clear head for what has to be done. Sawyer says she's free till the end of January and has even agreed not to return to school if I need her. Time now, Billie, is my enemy. I have to do this. I have to succeed. I'm realistic enough to know I may not make my deadline, and that's why I want your promise, yours and Sawyer's, that you'll finish it up for me."

"I promise. You look tired, Moss. Why don't you rest for a while? Amelia will be here soon and you're going to want to spend some time with her. Lay here on the sofa. I promise to wake you when they get here. I'll get a blanket."

Moss lay back on the sofa pillows, a grimace of pain stretching across his face. Billie returned with a colorful afghan Jessica had made and covered him. "Billie, I'm sorry."

There was no use pretending she didn't know what he was talking about. The time for pretense was gone. "I know you are, Moss. Sleep now."

"Billie . . ."

"Yes, Moss."

"I really am sorry. Somewhere I got off the track and couldn't get back on. Forgive me."

"There's nothing to forgive, Moss. It's past now. History, you always said. I have to be honest . . . I do forgive you; but I can't forget." She bent over and kissed his cheek. Through her tears she could see his pain-filled eyes.

"You'll make it, won't you, Billie?"

"You can count on it, Moss," she whispered as she brushed the hair back from her husband's forehead.

"What are you thinking, Billie? Not feeling pity for me, are you?" Moss asked after several quiet moments, watching Billie stare out into space.

"No, not pity. I was just thinking how this is really the first time you've ever talked with me this way. It's the first time you've come to me for help. After all these years."

"I always knew you were there for me, Billie. I always knew I could count on you from the first day we were married."

Billie turned her head, her eyes searching his. Her fingers had already found his hand and she willed some of her strength to pour into him. "In many ways, Moss, today is my wedding day. This is the day of commitment. We've shared something together, you and I. I've always loved you, Moss; I love you now, and if I could, I'd live it all again, even the bad times." Billie swallowed past the lump in her throat. Tears coursed down her cheeks.

"And Thad? You love him, don't you?"

Billie nodded. "Yes, Moss, I do. But there's one thing he can never give me, one thing that I need. My dream, Moss. Only you can give me that. The home, the family . . . our children. It's all I've ever wanted and it's what I still want." She was crying now, trembling with the force of her sobs. Moss took her into his arms, sharing her tears, grieving for the past.

"I don't deserve what you're doing for me, Billie. I've never deserved you. I knew it then and I know it now. I'll confess something to you, Billie. Whenever I would think about dying I always knew I wanted it to happen while I was in your arms." His lips brushed her cheek and their tears mingled.

Sawyer Coleman dug her hands deep into the pockets of her ranch mink jacket, a gift from Moss. The holiday atmosphere of Austin's airport was gone, leaving only a few disgruntled, weary travelers who kept their eyes on the clock and their ears tuned for flight announcements.

Pan American's flight 691 had landed and the passengers were deplaning. Aunt Amelia had said she and Rand would clear customs in New York when they changed flights for Austin. Sawyer watched now as a column of passengers made their way up the long carpeted ramp to the main terminal, struggling with their carry-on luggage as they maneuvered to the escalator. She spotted Aunt Amelia and Rand almost immediately and waved. Her mouth felt dry and she could feel a warm flush on her cheeks as Rand scooped her into his arms. "Little Sawyer, all grown up," he teased with a glint in his deep brown eyes.

"Sawyer, you gorgeous creature!" Amelia trilled. "Didn't I tell you she was beautiful?" she said to Rand. "Now unhand that girl so she can give me a proper kiss."

"You should have said ravishing," Rand corrected Amelia as he released Sawyer. "You were only a tad when I saw you last. Let's see, you must be all of eighteen or so. Am I correct?"

Sawyer bristled. "I'm past twenty-one, if you must know." She kissed Amelia soundly on the cheek and offered her own cheek to Rand, who turned her around and kissed her full on the mouth. Sawyer gasped, half in delight and half in annoyance.

"Pretty girls are my downfall."

"He's telling you the truth, Sawyer. Beware of him, he has a young woman hiding behind every pole and bush. My son is very handsome; he looks like Robert Redford, don't you think?"

It was Rand's turn to look uncomfortable and Sawyer pressed her advantage. "Oh, I don't know, Aunt Amelia. Perhaps, in a certain light."

"Why does one simple statement make me sound as though I've a wart on the end of my nose?" Rand asked coolly. Brazen, a little brash, but oh, so feminine. She was beautiful and she could blush so prettily. Aunt Billie had described Sawyer as being independent as hell and he had to agree as he met her level gaze and the slightly insolent curve of her smile.

"You said it, not I," Sawyer bantered lightly. "Look, the baggage is starting to come up. Get it together and I'll get a porter. My car is out front."

"Isn't she a darling child, Rand?" Amelia prompted as she and Rand walked to the baggage area. "I can't believe she's twenty-two, or soon will be. That's old enough to be married. Brainy, too. Runs in the Coleman family. Billie did an amazing job of raising her. Almost as good as I did with you," she said fondly.

"She's not a child, Mother. Those aren't the eyes of a child," Rand said knowledgeably.

"She'll always be a child to me, as will you, here in my heart. Sawyer is the last of the Colemans, and from what Billie tells me, she's taken Riley's place in many ways with her grandfather."

Amelia settled herself in the backseat of Billie's Mercedes while Rand slipped in beside Sawyer. Checking for traffic, Sawyer gunned the engine and the luxurious sedan growled to life as it spewed snow and ice in its wake. Rand closed his eyes in mock horror. Amelia smiled. This grandniece of hers was just what Rand needed. Wait till she told Billie.

"Where did you learn to drive?" Rand demanded as Sawyer narrowedly missed a snow plow and a pickup truck stuck on the side of the road.

"Actually, I taught myself. I do better flying. Don't tell me you're nervous driving with me."

"Nervous? Petrified would be more like it," Rand said through clenched teeth.

The heavy car ground to a halt, narrowly missing a snowbank, its tires spinning on an ice patch. Sawyer clenched the wheel in her gloved hands. She turned slightly to face Rand. "The way I see it, Rand, you have two choices. You can either walk the rest of the way to Sunbridge or you can sit there quietly. Make your choice."

"How far is it to Sunbridge?" Rand asked.

Sawyer burst out laughing. "Forty miles, the way the crow flies. That tender English skin of yours will freeze right up. What's it going to be?"

Rand threw up his hands. The laughter was there, the tone was half-teasing, but the eyes were something else. She would have booted his tail out of the car. Goddamn it, where had this one been all his life? Growing up. He decided he liked the finished product. "Drive."

The rearview mirror told Sawyer her aunt approved. Why was her heart beating so fast and why was her mouth so dry? This man was having an effect on her she didn't like. He was too damn handsome, too damn knowing, too damn observant. It was obvious she wasn't what he'd expected, just as he wasn't quite what she had expected. She wasn't in the market for a fling or any kind of a relationship. She had things to do and she was totally committed to Billie and Moss. Whatever feelings she was experiencing for this man would only clutter things up. Besides, he probably thought she was too young for him.

Most of the trip was made in silence. Amelia dozed occasionally in the corner of the warm car. Rand sat with his arms crossed against his chest, a grim look on his face. Finally he spoke. "You have a pilot's license?"

Sawyer nodded. "I will also soon have a degree in aeronautical engineering."

Rand's eyes glowed. It was obvious he approved of what he saw, what he heard. "Shall we call a truce?" he asked, smiling.

Sawyer looked over at him. "What you see is what you get. Don't interfere in my life. Don't for one minute think I can't cut it because I'm a woman." She paused. "Truce."

Amelia smiled contentedly. She'd known all along these two would like each other. These little spats, these little declarations and assertions, were all part of getting acquainted. If there was one person she knew in this world, it was Rand, and Rand's eyes were telling her something was happening to him.

The crunch of tires on the hard-packed snow alerted Billie that Sawyer was back from the airport. She felt suddenly old and brittle when she got up from the comfortable chair. She checked on Moss, then went to the foyer to meet the new arrivals, careful to close the door behind her. Moss needed his rest and from now on she would see that he got it.

"Amelia, how wonderful you look!"

Amelia wrapped her arms around Billie and hugged her. "This is where we both lie to each other and say how neither of us has changed."

"It's not a lie. You look the same, but older."

"How's that for flattery?" Amelia laughed. "You remember Rand?"

Billie held out her hand to the tall, handsome young man standing beside Sawyer. "It's been a long time. The last time I saw you, you were clutching Sally Dearest for dear life."

Sawyer hooted with laughter. "Sally Dearest? Who or what was Sally Dearest?"

Rand threw back his head and laughed. It was a pleasant sound and Billie liked him instantly. "Sally Dearest was my cat when I was three years old. She died when I was twelve."

"That's sad." Sawyer gurgled.

"They've been baiting each other all the way from the airport," Amelia said happily. Billie grinned. Amelia was already matchmaking. Sawyer, too, had a gleam in her eye. The look on Rand's face was appreciative.

"How's Moss?" Amelia asked anxiously.

{ 524 }

Billie shook her head. "Not too well. He's sleeping right now. Let's go into the library. I had fire going a while ago and we can replenish it."

"I'm going to take Rand to the workroom to show him the plane. If Grandpap wants me, that's where I'll be."

Settled in the library alone with Amelia, Billie handed her a glass of sherry. "That's quite a young man you've raised, Amelia. You're very good with children. Rand and then Susan."

"I think it was simply that they were good children to begin with." She laughed lightly. "I know how difficult it must have been for you to turn Susan over to me that way."

"There was little else to do at the time, considering the mess Maggie had created. We all felt it would be better for Susan, although I must admit, I never dreamed she would take to you and England like a duck to water. I'm proud of her, Amelia. She's made quite a name for herself and she seems very happily married. Even if we're not close as some mothers and daughters, that doesn't mean I can't admire her. And I always had Sawyer. It was like having a second chance."

"She's wonderful. But then, she always was. And she certainly enjoys all the beauty in this family. No, I take that back. You still lay claim to quite a bit of it yourself, Billie. When I look at Sawyer I see you thirty years ago. She's as much like you as Rand is like his father. Spitting image."

"Then I can see why you fell head over heels in love with Rand's father. Such wonderful blond good looks. He must be thirty-five, thirty-six?"

"He's thirty-eight and please don't remind me! The plastic surgeons tell me I've only one more face lift left in this lifetime! God, I wish I had your skin."

Billie laughed and refilled Amelia's glass. The conversation became serious. "I have something to tell you, Amelia. You're going to have to be strong. It's Moss. He has leukemia. There's not much time left."

It took several minutes of disbelief and intense questioning before Amelia seemed to accept the truth. "I can't believe it," she cried. "Not Moss. He's all I have left, Billie." Hard sobs tore at her body.

"That's not true. You've Rand and Susan and me. We've still got one other. Amelia, you must be strong. Don't make this any harder for Moss than it already is. Promise me you'll get hold of yourself." She gathered the woman into her arms,

{ 525 }

comforting her. Poor Amelia. Poor, lonely Amelia. Throughout her life Moss's love and approval had always been there for her, steadying her.

"You know, Billie"—Amelia blew her nose and wiped her eyes—"when things were roughest when I was growing up here at Sunbridge under Pap's disapproving eyes, it was always Moss I could go to with my troubles. He stood up to Pap for me, protected me. And even when I made a shambles of my life, I always knew I could count on him to love me."

"I know, I know," Billie soothed.

"When I see him, he'll know I've been told. He'll see it. There's no way I can hide it."

"I'm not asking you to hide your feelings, Amelia. Of course you should let Moss know how much you love him, how much you'll miss him. Tell him how much he's meant to your life. You're his sister, the two of you have shared the same beginnings and memories. All I'm asking of you is that you accept his decision to refuse treatment. Allow him his dignity. Don't press him, Amelia. Think of his suffering before you think of your own."

Amelia squeezed Billie's hand. "Of course you're right. You know me so well. When you told me that he was refusing treatment I'd already decided that I was going to force him to go to a hospital. Now I'll simply let him know I'll always be here if he needs me."

"He'll need you, Amelia. He'll always need you."

The days that followed were intense and frenzied. Moss's eyes followed Billie constantly. He'd never in all the years they'd been married paid this much attention to her. Now his unwavering gaze was direct and speculative. She sensed he was assessing, gauging, measuring, and *liking* what he saw. While this pleased her, it didn't mean half of what she'd thought it would. She no longer *needed* his approval; but it was nice to know it was there. How ironic.

It was the evening of the last full day of Amelia and Rand's visit. Arm in arm, Sawyer and Rand burst into the sunroom, where Billie, Amelia, and Moss were deep in conversation. "If there are no objections," Sawyer interrupted, "Rand is taking me to dinner in town. Auntie Amelia, it's all right with you, isn't it?"

Amelia nodded agreeably. "Go along. But"—she held

up a warning finger—"our flight leaves at seven in the morning, so try and get back before then. It's a long ride to the airport."

"We'll bloody well be back by then," Rand replied. "After dinner this child insists we dance the night away. Texas style." He grimaced. "She's taking me to a place called Dirty Nellie's." Rand looked at Billie. "Will I come out alive?"

"Good question." Billie laughed. "Trust Sawyer."

When the couple left the sunroom, Moss turned to Billie and Amelia with a strange look on his face. "Isn't he a little old for Sawyer?"

Amelia's jaw dropped. Billie blinked. "Old?" she echoed. "Moss, they're only going out to dinner. Rand is leaving in the morning. I wouldn't worry."

"Rand has scores of young women fawning over him back home." Amelia smiled. "Don't rattle yourself over this little harmless dinner."

Moss snorted. "Women are supposed to be astute where romance is concerned. Why haven't either of you picked up on Rand's feelings for Sawyer? I certainly saw it. Or does it take a man to recognize the symptoms?" he asked irritably. "Take him home tomorrow, Amelia, and don't bring him back until this project is finished. Sawyer has things to do now and I don't want her distracted."

Billie's gaze flew to Amelia. "We'll deal with it, Moss," Amelia said briskly. "They're sensible adults, and Sawyer knows what's at stake. . . . Why don't you relax and take a small nap. Billie, I could use some help in packing. This way, if everything is done, all we'll have to do is hop out of bed, dress, and be on our way."

Moss nodded and closed his eyes. Christ, how he hated these forced naps his body demanded of him. So little time and he had to sleep five times a day. He was half-aware of Billie and Amelia leaving the room. Once he tried to open his heavy lids. He loved to see Billie walk, that charming, crooked little walk that made her rear end sway from side to side. But he was just too tired. He would make a point of watching her tomorrow.

Sawyer was uneasy. Had it been a mistake to spend this last evening alone with Rand? Perhaps she should have said she was busy. But she wanted to be with him, wanted to sit across from him and feel those dark eyes warm her. It was just as well he was leaving in the morning. But these last few hours tonight were hers.

Rand's capable square hand reached for Sawyer's across the tabletop. His golden handsomeness was illuminated by the tapered candles and the reflected light of the chandeliers. "I've always loved England, and no matter where I was I couldn't wait to return. This time it's different. I don't want to go back. You're quite a girl, Sawyer Coleman, and I think—no, I know that if I stayed I would . . . Do you believe I can't get the words out?"

Sawyer tried for a good-natured smile. "I'm sorry you're leaving. We just got to know each other. I've enjoyed the time we spent together in my grandfather's workroom."

"I'm more than a little in love with you, Sawyer. We've both skirted around it, but Christ, I'm leaving tomorrow."

"I know. I know. I can't get involved. I have a commitment to my grandparents. What kind of person would I be if I turned my back on my responsibilities?"

"I'm not asking you to do that."

"Listen to me, Rand," Sawyer said, leaning over the table, both hands clasped in his. "I'm one of those people who can only do one thing at a time. This project has top proprity. If I slip or deviate even a little, I won't be able to get back on track. It wouldn't be fair to you, either. By now you must know I don't do things halfway. It's one hundred percent or not at all."

Rand nodded. "For a while I thought it was my age. What you're telling me is it's chin up and all that English rubbish. I thought you wild-west characters didn't deny your feelings."

"I'm not denying my feelings. I'm saying I can't act on them. I want you to come back. I know you promised my grandmother you would come if she needed you. I'd like to think that holds for me, too." Rand's answer was in his eyes. Sawyer swallowed hard and squeezed his hand.

"Grand has taken on quite a challenge seeing that Pap's plane gets off the ground. I just hope and pray we haven't bitten off more than we can chew. Oh, Rand, it's simply horrible, but I don't think he'll ever see his dream become a reality. Every day takes its toll on him. I'm sure you've noticed. I can see the day-to-day changes in him and it breaks my heart. I have to stay here and do what I can."

"Moss's dream has been shared by many others. There's been talk of a slant-wing craft for as long as I can remember.

I want to go on record right now, Sawyer: That specification we've been fighting over the past few days isn't going to work." Rand reached for a pen out of his breast pocket and made scratches on the back of the menu.

"I think this design has a good chance, Sawyer. Other oblique-winged craft have been tried, but as far as I know, no one has tried cantilevering the wing span, as you want to do."

Rand scratched a detailed design, one that had become very familiar to Sawyer over the past two weeks. The craft was a long needle-nose design with a single wing positioned above the fuselage. For operation at low speeds or takeoff and landings, the wing would be positioned conventionally, at right angles to the craft. For flight at higher speeds, the wing pivoted at an oblique angle of up to sixty degrees with the fore and aft centerline of the fuselage, reducing drag and promising greater speed and range without an increase in fuel consumption.

"Damn you, that cantilevering will work!" Sawyer cried. "I had the best engineers working on it. Why are you being so stubborn? You haven't been able to give me one good, justifiable reason except gut instinct that it won't work. That isn't good enough. I deal in facts and figures. I thought intuition was a female trait."

Rand held up his hand. "Okay, okay, you win. The specification stays. What I think Moss is really on to is the unusual composite material. Strong and lightweight. The foam core he's developed is revolutionary. He's quite a man, your grandfather. I wish I'd known him better all these years."

Sawyer felt momentarily drained. Arguing with Rand over something so important made her feel terrible. She was right; she *had* to be right. Every engineer in the plant said so. Yet she trusted Rand's opinions and knew he wasn't just trying to be difficult. "There's not a chance in hell that that plane could go down. I'd stake my life on it," Sawyer said forcefully.

"It won't be your life, Sawyer; it will be the life of the test pilot."

"I'll take that responsibility."

"Taking responsibility is one thing; living with the result is something else entirely."

"Damn you, Rand, don't keep doing this to me. You can't shake my confidence. Pap trusts me and so do all the other engineers."

"They don't love you the way I do," Rand murmured.

{ 529 }

There was a pause. Then Sawyer said quietly, "This isn't supposed to happen."

"The one thing you can't count on in this world is emotion."

"Maybe you can't count on it, but you can control it," Sawyer countered desperately.

"I hope you do better at it than I'm doing."

"I won't let *anything* interfere or stop me. Accept that, Rand."

"I have. Why do you think I'm leaving tomorrow? But I'll be back. Now *that's* something you can count on."

Sawyer nodded miserably. The tears glistening on her lashes tore at Rand. "Shall we order?" she said with false bravado. "I'm starving!"

"I'll bet you are, you little savage." He laughed, trying for levity. "You're always hungry."

"Don't blame me," she chided, looking up at him with mischief in her eyes. "If I can't nourish my soul, then my stomach takes precedence."

"Sometimes, Sawyer, I think you need a good spanking just to remind you to behave like a lady. And watch those devilish eyes. I just might change my mind about leaving tomorrow."

CHAPTER
{{{{{{{{ THIRTY-EIGHT *}}}}}}}}*

The long days of winter were upon them. Moss's workroom was cramped and on the dark side of the house, so Billie demanded that he move everything out to her studio, where the sun could shine through the glass doors and there was enough space for the technical engineers and designers in Moss's employ to move about freely. Moss's oblique-winged aircraft was becoming a reality. Manufacture of component parts and the construction of the plane itself had been under way in one of the old Coleman Aviation hangars since early last summer. All systems were go.

Billie set aside her own business, completing only the work for which she was already under contract. Now she spent her days and many of her evenings working beside Moss, answering the telephone, setting up schedules, and doing general dogwork. The studio was also ideal because of the proximity of the bedroom. In the big house the bedrooms were far removed from the workroom, and Moss could not be persuaded to leave his work and lie down. Here, with the work proceeding just outside the door, Billie could more easily cajole him into taking a nap. The little kitchen in the studio became a central hub from which delicious aromas of freshly brewed coffee, soups, stews, and snacks could tempt Moss's appetite. So much activity, so much work, yet nothing could forestall the ravages of the disease attacking his body. By will alone, Moss presented himself each day to his men, never allowing his optimism to flag. He worked them hard, praised them often, and was genuinely grateful for their energy and loyalty. It was when he was alone with Billie that he allowed his doubts to show. "You'll see it's finished, won't you, Billie?" he would plead. And always she would promise.

One afternoon in early May, Moss went into the bedroom without prompting. Billie called the crew chief over, worry darkening her eyes. "I think you and the men should make an early day of it, Joe. Things aren't good with Moss."

"We'll leave as soon as we clear up a little, Billie. He's been looking bad all week." The burly man shook his head, already grieving. "Don't you think you should get him to a hospital or something?"

"No, Joe. He doesn't want that. Dr. McDermott comes out every other day to check on him and keep him comfortable. He told me just yesterday that Moss was already in renal failure. It won't be long now."

"Go to him, Billie. I'll take care of things out here and before we leave I'll take the phone off the hook so he won't be disturbed."

"Thanks, Joe." Her eyes were already wandering to the closed bedroom door. "Tell the men thanks for everything and I think they should take the next few days off. I'll keep in touch."

For the next three days Billie remained at Moss's side. He was no longer able to get out of bed and he made feeble jokes about being as weak as a kitten. Paul McDermott had told Billie what to expect and wanted to send out a nurse to help her. Billie rejected the offer. "I'll let you know if I need help. Right now, I'm certain I can manage."

"I wish you'd let me put him in the hospital. He's in no condition to object. It would make it easier on everyone."

"Perhaps on everyone else, but not on Moss, and he's the only one who counts now."

Moss lay in Billie's bed, late-afternoon sun filtering through the draperies. Dark shadows stained his cheeks beneath his eyes. He'd lost a great deal of weight during the past months, but he was still handsome, and fire and purpose burned in those summer-blue eyes. Billie sat in her chair quietly while he slept, studying his face, committing it to memory. Death stalked outside the door and neither prayer nor denial would chase it away.

"Billie . . ." The sound of her name in the quiet of the room startled her. His voice seemed stronger, some of the old vitality singing in it. "Billie, come and lie down beside me." It was a question; it was a plea.

She settled herself on the bed beside him, resting her head against his shoulder, her arm wrapped around his middle, holding him. "This is a hell of a way to say good-bye, isn't it? I hate leaving you, Billie. These past months have shown me what we could have had all these years. If only I'd allowed you into my life."

"Shhh. You don't have to say these things. I already know them. There's so little I don't know, darling."

"Am I? Am I your darling?"

"You're my first love, Moss. You know what they say, don't you? First love, last love."

He nodded his head, not trusting his voice. After a moment: "But there are other loves, Billie. Different loves, and that's what I want for you. I know what you and Thad mean to each other and I want you both to be happy. I've been a bitter, foolish man, and I'm so sorry."

"There's no forgiveness needed, Moss. I'm so glad we've had this time together, this time to know each other and rediscover the reasons we ever loved each other."

Long moments. Eternities. "Billie?" Moss whispered. "I'm afraid. I don't know what's waiting for me . . . there."

Billie bit her lips, wincing back tears, choking back sobs. She stroked his cheeks, pretending not to feel the moisture beneath her fingers. "Don't be afraid, Moss. Have faith. There are so many whom we know, whom we've loved, waiting to help you, to meet you."

"Do you believe that?" His breathing was labored; he couldn't seem to catch his breath. "Tell me."

"I believe, darling. I believe one day I'll see Riley again. And Seth and my mother. All those who have gone before, waiting."

Moss nodded, accepting her faith as his own. Quietly, he repeated each of the names, always coming back to Riley. "Pray for me, Billie. Pap always had a lot to say about a good woman's prayers."

Again silence. Moss's breathing became rhythmical, long and deep, skittering quickly to short, shallow breaths, and then becoming long and deep again. Even as she held him she sensed the life force leaving him. His eyes fluttered; it was as though he were pulling himself back for one last moment.

"I love you, Billie, with all my heart."

"I know you do, Moss. I know."

They were the last words he ever spoke to her. Words she would remember for the rest of her days. Words that should have been spoken so many years ago. At last he had said them.

Dudley Abramson, the Coleman family lawyer, had to be almost as old as Moses, Billie thought as she watched him make a production out of opening his briefcase. His bony fingers clawed at the stiff crackling papers, finally separating them in the order he wanted. Small eyes crowned by bushy snow-white brows scanned the room. Wills were his favorite legal transaction. He loved watching greedy faces, disappointed faces, faces lit up with genuine surprise. This assemblage would offer no surprises. Moss Coleman's will was cut and dried; there would be nothing to contest. He felt a little disappointed. Still, a will was a will, and he'd best get on with it and put all of them out of their misery. He cleared his rattly throat and took a swipe at his few thinning hairs.

"Are we all gathered here today, all those I sent letters to?" He ran down the list: Billie, Maggie, and Susan; then after a second, Sawyer. He could feel Maggie's tension and bristled. Everyone knew that Sawyer Coleman was Maggie's illegitimate daughter. He sniffed. They weren't going to like this one bit. No sir, not one little bit. He felt better. His voice, when he continued, was still reedy and thin, but feisty somehow, as if daring one of them to object. He glossed over the sound mind bit and got to the heart of the matter. He read off the small bequests and token gifts, then paused for a dramatic effect, pushed his wire-frame glasses higher on his bony nose, and proceeded. "To my daughter Maggie, the sum of ten thousand dollars. A like amount of ten thousand dollars to my daughter Susan. The balance of my estate to my wife, Billie."

"That's it, ladies and gentlemen. Are there any questions?" He always liked this part, because there were always questions. He leaned back in the leather swivel chair and waited.

Maggie could feel her insides start to churn. She had hoped that things would go right today. She should have known better, she thought bitterly. How dare he? To be sloughed off with ten thousand dollars was more than she could bear. Was that what she was worth in her father's eyes? All those years, all those tears, all that hate . . . for what? For ten thousand dollars and the opportunity to visit her father's grave whenever she felt like it. Goddamn you, Mam, how could you have let him do this to me? All that talk you used to give me was just talk. You never cared, because if you had, you wouldn't have allowed this to happen. Well, from here on it's war. One of us is going to get bloodied and it isn't going to be me.

Billie watched the slight hand movement of Maggie's husband as he nudged her to get up and speak. Maggie shrugged off his hand. "Yes, I do have a question. What exactly does that mean? The statement that all the estate goes to mother? Does that mean we have to wait for her to die before Susan and I can inherit our share? If so, I don't think it's fair and I don't like it one bit. What about you, Susan?"

Susan flushed. "It doesn't seem fair to me. Maggie and I certainly deserve more than ten thousand dollars. That doesn't go very far these days. I don't like being dependent on my mother. Can't she distribute it to us if she wants?" Her husband wasn't going to like this. He'd been counting on a really large settlement to start his own music academy. "It's not fair," she repeated loudly.

"Fair or not, it's what your father wanted." He couldn't help but wonder which of the two girls would bring up the matter of contesting the will. The older one, Maggie, probably. She'd always been a handful and that husband of hers looked as though he had his own ideas. The old lawyer leaned over the desk when he saw Maggie turn to face her mother. Sawyer moved to stand protectively behind her grandmother's chair. So, the lines had already been drawn. Susan turned, too, and half rose out of her chair. It was Maggie who spoke.

"Well, Mother, are you going to let this ridiculous will stand or are you going to make some serious distributions? What about my son, Coleman? This isn't right and you know it." And then so cruelly that Billie bit down on her lip: "How is your will going to read? All of the estate to Sawyer? Why aren't you saying something, Mother? I want to know now. I want my share now. I don't want to have to wait for you to die and then fight with my own daughter over what should be mine. All my life I've been cheated. You know it, Mother!" Maggie's voice was a shrill scream.

Susan nodded her head and narrowed her eyes. How in the world was she going to explain this to her husband? she wondered frantically. What could you do with ten thousand dollars? Jerome needed ten times that much to get his music academy under way. How could Pap cheat her this way? It had to be Mam's fault. Pap was ill and didn't know what he was doing. Mam could have seen to it that the money was distributed fairly. Now she was going to have to get involved in a nasty suit; she could see it in Maggie's eyes. Why couldn't she just get her inheritance and walk away? Oh, no, that was too simple. Fight, choose up sides, go against her mother. It was disgusting. Well, this was one time she wasn't going to back off and take a wait-and-see attitude. She would fight with Maggie. By God, she was entitled. Someone was going to have to pay and it might as well be Mam.

"I agree with everything Maggie said," she cried angrily. "It should be divided evenly and I want mine now, too!"

Billie thought her head was going to explode. It was Sawyer's firm grip on her shoulders that calmed her. Billie's back stiffened. "No. Your father made this will and it will stand as is. If you need—"

"Need?" Maggie screeched. "Need? And then after you review our needs, our requests, you'll make the final decision. . . . You'll dole it out to us in dibs and dabs, is that it? Well, I don't want it that way."

"I don't, either," Susan said petulantly.

"You both have husbands to take care of you. Perhaps it's time you tried earning a living. Make something of your life."

"Stuff it, Mother. I'm entitled and so is Susan. Is that your final word?"

Billie drew a deep breath. "Yes, it's my final word. It's what your father wanted. What do you think he would do if he could see the way you're acting? Both of you should be ashamed of yourselves."

"It's so easy to be shame free when you're sitting on millions

{ 535 }

and millions of dollars, isn't it, Mother? Well, that isn't good enough. You had best revise your thinking or I'll engage a lawyer of my own. Susan?" Susan nodded agreement.

"Hold on a minute here," Billie protested. "There's something you must understand. First of all, I'm not sitting on millions and millions, as you put it. Your father was up to his neck in debt." She waited for the realization to sink in.

"That's impossible!" Maggie protested. "You're lying!"

"No, Maggie, I'm not. You both know that your father was in the midst of seeing his dream come true with his plane. Dreams cost money, lots of money."

"Pap built planes before and it only made him richer," Susan countered.

"That's true, but that was when the government subsidized him. This time Moss wanted no governmental interference. This time he was going it alone. Because of his health, he practically shut down every other enterprise. Sunbridge no longer provides beef for the military, and in truth, I doubt that there's fifty head of cattle left on the ranch. He poured everything into this plane and I'm not even certain there's enough to see the project through."

"So don't see the project through. What can you know about planes, anyway?" Maggie said rudely. "Take my advice and get out from under. Pap's dead and buried. Sell what you've got to the government and let them handle it from there. At least we won't be paupered by it."

"I promised your father and it's a promise I intend to keep."

Billie felt as though her innards were shriveling up. She thought she had prepared herself to explain things to Maggie and Susan. But they would never understand. And telling Maggie now about Moss's last, bedside bequest to her would not be a good idea. The Sunbridge house and ranch were to go to Maggie—but only after Billie had completely financed the project; if necessary, however, she was to place Sunbridge on the auction block. "Do your damnedest, Billie, to see that Maggie gets it," Moss had said. "But if your back is to the wall and you have to sell or mortgage, then do it." Would Maggie accept and understand the stipulation? Right now, Billie just didn't have the stomach to find out. Such naked hatred on both her children's faces. Hatred that was directed at her, not Moss. Dear God, what do I do now? she cried to herself. Her shoulders slumped in defeat. It was the slight pressure Sawyer exerted that made Billie sit up straight and look her daughters in the eye. "Do you hear me?" she said quietly, firmly. "I intend to honor that promise."

"If I may interject..." Dudley Abramson cleared his throat importantly. "If anyone here intends to contest this will, I will testify that Mr. Coleman knew of his illness almost two years ago. That was the main reason he did what he could to delay a divorce. He wanted to be certain your mother was his legal heir under the law of the state, not merely a beneficiary named to his estate. And if I might say"—his hawk eyes impaled Maggie and Susan—"it seems he was quite right in doing so. Since your mother and father were never divorced, your claims to the estate cannot take precedence over hers. And if it will comfort you, it is in my knowledge that the Coleman assets have been greatly reduced to less than a third of what they once were."

"And that's supposed to be a comfort? Mother"—Maggie turned her wrath on Billie—"you simply cannot proceed with this foolishness! Damn the plane. I, for one, cannot allow you to squander the rest of Pap's estate on something so ridiculous."

"Maggie, you heard Mr. Abramson. You and Susan have been given your share; the rest is mine to do with as I please. And I please to continue your father's work to its completion."

"Oh, no, you won't, Mother." Maggie jumped from her chair and towered over Billie. Susan seemed horrified by this aggression. "I happen to know a little something about the law. Susan and I have every right to protect the inheritance we can expect to inherit from *you*! We won't allow you to squander what's left."

Sawyer stared at Maggie in disbelief. This was her mother! The sudden urge to throttle her was so intense she bit into her lip. She'd never witnessed such hatred. Any leftover childish yearning for her mother evaporated at that moment. It was her and Grand against Maggie and Susan. She'd fight them both until there wasn't a breath left in her body. She was a Coleman, and by God, she was going to act like one.

Maggie and Susan were as good as their word. Four weeks later the Coleman assets were frozen by court order. Billie took the news badly. Sawyer tried to bolster her by showing her a list of names and banking institutions she planned to go to for financing.

Billie tried to swallow past the lump in her throat. Sawyer stood in front of her dressed in a tailored business suit with a light cashmere coat over her shoulders. Each hand gripped a briefcase. She was going out to make Moss's dream come true. Her travels would take her from one end of the world to the other. How young she looked. How vulnerable. "I should be coming with you," Billie said anxiously. "You can't do this alone. We need more help, Sawyer."

Sawyer set the cases down and put her hands on her grandmother's shoulders. "Look at me. We can do this; we'll find private investors. I have all the letters, all the specifications, and I know what I'm talking about. If you've lost faith in me, now's the time to say so."

"It's nothing like that, Sawyer. It's just that it's so much to ask of you. Promise me you're going to take it one step at a time."

"I promise. You take care of yourself and I'll call over the weekend. Don't wish me luck. Say a few prayers." Billie nodded.

While Sawyer was winging her way to California, Billie was placing a call to Thad. She almost fainted with relief when his voice came over the wire. "Thad . . . Sawyer left this morning. I need my one-man support system. Can you come?"

"Give me a day to clear the decks and I'll be on your doorstep before you know it. Are you all right?" The genuine concern in Thad's voice brought tears to Billie's eyes.

"I need you, Thad. I need someone besides Sawyer to tell me I can do this. I've never had such an awesome responsibility before. I'm beginning to doubt myself."

"Well, don't. Stop right now and start thinking positively. Lay in some supplies and begin cooking up a storm." He rattled off a list of things he wanted to eat. "Real American food. Go easy on the rice and make lots and lots of spuds."

Billie laughed. Already she felt better. Dear God, thank you for creating such a wonderful human being. "Thad, I can hardly wait to see you."

"The feeling is mutual. Keep busy and I'll be there before you know it."

Billie was sure the entire airport could tell how happy she was to see her old and dear friend. Her love. Thad's presence was her magic elixir, her security blanket, her safety net.

He held out his arms and Billie melted into them, her head resting against the rough navy wool. "I'm so glad you could come. So very glad," Billie whispered.

"I'm all yours. I've always been yours," Thad said huskily against her hair.

Billie raised her head to stare up at Thad, oblivious to the milling inbound and outbound passengers. Airports were places for good-byes and hellos. No one paid them the slightest bit of attention. They had more privacy here than at a secluded restaurant behind a wooden trellis and a potted plant.

"Let's get a drink, Thad. There's a small cocktail lounge to the left. I want to sit and look at you."

"I'm all for that, but you stole my line. I want to sit and look at you."

"Good. Then let's sit and look at each other. You look wonderful. You never seem to change, Thad."

"She can lie with a straight face, too." Thad grinned. "Okay, what'll it be?" he asked once they'd been seated and the waitress had approached.

"Whiskey sour."

"I'll have a double bourbon on the rocks."

"Was it difficult to get the time off, Thad? I should have given you more notice, but I panicked. I'm so glad you're here. I need your stability and your good common sense. Tell me I'm doing the right thing."

"You're referring to the plane, of course." Billie nodded. "Of course you're doing the right thing. You're honoring your commitment to your husband and to his dream. It's right, Billie."

"If it's so right, why are you, Sawyer, and I the only ones who think so? Maggie and Susan are Moss's children and they aren't looking at it that way. They won't even speak to me. All they want is the money."

Thad's next words caught Billie off guard. "The mother in you should recognize that that's all they have left of their father. They're both hurt, sore and bruised. It's the last thing they can do to get even—not with you, Billie, but with Moss—for all those hurts, all those slights, the lack of the love they both wanted. Maggie especially. I think Susan is just going along with Maggie because she thinks it's the thing to do. Greed is a powerful motivator. To destroy or prevent Moss's dream is all they really want. At least that's my opinion."

"I never wanted it to end like this. I tried to talk to the girls, but it did no good. Maggie was so cruel. Susan was...she just looked at me with a blank stare and didn't say anything. She was actually mute. Without Maggie behind her she's lost.

I didn't want to divide us. Maggie was unbelievably cruel to Sawyer when the girl stood up for me."

"How are things going?"

"Sawyer has taken to the road to see if she can get financial help. The men helped her, the crew Moss hand-picked to work on this project. Right now morale is low. Wages haven't been paid. I've gone through all the cash I could get my hands on before the court freeze. I've even used up Mother's inheritance. Amelia has helped out, but that's a drop in the bucket. We're talking dollars when we need millions. It doesn't look as though the courts are going to be in any hurry to speed things up, either. Maggie managed to get herself one terrific lawyer. He can make his reputation on this case. The longer it's dragged out, the more publicity he gets."

"There's no deadline, is there?"

"Not a date with a red circle on a calendar, if that's what you mean. But how long will those men continue to work without pay? Costs are mounting every day. Coleman credit is topnotch, but Moss was Coleman Aviation; I'm unproven, and investors and banks have little faith in me. I don't know where to turn."

"I have some money. It will just be another drop in the bucket, but if we keep filling that bucket with drops, sooner or later it will fill up."

"Thad, I can't let you do that. The money goes out faster than it comes in. And if the courts decide in favor of Maggie and Susan, this will all have been for nothing. . . . I'll never be able to complete Moss's dream. Never."

"Do you have a dollar-and-cents figure of what it will take to get this project into the air?"

Billie laughed bitterly. "I have it in every language and in every color. It's all back at the house. Will seeing it make a difference?"

"It might. Drink up and let's get out of here." There had to be a way. Thad's mind clicked away as he paid the check and guided Billie to the baggage area.

His luggage in tow, Thad and Billie left the airport and returned to Sunbridge. Within an hour Thad was settled in Moss's workroom, poring over ledgers and specifications. When he was finished he put on his cap and jacket. "Let's go out to the hangar and have a look-see." Billie obliged. Thad would know what to do.

It was a little after six in the evening when Billie and Thad returned once again to Sunbridge. She fixed them both some scrambled eggs, toast, and coffee, then sat down at the kitchen table to talk.

"Well, what do you think?" she asked anxiously.

Thad's brow was furrowed. "There might be a way. I'm just not sure." With long, thin fingers he raked through his sparse hair, seemingly lost in thought.

Billie sensed some inner conflict, something tearing at Thad. Unsure of what she should do or say, she carried the dishes to the sink and started to wash them. When she'd finished, Thad was still sitting hunched over the table, wearing the same intense look on his face.

"Thad? Is something wrong? You don't look right. Please tell me what it is."

Thad's tormented eyes lifted to meet Billie's worried gaze. He didn't know what to do, what to say. By tomorrow, he could be in Japan talking to Otami's father. Shadaharu Hasegawa had the money to help Billie. If Thad presented the case properly, there was every possibility that Moss's dream could come true. But in order to do that, he would have to break his promise and tell Billie about Riley's marriage . . . and his son. All the years of silence . . . what would Billie say when she found out she had a grandson? How would she feel? Thad groaned aloud.

"Thad, what is it? Are you ill?" Billie asked in concern.

"Make us some more coffee, Billie. Then I want you to sit down. I have something to tell you."

Billie sat silently at the table, listening intently, not touching her coffee. When Thad finished she had to wet her lips twice and force the words from her throat. "A grandson? Riley had a son and Moss didn't tell me? Oh, Thad, why didn't you tell me? What must that girl think of me? Of Moss? Riley . . . poor Riley."

"He loved Otami very much, Billie. And she loved him. It was what he wanted. He made me swear that I wouldn't confide in either of you. I had to do it, Billie. For Riley. Please, tell me you understand."

Billie's gazed eyes stared at Thad. "It seems so unreal. How could Moss not have told me? A grandson . . . Riley's son. So many years lost to all of us. Do you think Riley's wife will see me? The boy, too?"

"Of course. Billie, you have to understand that Otami would have made some overture to you sooner or later, or convinced

Riley to do so. Unfortunately, the boy was killed before he could release her from her promise to keep the marriage secret. The Japanese are a very honorable people, and Otami was duty-bound to honor her husband's wishes. She's a wonderful girl, Billie. You'll love her."

"I'm sure I will. It's Moss's not telling me that I'm having trouble with," Billie said wretchedly. "How could he keep that from me, Thad? Even when he was dying he didn't tell me. We'd come to terms with so many things in our lives. That was the time for him to tell me, for him to be honest. I don't understand. I'll never to able to forgive him if I don't understand."

"I can tell you Otami's side of it. Moss never chose to tell me about his visit to Japan. Otami's father wanted me to know, in case questions ever came up later."

"Tell me what happened, Thad."

Thad squirmed in his chair, dreading what he was going to have to say. "Moss went to Japan believing Otami was some sort of tart who'd gotten her hooks into Riley. I think he had a vision of her living in a rice paddy with the baby strapped to her back. When he arrived, he must have been shocked. The family home is equal, if not superior, to Sunbridge. Well, anyway, Moss made a mistake of demanding the child—he made all manner of threats."

"Oh, my God!" cried Billie.

"I understand from several letters I received from Otami that her father was frightened for his family. He hired guards to protect her and the boy. He wasn't sure what Moss would do."

"Thad, I have to go to Japan. Should we call first? Will they welcome us?"

"With open arms, Billie."

"Make arrangements, please, Thad. I'll go upstairs and pack. And Thad, we can't ask them for financing for this plane. It wouldn't be right. They might think that was the only reason we're making the trip, and it isn't. We'll find our financing some other way."

Thad poured himself a drink and picked up the phone. Inside of thirty minutes he had confirmed reservations to Tokyo via San Francisco, Hawaii, and Guam. He leaned back in the swivel chair, debating whether or not to call Otami. Would a surprise be best, or should he do the decent thing and call? The decent thing, of course.

Otami's voice was just as sweet as ever. "Uncle Thad, how nice of you to call. Are you planning on coming for a visit? My family would be honored. My father constantly asks about you."

"Yes, Otami, I am coming for a visit. I want to bring Riley's mother with me. It was necessary to tell her about you and your son. I will explain later, but I had no other choice. I hope you will forgive me."

"There is nothing to forgive. I'm sure you did what you believed was right. We will understand."

"We'll be there in less than twenty-four hours. Otami, Riley's mother needs you."

"Uncle Thad, I, too, need Riley's mother. More than you know. My son will be told and I will arrange for him to take time off from school. Is it not strange that Riley loves airplanes?"

"Not so strange, Otami. Preordained, I should think."

{{{{{{{{{ CHAPTER THIRTY-NINE }}}}}}}}}

Billie and Thad walked through Guam's new airport. Thad looked around, hardly believing his eyes. "This rivals anything we have in the States. You should have seen it in the old days."

"So much marble," Billie said, looking around.

"Come along, Billie. The commander at the Naval Air Station has arranged for a car. I'm going to take you around Guam and show you where your son lived and was happy. I owe that to you. We only have a few hours, but the island is small. Can you handle it?"

"I can handle it."

As Thad drove the car along Marine Drive he and Billie oohed and aahed. "Ten years makes one hell of a difference. I understand that Guam is now *the* Japanese honeymoon resort. There's a shopping center in Agana now. When Riley was here there were tiny little stores and I assume he did most of his shopping at the commissary. Things are so different."

"It rather looks like Hawaii. Where are we going first, Thad?"

"I want to show you the church where Riley was married and the little house he lived in with Otami."

As the navy car ate up the miles Billie craned her neck, not wanting to miss seeing anything her son might have lived with. After a short while, Thad slowed the car and turned. "The church on the right is where Riley was married. It's open, if you'd like to go in. They had it decorated that day with plumeria and orchids. It was beautiful. Otami has pictures of the wedding. I'm sure she'll share them with you."

"No, Thad, I don't want to go in. It's enough that I see it. San Juan deBautiste Church," Billie said softly. "What a lovely name."

"Start counting now. The little house where Riley and Otami lived can be seen from the road. Eight buildings including the dental clinic."

Billie drew in her breath. Why this was so important, she didn't know. A piece of her son's life. The last piece. "There it is!" Tears misted Billie's eyes as she stared at the small stucco house that was painted white with what looked like burgundy trim. A spanking new yellow Suzuki pickup truck stood in the driveway. "I wonder who lives here now," Billie whispered hoarsely.

"The sign on the tree says Deo. Riley and Otami had a sign, too. It said Riley and Otami Coleman. Rather like the plaque at Sunbridge. I know one thing, though."

"What's that?" Billie asked, dabbing at her eyes.

"If the people living here now are one-tenth as happy as Riley and Otami were, they've got all there is to have in life. Have you seen enough?"

"It's all so beautiful." Billie's eyes misted over again. "I'm so glad you brought me here, Thad. Thank you."

"I have to be honest. I did it as much for myself as for you."

Billie's smile was wan. "I know."

"Back to the airport. If we burn rubber, we'll just make it."

It was cold and blustery when Thad and Billie descended the portable stairway on the Continental jet. The minute Billie's feet touched solid ground, her shoulders slumped. Jet lag had finally caught up with her. Try as she would, she could barely keep her eyes open. Customs and baggage, and then she could check into the hotel and take a shower. She'd need some good strong coffee before she could even think about going to see her daughter-in-law. Her heart was pumping furiously. She couldn't help but wonder whether it was from bone weariness or wild anticipation.

Thad's face showed his concern as he ushered Billie through customs. "If you're half as tired as you look, you have to feel the way I do. I think we should go to the hotel and get some sleep. It's early and we have plenty of time. Otami will certainly understand. You look done in, Billie."

"I am. I agree. We both need sleep. A few hours, anyway. I can't believe I'm really here and that I'm going to see my daughter-in-law and grandson in a short while. It's so over-whelming, I don't think I'm over the shock. Do you think they'll like me, Thad?" Billie asked anxiously. "I'm not like Moss. I don't ever want them to think I am. But I have to try to explain to them why he acted the way he did. It's all right to do that, isn't it?"

"Of course it is. Otami and her family are wonderful people. They'll understand. They bear no malice toward you and I'm sure there was none for Moss. Be yourself, Billie. That's the best advice I can give you."

"I brought Riley's baby pictures," Billie blurted. "As a matter of fact I brought all his pictures for Otami to see. And I . . . I brought his baseball mitt and his ball that Hank Aaron autographed. The Japanese have a great love of baseball. As a matter of fact I just recently read an article about the Tokyo Yomiuri Giants. They're known for their hitting and fielding. I read the article, I don't know why. At least I'll have something to talk about with my grandson."

Thad raised startled eyes to meet Billie's tired gaze. "I'm sure you will. Most Japanese boys grow up playing baseball."

"Hopefully I'm going to be able to show you Mount Fuji before we leave. In all my visits to this wonderful city I've only seen it twice myself. It's quite awesome. The clouds are usually too low to see the snow peak. For you, Billie, I have a feeling the cloud cover will lift."

Billie forced a smile. She had never in her life been so exhausted. "How long are we going to be here? I never thought to ask."

"Five days. It was the best I could do. Enough time for you to get acquainted with Riley's family. I'm sure that Otami will want to show you her beloved city. It's a far cry from Texas. Ten million people live in Tokyo."

One eye was drooping sleepily. Thad smiled at the valiant effort Billie was putting forth. "I would like to shop on the

Ginza," she said, yawning. "Sawyer will be so impressed with me."

"I think Sawyer will be more impressed if you tell her you got up the nerve to take a ride on the Shinkansen Super Express. It is called the bullet train and supposedly it's the speediest in the world, traveling one hundred thirty miles per hour. Her technical mind will want to know everything, so it might be wise if we got some brochures for her."

"That sounds good to me, Thad." An instant later Billie was asleep.

Thad shifted his weight slightly so that Billie's nodding head would rest comfortably against his shoulder. He spent the remainder of the long ride from Narita to Tokyo rehearsing what he was going to say to Otami's father. Billie was caught up in emotionalism and rightly so. It would rest with him to bring up the matter of the plane and what had to be done. A pity Sawyer wasn't here. The fact that he had a good rapport with the Japanese would certainly help. He didn't think he would have to talk too long or too loud to get his point across. Riley's grandfather would understand what was happening. The man would listen, tilt his head to the side, and then say, How can I help? How much do you need? And that would be the end of it.

Thad shook Billie's shoulder gently. "Wake up, Billie, we're at the hotel."

Billie was too groggy to appreciate the beauty of the Asian hotel as she followed Thad and the diminutive Oriental carrying their bags. She needed sleep and she wanted to be at her best when she met Otami and her grandson.

"Here's your room, Billie. I'm down the hall in fifteen-oh-eight. Sleep now and ring my room when you wake." He kissed her lightly on the cheek and walked on down the hall, leaving Billie to herself. She immediately took off her coat, drew the draperies, and crawled into bed fully clothed.

She slept deeply and soundly for twelve hours, hardly disturbing the bright blue covers.

While Billie slept, Thad headed for the Virgo dining room with its French cuisine and panoramic view of Tokyo. While he ate he rehearsed the talk he was going to have with Otami's father, rejected some ideas and expanded on others. Finally satisfied, he gulped his tea, paid the bill, and left the restaurant.

Once Thad was outside, his step was springy, his bearing

more military. When things were going right, it was easier to stand tall. It was easier to do a lot of things. Simple everyday living was a delight; anything beyond that a bonus.

Mr. Hasegawa welcomed Thad in the Western manner. They shook hands and then bowed to each other.

"Welcome, Thaddeus. It has been a long time since you honored me with a visit. My daughter and wife are in a state of delirium that Mrs. Coleman is here. After all these years we thought it would never come to pass. My sorrow was yours at the news of Mr. Coleman's death. On many occasions my family prayed that he would one day return and make my grandson his. We wanted to share our good fortune with him. I know it was your sorrow, also. Tell me, quickly, do you bring news of the film stars for my wife? She has called me twice already today to see if you had been in touch. She is particularly taken with . . . one moment, I wrote down the name. Aah, here it is: Tom Selleck. Yes, Tom Selleck. Do you know much about this film star?"

"He's the eighties heartthrob. I think I can give her a few highlights. How is the boy?"

"Young Riley makes me more proud each day. I believe he follows in his father's footsteps. He thinks of nothing but planes and flying. We have our own jet and he is forever begging to go with me. Unfortunately, I like to keep my feet on the ground as much as possible. It is the miracle of progress. Sit down, Thaddeus, and we will have some Scotch and one of those fine Havana cigars you brought on your last visit. Then we will talk. I wish to know how all this came about."

Thad waited until the room was blue gray with smoke and the Scotch bottle was nearly empty before he began his speech. It all came out neatly, slow and easy.

"So . . . Mrs. Coleman needs my help. That is clear. Tell me what you want me to do. I will need at least a week with my bankers. Is my presence in America essential?" the old man asked anxiously.

"Only if you wish to be there."

They talked for hours, these two old friends. When the room became too foul with cigar smoke they adjourned to another. They talked of the old days, his daughters, and his grandchildren. Moss Coleman's dream would be backed by Hasegawa money. How ironic, Thad thought, that this beautiful human being whom Moss Coleman had detested was going to make his last dream a reality.

"I don't know how to thank you for your generosity. The return on your investment will be substantial. I guarantee it."

Hasegawa waved his hand to negate Thad's words. "Sometimes, Thaddeus, a man's dreams are all he has. When they are not fulfilled it is most sad. I, for one, never had much use for people who had the power to shatter a man's dreams. We are to build, to create, to finish. If one cannot do it, then it is up to another to carry on. I do this for Moss Coleman, for his son, whom he loved with all his heart, and for my grandson, whom I love with all my heart. Cannot we say that finally the East has met the West and let it go at that?"

"Very well said," Thad replied with a catch in his throat. "I think it's time for me to return to the hotel. Mrs. Coleman might wake and she is most anxious to see her family."

"Regardless of the time, you are to bring her immediately. She must not wait one minute longer than she must meet her family. Are they not wonderful words?" Shadaharu Hasegawa asked with a twinkle in his eye. "Your promise, Thaddeus."

"Yes. Until later, old friend."

"Until later." Hands were shaken and bows were made.

It was done.

When Billie woke, she lay for long moments thinking about where she was and why she was here in this strange land so far from Sunbridge and Moss's dream. When her eyes became accustomed to the darkness around her, she reached toward the bedside lamp and turned it on. The digital watch, Japanese-made, read 5:05. The sun would be up soon. She lay still a few moments longer, rested now and in control. She'd shower, dress, apply her makeup, and then call Thad. They could have coffee in the hotel dining room and then make an appearance at her daughter-in-law's home. At a respectable hour. The Japanese were very particular about the social amenities, or so she had read.

On her way to the bathroom thoughts of Moss skittered through her mind. Later she would have to sort them all out. Betrayal wasn't something to take lightly. She would get her perspective and deal with it all sometime soon. Nothing was going to mar this visit if she could help it.

The stinging shower woke Billie completely. She wrapped herself in one of the hotel's plum-colored bath sheets and applied makeup sparingly but deftly.

She called Thad and they agreed to meet in twenty minutes. He sounded wide awake—he'd probably been up for hours, Billie reflected, waiting for her to wake and call him.

Billie shook out the mauve silk dress and hung it in the bathroom to smoothe away the wrinkles. She could dry her hair in five minutes, then dress and be ready to leave.

"Do I look all right, Thad? Am I too dressy or do you think I should wear a suit? I brought one. I don't want to look overdone but more done, if you know what I mean," Billie babbled.

"Believe me, you look fine. Beautiful, in fact. The dress is perfect. Now stop worrying. If you keep frowning like that you're going to get wrinkles, and then what will you do?" Thad said lightly.

Billie stopped in midstride. "But Thad, I already have a few wrinkles."

"Do you? I hadn't noticed. To me you look the way you did when I first met you. I'm the one who's aged. You want wrinkles, you can have all of mine. I'll gladly share."

"I really hadn't noticed," Billie said seriously as she peered closely at Thad's face. She laughed nervously and Thad joined in. "I'll tell you what. You keep yours and I'll keep mine and then we can both forget about them. I need coffee, Thad. I'm too nervous to eat, though."

Ninety minutes later the huge iron gate opened to admit Billie and Thad. They were ushered into the house and immediately taken to a formal sitting room where Otami, her parents, and two of her sisters waited. There were greetings and introductions all around. Billie stood rooted to the floor, unable to move in Otami's direction. A vision of Jessica Coleman holding out her arms to welcome her so long ago flashed before her. A radiant smile and outstretched arms were all Otami needed. She forgot the Japanese way for a moment and ran to Billie. Tears burned Billie's eyes as she wrapped her arms around Otami. Was it Otami trembling or was it Billie herself? Was that Otami's heart pounding or her own? Did it matter?

"Please forgive me, Mother Coleman. I have prayed for this moment for so long and now that it is here I am so overcome I have forgotten my manners. Welcome to my home. Riley is on his way from school and will join us within the hour. We wish, my family and I, that you and Uncle Thad will join us for breakfast."

"There is nothing to forgive. It is I who must ask forgiveness for my husband and myself. I didn't know. I would never . . . I didn't know, Otami."

"I know that, Mother Coleman. You're here now and that's all that matters. After breakfast you and I and Riley will talk of your son and my son." Impulsively, Otami threw her arms around Billie a second time and this time wept openly with happiness. Billie drew her close and kept her arm around Otami's waist as they made their way to a formal dining room whose table was set Western style.

"In your honor, Mrs. Coleman, we will breakfast in the American manner. My cook is preparing eggs Benedict, pancakes with Vermont maple syrup. Real maple syrup, Thad." Mr. Hasegawa chuckled.

"You are indeed a man after my own heart. Are you serving that awful green tea or are we having coffee?"

"For you, nothing but the best. I believe it is called Crock of Nuts or some other ridiculous name."

Otami laughed. "Father, it is Chock Full o' Nuts. Riley taught me to drink coffee, and when I returned home I had my father import the coffee for us. We drink it all the time. My father is teasing you, Uncle Thad, as you well know." Her words were directed to Thad but her gaze never left Billie.

"All these females I surround myself with are outnumbering me. Now, before my wife goes up in a puff of smoke, we will talk of the American film stars and what is going on in tissue town."

"Tinsel town, Father. It is Mother's only vice. She is perfect in every other way." Otami smiled. "She has an obsession with the film stars," she explained to Billie. "Uncle Thad keeps us abreast of what is going on in Hollywood. He sends magazines and pictures and movie reviews. My mother does not speak English but she can understand when Uncle Thad talks of the stars."

Billie laughed. "Thad, you never told me. What else haven't you told me?" Instantly she was sorry for the words, even though her tone was light and teasing.

Billie and Otami had eyes only for each other. It was as though neither could get her fill of the other. Thad droned on about Tom Selleck and Kenny Rogers, and both Otami and Billie grinned conspiratorially when Thad started to describe the endowments of Jacqueline Bisset and Dolly Parton. Caught up in the moment, Thad was unaware of the silence at the table and flushed sheepishly when his host clapped his hands loudly. Otami giggled and Billie lowered her eyes so Thad wouldn't see the laughter in them.

Breakfast progressed slowly. They started with juice and fruit, then followed with toast and small muffins. Coffee was liberally poured by a small girl dressed in a sky-blue kimono. The eggs Benedict were perfect and Billie ate heartily, while Thad did justice to the buckwheat pancakes with maple syrup. Without looking at her watch, Billie knew the hour was almost up. Her grandson should be arriving shortly. She took a deep breath and looked at Otami.

"It is understandable for you to be anxious about meeting Riley. He is anxious, too. He tries so hard to be all things to all of us. He is very much like his father, as you will see. He did inherit one thing from my family and that is his love of the entertainment business. He adores American music. He will be here soon, Mother Coleman. We are finally a family. It is all I ever wanted for my son and now it has come to pass. My father, who is wise in so many ways, thought this would happen someday. You were so right, my honorable father."

"Do you hear that, Thad? She called me her honorable father. I can't remember the last time she did that. We are joking, Mrs. Coleman, to put you at your ease. I see we are not succeeding. We understand. Otami, take Mrs. Coleman into the library and I will send Riley to you when he arrives."

Billie's eyes shone with relief. It wasn't that she didn't want to meet her grandson in front of the entire family, but she needed to get herself and her emotions under control.

Otami linked her arm through Billie's and led her to her father's library. "This room has many chairs for our Western visitors. My father thought you would be more comfortable here. We have so much to talk about. So many years to compare. I want to share what Riley and I had with you. In his heart he would want me to do this."

"Why have you never remarried, Otami?"

"There is only room in my heart to love one man. Riley is dead, but his son is alive. He is never far from me. I am content. But to answer your question, I could never find anyone I could love the way I loved Riley," Otami said softly. "Tell me, Mother Coleman, will you be able to marry another?"

"Yes, Otami."

"Would I be forward in asking if Uncle Thad is the person you would consider sharing your heart with?"

{ 551 }

"You wouldn't be forward at all. Yes, Thad is the person I would share my heart with. I think I've been sharing it for years."

"We will share all these things later, if you are agreeable. There is so much I want to know. There is so much I want to share with you. I think all my life—and I mean that part of my life with Riley and afterward—I thought your family would not welcome me. I never got beyond the welcome part, but I wanted you to love me. I wanted all of Riley's family to love me. In his own way I think Riley was trying to tell me this wouldn't be possible and that's why he made me agree not to get in touch with you. He didn't want me to be hurt."

Oh, damn you, Moss. Damn you. Billie reached out her hand to Otami. She would neither defend nor chastise her husband's memory. It was history. This was now. This beautiful woman would have to decide for herself what was real and what was true.

Otami's grip on Billie's hand tightened when the knock sounded on the library door. "My son is here to meet his grandmother at last."

Billie took a deep breath and stood next to Otami. Through her blurred vision she watched Riley's likeness walk toward her. Incredible dark eyes drank in the sight of her as his arms shot out and Billie found herself in her grandson's embrace. She rested her cheek on the top of his dark head and squeezed the tears back from her eyes. When young Riley released her he was embarrassed, as any ten-year old would be by the sudden display of his emotions. Clear, intelligent eyes, not the same summer blue as his father's but a dark, deep ebony, shone up at her.

"Hello, Grandmam." He smiled but kept his arm around her to steady her. "Welcome to our home. My mother and I have waited a long time for this day."

"And then you nearly crush the breath from her!" Otami said sternly. "Apologize."

"But Mother, that's what you said Father used to do to you. You said his father did it to his mother. I wanted to welcome Grandmam Texas-style. I didn't mean to offend you," Riley said anxiously, his eyes on his frowning mother.

"You didn't. I loved every minute of it, and yes, Otami, Riley was right. It is an exuberant Texas custom. I want you to be yourself; otherwise we'll never get to know each other."

"We have the advantage, Grandmam. Mama has told me

all about you and the Coleman ranch, and Texas and American airplanes. I intend to be an aeronautical engineer."

"My granddaughter, Sawyer, is doing the same thing. You would make some team." Billie laughed. "I brought pictures. Actually, I brought several family albums for you and your mother to see. We can have prints made from any of the pictures you might care to have. There's one in particular of your father on his first pony. Perhaps that isn't quite true; he was falling off the pony when I snapped the picture."

Otami laughed delightedly. "Riley used to tell me that the horse hadn't been born that could throw him."

"Not quite true. Riley tended to exaggerate when it came to horses. He was more at home around planes. In all fairness to Riley, he more or less slid off the pony. But he was thrown more times than I can remember, and he always got right back on. His grandfather insisted. Your father always tried to do what was expected of him."

"Until he met me," Otami said sadly.

"No, no, no, you must never say that. You must not even think such a thing," Billie said, moving closer to Otami and putting her arms around her. "Riley loved you and it was inevitable that he marry you. It's just that he was unwilling to take even the slightest chance that his family might . . . might not see things his way. I regret his decision, but I understand it. As my father-in-law, my husband, and my son used to say, it's history now. What we have now are our memories. Some of them aren't too pleasant and others will be with us for the rest of our lives. However, one cannot live on memories. I have my philosophy where memories are concerned."

"What are they, Grandmam?" Riley asked curiously.

"Memories have a place in all our lives. They dull and they fade with time, and that's as it should be. Only cowards live on memories day after day because they're afraid to reach out for life." At Riley's solemn nod, Billie glanced at Otami's stricken face. "No, no, Otami, I didn't mean you."

"But it's true. My family has been telling me that for years. My son manages to tell me that at least once a day when he is home. I never thought of it in terms of cowardice before. You must not be sorry for your words, because they are true. Do you see my son shake his head? At last he has an ally. You are of one thought. Even my father chastises me from time to time." A beautiful smile lightened her serious features. "I promise to work on it."

{ 553 }

"We'll hold you to it, Mama. Between the two of us, Grandmam, perhaps we can convince my mother that there is a world outside the gates of this house."

"Then there is no hope for me." Otami sighed.

"Ah, but there is. Now we can go to America and see where my father lived. You promised me that if Father's side of the family ever recognized us, you would take me to Texas. A promise, Mama, that must now be honored."

"We haven't been invited, Riley. Where are your manners?"

"But of course you're invited. Anytime. I would love to have your entire family come to Sunbridge. Riley, you will have so much in common with my granddaughter. She'll share the Coleman dream with you. A dream that you'll understand and perhaps want to work on. Later, we can discuss what's going on back in Texas. I brought something for you, Riley. It's in a package by the front door. Will you fetch it?"

Riley loped off to do his grandmother's bidding. Otami raised questioning eyes to Billie.

"I . . . I brought Riley's baseball and mitt for young Riley. The family albums are in the package, also. At the last minute I stuck in Riley's baseball cap. Was it a mistake, do you think?"

"Never. My son doesn't have much from his father. The few belongings that were returned to me by the navy were . . . what I mean is, he will appreciate these things because they are from his father's boyhood and his home."

Riley returned carrying the package, his gaze anxious as Billie unwrapped the string and held out the contents of the box. "I think you should have these things. There are others at Sunbridge that you might . . . that you . . ."

Riley looked down into the box and dropped to his knees. His touch was gentle as he lifted out the worn mitt and the ball. The little league cap went onto his shiny black head immediately. The baseball was brought lovingly to his cheek. "Was this the way my father smelled?" he asked, handing the hat to Billie, who sniffed obligingly. She nodded, a lump settling in her throat.

"It's right and fitting that you have what belonged to your father. I don't think this is the time to discuss it, but you and your mother also are entitled to Riley's inheritance. I'll have to have my lawyers work on that. I didn't know about you and your mother until a few days ago."

"Do you think Uncle Thad would like to field a few balls, Grandmam?"

"I think so. Why don't you go ask him? Your mother and I have a lot of talking to do."

Riley bent over to kiss his mother and Billie. His dark eyes lingered on Billie's face for a long time. "My father looked like you."

"Yes, he did a little. But he had a lot of Coleman in him, too. He was a wonderful man, Riley. He was a father for you to be proud of."

"Thank you for the gifts. I'll treasure them always."

Otami turned to Billie. "That was most kind of you. I often regretted I had nothing to give the boy but a few old clothes that were returned to me. You have made my son very happy and that makes me happy. I promise you I will give serious thought to the discussion on memories."

"You aren't offended?"

"No. You spoke the truth. It took courage for you to do that. Now, can we look at the photographs you brought along? I would like to see the comparison to my son." Billie nodded as she lifted the albums from the bottom of the carton she had brought from Texas.

The pictures were shared with Otami and then with Riley and Thad, and yet again with Otami's parents. When Billie looked at her watch it was late afternoon.

Wonderful, meaningful days passed with Billie and her new family. Riley insisted on a tour of the university and Otami made sure that a walk down the Ginza at dawn was as memorable as Billie knew it would be. Kabuki drama was Mr. Hasegawa's contribution. It was an experience Billie knew she would never forget.

It was agreed that Otami and Riley would journey to Texas as soon as the school semester ended in a month's time.

The entire Hasegawa family saw Thad and Billie off at the airport. Minutes before boarding, on Thad's advice, Mr. Hasegawa pressed an envelope into Billie's hand. "For the dream," the old man whispered as he kissed her lightly on the cheek and then bowed low. Billie swallowed hard and nodded, unsure of what he meant. One last, long look at her daughter-in-law and grandson and she was ushered through the turn-stile.

"What do you suppose Mr. Hasegawa meant when he said this envelope was for the dream?" Billie asked Thad as she buckled her seat belt.

{ 555 }

A smug look settled on Thad's face. "Why don't you open it and see?"

Billie slit the envelope with her nail and pulled out the contents. Her face drained of all color as she looked at the oblong pieces of paper. All checks drawn on the Tokyo bank. Blank except for a signature. A square of crackly, cream-colored paper was enclosed and Billie unfolded it with trembling hands. Dabbing at her eyes, she thrust the paper at Thad. "Please, read it to me."

My dear Mrs. Coleman:

It is unbearable to me that your husband's dream be shattered for lack of financing. You and your family will honor my family if you will accept our help in this endeavor. My only request is that you allow our grandson to share in the fulfillment of his grandfather's dream.

May good fortune smile upon you always.

With much affection and understanding, I remain,

Shadaharu Hasegawa

Billie blew her nose lustily. "I can't believe this. Thad, I didn't want you to ask him, to even discuss it. What must the man think?"

"What he thinks is obvious if you read this letter. I've known the man for years, Billie. I knew he would want to help. If you'll notice, there are no legal papers, no strings, no terms. He trusts you. He wants to do this. Accept it, Billie, in the spirit it's meant. He would die of shame, and I mean that literally, if you refuse."

"But Thad, blank checks? What does that mean? How are we to know what is too much? How can I just fill in amounts?"

"As much as it takes. It's that simple. Or, if you prefer it another way, unlimited funds."

"What if things go wrong again and the money goes down the drain like the last time?"

"It won't happen, Billie. But if it should, there will be another batch of checks. It's done."

"The man never laid eyes on me until five days ago and he's giving me carte blanche with his money. Thad, it isn't done."

"I beg to differ. And the man knows you better than you think. I told you we've been friends for years. Allow him the honor of helping you. He wants to do it."

"I'll never get over this. I didn't know there were people like that in this world."

"If the situation were reversed, what would you do?"

Billie laughed, a delightful sound that sent shivers up Thad's spine. "I'd do the same, I guess. Thank you, Thad. I think I'm glad that you didn't listen to me. I have a lot of thinking to do. What do you think of young Riley? He's such a marvelous young man. So like Riley in many ways and yet he has the Eastern culture that makes him what he is. My Amerasian grandson. So much has happened to me in these last days."

"Why don't we both try to get some sleep? You're going to be one busy lady when you get back to Texas, and I have to get back to the navy before they send out a search party for me."

"That's one of your better ideas. I'm still waiting for your best one yet."

"It's coming. Count on it."

"I will."

{{{{{{{{{{ CHAPTER FORTY }}}}}}}}}

The months flew by with Sawyer and Billie at the helm of Moss's dream.

Otami and young Riley settled into Sunbridge as though they'd been born to the place. There wasn't a nook or cranny that Otami didn't explore. Her dark eyes took on life and she smiled constantly. Her husband's home. She was finally seeing what he had spoken of so often. She was feeling what he felt, loving what he loved. The sadness was gone and was replaced with optimism.

Eight months after Otami and Riley's arrival, the project hit one snag after another. Money seemed to evaporate into thin air. When the phone shrilled at Billie's elbow, she had a feeling it was going to be more bad news. She wasn't disappointed.

"I could tell you this at home," Sawyer said tightly, "but I didn't want to upset Otami. I know you'll take it all in stride, Grand. We blew it. We were so damn close and we blew it. We're ninety-one million dollars down."

"Ninety-one million down! Does that mean . . ." Billie's voice was full of awe and fear.

"That's exactly what it means. This plane doesn't just eat money; it gobbles it up. I spoke to Grandpap's advisers, and if you're agreeable, we want to take this project to Japan. Mr. Hasegawa insists he can find financial backing for us over there. It's the only way, Grand."

"What went wrong?" Billie asked grimly. "Give me a reason, something to chew on."

"We didn't trim enough weight. We're not meeting specifications for fuel consumption. I knew it. I'm losing control, Grand. We have to go on the road with this. Otherwise we lose everything, and I, for one, don't want that to happen. Give me a yes or a no."

Billie felt light-headed as her granddaughter waited for her answer. Otami's puzzled face was staring at her. "Go for it, Sawyer. You have my approval. Just give Otami and me enough time to get packed."

The laughter in the background made Billie raise her eyebrows. "Grand, Riley just told me his grandfather has things under control. The hangar will be ready, the engineers and crew ready for work. All we have to do is pack our duffel bags and blow this place."

"Are you taking the entire project team?" Billie asked hesitantly.

"Only those who don't fight me every step of the way. I've been right all the way down the line, Grand. I'm not being cocky. You have to believe that." The desperate tone in Sawyer's voice made Billie's thoughts race back in time to hear Moss's hoarse whisper: *Give Sawyer her head, Billie. Stand behind her and give her all your encouragement. She can do it. If she makes a mistake, and she will, she won't make it a second time. Promise me.*

"Darling, I do believe you," Billie replied warmly. "Do what you have to do. If at all possible, we want to keep this in the family. The Hasegawas are family. If it isn't possible, have Riley's grandfather bring in whoever he thinks can help us."

The relief in Sawyer's voice made Billie feel faint. "You are the grand in grandmother," Sawyer cried exuberantly.

After she'd hung up, Billie quickly explained the situation to Otami, who listened, nodding. "Riley spoke to me of this just last week," she said. "He wanted to talk to you about it and so did I, but I know nothing of airplanes. . . . It is only money, Mother Coleman. My father will see to it that the plane stays in the family, our family."

"But to start over! So much money, so much time. I didn't know . . . I had no idea . . ."

"Dreams don't just happen, Mother Coleman; they are created. Your God's creation took six days. This will take just a little longer. When are we leaving?" she asked.

"Day after tomorrow. Is that too soon?"

"I am already packed."

"I have to call Thad and tell him."

"He knows. I think he and my father have had their heads together. Neither man wanted to suggest . . . what I'm saying is . . ."

"It had to come from Sawyer. She had to admit she needed help, the kind of help the men aren't giving her. I suppose it's natural that they resent her. I have so much faith in that girl. Moss would never have turned this over to her if he didn't think she was more than capable."

"We're a shoo-in." Otami giggled.

Billie hugged her daughter-in-law. "My world is right-side up now. Do you feel it, Otami?"

"Yes, I do. This is right."

"I know. I feel it here. Did they say anything about a deadline?" Billie asked anxiously. "Investors and governments always talk of deadlines. You can . . . you can lose everything on a deadline. They're going to start from square one and . . . is there going to be some kind of deadline?"

"I don't know."

"If there is, we aren't going to worry about it. Sawyer will handle it. She's so young, Otami,"

"Only in numbered years. In here," Otami said, pointing to her heart, "she is ageless. Her grandfather would not have entrusted his dream to a child."

Eleven months after moving into the Hasegawa household Billie felt more at home than she had ever felt at Sunbridge. She was glad now that she would soon be able to turn Sunbridge over to Maggie. Any monies she might have realized from the sale of the valuable property would have gone unnoticed in this war of megadollars. It would be better for Maggie, better for everyone.

It was late and for some reason she couldn't sleep. No doubt Thad's impending arrival had something to do with it. Billie decided that a stroll in the Hasegawa garden would settle her nerves.

How beautiful this was, so far removed from cactus and sagebrush. Everything was of the dwarf variety, even the statuary. The sparkling ponds and scaled-down bridges were so pleasing to her eye that Billie sat down on an iron bench to look around her. For some reason she suddenly felt Moss's presence. Nervously, she raised her eyes upward. "She's doing it," Billie whispered. "This was the only way. Soon, Moss, your dream will take wing and then it will all be over and you can rest in peace."

From his place in eternity he had interfered again. Now she was openly jittery. Things were going well—everyone said so. Six more weeks, two months at the most, and the plane would be ready to test. Sawyer seemed confident. Riley was openly jubilant.

She should be walking off some of her uneasiness. A stroll through the beautiful garden might ease her jumpy nerves. If Thad were here, she would be fine. Her reason for living . . . Thad.

Billie's stroll took her around the garden to the back level of the Hasegawa house. Sawyer's windows were open and Billie could see her silhouette in the dimness of the room. She looked as though she were talking on the phone. At this hour! Billie walked over slowly, taking the time to smell a bloom or pick a budding flower from the round, manicured beds.

How easily Sawyer had adapted to this new environment. To the men at the plant she wasn't an American female with a know-it-all attitude; she was just another worker in a grease-stained coverall and billed cap. She listened to them and they listened to her. There was no fight for control, no manipulating for power, none of the double-dealing so rampant back in the States. This was a joint effort and each man carried his share. At the end of the long work day they bowed to one another and returned to their families. Many returned after the dinner hour to rehash the day's events one last time and set up for the following morning so things would move along faster. It was dedication of the first order.

"Rand, I'm telling you, it will work," Sawyer was saying.

"I managed to shave off another two hundred pounds. I feel you're wrong. This plane has to go with a maximum T-O weight. I'm that close. Stop being so damn pigheaded and listen to me. I know what I'm doing.

"Let's talk about something else for a moment. I miss you. I really do. Did you get my last letter? . . . What do you mean *I'm* a piece of work? That's American slang. It *was* a compliment, wasn't it?"

Billie tapped on the windowsill. Sawyer motioned her to walk around to the sliding doors. She kept on with her conversation while her grandmother settled herself in the one comfortable chair in the room. She hugged the sound of her granddaughter's happy voice to her heart. Sawyer might not know it, but there was that special tone in her voice that only lovers used. The sparkle in her eyes was something Billie recognized from her own youth and could still see in the mirror when Thad was about to make an appearance.

"I need a test pilot. Do you think I should advertise in the *New York Times*?" The mock horror on Sawyer's face made Billie laugh. "You! I never thought of you, Rand. . . . The hell you say. You bloody Englishmen are touchy, aren't you? Listen, if you want to take a shot at it, the job is yours. How soon can you be here? . . . No good. What about day after tomorrow? . . . Me, set you up! How could you even think such a thing? I'd never trade on our friendship. I'll take you to dinner. . . . You're on. Good night, Rand."

"Did you set him up, Sawyer?" Billie asked.

Sawyer grimaced. "Sort of. Look, Grand, he's the best in the business. We need the best. He knows this plane's design as well as I do. Aside from a minor point or two we agree on everything. He trusts me. He wouldn't agree to test this baby if he didn't trust me. Right, Grand?"

"Right."

"If I'm so right, why do I feel so . . . so . . . uneasy?"

"Could it be because you care for him more than you'll admit? Is it possible that the things you're arguing about are more important than you think? He's laying his life on the line to test this plane for you. That's trust of the first order. You have to be sure, Sawyer."

"I am sure, Grand. But so many things could still go wrong. I could go over this six ways to Sunday and some piddly little thing could go wrong and Rand's life could hang in the balance."

"It's up to you to see that nothing goes wrong."

"It's such a terrible responsibility. Sometimes, Grand, I feel as though I'm a hundred years old. I'm glad Rand is coming. I need to know who I am again, for a little while. I do care for him, Grand, maybe too much. We write, you know, and talk every so often. He rings me on the telly. Isn't that quaint?"

"About as quaint as talking on the horn. Isn't that what your generation says?" Sawyer laughed.

"Thad is coming in a day or so," Billie volunteered. "Maybe even tomorrow if things go right."

"When are you two getting married?"

"Just as soon as this plane gets airborne. We're going to Hong Kong, and when it's right we'll, as you say, tie the knot."

"I'm so happy for you. You've been a brick through all this. Grandpap sure picked himself a winner when he picked you."

"I always thought so." Billie laughed. "Time for bed. You have an early day and I need my beauty sleep."

The following two months were the happiest Billie had ever known. She was drawn into the Hasegawa family and basked in their loving acceptance of her. Thad drew on his leave and visited for days at a time, making her happiness total and complete.

Otami and Billie watched the romance between Rand and Sawyer blossom. It was obvious to anyone who cared to observe the young girl that the commitment to her grandfather's dream came first. Rand appeared to understand . . . for now.

They were all seated around the Hasegawa dining room table having cake and coffee. The test flight, Sawyer had just said, was scheduled for March 31, the last day of the last month granted them by their investors to come up with a marketable product. Rand was scowling. Sawyer looked gloomy, and Riley sat with his hands propping up his face. The elder Hasegawa let his glance stray to the young people and then to Billie. He clearly wanted to know what the problem was.

Suddenly Rand spoke. "I'm telling you, Sawyer, a sixty-degree angle on the wing sweep is too steep. Either you bring it back to fifty-five degrees or you get yourself another test pilot. There're a lot of things I'll do for you, but killing myself isn't one of them."

"I'm telling you sixty degrees was one of Grandpap's original specifications," Sawyer argued heatedly. "I've lived with this plane for two solid years. I know what I'm doing. The others agree. You're the only dissenter."

"Maybe I'm the only dissenter because I'm the only one who's going to fly that bird. I want to come back in one piece. Fifty-five degrees!"

"No! We'll lose efficiency."

"Yes!"

Sawyer got up and walked around the table till she was facing Rand. "Do you think for one minute that I'd let you fly the dream if I had one iota of doubt?...Well, you bloody Englishman? Answer me—but before you do, you should know something else: I love you. Now think long and hard before you give me your answer."

Billie's eyes widened. She'd never seen Sawyer so adamant. Otami was busy picking at her nails and Shadaharu was staring intently at a spot on the immaculate linen tablecloth. Only Riley stared at the couple.

Rand's brain clicked, reeling off the plane's specifications. Twice he frowned. Sawyer's penetrating, demanding gaze forced him to make an immediate decision. The niggling doubt would have to be shelved. He'd go over it again on the drawing board and then inch by inch in the hangar. Sawyer wasn't stubborn just for the sake of being stubborn. She'd made a believer of him on more than one occasion. Her gaze was clear and steady, defiant. He nodded. He was rewarded with a bone-crushing hug.

"You aren't humoring me, are you? You know I'm right. I haven't taken a chance or a gamble yet. I would never play with your life, Rand, not for anything. Tell me you trust me, that you trust what I've done," Sawyer demanded passionately.

Rand nodded again, unable to speak. His tongue was so thick he had trouble swallowing. Neither noticed as the others got up from the table. It was Sawyer who later ran into the hall to call them all back to the dining room.

Sawyer stood next to Rand, her eyes apologetic. "Mr. Hasegawa, the plane won't be ready March thirty-first. We need an extra day, possibly two. What will that mean to your people?"

How like Sawyer not to apologize. They'd all given it their best shot and failed to come in on schedule. One day, two, what difference could it make? A lot, according to the investors. Their contract gave them until the last day in March to prove

{ 563 }

themselves . . . or lose everything. And a contract was a contract. If April first arrived before the project's completion the contracts would be in breach.

"I can't ask more of the men than they've given. To come so close, so far, and not be able—"

"Grandfather, do something," Riley cried. "Make it right."

The elder Hasegawa placed a gentle hand on his grandson's shoulder. "It is out of my hands, my grandson."

"I don't believe that, Father. There must be something. You have always been the perfect father with the perfect solution for everything. It can't all have been for nothing. We can't lose now," Otami cried as she clutched at her father. "Please, think of something."

"We need an extra day in March. Just twenty-four hours. That's all," Riley cried childishly.

"Enough! I will look into the matter but can make no promises," the Japanese said formally as he withdrew from the room.

"Why do I feel as though I've failed?" Sawyer cried brokenly.

"You didn't fail. Things got in the way. You did magnificently," Rand said loyally. The others chorused their agreement. "Come along, back to the hangar. We have work to do. No one went home tonight. The crew is sleeping in three-hour shifts."

Billie sat down with a thump and buried her face in her hands. Surely they couldn't lose now. Otami put her arms around Billie's shoulders. Riley sat across from her. "Grandfather will find a way. I know he will."

"My father is a remarkable man, Mother Coleman. If it is humanly possible to make this right, he will. He will feel he must do it for our honor. We must all think positively."

Billie nodded.

They worked like Trojans for the remaining days. Thad arrived to offer his help and input. Billie rarely saw him and when she did he was so tired she could do no more than kiss his cheek and cover him with a blanket while he slept his allotted shift. Everything was the dream now. Nothing else mattered.

March 31 arrived all too soon. Sawyer was gaunt and red-eyed. Rand, at her side, looked no better. Everyone seemed to move in slow motion, Billie thought as she entered the hangar to seek out Sawyer. "Will you make it?"

"No. We need another two shifts. I did everything by the

book. We didn't allow for the human element. . . . Grandpap didn't tell me that. Eighteen hours, that's all. My God, Grand, I can't believe it."

At six o'clock that evening Shadaharu Hasegawa entered the hangar, a smile on his face. He closeted himself with Riley and Sawyer in her makeshift office for eight minutes, and when they emerged Sawyer's red eyes were sparkling as she waved an airy arm in Billie's direction. It was going to be all right.

"Thank you, God," Billie whispered. "Thank you."

The time was one hour past dawn. The calendar said it was April 1, but Riley's grandfather had proclaimed an extra day in the month of march. The Hasegawa newspapers in Tokyo carried the date of March 32, and newspapers didn't lie.

It seemed the world watched Moss Coleman's dream that day. Present were the Hasegawa family, the entire crew, Sawyer, Billie, and Thad. The media stood in a roped-off area ready to record the progress of the slant-winged silver bird.

Sawyer in her greasy coverall and visored cap stared into the sun. She ran half the distance to the runway and gave Rand a thumbs-up salute. Rand blew her a kiss and climbed into the cockpit.

As the plane started its glide down the runway, Billie blessed herself and whispered, "Rest easy, Moss. In a few minutes it will be history."

Strong arms enveloped her and she leaned back against Thad's chest. "Remember your promise," he said close to her ear. "Win or lose, fly or not, we get married tomorrow."

"I've been dreaming about my promise for a lifetime," she told him.

The dull roar of the engines exploded in the air as Rand taxied onto the far end of the runway. Billie stood in the circle of Thad's arms, fingers crossed, eyes lifted heavenward. "In just a few minutes we'll know."

"Do you mean we'll know if it was all worth it?"

"No. Everything, every joy, every tear, has been worth it for my whole life to bring me here with you today."

He kissed her cheek, holding fast to this woman whom he had loved for the whole of his life.

Billie turned to face Thad, her hazel eyes smiling into his. Overhead, Rand was airborne and holding steady. "Sometimes, Thad, I see questions in your eyes. Don't you know that some loves are for yesterday and others are forever?"

The light from her smile obliterated the shadows in his heart. "That's how I love you, Billie. Yesterday and forever."

{{{{{{{{ CHAPTER FORTY-ONE }}}}}}}}

Maggie Coleman caught a glimpse of her reflection in the pier glass. The image staring back at her made her gasp. She looked like a bag lady without the shopping bags. Her hand went to her hair and then to her cheek. What day was it? She had to stop and think, to try to calculate the month as well as the day.

How long ago had it been since her husband had left her? A year, six months? She didn't know and didn't care. She didn't feel his loss, would never feel it. It was over.

Pap's dream, that was over, too. The silver bird had flown beautifully off into the wild blue yonder with Rand at the controls. Sawyer must have convinced him to test the plane. Hate rushed through her veins at the knowledge that Sawyer had been the one responsible for making Pap's dream come true. Mam had called her excitedly from Japan, expecting Maggie to rejoice with her. Despite everything—the court injunctions and legal blockades to prevent Mam from squandering everything on that damn plane—she still expected her daughters to share in the glory. The lady certainly knew how to dish out the guilt.

Everyone was gone now. Pap was gone, Mam was gone, Sawyer was gone, her husband was gone. Coleman was away at military school, and she only saw him at Christmas and for the last two weeks in August. Stolen from her; everything in her life that should have been hers had been stolen from her. It hurt, and she had cried—for days, for weeks, for months. She was still crying, still trying to bandage her wounds, but there wasn't a Band-Aid large enough to ease the monstrous pain that attacked her twenty hours out of every day. The years, where had they gone? How had she lived through them?

Maggie's vision blurred momentarily as she looked around frantically for the vodka bottle. The clear liquid always made things better, or at least dulled the pain so that it didn't hurt quite so much.

There it was, on the night table, right next to the letter from old Dudley Abramson that had been sitting unopened for several days. She filled the tumbler to the rim and stared at the stark white envelope for a long moment before tossing it into the wastebasket. She didn't need his advice, or his criticism! She didn't care what he had to say. "You just wasted a stamp, you old buzzard," she said aloud.

A few minutes later she fished in the wastebasket and withdrew the letter. Maybe she should open it and see what it said. She was practically sober; she could handle it. She took a deep breath, ripped the envelope open, and stared with unbelieving eyes at the three pieces of paper in her hand. It was the key taped to the deed to Sunbridge that made her sink to the bed. The letter itself was short:

Dear Mrs. Tanner:

As per your parents' instructions, I am forwarding to you a fully executed deed to Sunbridge. The key is taped to the deed. Sunbridge now legally belongs to you.

I would like to take this time to remind you the taxes were due the first of April.

If there is anything the firm can do for you, please feel free to call upon us.

Yours truly,
Dudley Abramson

Maggie's hands were shaking so badly she could barely get her father's letter out of the unsealed envelope. It was handwritten, a jerky, uneven scrawl. The date on the single sheet of paper showed it had been written a week before his death.

Dear Maggie,

I can't go to that unknown place that awaits all of us until I do this one last thing. I hope and pray the time comes when Mr. Abramson will feel confident enough to forward this, my last word, to you. Your mother and I have spoken at great length about my intention of deeding Sunbridge to you. She has promised that if at all possible, she will not put Sunbridge up for auction but will turn it over to you. If, for some reason, it does have

{ 567 }

to be sold, I wanted you to know of my intentions. Our lives are full of uncertainties these days, but we must not dwell on them; we must all move forward, you most of all, Maggie.

Soul-searching has become a necessary pastime these last weeks. Old hurts can never be rectified. The ache in me for what I missed is more painful than the illness controlling my body. Forgiveness is something I have always taken for granted. I find it impossible to believe you will forgive me, but your mother assures me you will. I truly regret, dear Maggie, that I was so blind to your needs. I will carry that regret with me to eternity.

Only you, Maggie, can fill Sunbridge with love, life, humor, beautiful music, and wondrous words, because you care. Bring your son here, Maggie, and make a new life for yourself. I know a Higher Being will allow me to watch over you here in this place we call Sunbridge. Trust me, Maggie. You are part of my life, my love, my daughter. Be happy.

Pap

Maggie threw herself on the bed and howled. The huge four-poster rocked with the force of her sobs. When her release was complete she wiped her face with the corner of the bedspread. Her smile, when it came, was as radiant as the first golden sun of summer.

Four hours later Maggie Coleman Tanner was Texas bound. She was going home.

The key clenched in her hand was all the proof she needed that this wasn't all some kind of dream.

The rental car ground to a stop and Maggie was out in an instant. There it was. Home. What a wonderful, glorious word.

The key slid into the lock. She turned the handle and the door swung open. The first thing her tired eyes saw was the four-peg hatrack holding three Stetsons. Seth, Pap, Riley. She knew in her heart that the last peg had been ordained for her son, Coleman. His Stetson would hang there just as soon as that military school could send him here.

Home to Sunbridge.